LOOSED UPON THE WORLD

LOOSED
UPON THE
WORLD

THE SAGA
ANTHOLOGY OF
CLIMATE FICTION

EDITED BY JOHN JOSEPH ADAMS

SAGA PRESS

LONDON SYDNEY **NEW YORK** TORONTO NEW DELHI

SAGA PRESS

AN IMPRINT OF SIMON & SCHUSTER, INC.

1230 AVENUE OF THE AMERICAS, NEW YORK, NEW YORK 10020

FOR GRACE,

WHO I HOPE WILL INHERIT A BETTER WORLD

THAN THE ONES DEPICTED HERE.

CONTENTS

INTRODUCTION

JOHN JOSEPH ADAMS

Welcome to the end of the world, already in progress.

Apocalypses are something of a specialty of mine, having edited five anthologies on the subject so far, and it is extraordinarily clear to me that climate change is nothing short of an apocalypse in action. And when the head of the Senate Environment and Public Works Committee is the author of a book calling climate change "the greatest hoax" and says things like "Man can't change climate [only God can]," it brings to mind the dystopian volumes I've edited as well.

One of the many problems we face is simply in popular comprehension. It's hard to imagine how a two-degree increase in the average global temperature could possibly affect you or me, or why a three-foot rise in sea level would matter to someone who doesn't live on a coastline. We might hear about the rapid extinction of fauna in some far-off place and respond with nothing more than, "That's a shame . . ."; or complain to our neighbors when beach access is closed to us because some small sea bird is nesting. It all feels distant, either in space or in time—something that's affecting someone somewhere far away, or will affect a future generation as yet unborn.

But that sense of distance is a false one. It's happening now, and we will feel the affects in our lifetime. As I write this, my home state of California is in its fourth year of drought. The snowpack that we rely on every winter to sustain our water supplies throughout the year never came.

Better minds than mine are working on solutions to the problem of climate change, some of whom have applied their expertise in the stories in this volume. It's an enormous problem with ramifications for every species on Earth. It will require the cooperation of every nation that shares this fragile globe.

Fiction is a powerful tool for helping us contextualize the world around us. By approaching the topic in the realm of fiction, we can perhaps humanize and illuminate the issue in ways that aren't as easy to do with only science and cold equations.

It's my hope that this anthology will serve as a warning flare, to illustrate the kinds of things we can expect if climate change goes unchecked, but also some of the possible solutions, to inspire the hope that we can maybe still do something about it before it's too late.

FOREWORD

PAOLO BACIGALUPI

If I were to tell you that Lake Mead is setting record lows for its water reserves, or that Las Vegas is currently tunneling under the lake, in a multi-billion-dollar mega-project pursuit of this dwindling supply, it may not mean much to you. You don't live in Las Vegas, or, even if you do, it's a little hard to get worked up over the sight of a serene blue artificial lake with only a white bathtub ring around its edge to mark its shrinkage.

But what if I were to drop you into a life where your house was suddenly valueless? A place where your neighborhood had emptied of people overnight? A world where your polished granite counter tops and maple cabinets and marble-tile bathrooms can't be sold to a new buyer, because no one would be stupid enough to buy a house where no water comes out of the faucet and no toilet flushes. If you were to live in that world, where your five bed/three bath house and crushing mortgage were suddenly the value equivalent of owning a cave, *that* might make an impact.

It would for me, at least.

Theories and ideas and infrastructure versus visceral experience. Human beings are wired to react quickly and exquisitely when it comes to the visceral, but we remain primitive as apes when it comes to the abstract, the complex, and the long-term. This gap, between what we flee on the savannah and what might destroy us completely in thirty years, is where I make my writer's home. Sometimes, I've discovered, it's possible for a fiction writer to perform a kind of hack on a reader's mind, making them feel things that do not yet exist. And if we writers do our jobs well, when the reader closes a book, they will see the world differently. They will see low water levels in Lake Mead and connect them to catastrophic loss, to forced migration, to uncertainty.

It's interesting that by creating a made-up world, you can show the *real* world more sharply and clearly, and in that process, you have the chance of making people engage not with the future, but with the intense realities of our present—the realities that were previously passing them by. Suddenly, when someone is watering a lawn, or a news magazine prints a drought map, you can experience not abstractly and theoretically, as before, but *viscerally*, as we must, if we ever are to think long-term effectively.

But which long-term? What future waits for us? If you pick up an environmental news magazine, you'll see one set of storylines telling you that the destruction of the Earth is imminent; if you read *Popular Science*, you're going to see another set of storylines that say, "Look at the cool gadgets that could change the game for climate."

As writers, we decide which storylines matter—which ones we give weight to, with our attention. I can't say that we'll never discover some fabulous way to scrub carbon out of our coal-burning power plants and sequester it—but I can say that I haven't seen it make any impact yet.

The reality is, from what I understand about our current climate situation, we've already skipped merrily past the point of causing immense damage, and now we're headed for a more final cliff. That is fact. Carbon in the atmosphere has hit 400ppm and we still don't have a serious plan to stop it. So when a feel-good technology magazine talks about the possibility of a technology like carbon sequestration, that's all it is: a possibility. The fact of 400ppm remains, uncombatted.

Ultimately what all these feel-good technology stories add up to, is "Oh, we'll fix that problem *somehow*" and how that plays out is "Let's just go on, conducting business as usual." The idea is that *somehow* we're going to get out of it with a clever techno-fix, but because there are no technologies that are proven, nor any technologies that are in wide use, these are "idea" technologies. They are, in fact, *fiction*, or if you really want to stick the knife in—fantasy.

Of course, there *is* a solution for sequestering carbon—it's to not burn the goddamn stuff in the first place. But that's not as sexy. That's not a techno-fix; it's a social fix, and social fixes are hard, and complicated, and require human cooperation and restraint, whereas fantasy techno-fixes are easy. We can just lie back and dream about them. So easy.

At root, the "Techno-optimist" argument says that we are an innovative species and whenever we face a problem we will innovate. Our entire history proves it. And yet . . . just because we are innovative, it doesn't necessarily mean we are wise. If our food sources are tainted with mercury, perhaps we conclude that the solution is to make ourselves immune to mercury-poisoning, which would then allow us to dump as much mercury into the air and water as we like. It might screw up the whales, but hell, we don't need whales, so why should we care? Similarly, if we could make it so that factory pollution didn't cause asthma, would we care about air quality much? Probably not. We could make the air as thick as soup, while our factories cranked out another round of iWatches, or smartphones, or dumb rubber chickens.

All of these fixes are symptomatic of a solution-set that is seldom holistic and utterly disinterested in root causes. We're just clever enough to say, "The problem is pollution." But we're not clever enough to say, "Let's stop polluting." Or, rather, we *are* that clever, but given that so many people get short-term profit from activities that generate pollution, we never go there. So instead we hunt for a cheap techno-fix. So we'll hunt for a way to regenerate people's lungs, or we'll invest in desalinization for California in the face of water scarcity, or we'll invest in bioengineered crops to weather the droughts and hurricanes that will become more common as our climate-wrecked future becomes more inescapable.

This lust for the techno-fix is on full display in our fetish for space travel, the idea that humanity's best chance of survival is to get off our blue marble and go . . . elsewhere. In stories on the subject, the Earth is almost always used up, polluted, broken, nuked—but whatever, that's fine, because we're going to *Mars!*

Ahem.

I'm not sure why we think that Mars, or any other planet, would be such a great destination for us. Here we are on a planet that gives us free water, free air, even free food, essentially—a place where I can literally drop seeds on the ground, add water, and make food for myself—and yet we think our best hope lies on a planet where none of these things exist.

It boggles the mind. We have a hard time surviving on Antarctica, and at least there you've got air and water and penguins. So sure, Elon, you go ahead and give that Mars thing a shot, but don't try to tell me that's a good survival tactic.

Engineers don't grow up thinking about building a healthy soil ecosystem, or trying to restore some estuary, or making sure that migratory bird patterns remain undisturbed. They don't spend their time trying to turn people into better long-term planners, or better educated and informed citizens, or creating better civic societies. That's not where our techno-fix obsession goes; it's toward making an internal combustion engine work better and go faster, or swapping it out for an electric one. It's toward making things go up, go boom, go fast, go digital, go go go . . .

The reality is that bundling humanity into rocketships to take us off to find Earth 2.0 is a fantasy. It's easy to see why our love affair with that fantasy is so seductive—it embodies so many powerful mythic concepts: adventure, frontier, reinvention. And yet, it also embodies the idea that our salvation lies on planets that lack, well, *everything* really.

And while we're staring up at the stars, we're distracted from the real work at our feet—making this place that nurtured us whole and healthy enough to sustain our children and grandchildren and their children after them, so that they can thank us, instead of cursing us for the ruins we leave to them.

Ultimately the argument over whether we write about and imagine positive or negative futures is a straw man. The important thing to understand is that imaginative literature is mythic. The kinds of stories we build, the way we encourage people to live into those myths and dream the future—those stories have power. Once we build this myth that the rocketship and the techno-fix is the solve for all our plights and problems, that's when we get ourselves into danger. It's the one fantasy that almost certainly guarantees our eventual self-destruction.

One hopes that as we go about constructing our many theories of how the future will unfold and what part we will play in it, that we look not to the simple escape myth of last-minute innovation that gets us only out the frying pan of one disastrous scenario while landing us in the fire of another, but instead look to the root causes of each desperate techno-fix action, and instead of reaching for the simple tool, and fantasizing about quick and easy escape from our responsibilities via rocketship or desal plant or GMO, that we reach instead for the wisest tool.

What if we dreamed a different future, one where did this profoundly unsexy thing, and actually cared for the garden that we evolved within? It seems to me that this is a future with potential . . . and maybe a myth worth dreaming.

LOOSED

UPON

THE

WORLD

SHOOTING THE APOCALYPSE

PAOLO BACIGALUPI

If it were for anyone else, he would have just laughed in their faces and told them they were on their own.

The thought nagged at Timo as he drove his beat-up FlexFusion down the rutted service road that ran parallel to the concrete-lined canal of the Central Arizona Project. For any other journo who came down to Phoenix looking for a story, he wouldn't even think of doing them a favor.

All those big names looking to swoop in like magpies and grab some meaty exclusive and then fly away just as fast, keeping all their page views and hits to themselves . . . he wouldn't do it.

Didn't matter if they were *Google/NY Times*, Cherry Xu, *Facebook Social Now*, Deborah Williams, *Kindle Post*, or *Xinhua*.

But Lucy? Well, sure. For Lucy, he'd climb into his sweatbox of a car with all his camera gear and drive his skinny brown ass out to North Phoenix and into the hills on a crap tip. He'd drive this way and that, burning gas trying to find a service road, and then bump his way through dirt and ruts, scraping the belly of the Ford the whole way, and he still wouldn't complain.

Just goes to show you're a sucker for a girl who wears her jeans tight.

But it wasn't just that. Lucy was fine, if you liked a girl with white skin and little tits and wide hips, and sometimes Timo would catch himself fantasizing about what it would be like to get with her. But in the end, that wasn't why he did favors for Lucy. He did it because she was scrappy and wet and she was in over her head—and too hard-assed and proud to admit it.

Girl had grit; Timo could respect that. Even if she came from up north and was so wet that sometimes he laughed out loud at the things she said. The girl didn't know much about dry desert life, but she had grit.

So when she muttered over her Dos Equis that all the stories had already been done, Timo, in a moment of beery romantic fervor, had sworn to her that it just wasn't so. He had the eye. He saw things other people didn't. He could name twenty stories she could still do and make a name for herself.

But when he'd started listing possibilities, Lucy shot them down as fast as he brought them up.

Coyotes running Texans across the border into California?

Sohu already had a nine-part series running.

Californians buying Texas hookers for nothing, like Phoenix was goddamn Tijuana?

Google/NY Times and *Fox* both had big spreads.

Water restrictions from the Roosevelt Dam closure and the drying-up of Phoenix's swimming pools?

Kindle Post ran that.

The narco murders that kept getting dumped in the empty pools that had become so common that people had started calling them "swimmers"?

AP. Fox. Xinhua. LA Times. The Talisha Brannon Show. Plus the reality narco show *Hard Bangin'.*

He kept suggesting new angles, new stories, and all Lucy said, over and over was, "It's been done." And then she'd rattle off the news organizations, the journos who'd covered the stories, the page hits, the viewerships, and the click-thrus they'd drawn.

"I'm not looking for some dead hooker for the sex and murder crowd," Lucy said as she drained her beer. "I want something that'll go big. I want a scoop, you know?"

"And I want a woman to hand me a ice-cold beer when I walk in the door," Timo grumped. "Don't mean I'm going to get it."

But still, he understood her point. He knew how to shoot pictures that would make a vulture sob its beady eyes out, but the news environment that Lucy fought to distinguish herself in was like gladiatorial sport— some winners, a lot of losers, and a whole shit-ton of blood on the ground.

Journo money wasn't steady money. Wasn't good money. Sometimes, you got lucky. Hell, he'd got lucky himself when he'd gone over Texas way and shot Hurricane Violet in all her glory. He'd photographed a whole damn fishing boat flying through the air and landing on a Days Inn, and in that one shot he knew he'd hit the big time. Violet razed Galveston and blasted into Houston, and Timo got page views so high that he sometimes imagined that the cat 6 had actually killed him and sent him straight to Heaven.

He'd kept hitting reload on his PayPal account and watched the cash pouring in. He'd had the big clanking *cojones* to get into the heart of that clusterfuck, and he'd come out of it with more than a million hits a photo. Got him all excited.

But disaster was easy to cover, and he'd learned the hard way that when the big dogs muscled in, little dogs got muscled out. Which left him back in sad-sack Phoenix, scraping for glamour shots of brains on windshields and trussed-up drug bunnies in the bottoms of swimming pools. It made him sympathetic to Lucy's plight, if not her perspective.

It's all been done, Timo thought as he maneuvered his Ford around the burned carcass of an abandoned Tesla. *So what if it's been motherfucking done?*

"There ain't no virgins, and there ain't no clean stories," he'd tried to explain to Lucy. "There's just angles on the same-ass stories. Scoops come from being in the right place at the right time, and that's all just dumb luck. Why don't you just come up with a good angle on Phoenix and be happy?"

But Lucy Monroe wanted a nice clean virgin story that didn't have no grubby fingerprints on it from other journos. Something she could put her name on. Some way to make her mark, make those big news companies notice her. Something to grow her brand and all that. Not just the day-to-day grind of narco kills and starving immigrants from Texas, something special. Something new.

So when the tip came in, Timo thought what the hell, maybe this was something she'd like. Maybe even a chance to blow up together. Lucy could do the words, he'd bring the pics, and they'd scoop all the big-name journos who drank martinis at the Hilton 6 and complained about what a refugee shit hole Phoenix had become.

The Ford scraped over more ruts. Dust already coated the rear window of Timo's car, a thick beige paste. Parallel to the service road, the waters of the Central Arizona Project flowed, serene and blue and steady. A man-made canal that stretched three hundred miles across the desert to bring water to Phoenix from the Colorado River. A feat of engineering, and cruelly tempting, given the ten-foot chain link and barbed wire fences that escorted it on either side.

In this part of Phoenix, the Central Arizona Project formed the city's northern border. On one side of the CAP canal, it was all modest stucco tract houses packed together like sardines stretching south. But on Timo's side, it was desert, rising into tan and rust hill folds, dotted with mesquite and saguaro.

A few hardy subdivisions had built outposts north of the CAP's moat-like boundary, but the canal seemed to form a barrier of some psychological significance, because for the most part, Phoenix stayed to the south of the concrete-lined canal, choosing to finally build itself into something denser than lazy sprawl. Phoenix on one side, the desert on the other, and the CAP flowing between them like a thin blue DMZ.

Just driving on the desert side of the CAP made Timo thirsty. Dry mouth, plain-ass desert, quartz rocks, and sandstone nubs with a few creosote bushes holding onto the dust and waving in the blast furnace wind. Normally, Timo didn't even bother to look at the desert. It barely changed. But here he was, looking for something new—

He rounded a curve and slowed, peering through his grimy windshield. "Well, I'll be goddamned. . . ."

Up ahead, something was hanging from the CAP's barrier fence. Dogs were jumping up to tug at it, milling and barking.

Timo squinted, trying to understand what he was seeing.

"Oh, yeah. Hell, yes!"

He hit the brakes. The car came grinding to a halt in a cloud of dust, but Timo was already climbing out and fumbling for his phone, pressing it to his ear, listening to it ring.

Come on, come on, come on.

Lucy picked up.

Timo couldn't help grinning. "I got your story, girl. You'll love it. It's *new*."

The dogs bared their teeth at Timo's approach, but Timo just laughed. He dug into his camera bag for his pistol.

"You want a piece of me?" he asked. "You want some of Timo, bitches?"

Turned out they didn't. As soon he held up the pistol, the dogs scattered. Animals were smarter than people that way. Pull a gun on some drunk California frat boy and you never knew if the sucker was still going to try and throw down. Dogs were way smarter than Californians. Timo could respect that, so he didn't shoot them as they fled the scene.

One of the dogs, braver or more arrogant than the rest, paused to yank off a final trophy before loping away; the rest of the pack zeroed in on it, yipping and leaping, trying to steal its prize. Timo watched, wishing he'd pulled his camera instead of his gun. The shot was perfect. He sighed and stuffed the pistol into the back of his pants, dug out his camera, and turned to the subject at hand.

"Well, hello, good-looking," he murmured. "Ain't you a sight?"

The man hung upside down from the chain link fence, bloated from the Phoenix heat. A bunch of empty milk jugs dangled off his body, swinging from a harness of shoelace ties. From the look of him, he'd been cooking out in the sun for at least a day or so.

The meat of one arm was completely desleeved, and the other arm . . . well, Timo had watched the dogs make off with the poor bastard's hand. His face and neck and chest didn't look much better. The dogs had been doing some jumping.

"Come on, *vato*. Gimme the story." Timo stalked back and forth in front of the body, checking the angles, considering the shadows and light. "You want to get your hits up, don't you? Show Timo your good side, I make you famous. So help me out, why don't you?"

He stepped back, thinking wide-frame: the strung-up body, the black nylon flowers woven into the chain link around it. The black, guttered candles and cigarettes and mini liquor bottles scattered by the dogs' frenzied feeding. The CAP flowing behind it all. Phoenix beyond that, sprawling all the way to the horizon.

"What's your best side?" Timo asked. "Don't be shy. I'll do you right. Make you famous. Just let me get your angle."

There.

Timo squatted and started shooting. *Click-click-click-click*—the artificial sound of digital photography and the Pavlovian rush of sweaty excitement as Timo got the feel.

Dead man.

Flowers.

Candles.

Water.

Timo kept snapping. He had it now. The flowers and the empty milk jugs dangling off the dude. Timo was in the flow, bracketing exposures, shooting steady, recognizing the moment when his inner eye told him that he'd nailed the story. It was good. *Really* good.

As good as a cat 6 plowing into Houston.

Click-click-click. Money-money-money-money.

"That's right, buddy. Talk to your friend Timo."

The man had a story to tell, and Timo had the eye to see it. Most people missed the story. But Timo always saw. He had the eye.

Maybe he'd buy a top-shelf tequila to celebrate his page-view money. Some diapers for his sister Amparo's baby. If the photos were good, maybe he'd grab a couple syndication licenses, too. Swap the shit-ass battery in the Ford. Get something with a bigger range dropped into it. Let him get around without always wondering if he was going to lose a charge.

Some of these could go to *Xinhua*, for sure. The Chinese news agencies loved seeing America ripping itself to shit. BBC might bite, too. Foreigners loved that story. Only thing that would sell better is if it had a couple guns: *America, the Savage Land* or some shit. That was money, there. Might be rent for a bigger place. A place where Amparo could bail when her boyfriend got his ass drunk and angry.

Timo kept snapping photos, changing angles, framing and exposure. Diving deeper into the dead man's world. Capturing scuffed-up boots and plastic prayer beads. He hummed to himself as he worked, talking to his subject, coaxing the best out of the corpse.

"You don't know it, but you're damn lucky I came along," Timo said. "If one of those citizen journalist *pendejo* lice got you first, they wouldn't have treated you right. They'd shoot a couple shitty frames and upload them social. Maybe sell a Instagram pic to the blood rags . . . but they ain't quality. Me? When I'm done, people won't be able to *dream* without seeing you."

It was true, too. Any asshole could snap a pic of some girl blasted to pieces in an electric Mercedes, but Timo knew how to make you cry when you saw her splattered all over the front pages of the blood rags. Some piece of narco ass, and you'd still be bawling your eyes out over her tragic death. He'd catch the girl's little fuzzy dice mirror ornament spattered with blood, and your heart would just break.

Amparo said Timo had the eye. Little bro could see what other people didn't, even when it was right in front of their faces.

Every asshole had a camera these days; the difference was that Timo could *see.*

Timo backed off and got some quick video. He ran the recording back, listening to the audio, satisfying himself that he had the sound of it: the wind rattling the chain link under the high, hot Arizona sky; meadowlark call from somewhere next to the CAP waters; but most of all, the empty dangling jugs, the three of them plunking hollowly against each other—a dead man turned into an offering and a wind chime.

Timo listened to the deep *thunk-thunk-thunk* tones.

Good sounds.

Good empty desert sounds.

He crouched and framed the man's gnawed arm and the milk jugs. From this angle, he could just capture the blue line of the CAP canal and the leading edge of Phoenix beyond: cookie-cutter low-stories with lava-rock front yards and broke-down cars on blocks. And somewhere in there, some upstanding example of Arizona Minuteman militia pride had spied this sucker scrambling down the dusty hillside with his water jugs and decided to put a cap in his ass.

CAP in his ass, Timo chuckled to himself.

The crunch of tires and the grind of an old bio-diesel engine announced Lucy's pickup coming up the dirt road. A trail of dust followed. Rusty beast of flex fuel, older than the girl who drove it and twice as beat-up, but damn, was it a beast. It had been one of the things Timo liked about Lucy soon as he met her. Girl drove a machine that didn't give a damn about anything except driving over shit.

The truck came to a halt. The driver's side door squealed aside as Lucy climbed out. Army green tank top and washed-out jeans. White skin, scorched and bronzed by Arizona sun, her reddish brown hair jammed up under an ASU Geology Department ball cap.

Every time he saw her, Timo liked what he saw. Phoenix hadn't dried her right, yet, but still, she had some kind of tenacious-ass demon in her. Something about the way her pale blue skeptical eyes burned for a story told you that once she bit in, she wouldn't let go. Crazy-ass pitbull. The girl and the truck were a pair. Unstoppable.

"Please tell me I didn't drive out here for a swimmer," Lucy said as she approached.

"What do you think?"

"I think I was on the other side of town when you called, and I had to burn diesel to get here."

She was trying to look jaded, but her eyes were already flicking from detail to detail, gathering the story before Timo even had to open his mouth. She might be new in Phoenix, but the girl had the eye. Just like Timo, Lucy saw things.

"Texan?" she asked.

Timo grinned. "You think?"

"Well, he's a Merry Perry, anyway. I don't know many other people who would join that cult." She crouched down in front of the corpse and peered into the man's torn face. Reaching out, she caressed the prayer beads embedded in the man's neck. "I did a story on Merry Perrys. Roadside spiritual aid for the refugees." She sighed. "They were all buying the beads and making the prayers."

"Crying and shaking and repentance."

"You've been to their services, too?"

"Everybody's done that story at least once," Timo said. "I shot a big old revival tent over in New Mexico, outside of Carlsbad. The preacher had a nasty-ass thorn bush, wanted volunteers."

Timo didn't think he'd ever forget the scene. The tent walls sucking and flapping as blast-furnace winds gusted over them. The dust-coated refugees all shaking, moaning, and working their beads for God. All of them asking what they needed to give up in order to get back to the good old days of big oil money and fancy cities like Houston and Austin. To get back to a life before hurricanes went cat 6 and Big Daddy Drought sucked whole states dry.

Lucy ran her fingers along the beads that had sunk deep into the dead man's neck. "They strangled him."

"Sure looks that way."

Timo could imagine this guy earning the prayer beads one at time. Little promises of God's love that he could carry with him. He imagined the man down in the dirt, all crying and spitty and grateful for his bloody back and for the prayer beads that had ended up embedded in his swollen, blackening neck, like some kind of Mardi Gras party gone wrong. The man had done his prayers and repentance, and this was where he'd ended up.

"What happened to his hand?" Lucy asked.

"Dog got it."

"Christ."

"If you want some better art, we can back off for a little while, and the dogs'll come back. I can get a good tearaway shot if we let them go after him again—"

Lucy gave Timo a dirty look, so he hastily changed tacks. "Anyway, I thought you should see him. Good art, and it's a great story. Nobody's got something like this."

Lucy straightened. "I can't pitch this, Timo. It's sad as hell, but it isn't new. Nobody cares if Old Tex here hiked across a thousand miles of desert just to get strung up as some warning. It's sad, but everyone knows how much people hate Texans. *Kindle Post* did a huge story on Texas lynchings."

"Shit." Timo sighed. "Every time I think you're wise, I find out you're still wet."

"Oh, fuck off, Timo."

"No, I'm serious, girl. Come here. Look with your eye. I know you got the eye. Don't make me think I'm wasting my time on you."

Timo crouched down beside the dead man, framing him with his hands. "Old Tex here hikes his ass across a million miles of burning desert, and he winds up here. Maybe he's thinking he's heading for California and gets caught with the State Sovereignty Act, can't cross no state borders now. Maybe he just don't have the cash to pay coyotes. Maybe he thinks he's special and he's going to swim the Colorado and make it up north across Nevada. Anyways, Tex is stuck squatting out in the hills, watching us live the good life. But then the poor sucker sees the CAP, and he's sick of paying to go to some public pump for water, so he grabs his bottles and goes in for a little sip—"

"—and someone puts a bullet in him," Lucy finished. "I get it. I'm trying to tell you nobody cares about dead Texans. People string them up all the time. I saw it in New Mexico, too. Merry Perry prayer tents and Texans strung up on fences. Same in Oklahoma. All the roads out of Texas have them. Nobody cares."

Wet.

Timo sighed. "You're lucky you got me for your tour guide. You know that, right? You see the cigarettes? See them little bitty Beam and Cuervo bottles? The black candles? The flowers?"

Timo waited for her to take in the scene again. To see the way he saw. "Old Tex here isn't a *warning.* This motherfucker's an *offering.* People turned Old Tex into an offering for Santa Muerte. They're using Tex here to get in good with the Skinny Lady."

"Lady Death," Lucy said. "Isn't that a cult for narcos?"

"Nah. She's no cult. She's a saint. Takes care of people who don't got pull with the Church. When you need help on something the Church don't like, you go to Santa Muerte. The Skinny Lady takes care of you. She knows we all need a little help. Maybe she helps narcos, sure, but she helps poor people, too. She helps desperate people. When Mother Mary's too uptight, you call the Skinny Lady to do the job."

"Sounds like you know a lot about her."

"Oh, hell, yes. Got an app on my phone. Dial her any time I want and get a blessing."

"You're kidding."

"True story. There's a lady down in Mexico runs a big shrine. You send her a dollar, she puts up an offering for you. Makes miracles happen. There's a whole list of miracles that Santa Muerte does. Got her own hashtag."

"So what kind of miracles do you look for?"

"Tips, girl! What you think?" Timo sighed. "Narcos call on Santa Muerte all the time when they want to put a bullet in their enemies. And I come in after and take the pictures. Skinny Lady gets me there before the competition is even close."

Lucy was looking at him like he was crazy, and it annoyed him. "You know, Lucy, it's not like you're the only person who needs an edge out here." He waved at the dead Texan. "So? You want the story or not?"

She still looked skeptical. "If anyone can make an offering to Santa Muerte online, what's this Texan doing upside down on a fence?"

"DIY, baby."

"I'm serious, Timo. What makes you think Tex here is an offering?"

Because Amparo's boyfriend just lost his job to some loser Longhorn who will work for nothing. Because my water bill just went up again, and my rationing just went down. Because Roosevelt Lake is gone dry, and I got Merry Perrys doing revivals right on the corner of 7th and Monte Vista, and they're trying to get my cousin Marco to join them.

"People keep coming," Timo said, and he was surprised at the tightness of his throat as he said it. "They smell that we got water, and they just keep coming. It's like Texas is a million, million ants, and they just keep coming."

"There are definitely a lot of people in Texas."

"More like a tsunami. And we keep getting hit by wave after wave of them, and we can't hold 'em all back." He pointed at the body. "This is Last Stand shit here. People are calling in the big guns. Maybe they're praying for Santa Muerte to hit the Texans with a dust storm and strip their bones before they get here. For sure they're asking for something big."

"So they call on Lady Death." But Lucy was shaking her head. "It's just that I need more than a body to do a story."

"But I got amazing pics!"

"I need more. I need quotes. I need a trend. I need a story. I need an example. . . ."

Lucy was looking across the CAP canal toward the subdivision as she spoke. Timo could almost see the gears turning in her head. . . .

"Oh, no. Don't do it, girl."

"Do what?" But she was smiling already.

"Don't go over there and start asking who did the deed."

"It would be a great story."

"You think some motherfucker's just gonna say they out and wasted Old Tex?"

"People love to talk, if you ask them the right questions."

"Seriously, Lucy. Let the cops take care of it. Let them go over there and ask the questions."

Lucy gave him a pissed-off look.

"What?" Timo asked.

"You really think I'm that wet?"

"Well . . ."

"Seriously? How long have we known each other? Do you really think you can fool me into thinking the cops are gonna give a shit about another dead Merry Perry? How wet do you think I am?"

Lucy spun and headed for her truck.

"This ain't some amusement park!" Timo called after her. "You can't just go poke the Indians and think they're gonna native-dance for you. People here are for *real!*" He had to shout the last because the truck's door was already screeching open.

"Don't worry about me!" Lucy called as she climbed into the beast. "Just get me good art! I'll get our story!"

"So let me get this straight," Timo asked for the fourth or fifth time. "They just let you into their house?"

They were kicked back on the roof at Sid's Cafe with the rest of the regulars, taking potshots at the prairie dogs who had invaded the half-finished subdivision ruins around the bar, trading an old .22 down a long line as patrons took bets.

The subdivision was called Sonora Bloom Estates, one of those crap-ass investments that had gone belly-up when Phoenix finally stopped bailing out over-pumped subdivisions. Sonora Bloom Estates had died because some bald-ass pencil-pusher in City Planning had got a stick up his ass and said the water district wasn't going to support them. Now, unless some company like IBIS or Halliburton could frack their way to some magical new water supply, Desert Bloom was only ever going to be a town for prairie dogs.

"They just let you in?" Timo asked. "Seriously?"

Lucy nodded smugly. "They let me into their house, and then into their neighbors' houses. And then they took me down into their basements and showed me their machine guns." Lucy took a swig of Negra Modelo. "I make friends, Timo." She grinned. "I make a *lot* of friends. It's what I do."

"Bullshit."

"Believe it or don't." Lucy shrugged. "Anyway, I've got our story. 'Phoenix's Last Stand.' You wouldn't believe how they've got themselves set up. They've got war rooms. They've got ammo dumps. This isn't some cult militia; it's more like the army of the apocalypse. Way beyond preppers. These people are getting ready for the end of the world, and they want to talk about it."

"They want to talk."

"They're *desperate* to talk. They *like* talking. All they talk about is how to shove Texas back where it came from. I mean, you see the inside of their houses, and it's all Arizona for the People, and God and Santa Muerte to back them up."

"They willing to let me take pictures?"

Lucy gave him another smug look. "No faces. That's the only condition."

Timo grinned. "I can work with that."

Lucy set her beer down. "So what've you shot so far?"

"Good stuff." Timo pulled out his camera and flicked through images. "How about this one?" He held up the camera for her to see. "Poetry, right?"

Lucy eyed the image with distaste. "We need something PG, Timo."

"PG? Come on. PG don't get the hits. People love the bodies and the blood. *Sangre* this, *sangre* that. They want the blood, and they want the sex. Those are the only two things that get hits."

"This isn't for the local blood rags," Lucy said. "We need something PG from the dead guy."

She accepted the rifle from a hairy biker dude sitting next to her and sighted out at the dimming landscape beyond. The sun was sinking over the sprawl of the Phoenix basin, a brown blanket of pollution and smoke from California wildfires turning orange and gaudy.

Timo lifted his camera and snapped a couple quick shots of Lucy as she sighted down the rifle barrel. Wet girl trying to act dry. Not knowing that everyone who rolled down to Phoenix tried to show how tough they were by picking up a nice rifle and blasting away at the furry critters out in the subdivisions.

The thought reminded Timo that he needed to get some shots of Sumo Hernandez and his hunting operation. Sucker had a sweet gig bringing Chinese tourists in to blast at coyotes and then feed them rattlesnake dinners.

He snapped a couple more pictures and checked the results. Lucy looked damn good on the camera's LCD. He'd got her backlit, the line of her rifle barrel across the blaze of the red ball sun. Money shot for sure.

He flicked back into the dead Texan pictures.

"PG, PG . . . ," Timo muttered. "What the fuck is PG? It's not like the dude's dick is out. Just his eaten-off face."

Lucy squeezed off another shot and handed the rifle back.

"This is going to go big, Timo. We don't want it to look like it's just another murder story. That's been done. This has to look smart and scary and real. We're going to do a series."

"We are?"

"Hell yes, we are. I mean, this could be Pulitzer-type stuff. 'Phoenix's Last Stand.'"

"I don't give a shit about Pulitzers. I just want good hits. I need money."

"It will get us hits. Trust me. We're onto something good."

Timo flicked through more of his pictures. "How about just the beads in the guy's neck?" He showed her a picture. "This one's sweet."

"No." Lucy shook her head. "I want the CAP in it."

Timo gave up on stifling his exasperation. "PG, CAP. Anything else, ma'am?"

Lucy shot him a look. "Will you trust me on this? I know what I'm doing."

"Wet-ass newcomer says she knows what she's doing."

"Look, you're the expert when it comes to Phoenix. But you've got to trust me. I know what I'm doing. I know how people think back East. I know what people want on the big traffic sites. You know Phoenix, and I trust you. Now you've got to trust *me*. We're onto something. If we do it right, we're going to blow up. We're going to be a phenomenon."

The hairy biker guy handed the rifle back to Lucy for another shot.

"So you want PG, and you want the CAP," Timo said.

"Yeah. The CAP is why he died," she said absently as she sighted again with the rifle. "It's what he wanted. And it's what the Defending Angels need to protect. It's what Phoenix has that Texas doesn't. Phoenix is alive in the middle of a desert because you've got one of the most expensive water transport systems in the world. If Texas had a straw like the CAP running to some place like the Mississippi River, they'd still be fine."

Timo scoffed. "That would be like a thousand miles."

"Rivers go farther than that." Lucy squeezed off a shot and dust puffed beside a prairie dog. The critter dove back into its hole, and Lucy passed the rifle back. "I mean, your CAP water is coming from the Rockies. You've got the Colorado River running all the way down from Wyoming and Colorado, through Utah, all the way across the top of Arizona, and then you and California and Las Vegas all share it out."

"California doesn't share shit."

"You know what I mean. You all stick your straws in the river; you pump water to a bunch of cities that shouldn't even exist. CAP water comes way more than a thousand miles." She laughed and reached for her beer. "The irony is that at least Texans built where they *had* water. Without the CAP, you'd be just like the Texans. A bunch of sad-ass people all trying to move north."

"Thank God we're smarter than those assholes."

"Well, you've got better bureaucrats and pork barrels, anyway."

Timo made a face at Lucy's dig but didn't bother arguing. He was still hunting through his photos for something that Lucy would approve of.

Nothing PG about dying, he thought. *Nothing PG about clawing your way all the way across a thousand miles of desert just to smash up against chain link. Nothing PG about selling off your daughter so you can make a run at going north, or jumping the border into California.*

He was surprised to find that he almost felt empathy for the Texan. Who knew? Maybe this guy had seen the apocalypse coming but he'd just been too rooted in place to accept that he couldn't ride it out. Or maybe he'd had too much faith that God would take care of him.

The rifle was making the rounds again. More sharp cracks of the little .22 caliber bullets.

Faith. Maybe Old Tex's faith had made him blind. Made it impossible for him to see what was coming. Like a prairie dog who'd stuck his head out of his burrow and couldn't quite believe that God had put a bead on his furry little skull. Couldn't see the bullet screaming in on him.

In the far distance, a flight of helicopters was moving across the burning horizon. The *thud-thwap* of their rotors carried easily across the hum of the city. Timo counted fifteen or twenty in the formation. Heading off to fight forest fires, maybe. Or else getting shipped up to the Arctic by the Feds.

Going someplace, anyway.

"Everybody's got some place to go," Lucy murmured, as if reading his mind.

The rifle cracked again, and a prairie dog went down. Everyone cheered. "I think that one was from Texas," someone said.

Everyone laughed. Selena came up from below with a new tray of bottles and handed them out. Lucy was smirking to herself, looking superior.

"You got something to say?" Timo asked.

"Nothing. It's just funny how you all treat the Texans."

"Shit." Timo took a slug from his beer. "They deserve it. I was down there, remember? I saw them all running around like ants after Hurricane Violet fucked them up. Saw their towns drying up. Hell, everybody who wasn't Texas Forever saw that shit coming down. And there they all were, praying to God to save their righteous Texan asses." He took another slug of beer. "No pity for those fools. They brought their apocalypse down on their own damn selves. And now they want to come around here and take away what we got? No way."

"No room for charity?" Lucy prodded.

"Don't interview me," Timo shot back.

Lucy held up her hands in apology. "My bad."

Timo snorted. "Hey, everybody! My wet-ass friend here thinks we ought to show some charity to the Texans."

"I'll give 'em a bullet free," Brixer Gonzalez said.

"I'll give 'em two!" Molly Abrams said. She took the rifle and shot out a distant window in the subdivision.

"And yet they keep coming," Lucy murmured, looking thoughtful. "They just keep on coming, and you can't stop them."

Timo didn't like how she mirrored his own worries.

"We're going to be fine."

"Because you've got Santa Muerte and a whole hell of a lot of armed lunatics on your side," Lucy said with satisfaction. "This story is going to make us. 'The Defending Angels of Phoenix.' What a beautiful scoop."

"And they're just going to let us cover them?" Timo still couldn't hide his skepticism.

"All anyone wants to do is tell their story, Timo. They need to know they matter." She favored him with a sidelong smile. "So when a nice journo from up north comes knocking? Some girl who's so wet they can see it on her face? They love it. They love telling her how it is." Lucy took a sip of her beer, seeming to remember the encounter. "If people think you're wet enough, you wouldn't believe what they'll tell you. They've got to show how smart and wise they are, you know? All you need to do is look interested, pretend you're wet, and people roll right over."

Lucy kept talking, describing the world she'd uncovered, the details that had jumped out at her. How there was so much more to get. How he needed to come along and get the art.

She kept talking, but Timo couldn't hear her words anymore because one phrase kept pinging around inside his head like a pinball.

Pretend you're wet, and people roll right over.

"I don't know why you're acting like this," Lucy said for the third time as they drove out to see the Defending Angels.

She was driving the beast, and Timo was riding shotgun. He'd loaded his gear into her truck, determined that any further expenses from the reporting trip should be on her.

At first, he'd wanted to just cut her off and walk away from the whole thing, but he realized that was childish. If she could get the hits, then fine. He'd tag along on her score. He'd take her page views, and then he'd be done with her.

Cutting her off too soon would get him nothing. She'd just go get some other *pendejo* to do the art, or else she might even shoot the pictures herself and get her ass paid twice, a prospect that galled him even more than the fact that he'd been manipulated.

They wound their way into the subdivision, driving past ancient Prius sedans and electric bikes. At the end of the cul-de-sac, Lucy pulled to a halt. The place didn't look any different from any other Phoenix suburb. Except apparently, inside all the quiet houses, a last-battle resistance was brewing.

Ahead, the chain link and barbed wire of the CAP boundary came into view. Beyond, there was nothing but cactus-studded hills. Timo could just make out the Texan on the far side of the CAP fences, still dangling. It looked like the dogs were at him again, tearing at the scraps.

"Will you at least talk to me?" Lucy asked. "Tell me what I did."

Timo shrugged. "Let's just get your shoot done. Show me these Angels of Arizona you're so hot for."

"No." Lucy shook her head. "I'm not taking you to see them until you tell me why you keep acting this way."

Timo glared at her, then looked out the dusty front window.

"Guess we're not going to see them, then."

With the truck turned off, it was already starting to broil inside. The kind of heat that cooked pets and babies to death in a couple hours. Timo could feel sweat starting to trickle off him, but he was damned if he was going to show that he was uncomfortable. He sat and stared at the CAP fence ahead of them. They could both sweat to death for all he cared.

Lucy was staring at him hard. "If you've got something you want to say, you should be man enough to say it."

Man enough? Oh, hell, no.

"Okay," Timo said. "I think you played me."

"Played you how?"

"Seriously? You going to keep at it? I'm on to you, girl. You act all wet, and you get people to help you out. You get people to do shit they wouldn't normally do. You act all nice, like you're all new and like you're just getting your feet under you, but that's just an act."

"So what?" Lucy said. "Why do you care if I fool some militia nutjobs?"

"I'm not talking about them! I'm talking about me! That's how you played me! You act like you don't know things, get me to show you around. Show you the ropes. Get you on the inside. You act all wet and sorry, and dumbass Timo steps in to help you out. And you get a nice juicy exclusive."

"Timo . . . how long have we known each other?"

"I don't know if we ever did."

"Timo—"

"Don't bother apologizing." He shouldered the truck's door open.

As he climbed out, he knew he was making a mistake. She'd pick up some other photographer. Or else she'd shoot the story herself and get paid twice for the work.

Should have just kept my mouth shut.

Amparo would have told him he was both dumb and a sucker. Should have at least worked Lucy to get the story done before he left her ass. Instead he'd dumped her and the story.

Lucy climbed out of the truck, too.

"Fine," she said. "I won't do it."

"Won't do what?"

"I won't do the story. If you think I played you, I won't do the story."

"Oh, come on. That's bullshit. You know you came down here for your scoop. You ain't giving that up."

Lucy stared at him, looking pissed. "You know what your problem is?"

"Got a feeling you're going to tell me."

"You're so busy doing your poor-me, I'm-from-Phoenix, everyone's-out-to-get-me, we're-getting-overrun, wah-wah-wah routine that you can't even tell when someone's on your side!"

"That's not—"

"You can't even tell someone's standing right in front of you who actually gives a shit about you!" Lucy was almost spitting, she was so mad. Her face had turned red. Timo tried to interject, but she kept talking.

"I'm not some damn Texan here to take your water, and I'm not some big-time journo here to steal your fucking stories! That's not who I am! You know how many photographers I could work with? You know how many would bite on this story that I went out and got? I put my ass on the line out here! You think that was easy?"

"Lucy. Come on . . ."

She waved a hand of disgust at him and stalked off, heading for the end of the cul-de-sac and the CAP fence beyond.

"Go find someone else to do this story," she called back. "Pick whoever you want. I wouldn't touch this story with a ten-foot pole. If that's what you want, it's all yours."

"Come on, Lucy." Timo felt like shit. He started to chase after her. "It's not like that!"

She glanced back. "Don't even try, Timo."

Her expression was so scornful and disgusted that Timo faltered.

He could almost hear his sister Amparo laughing at him. *You got the eye for some things, little bro, but you are blind, blind, blind.*

She'll cool off, he thought as he let her go.

Except maybe she wouldn't. Maybe he'd said some things that sounded a little too true. Said what he'd really thought of Lucy the Northerner in a way that couldn't get smoothed over. Sometimes, things just broke. One second, you thought you had a connection with a person. Next second, you saw them too clear, and you just knew you were never going to drink a beer together, ever again.

So go fix it, pendejo.

With a groan, Timo went after her again.

"Lucy!" he called. "Come on, girl. I'm sorry, okay? I'm sorry . . ."

At first, he thought she was going to ignore him, but then she turned.

Timo felt a rush of relief. She was looking at him again. She was looking right at him, like before, when they'd still been getting along. She was going to forgive him. They were going to work it out. They were friends.

But then he realized her expression was wrong. She looked dazed. Her sunburned skin had paled. And she was waving at him, waving furiously for him to join her.

Another Texan? Already?

Timo broke into a run, fumbling for his camera.

He stopped short as he made it to the fence.

"Timo?" Lucy whispered.

"I see it."

He was already snapping pictures through the chain link, getting the story. He had the eye, and the story was right there in front of them. The biggest, luckiest break he'd ever get. Right place, right time, right team to cover the story. He was kneeling now, shooting as fast as he could, listening to the digital report of the electronic shutter, hearing money with every click.

I got it, I got it, I got it, thinking that he was saying it to himself and then realizing he was speaking out loud. "I got it," he said. "Don't worry, I got it!"

Lucy was turning in circles, looking dazed, staring back at the city. "We need to get ourselves assigned. We need to get supplies. . . . We need to trace this back. . . . We need to figure out who did it. . . . We need to get ourselves assigned!" She yanked out her phone and started dialing madly as Timo kept snapping pictures.

Lucy's voice was an urgent hum in the background as he changed angles and exposures.

Lucy clicked off the cell. "We're exclusive with *Xinhua*!"

"Both of us?"

She held up a warning finger. "Don't even start up on me again."

Timo couldn't help grinning. "Wouldn't dream of it, partner."

Lucy began dictating the beginnings of her story into her phone, then broke off. "They want our first update in ten minutes; you think you're up for that?"

"In ten minutes, updates are going to be the least of our problems."

He was in the flow now, capturing the concrete canal and the dead Texan on the other side.

The dogs leaped and jumped, tearing apart the man who had come looking for water.

It was all there. The whole story, laid out.

The man.

The dogs.

The fences.

The Central Arizona Project.

A whole big canal, drained of water. Nothing but a thin crust of rapidly drying mud at its bottom.

Lucy had started dictating again. She'd turned to face the Phoenix sprawl, but Timo didn't need to listen to her talk. He knew the story already—a whole city full of people going about their daily lives, none of them knowing that everything had changed.

Timo kept shooting.

ABOUT THE AUTHOR

Paolo Bacigalupi is the bestselling author of the novels *The Windup Girl, Ship Breaker, The Drowned Cities, Zombie Baseball Beatdown,* and the collection *Pump Six and Other Stories.* He is a winner of the Michael L. Printz, Hugo, Nebula, Locus, Compton Crook, and John W. Campbell Memorial awards, and was a National Book Award finalist. A new novel for young adults, *The Doubt Factory,* came out in 2014, and a new science fiction novel dealing with the effects of climate change, *The Water Knife,* was published in May 2015.

THE MYTH OF RAIN

SEANAN McGUIRE

Female spotted owls have a call that doesn't sound like it should come from a bird of prey. It's high-pitched and unrealistic, like a squeaky toy that's being squeezed just a little bit too hard. Lots of people who hear them in the woods don't even realize that they've heard an *owl*. They assume it's a bug, or a dog running wild through the evergreens, beloved chewy bone clenched tightly in its jaws.

I held tight to the branch beneath me and adjusted my binoculars, trying to find the telltale barred plumage. The night scope I had was good, but I needed a positive ID before I moved. I had been tracking this female for the better part of two days. I was tired, and muddy, and covered in mosquito bites. Kathy had already radioed in to confirm that her team was done scooping, tagging, and crating all the Western pond turtles in her sector. They were moving on to assist Benet and his team with the search for Beller's ground beetles. The stress there really belonged on the word "ground." They were going to be on the *ground*. And I, and my team, would be staying in the trees for the foreseeable future.

"Do birds, Julie," I muttered, adjusting my binoculars again. "You like birds. You think they're pretty. You should do birds. That way, you'll be less miserable thinking about how all this is going to *burn*."

There was a flash of barred wings in the tree in front of me, feathers ruffled out as the female owl I had been tracking settled on the branch. I stopped talking and held my breath, tracking her slow, bobbing walk as she moved toward the main body of the tree.

Come on, sweetheart, I thought, so fiercely that if I could have developed telepathy in that moment, I would have done it. *Show me that you're going home.*

The owl paused, looking around herself with a predator's wariness. She didn't need to wonder what kind of monsters lurked in the woods: she knew, because she was one of them. Her wings were silent and her talons were sharp, but there were still things that could hurt her.

She had no idea how many things there were that could hurt her.

Finally, the owl vanished into her tree, and I lowered my binoculars, beginning to inch my way back along the branch I had been perched upon. I knew where her nest was now. I could come back any time I needed to.

There were monsters coming to these woods. I was going to do my best to save her.

When the droughts hit the West Coast in the early teens, everyone said, "This too will pass." Climate change was still up for debate in those days, at least in the eyes of people who had everything to gain by keeping the argument going for just a little longer, long enough for them to make their money and get the hell out of Dodge. Lots of beach houses got quietly sold during the back half of the decade. Lots of island resorts were traded in for ski lodges and mountain getaways. The signs were there, if you knew where to look for them.

Trouble was, the spin machine was spinning as fast as it could, and when people pointed to the signs, the pundits said we were fear-mongering and telling lies and trying to discredit good American businessmen who were only doing what they did for the good of the country. A lot of money traded hands in those days, and even as people were starting to focus on eating local and recycling, they ignored the fact that the lakes were drying and the hills were burning and the whole great stretch of green that we had all depended upon for so long was becoming a fairy tale. The myth of rain in California.

Thing about lies is that no matter how often you tell them and how much you believe them, they're not going to become true. "Fake it until you make it" may work for public speaking and falling in love, but it doesn't stop climate change. By 2017, it was pretty clear who the liars were, and they weren't the scientists holding up their charts and screaming for the support of the public. By 2019, it was even clearer that we'd listened to the lies too long. The tipping point was somewhere behind us, overlooked and hence forgotten. Maybe there had been a time when we could have reversed the damage and restored our planet to its natural equilibrium. Maybe not. It didn't really matter anymore.

The rich fled the places where the sun was too bright and the rain was too rare, and when the places they fled to dried up in turn, the rich fled farther, looking for some promised land that had managed to remain pristine while they were busy wrecking the world the rest of us had to live in. It was inevitable that their eyes would settle on the Pacific Northwest, where the trees were still green and the rain was still coming down.

Global climate change hadn't spared the Pacific Northwest. Everyone I knew from Seattle complained about how hot it was, even breaking seventy degrees in October. They complained about how blue their skies were and how much they missed the rain. And a few of them—the ones who understood what was about to happen—complained about the way the big corporations were sniffing around, the maggots moving on from the corpse of San Francisco, which they had already stripped down to dry bones.

Without its ever-present rain, Seattle was a beautiful, tempting target, and Portland was even more so. They were still cool. They were still green. The changes that had done so much damage to the rest of the country had just made them more attractive to everyone else—especially the parts of everyone else who could afford to move on a whim. Forget the poor. Forget the disenfranchised. They were the ones who had done the least to destroy the world as we'd known it for so long, and now they were the ones being left behind.

Oh, we fought. Because the thing was, Portland and Seattle and Vancouver, they were beautiful cities, with their own positive qualities . . . but what they weren't was infinitely capable of expansion. There were protected wetlands and forests to every side, mountain microclimates and endangered species under the protection of the federal government. The Pacific Northwest was already full, sorry, and it wasn't looking to double its population any time soon.

But it was also the home to several large, thriving tech firms, which between them controlled more of the political figures in the area than anyone had ever considered. Some of these men and women had been the ones to put us into our current predicament, continuing to throw their money into economically and environmentally unsound practices because it was cheaper than the alternatives. Who cared if a few newts died when their ponds dried up, if it meant that microchip manufacturing could be outsourced for just a little bit longer? Who cared if a few houses wound up literally underwater, if it meant they could keep paying fines instead of fixing problems?

And then, when they had to stop paying fines, when they had to start fixing problems, those same brave men and women turned their attention to getting rid of laws they didn't like. Why did owls need entire forests for themselves? Yes, it was important to preserve species diversity, but that land was needed by humans, who would do more with it than simply leave it untouched and growing wild. There were DNA banks now, there were zoos and private collections, there were a hundred ways to wipe a creature out of the natural world without losing it forever. It was cruel, yes, but it was also necessary. How could they leave so much green and verdant land unused, when so many people were wanting?

The environmentalists had lost the fight against industry and fossil of tea slowly cooling next to his hand. A small plastic tank rested on the table in front of him. Something moved inside. I squinted. Three large skink-like lizards were stacked atop each other like children's toys, their spade-shaped heads twitching from side to side as they watched for danger.

"Alligator lizards?" I asked.

"Northern alligator lizards," said Benet. He didn't open his eyes. "They don't like deserts. They do like streams and mud. No one's seen one in California for ten years. They went from Least Concern to Presumed Extinct in less than a decade."

Crap. "Where did you find them?"

"I flipped over a log looking for beetles, and there they were. They must have been eating the things I was supposed to save." He opened his eyes, fixing me with a look that was equal parts misery and despair. "I didn't know that they were here. I haven't been watching for them—no one has. Their habitat never extended this far up before. How are we supposed to save this ecosystem if we don't even know what's in it? We're going to fail."

"We've known that since day one," I said. He blinked, expression shifting toward betrayal, and I sighed. "There was no way we could save everything that needed to be saved. We'd need a country, not just a compound. The Arks will preserve, but they'll be incomplete. We know that. Maybe in three generations, the people working them will be able to pretend that they give an accurate look at what life was like before we clear-cut the planet. Maybe in six generations, we'll be planting again, and this will be the basis for an ecosystem all its own. But we're *going* to fail, if you define success as 'we saved everything.'" I shook my head. "Something has to burn. When the world catches fire, something has to burn."

"You're our resident little ray of sunshine, aren't you?" asked Kathy, walking in with a crate under her arm. She deposited it in the cryo freezer next to the door. Those poor turtles would never know what had hit them. "How went the owl search?"

"I finally found out where the last lady owl has been nesting during fuel and men who spoke in voices that dripped money. They had failed to stop climate change in its infancy, and failed again in its childhood, and now that it was an angry adult, slamming its fists into every country in the world, there was no stopping it. They looked upon this newest fight, and knew they couldn't win.

Still, they fought—*we* fought. We used every delaying tactic in the world, and a few more that we made up on the spot. They played dirty, and so we played dirty. And in the end, they had more money and fewer morals, and they won. They won everything.

Protection for endangered species and habitats wasn't as important as space for homes and cities and jobs. Commerce and trade were coming to the Pacific Northwest whether we wanted them or not, despite our protests that they had been here all along. State legislators looked at a sky that was black with crows and said, "The wildlife is doing fine without our help." They didn't see the complicated web of systems that set those crows in flight.

We argued. We bartered. We stalled.

We won. A small battle, not the war; a small victory, more of a sop to bleeding-heart environmentalists than anything real.

We got a year.

I reached base camp two hours after sunrise. My owl was long since asleep in her hole, waiting out the hours of daylight. Hunting nocturnal predators means late nights followed by long days: I'd go back around noon with a team, and we'd extract her from her nest, stuffing her into a carrier that was more than large enough for her needs, but that would seem too small to a creature who was used to having the entire sky beneath her wings. I wondered if owls were claustrophobic. I forced myself to stop just as quickly. It didn't matter—it couldn't matter—because we were running out of time.

Benet sat at one of the camp tables with his eyes closed and a mug the day; I'm going to grab the extraction team and go pry her out around noon," I said. The skin around Kathy's eyes tightened, her lips thinning as she pressed them together in an expression that was not a frown, not quite; she wasn't letting it get that far.

I had no such restraint. I frowned, eyeing her sidelong. "What's wrong?"

"Remember last week's report, where you confirmed removal of eight owls from the sectors you'd been assigned?"

"Uh-huh," I said, feeling my heart sink toward my toes.

"Some people think that's sufficient genetic diversity to preserve the species," she said. "Julie, I'm so sorry."

My heart sank further. "How much of my territory are they seizing early?"

She shook her head. That was enough of an answer, really, but I still wanted to hear her say it; I wanted to *know* how shortsighted the people who were supposedly in charge were going to be. So I waited, just looking at her, until she said, "They're taking the whole thing. They say that the construction crews are running ahead of schedule, and we've taken in so many refugees from Southern California—"

"Vultures, you mean," I said, breaking in. "They killed their state, and now they're coming for ours. This should be against the law."

"It was against the law, remember?" She didn't bother to conceal her bitterness. We were all among friends there. There had been some concern about spies initially, the environmental equivalent of industrial espionage, but we had all eventually realized that we didn't care. If they were getting their hands dirty with the rest of us, they could carry as many tales of angry, resentful environmentalists back to their bosses as they liked. It wasn't like anyone was going to be shocked by the depths of our anger. We were trying to save the remains of the natural world, and they were still lighting matches.

"Fine," I said. That didn't seem like enough, so I repeated it: "*Fine.* How long do we have? The insect teams have barely started their sweeps, and you know the remaining mammalian populations are migratory; we need to do a full underbrush check to make sure they're not in my territory."

"There isn't going to be time for that."

The world seemed to slow and crystallize. I heard Benet's chair scrape against the floor as he rose and moved to stand beside me, leaving his alligator lizards on the table. Kathy looked at me solemnly, and the pity in her eyes was one more match for the pyre that was being built, one fallen evergreen at a time, in the wasteland of my soul.

"How long?" I whispered.

"The construction crews will arrive to start the clear-cutting today at eleven," said Kathy. "I'm so, so sorry."

I stared at her for a moment. Then I whirled, turning to Benet and jabbing a finger at his chest. "Get on the com and call *everybody*. I don't care if they're ass-deep in pine martens; they get here *now*. We have four square miles to clear, and we have four hours to do it."

"We're not going to make it," said Benet, and he was right, and *I didn't care.*

"We'll get the owl, and we'll get whatever else we can find, and we'll save them, do you hear me? We're going to save them. Now move." I moved. So did he.

We had a world to save.

I grew up in northern California, at the foot of Mount Diablo, which teemed with tarantulas and rattlesnakes. It wasn't uncommon to look out the window in the early morning and see coyotes in the yard, moving like pale ghosts through the fog. I was lucky. I was born in the last of the good decades, when it still rained, when the puddles still iced over in the winter months. Maybe I never saw snow on the ground, but I knew the sound of my feet crunching through frozen grass, and I knew all the cycles and seasons of the natural world.

I know the exact day the frogs stopped singing for the last time in the dry creekbed that ran behind my childhood home. I could remember the hour and minute, quote it like scripture. It had been years since I'd actually seen a bullfrog by that point, and I was a grad student in environmental science, marching in climate awareness parades on the weekends, writing impassioned op-eds about recycling and ecological sustainability. I preached the gospel of the carrier bag and the compost heap, and it all amounted to nothing, because the rain stopped, and the frogs stopped, and one night the mountain burned and swallowed my parents and the house where I'd grown up in a single brilliant gulp. They were killed by climate change, even if no murder charges were ever going to be brought against a human agency.

We'd known by then that our last stand would be the Pacific Northwest. It was mountainous enough that the change in sea level wasn't projected to be completely disastrous for human life. All we had to do was keep human life from being completely disastrous for everything else. And we had failed. Maybe we'd been doomed to fail from the very beginning. It was honestly hard to know one way or the other, and the burning was upon us.

Our camp was one of fifteen scattered through the Olympic Peninsula. Two hundred and fifty people were distributed between them, each fighting the same hopeless fight. Some of those people were fighting it for good reasons and some were fighting it for bad ones, and in the end, it didn't matter. You don't question the motives of the firebreak. You're just grateful when it gives you a little bit longer before you go up in flames.

Benet was by my side as I plunged back into the forest, a carrier in my arms and a pair of falconer's gloves clipped to my waist. The people who had decided my time was up only looked at numbers. They had a bunch of columns on a page that said "owls normally nest in pairs" and "an even number of owls has been extracted from this territory." They had paid biologists who would look at the samples we'd sent in and claim that we'd preserved sufficient genetic diversity, even if we hadn't, because bringing back the owls was a problem for another time, another generation—another world. We were up against people who had shown time and again that they were happy to destroy whatever they needed to in order to line their own pockets just a little more. They were always "saving for a rainy day."

Well, the world was out of rainy days, and still those assholes kept on saving, while we were out here in the trenches, saving everything that really mattered. We deserved what we'd brought down on our heads. Humanity was the architect of its own destruction—and I don't give a shit if that sounds callous. There were the ones who lied and the ones who died, and we made this mess for ourselves. The frogs didn't. The beetles and the turtles and the lizards didn't. And right now, most of all, the owls didn't. We deserved damnation. They deserved a second chance.

The remains of a large fallen tree—now just trunk and major bearing branches—lay off to one side of our makeshift path, decaying gently back into the forest floor. Benet shot it a longing look. I smiled, just a little. Just enough to let him know I understood.

"Grab three people and take it apart," I said. "There's no telling what you'll find."

"I can see three species of moss, two lichens, and signs of burrower beetles," he said. "We're going to find a *world*." Then he was gone, waving for the nearest members of the team to join him as he dropped to his knees next to the log and started digging.

The rest of us kept moving, although I knew full well that this was a scenario that would be playing out over and over again now that I had given permission for it to happen once. We each had our own areas of focus and obsession, scattered across the natural world like Legos on a bedroom floor at midnight. If we stepped on one of them—a fallen log, a frog calling from a hidden stream, even a rare or threatened mushroom— we would have to stop and deal with the pain, because there just wasn't another option. All of us were what we were. We had to save what we could. Otherwise, there'd be nothing to distinguish us from the ones who'd sent us there, scrambling to put our toys away before the house went up in flames.

The trees were dense there, barely touched by human hands. I'd always come through carefully before, picking my way between the saplings, doing as little damage as I could. It was an old, useless habit; I could have cut each tree down and thrown it away as soon as I was sure it didn't contain something worth saving. But the part of my soul that had been involved in conservation since I was in my teens chafed at the idea that anything *wasn't* worth saving; that we couldn't find a way to somehow remove every tree from this soil and carry it away to a place where it could keep on growing, safe and sheltered in the welcoming earth. I had listened to that part of my soul. I shouldn't have, because now I was crashing through the forest like an intruder, and the forest was responding by crashing back.

My owl's tree was just ahead. I shoved a branch out of my way, hearing the crack as it was bent too far, and took a hasty count of my remaining assistants. There were only six of them, and only one was someone I recognized as working with birds, although his specialization was in corvids, not owls. "I'm heading up," I shouted, indicating the tree. "You start searching down here, look for anything else that needs extraction."

"What if you fall?" asked one of the women. I didn't recognize her.

"Then I fall," I said. There was no time to set up a proper rig; I pulled the climbing clamps from my belt, jammed them into the tree, and started my ascent.

The higher I got, the more I understood what we were about to lose. Mount Rainier gleamed in the far distance, Grandfather coming out from behind the increasingly uncommon clouds to watch solemnly as we stripped the world around him. Everywhere I looked, there were trees. Sometimes they surrounded islands of steel and glass, or were split by the black ribbons of the highway system, but they were alive, and they were there, and they deserved this land as much as we did. Maybe more.

I pulled myself higher, feeling the clamps flex beneath my hands as the servos adjusted, recalibrated, and locked in. They were designed to handle my weight plus or minus forty pounds—more than that and

I would have needed a second set of hands to safely make the descent. There's not an owl in this world that weighs that much, thankfully.

Every inch of my ascent brought another strip of forest into view, until finally I could see where it ended. The land there had already been clear-cut and prepared for development, centuries of growth stripped away in favor of concrete foundations and—eventually—perfectly manicured, perfectly controlled little lawns, one strip to a home, so that people could pretend that they hadn't destroyed the natural world for their own benefit. Some of them would plant wildflowers that used to grow there naturally. I was sure of it. They'd fill their tiny yards with color and pat themselves on the back when bees or butterflies appeared, pretending that those sightings weren't rarer than they used to be, pretending that they'd never done anything wrong.

And in a generation, when their kids had grown up thinking "the great outdoors" meant a paved cul-de-sac and a few sad cabbage butterflies, all those mistakes and misdemeanors would be forgotten, swept under the rug of history and never discussed in polite company. The Arks would be up and running by then. It would be easy to say "oh, it's better like this" and "oh, they would never have survived in the wild." There would be the gene banks to fall back on once the live displays were out of favor—and they would be. Zoos had been viewed as the best form of conservation once, and look where that ended.

I wasn't saving these animals. I was buying them a stay of execution; that was all. They would die in cages, never seeing the open sky or feeling the warm, welcoming soil beneath their claws. I was turning them into artifacts, and they'd never been given a choice in the matter. Even now, it wasn't like we were *asking* them whether they wanted to be saved, when "safe" meant captive and confined. We'd taken gene samples from every individual we could find. We could have released them back into the world, letting them die with the habitats that had sustained them for so long. Was it mercy or arrogance that led us to stay our hands and keep them caged? Did we have the right?

The owl's hole loomed dark in the trunk above me. It was a good location, sheltered from the wind and rain, sufficiently concealed by the nearby branches that no competing predators were likely to find it by mistake. I wondered what had happened to her mate. She was a mature female with a good nesting place, and we hadn't caught a solo male in this territory; she had been widowed somehow, probably by human hands, and now I was coming to take away her freedom.

But I had to. I had to, or she was going to die. I could see the wood's edge from where I hung suspended against the tree, see the great construction equipment rolling into place, ready to begin the burn. There was no future there.

Pulling on the falconer's gloves, I eased myself closer to the hole, until I could see the silent lump of feathers that was my owl. She might be awake by now: I hadn't been silent in my ascent, and birds of prey have excellent hearing. She wasn't fleeing because I had blocked the exit, and because sometimes, stillness was the best defense something like her could have.

It wasn't going to save her this time. I plunged my hands into the darkness, seizing the owl and pulling her out into the light.

She fought. She flapped and struggled and screamed her indignation into the air, glaring at me with her bright black eyes, gnashing her beak as she fought to reach me. When she cried, it was like her entire face opened, blossoming into a flower formed from terrible anger and betrayal. She screamed. I struggled to hold her, gathering her as close as I dared before switching my grip to let me open the carrier. I was careless. That was the only explanation. I was careless, and I was conflicted, and I took my eyes off the owl for a heartbeat.

That was long enough.

When she moved, it was like a storm: swift and unforgiving and inescapable. Her beak sliced into the flesh above my collarbone, opening it wide. It happened so fast that for a moment, there was no pain. There was only the shock of beak against bone, and the red smell of blood mixing with the green smell of the trees.

My clamps were designed to keep me from falling, but they couldn't do much when they were disengaged. I fell. Twisting hard against the pain in my chest, I managed to wrap the clamps around a branch and hit the switch to auto-engage. They pulled me up hard, knocking the wind out of my lungs and leaving me dangling, helpless, as the owl I'd come to save took flight and winged away into the forest, white wings against black branches and blue, blue sky.

"Dammit," I whispered—but maybe it was better this way. Maybe some things were never meant to be caged, nevermore to see the land to which they'd been born. The owl flew, and I hung suspended, granting myself a moment before I disengaged the clamps and went back to fighting to hold the fire back for just those few precious moments longer.

All we could do was save what little we could put our hands on, and remember the things we had to leave behind. We owed the world we had destroyed that, at least. We owed it so much more.

Maybe someday, our children would see owls in the world again.

ABOUT THE AUTHOR

SEANAN MCGUIRE was born and raised in Northern California, resulting in a love of rattlesnakes and an absolute terror of weather. She shares a crumbling old farmhouse with a variety of cats, far too many books, and enough horror movies to be considered a problem. Seanan publishes about three books a year, and is widely rumored not to actually sleep. When bored, Seanan tends to wander into swamps and cornfields, which has not yet managed to get her killed (although not for lack of trying). She also writes as Mira Grant, filling the role of her own evil twin, and tends to talk about horrible diseases at the dinner table.

OUTER RIMS

TOIYA KRISTEN FINLEY

out'er rims, *n.* *1*. areas of continents flooded in 2014 by rising sea levels due to climate change; the resulting regions.

Why she brought the kids one last time would be the question always troubling her, never finding its reasonable answer. She told herself she wanted them to see the shore before the world changed again. After all, no one regretted last chances unless they weren't taken. Six years earlier, she'd thought of visiting NYC, the bistro where she met her husband, to honor his memory. But she fussed over the budget. Her last chance passed her by, after half of New York City had eventually been submerged by the encroaching Atlantic.

She wouldn't rob her children of one last stay at the place they spent summers with their father. Branden and Shannon were more excited about the world changing than losing the shoreline. *Where will the land be next year? One day, the whole world'll be underwater!* they said, but they could imagine such things because they would be far from there when the storm's eye came roaring up from the gulf.

Shannon's head lolled against the door crushing her afro puffs, and her neck bent down on her shoulder. Yet she could sleep anywhere at any time, even during the biggest move of her life, and dozed in the back. Branden popped gum in the front passenger seat. He leaned his chin on his sharp knee and looked out the window at the highway. Normally, she would tell him to keep his shoes off the seat, but he was relaxed when he talked about things she thought should unnerve an eleven-year-old boy.

"Where's everybody gonna live?"

"Good question. Maybe they'll stay with family or friends like us before they find their own place."

"Everything's gonna get crowded real fast," he said. "The country keeps getting smaller and smaller. One day, there won't be room left."

"Well, when that time comes, maybe we'll live on the moon," she said.

He twirled the bubble gum around his tongue and smiled and went back to the view outside. "All those trees'll be gone." No sadness. No longing. Just a fact.

They were minutes away from the shore when she saw a figure laboring with a sedan on the shoulder of the road. The car slowed and she pulled over. Branden spun away from the window. Under those long, straight lashes, his eyes bulged with disbelief. "But he's a stranger!"

She violated every rule she'd given her children about people they didn't know. "He's having car trouble. I'm sure he's trying to get out of here, too."

She lowered the front passenger's window. Branden slinked down in the seat. "You need help?"

A young man emerged from under the hood. In the humidity and car's heat, sweat sealed his hair to his forehead. Trees shadowed him, but the redness around his pupils made the blue look like marbles protruding from his eyes. He glanced away from her and down the road, as if he couldn't believe she'd pulled over, either. "There's a parts place off exit six. If you could take me, I'd be much obliged."

Branden pouted and rolled up the window.

"Act right," she said.

"Ma'am, I really, really appreciate this," the young man said from the backseat. "Especially with the flooding coming."

"Where you headed?" she said.

"I don't know. Midwest somewhere, I guess. I'm tired of hangin' around the outer rims. Who knows when the next bad storm's comin'."

"I heard that." Her son wouldn't stop staring at the young man. "Turn around, Branden," she said under her breath.

In the rearview mirror, the young man closed his eyes. He leaned back and angled his face toward the roof, maybe to pray. With eyes wide, his lips parted.

"Mom," Branden said, "he's shivering."

The young man complained of a headache. He scratched his chest until his arms weakened and fell at his sides. But the guilt hadn't come to her yet. She'd take him to a hospital. If she hadn't picked him up, he'd be lying on the side of the highway. The worst that could happen, he'd be admitted; they'd make sure he was evacuated as a patient. But he could be discharged before then. It could be simple heat exhaustion. He'd walk out of the ER in a few hours and be on his way.

Guilt didn't catch up with her until she saw the white tent in the hospital parking lot and the officers directing traffic. A policeman wearing a surgical mask stopped her. He grabbed his walkie-talkie when he saw the young man in the back.

"Can I get you to park over here, ma'am?" Park away from the ER, where doctors in blue suits and large square hoods waited with pens and clipboards.

She nodded at the policeman. Her son sat up. He put his feet on the floor. "I'm sorry," she said.

2. an area at the edges of a greater part or whole: He banished the thought to the outer rims of his mind.

This woman beyond Cantor's hood respirator did her best to force a polite smile. She rubbed her left thumb with the cracked nail of her right index finger. A bit of dirt clung to the cuticle. Dr. Cantor would rather have a child sitting in front of her, or at least a teenager. She could tell them she was a disease detective who got to wear moon gear, watch them grin or giggle in respect, and downplay the impending rage of water and sickness. But this was her first time wearing the level-4 suit. This woman, with her teeth set firmly against her lips, felt the threat of the hood and the mask.

Cantor felt pushed to find any hint or clue before these people were forced to evacuate, mixing with another population. And already the disease was spreading. This illness that looked like malaria and blossomed in the warm climate. This illness with seemingly airborne transmission and no mosquito bites. The woman in front of her tried to keep her stare on the table, but she'd glance at Cantor's rubber gloves. Crease her eyebrows at the hood and respirator protecting Cantor from the air she breathed.

She thought of all the ways she could make this woman less uneasy, help her drop her guard in this atmosphere. Make her more relaxed so they'd have some flow to the conversation, a greater chance to suss out an answer in an insignificant detail she wouldn't share otherwise. The only way she could consider them connecting was as black women with so few of them living here now. But they weren't sisters talking over coffee. From the stiffness in her shoulders and the frantic tapping of her heel to the floor, the woman made it clear that Cantor was not on her side.

"I'm . . . sorry we've made you wait," Dr. Cantor said. "Lots going on." The left corner of her mouth crinkled up, but she didn't know if the woman could see it.

"It hasn't been a fun few hours, I'll admit." She leaned in and raised her eyebrows with her voice. Cocked her chin.

"It's all right. I can hear you fine." It was Cantor who sounded hollow.

The woman leaned back, but her shoulders were still stiff.

Cantor glanced over the pages on the clipboard. "Ms. Burrell, you're from Portland, Tennessee, correct?"

"Yes. We're planning to go up to Ohio."

Cantor grinned like a fool. Burrell's eyelashes fluttered and her eyebrows frowned.

"My aunt lived in Clarksville," Cantor said. "I don't run into many people from the area. I used to spend summers there. My mom put me and my brothers on the 9-Rail."

"9-Rail?" Burrell shook her head. She managed her first real smile. Of fondness. "Haven't thought about the 9-Rail since it went underwater."

"Yeah. Guess you can tell I haven't been home in years."

"Where was home?"

"Alabama. Mobile," Cantor said. "Yeah . . . Went to school in Milwaukee and decided to stay. But Clarksville, I don't think I've been there in fifteen years."

"You wouldn't recognize it. It turned into a real city almost overnight."

Cantor laughed. "Man, I loved my aunt, but being trapped in that podunk town?" Burrell laughed with her.

"I'll miss it," Burrell said.

And Cantor composed herself. "Where'd you meet Don Jackson?"

"Is he . . . ?"

"He has a very high fever."

Burrell unclasped her hands and pushed herself forward. "We were on our way back from the shore. His car broke down. I just wanted to help him out, especially with everything going down. I didn't want him to get stuck or worse."

"When did you notice he was sick?"

She shrugged. She looked down, grinded her lips together like she was having a conversation with herself. "He was working under the hood, you know? And it was hot. He was sweating, and his face was red, but . . . I don't know. He was in the car maybe ten minutes? He seemed really tired."

"Did he tell you how he was feeling?"

"He said he felt really hot and he was getting a headache. He really couldn't say much."

"And how are you feeling?"

"Fine, considering. Can you tell me anything? When can I get my kids out of here?"

The clipboard fell against the desk. Cantor couldn't look at her head-on. Her eyes darted back and forth, back and forth, seeking the response that would give Burrell some comfort knowing she and her children would be okay. Burrell stared, demanded an answer from her. "I understand how difficult the circumstances are, but you'll have to stay for observation." And that was the most Cantor would force herself to say. She wouldn't let this woman know that her good deed could leave her whole family dead in a day.

Only Dr. Alagiah was in the makeshift lab. When the disease first manifested malaria symptoms, he'd kept his team optimistic. But as it proved itself to be contagious, the lab became haunted. A place they wished they could avoid. A place for work in silence as the weather reports hung over their heads.

Dr. Alagiah's expressions, even behind the protective hood, were clear. "We've received . . . We need to . . ." He dropped his head.

"Dr. Alagiah?" Cantor said.

He closed his eyes. "We got word we're to pack."

When his eyes opened, Cantor found the filtering around her face insufficient. She choked on the fresh air. "We have no idea—"

"We don't get more time. This didn't come from the CDC."

"We're going to *abandon* them?"

Dr. Alagiah cupped her left elbow in his palm. His arm stayed steady, but the rest of him shook. "They're hoping . . . it'll be the end of the disease. It's spreading too quickly in this heat—"

"With everybody evacuating, they're assuming everyone who's infected is here . . . or dead already."

He was still shaking. "But we'll have more time after the storms."

She threw the clipboard to the asphalt.

* * * *

Already, the exposed had been pushed deeper into the hospital. Precautionary measures, they'd been told, to protect non-infected patients. No windows here. A vast, cavernous waiting area with the TVs turned off. To conserve power, they were told, in case there were difficulties during the evacuation.

Cantor and her colleagues collected some samples to take with them. Maybe the blood would reveal answers after the flood, once the disease had been drowned in this outer rim. And the CDC would have a point of attack should it rise again and make its way north. These people were helpful, all things considered. They'd laugh at themselves for being afraid of the needle or picking the worst time to be stuck in a hospital. But when they looked at Cantor, she could feel them screaming, *Please, please let me go now. I'm not sick.*

And at what point would they realize no one would come for them? The doctors and nurses would no longer check on them. The disease detectives would be gone, too. What then? As they realized they'd be left to go under?

Her colleagues didn't make eye contact as they worked as quickly and methodically as they could. They sweated behind their hoods. They said as little as possible. Cantor began to entertain a thought pricking her conscience—*what will happen will happen.* She could ignore it at first. Kept it at bay with rationalizations about her job and the nature of the disease. But these people . . . She saw the moment when they realized they were alone. When they freed themselves from this room, but all transportation was gone. When the tidal waves rose up to devour them. Worst-case scenario, she told herself, she at least tried to do something. She wondered if she were being selfish, but she didn't let that bother her for long.

Her daughter draped across her knee asleep and her son sitting next to her vacant-eyed and kicking the wall beneath his chair, she watched Cantor approach her with detached weariness.

"Ms. Burrell, may I speak with you alone?"

* * * *

3. OUTCASTS; forgotten or unseen persons.

Did he ask about them? He'd meant to. But he couldn't remember. Now he was sure he was awake, because he wasn't shaking like this a minute ago. He came in and out, in and out, until being asleep was like consciousness. Then he'd open his eyes and find he'd been to another world and just returned to this bed. When the pain from the headache let him turn his head, he saw all the people in the room like him, stuck in hospital beds, infected with the same damn thing. But they'd multiplied. There was more sobbing. More vomiting. Did he ask about them? Did he find out if they were okay? She had been so kind to give him a lift. Were they still here? Did they get away from the storm, or had the storm passed? The CDC people, he didn't see any now. They were never not around, giving him their "Don, how're you doing?" even in his sleep. Perhaps he'd asked one of them about that family in his dreams. He would ask now if he could find anyone. At one point, when he could recall being awake, the CDC angels swarmed the room. Their bulbous heads peered into him. Their vacuum-hose wings swooshed even when they stood still. They poked him with their plastic blue skin, asked him lots of questions. He didn't remember a mosquito bite. He didn't feel any, anyway. He was thankful for that. Mosquito-bite itches drove him crazy, and his arms were jelly now. He wondered if some other insect had done this. Mites seemed to be running up and down his arms, his legs, his chest, under his skin when he was in the backseat. And the little boy was angry with him for getting in the car. They were on their way out of that place, and then he came along with his bugs. Did the insects jump off him and onto that little girl? To their mother? To the boy? A woman whimpered and moaned across the room. He listened to his own bed twitch as his limbs rumbled and threatened to snap at the elbows and knees. He wished they would. Then he couldn't feel them anymore. He wanted to apologize. He really should apologize. He killed them. The blues said the family was still here. They were being checked on and poked up, too. If he didn't make them sick, he'd forced the storm on them. Perhaps this was the storm raging in his bones. Like old people used to say they could tell a storm was coming by the creakiness in their joints. He wished it would hurry. He waited for the waters. In this bed he was alone. But if he was going to die, he wanted the sea to pick him up and carry him out where he could drown with everyone else.

4. ANATHEMA; the accursed. [2014-15]

He pushed his sister's head off his shoulder. She slapped his arm. Her eyes were still closed. "Quit it."

"You're hot," he said.

"I'm not, Branden," she said.

"You're heavy."

Mom talked with adults in the chairs near the corner. Three men and a woman. They were strangers. He didn't understand why she trusted them all of a sudden.

"When we leaving?" his sister asked. She put her elbow on the armrest and used her hand for a pillow.

"Be right back, Shannon."

Mom and the adults shook and nodded their heads at each other. All talked at the same time. Their arms swirled and chopped at the air. Their fingers pointed to interrupt.

". . . if we're sick? We get outta here We'll just make everybody sick and spread it—"

"But there's no reason to know that we are. We won't make it if we don't leave—"

"Go to the media. There's got to be a reporter following a storm here."

"You're crazy," Mom said. "I'm sure they're outside somewhere, on high ground."

"Why'd you tell us if you don't expect us to do anything?"

"I'm confused about the options," Mom said.

"Only one option we—"

"Mom?"

A shock spread through all five of them. Like the worst secret in the world got told and everybody was gonna get in trouble for it. They were scared. Adults. In a panic.

Mom jumped from her seat and grabbed his hand. "I need you to go wait with Shannon." Her eyes were shiny. The little lines around her mouth got deeper.

"Is that man dead?"

"I don't know."

"Are we sick?"

She didn't say anything for a moment. "I don't know."

Branden tried to free his hand from hers. She shuddered and let him go. "Please, just wait with your sister. Don't tell her. Don't tell anybody."

His chest itched. The itch crawled all over his stomach and his arms. He scratched, but he knew it wouldn't go away. Whatever that man had, whatever those weird doctors asked him about, he had it, too. He wanted to get away from here. But did he want to give the rest of the world *this*? It jumped onto him from that man. And it would jump from him to person to person to person until everybody on the planet died.

"You know you're not supposed to be in grown-ups' business," Shannon said.

"Stay away from me!" he said.

Shannon rolled her eyes. She crossed her arms and looked at Mom.

"I'm sorry," Branden said. He sat next to Shannon, but he pulled his arms and legs close to his body.

All the adults came together. Branden watched them get angry and sad. Some of them cried. They hugged. Then they tore pieces of paper and handed them around. They all wrote on the bits of paper and handed them to an old Latino man. They talked some more, and the next thing Branden knew, Mom got him and Shannon and told them to stay with the other kids no matter what.

The quiet boredom in the room was gone. Branden immediately wanted it back. The men picked up couches. They ran towards the exits with them and rammed them into the doors. Shannon wrapped her arms around Branden's neck. Kids cried for their parents. They huddled into each other and screamed with each *bang*. Adults shouted directions at each other. They told their children to stop yelling because everything was going to be okay.

Hot breath and tears slid under his collar. Hair got in his mouth as kids held onto him and rubbed their faces on his shirt. The sickness hopped from person to person, and it wouldn't matter if they got out of the building or not, if they got away from the storm. Mom watched them bust the doors open. She rubbed her chin when the chains fell, staring out with that same look she had when the man in the backseat started to shiver.

The adults grabbed tables and chairs and pounded through the doors. They pulled their kids from the pack crying in the corner and threw them over their shoulders or ran so hard, they dragged them across the floor.

"Mom!" Shannon said.

She turned to them and frowned. "Hurry! Stay with me."

Outside the waiting room, furniture crashed through windows. The hallways burst in shards. Mom pressed Branden and Shannon to her sides, hunched over them and kept them near the back of the group. "Shouldn't have told them. Shouldn't have told them," she said to herself.

Parents pushed their kids through the windows. But their clothes and skin snagged on the glass. Some pounded on the walls until the walls turned red. "Don't look don't look don't look don't look!" Mom said, and they fell to their knees at the sound of heavy boots.

"Don't make me go through the window!" Shannon screamed, and she cried.

Men with thudding voices yelled in the halls. They said they'd shoot. They said to get down. They said to move back in the room, and Branden heard their fists hit cheeks and chins.

"Were they gonna shoot us anyway?" he said.

"Just get down," Mom said. "Just stay here."

"*Were they?*" Branden said.

"I don't know."

"We're not sick. They have to let us go," Shannon said. "Make them, Mom."

"We *are* sick. We're gonna kill people. But I don't wanna stay. Should we stay?"

"Mom—" Shannon said, but Mom was staring down the hall at the men with guns. She mouthed something to herself. Her lips moved faster than the words could make sense.

She pressed them to the floor. Then she bowed her head, too. With his eyes tight to the floor, not seeing anything, he heard Mom say, "I thought it was important; that's all. You didn't need to see it. *We* wouldn't have changed. . . . We make it out of here, you take care of you. Can't be any other way."

He thought the adults had figured it out. He thought Mom told them what they should do. He wanted her to say, *We're sick, but we can still live.* But he lied to himself. He wondered why *you take care of you* couldn't keep her from giving that man a ride.

Branden shivered again. He wasn't sure if the sickness made him do it, or Mom's fear rubbing up against him. But the cold and wet tickled his scalp, and he knew it was the wind bringing the rain through the broken windows.

ABOUT THE AUTHOR

Nashville native TOIYA KRISTEN FINLEY is a writer, editor, game designer, and narrative designer/game writer. Her fiction has been published in *Nature, Fantasy Magazine, Daily Science Fiction, The Best of Electric Velocipede,* and *The Year's Best Science Fiction & Fantasy, 2010.* She is the Founding and former Managing/Fiction Editor of Harpur Palate and a Co-Founder and instructor at GDC Online's Game Writing Tutorial. Her work in games includes *Academagia: The Making of Mages* and its DLC, *Fat Chicken,* and a list of unannounced/suspended-production social-network RPGs and mobile games whose existence shall remain forever a secret (hey, that's the game industry for ya). *The Game Narrative Toolbox* (Focal Press), a book on narrative design she's co-authored with Jennifer Brandes Hepler, Ann Lemay, and Tobias Heussner was published in 2015.

KHELDYU

KARL SCHROEDER

The truck crested a hill and Gennady got his first good look at the Khantayskoe test site. He ground to a stop and sat there for a long time.

Spreading before him were thirty square kilometers of unpopulated Siberian forest. Vast pine-carpeted slopes ran up and up into impossible distance to either side, yet laid over the forest of the south-facing rise was a gleaming circle six kilometers in diameter. It was slightly crinkly, like a giant cellophane disk or parachute that had been dropped there by a passing giant. Its edges had been perfectly sharp in the photos Gennady had seen, but they were ragged in real life. That circle was just a vast roof of plastic sheeting, after all, great sections of which had fallen in the past several winters. Enough remained to turn the slope into a glittering bull's-eye of reflecting sheets and fluttering, tattered banners of plastic.

Underneath that ceiling, the dark, low forest was a subdued shade of gray. That gray was why Gennady was now putting on a surgical mask.

Standing up out of the top quarter of the circle was a round, flat-topped tower, like a smokestack for some invisible morlock factory. The thing was over a kilometer tall, and wisps of cloud wreathed its top.

He put the truck into gear and bumped his way toward the tumbled edges of the greenhouse. There was no trick to roofing over a whole forest, at least around there; few of the gnarled pines were more than thirty feet tall. Little grew between them, the long sight lines making the northern arboreal forest a kind of wall-less maze. Here, the trees made a perfect filter, slowing the air that came in around the open edges of the greenhouse and letting it warm slowly as it converged on that distant tower.

"There's just one tiny problem," Achille Marceau had told Gennady when they'd talked about the job, "which is why we need you. The airflow stopped when we shut down the wind turbines at the base of the solar updraft tower. It got hot and dry under the greenhouse, and with the drought—well, you know."

The tenuous road wove between tree trunks and under the torn translucent roof whose surface wavered like an inverted lake. For the first hundred meters or so, everything was okay. The trees were still alive. But then he began passing more and more orange and brown ones, and the track became obscured by deepening drifts of pine needles.

Then these began to disappear under a fog of grayish-white fungus.

He'd been prepared for this sight, but Gennady still stopped the truck to do some swearing. The trees were draped in what looked like the fake cobwebs kids hung over everything for American Halloween. Great swathes of the stuff cocooned whole trunks and stretched between them like long, sickening flags. He glanced back and saw that an ominous white cloud was beginning to curl around the truck—billions of spores kicked up by his wheels.

He gunned the engine to get ahead of the spore clouds, and that was when he finally noticed the other tracks.

Two parallel ruts ran through the white snow-like stuff, outlining the road ahead quite clearly. They looked fresh and would have been made by a vehicle about the same size as his.

Marceau had insisted that Gennady would be the first person to visit the solar updraft plant in five years.

The slope was just steep enough that the road couldn't run straight up the hillside but zigzagged, so it took Gennady a good twenty minutes to make it to the tower. He was sweating and uncomfortable by the time he finally pulled the rig into the gravel parking area under the solar uplift tower. The other vehicle wasn't here, and its tracks had disappeared on the mold-free gravel. Maybe it had gone around the long curve of the tower.

He drove that way himself. He was supposed to be inspecting the tower's base for cracks, but his eyes kept straying, looking for a sign that somebody else was here. If they were, they were well hidden.

When he got back to the main lot, he rummaged in the glove compartment and came up with a flare gun. Wouldn't do any good as a weapon, but from a distance, it might fool somebody. He slipped it into the pocket of his nylon jacket and climbed out to retrieve a portable generator from the bed of the truck.

Achille Marceau wanted to replace 4 percent of the world's coal-powered generating plants with solar updraft towers. With no fuel requirements at all, these towers would produce electricity while simultaneously removing CO_2 from the air. All together they'd suck a gigaton of carbon out of the atmosphere every year. Ignoring the electricity sales, at today's prices the carbon sales alone would be worth forty billion dollars a year. That was twenty-four million per year from that tower alone.

Marceau had built this tower to prove the plan by producing electricity for northern China while simultaneously pulling down carbon and sequestering it underground. It was a brilliant plan, but he'd found himself underbid in the cutthroat post-carbon-bubble economy, and he couldn't make ends meet on the electricity sales alone. He'd had to shut down.

Now he was back—literally, a few kilometers back, waiting for his hazardous-materials lackey to open the tower and give the rest of the trucks the all-clear signal.

The plastic ceiling got higher the closer you got to the tower, and now it was a good sixty meters overhead. Under it, vast round windows broke the curve of the wall; they were closed by what looked like steel venetian blinds. Some portable trailers huddled between two of the giant circles, but these were for management. Gennady trudged past them without a glance and climbed a set of metal steps to a steel door labeled Небезпеки—"HAZARD," but written in Ukrainian, not Russian. Marceau's key let him in, and the door didn't even squeak, which was encouraging.

Before he stepped through, Gennady paused and looked back at the shrouded forest. It was eerily quiet, with no breeze to make the dead trees speak.

Well, he would change that.

The door opened into a kind of airlock; he could hear wind whistling around the edges of the inner portal. He closed the outer one and opened the inner, and was greeted by gray light and a sense of vast emptiness. Gennady stepped into the hollow core of the tower.

The ground was just bare red stone covered with construction litter. A few heavy lifters and cranes dotted the stadium-sized circle. Here there was sound—a discordant whistling from overhead. Faint light filtered down.

He spent a long hour inspecting the tower's foundations from the inside, then carried the little generator to the bottom of another flight of metal steps. These zigzagged up the concrete wall. About thirty meters up, a ring of metal beams held a wide gallery that encircled the tower, and more portable trailers had been placed on that. The stairs went on past them into a zone of shifting silvery light. The stuff up there would need attending to, but not just yet.

Hauling the generator up to the first level took him ten minutes; halfway up, he took off the surgical mask, and he was panting when he finally reached the top. He caught his breath and then shouted, "Hello?" Nobody answered; if there was another visitor here, they were either hiding or very far away across—or up—the tower.

The windows of the dust-covered control trailer were unbroken. The door was locked. He used the next key on that but didn't go in. Instead, he set up the portable generator and connected it to the mains. But now he was in his element and was humming as he pulled the generator's cord.

While it rattled and roared, he took another cautious look around, then went left along the gallery. The portable trailer sat next to one of the huge round apertures that perforated the base of the tower. Seated into this circle was the biggest wind turbine he'd ever seen. The gallery was right at the level of its axle and generator, so he was able to inspect it without having to climb anything. When Marceau's men mothballed it five years ago, they'd wrapped everything vulnerable in plastic and taped it up. Consequently, the turbine's systems were in surprisingly good shape. Once he'd pitched the plastic sheeting over the gallery rail, he only had to punch the red button at the back of the trailer, and somewhere below, an electric motor strained to use all the power from his little generator. Lines of daylight began to separate the imposing venetian blinds. With them came a quickening breeze.

"Put your hands up!"

Gennady reflexively put his hands in the air, but then he had to laugh.

"What are you laughing at?"

"Sorry. Is just that last time I put my hands up like this was for a woman also. Kazakhstan, last summer."

There was a pause. Then: "Gennady?"

He looked over his shoulder and recognized the face behind the pistol. "Nadine, does your brother know you're here?"

Nadine Marceau tilted her head to one side and shifted her stance to a hipshot, exasperated pose as she lowered the pistol. "What the hell, Gennady. I could ask you the same question."

With vast dignity, he lowered his hands and turned around. "I," he said, "am working. You, on the other hand, are trespassing."

She gaped at him. "You're *working*? For *that* bastard?"

So, then it wasn't just a rumor that Achille and Nadine Marceau hated each other. Gennady shrugged; it wasn't his business. "Cushy jobs for the IAEA are hard to come by, Nadine; you know that. I'm a freelancer, I have to get by."

"Yeah, but—" She was looking down, fumbling with her holster, as widening light unveiled behind her the industrial underworld of the solar uplift tower. Warm outside air was pouring in through the opening shutters now, and, slowly, the giant vanes of the windmill fixed in its round window began to turn.

Nadine cursed. "You've started it! Gennady, I thought you had more integrity! I never thought you'd end up being part of the problem."

"Part of the problem? God, Nadine, is just a windmill."

"No, it's not—" He'd turned to admire the turning blades but, looking back, saw that she had frozen in a listening posture. "Shit!"

"Don't tell him I'm here!" she shouted as she turned and started running along the gallery. "Not a word, Gennady. You hear?"

Nadine Marceau, UN arms inspector and disowned child of one of the wealthiest families in Europe, disappeared into the shadows. Gennady could hear the approaching trucks himself now; still, he spread his hands and shouted, "Don't you even want a cup of coffee?"

The metal venetian blinds clicked into their fully open configuration, and now enough outside light was coming in to reveal the cyclopean vastness of the tower's interior. Gennady looked up at the little circle of sky a kilometer and a half overhead and shook his head ruefully. "It's not even radioactive."

Why was Nadine here? Some vendetta with her brother, no doubt, though Gennady preferred to think it was work-related. The last time he'd seen her was in Azerbaijan, two years ago; that time, they'd been working together to find some stolen nukes. A nightmare job but totally in line with both their professional backgrounds. This place, though, it was just an elaborate windmill. It couldn't explode or melt down or spill oil all over the sensitive arboreal landscape. No, this had to be a family thing.

There were little windows in the reinforced concrete wall. Through one of these he could see three big trucks, mirror to his own, approaching the tower. Nadine's brother Achille had gotten impatient, apparently. He must have seen the blinds opening, and the first of the twenty wind turbines that ringed the tower's base starting to move. A legendary micro-manager, he just couldn't stay away.

By the time the boss clambered out of the second truck, unsteady in his bright-red hazmat suit, Gennady had opened the office trailer, started a HEPA filter whirring, and booted up the tower's control system. He leaned in the trailer's doorway and watched as first two bodyguards, then Marceau himself, then his three engineers, reached the top of the stairs.

"Come inside," Gennady said. "You can take that off."

The hazmat suit waved its arms and made a garbled sound that Gennady eventually translated as "You're not wearing your mask."

"Ah, no. Too hard to work in. But that's why you hired me, Mr. Marceau. To take your chances."

"Call me Achille! Everybody else does." The hazmat suit made a lunging motion; Gennady realized that Nadine's brother was trying to clap him on the shoulder. He pretended it had worked, smiled, then backed into the trailer.

It took ten minutes for them to coax Marceau out of his shell, and while they did, Gennady debated with himself whether to tell Achille that his sister was there too. The moments dragged on, and eventually Gennady realized that the engineers were happily chattering on about the status of the tower's various systems, and the bodyguards were visibly bored, and he hadn't said anything. It was going to look awkward if he brought it up now . . . so he put it off some more.

Finally, the young billionaire removed the hazmat's headpiece, reveal-ing a lean, high-cheekboned face currently plastered with sweat. "Thanks, Gennady," he gasped. "It was brave of you to come in here alone."

"Yeah, I risked an epic allergy attack," said Gennady with a shrug. "Nothing after camping in Chernobyl."

Achille grinned. "Forget the mold; we just weren't sure whether open-ing the door would make the whole tower keel over. I'm glad it's structur-ally sound."

"Down here, maybe," Gennady pointed out. "There's a lot up there that could still fall on us." He jerked a thumb at the ceiling.

"You were with us yesterday." They'd done a visual inspection from the helicopters on their way to the plateau. But Gennady wasn't about to trust that.

Achille turned to his engineers. "The wind's not cooperating. Now they're saying it'll shift the right way by two o'clock tomorrow afternoon. How long is it going to take to establish a full updraft?"

"There's inertia in the air inside the tower," said one. "Four hours, granted the thermal difference . . . ?"

"I don't think we'll be ready tomorrow," Gennady pointed out. He was puzzled by Achille's impatience. "We haven't had time to inspect all the turbines, much less the scrubbers on level two."

The engineers should be backing him up on this one, but they stayed silent. Achille waved a hand impatiently. "We'll leave the turbines parked for now. As to the scrubbers . . ."

"There might be loose pieces and material that could get damaged when the air currents pick up."

"Dah! You're right, of course." Achille rubbed his chin for a second, staring into space. "We'd better test the doors now . . . might as well do it in pairs. Gennady, you've got an hour of good light. If you're so worried about them, go check out the scrubbers."

Gennady stared at him. "What's the hurry?"

"Time is money. You're not afraid of the updraft while we're testing the doors, are you? It's not like a hurricane or anything. We walk all the time up there when the unit's running full bore." Achille relented. "Oh, take somebody with you if you're worried. Octav, you go."

Octav was one of Achille's bodyguards. He was a blocky Lithuanian who favored chewing tobacco and expensive suits. The look he shot Gennady said, *This is all your fault.*

Gennady glanced askance at Octav, then said to Achille, "Listen, is there some reason why somebody would think that starting this thing up would be wrong?"

The boss stared at him. "Wrong?"

"I don't mean this company you're competing with—GreenCore. I mean, you know, the general public."

"Don't bug the boss," said Octav.

Achille waved a hand at him. "It's okay. A few crazy adaptationists think reversing climate change will cause as many extinctions as the temperature rise did in the first place. If you ask me, they're just worried about losing their funding. But really, Malianov—this tower sucks CO_2 right out of the air. It doesn't matter where that CO_2 came from, which means we're equally good at offsetting emissions from the airline industry as we are from, say, coal. We're good for everybody."

Gennady nodded, puzzled, and quickly followed Octav out of the trailer. He didn't want the bodyguard wandering off on his own—or maybe spotting something in the distance that he shouldn't see.

Octav *was* staring—standing in the middle of the gallery, mouth open. "Christ," he said. "It's like a fucking cathedral." With light breaking in from the opening louvers, the full scale of the place was becoming clear, and even jaded Gennady was impressed. The tower was a kilometer and a half tall, and over a hundred meters across, its base ringed with round wind turbine windows. "But I was expecting some kinda machinery in here. Is that gonna be installed later?"

Gennady shook his head, pointing at the round windows. "That's all there is to it. When those windows are open, warm air from the greenhouse comes in and rises. The wind turbines turn, and make electricity."

Gennady began the long climb up the steps to the next gallery. His gaze kept roving across the tower's interior; he was looking for Nadine. Was Octav going to spot her? He didn't want that. Even though he knew Nadine was level-headed in tight situations, Octav was another matter. And then there was the whole question of why she was out here to begin with, seemingly on her own, and carrying a gun.

Octav followed on his heels. "Well, sure, I get the whole 'heat rises' thing, but why'd he build it *here*? In the middle of fucking Siberia? If it's solar-powered, wouldn't you want to put it at the equator?"

"They built it on a south-facing slope, so it's 85 percent as efficient as it would be at the equator. And the thermal inertia of the soil means the updraft will operate twenty-four hours a day."

"But in winter—"

"Even in a Siberian winter, because it's not about the absolute temperature, it's about the *difference* between the temperatures inside and outside."

Octav pointed up. "Those pull the CO_2 out of the air, right?"

"If this were a cigarette of the gods, that would be the filter, yes." Just above, thousands of gray plastic sheets were stretched across the shaft of the tower. They were stacked just centimeters apart so that the air flowed freely between them.

"It's called polyaziridine. When the gods suck on the cigarette, this stuff traps the CO_2."

They'd come to one of the little windows. Gennady pried it open and dry summer air poured in. They were above the greenhouse roof, and from here you could see the whole sweep of the valley where Achille had built his experiment. "Look at that."

Above the giant tower, the forested slope kept on rising, and rising, becoming bare tanned rock and then vertical cliff. "Pretty mountains," admitted Octav.

"Except they're not mountains." Yes, the slopes rose like mountainsides, culminating in those daunting cliffs. The trouble was, at the very top, the usual jagged, irregular skyline of rocky peaks was missing. Instead, the cliff tops ended in a perfectly flat, perfectly horizontal line—a knife-cut across the sky—signaling that there was no crest-and-fall down a north-facing slope up there. Miles up, under a regime of harsh UV light and whipping high-altitude winds, clouds scudded low and fast along a nearly endless plain of red rock. Looking down from up there, the outflung arms of the Putorana Plateau absolutely dwarfed Achille's little tower.

"I walked on it yesterday when we flew up to prime the wells," said Gennady. Octav hadn't been along on that flight; he hadn't seen what lay beyond that ruler-straight crest. "That plateau covers an area the size of

Western Europe, and it's so high, nothing can grow up there. This whole valley is just an erosion ditch in it."

Octav nodded, reluctantly intrigued. "Kinda strange place to build a power plant."

"Achille built here because the plateau's made of basalt. When you pump hot carbonated water into basalt, it makes limestone, which permanently sequesters the carbon. All Achille has to do is keep fracking up top there and he's got a continent-sized sponge to soak up all the excess CO_2 on the planet. You could build a thousand towers like this all around the Putorana. It's perfect for—" But Octav had clapped a hand on his shoulder.

"Shht," whispered the bodyguard. "Heard something."

Before Gennady could react, Octav was creeping up the steps with his gun drawn. "What do you think you're doing?" Gennady hissed at the Lithuanian. "Put that thing away!"

Octav waved at him to stay where he was. "Could be bears," he called down in a hoarse—and not at all quiet—stage whisper. The word *bears* seemed to hang in the air for a second, like an echo that couldn't find a wall to bounce off.

Gennady started up after him, deliberately making as much noise as he could on the metal steps. "Bears are not arboreal; much less likely will they be foraging up in the scrubbers—" Octav reached the top of the steps and disappeared. Here, the hanging sheets of plastic made a bizarre drapery that completely filled the tower. Except for this little catwalk, the entire space was given over to them. It was kind of like being backstage in a large theater, except the curtains were white. Octav was hunched over, gun drawn, stepping slowly forward around the slow curve of the catwalk. This would have been a comical sight except that, about eight meters ahead of him, the curtains were swaying.

"Octav, don't—" The bodyguard lunged into the gloom.

Gennady heard a scuffle and ran forward himself. Then, terribly, two gunshots like slaps echoed out and up and down.

"No, what have you—" Gennady staggered to a stop and had to grab

the railing for support; it creaked and gave a bit, and he suddenly realized how high up they were. Octav knelt just ahead, panting. He was reaching slowly out to prod a crumpled gray-and-brown shape.

"*Jssht!*" said the walkie-talkie on Octav's belt. More garbled vocal sounds spilled out of it, until Octav suddenly seemed to realize it was there and holstered his pistol with one hand while taking the walkie-talkie out with the other.

"Octav," he said. The walkie-talkie spat incoherent staticky noise into his ear. He nodded.

"Everything's okay," he said. "Just shot a goose, is all. I guess we have dinner."

Then he turned to glare at Gennady. "You should have stayed where I told you!"

Gennady ignored him. The white curtains swung, all of them now starting to rustle as if murmuring and pointing at Octav's minor crime scene. More of the louvered doors had opened far below, and the updraft was starting. Shadow and sound began to paint the tower's hollow spaces.

Nadine would be hard to see now and impossible to hear. Hopefully, she'd noticed Octav's shots; even now, if she had a grain of sense, she'd be on her way back to her truck.

Gennady brushed past Octav. "If you're done murdering the locals, I need to work." The two did not speak again as Gennady tugged at the plastic and inspected the bolts mounting the scrubbers to the tower wall.

A Siberian summer day lasts forever; but there came a point when the sun no longer lit the interior top of the tower. The last hundred meters up there were painted titanium white and reflected a lot of light down. Now, though, with the sky a dove gray shading to nameless pink, and the sun's rays horizontal, Achille's lads had to light the sodium lamps and admit it was evening.

The lamps were the same kind you saw in parking lots all over the world. For Gennady, they completely stole the sense of mystery from the tower's interior, making it as grim an industrial space as any he'd seen. For a while, he stood outside the control trailer with Octav and a couple of the engineers, trying to get used to the evil greenish yellow cast that everything had. Then he said, "I'm going to sleep outside."

One of the engineers laughed. "After your run-in with the climbing bears? And you know, there really are wolves in this forest."

"No, no, I will be in one of the admin trailers." Nobody had even opened those yet, and besides, he needed to find a spot where late-night comings and goings wouldn't be noticed by these men.

"First, you must try the goose!" While the others inspected and tested, Octav had cooked it over a barrel fire. He'd only made a few modest comments about the bird, but Gennady knew he was ridiculously proud of his kill, because he'd placed the barrel smack in the center of the hundred-meter-wide floor of the tower. He'd even dragged over a couple of railroad ties and set them up like logs around his campfire.

Achille was down there now, peering at his air quality equipment, obviously debating whether he could lose his surgical mask. He waved up at them. "Come! Let's eat!"

Gennady followed the others reluctantly. He knew where this was headed: to the inevitable male bonding ritual. It came as no surprise at all when, as they tore into the simultaneously charred and raw goose, Achille waved at Gennady and said, "Now, this man! He's a real celebrity! Octav, did you know what kind of adventurer you saved from this fierce beast?" He waved his drumstick in the air. Octav looked puzzled.

"Gennady, here. Gennady fought the famous Dragon of Pripyat!" Of course the engineers knew the story, and smiled politely; but neither Octav nor Bogdan, the other bodyguard, knew it. "Tell us, Gennady!" Achille's grin was challenging. "About the reactor and the devil guarding it."

"We know all about that," protested an engineer. "I want to know about the Kashmiri incident. The one with the nuclear jet. Is it true you flew it into a mine?"

"Well, yes," Gennady admitted, "not myself, of course. It was just a drone." Of course the attention was flattering, but it also made him uncomfortable, and over the years, he'd learned that the discomfort outweighed the flattery. He told them the story, but as soon as he could, he found a way to turn to Achille and say, "But these are just isolated incidents. Your whole career has been, well, something of an adventure itself, no?"

That burst of eloquence had about exhausted his skills of social manipulation; luckily, Achille was eager to talk about himself. He and Nadine had inherited wealth, and Gennady had sensed yesterday that this weighed on him. He wanted to be a self-made man, but he wasn't, so, he was using his inheritance recklessly, to see if he could achieve something great. He also had an impulsive urge to justify himself.

He told them how, when he'd seen the sheer scale of the cap-and-trade and carbon-tax programs that were springing up across the globe, he'd decided to put all his chips into carbon air capture. "Because," he explained, "it was a completely discredited approach."

"Wait," said Octav, his brow crinkling. "You went into . . . that . . . because it had no credibility?" Achille nodded vigorously.

"Decades of research, patents, and designs were just lying around, waiting to be snapped up. I was already building this place, but the carbon bubble was bursting as governments started pulling their fossil fuel subsidies. Here, the local price of petrol had gone through the roof as the Arctic oilfields went from profitable to red. But, you see, I had a plan."

The plan was to offer to offset CO_2 emissions of industries anywhere on the planet from right there. Since Achille's giant machines harvested greenhouse gases from the ambient atmosphere, it didn't matter where they were—which meant he could sell offsets to airlines, mines in South America, or container ships burning bunker oil with equal ease.

"But then Kafatos stole my market."

The Greek industrialist's company, GreenCore, had bought up vast tracts of Siberian forest and had begun rolling out a cheaper biological alternative to Achille's towers.

"They do what? Some kind of fast-growing tree?" asked Gennady. He knew about the rivalry between Achille and Kafatos. It wasn't just business; it was personal.

Achille nodded. "Genetically modified lodgepole pines. Super-fast-growing, resistant to the pine beetle. They want to turn the forest itself into a carbon sponge. It's as bad an idea as tampering with Mother Nature was—as oil was—in the first place," he said, "and I intend to prove it."

The conversation wound down a bit after this motivational speech, but then one of the engineers looked around at the trembling shadows of the amphitheater in which they sat, and said, "Pretty spooky, eh?"

"Siberia is all spooky," Bogdan pointed out. "Never mind just here."

And that set them all off on ghost stories and legends of the deep forests. The locals used to believe Siberia was a middle world, halfway up a vast tree, with underworlds below and heavens above. Shamans rode their drums between the worlds, fighting the impossible strength of the gods with dogged courage and guile. They triumphed now and then, but in the end, the deep forest swallowed all human achievement like it would swallow a shout. What was human got lost in the green maze; what came out was changed and new.

Bogdan knew a story about the "valley of death" and the strange round *kheldyu*—iron houses—that could be found half-buried in the permafrost here and there. There was a valley no one ever returned from; *kheldyu* had been glimpsed there by scouts on the surrounding heights.

The engineers had their own tales, about lost Soviet-era expeditions. There were downed bombers loaded with nukes on hair trigger, which might go off at any moment. There were Chinese tunnel complexes, and lakes so radioactive that to stand on their shores for a half an hour meant dying within the week. (Well, that last story, at least, was perfectly true.)

"Gennady, what about you?" All eyes turned to him. Gennady had relaxed a bit and was willing to talk; but he didn't know any recent myths or legends. "All I can tell you," Gennady said, "is that it'll be poetic justice if we save the world by burying all our carbon here. Because what's in this place nearly killed the whole world through global warming once already."

The engineers hadn't heard about the plateau's past. "This place—this *thing*," said Gennady in his best ghost-story voice, "killed ninety percent of all life on Earth when it erupted. This supervolcano, called the Siberian Traps, caused the Permian extinction two hundred and fifty million years ago. Think about it: the place was here before the dinosaurs and it's still here, still taller than mountain ranges and as wide as Europe." There was nothing like it on Earth—older than the present continents, the Putorana was an ineradicable scar from the greatest dying the world had ever seen.

So then they had to hear the story of the Permian extinction. Gennady did his best to convey the idea of an entire world dying, and of geologic forces so gargantuan and unstoppable that the first geologists to find this spot literally couldn't imagine the scale of the apocalypse it represented. He was rewarded by some appreciative nods, particularly for his image of a slumbering monster that could indifferently destroy all life on the planet by just rolling over. The whole thing was too abstract for Octav and Bogdan, though, who were yawning.

"Right." Achille slapped his knees. "Tomorrow's another busy day. Let's turn in, everybody, and get a start at sun-up."

"Uh, boss," said an engineer, "sunrise is at three a.m."

"Make it five, then." Achille headed for the metal steps.

Gennady repeated his intent to sleep in the admin trailer; to his relief, no one volunteered to do the same. When he stepped through the second door of the tower's airlock, it was to find that although it was nearly midnight, the sun was still setting. He remembered seeing this effect before: the sun might dip below the horizon, but the lurid peach-and-rose-colored glow it painted on the sky wasn't going to go away. That smear of dusk would just slide up and across the northern horizon over the next few hours, and then the sun would pop back up once it reached the east.

That was helpful. The administration trailer needed a good airing-out, so he opened all its windows and sat on the front step for a while, waiting to see if anybody came out of the tower. The sunset inched northward. He checked his watch. Finally, with a sigh, he set off walking around the western curve of the structure. A flashlight was unnecessary, but he did bring the flare gun. Because, well, there might be bears.

Nadine had done a pretty good job of hiding her truck among gnarled cedars and cobwebs of fungi on the north side of the tower. Either she'd been waiting for him, or she had some kind of proximity alarm, because he was still ten meters away when he heard the door slam. He stopped and waited. After a couple of minutes, she stood up out of the bushes, a black cutout on the red sky. "It's just you," she said unnecessarily.

Gennady shrugged. "Do I ever bring friends?"

"Good point." The silhouette made a motion he interpreted as the holstering of a pistol. He strolled over while she untangled herself from the bushes.

"Come back to the trailer," he said. "I have chairs."

"I'm sleeping here."

"That's fine."

". . . Okay." They crunched back over the gravel. Halfway there, Nadine said, "Seriously, Gennady. You and Achille?"

"What is the problem?" He spread his hands, distorting the long shadow that leaned ahead of him. "He is restarting his carbon air capture project. That's a good thing, no?"

She stopped walking. "That's what you think he's doing?"

What did that mean? "Let's see. It's what he says he's doing. It's what the press releases say. It's what everybody else thinks he's doing. . . . What else *could* he be up to?"

"Everybody asks that question." She kicked at the gravel angrily. "But nobody sees what he's doing! You know—" She laughed bitterly. "When I told my team at the IAEA what he was up to, they just laughed at me. And you know what? I thought about calling you. I figured, *Gennady knows how these things go. He'd understand.* But you don't get it either, do you?"

"You know I am not smart man. I need thing explained to me."

She was silent until they reached the admin trailer. Once inside, she said, "Close those," with a nod at the windows. "I don't want any of that shit in here with us."

She must mean the mold. As Gennady went around shutting things up, Nadine sat down at the tiny table. After a longing look at the moth-balled coffee machine, she steepled her hands and said, "I suppose you saw the pictures."

"That the paparazzi took of you two at the Paris café? There were a few, if I recall."

She grimaced. "I particularly like the one that shows Kafatos punching Achille in the face."

Gennady nodded pensively. It had been two years since Achille came across his sister having dinner with Kafatos, his biggest business rival. The punch was famous, and the whole incident had burned through the internet in a day or two, to be instantly forgotten in the wake of the next scandal.

"Achille and I haven't spoken since. He's even taken me out of his will— you know he was the sole heir, right?"

Gennady nodded. "I figured that was why you went to work at the IAEA."

"No, I did that out of idealism, but . . . Anyway, it doesn't matter. I knew all about Achille's little rivalry with the Greek shithead, but something about it didn't add up. Achille was lying to me, so I went to Kafatos to see if he knew why. He didn't, so the whole café incident was a complete waste. But I eventually *did* get the story from one of Achille's engineers."

"Let me guess. It's something to do with the tower?"

She shrugged. "It never crossed my mind. When Achille came up with the plan for this place, I guess it was eight years ago, it seemed to make sense. He knew about the Permian, and he talked about how he was going to 'redeem' the site of the greatest extinction in history by using it to not just stop but completely reverse global warming. The whole blowup with Kafatos happened because GreenCore bought up about a million square kilometers of forest just east of Achille's site. Kafatos has been genetically engineering pines to soak up the carbon, but you know that." She took a deep breath. "You also know there's no economic reason to reopen the tower."

Gennady blinked at her. "They told me there was; that was why we were here. Told me the market had turned . . ."

She sent him a look of complete incredulity, then that look changed, and suddenly Nadine stood up. Gennady opened his mouth to ask what was wrong, just as one of the windows rattled loosely in its mount. Nadine was staring out the window, a look of horror on her face.

A deep vibration made the plywood floor buzz. The glass rattled again.

"He's opening the windows!" Nadine ran for the door. Gennady peered outside.

"Surely not all of them . . ." But all the black circles he could see from here were changing, letting out a trickle of sodium-lamp light.

By the time he got outside, she was gone—off and running around the tower in the direction of her truck. Gennady shifted from foot to foot, trying to decide whether to follow.

Her story hadn't made sense, but still, he paused for a moment to gaze up at the tower. In the deep sunset light of the midsummer night, it looked like a rifle barrel aimed at the sky.

He slammed through the airlocks and went up the stairs. All around the tower's base, the round windows were humming open.

Gennady fixed an empty smile on his face and deliberately slowed himself down as he opened the door to the control trailer. He was thinking of radioactive lakes; of the Becquerel Reindeer, an entire radioactive herd he'd seen once, slaughtered and lying in the back of a transport truck; of disasters he'd cleaned up after, messes he'd hidden from the media—and the kinds of people who had made those messes.

"Hey, what's up?" he said brightly as he stepped inside.

"Close that!" Achille was pacing in the narrow space. "You'll let in the spores!"

"Ah, sorry." He sidled around the bodyguards, behind the engineers who were staring at their tablets and laptops, and found a perch near an empty water cooler. From there, he could see the laptop screens, though not well.

"What's up?" he said again.

One of the engineers started to say something, but Achille interrupted him. "Just a test. You should go back to bed."

"I see." He stepped close to the table and looked over the engineer's shoulder. One of the laptop screens showed a systems diagram of the tower. The other was open to a satellite weather map. "Weather's changing," he muttered, just loud enough for the engineer to hear. The man nodded.

"Fine," Gennady said more loudly. "I'll be in my trailer." Nobody moved to stop him as he left, but outside he paused, arms wrapped around his torso, breath cold and frosting the air. Already he could feel the breeze from below.

Back in Azerbaijan, Nadine had been one of the steadiest operatives during the Alexander's Road incident; they had talked one evening about what Gennady had come to call "industrial logic." About what happened when the natural world became an abstraction, and the only reality was the system you were building. Gennady had fallen for that kind of thinking early in his career, had spent the rest of his life mopping up after other people who'd never gotten out from under it. He couldn't remember the details of the conversation now, but he did remember her getting a distant expression on her face at one point and muttering something about Achille.

But it wasn't just about her brother; all of this had something to do with Kafatos, too. He shook his head, and turned to the stairs.

A flash lit the inside of the tower and seconds later, a sharp *bang!*

echoed weirdly off the curving walls. The grinding noise of the window mechanisms stopped.

A transformer had blown. It had happened on the far side of the tower; he started in that direction but had only taken a couple of steps when the trailer door flew open and the engineers spilled out, all talking at once. "Malianov!" one shouted. "Did you see it?"

He shook his head. "Heard it, but not sure where it came from. Echoes . . ." Let them stumble around in the dark for a while. That would give Nadine a chance to get away. Then he could find her again and talk her out of doing anything further.

Octav and Bogdan had come out, too, and Bogdan raced off after the engineers. Gennady shrugged at Octav and said, "I am still going back to bed." He'd gone down the stairs, reached the outer door, and actually put his hand on the latch before curiosity overcame his better judgment, and he turned back.

He came up behind the engineers as they were shining their flashlights at the smoking ruin that used to be a transformer. "Something caused it to arc," one said. Bogdan was kneeling a few meters away. He stood up and dangled a mutilated padlock in the beam of his flashlight. "Somebody's got bolt cutters."

All eyes turned to Gennady.

He backed away. "Now, wait a minute. I was with you."

"You could have set something to blow and then come back to the trailer," said one of the engineers. "It's what I would have done."

Gennady said nothing; if they thought he'd done it, they wouldn't be looking for Nadine. "Grab him!" shouted one of the engineers. Gennady just put out his hands and shook his head as Bogdan took hold of his wrists.

"It's not what *I* would have done," Gennady said. "Because this would be the result. I am not so stupid."

"Oh, and I am?" Bogdan glared at him. At that moment, one of the engineers put his walkie-talkie to his ear and made a shushing motion. "We found the—what? Sir, I can't hear what—"

The distorted tones of the voice on the walkie-talkie had been those of Achille, but suddenly they changed. Nadine said, "I have your boss. I'll kill him unless you go to the center of the floor and light the barrel fire so I can see you."

The engineers gaped at one another. Bogdan let go of Gennady and grabbed at the walkie-talkie. "Who is this?"

"Someone who knows what you're up to. Now move!"

Bogdan eyed Gennady, who shrugged. "Nothing to do with me."

There was a quick, heated discussion. The engineers were afraid of being shot once they were out in the open, but Gennady pointed out that there was actually more light around the wall, because that's where the sodium lamps were. "She doesn't want to see us clearly; she just wants us where it'll be obvious which way we're going if we run," he said.

Reluctantly, they began edging toward the shadowed center of the tower. "How can you be so sure?" somebody whined. Gennady shrugged again.

"If she'd wanted to kill her brother, she would have by now," he pointed out.

"Her *what*?"

And at that moment, the gunfire started.

It was all upstairs, but the engineers scattered, leaving Gennady and Bogdan standing in half shadow. Had Octav stayed up top? Gennady couldn't remember. He and Bogdan scanned the gallery, but the glare from the sodium lamps hid the trailer. After a few seconds, Gennady heard the metallic bounce of feet running on the mesh surface overhead. It sounded like two sets, off to the right.

"There!" Gennady pointed to the left and began running. Bogdan ran too, and quickly outpaced him; at that point, Gennady peeled off and headed back. There was another set of stairs nearby, and though the engineers were there, they were huddling under its lower steps. He didn't think they'd stop him, nor did they as he ran past them and up.

Bogdan yelled something inarticulate from the other side of the floor. Gennady kept going.

"Nadine? Where are you?" She'd been running in a clockwise direction around the tower, so he went that way too, making sure now that he was making plenty of noise. He didn't want to surprise her. "Nadine, it's me!"

Multiple sets of feet rang on the gallery behind him. Gennady took the chance that she'd kept going up, and mounted the next set of steps when he came to them. "Nadine!" She'd be among the scrubbers now.

He reached the top and hesitated. Why *would* she come up here? It was the cliché thing to do: in movies, the villains always went up. Gennady tried to push past his confusion and worry to picture the layout of the tower. He remembered the two inspection elevators just as a rattling hum started up ahead.

By the time he reached the yellow wire cage, the car was on its way up. Next stop, as far as he knew, was the top of the tower. Nadine could hold it there, and maybe that was her plan. There wouldn't be just the one elevator, though, not in a structure this big. Gennady turned and ran away from the sound of the moving elevator.

He could hear somebody crashing up the steps from the lower levels. "Malianov!" shouted Octav.

He was a good quarter of the way around the curve from Gennady, so Gennady paused and leaned on the rail to shout, "I'm here!"

"What are you doing?"

"I'm right on her heels!"

"Stop! Come down! Leave it to us."

"Okay! I'll be right there." He ran on, and reached the other elevator before Octav had reached the last flight of steps. Gennady wrenched the rusty outer cage door open but struggled with the inner one. He got in and slammed it just as Octav thundered up. Gennady hit the UP button while Octav roared in fury; but three meters up, he hit STOP.

"Octav. Don't shoot at me, please. I'll send the cage back down when I get to the top. I just need a minute to talk with Nadine, is all."

In the movies, there'd be all kinds of wild gunplay happening right now, but Octav was a professional. He crossed his arms and glowered at Gennady through the grid flooring of the elevator. "Where's she going?" he demanded.

"Damned if I know. Up."

"What's up?"

"Someplace she can talk to her brother alone, I'm thinking. Reason with him, threaten him, I don't know. Look, Octav, let me talk to her. She might shoot you, but she's not going to shoot me."

"It really is Nadine? Achille's sister? Do you know her?"

"Well, remember that story I told last night about Azerbaijan and the nukes? We worked together on that. You know she's with the IAEA, too. You never met her?"

There was an awkward pause. "What happened in the trailer?" Gennady asked. "Did she hurt him?" Octav shook his head.

"She was yelling," he said. "I snuck around the trailer and came in through the bathroom window. But I got stuck."

Gennady stifled a laugh. He would have paid to see that; Octav was not a small man.

"I took a shot at her but she ran. Might have winged her, though."

Gennady cursed. "Octav, that's your boss's sister."

"He told me to shoot!"

There was another awkward pause.

"I'm sure she doesn't mean to harm him," said Gennady, but he wasn't so sure now.

"Then why's she holding him at gunpoint?"

"I don't know. Look, just give me a minute, okay?" He hit UP before Octav could reply.

He'd gotten an inkling of the size of the tower when they'd inspected it by helicopter, but down at the bottom, the true dimensions of the place were obscured by shadow. Up here, it was all vast emptiness, the walls a concrete checkerboard that curved away like the face of a dam. It was all faintly lit by a distant, indigo-silver circle of sky. On the far side of this bottomless amphitheater, the other elevator car had a good lead on him. Nadine probably wouldn't hear him now if he called out to her.

The elevator frameworks ended at tiny balconies about halfway up the tower. Nadine's cage was slowing now as it neared the one on the far side.

Gennady shivered. A cool wind was coming up from below, and it went right through the gridwork floor and flapped his pant legs. There wasn't much to it yet, but it would get stronger.

He watched as Nadine and Achille got out of the other elevator. A square of brightness appeared—a door opening to the outside—and they disappeared through it.

When his own elevator stopped, he found he was at a similar little balcony. There was nothing there but the side rails and a gray metal utility door with crash bars in the outer concrete wall. The sense of height there was utterly physical; he'd sense it even if he shut his eyes, because the whole tower swayed ever so gently, and the moving air made it feel like you were falling. Gennady sent the elevator back down and leaned on the crash bar.

Outside, it was every bit as bad as he'd feared. The door let onto a narrow catwalk that ran around the outside of the tower in both direc- tions. He remembered seeing it from the helicopter, and while it had looked sturdy enough from that vantage, in the gray dawn light he could see long streaks of rust trailing down from the bolts that held it to the wall.

He swallowed, then tested the thing with his foot. It seemed to hold, so he began slowly circling the tower. This time, he tried every step before committing himself and leaned on the concrete wall, as far from the rail- ing as he could get.

Now he could hear a vague sound, like an endless sigh, rising from below. That, combined with the motion of the tower, made it feel as if something were rousing down in the wall-less maze that filled the black valley.

After a couple of minutes, the far point of the circle hove into view.

Here was something he hadn't seen from the helicopter: a broadening of the catwalk on this side. Here it became a wide, reinforced platform, and on it sat a white-and-yellow trailer. That was utterly incongruous: Gennady could see the thing's undercarriage and wheels sitting on the mesh floor. It had probably been hauled up there by helicopter during the tower's construction.

A pair of parachutes was painted on the side of the trailer. They were gray in this light but probably pink in daylight.

Now he heard shouting—Achille's voice. Gennady tried to hurry, but the catwalk felt flimsy and the breeze was turning into a wind. He made it to the widened platform, but that was no better, since it also had open gridwork flooring and several squares of it were missing.

"Nadine? It's Gennady. What're you doing?"

"Stop her!" yelled Achille. "She's gone crazy!"

He took the chance and ran to the trailer, then peeked around its corner. He was instantly dazzled by intense light—flare light, in fact—lurid and almost bright green. He squinted and past his sheltering fingers saw it shift around, lean up, and then fade.

"Stop!" Achille sounded desperate. Gennady heard Nadine laugh. He edged around the corner of the trailer.

"Nadine? It's Gennady. Can I ask what you're doing?"

She laughed, sounding a little giddy. Gennady blinked away the dazzle dots and spotted Achille. He was clutching the railing and staring wide-eyed as Nadine pulled another flare out of a box at her feet.

She'd holstered her pistol and now energetically pulled the tab from the flare. She windmilled her arm and hurled it into the distance, laughing as she did it. Gennady could see the bright spark following the last one down—but the vista there was too dizzying and he quickly brought his eyes back to Nadine.

"Found these in the trailer," she said. "They're perfect. Want to help?" She offered one to him. Gennady shook his head.

"That's going to cause a fire," he said. She nodded.

"That's the idea. Did you bring a radio? We dropped ours. Achille here has to radio his people to shut down the tower." She looked hopeful, but Gennady shook his head. "We'll have to wait for that new bodyguard, then," she said. "He's sure to have one. Then we can all go home."

The good news was, she didn't look like she was on some murderous rampage. She looked determined but no different from the Nadine he'd known five years ago. "We can?" said Gennady. "This is just a family fight, is that it? Achille's not going to press charges, and the others aren't going to talk about it?"

She hesitated. "Come on, can't you let me have my moment? You of all people should be able to do that."

"Why me of all people?"

She smiled at him past smoke and vivid pink light. "'Cause you've already saved the world a couple times."

She turned to throw another flare.

"Not the world," Gennady said—only because he felt he had to say something to keep her talking. "Azerbaijan, maybe. But . . . all this"— he gestured at the falling flares—"seems like a bit much for having your brother get into a fight with your date."

"No. *No!*" She sounded hugely disappointed in him. "This isn't about that little incident with Kafatos, is it, Achille?" Achille flung up his free hand in exasperation; his other still tightly held the rail. "Although," Nadine went on, "I'm afraid I might have given brother dear the big idea myself, a couple of days before."

"What idea?" Gennady looked to Achille, who wouldn't meet his eyes.

"When he told me about the tower project and said he wanted to use the Putorana Plateau as a carbon sink, I told him about the Permian extinction. He was fascinated—weren't you, Achille? But he really lit up when I told him that though it was heat shock that undoubtedly killed many of the trees on the planet, it was something else that finished off the rest."

"What are you talking about?"

Nadine pointed down at the disc of plastic-roofed forest below them. "You drove through it on the way up here. It's out there, trying to get into our lungs, our systems. . . ."

"The *fungus*?"

She nodded. "A specific breed of it. It covered Earth from pole to pole during the Permian. It ate all the trees that survived the heat . . . *conifer* trees, tough as they were. And here's the thing: it's still around today." Again she nodded at the forest. "It's called *Rhizoctonia*, and Achille's been farming a particularly nasty strain of it here for two years."

Gennady looked at Achille. He was remembering how the day had gone—how Achille seemed to be building his restart schedule around prevailing winds rather than the integrity of the tower's systems.

If you wanted to cultivate an organism that ate wood and thrived in dry heat, you'd want a greenhouse. They were perched above the biggest greenhouse in central Asia.

Nadine hoisted up the box of flares and stalked off along the catwalk. "I need to make sure the whole fungus crop goes up. *You* need to make sure Achille's engineers close the windows, or the heat's all going to come up here. See you in a bit." She disappeared around the curve of the tower; a short time later, Gennady saw a flare wobble up and then down into the night.

He turned to Achille, who had levered himself onto his feet. "Is she crazy? Or did we really come here to bomb Kafatos's forest with spores?"

Achille glared defiantly back. "So what if we did? It's industrial espionage, sure. But he screwed me over to start with, made a secret deal with the oligarchs to torpedo my bid. Fair's fair."

"And what's to prevent this rhyzocti-thing from spreading? How's it supposed to tell the difference between Kafatos's trees and the rest of the forest?" Achille looked away, and suddenly Gennady saw it all—the whole plan.

"It can't, can it? You were going to spread a cloud of spores across the whole northern hemisphere. Every heat-shocked forest in Asia and North

America would fall to the *Rhizoctonia*. Biological sequestration of carbon would stagger to a stop, not just here but everywhere. Atmospheric carbon levels would shoot up. Global warming would go into high gear. No more talk about mitigation. No more talk about slowing emissions on a schedule. The world would have to go massively carbon-negative immediately. And you own all the patents to that stuff."

"Not all," he admitted. "But for the useable stuff, yeah."

A metallic *bong bong bong* sound came from the catwalk opposite the direction Nadine had taken. Moments later, Octav showed up. He was puffing, obviously spooked by the incredible drop but determined to help his boss. "Where is she?"

"Never mind," said Achille. "Have you got a walkie-talkie?" Octav nodded and handed it over.

"Hello, hello?" Achille put the thing to his ear, other hand on his other ear, and paced up and down. Octav was staring at the balloons painted on the trailer.

"What is that?" he said, assuming, it seemed, that Gennady would know.

"Looks like they were expecting tourists. Base jumping off a solar updraft tower?" From up there, you'd be able to slide down the valley thermals to the river far below. "I guess it could be fun."

"I can't get a signal," said Achille. "You," he said to Octav, "go after her!"

"You can't get a signal because you're outside. They're inside." Gennady pointed at the door in the side of the tower as Octav pounded away along the catwalk. "Try again from next to the elevator." Achille moved to the door and Gennady made to follow, but as Achille opened it, a plume of smoke poured out. "Oh, shit!"

The tower had been designed to suck up air from the surrounding forest. It was already pulling in smoke from the fires Nadine had lit with her flares. And she was moving in a circle, trying to ensure that the entire bull's-eye of whitened pines caught.

"Yes! Yes!" Achille was gasping into the radio, ducking out of the smoke-filled tower every few seconds to breathe. "You have to do it now! The whole forest, yes!" He glanced at Gennady. "They're trying to get to the trailer, but they'd have to fix the transformer first and there's too much smoke, I don't know if they're going to make it."

Gennady looked down at the forest; lots of little spot fires were spreading and joining up into larger orange smears and lozenges. If Nadine made it all the way around, they'd be trapped at the center of a firestorm. "We're stuck too."

"Maybe not." Achille ran to the trailer, which turned out to be full of cardboard boxes. They rummaged among them, finding more flares—not useful—and safety harnesses, cables and crampons and—"Ha!" said Achille, holding up two parachutes.

"Is that all?"

The billionaire kicked around at the debris. "Yeah, you'd think there'd be more, but you know we never got this place up and running. These are probably the test units. Doesn't matter; there's one for me, one for you."

"Not Nadine?" Achille shot him an exasperated look. She was his own sister, but he obviously didn't care. Gennady took the chute he offered, with disgust. He would, he decided, give it to Nadine when she came back around—if only to see the expression on Achille's face.

Achille was headed out the door. "What then?" asked Gennady. Nadine's brother looked back, still exasperated. "Are you just going to walk away from your dream?"

Achille shook his head. "The patents and designs are all I've got now. I can't make a go selling the power from this place. It's the fungus or nothing. So, look, this fire might eat the tower, but the wind is blowing *in*. The *Rhizoctonia* on the fringes will be okay. As soon as we're on the ground, I'm going to bring in some trucks and haul away the remainder during the cleanup. I can still dump that all over Kafatos's Goddamned forest. We lost the first hand, that's all."

"But . . ." Gennady couldn't believe he had to say it. "What about Nadine?"

Achille crossed his arms, glowering at the fires. "This has been coming a long time. You know what the worst part is? I'd made her my heir again. Lucky thing I never told her, huh."

As they stepped outside, a deep groan came from the tower, and Gennady's inner ear told him he was moving, even though his feet were firmly planted on the deck. Looking down, he saw they were ringed by fire now. The only reason the smoke and heat weren't streaming up the side of the tower was because they were pouring through the open windmill apertures. Past the open door he could see only a wall of shuddering gray inside. The engineers and Bogdan must already be dead.

The tower twisted again, and with a popping sound, sixteen feet of catwalk separated from the wall. It drooped, and just then, Nadine and Octav came around the tower's curve, on the other side of it.

Achille and Nadine stared at one another over the gap, not speaking. Then Achille turned away with an angry shrug. "We have to go!" He began struggling into his parachute.

Octav waved at Gennady. "Got any ideas?" Neither he nor Nadine was holding weapons. They've obviously realized their best chance for survival lay with one another.

Gennady edged as close to the fallen section of catwalk as he dared. "Belts, straps, have you got anything like that?" Octav grabbed at his waist, nodded. "The tower's support cables!" Gennady pointed at the nearest one, which leaned out from under the door. "We're going to have to slide down those!" He could see that the cables' anchors were outside the ring of fire, but that wouldn't last long. "Pull up the floor mesh over one, and climb down to the cable anchor. Double up your belt and—hang on a second." Octav's belt would be worn through by friction before they got a hundred feet. Gennady ran into the trailer, which was better lit now by the rising sun, and tossed the boxes around. He found some broken metal strapping. Perfect. Coming out, he tossed a piece across to Octav. "Use that instead. Now get going!"

As they disappeared around the curved wall, Achille darted from behind the trailer. "Coming?" he shouted as he ran to the railing.

Gennady hesitated. He'd dropped his parachute by the trailer steps.

It was clear what had to be done. There was only one way off this tower. Still, he just stood there, watching as Achille clumsily mounted the railing.

Achille looked back. "Come on, what are you waiting for?"

Images from the day were flashing through Gennady's mind—and more, a vision of what could happen after the fire was over. He turned to look out over the endless skin of forest that filled the valley and spread beyond to the horizon.

He'd spent his whole life cleaning up other people's messes. There'd been the Chernobyl affair and that other nuclear disaster in Azerbaijan. He'd chased stolen nukes across two continents, and only just succeeded in hiding from the world a discovery that would allow any disgruntled tinkerer to build such weapons without needing enriched uranium or plutonium. He'd told himself all the while that he did these things to keep humanity safe. Yet it had never been the idea that people might die that had moved him. He was afraid for something else, and had been for so long now that he couldn't imagine living without that fear.

It was time to admit where his real allegiance lay.

"I'm right behind you," he said with a forced smile. And he watched Achille dive off the tower. He watched Nadine's brother fall two hundred feet and open his chute. He watched the vortex of flame around the tower's base yank the parachute in and down, and swallow it.

Gennady picked up the last piece of metal strapping and, as the tower writhed again, ran along the catwalk opposite to the way Nadine and Octav had gone.

He rolled over and staggered to his feet, coughing. A cloud of white was churning around him, propelled by a quickening gale. Overhead, the plastic sheeting that covered the dead forest flapped where he'd cut through it. The support cable made a perfectly straight line from the concrete block at his feet up to the distant tower—or was it straight? No, the thing was starting to curve. Achille's tower, which was now in full sunlight, was curling away from the fire, as if unwilling to look at it anymore. Any second now, it might fall.

Gennady raced around the perimeter of the fire as the sun touched the plastic ceiling. The flames were eating their way slowly outward, pushing against the wind. Gennady dodged fallen branches and avoided thick brambles, pausing now and then to cough heavily, so it took him a few minutes to spot the support cable opposite the one he'd slid down. When it appeared, it was as an amber pen stroke against the predawn sky. The plastic greenhouse ceiling was broken where the cable pierced it, as it should be if bodies had broken through it on their way to the ground.

As he approached the cable's concrete anchor, he spotted Octav. The bodyguard was curled up on the ground, clutching his ankle.

"Where's Nadine?" Octav looked up as Gennady pounded up. He blinked, looked past Gennady, then they locked eyes.

That look said, *Where's Achille?*

Neither said anything for a long moment. Then, "She fell off," said Octav. "Back there." He pointed into the fire.

"How far—"

"Go. You might find her."

Gennady didn't need any more urging. He let the white wind push him at the shimmering walls of orange light. As the banners of fire whipped up, they caught and tore the plastic sheeting that had canopied the forest for years, and they angrily pulled it down. Gennady looked for another break in that upper surface, hopefully close to the cable's anchor, and after a moment, he spotted it. Nadine had left a clean incision in the plastic but had shaved a pine below that; branches and needles were strewn across the white pillows of *Rhizoctonia* and made Nadine herself easy to find.

She blinked at him from where she lay on a mattress of fungi. She looked surprised, and for a moment, Gennady had the absurd thought that maybe his hair was all standing up or something. But then she said, "It doesn't hurt."

He frowned, reached down, and pinched her ankle.

"Ow!"

"Fungus broke your fall." He helped her up. The flames were being kept at bay by the inrushing wind, but the radiant heat was intense. "Get going." He pushed her until she was trotting away from the fire.

"What about you?"

"Right behind you!"

He followed, more slowly, until she disappeared into the swirling *Rhizoctonia*. Then he slowed and stopped, leaning over to brace his hands on his knees. He looked back at the fire.

Sure, if Achille had been thinking, he would have known that the fire would suck in any parachute that came off the tower. Yet Gennady could have warned him, and didn't. He'd murdered Achille; it was that simple.

The wall of fire was mesmerizing and its heat like a wall pushing Gennady back. There must have been a lot of fires like this one the last time the *Rhizoctonia* roused itself to make a meal of the world. Achille had engineered special conditions under his greenhouse roof, but it wouldn't need them once it got out. The whole northern hemisphere was a tinderbox, a dry feast waiting for the guest who would consume it all.

Gennady squinted into the flames, waiting. He didn't regret killing Achille. Given the choice between saving a human, or even humanity itself, and preserving the dark labyrinth of Khantayskoe, he'd chosen the forest. In doing that, he'd finally admitted his true loyalties and stepped over the border of the human. But that left him with nowhere to go. So, he simply stood and waited for the fire.

Somebody grabbed his arm. Gennady jerked and turned to find Octav standing next to him. The bodyguard was using a long branch as a crutch. There was a surprising expression of concern on his face. "Come on!"

"But, you see, I—"

"I don't care!" Octav had a good grip on him and was stronger than Gennady. Dazed, Gennady let himself be towed away from the fire, and in moments, a pale oval swam into sight between the upright boles of orange-painted pine: Nadine's face.

"Where's Achille?" she called.

Gennady waited until they were close enough that he didn't have to yell. "He tried to use a parachute. The fire pulled him in."

Nadine looked down, seeming to crumple in on herself. "Oh, God, all those men, and, and Achille . . ." She staggered, nearly fell, then seemed to realize where they were. Gennady could feel the fire at his back.

She inserted herself between Octav and Gennady, propelling them both in the direction of the lake at the bottom of the hill. "I'm sorry; I never meant any of this to happen," she cried over the roar of the fire. "All I wanted was for him to go back to his original plan! It could still work." She meant the towers, Gennady knew, and the carbon-negative power plants, and the scheme to sequester all that carbon under the plateau. Not the *Rhizoctonia*. Maybe she was right, but even though she was Achille's heir and owner of the technologies that could save the world, she would never climb out from under what had just happened. She'd be in jail soon, and maybe for the rest of her life.

There were options. Gennady found he was thinking coolly and rationally about those; his mind seemed to have been miraculously cleared, and of more than just the trauma of the past hour. He was waking up, it seemed, from something he'd thought of as his life, but which had only been a rough rehearsal of what he could become. He knew himself now, and the anxiety and hesitation that had dogged him since he was a child was simply gone.

What was important was the patents, and the designs, the business plan, and the opportunities that might bring another tower to the plateau. It might not happen this year or next, but it would have to be soon.

Someone had to take responsibility for the crawling disaster overtaking the world and do something about it.

He would have to talk to Nadine about that inheritance, and about who would administer the fortune while she was in prison. He doubted she would object to what he had in mind.

"Yes, let's go," he said. "We have a lot to do and not much time."

ABOUT THE AUTHOR

KARL SCHROEDER (kschroeder.com) was born into a Mennonite community in Manitoba, Canada, in 1962. He started writing at age fourteen, following in the footsteps of A. E. van Vogt, who came from the same Mennonite community. He moved to Toronto in 1986, and became a founding member of SF Canada (he was president from 1996–97). He sold early stories to Canadian magazines, and his first novel, *The Claus Effect* (with David Nickle) appeared in 1997. His first solo novel, *Ventus*, was published in 2000, and was followed by *Permanence and Lady of Mazes*. His most recent work includes the Virga series of science fiction novels (*Sun of Suns, Queen of Candesce, Pirate Sun*, and *The Sunless Countries*) and hard SF space opera *Lockstep*. He also collaborated with Cory Doctorow on *The Complete Idiot's Guide to Writing Science Fiction*. Schroeder lives in East Toronto with his wife and daughter.

THE SNOWS OF YESTERYEAR

JEAN-LOUIS TRUDEL

Northern Kujalleq Mountains

What would they do without the guy from northern Ontario? Paul's thoughts were stuck in a loop. The same question was popping up every few seconds, probably because his leg muscles were gobbling up most of his body's oxygen. His brain just couldn't phrase a proper answer when the cold September wind was freezing his cheekbones, his breath burned in his throat, and his legs drove him up the snowy slope. The bag with the medikit seemed to grow heavier with every step. Soon, it would drag him all the way back down the mountain.

What would they do without the guy from northern Ontario? The others had nominated him on the spot. Sure, send Paul, he's Canadian, he knows how to ski! Yeah, and he likes to play in the snow too. In the end, Francine had looked at him with those big, dark eyes of hers, and he'd been unable to say no.

He couldn't complain, not really. The Martian Underground had had its pick of young bacteriologists, but they wanted the one with actual winter experience. The guy from northern Ontario. He'd said yes, to the job in Greenland and to the rescue mission.

Even with lightweight snowshoes, he sank a bit in the fresh snow as he leaned into the climb. Tomorrow, his muscles would ache. They didn't use to, not when he snowshoed through the woods of Killarney Park or skied cross-country in the hills outside Sudbury. But he was almost thirty and he'd spent more time in the lab lately than in the field.

He did wonder how the Old Man had fared coming out this way. He must have taken the long way around, down to Narsarsuaq, and then down the coast, skirting the fjord, until he could walk up the valley formerly occupied by the Ikersuaq glacier. Four days at least. A long hike, but not a hard one even for Professor Emeritus Donald B. Hall, who was so old he remembered the twentieth century. Very little of it, actually, but enough to spin unlikely stories that entranced his graduate students.

Early on, Paul had looked up some history sites and decided Old Man Hall was repeating tales he'd heard from his own teachers. Passing joints at a Beatles concert? Flying to Berlin to help tear down the Wall? His date of birth was confidential, but he couldn't be that old, even with stem cell therapies.

Not that he was going to get the chance to beat any records if Paul didn't reach him in time. Every time Paul looked back, the sun seemed closer to the horizon. He only stopped once, to catch his breath. If he saved the Old Man's life, he swore he would get the truth out of him about the one story he'd never managed to disprove or disbelieve.

His heart pumping, Paul started to climb again. He still found patches of snow to plant his snowshoes in, but he was nearing the windswept summit. Sometimes, the synthetic treads clanked and slipped on the bare rock, and he lost his balance for a second, his arms windmilling.

He was pondering whether or not to take off the snowshoes and rely on his boots the rest of the way when he saw the sign.

PRIVATE PROPERTY.

Paul frowned, worry fighting it out with disgust. The valley floor had been buried under the ice for millennia, and it had remained so well into the twenty-first century. And now, as stunted trees grew among the glacier rubble, it had already been claimed by outside interests. The sign was labeled in English, not in Kalaallisut or Danish. A number in a corner identified one of the companies owned by the Consortium that ran the seaports catering to the trans-Arctic trade.

Despite the sign, the new owners probably hadn't bothered with a full surveillance grid. Otherwise, the Old Man would already have been picked up, flown to a hospital, and fined.

Paul should be safe as well from prying eyes. Beyond the sign, the peak was in sight. After putting away his snowshoes, the bacteriologist clambered up the last few meters and mounted a small repeater on top of a telescopic pole. He wedged the pole into place with a few rocks. The small device hunted around for a few seconds and then locked on the signal of its companion a couple of kilometers away, within sight of the Martian Underground base camp.

"I'm at the boundary," Paul rasped into his mike. "A bit past it, in fact. I'll be starting the downhill leg now."

"We're here if you need us," answered the sweet voice of Francine. "You're running behind schedule, but just be careful."

"I intend to."

"And, Paul," cut in the voice of the director, "try and find out why Professor Hall ended up where he did."

"I definitely intend to."

"I know he left before you announced your latest results, but if this was all a ruse to allow him to rendezvous with outsiders . . ."

"I don't see how he could have known before me or swiped a DNA sample. But I'll ask."

He strapped on his skis and launched a small drone to act as an extra pair of eyes for him. As he set off, the drone's-eye view was relayed to his ski goggles and helped him avoid several literal dead ends. Slopes leading to unseen cliffs, rocks hiding around a curve, and other places where he would have ended up dead. Though his exposed skin stung from the wind chill, he enjoyed the descent along the slope of new powder, its blank whiteness marred only by animal tracks. A slope never skied before.

Mid-September wasn't supposed to be this cold in southern Greenland. Yet, temperatures had dipped as they once did in the twentieth century and preserved a couple of recent snowfalls. In Sudbury, Paul had played in snowdrifts that were much thicker when his mother sent him outside because she didn't want to see him at home. He looked too much like his father and she didn't care for the constant reminder. So, yeah, he really liked the snow. It had done such a great job of replacing the home he couldn't have.

The local forecast wasn't calling for more, but Paul tracked warily the oncoming cloud banks, massed so thickly over Niviarsiat Mountain that they threatened to blot out the late-afternoon sun.

The Old Man's camp was putting out an intermittent signal, just strong enough to reach his drone still circling above the valley. By the time Paul was halfway down the mountain, he knew in which direction he would have to head. Toward the ice dam and the lake.

It was almost dark when he found the tent. It was white, propped up by a glacial erratic, and set in the middle of an expanse of fresh snow. Perfectly camouflaged.

"Professor Hall?" Paul called, his voice reduced to a hoarse croak.

"Don't bother knocking."

Hall was lying on an air mattress, bundled up in a sleeping bag. Prompted by the voice in his earbud, Paul hastened to check the Old Man's vital signs.

"His temperature is slightly elevated."

"Perfectly normal for a fracture. Carry on. Anything else?"

The professor endured Paul's amateurish inspection without a complaint. He unzipped the sleeping bag himself, revealing his bare legs. A large, purplish swelling ran around the middle of his left shin. The skin was mottled and bruised but unbroken. Paul swept his phone, set for close focus, over most of the injury.

The base camp's doctor did not hide her relief.

"Not an open break, then. This will make things easier. Give him pain-killer number four and take a breather. Do not try moving him or putting on the exolegs for another fifteen minutes at least."

Paul took out the hypo from the medikit and loaded the designated ampoule. As soon as the painkiller hit the Old Man's bloodstream, a couple of deeply etched lines on his face relaxed and vanished.

The bacteriologist settled down on the tent's only stool. He was breathing more easily, but his shoulders felt like tenderized meat. When he undressed to put on a dry shirt, he found that the skin chafed by the pack's shoulder straps had turned an angry red.

"So, what was so urgent?" he asked. "I thought you were dying."

"I may have exaggerated slightly the gravity of my condition."

"Why?"

"Because it wasn't a secure link. However, I assume you've set up a secure line of relays, as I asked."

"As secure as we could make it, using the same repeaters we use in our glacier tunnels. Narrow beams once the lock is made."

"Good boy."

"Well, tell me now, why couldn't Francine just fly in with the chopper to get you?"

"Any craft big enough to take both of us out of here would have been detected."

"I could have died out there on the mountain, Professor. Were you that afraid of being busted for trespassing?"

Hall responded by pointing his phone at the tent wall. A low-resolution video played on the billowing canvas. The first pictures were blurry, but they seemed to show a small ground-hugging plane, its wings flapping occasionally to detour around a rocky outcrop. It flew above the shadowed southern valley flank, heading straight for the ice dam, and stopped so suddenly that it dropped out of the screen.

"I thought it had crashed. So, I sent up my emergency drone to see if the flyer needed any help. But you know what they say about good deeds . . ."

Wormhole Base, Northern Greenland

The ice was a creaking, shifting presence. Dylan didn't like to dwell on the audible reminders that a substance so hard could be so dynamic that it would slowly fill any tunnel bored through it, given time.

"Was this part of the American base?" Kubota asked.

The businessman from somewhere in Asia—the name sounded Japanese to Dylan, but he hadn't inquired—was casting eager looks at the mechanical debris mixed in with the icy rubble left along the foot of the newly carved wall. Dylan hurried him along and opted for enough of an explanation to keep him happy.

"In a sense, yes. The Americans were thought to have cleaned out all of Project Iceworm's stuff when they left back in 1966, but we're still finding their scraps. Looks like they just didn't bother dragging out various pieces of broken-down machinery or equipment. We've also come across furniture and remnants of the theater. Or perhaps it was the church. Everything got trapped inside the ice sheet when it closed in."

"So then, this tunnel isn't one of the original diggings?"

"No."

"Did you find any missiles?"

Dylan glanced at Kubota without managing to spot the twinkle in his eye that had to be there.

"No," he said curtly. "And the nuclear reactor was decommissioned and removed."

"Good. So then, this is a safe place."

Maybe he was radiation-shy. Given the effects of the Taiwan nuclear exchange on the entire region he came from, that wouldn't be surprising.

"The safest," Dylan confirmed. "Part of the Consortium's cover here is the Extragalactic Neutrino Observatory. The deep ice is clean enough for Cerenkov radiation to shine through quite a large volume. Not as good as in Antarctica, but at least we're looking in the opposite direction. The detectors point down, of course, to use the Earth itself as a gigantic shield and filter, but they're also protected to some extent by the bulk of the ice over them. We're not as far down, with only ninety meters of ice above us, but it's still a nicely rad-free environment."

"A one-time creation."

"The whole point," Dylan agreed.

The Consortium offered visitors with a need for utmost confidentiality the most private facilities ever built. Every meeting room was freshly dug out of millennia-old ice. The only manufactured objects brought in—chairs, tables, infrared lamps—were so basic as to be easily searched for even nanotech bugs. Nobody else had used a given room before and nobody else would afterward.

This time, the Consortium itself had called the meeting. Secrecy would be absolute. Dylan had heard that all of the furniture would be made of particleboard produced on the premises with lumber harvested from a submerged forest in an African lake. The whole idea being that no hidden transmitter or recorder could have been included decades ago within the trunks of a soon-to-be-drowned grove, or would have survived the chipping process . . . Dylan could think of a few flaws with this assumption, but as long as it served its purpose of setting suspicious minds at ease, he wouldn't quibble.

"Here we are," he said.

Kubota went in first and Dylan followed, finding his way to the side of Brian McGuire. As head manager of the local Consortium office, McGuire would chair the meeting. As the brightest of the bright young interns, Dylan would supply specifics if required.

The room was large and freezing cold until one entered the enchanted ring of infrared lamps.

The tables were set in a hollow square, with enough seating for twenty people: an eclectic mix of owners, executives, and highly trusted assistants.

"No names," McGuire announced in a booming voice. "Names are too easy to remember. Faces just slip away. Or change."

Not that individual names really mattered. The only names that counted were displayed on yellow cardboard squares, and they identified the companies or industrial concerns represented by the people around the table.

"Notes?" asked a woman with a slight Scandinavian accent.

"You may use papers or internal electronics. If you managed to sneak in any external electronics, my congratulations to your technical staff, but you'll still have to sneak them out and their contents will have to survive a low-level electromagnetic pulse."

The woman nodded. McGuire added:

"At the end of the meeting, I will offer a road map, boiled down to six main points. We worded them to be easy to memorize. In many instances, details will come later. We are here to ask and to answer questions. If the answers aren't satisfactory, we won't go forward. But I truly believe that we are standing on the ground floor of something big."

Heads nodded. The Consortium had already proved it could place big bets when it had built up Qaqortoq from a sleepy fishing village into a major port for container ships coming or going from Asia, Europe, or North America, and needing to swap containers before heading to their ultimate destination. In the broader context, Wormhole Base was a side project catering to a few thousand people a year, though it also served to demonstrate the Consortium's commitment to Greenland. But McGuire was willing to go slow and build his case first.

"Global warming is the new industrial frontier. Mitigation and adaptation are already huge and are going to become even huger. We'll have to beat back deserts, move cities to higher ground, and re-create whole new species."

"I thought the Loaves and Fishes group was cornering the market for new heat-tolerant crops and pollution-resistant fish," said an older man whose spot at the table bore the name of a well-known Canadian nanotech company.

"Perhaps, but they're not turning a profit," Dylan objected.

McGuire threw him a menacing look, but his voice remained smooth and practiced as he ignored the double interruption.

"Everybody here has a finger in the pie and a stake in the result, but we want more. Greenland is the first new piece of prime real estate completely up for grabs since humans arrived in North America—unless that first wave actually beat the one that went to Australia."

"Rather barren real estate."

"It'll get better."

"And not entirely deserted."

"The current population is just hanging off the edges of the landmass, so it will only be a factor if we let it. Our new facilities have attracted so many immigrants that they're swamping the locals. One way or another, we don't expect the Nuuk government to be a worry."

The man identified as Toluca nodded, apparently willing to concede the point. His own face bore a distant family resemblance to that of the Greenland Inuit.

"As part of your invitation, we included a topographic map of Greenland without the ice sheet," McGuire added. "It must have struck you, looking at the map, that there are only a few major glacial outlets. Plug them up and the Greenland ice sheet will no longer contribute anything to sea level rise."

There were blank looks all around the table. Preventing sea level rise was not an obvious source of profits. Saving the world would have to yield dividends to catch this group's attention.

"Where will the water go?"

"Nowhere. It'll stay where it is. Part of Greenland lies below sea level. Up to three hundred meters. The central part of the continent can easily contain a major inland sea."

"Isn't the crust depressed under the weight of all that ice? Won't it rebound?"

The woman from Scandinavia probably knew something about postglacial rebound. Dylan looked expectantly at McGuire, but the Consortium manager did not need to consult his assistant.

"Come on, think! If the water is contained when the ice melts, it won't go anywhere. The overburden remains nearly the same. The meltwater will be quite sufficient to prevent isostatic rebound."

The woman did not yield as easily as Toluca and probed further.

"I did look at the map. The central ice sheet is over three kilometers high; most of the surrounding mountains are no more than hills. The peaks reach up to two kilometers on the eastern coast, but most of the western hills are only half a kilometer high. Even if you could turn most of central Greenland into an enclosed basin, something like half the ice is still going to melt and add to sea level rise."

"Half is better than none. And the half flowing out can be turned to good use."

"Such as?"

"No mean bonus. If you plug the outlets and water rises behind the walls, we will be able to use some of it to power hydroelectric plants."

Dylan hid a smile as backs straightened, chair legs scraped along the roughened ice of the floor, and gazes fastened on McGuire.

"White coal," Kubota said, his eyes narrowing.

"Enough to power whole new cities, yes."

"The gaps between the hills are huge," the Scandinavian woman noted.

"All the more work for us. If this is sold as a way to control water outflow, we can get government money to help with the construction. And we can start with the smallest outlets, the ones that will cost least to plug and will be all the more profitable."

"So then, assuming there is money to be made, I think we would like to be a part of it," Kubota said slowly. "We can talk about the technical issues later. Plenty of time for that. What I would like to know is how you intend to tackle the political side. Sea levels have risen a meter since the beginning of the century, but most governments haven't budged or tried seriously to slow the warming. So then, why would they act now?"

"Floods."

"As in glacial lake outburst floods?" the Scandinavian woman asked. "Those can be cataclysmic!"

Dylan had researched the Missoula floods that had devastated eastern Washington State at the end of the last glacial period. The lake had been gigantic. The collapse of an ice dam had unleashed a flood with more water than all of the planet's rivers put together, flowing with a speed rivaling that of a car on a highway. The flood had scoured riverbanks down to bedrock and carried chunks of glacier for kilometers downstream. He expected to answer questions later, but it was still McGuire's show for now.

"Precisely," the Consortium manager confirmed. "Take Niviarsiat Lake in Kujalleq. Fifty years ago, there was a glacier half a kilometer high in the same spot. Now it's a meltwater lake dammed by leftover ice. If the dam broke, the water would rush down Ikersuaq Fjord and destroy everything within reach."

"Is this what you're proposing to do?" the Canadian asked.

Some of the attendees glanced at the icy walls and ceiling, as if to reassure themselves they were as safe from espionage as could be.

"Does anybody live in Ikersuaq Fjord?" Toluca asked.

"Most of the valley near the lake actually belongs to a Consortium company and access is forbidden. Once you reach the actual fjord, there's a small settlement at Niaqornaq and the town of Narssaq is found on the next fjord over, though it is connected to Ikersuaq by a strait. Many buildings have already been moved to higher ground, but the docks would certainly be swamped. Let's be frank, people. Casualties would help us make our case to the government."

"Is this a hypothetical discussion?" the Canadian insisted.

McGuire held the eyes of the owners and executives around the table. Dylan noticed some of the assistants closer to his own age looked uneasy, but they weren't involved. McGuire challenged his peers when he answered, his voice dropping to a lower tone.

"Last winter, one of our best men set off explosives underneath the glaciers feeding the lake. There were no visible effects, and the blasts could be confused with an icequake, but the ice beneath the glaciers was turned into Swiss cheese. Throughout the summer, the glaciers calved several times, shedding huge chunks of ice that melted in the sun. The lake level has risen so far and so fast that pressure near the bottom should have pushed the freezing point below the temperature of the ice. The water should already be eating away at the base of the dam."

"When will it break?"

"Two weeks from now. Mid-September."

Nobody asked how he could be so certain of the timing. Faces closed while minds readied to grapple with technical details as a way of forgetting what had just been discussed. Dylan suspected that all they cared about now was that the meeting room be blown up as promised after they left, tons of ice crushing the furniture and burying the very memory of the dangerous words they had heard.

Niviarsiat Lake, Southern Greenland

Old Man Hall had slipped just as he was launching the drone into the air, banging his leg hard on a boulder in the wrong place at the wrong time. He said drily that he'd known right away that it was a break, not just a bruise. Paul didn't ask how. Unable to put any weight on it, he'd managed to hop and crawl back to his tent, where he'd waited for the return of the drone.

The drone's video was much clearer than the phone pictures. The small plane seen earlier had found a smooth stretch of gravel by the fan of rivulets streaming out of the ice dam base. Paul would have liked to freeze the frame, but the professor was still holding his phone. The gravel looked suspiciously smooth and uniform, devoid of any larger rocks or significant dips. A previously used landing strip, perhaps?

"This is where it gets interesting," the Old Man whispered.

The plane had come to a quick stop close to the foot of the ice dam. A man stepped out, looked around, but did not look up. He opened a cargo compartment, took out a heavy rucksack, and walked over to the dam, bent under the weight of his load. He was using what looked like a ski pole as a walking stick. He took his time climbing up the bumpy outward surface of the dam. When he was about two-thirds of the way to the top, the man knelt by a narrow crevasse and probed with his pole. He got up and tried another crevasse a few meters away. It took him two more tries to find what he was looking for.

This time, he pulled out of his bag four long, boxlike objects linked by cables. He lowered them inside the crevasse, using a rope clipped to one of the boxes, and then rose to his feet. The rucksack was much lighter now. The man checked his phone, walked down a few meters, checked it again, walked back to the plane, and checked it one last time before taking off.

"Any chance those wouldn't be high explosives?" Paul asked hollowly.

"A very small one. I've been in the field for decades; I've seen geologists at work, glaciologists, bacteriologists, paleontologists. . . . I can't say why exactly, but the man's behavior just doesn't fit. He was too hasty, didn't take any measurements. . . . Perhaps he was dropping off an instrument package for somebody else, but I don't buy it. It's a good thing I didn't look at the video for a couple of hours. Too busy trying to take care of my leg, so it was already dark when I watched it."

"And that's when you called base camp."

"Right away. And I didn't sleep much that night."

"Why do you think they would want to blow it up?"

"Unsure. The lake behind it is not that big, but the flood would rush down to the fjord and threaten Narssaq. I think Narsarsuaq would be safe from any kind of backwash. If it's some sort of terrorist plot, I fail to see the logic of it."

"What about the Loaves and Fishes people?"

"They're into radical adaptation. New heat-tolerant crops. New marine life forms engineered to withstand the acidic seas. If they can thrive on a plastic-enriched diet, even better, since the oceans aren't going to run out of plastic for centuries . . . But terrorism on this scale? I know they've sabotaged some bottom trawlers to make a point about disappearing fish stocks. And they've been strident about highlighting the shifting land and ocean conditions due to climate change. Still, why would they be behind this?"

Paul shook his head, unable to offer a rationale. The Old Man had been thinking it over for hours, after all.

"How about the Sunscreen Lobby? They've been looking for a way to convince governments to fund their orbital shield for years."

The professor shrugged. "Sure, extreme environmentalists of all stripes might go for it as a reminder of the dangers of global warming, but casualties are going to be low even if they blow it at night. And there's so much happening elsewhere that I doubt it would grab the world's attention."

"If it's that unlikely, it might not be a bomb. I should go and check before we panic."

"Now? It's dark and you won't see anything."

"I've got a good lamp. I watched the video carefully. I think I can find the right crevasse."

"How will you fish the package out? It looks like he picked the deepest crevasse he could find."

"But he didn't recover the rope he used to lower the package. With a bit of luck, I can use the rope to pull it back up."

The professor half rose, stretching out his arm as far as he could.

"Don't go. If the dam blows while you're out there, I won't have a chance. The flash flood will just roll over me."

"And I'll be dead. In that case, you might as well tell me now why you came to be here."

"What I do on my own time is none of your business."

Paul stood and zipped up his coat.

"If that's how you feel, Professor, we'll have to discuss this when I come back. I've come over the mountain to help you, and that was hard enough. But I've spent years working on the identification of bacteria preserved in the ice or beneath the ice. I've examined I don't know how many samples taken out of tunnels dug with hot water hoses or brought back by icebots from the deepest layers of the ice sheet. I've helped to isolate bacteria able to repair their DNA in freezing conditions for over a million years. I've found two new strains that synthesize methane in brutally cold conditions to help the Martian Underground plan for the global warming of Mars. And I've . . . So, if you think I don't care that my work may benefit somebody who didn't pay for it, you need more time to rethink your assumptions."

"All work that I taught you how to do."

"Don't flatter yourself. I had other professors. But I did look up to you for one thing."

"What?"

"Ethics."

The Old Man grabbed for the stool and tried to lever himself upright without using his leg. Paul shouldered his backpack again, wincing slightly, and opened the tent slit.

"No, Paul, wait. It's not what you think. I was freelancing, but it had nothing to with the Martian Underground or with your work."

"What, then?"

"I had a contract with the Pliocene Park Foundation. I was supposed to sample Niviarsiat Lake, or the glaciers upstream ideally, for ancient DNA."

Paul turned around.

"The Pliocene Park project? I've heard of it. Doesn't it involve buying land for a nature preserve that will re-create the environment of the Pliocene?"

"More than that. It will be stocked not only with surviving species of the Pliocene but with ones we've been able to resurrect from past extinction. In Siberia, the melting permafrost has released carcasses from the last interglacial. Reviving mammoths was only a start. The Russians are working on mastodons and stegodons and chalicotheres. But one of the best places for finding relics is underneath the Greenland ice sheet. There may be fossils once we access the underlying rocks. And there are certainly DNA remains in the lowest strata of the ice, some of which should date back to the Pliocene. Mostly plants, we expect, but also some northern animals."

"So, you were working for a zoo. I guess we can all sleep easier."

"There's more to it than that. Global warming is a time machine back to the Pliocene. The whole project is about reminding people of that."

Paul sighed. "Your generation is still trying, isn't it?"

"And yours has given up."

"Perhaps because we saw how far you got. The sins of our fathers passed down to us, but we don't have to repeat the errors of our fathers."

"At least we tried to slow down the warming. Our generation threw everything at the problem. Finally cut back on total emissions even as the population kept rising to ten billion. But the seas got warmer and no longer absorbed as much carbon dioxide. So, we seeded the ocean deserts with iron dust and made them bloom with phytoplankton. Carbon dioxide uptake increased but ocean acidification too. The coral reefs died and fisheries declined. People starved and turned to coastal fish and shrimp farms. Without the mangroves they cut down and the sandbars drowned by rising seas, hurricanes swept in and tidal surges wiped out many of the farms. . . . More people starved. In the end, we went back to farming where the rains still came, even if forests had to be cleared, even if synthetic fertilizers were needed, and even if transportation costs ballooned as such farms got too far from the mouths to feed. But pulping the forests returned carbon to the atmosphere and transportation still burned up too much carbon, although far less than in the days of gas-guzzlers."

Paul had let him speak, thinking of the world beyond the small tent, beyond the deserted valley in southern Greenland. Drowned cities, burning forests, shifting sand dunes in Iowa, and the poor dying of thirst in

India. What could a guy from northern Ontario do about it all? He'd stopped loving the snow when he'd realized it was an illusion. It only covered up the same landscape as before. In the end, it changed nothing. "And, in the end," Paul said quietly, "every route took you back to your starting point, leaving us to live in a warming world or die."

"So, what did you do?"

"We faced reality. My generation intends to live. On this world or another."

Paul stalked out, leaving his mentor speechless. He stood in darkness for a moment, listening for any sound other than his quickened breathing. If there was a bomb, it could be set off by a signal sent from a satellite passing overhead. The man in the plane wouldn't come back. There would be no warning.

He went back inside the tent and took out from his bag another earbud as well as the medikit. He displayed the exolegs, which looked like pieces of bulky black hose connected to shapeless shoes.

"The earbud, you know to use. If you haven't used exolegs before, pay attention to our doctor's instructions. The main thing is not to try to pull them on. Even with the painkiller, you'd feel the bones grinding together. If you do it right, they will split lengthwise so that you can wrap the covering around your leg. The smart material will exert the right amount of pressure to set and immobilize the bones. Afterward, if you lead with your good leg, the artificial muscles will also walk your legs for you. The exoskeleton will take up most of the pounding, but you'll feel it when the painkiller wears off. It will hurt like hell."

He grinned evilly, thinking of his own battered flesh, then pointed in the general direction he'd come from.

"Head south, up the valley flank. The summit repeater will act as your beacon. But stop when you've reached an altitude one hundred meters above sea level. There's a terrace Francine can land the chopper on to take us out. If you don't run across it, stay put, and I'll find you later. Or Francine will find you in the morning."

"Paul, wait, please. Come with me. You don't need to go."

"I still think it might not be a bomb. And if it's a bomb, there might be clues as to its maker."

"If it's a bomb, there's a good chance that it will blow tonight."

"It's still early. I'm betting that they'll wait till midnight, whoever they are."

This time, when he stepped outside, he kept going. Clouds hid most of the stars, so he turned on a flashlight. Gravel crunched under his boots and he thought of his old dream of walking on Mars. Nobody could work for the Martian Underground and not think of the possibilities.

Colonizing Mars was another long shot, like the orbital sunscreen intended to cool Earth. The methanogenic bacteria found in cold, light-less, microscopic pockets at the base of ancient Earth glaciers might serve to hasten the terraformation of Mars. They might even prove to be of Martian origin. On Earth, they were part of a slow-paced, long-lived sub-glacial ecosystem still dining off leftover biomass from earlier thaws.

Sown across the Martian surface, they would belch, under the right conditions, enough methane to start creating a future haven for human-ity. Within the Martian Underground, fans of the idea sometimes called themselves the Young Farts of Mars, if only to make it clear they wouldn't be happy with just going to Mars, like previous generations. Francine's voice suddenly blared into his ear.

"Paul Weingart, what are you doing?"

"What a guy from northern Ontario can do. No more, no less."

"We heard everything. We think it's a bomb and that you should get the hell out of the way. Both of you."

"I won't be long. Just keep track of Professor Hall for me."

"Paul, please, wait!"

"Too late. Now please give me some quiet; I need to concentrate."

He had reached the foot of the dam. The flashlight's beam played over the icy slope. He hadn't been boasting. He had a good memory for weird surfaces, trained perhaps by his work in the lab, and it only took him a quarter of an hour to find the spot where the man had left the package.

He swore when he discovered that the rope had slipped, falling into the crevasse. However, the beam picked up the yellow nylon rope only a meter or so below the lip of the crevasse. Paul threw himself flat on the ice, extended his arm, and grabbed the end of the rope.

And swore again when he realized he could do nothing with it. The load at the far end of the rope was too heavy. With one arm fully outstretched and the other braced at an angle against an ice boulder to keep himself from slipping forward, he lacked the leverage needed to pull up the package.

He pondered his next move for a moment, fully aware of the ticking minutes that brought midnight closer. He finally took his other hand away from its hold and gently teased one of his snowshoes out of his pack. The friction between the main mass of his body and the snow-dusted ice was all that was keeping him in place. He lowered the snowshoe within reach of his right hand, using it to thread the rope between the frame and the decking before tying a quick lasso knot. He pulled back his free hand and groped for a hold.

Paul thought of Francine before trying to rise. She'd sounded worried about him. Was she still listening in? Trying to guess what was happening to him from his breathing?

Exhaling sharply, he pulled himself back from the brink in one go. He stayed in a crouch for a moment, his heart pounding, and then pulled out the snowshoe as slowly as possible. He was afraid that the knot might slip when placed under tension, but all he did was pick up the slack in the rope.

Once he had the rope well in hand, he wasted no time in lifting the package out of the crevasse. A grunt escaped his lips. The package was heavy.

"All's well," he announced. "I've got the . . ."

He hesitated. Shone the light on the objects from the crevasse. Noted the absence of any dials, gauges, or markings. Started walking suddenly with a faster stride.

"I think it's a bomb, after all."

"Leave it, then," the director said.

"Not yet."

He backtracked all the way to the Old Man's tent. He checked it was empty and left the explosives inside. The farther he got from the tent, the harder it was to breathe. What if they blew *now*? He would feel really silly.

Yet the bomb hadn't blown when he reached the side of the valley and began climbing immediately. Soon, he spotted the trail left by Old Man Hall, the trampled snow almost silvery in the light. He made quick work of following in the professor's footsteps and soon discerned the man's silhouette ahead of him. Just as he was on the verge of hailing him, the bomb blew.

The noise was surprisingly loud and the flash illuminated the entire nightscape, the dam dazzlingly white, the evergreen saplings thrown in sharp relief, and every rock of the valley floor clearly outlined. A few seconds later, gravel pattered down like a hard rain.

Paul wheezed helplessly for a moment, his ears ringing. He couldn't remember breathing since leaving the crevasse, but relief now unclenched some of the muscles he had tensed. The flash had shown him the terrace was within sight. Old Man Hall had found the edge of the flatter ground and was just waiting for him. He was an experienced hiker, after all.

The explosion had also caused the professor to turn around and locate the younger man. Once Paul caught up to him, the first thing out of the professor's mouth was a warning.

"They'll come and see why the dam didn't collapse. Whoever did this isn't going to be happy with us."

"I know. But we'll be gone. And your camp has been blown to bits. We'll be hard to track."

"But completely exposed until we get back."

"Look up."

The Old Man blinked and glanced at the clouds overhead, the light clipped to his head sweeping up. Whitish stars were falling from the sky and crowding into the beam. Snowflakes.

"It's snowing."

"As expected. The snow will hide our tracks, cover what's left of your tent, and make it more difficult for others to follow the helicopter."

"What helicopter?"

Paul raised his hand and waved at the shape emerging out of the flurries. He'd cheated. His younger ears had picked up the sound of the approaching aircraft before his mentor.

The professor's shoulders slumped as the man relaxed. He'd held up surprisingly well, given his age. This reminded Paul of the question he'd wanted to ask.

"Hey, prof, there's one thing I always wanted to know. Did you really work on the DNA profiling of OJ Simpson?"

Hall stared at him and then smiled slowly.

"I'll tell you in the helicopter if you tell me why you were so sure that it was going to snow."

Paul nodded. He'd given him a few clues, but Old Man Hall was still a sharp one. "You know what many of us are looking for. Sure, the Martian Underground puts up the funding for bacteria that can survive on Mars, whether they're simple extremophiles or highly durable methanogens. But that won't help us on Earth. Except that, as you said, global warming is taking us back to the Pliocene."

"You've found something from the Pliocene!"

"Ironic, isn't it, that you came hunting here for Pliocene relics just as I was able to announce that I'd isolated a new strain of ice-forming bacteria in a sample from deep below the ice sheet."

"Rainmakers?"

"Exactly. We've always thought that bacteria from a warmer age might be more effective in our warming world than current strains. Pliocene microorganisms adapted to a warmer climate over millions of years, not the ten thousand years or so since the last freeze-up. The strain I found is related to modern-day varieties that promote ice nucleation in clouds."

"And now you've released it in the wild?"

The professor looked up again, his mouth closed firmly to resist the temptation of sticking out his tongue and tasting bacteria from another geological age.

"Whose fault is that?" Paul asked. "Don't worry; there's some left for further study, but I cultured enough to leave a flask with Francine. We agreed that she could use a drone to seed any likely cloud mass if it seemed necessary."

"That wasn't very ethical," the Old Man said, eyes downcast.

"But it may save our lives until we can report the sabotage to authorities."

The professor nodded, any further comment cut off by the roar of the helicopter landing at the far end of the terrace. Paul knew that he would soon work out the other implications of the discovery. The new bacteria heralded a wave of other discoveries that might help with humanity's adaptation to a warmer world. Might even help to control warming, if that wasn't too much to hope for.

Old Man Hall headed for the craft, walking stiffly. Paul followed, but he didn't make it all the way. The helicopter's pilot had jumped out in the snow and she ran to meet him. It was Francine.

She threw her arms around him, hugged him, and kissed him. When they stopped to breathe again, he smiled and asked, "Francine Pomerleau, what are you doing?"

"The only thing possible under the circumstances. You've forced me to ask a question that I don't know the answer to. What would I do without my guy from northern Ontario?"

ABOUT THE AUTHOR

Born in Toronto, JEAN-LOUIS TRUDEL now lives in Québec City, Canada. He holds degrees in physics, astronomy, and the history of science, capping his education with a doctorate in history. Jean-Louis now teaches history part-time at the University of Ottawa. He is the author of twenty-eight books in French, including novels, collections, and YA fiction, one anthology in English (*Tesseracts7*), and more than one hundred short stories in French and English. His publications have won him several Prix Aurora Awards. He also writes with Yves Meynard under the name Laurent McAllister, accounting for five more books and a handful of short stories. Their 2009 novel *Suprématie* won plaudits, nominations, and Canada's top science fiction awards.

THE RAINY SEASON

TOBIAS S. BUCKELL

Elaine grabbed her duffel bag and wrestled it down from the overhead rack, and looked out the windows of her stopped train at the new station's winglike roofs curving overhead. She didn't recognize any of the waiting faces in the Encinitas terminal, though it was hard to tell by just the eyes. So many people wore surgical masks.

Which reminded her. She pulled hers on. The air was slightly hazy today.

She wondered idly if she should consider a full respirator. Back in Michigan, Kenneth certainly seemed to consider it a good idea. "You can't risk breathing in that coastal air," he said. "Who knows what's in it?"

"Only tourists wear full respirators," she'd protested.

"You're not that different," Kenneth said. "You don't live there anymore. You haven't for a very long time."

Fair enough. Still. People wearing full respirators were something to chuckle at. Out-of-towners. She'd be inside soon enough, Elaine thought. And stepped out of the train into the bright sun.

A few minutes of meandering around the slowly thinning crowd, and she realized that no one would be there to pick her up as promised. She relented and got into a cab.

She should have known better than to trust that Beverly and Jackson would actually pick her up as promised. *Welcome home, Elaine,* she thought.

Everything had changed. That she expected, but it still hit her. When you lived somewhere, you slowly saw the raw physical nature of the world shift. A building here or there. Starts scattered across locations.

But when you came back to somewhere you lived after an absence, it all happened at once. Your brain had to process and work hard to update that model of realness minute after minute as you looked around and saw change after change. The place wasn't the same. The place you lived no longer existed. In the same geographical location is a new place, with some traces of the things that you used to consider that location still surviving.

And there was no driver up front to ask questions like "what happened to the chicken place that used to be on this corner?"

Well, that was a stupid question, wasn't it? It was gone. It didn't matter anymore. She hadn't been there to see it go. It didn't care that she cared that it was gone. And probably neither did anyone else.

She stopped trying to catalogue the differences, to expect certain signs and buildings at certain points. This was a new city. This wasn't really coming back; this was arriving for the first time. She was different. Encinitas was different.

Deal with it, she told herself.

As the car drove itself down the 101, winding along the coast, she caught glimpses of people laid out on the beach, their faces hidden behind bug-like gas masks. It was like an invasion of the rubbery sea-people, Elaine thought to herself.

It had all been perfectly normal to her once.

Beverly and Jackson stared at her when they opened the door. Their eyes had a dull haze to them as they just stared at her, reaching for some memory.

"Hello?" Elaine prompted.

The words were a spark to their fuel. They suddenly moved into action. "When did you get in?" Beverly asked.

"You came?" Jackson said, nodding his head slowly in that bird-like way Elaine had always hated.

"Of course I fucking came," Elaine snapped.

Beverly stepped between the two of them. Ostensibly to grab the canvas duffel bag Elaine shouldered. But it was a shielding move. "It's an honest question," Beverly muttered. "It's been six years. We haven't seen you in *six* years."

"I sent an email," Elaine said. "I sent texts. I explained I'd be taking the train up from San Diego after flying in."

Jackson scratched at bleach-blond hair and looked pained. "Email?"

"Jackson isn't good at checking that stuff; you know that," Beverly said, a hint of accusation in her tone.

"I sent *you* a message," Elaine said.

Beverly bit her lip. "It's not a good time right now, and a lot of people sent me messages. I'm sorry we weren't there to pick you up."

They locked eyes for a second. And Elaine decided a fight over not being picked up would get them nowhere. *We're all adults here,* she thought. All on the edge. Elaine stepped over plastic toys and metal cars as Beverly shuffled her in and quickly closed the door.

"We weren't expecting you. Tomorrow we can put together the bunks for the kids; they're already in bed, though. I don't want to wake them up. Unless you want to sleep in . . ."

Elaine shook her head and looked down the tiny hallway. "No," she said quickly. "No. The couch is fine."

She'd left home in the silent, groggy morning hours. Crisp fall air and the smell of coffee. Quiet kisses goodbye and feeling of . . . something like a reddened, dead leaf spinning slowly as it wafted to the ground. She'd been balled up tight inside for the whole trip, getting tenser as she got closer to the coast.

Now she was a spring-tight wad of self-control as she put her bag down next to the couch. "I could get a room. At a hotel."

"Oh, Jesus Christ," Beverly snapped. "I'm sorry we weren't ready for you. I'm sorry we don't have a room yet. I can go get the kids up . . ."

"Bev!" Jackson pleaded. "Bev."

Elaine sank onto the couch. "The couch is fine. I've been in cramped seats all day. It's just fine. I just need to wash my face."

Beverly hovered over the couch, and then banked off toward the kitchen to angrily clean up. Through the cutout in the wall Elaine saw several carefully wrapped casseroles and lots of other plastic dishes. Offerings from neighbors. Food to get you through a hard time.

The house reeked of melted cheese and pasta.

In the toothpaste- and hard-soap-encrusted bathroom, Elaine pushed aside shaving cream and cologne to perch her old leather travel bag on the marble sink top so she could wash her face and brush her teeth.

She looked in the mirror, past her flyaway hair and to the room on the other side of the hall. The door was open. An old plastic rocking chair anxiously leaned forward in the late evening light. Elaine stared at it until she realized she'd stopped brushing her teeth.

That absence. The lack of something in the house. It kept pricking the back of her neck.

An empty rocking chair.

One of her favorite spots had always been the deck. They were close to the edge of the state park, and everything had been built up around them. The richer folk carving elaborate space out so they could have their ocean views. But their ancient little beach house creaked on.

If you looked straight ahead and paid no attention to the noise, it was you, the rocks, and then ocean going on for ever and ever.

The sun glinted over the gray surface, and Elaine scratched at the edge of her gas mask, then slipped it up to sip coffee.

Jackson joined her, slipping in right next to her. "Didn't think you'd be up this early," he said. "Jet lag and all."

"The couch is shit for sleeping on," Elaine said. "My back is twisted. I barely slept."

"She'll get you in a real bed tomorrow."

"Doesn't matter." Elaine sighed, the sound louder than it needed to be, thanks to the mask. "It isn't important."

Jackson nodded. "She's real angry."

"I know. Six years. I'm sorry. It just . . . It wasn't easy. I never fit. I forgot to call. And then it felt like it would be awkward if I did. And then it got easy to not call. Because I wasn't here. And I didn't have to."

"That's not why she's angry," Jackson said softly.

Elaine heard something in his voice that signaled that she needed to pay attention. Jackson had always been more in tune with Bev. If he felt like he needed to say something, she should listen.

"It's the will," Jackson said.

"What about it?"

He rubbed his forehead, tapped his feet. Avoided her eyes. "You didn't come back because of the will?"

"I haven't seen the will. Damn, Jackson, I haven't even thought about the will." Elaine put the coffee down on the deck.

"Never even wondered about the beach house?" Jackson looked around.

"Figured it was Bev and you. You moved in with him." It made sense to her. And after she'd legged it for the Midwest, she figured she'd all but divorced her own family. They'd raised her. But they weren't really blood. She hadn't expected anything.

Jackson shook his head and looked down between the slats of wood at the sandy ground below. "Nah." He snorted. "The old man left it all to you, Elaine."

Elaine suddenly felt like she'd had the world yanked out from underneath. "The fuck?"

"All that's left is the house and a few dollars in savings. But he left it all to you."

She stared at Jackson. "Why?"

He shrugged bony shoulders. "Figured you to be the more mature one. Will says you get to decide what's done. Think he was never really happy about the fact that we both had to move back in."

Elaine pulled her knees up to her chin. She didn't want to have to think about what happened with the house. Or what to do. Or what was fair. "Bev isn't mad; she's scared," she whispered.

Jackson said nothing.

The door to the deck slid open with a loud thunk. Bev stood in the frame, one of her sons in one arm half dressed in black, a clip-on bowtie dangling from his neck. "Are you my aunt?" he asked loudly.

"We don't have much time," Bev said. "Hannes says the storm's going to hit soon. We need to get to the lagoon or it'll be canceled."

Elaine stared for a moment at the formal tux on her nephew and struggled to remember the five-year-old's name.

Wow. She'd really yanked the string and bugged out, hadn't she? No standing bridges left.

Alec, she thought. His name was Alec.

"Wear something nice," Bev warned them both before retreating back inside.

Elaine looked out to the ocean and saw darkness on the edge of the horizon. She hadn't bothered to check the weather report.

The edge of the storm hit in the middle of the ceremony. Three men in their seventies had turned up to pay their respects, wearing bright floral shirts and baggy pants. They stepped forward and fondly remembered out loud the old days and surfing off the coast. Late nights on the beach. Driving up and down the coast.

Offshore fishing.

It was a litany of familiarity.

And before Beverly, Jackson, or Elaine could step forward, it began to rain. Elaine pulled the mask out of her purse and fastened it over her face. Jackson looked up at the clouds and stuck out his tongue.

Beverly slapped his hand. "Empty the ashes, Jackson. We need to leave. Alex, do *not* imitate your uncle."

Alex. Of course. I'd been one letter off.

"Shouldn't we . . ." Jackson waved a hand around. "You know? Say something?"

Beverly looked at the clouds. "We need to leave. It's going to get bad."

The rain thickened. The old men trundled off, slapping each other on the back. I pushed the mask hard against my nose for a better seal.

"Good-bye, dad," Jackson said, and began to scatter his ashes.

The rain spread his remains into the mud.

I had no idea if this was what he had wanted, but I wasn't going to ask or second-guess. I stood and thought about the emptiness in the house, and tried to engage with the fact that he just *wasn't here* anymore.

We did stand in silence for a bit and then returned to the car.

As everyone piled back in, I pulled my mask off and stood behind Beverly. "Bev?"

She turned around. The rain plastered her carefully styled hair flat to her forehead. I shivered. I'd run away from this intensity. But standing in front of her, I wanted to reach forward and dive back in. Build that bridge.

No no no, shut up, leave it alone, shouted another dwindling voice further inside me.

I blinked. "I didn't know about the will," I said. "I didn't want to cause trouble."

"You didn't know?" Beverly looked incredulous.

"Not until Jackson told me."

"He didn't talk to you? You two didn't plan this?"

I stepped back. "Why would I plan this? What is *this*?"

"You know."

"No, Bev, I don't. I don't know." I was breathing heavily now, my face streaming wet with rain. The words flowed. "So why don't you tell me?"

Her lips curled slightly. "It's even worse, then. If you never talked. He just died, never hearing again from you. And still he did this. Left you the house. And you can't even appreciate it."

"I didn't *want* it." Elaine stepped closer. "I swear."

"You *should* want it," Bev said. "Because it is the family's. The house has been in the family for four generations now. But you could care less. Because you aren't really a part of the family. You don't want it or us. You found out you were adopted, and since then, you didn't want jack shit to do with us. You don't even want the greatest gift our father could give any of us."

The rain smelled sharp. Chemical sharp.

Pull it in, Elaine urged herself. *Take control, mollify her, and get in the damn car.* But in the rain, she could see the outline of Bev's attitude. She could read that her body language signaled "ungrateful bitch" in bright red.

And as prickly as she was, Elaine usually stepped back from the cliff. Usually walked away.

Or even ran away entirely from it all.

She stepped forward. "Maybe," she gritted. "Maybe he gave it to me because he didn't think his own daughter could keep it together enough to make the right call. Between both of you moving back in with him, he had time to get a real close read on you both, right?"

Bev's eyes widened and she slapped Elaine.

They both stood and stared at each other.

Then Bev got in the car and shut the door. "Maybe you're right," she shouted from inside. "So why don't you get your own damn ride back to the house."

Elaine's mouth was half open, cheek still stinging.

Jackson was in the back with the kids, and he had a "what the fuck?" expression on his face. He slid the window down as Bev started to pull away. "You're tripping, Elaine!"

"I know," Elaine said, still stunned by what she'd said. Sure, she'd thought things like that. Unvoiced suspicions, old family wounds. Festering.

Jackson threw her gas mask out of the window at her. "The rain, idiot. You're tripping."

They shot away, bouncing over the dirt road, headed back toward asphalt. Elaine leaned over and picked up the mask. It had broken against a rock.

"Shit," she whispered, feeling a bit dizzy from the fumes around her. Shit. What pyschotropics were falling out of the sky today? What was she inhaling? Something that had dropped her barriers to saying what was on her mind.

Shit.

"This is *why* I left," she shouted at the darkening sky. She looked back toward the muddy spot where they'd scattered the ashes, and then stumbled back toward it. "I didn't deserve the slap. But I think I needed to be yelled at. That wasn't very nice of me."

Oh, Dad, she thought, looking down at the ground. *But you'd know that.* He hadn't slapped her after she'd come in from a heavy storm, high out of her mind because she was local and wouldn't be bothered to wear a mask. She'd laid it all out there. Called him a deadbeat loser surfer who'd been lucky enough to be given a house so he could burn out slowly by the beach.

And more. The stuff ambitious young people say when the light in their eyes was still unbridled and unblunted by a wider world.

Loser.

Elaine started to cry over the mud. "I'm sorry I didn't call. I was too damn stubborn."

She could feel the storm eating at her from the inside. Dissolving through her skin, her leaking eyes.

"Elaine?"

Her fingertips tingled as the rain lashed at them.

"Elaine!"

She held them up in the air as the wind slapped at her jacket, trying to rip it away from her shoulders like a desperate lover.

Hands grabbed her shoulders and twisted her around. She stared at the man in front of her without understanding for a moment that she was looking at a face. Weathered and leathery, with gray-green eyes and faded blond hair.

"Elaine," he said again. "You shouldn't be out in this. We need to get to shelter."

"I recognize you," she said, dazed. "You look familiar."

"Hannes," he shouted over the increasing wind and rain. The sound of droplets striking the mud and puddles was overwhelming. Thunder cracked. The world split itself apart with light and then faded back to normal.

"Hannes," Elaine said.

He had taken off a mask, which he now slid over her face as he steered through the mud. His shoulders were firm. She hung onto them. A stable foundation in the gusting winds.

"Why are you here?" she asked.

"Used to come out here drinking with him and your brother," Hannes said. He steered her into a strange-looking car with giant wheels. "Though we were not supposed to. They liked having me along; I could tell them what best to buy to go with the rain."

Inside, once the doors shut, the wail of the storm muted, Elaine found a curious calm. There was space to think as the effects of the storm trickled down through skin contact and deeper into the space under her skin.

She looked out at the gray darkness and wet.

Chemicals. She remembered when the rain had started causing side effects, and people started analyzing it. Realizing that the genetically engineered organism let loose to gobble up the miles of plastic trash floating in the Pacific had somehow gotten signals crossed and instead began pumping out a cocktail of modern pharmaceuticals before they were sucked up into the clouds.

Or maybe that had even been on purpose.

Conspiracy theories always had seemed silly, but right now, staring out of the window, nothing seemed out of reach.

Hannes got in, exposing the inside of the car to the maelstrom outside.

"This is intense," Elaine told him. She probably needed to go to the emergency room. But then she remembered something. "You're Hannes!"

He laughed. "It's intense for me too, and I'm used to it. Yes, I'm Hannes."

"The weather guy."

He smiled at her. "Psychopharmacological weatherman, yep." He started the car and they bumped along the sand and mud, balloon tires carefully moving them along. "I was going to turn back when I saw your sister whip past, but then I saw you standing there in the rain. The storm's going to get worse."

"Worse?" She couldn't imagine worse.

"There's a microburst about to hit," he said. "We should take shelter."

"You can tell that?" She was suitably impressed. "I thought you were just sensitive to what moods the storm would bring. What is this one going to bring?"

"It's an MDMA riff," Hannes said.

"What?"

"There was a low-pressure front of a very mild hallucinogenic at the start. Maybe some feel-goods. Now there's some other contaminants, but it's basically raining ecstasy right now. I don't know what's coming in the microburst. That's why I want to take shelter."

"You don't know?"

He looked at her and grinned. "Storm's too big, too complex. It's passed over huge chunks of the ocean out there. It could have picked up anything. It might have picked up a little of everything."

* * * *

The road back was washed out. Hannes eyed the muddy water sluicing past the dip, guardrails buried under the chocolate milkshake of flood, then shook his head and turned them around.

"This would be a horrible place to die," Elaine said. "After all the work I did leaving, and building a life in Michigan, I still end up caught by a storm here in Cali."

"There's a small welcome building up here with some exhibits inside," Hannes said. "As long as we reach it in five minutes, we're fine."

"They think I'm stuck up and unhappy," Elaine told him. "Bev and Jackson. They think I stayed away because I'm dry and hiding. But the truth is, I'm on a mission. I'm focused. And I'm happy back there. I run my own goddamn business. And it's going well. They don't understand that people who know what they want, and are on a mission for it, they're in good shape."

"Jackson doesn't think you're unhappy," Hannes said, veering off down a gravel road as debris struck the side of the vehicle.

"He was like Dad. He was good to me. And he just wanted to live on the beach. Leave people to be themselves."

Hannes smiled, tanned skin creasing in the corners of his eyes. "And there's something wrong with that?"

"No." She didn't think that anymore. She knew that was just a way of knowing what you wanted. "I used to think they were directionless and didn't have a fire in them like I did. But it's a different fire."

Hannes nodded and wiped greenish-tinged water away from his forehead. "Why'd you leave? No one would ever talk about it." He looked over at her. "Some of us missed you."

Hannes missed her? He'd lived four blocks down and been a year behind. She barely remembered him as one of Jackson's beach buddies that wandered in and out of the house. There'd always been other itinerant friends Jackson adopted, living on his floor or passed out on the deck with a blanket.

"I was offered a buyout," Elaine said to Hannes.

"What?"

"A buyout. Someone wants to give me millions to sell my business."

"I didn't know you had a business." They stopped in front of a stone building with overhanging terra-cotta eaves.

"I built an intellectual property rights firm that manages off-brand three-dimensional plans for desktop printers."

Hannes looked over at her, bemused. "Are you going to sell?"

Elaine looked out at the sheets of pelting rain. "I don't have a fucking clue." But it was nice to let that secret out into the muted space inside the vehicle, where the words could settle into the soft plastic of the dashboard.

It made them real for the first time, instead of a secret ghost following her that even she hadn't acknowledged.

The visitors' center was locked down, so Hannes came back with a crowbar and broke the lock as the storm seemed to double and then triple its intensity. The entire world smelled like the back of a pharmacy now. Suffocatingly chemical.

When she stepped inside the protected air of the center, protected by stone walls, the clean air felt like a vacuum sucking her lungs out.

She coughed and staggered. Held onto Hannes.

"Hannes?" she asked in the dark once he shut the solid wooden doors behind them. "Did you really miss me?"

The idea that the historical, absent space she'd tried to create still had some reach surprised her.

Hannes looked down at her. "Of course. You had a fire. Energy. Purpose."

"Purpose?"

"You were always looking at the future. Planning. You would talk to people about what was going to happen when desktop fabrication became common. You would talk about things like 'disruption' and 'intellectual property' and most of us didn't even know what the hell you were talking about. But you were smart."

"I geeked out on that shit. I didn't think anyone paid attention," Elaine said, shaking sharp-smelling rainwater off her skin.

"I became a pharmacological forecaster because of you," Hannes said. He stepped closer. The rain-soaked shirt clung tight to his abs. They were as rocklike as his shoulders had been.

Statuesque.

A lot of fine marble, she thought.

"Because of me?" she asked.

There were zones here, she realized. The world. And inside of that, the town around them. The storm. Inside the storm, the visitors' center. And inside the center, they'd just stepped forward into a tiny little world that just contained the two of them, dripping wet.

It made sense that they'd end up there, she thought muzzily. They'd affected each other before she'd attained escape velocity and gotten away.

Now she was back.

Closer and closer. The center spinning around them both. She reached up and kissed him. Their tongues sparked with what felt like leftover lightning. She grabbed his shirt and ripped, and the tearing sound continued, gathering in tone and intensity.

The entire room shook. She staggered back, and looked up to see the roof peeling away.

Invaders from another world descended with flashing lights and machines and ripped them apart. Elaine held onto his hand as hard as she could but didn't have the strength.

"Hannes!"

She threw up all over herself and pulled at something jabbing deep into her forearm. Machines beeped warnings, and something pricked her.

"No insurance?" Elaine couldn't parse those words. "None?"

"Dad." Bev tapped the tray with the half-eaten food on it.

"Dad." Elaine bit her lip.

She asked after Hannes, and one of the nurses took her to a door propped open with a chair. Hannes sat on a bench outside with a half-burned cigarette held delicately between his fingertips.

"You're kidding me," she said, sitting next to him. "You smoke? Who does that?"

"The few, the ashamed, but belligerent," he said.

"I can't believe I kissed a smoker," Elaine said, deciding to storm the hill of awkwardness.

Hannes actually blushed. "Look, about that, I'm really sorry. We were out of our minds back there in the storm. It was raining chemicals. We would have been . . ."

"It's okay," Elaine said. "I understand. But, Hannes, what were you really doing coming up there? You're weather-sensitive; you predict storms. And you weren't all that close to my family."

He dropped the cigarette and stubbed it out with the tip of his hospital flip flops. "I was doing the whole 'what if' thing," he admitted. "For so long, I had this image in my head of what you had become, based on a sort of idea I thought I had of who you were."

"So you came to the funeral to connect with a high school crush?" Elaine asked.

Hannes laughed. "You make it sound worse than it was. Look, I really did know your dad pretty well, and I was just . . . I don't know. But I'm glad I went. I'm not going to say I learned something about myself in that storm, but it certainly helped me prioritize."

"Near-death experience framed everything for you?" Elaine asked with a bit of sarcasm.

"Something like that."

Elaine sighed and rode out into the ocean, letting herself spi
in circles and dissolve into the foam of the receding waves. She
happily as she spilled between the grains of sand.

The sun cut the room into bright and shadow, and Elaine blinke
eaten breakfast tray caught her attention. Had she eaten that?

Her memories skipped and warbled about like a flock of happy

"Oh, thank God." Bev stood up and walked over. "You overc
the storm. They found you and Hannes sheltering in the Visitor'

She looked like walking guilt.

Elaine wanted to believe that. But then, who had decided to co
to the funeral when she'd abandoned the family? And who had
to do that to avoid a hard decision? And . . . it didn't really matt

Elaine took a deep breath. "About the house . . ."

Bev waved her quiet. "The storm took it."

"What? Was it that bad?"

"Other than the roof to the center you were in and some mino
no. Hannes knew the microburst was coming, but it wasn't that
told us he fixed the termite problem we'd been having with sor
friend of his gave him. But he was wrong."

Elaine sat up, and the room wavered a bit. She took a deep b
everyone okay?"

Bev nodded. "We went next door."

"So there's no house?"

"It's all a heap." She folded her arms. And then, to Elaine'
started laughing. "Fucking Dad, right? Of course it was riddle
mites. Shit."

"We'll use the insurance money to rebuild it," Elaine said. 1
came out strong and sure. She could see the path in front of her.
what came next.

Bev laughed sadly. "No insurance."

She put her elbows on her knees. "I had an epiphany."

He looked over. "Really?"

Elaine smiled. "When the roof ripped off. I'm angry about that. Been thinking about it ever since I woke up. I'm going to sell my business. And create a larger fabrication business, one that just prints out whole houses that can withstand hurricanes, microbursts, earthquakes, floods. Whatever. Because this heavy-weather shit is getting more and more common." With walls that filtered air, she thought.

"I believe you'll do it," Hannes said.

"And I need to tell Bev I'll use the money I make off the sale to rebuild Dad's house again for us."

"You thinking of staying?" Hannes asked.

"No." She looked at him, answering a question he hadn't voiced. "I have a life back where I came from. A life I love. A whole world. But I want this to be here. It should be here. You know?"

A tiny trace of disappointment flicked across his eyes. But he understood and nodded. "It'll be nice to have the old beach house in some form still up there. The rich folk hate it."

She laughed. "That'll be half the fun in rebuilding it more or less like it was."

He stood up. Elaine did to, crinkling her nose at the acrid smell of smoke on him. "You'll want to leave by tomorrow afternoon to get home. In the afternoon, there's an eighty percent chance of stimulants. You don't need that after your overdose."

She smiled. "Thanks, Hannes." She hugged him. Impulsive but happy. He walked inside, not looking back.

For a moment, she stood out there in the dry heat, looking around at the parking lot and a set of alien-looking palms. And then it was time to move and go back inside to be with her family again, really, for the first time since she'd left.

ABOUT THE AUTHOR

TOBIAS S. BUCKELL is a Caribbean-born speculative fiction writer who grew up in Grenada, the British Virgin Islands, and the U.S. Virgin Islands. He has written several novels, including the *New York Times* bestseller *Halo: The Cole Protocol*, the Xenowealth series, and *Artic Rising* and *Hurricane Fever*. His short fiction has appeared in magazines such as *Lightspeed, Analog, Clarkesworld,* and *Subterranean,* and in anthologies such as *Armored, Under the Moons of Mars, Operation Arcana,* and *The End is Nigh.* He currently lives in Ohio with a pair of dogs, a pair of cats, twin daughters, and his wife.

A HUNDRED HUNDRED DAISIES

NANCY KRESS

I hear him go out the front door. The wind had stopped, like it always does at sundown, and even though he was moving quiet as a deer, I'd been lying awake for this. My clock says two thirty a.m. The hot darkness of my bedroom presses all around me. The front door closes and the motion-detector light on the porch comes on. We still have electricity. The light stays on ten full minutes in case of robbers.

Like we have anything left to steal.

I'm ready. Shoes and jacket on, window open. After supper, I took the sensor out of the motion light on the west side of the house. My father doesn't notice. He's headed the other way, toward the road.

Out the window, down the maple tree, around the house. He'd parked the truck way down the road, clear past the onion field. What used to be the onion field. Quietly, I pull my bicycle, too old and rusty to sell, out from my mom's lilac hedge. No flowers again this year.

The truck starts, drives away. I pedal along the dark road, losing him at the first rise. It doesn't matter. I know where he's going, where they're all going, where he thought he could go without me. No way. I'm not a child, and this is my future, too.

Somewhere in the roadside scrub, a small animal scurries away. An owl hoots. The night, so hot and dry even though it's only May, draws sweat from me, which instantly evaporates off my skin. There are no mosquitoes. I pedal harder.

Allen Corporation has posted a guard at the construction site, where until now there has been no guard, nor a need for one. Did someone tip them off? Is the law out there, with guns? I've beaten my father to the site, which at first puzzles me, and then doesn't. He would have joined up with the others somewhere, some gathering place to consolidate men and equipment. You couldn't just roar up here in a dozen pickups and SUVs, leaving tracks all over the place.

A single floodlight illuminates the guard, throwing a circle of yellow light. He sits in a clear, three-sided shack like the one where my sister Ruthie waits for the school bus with her little friends. I can see him clearly: a young guy, not from here. At least, I don't recognize him. He's got on a blue uniform and he's reading a graphic novel. He lifts a can to his mouth, drinks, goes back to the book.

Is he armed? I can't tell.

A thrill goes through me, starting at my belly and tingling clear up to the top of my head. I can do this. My father and the others will be here soon. I can get this done before they arrive.

"Hey, man!" I call out, and lurch from the darkness. The guard leaps to his feet and pulls something from his pocket. My heart stops. But it's not a gun—too small. It's a cell phone. He's supposed to call somebody else if there's trouble.

"Stop," he says in a surprisingly deep voice.

I stop, pretend to stagger sideways, and then right myself and put on what Ruthie calls my "goofy head"—weird grin, wide eyes. I slur my words. "Can I ha' one o' those beers? You got more? I'm fresh out!"

"You are trespassing on private property. Leave immediately."

"No beer?" I try to sound tragic, like somebody in a play in English class.

"Leave immediately. You are trespassing on private property."

"Okay, okay, sheesh, I'm going already." Now I can make out the huge bulk of the pipeline, twenty feet beyond the guard shack. I stagger again and fall forward, flat on my face, arms extended way forward so he can see that my hands are empty. "Aw, fuck."

The guard says nothing. At the edge of my vision I see him finger the cell. He doesn't want to look like a fool, calling in about one drunken kid, waking up Somebody Important at three in the morning. But he doesn't want to make a mistake, either. I help him decide. I turn my head and puke onto the ground.

This is a thing I learned to do when I was Ruthie's age: vomit at will without sticking a finger down my throat. I practiced and practiced until I could do it anytime I wanted to impress my friends or get out of school. So, I lay there hurling my cookies, and I'm not a big guy: five-nine and 145 pounds. Middleweight wrestling class.

The guard makes a sound of disgust and moves closer. Clearly, I'm no threat. "Get out of here, you fag. Now!"

I flail feebly on the ground.

"I said get out!" He yells louder, like that might sober me, and moves in for a kick. When he's close enough, I spring. He's bigger and older, but I was runner-up for state wrestling champion. Before he knows it, I've got him on the ground. Illegal hold, unnecessary roughness, unsportsmanlike conduct: two penalty points.

He shouts something and fights back, even though that increases his pain. I'm not sure I can hold him; he's *strong*. I hear a truck in the distance.

The guy is going to get free.

My father will be here any minute.

Adrenaline surges through me like a tsunami.

The ground is littered with construction-site rubble. I pick up a rock and bash him on the head. He drops like a fifty-pound sack of fertilizer, and that throws me off balance. I go down, too, and my head strikes some random piece of metal. Everything blurs except the thought *Oh, God, what if I killed the fucker?* When I can see again, I drag myself over to him. Blood on his head, but he's breathing. I've dragged myself through my own vomit. The truck halts.

Men rush forward. My father says, *"Danny?"*

"Christ, Larry, what is this?" Mr. Swenson, who farms next to us. Used to farm next to us.

I gasp, "Took . . . out guard . . . for you."

"Oh, *fuck*," somebody else says. And then, "Kid, did he see your face?"

The answer must have been on my own face, because the man snaps, "You couldn't have worn a ski mask?"

"Shut up, Ed," Mr. Swenson says. I can't get out my answer: *I didn't know there'd be a guard!* Someone is bending over the guard, lifting him in a fireman's carry. Someone else is pulling back my eyelids and peering at my eyes—a doctor? Is Dr. Radusky here? No, he wouldn't . . . he can't . . . Things grow fuzzier. I lose a few minutes, but I know I'm not passed out, because I'm aware of both my father kneeling beside me and parts of the argument floating above:

"—do it anyway!"

"—Larry's kid screwed us and—"

"We came here to—"

"The law—"

"I'm not leaving until I do what I come for!"

They do it, all of them except Dad. Quick and hard, panting and grunting. The night shrieks with pickaxes, chainsaws, welding torches. Someone moves the floodlight pole closer to the pipeline.

The huge pipe, forty-eight inches in diameter and raised above the ground on stanchions to let animals pass underneath, is being wrecked. Only a thirty-foot section of its monstrous and unfinished length, but that's enough. For now. I hear a piece of heavy equipment, dozer or backhoe, start up, move. A moment later, a crash.

More pipe down.

It's over in twenty minutes, during which I vomit once more, this time unwilled. Puking again blurs my vision. When it clears, my father is pull-ing me to my feet. I stagger against him. Before someone kills the flood-light, I see the Allen Corporation Great Lakes Water Diversion Pipeline lying in jagged pieces. I see dust covering everything to an inch thick and still falling from the sky, like rain. I see the farm the way it was when I was Ruthie's age, the corn green and spiky, Mom's lilacs in bloom, the horse pasture full of wildflowers. I see my dead grandfather driving the combine. I know then that my head hasn't cleared at all, and that I am hallucinating.

But one thing I see with total clarity before I pass out: my father's grim, tight-lipped face as he half carries me to the pickup full of men.

The law is at our house by six thirty a.m.

Before that, Dr. Radusky came by. He made me do various things. "Concussion," he said, "consistent with falling off his bicycle and hitting his head. Keep him awake, walking around as much as you can, and bring him to my office tomorrow for another look-see. No school today or tomorrow, and no wrestling for longer than that." He didn't look at my father, but Dr. Radusky knew, of course. The whole town knew.

"Larry," my mother says in the hallway beyond my bedroom. They're taking turns making sure I sit up, walk around, and don't sleep. "Sheriff is downstairs."

"Uh-huh." My father leaves.

My mother comes into my room and snaps, not for the first time, "What in Christ's name were you thinking?"

I don't answer. If they don't see that I'm a hero, the hell with them.

"I'm going downstairs," she says. "Don't lie down, Danny. Promise me."

I nod sullenly. As soon as she's gone, Ruthie slides in. She's dressed for school in jeans and an old green blouse that used to be Mom's. It's been cut down somehow to sort of fit her. "Danny," she whispers, "what did you *do*?"

"Nothing, squirt."

"But everybody's mad at you!"

"I was out riding my bike and fell off it and hit my head. That's all."

"Out riding in the night? Why?"

"You wouldn't understand." My head throbs and aches.

"Were you going to see a girl?"

I wish. "None of your business."

"Was it Jenny Bradford?"

"Beat it, squirt."

"I'm going to go downstairs and listen."

"No, you're not!"

"If I don't, then will you tell me another picture?"

Ruthie scavenges photographs. She ferrets them out of the boxes and envelopes where Mom has shoved them, hidden all over the house because Mom can't bear to look at them anymore. I remember her doing it, crying as she ripped some from their frames—there used to be a lot of framed pictures all over the place—and tossed the silver frames into the box for the pawnshop. Now Ruthie finds them and brings them to me to identify things: *That's Great-Uncle Jim in front of the barn we sold to the Allen people; that's Grandpa driving the combine.* She doesn't remember any of it, but I do.

She pulls a picture from under her blouse and holds it out to me. This one is newer than most of her stash, printed on a color printer from somebody's digital camera. I remember that printer. We sold it long ago, along with everything else: the antiques handed down from Great-Grandma Ann, the farm equipment, the land. None of it was enough. The house is in foreclosure.

I say, "That's our old horse pasture."

"We had horses?"

"One horse." White Foot. He'd been mine.

"Where's the horse?"

"Gone."

"Where's the pasture? Is it the dirt field over by the falling-down fence?"

"Yeah."

"But what are those?" She points at the photograph.

In the picture, the pasture, its fences whole and whitewashed, is full of wildflowers, mostly daisies. Wave after wave of daisies in semi-close-up, their centers bright yellow like little suns, their petals almost too white, maybe from some trick of the camera. When was the last time I saw a daisy? Had Ruthie ever seen one?

I say, "Fuck, fuck, fuck."

"You just said bad words!"

"They're called 'daisies.' Now go away, brat."

"You said bad words! I'm telling!"

Heavy footsteps on the stairs. Ruthie, looking close to tears, thrusts the photo under her blouse and skitters out the door. It isn't the tears that do me in, it's the blouse.

My parents come in with Sheriff Buchmann. The room is too full. I know from her face that Mom hates Buchmann seeing my patched bed-spread, faded curtains, sparse furniture. Me, I just hate the sheriff.

He says, "Daniel, did you go last night to the site of the Allen Corporation's pipeline?"

"No, sir."

"How'd you get that bandage on your head?"

"Tripped in the dark and fell off my bike."

"Where?"

"Corner of Maple and Grey."

"And what were you doing down there?"

"I had a fight with my father and wanted to get away."

"What was the fight about?"

"My grades. My teacher called yesterday. My math grade sucks." Could Buchmann tell I'd been rehearsed? He'd check, but Mr. Ruhl did call yesterday, and my math grade does suck. My parents gaze at me steadily, without emotion. They're good at that. So is Buchmann. I want to ask if the pipeline guard is okay, but I can't. I wasn't there. It never happened. Unless the guard can ID me.

I gaze back, emotionless, my father's son.

Ruthie is drawing daisies. I don't know where she got the paper. Her crayons are only what's been hoarded for years, now stubby lengths of yellow and green laid carefully on the kitchen table. So far, she's covered three sheets of thin paper with eight daisies each, every flower in its own little box. They have yellow centers, green leaves, and petals that are the white of the paper outlined in green.

"Hi, Danny! Is your head better?"

"Yeah. What are these?"

"Daisies, stupid."

"I mean, why are you making them?"

"I want to." She looks up at me, crayon stub in her fist, her face all serious. "Do you know what my teacher taught us in school today?"

"How would I know? I'm not in the second grade." Unlike me, Ruthie likes school and is good at it.

"She taught us about the pipeline. Some people broke it Monday night."

My hand stops halfway to the fridge handle, starts again, opens the fridge door. Nothing to eat but bread, leftover potatoes, drippings, early strawberries Mom picked today. She will be saving those.

Ruthie says, "The pipeline people are fixing it. It's supposed to carry water to 'The Southwest.'" She says the words carefully, like she might say "Narnia" or "Middle-earth."

"Is that so," I say. I take bread and drippings from the fridge.

"Yes. The water will come from 'Lake Michigan.' That's one of the Great Lakes."

"Yeah, I know."

"There are five Great Lakes, and they have four-fifths of the fresh water in the world. That means that if you put all the fresh water in the world into five humongous pots, then four—"

I stop listening to her math lesson. The guard couldn't ID me. I watched him on TV—we still have a TV, so old that nobody wants it, but no LinkNet for any good programs. The guard looked even younger than I remembered, no more than a few years older than me. He also looked more scared than I remembered. I spread drippings on my bread.

Ruthie is still reciting. "The water is supposed to go to farms around the 'Great Lakes Basin,' but it's not. It's going to go through the big pipe to 'The Southwest.' Danny, why can't we have some of that water to make our farm grow again?"

"Bingo."

"Answer me!" Ruthie says, sounding just like Mom.

"Because the Southwest can pay for it and we can't."

Ruthie nods solemnly. "I know. We can't pay for anything. That's why we have to move. I don't wanna move. Danny—where will we go?"

"I don't know, squirt." I no longer want my bread and drippings. And I don't want to talk about this with Ruthie. It fills me with too much rage. I put the half-eaten bread in the fridge and go upstairs.

The next night, the pipeline is attacked in Fuller Corners, twenty miles to the south. There were two guards, both armed. One is killed.

"Daniel Raymond Hitchens, you are under arrest for destruction of property, trespass, and assault in the first degree. You have the right to remain silent. Anything you say can and will be used against you in a court of law. You have the right to an attorney—"

The two cops, neither from here, have come right into math class during final exams. They cuff me and lead me out, my test paper left on my desk, half the equations probably wrong. My classmates gape; Connie Moorhouse starts to cry. Mr. Ruhl says feebly, "See here, now, you can't—" He shuts up. Clearly, they can.

Outside the classroom, they frisk me. I bluster, "Aren't I supposed to get one phone call?"

"You got a phone?"

I don't, of course—gone long ago.

"You get your call at the station."

They take me to the police station in Fuller Corners. There is a lot of talking, video recording, paperwork. I learn that I am suspected of killing the guard in the Fuller Corners attack. The surviving guard identified me. This is ridiculous; I have never even been to Fuller Corners. That doesn't stop me from being scared. I know that something more is going on here, but I don't know what. When I get my phone call to my father, I am almost blubbering, which makes me furious.

My parents come roaring down to Fuller Corners like hounds on a deer. Along with them come more TV cameras than I can count. More shouting. A lawyer. I can't be arraigned until tomorrow. What is *arraigned*? It doesn't sound good. I spend the night in the Fuller Corners lockup because I'm seventeen, not sixteen. The jail has two cells. One holds a man accused of raping his wife. The other has me and a drunk who snores, sprawling across the bottom bunk and smelling of booze and piss. He never wakes the entire time I'm there.

Dad drives me home after the arraignment. I am out on bail. More TV cameras, even a robocam. I recognize Elizabeth Wilkins talking into a microphone on the courthouse steps. She looks hot. Everyone follows my every move, but in the truck, it's just my father and me, and he doesn't look at me.

He doesn't say anything, either.

We drive through the ruined land, field after field empty of all but blowing dust. The thing that gets me is how fast it happened. We learned in school about the possible desertification of the Midwest from global warming. But it was only one possibility, and it was supposed to take decades, maybe longer. Then some temperature drop somewhere in the Pacific Ocean—the *Pacific Ocean*, for fuck's sake—changed some ocean currents, and that brought years of drought ending in dust that blew around from dawn to sundown. Ending in grass fires and foreclosures and food shortages. Ending in Fuller Corners.

Finally, my father says, "This is just the beginning." He keeps his eyes on the road. "But not for you, Danny. You're not going to prison. If that's what you're thinking, get it out of your mind right now. Not going to happen. They got nothing but made-up evidence that won't hold up."

"Then why was I arrested?"

"PR. Yeah, you're the poster boy for this. Bastards."

On the courthouse steps, Elizabeth Wilkins said into her microphone, "The protestors are even using their children in a shameful and selfish fight to stop the pipeline that will save so many lives in the parched and dying cities of Tucson and—"

I am not a child.

"Dad," I blurt out, "were you at Fuller Corners?"

His eyes never leave the road, his expression never changes, he says nothing. Which is all the answer I need.

I thought I knew fear before. I was wrong.

At home, Mom is frying potatoes for dinner. It's warm outside but all the windows are shut against the dust, and all the curtains are drawn tight against everything else. Ruthie lies on the kitchen floor, frantically coloring. I go upstairs and sit on the edge of my bed.

A few minutes later, Ruthie comes into my room. She plants herself in front of me, short legs braced apart, hands clasped tight in front of her. "You were in jail."

"I don't want to talk about it. Go away, squirt."

"I can't," she says, and the odd words plus something in her voice make me focus on her. When she was littler, she used to go stand on her head in the pantry and cry whenever anyone wouldn't tell her something she wanted to know.

"Danny, did you break the pipe?"

"No," I say, truthfully.

"Are more people going to break the pipe more?"

"Yes, I think so." *Just the beginning.*

"An 'eviction notice' came today while you were in jail. Does that mean we have to move right away?"

"I don't know." Is the timing of the eviction notice with my faked-up poster-boy arrest just coincidental? How would I even know? The people building the pipeline, which is going to be immensely profitable, are very determined. But so is my father.

Ruthie says, "Where will we go?"

"I don't know that, either." The Midwest is a dust plain, the Southwest desperate for water, the Great Lakes states and Northeast defending their great treasures, the lakes and the Saint Lawrence Seaway. Oregon and Washington have closed their borders, with guns. The South is already too full of refugees without jobs or hope.

Ruthie says, "I think we should go to Middle-earth. They have lots of water."

She doesn't really believe it; she's too old. But she can still dream it aloud. Then, however, she follows it with something else.

"It will be a war, won't it, Danny? Like in history."

"Go downstairs," I say harshly. "I hear Mom calling you to set the table."

She knows I'm lying, but she goes.

I go into the bathroom and turn on the sink. Water flows, brown and sputtery sometimes, but there. We have a pretty deep well, which is the only reason we're still here, the only reason we have electricity and pota- toes and bread and, sometimes, coffee. I've caught Mom filling dozens of plastic gallon bottles from the kitchen tap. Even our small town, smaller now that so many have been forced out, has a black market.

I turn off the tap. The well won't hold much longer. The Great Lakes–St. Lawrence River Basin Water Resources Compact won't hold, either. Lake levels have been falling for over a decade. There isn't enough, won't be enough, can't be enough for everybody.

I go down to dinner.

Exhausted from two nights of sleeplessness and two days of fitful naps, I nonetheless cannot sleep. At two a.m., I go downstairs and turn on the TV. Without LinkNet, we get only two stations, both a little fuzzy. One of them is all news all the time. With the sound as low as possible, I watch myself being led from the jail to the courthouse, from the courthouse to our truck. I watch film clips of the dead guard. I watch an interview with the guard I clobbered with a rock. He describes his "assailant" as six feet tall, strongly built, around twenty-one years old. Either he has the worst eyesight in the county or else he can't admit he was brought down by a high school kid who can't do algebra.

Not that I'm going to need algebra in what my future was becoming.

When I can't watch any more, I go into the kitchen. I gather up what I find there, rummage for a pair of scissors, and go outside. There is no wind. Dad's emergency light, battery-run and powerful enough to illuminate the entire inside of the barn we no longer own, is in the shed. When I've finished what I set out to do, I return to the house.

Ruthie is deeply asleep. She stirs when I hoist her onto my shoulder, protests a bit, then slumps against me. When I carry her outside, she wakes fully, a little scared but now also interested.

"Where we going, Danny?"

"You'll see. It's a surprise."

I'm forced to continue to carry her because I forgot her shoes. She grows really heavy but I keep on, stumbling through the dawn. At the old horse pasture, I set her on a section of fence that hasn't fallen down yet. I turn on the emergency light and sweep it over the pasture.

"Oh!" Ruthie cries. "Oh, Danny!"

The flowers are scattered all across the bare field, each now on its own little square of paper: yellow centers, white petals outlined in green, green leaves until the green crayon was all used up and she had to switch to blue.

"Oh, Danny!" she cries again. "Oh, look! A hundred hundred daisies!"

It will be a war, won't it? Yes. But not this morning.

The sun rises, the wind starts, and the paper daisies swirl upward with the dust.

ABOUT THE AUTHOR

NANCY KRESS is the author of thirty-two books, including twenty-five novels, four collections of short stories, and three books about writing. Her work has won two Hugos ("Beggars in Spain" and "The Erdmann Nexus"), six Nebulas (all for short fiction), a Sturgeon ("The Flowers of Aulit Prison"), and a John W. Campbell Memorial Award (for *Probability Space*). The novels include science fiction, fantasy, and thrillers; many concern genetic engineering. Her most recent work is the Nebula-winning and Hugo-nominated *After the Fall, Before the Fall, During the Fall* (Tachyon, 2012), a long novella of eco-disaster, time travel, and human resiliency. Intermittently, Nancy teaches writing workshops at various venues around the country, including Clarion and Taos Toolbox (yearly, with Walter Jon Williams). A few years ago she taught at the University of Leipzig as the visiting Picador professor. She is currently working on a long, as-yet-untitled SF novel. Nancy lives in Seattle with her husband, writer Jack Skillingstead, and Cosette, the world's most spoiled toy poodle.

THE NETHERLANDS
LIVES WITH WATER

JIM SHEPARD

A long time ago, a man had a dog that went down to the shoreline every day and howled. When she returned, the man would look at her blankly. Eventually, the dog got exasperated. "Hey," the dog said. "There's a shit-storm of biblical proportions headed your way." "Please. I'm busy," the man said. "Hey," the dog said the next day, and told him the same thing. This went on for a week. Finally, the man said, "If you say that once more, I'm going to take you out to sea and dump you overboard." The next morning, the dog went down to the shoreline again, and the man fol-lowed. "Hey," the dog said, after a minute. "Yeah?" the man said. "Oh, I think you know," she told him.

"Or here's another one," Cato says to me. "Adam goes to God, 'Why'd you make Eve so beautiful?' And God says, 'So you would love her.' And Adam says, 'Well, why'd you make her so stupid?' And God says, 'So she would love you.'"

Henk laughs.

"Well, he thinks it's funny," Cato says.

"He's eleven years old," I tell her.

"And very precocious," she reminds me. Henk makes an overly jovial face and holds two thumbs up. His mother takes her napkin and wipes some egg from his chin.

We met in the same pre-university track. I was a year older but hadn't passed Dutch, so I took it again with her.

"You failed Dutch?" she whispered from her seat behind me. She'd seen me gaping at her when I came in. The teacher had already announced that's what those of us who were older were doing there.

"It's your own language," she told me later that week. She was holding my penis upright so she could run the edge of her lip along the shaft. I felt like I was about to touch the ceiling.

"You're not very articulate," she remarked later on the subject of the sounds I'd produced.

She acted as though I were a spot of sun in an otherwise rainy month. We always met at her house, a short bicycle ride away, and her parents seemed to be perpetually asleep or dead. In three months, I saw her father only once, from behind. She explained that she'd been raised by depressives who'd made her one of those girls who'd sit on the playground with the tools of happiness all around her and refuse to play. Her last boyfriend had walked out the week before we'd met. His diagnosis had been that she imposed on everyone else the gloom her family had taught her to expect.

"Do I sadden you?" she'd ask me late at night before taking me in her mouth.

"Will you have children with me?" I started asking her back.

And she was flattered and seemed pleased without being particularly fooled. "I've been thinking about how hard it is to pull information out of you," she told me one night when we'd pitched our clothes out from under her comforter. I asked what she wanted to know, and she said that was the kind of thing she was talking about. While she was speaking, I watched her front teeth, glazed from our kissing. When she had a cold and her nose was blocked up, she looked a little dazed in profile.

"I ask a question and you ask another one," she complained. "If I ask what your old girlfriend was like, you ask what anyone's old girlfriend is like."

"So ask what you want to ask," I told her.

"Do you think," she said, "that someone like you and someone like me should be together?"

"Because we're so different?" I asked.

"Do you think that someone like you and someone like me should be together?" she repeated.

"Yes," I told her.

"That's helpful. Thanks," she responded. And then she wouldn't see me for a week. When I felt I'd waited long enough, I intercepted her outside her home and asked, "Was the right answer no?" And she smiled and kissed me as though hunting up some compensation for diminished expectations. After that, it was as if we'd agreed to give ourselves over to what we had. When I put my mouth on her, her hands would bend back at the wrists as if miming helplessness. I disappeared for minutes at a time from my classes, envisioning the trance-like way her lips would part after so much kissing.

The next time she asked me to tell her something about myself, I had some candidates lined up. She held my hands away from her, which tented the comforter and provided some cooling air. I told her I still remembered how my older sister always replaced her indigo hair bow with an orange one on royal birthdays. And how I followed her everywhere, chanting that she was a pig, which I was always unjustly punished for. How I fed her staggeringly complicated lies that went on for weeks and ended in disaster with my parents or teachers. How I slept in her bed the last three nights before she died of the flu epidemic.

Her cousins had also died then, Cato told me. If somebody even just mentioned the year 2015, her aunt still went to pieces. She didn't let go of my hands, so I went on, and told her that, being an outsider as a little boy, I'd noticed *something* was screwed up with me, but I couldn't put my finger on what. I probably wasn't as baffled by it as I sounded, but it was still more than I'd ever told anyone else.

She'd grown up right off the Boompjes; I'd been way out in Pernis, looking at the Caltex refinery through the haze. The little fishing village was still there then, huddled in the center of the petrochemical sprawl. My sister loved the lights of the complex at night and the fires that went hundreds of feet into the air like solar flares when the waste gases burned off. Kids from other neighborhoods never failed to notice the smell on our skin. The light was that golden sodium vapor light, and my father liked to say it was always Christmas in Pernis. At night, I was able to read with my bedroom lamp off. While we got ready for school in the mornings, the dredging platforms with their twin pillars would disappear up into the fog like Gothic cathedrals.

A week after I told her all that, I introduced Cato to Kees. "I've never seen him like this," he told her. We were both on track for one of the technology universities, maybe Eindhoven, and he hadn't failed Dutch. "Well, I'm a pretty amazing woman," she explained to him.

Kees and I both went on to study physical geography and got into the water sector. Cato became the media liaison for the program director for Rotterdam Climate Proof. We got married after our third International Knowledge for Climate research conference. Kees asked us recently which anniversary we had coming up, and I said eleventh and Cato said it was the one hundredth.

It didn't take a crystal ball to realize we were in a growth industry. Gravity and thermal measurements by GRACE satellites had already flagged the partial shutdown of the Atlantic circulation system. The World Glacier Monitoring Service, saddled with having to release one glum piece of news after another, had just that year reported that the Pyrenees, Africa, and the Rockies were all glacier-free. The Americans had just confirmed the collapse of the West Antarctic ice sheet. Once-in-a-century floods in England were now occurring every two years. Bangladesh was almost entirely a bay and that whole area a war zone because of the displacement issues.

It's the catastrophe for which the Dutch have been planning for fifty years. Or, really, for as long as we've existed. We had cooperative water management before we had a state. The one created the other; either we pulled together as a collective or got swept away as individuals. The real old-timers had a saying for when things fucked up: "Well, the Netherlands lives with water." What they meant was that their land flooded twice a day.

Bishop Prudentius of Troyes wrote in his annals that in the ninth century, the whole of the country was devoured by the sea; all the settlements disappeared, and the water was higher than the dunes. In the Saint Felix flood, North Beveland was completely swept away. In the All Saints' flood, the entire coast was inundated between Flanders and Germany. In 1717, a dike collapse killed fourteen thousand on Christmas night.

"You like going on like this, don't you?" Cato sometimes asks.

"I like the way it focuses your attention," I told her once.

"Do you like the way it scares our son?" she demanded in return.

"It doesn't scare me," Henk told us.

"It *does* scare you," she told him. "And your father doesn't seem to register that."

For the last few years, when I've announced that the sky is falling, she's answered that our son doesn't need to hear it. And that I always bring it up when there's something else that should be discussed. I always concede her point, but that doesn't get me off the hook. "For instance, I'm still waiting to hear how your mother's making out," she complains during a dinner when we can't tear Henk's attention away from the Feyenoord celebrations. If a team wins the Cup, the whole town gets drunk. If it loses, the whole town gets drunk.

My mother's now at the point that no one can deny is dementia. She's still in the little house on Polluxstraat, even though the Pernis she knew seems to have evaporated around her. Cato finds it unconscionable that I've allowed her to stay there on her own, without help. "Let me guess," she says whenever she brings it up. "You don't want to talk about it."

She doesn't know the half of it. The day after my father's funeral, my mother brought me into their bedroom and showed me the paperwork on what she called their Rainy Day Account, a staggering amount. Where had they gotten so much? "Your father," she told me unhelpfully. When I went home that night and Cato asked what was new, I told her about my mother's regime of short walks.

At each stage in the transfer of assets, financial advisors or bank officers have asked if my wife's name would be on the account as well. She still has no idea it exists. It means that I now have a secret net worth more than triple my family's. What am I up to? Your guess is as good as mine.

"Have you talked to anyone about the live-in position?" Cato now asks. I'd raised the idea with my mother, who'd started shouting that she never should have told me about the money. Since then, I'd been less bullish about bringing Cato and Henk around to see her.

I tell her things are progressing just as we'd hope.

"Just as we'd hope?" she repeats.

"That's it in a nutshell," I tell her, a little playfully, but her expression makes it clear she's waiting for a real explanation.

"Don't you have homework?" I ask Henk, and he and his mother exchange a look. I've always believed that I'm a master at hiding my feelings, but I seem to be alone in that regard.

Cato's been through this before in various iterations. When my mother was first diagnosed, I hashed through the whole thing with Kees, who'd been in my office when the call came in. And then later that night, I told Cato there'd been no change, so as not to have to trudge through the whole story again. But the doctor had called the next day, when I was out, to see how I was taking the news, and she got it all from him.

Henk looks at me like he's using my face to attempt some long division.

Cato eats without saying anything until she finally loses her temper with the cutlery. "I told you before that if you don't want to do this, I can," she says.

"There's nothing that needs doing," I tell her.

"There's plenty that needs doing," she says. She pulls the remote from

Henk and switches off the news. "Look at him," she complains to Henk. "He's always got his eyes somewhere else. Does he even know that he shakes his head when he listens?"

Pneumatic hammers pick up where they left off outside our window. There's always construction somewhere. Why not rip up the streets? The Germans did such a good job of it in 1940 that it's as if we've been competing with them ever since. Rotterdam: a deep hole in the pavement with a sign telling you to approach at your own risk. Our whole lives, walking through the city has meant muddy shoes.

As we're undressing that night, she asks how I'd rate my recent performance as a husband.

I don't know; maybe not so good, not so bad, I tell her.

She answers that if I were a minister, I'd resign.

What area are we talking about here, I wonder aloud, in terms of performance?

"Go to sleep," she tells me, and turns off the lamp.

If climate change is a hammer to the Dutch, the head's coming down more or less where we live. Rotterdam sits astride a plain that absorbs the Scheldt, Meuse, and Rhine outflows, and what we're facing is a troika of rising sea level, peak river discharges, and extreme weather events. We've got the jewel of our water defenses—the staggeringly massive water barriers at Maeslant and Dordrecht, and the rest of the Delta Works— ready to shut off the North Sea during the next cataclysmic storm, but what are we to do when that coincides with the peak river discharges? Sea levels are leaping up, our ground is subsiding, it's raining harder and more often, and our program of managed flooding—Make Room for the Rivers—was overwhelmed long ago. The dunes and dikes at eleven locations from Ter Heijde to Westkapelle no longer meet what we decided would be the minimum safety standards. Temporary emergency measures are starting to be known to the public as Hans Brinkers.

And this winter's been a festival of bad news. Kees' team has measured increased snowmelt in the Alps to go along with prolonged rainfall across northern Europe and steadily increasing wind speeds during gales, all of which lead to increasingly ominous winter flows, especially in the Rhine. He and I—known around the office as the Pessimists—forecasted this winter's discharge at eighteen thousand cubic meters per second. It's now up to twenty-one. What are those of us in charge of dealing with that supposed to do? A megastorm at this point would swamp the barriers from both sides and inundate Rotterdam and its surroundings—three million people—within twenty-four hours.

Which is quite the challenge for someone in media relations. "Remember, the Netherlands will always be here," Cato likes to say when signing off with one of the news agencies. "Though probably under three meters of water," she'll add after she hangs up.

Before this most recent emergency, my area of expertise had to do with the strength and loading of the Water Defense structures, especially in terms of the Scheldt estuary. We'd been integrating forecasting and security software for high-risk areas and trying to get Arcadis to understand that it needed to share almost everything with IBM and vice versa. I'd even been lent out to work on the Venice, London, and St. Petersburg surge barriers. But now all of us were back home and thrown into the Weak Links Project, an overeducated fire brigade formed to address new vulnerabilities the minute they emerged.

Our faces are turned helplessly to the Alps. There's been a series of cloudbursts on the eastern slopes: thirty-five centimeters of rain in the last two weeks. The Germans have long since raised their river dikes to funnel the water right past them and into the Netherlands. Some of that water will be taken up in the soil, some in lakes and ponds and catchment basins, and some in polders and farmland that we've set aside for flooding emergencies. Some in water plazas and water gardens and specially designed underground parking garages and reservoirs. The rest will keep moving downriver to Rotterdam and the closed surge barriers.

"Well, 'Change is the Soul of Rotterdam,'" Kees joked when we first looked at the numbers on the meteorological disaster ahead. We were given private notification that there would be vertical evacuation if the warning time for an untenable situation were under two hours, and horizontal evacuation if it were over two.

"What am I supposed to do," Cato demanded to know when I told her, "tell the helicopter that we have to pop over to Henk's school?" He now has an agreed-upon code; when it appears on his iFuze, he's to leave school immediately and head to her office.

But in the meantime, we operate as though it won't come to that. We think we'll come up with something, as we always have. Where would New Orleans or the Mekong Delta be without Dutch hydraulics and Dutch water management? And where would the US and Europe be if we hadn't led them out of the financial panic and depression just by being ourselves? EU dominoes from Iceland to Ireland to Italy came down around our ears but there we sat, having been protected by our own Dutchness. What was the joke about us, after all? That we didn't go to the banks to take money out; we went to put money in. Who was going to be the first, as economy after economy capsized, to pony up the political courage to nationalize their banks and work cooperatively? Well, who took the public good more seriously than the Dutch? Who was more in love with rules? Who tells anyone who'll listen that we're providing the rest of the world with a glimpse of what the future will be?

After a third straight sleepless night—"Oh, who gets any sleep in the water sector?" Kees answered irritably the morning I complained about it—I leave the office early and ride a water taxi to Pernis. In Nieuwe Maas, the shipping is so thick that it's like kayaking through canyons, and the taxi captain charges extra for what he calls a piloting fee. We tip and tumble on the backswells while four tugs nudge a supertanker sideways into its berth like puppies snuffling at the base of a cliff. The tanker's hull is so high that we can't see any superstructure above it.

I hike from the dock to Polluxstraat, the traffic on the A4 above rolling like surf. "Look who's here," my mother says instead of hello, and goes about her tea-making as though I dropped in unannounced every afternoon. We sit in the breakfast nook off the kitchen. Before she settles in, she reverses the pillow embroidered GOOD NIGHT so that it now reads GOOD MORNING.

"How's Henk?" she asks, and I tell her he's got some kind of chest thing. "As long as he's healthy," she replies. I don't see any reason to quibble.

The bottom shelves of her refrigerator are puddled with liquid from deliquescing vegetables and something spilled. The bristles of her bottle scraper on the counter are coated with dried mayonnaise. The front of her nightgown is an archipelago of stains.

"How's Cato?" she asks.

"Cato wants to know if we're going to get you some help," I tell her.

"I just talked with her," my mother says irritably. "She didn't say anything like that."

"You talked with her? What'd you talk about?" I ask. But she waves me off. "Did you talk to her or not?"

"That girl from up north you brought here to meet me, I couldn't even understand her," she tells me. She talks about regional differences as though her country's the size of China.

"We thought she seemed very efficient," I reply. "What else did Cato talk with you about?"

But she's already shifted her interest to the window. Years ago, she had a traffic mirror mounted outside on the frame to let her spy on the street unobserved. She uses a finger to widen the gap in the lace curtains.

What else should she do all day long? She never goes out. The street's her revival house, always showing the same movie.

The holes in her winter stockings are patched with a carnival array of colored thread. We always lived by the maxim that things last longer mended than new. My whole life, I heard that with thrift and hard work, I could build a mansion. My father had a typewritten note tacked to the wall in his office at home: LET THOSE WITH ABUNDANCE REMEMBER THAT THEY ARE SURROUNDED BY THORNS.

"Who said *that*?" Cato asked when we were going through his belongings.

"Calvin," I told her.

"Well, you would know," she said.

He hadn't been so much a conservative as a man whose life philosophy had boiled down to the principle of no nonsense. I'd noticed even as a tiny boy that whenever he liked a business associate, or anyone else, that's what he said about them.

My mother's got her nose to the glass at this point. "You think you're the only one with secrets," she remarks.

"What's that supposed to mean?" I ask, but she acts as though she's not going to dignify that with a response. Follow-up questions don't get anywhere, either. I sit with her a while longer. We watch a Chinese game show. I soak her bread in milk, walk her to the toilet, and tell her we have to at least think about moving her bed downstairs somewhere. The steps to her second floor are vertiginous even by Dutch standards, and the risers accommodate less than half your foot. She makes an effort to follow what I'm saying, puzzled that she needs to puzzle something out. But then her expression dissipates and she complains she spent half the night looking for the coffee grinder.

"Why were you looking for the coffee grinder?" I ask, a question I have to repeat. Then I stop, for fear of frightening her.

Henk's class is viewing a presentation at the Climate Campus—*Water: Precious Resource and Deadly Companion*—so we have the dinner table to ourselves. Since Cato's day was even longer than mine, I prepared the meal, two cans of pea soup with pigs' knuckles and some Belgian beer, but she's too tired to complain. She's dealing with both the Americans, who are always hectoring for clarification on the changing risk factors for our projects in Miami and New Orleans, and the Germans, who've publicly dug in their heels on the issue of accepting any spillover from the Rhine in order to take some of the pressure off the situation downstream.

It's the usual debate, as far as the latter argument's concerned. We take the high road—it's only through cooperation that we can face such monumental challenges, etc.—while other countries scoff at our aspirations toward ever more comprehensive safety measures. The German foreign minister last year accused us on a simulcast of acting like old women.

"Maybe he's right," Cato says wearily. "Sometimes I wonder what it'd be like to live in a country where you don't need a license to build a fence around your garden."

Exasperated, we indulge in a little Dutch-bashing. No one complains about themselves as well as the Dutch. Cato asks if I remember that story about the manufacturers having to certify that each of the chocolate letters handed out by Santa Claus contained an equal amount of chocolate. I remind her about the number one download of the year turning out to have been of *fireworks sound effects*, for those New Year's revelers who found real fireworks too worrisome.

After we stop, she looks at me, her mouth a little slack. "Why does this sort of thing make us horny?" she wonders.

"Maybe it's the pea soup," I tell her in the shower. She's examining little crescents of fingernail marks where she held me when she came. Then she turns off the water and we wrap ourselves in the bedsheet-sized towel she had made in Surinam. Cocooned on the floor in the tiny, steamy bathroom, we discuss Kees' love life. He now shops at a singles' supermarket, the kind where you use a blue basket if you're taken and a yellow if you're available. When I asked how his latest fling was working out, he said, "Well, I'm back to the yellow basket."

Cato thinks this is hilarious.

"How'd *we* get to be so lucky?" I ask her. We're spooning and she does a minimal grind that allows me to grow inside her.

"The other day, someone from BBC1 asked my boss that same question about how he ended up where he did," she says. She turns her cheek so I can kiss it.

"What'd he say?" I ask when I've moved from her cheek to her neck. She's not a big fan of her boss.

She shrugs comfortably, her shoulder blades against my chest. I wrap my arms tighter so the fit is even more perfect. The gist of his answer, she tells me, was mostly by not asking too many questions.

My mother always had memory problems, and even before my sister died, my father said that he didn't blame her; she'd seen her own brothers swept away in the 1953 flood and had been a wreck for years afterward. On January 31, the night after her sixth birthday, a storm-field that covered the entire North Sea swept down out of the northwest with winds that registered gale force eleven and combined with a spring tide to raise the sea six meters over NAP. The breakers overtopped the dikes in eighty-nine locations over a 170-kilometer stretch and hollowed them out on their land sides so that the surges that followed broke them. My mother remembered eating her soup alongside her two brothers, listening to the wind increase in volume until her father went out to check on the barn and the draft from the opened door blew their board game off the table. Her mother's Bible pages flapped in her hands like panicked birds. Water was seeping through the window casing, and her brother touched it and held out his finger for her to taste. She remembered his look when she realized that it was salty: not rain but spray from the sea.

Her father returned and said they all had to leave now. They held hands in a chain and he went first and she went second, and once the door was open, the wind staggered him and blew her off her feet. He managed to retrieve her, but by then, they couldn't find the others in the dark and the rain. She was soaked in ice and the water was already up to her thighs, and in the distance, she could see breakers where the dike had been. They headed inland and found refuge inside a neighbor's brick home and discovered that the back half of the house had already been torn away by the water. He led her up the stairs to the third floor and through a trapdoor onto the roof. Their neighbors were already there and her mother, huddling against the wind and the cold. The house west of them imploded but its roof held together and was pushed upright in front of theirs, diverting the main force of the flood around them like a breakwater. She remembered holding her father's hand so their bodies would be found in the same place. Her mother shrieked and pointed and she saw her brothers beside a woman with a baby on the roof of the house beyond them to the east. Each wave that broke against the front drenched her brothers and the woman with spray, and the woman kept turning her torso to shield the baby. And then the front of the house caved in and they all became bobbing heads in the water that were swept around the collapsing walls and away.

She remembered the wind finally dying down by midmorning, a heavy mist in the grey sky, and a fishing smack off to the north coasting between the rooftops and bringing people on board. She remembered a dog lowered on a rope, its paws flailing as it turned.

After their rescue, she remembered a telegraph pole slanted over, its wires tugged by the current. She remembered the water smelling of gasoline and mud, treetops uncovered by the waves, and a clog between two steep roofs filled with floating branches and dead cattle. She remembered a vast plain of wreckage on the water and the smell of dead fish traveling on the wind. She remembered two older boys sitting beside her and examining the silt driven inside an unopened bottle of soda by the force of the waves. She remembered her mother's animal sounds and the length of time it took to get to dry land, and her father's chin on her mother's bent back, his head bumping and wobbling whenever they crossed the wakes of other boats.

independently of the ground layer. Nine entire neighborhoods have been made amphibious, built on hollow platforms that will rise with the water but remain anchored to submerged foundations. And besides the giant storm barriers, atop our dikes we've mounted titanium-braced walls that unfold from concrete channels, leviathan-like inflatable rubber dams, and special grasses grown on plastic mat revetments to anchor the inner walls.

"Is it all enough?" Henk will ask whenever there's a day of unremitting rain. "Oh, honey, it's more than enough," Cato will tell him, and then quiz him on our emergency code.

"It's funny how this kind of work has been good for me," Cato says. She's asked me to go for a walk, an activity she knows I'll find nostalgically stirring. We tramped all over the city before and after lovemaking when we first got together. "All of this end-of-the-world stuff apparently cheers me up," she remarks. "I guess it's the same thing I used to get at home. All those glum faces, and I had to do the song and dance that explained why they got out of bed in the morning."

"The heavy lifting," I tell her.

"Exactly," she says with a faux mournfulness. "The heavy lifting. We're on for another simulcast tomorrow and it'll be three Germans with long faces and Cato the Optimist."

We negotiate a herd of bicycles on a plaza and she veers ahead of me toward the harbor. When we cross the skylights of the traffic tunnels, giant container haulers shudder by beneath our feet. She has a beautiful back, accentuated by the military cut of her overcoat.

"Except that the people you're dealing with now *want* to be fooled," I tell her.

"It's not that they want to be fooled," she answers. "It's just that they're not convinced they need to go around glum all the time."

"How'd that philosophy work with your parents?" I ask.

"Not so well," she says sadly.

We always knew this was coming. Years ago, the city fathers though
was our big opportunity. Rotterdam no longer would be just the u
port, or Amsterdam without the attractions. The bad news was going
impact us first and foremost, so we put out the word that we were looki
for people with the nerve to put into practice what was barely possil
anywhere else. The result was Waterplan 4 Rotterdam, with brand-n
approaches to storage and safety: water plazas, super cisterns, wa
balloons, green roofs, and even traffic tunnels that doubled as immen
drainage systems would all siphon off danger. It roped in Kees and Ca
and me, and by the end of the first week, had set Cato against us. H
mandate was to showcase Dutch ingenuity, so the last thing she need
was the Pessimists clamoring for more funding because nothing anyo
had come up with yet was going to work. As far as she was concerned, o
country was the testing ground for all high-profile adaptive measures ar
practically oriented knowledge and prototype projects that would attra
worldwide attention and become a sluice gate for high-tech exports. Sl
spent her days in the international marketplace, hawking the notion th
we were safe here because we had the knowledge and were using it to fir
creative solutions. We were all assuming that a secure population was
collective social good for which the government and private sector alil
would remain responsible, a notion, we soon realized, not universal
embraced by other countries.

Sea-facing barriers are inspected both by hand and by laser-imagir
Smart dikes schedule their own maintenance based on sensors that dete
seepage or changes in pressure and stability. Satellites track ocean cl
rents and water-mass volumes. The areas most at risk have been divide
into dike-ring compartments in an attempt to make the country a syster
of watertight doors. Our road and infrastructure networks now functic

We turn on Boompjes, which is sure to add to her melancholy. A seven-story construction crane with legs curving inward perches like a spider over the river.

"Your mother called about the coffee grinder," she remarks. "I couldn't pin down what she was talking about."

Boys in bathing suits are pitching themselves off the high dock by the Strand, though it seems much too cold for that and the river too dirty. Even in the chill, I can smell tar and rope and, strangely, fresh bread.

"She called you or you called her?" I ask.

"I just told you," Cato says.

"It seems odd that she'd call you," I tell her.

"What *was* she talking about?" Cato wants to know.

"I assume she was having trouble working the coffee grinder," I tell her.

"Working it or finding it?" she asks.

"Working it, I think," I suggest. "*She* called *you*?"

"Oh, my God," Cato says.

"I'm just asking," I tell her after a minute.

All of Maashaven is blocked from view by a giant suction dredger that's being barged out to Maasvlakte 2. Preceded by six tugs, it looks like a small city going by. The thing uses dragheads connected to tubes the size of railway tunnels and harvests sand down to a depth of twenty meters. It'll be deepening the docking areas out at Yangtzehaven, Europahaven, and Mississippihaven. There's been some worry that all of this dredging has been undermining the water defenses on the other side of the channel, which is the last thing we need. Kees has been dealing with their horseshit for a few weeks now.

We rest on a bench in front of some law offices. Over the front entrance, cameras have been installed to monitor the surveillance cameras, which have been vandalized. Once the dredger has passed, we can see a family of day campers on the opposite bank who've pitched their tent on a berm overlooking the channel.

"Isn't it too cold for camping?" I ask her.

"Wasn't it too cold for swimming?" she responds, reminding me of the boys we'd passed.

She says Henk keeps replaying the same footage on his iFuze of Feyenoord's MVP being lowered into the stadium beneath the team flag by a VSTOL. "So, here's what I'm thinking," she continues, as if that led directly to her next thought. She mentions a conservatory in Berlin, fantastically expensive, that has a chamber music program. She'd like to send Henk there during his winter break and maybe longer.

This seems to me to be mostly about his safety, though I don't acknowledge that. He's a gifted cellist but hardly seems devoted to the instrument.

With her pitchman's good cheer, she repeats the amount it will cost, which to me sounds like enough for a week in a five-star hotel. But she says money can always be found for a good idea, and if it can't, then it wasn't a good idea. Finally, she adds that as a hydraulic engineer, I'm the equivalent of an atomic physicist in technological prestige.

Atomic physicists don't make a whole lot of money either, I remind her. And our argument proceeds from there. I can see her disappointment expanding as we speak, and even as my inner organs start to contract, I sit on the information of my hidden nest egg and allow all of the unhappiness to unfold. This takes forever. The word in our country for the decision-making process is the same as the one we use for what we pour over pancakes. Our national mindset pivots around the word *but* as in *This, yes, but that, too.* Cato puts her fingers to her temples and sheathes her cheeks with her palms. Her arguments run aground on my tolerance, which has been elsewhere described as a refusal to listen. Passion in Dutch meetings is punished by being ignored. The idea is that the argument itself matters, not the intensity with which it's presented. Outright rejections of a position are rare; what you get instead are suggestions for improvement that, if followed, would annihilate the original intent. And then everyone checks their agendas to schedule the next meeting.

Just like that, we're walking back. We're single file again, and it's gotten colder.

From our earliest years, we're taught not to burden others with our emotions. A young Amsterdammer in the Climate Campus is known as the Thespian because he sobbed in public at a coworker's funeral. "You don't need to eliminate your emotions," Kees reminded him when the Amsterdammer complained about the way he'd been treated. "You just need to be a little more economical with them."

Another thing I never told Cato: my sister and I the week before she caught the flu had been jumping into the river in the winter as well. That was my idea. When she came out, her feet and lips were blue and she sneezed all the way home. "Do you think I'll catch a cold?" she asked that night. "Go to sleep," I answered.

We take a shortcut through the sunken pedestrian mall they call the Shopping Gutter. By the time we reach our street, it's dark, raining again, and the muddy pavement's shining in the lights of the cafes. Along the new athletic complex in the distance, sapphire blue searchlights are lancing up into the rain at even intervals, like meteorological harp strings. "I don't know if you *know* what this does to me, or you don't," Cato says at our doorstep, once she's stopped and turned. Her thick brown hair is beaded with moisture where it's not soaked. "But either way, it's just so miserable."

I actually *have* the solution to our problem, I'm reminded as I follow her up the stairs. The thought makes me feel rehabilitated, as though I've told her instead of only myself.

Cato always maintained that when it came to their marriage, her parents practiced a sort of apocalyptic utilitarianism: on the one hand, they were sure everything was going to hell in a handbasket, while on the other, they continued to operate as if things could be turned around with a few practical measures.

But there's always that moment in a country's history when it becomes obvious the earth is less manageable than previously thought. Ten years ago, we needed to conduct comprehensive assessments of the flood defenses every five years. Now safety margins are adjusted every six months to take new revelations into account. For the last year and a half, we've been told to build into our designs for whatever we're working on features that restrict the damaging effects *after* an inevitable inundation. There won't be any retreating back to the hinterlands, either, because given the numbers we're facing, there won't be any hinterlands. It's gotten to the point that pedestrians are banned from many of the sea-facing dikes in the far west even on calm days. At the entrance to the Haringvlietdam, they've erected an immense yellow caution sign that shows two tiny stick figures with their arms raised in alarm at a black wave three times their size that's curling over them.

I watched Kees' face during a recent simulation as one of his new configurations for a smart dike was overwhelmed in half the time he would have predicted. It had always been the Dutch assumption that we would resolve the problems facing us from a position of strength. But we passed that station long ago. At this point, each of us understands privately that we're operating under the banner of lost control.

The next morning, we're crammed together into Rotterdam Climate Proof's Smartvan and heading west on N211, still not speaking. Cato's driving. At 140 km/hr, the rain fans across the windshield energetically, racing the wipers. Grey clouds seem to be rushing in from the sea in the distance. We cross some polders that are already flooded, and there's a rocking buoyancy when we traverse that part of the road that's floating. Trucks sweep by backward and recede behind us in the spray.

The only sounds are those of tires and wipers and rain. Exploring the radio is like visiting the Tower of Babel: Turks, Berbers, Cape Verdeans, Antilleans, Angolans, Portuguese, Croatians, Brazilians, Chinese. Cato managed to relocate her simulcast with her three long-faced Germans to the Hoek van Holland; she told them she wanted the Maeslant Barrier as a backdrop, but what she really intends is to surprise them, live, with the state of the water levels already. Out near the Barrier, it's pretty dramatic. Cato the Optimist with indisputable visual evidence that the sky is falling: can the German position remain unshaken in the face of that? Will her grandstanding work? It's hard to say. It's pretty clear that nothing else will.

"Want me to talk about Gravenzande?" I ask her. "That's the sort of thing that will really jolt the boys from the Reich."

"That's just what I need," she answers. "You starting a panic about something that might not even be true."

Gravenzande's where she's going to drop me, a few kilometers away. Three days ago, geologists there turned up crushed shell deposits seven meters higher on the dune lines inland than anyone believed floods had ever reached, deposits that look to be only about ten thousand years old. If this ends up confirmed, it's seriously bad news, given what it clarifies about how cataclysmic things could get even before the climate's more recent turn for the worse.

It's Saturday, and we'll probably put in twelve hours. Henk's getting more comfortable with his weekend nanny than with us. As Cato likes to tell him when she's trying to induce him to do his chores: around here, you work. By which she means that old joke that when you buy a shirt in Rotterdam, it comes with the sleeves already rolled up.

We pass poplars lining the canals in neat rows, a canary-yellow smudge of a house submerged to its second-floor windows, and beyond a round-about, a pair of decrepit rugby goalposts.

"You're really going to announce that if the Germans pull their weight, everything's going to be fine?" I ask. But she ignores me.

She needs a decision, she tells me a few minutes later, as though tired of asking. Henk's winter break is coming up. I venture that I thought it wasn't until the twelfth, and she reminds me with exasperation that it's the fifth, the schools now staggering vacation times to avoid overloading the transportation systems.

We pass the curved sod roofs of factories. The secret account's not a problem but a solution, I decide, and as I model to myself ways of implementing it as such, Cato finally asserts—as though she's waited too long already—that she's found the answer: she could take that Royal Dutch Shell offer to reconfigure their regional media relations, they could set her up in Wannsee, and Henk could commute. They could stay out there and get a bump in income besides. Henk could enroll in the conservatory.

We exit N211 northwest on an even smaller access road to the coast, and within a kilometer, it ends in a turnabout next to the dunes. She pulls the car around so it's pointed back toward her simulcast, turns off the engine, and sits there beside me with her hands in her lap.

"How long has this been in the works?" I ask. She wants to know what I mean, and I tell her that it doesn't seem like so obscure a question; she said no to Shell years ago, so where did this new offer come from?

She shrugs, as if I'd asked if they were paying her moving expenses. "They called. I told them I'd listen to what they had to say."

"They called you," I tell her.

"They called me," she repeats.

She's only trying to hedge her bets, I tell myself to combat the panic. Our country's all about spreading risk around. "Do people just walk into this conservatory?" I ask. "Or do you have to apply?"

She doesn't answer, which I take to mean that she and Henk already have applied and he's been accepted. "How did Henk feel about this good news?" I ask.

"He wanted to tell you," Cato answers.

"And we'd see each other every other weekend? Once a month?" I'm attempting a version of steely neutrality but can feel the terror worming its way forward.

"This is just one option of many," she reminds me. "We need to talk about all of them." She adds that she has to go. And that I should see all this as being primarily about Henk, not us. I answer that the Netherlands will always be here, and she smiles and starts the van.

"You sure there's nothing else you want to talk to me about?" she asks.

"Like what?" I say. "I want to talk to you about everything."

She jiggles the gear shift lightly, considering me. "You're going to let me drive away," she says, "with your having left it at that."

"I don't want you to drive away at all," I tell her.

"Well, there is that," she concedes bitterly. She waits another full minute, then a curtain comes down on her expression and she puts the car in gear. She honks when she's pulling out.

At the top of the dune, I watch surfers in wet suits wading into the breakers in the rain. The rain picks up and sets the sea's surface in a constant agitation. Even the surfers keep low to stay out of it. The wet sand's like brown sugar in my shoes.

Five hundred thousand years ago, it was possible to walk from where I live to England. At that point, the Thames was a tributary of the Rhine. Even during the Romans' occupation, the Zuider Zee was dry. But by the sixth century BC, we were building artificial hills out of marsh grass mixed with manure and our own refuse to keep our feet out of the water. And then in the seventeenth century, Hulsebos invented the Archimedes screw, and water wheels could raise a flow four meters higher than where it began, and we started to make real progress at keeping what the old people called the Waterwolf from the door.

In the fifteenth century, Philip the Good ordered the sand dike that constituted the original Hondsbossche Seawall to be restored, and another built behind it as a backup. He named the latter the Sleeper dike. For extra security, he had another constructed behind that, calling that one the Dreamer dike. Ever since, schoolchildren have learned, as one of their first geography sentences, that *Between Camperduinen and Petten lie three dikes: the Watcher, the Sleeper, and the Dreamer.*

We're raised with the double message that we have to address our worst fears but that nonetheless they'll also somehow domesticate themselves. Fifteen years ago, Rotterdam Climate Proof revived "The Netherlands

Lives with Water" as a slogan, the accompanying poster featuring a two-panel cartoon in which a towering wave in the first panel is breaking before its crest over a terrified little boy, and in the second, it separates into immense foamy fingers so he can relievedly shake its hand.

When Cato told me about that first offer from Shell, I could *see* her flash of feral excitement about what she was turning down. Royal Dutch Shell! She would've been fronting for one of the biggest corporations in the world. We conceived Henk a few nights later. There was a lot of urgent talk about getting deeper and closer and I remember striving once she'd guided me inside her to have my penis reach the back of her throat. Periodically, we slowed into the barest sort of movement, just to further take stock of what was happening, and at one point we paused in our tremoring, and I put my lips to her ear and reminded her of what she'd passed up. After winning them over, she could have picked her city: Tokyo, Los Angeles, Rio. The notion caused a momentary lack of focus in her eyes. Then as a response, she started moving along a contraction, and Shell and other options including speech evanesced away.

If she were to leave me, where would I be? It's as if she was put here to force my interaction with humans. And still I don't pull it off. It's like that story we were told as children, of Jesus telling the rich young man to go and sell all he has and give it to the poor, but instead, the rich man chose to keep what he had and went away sorrowful. When we talked about it, Kees said he always assumed the guy had settled in Holland.

That Monday, more bad news: warm air and heavy rain have ventured many meters above established snowlines in the western Alps, and Kees holds up before me with both hands GRACE's latest printouts about a storm cell whose potential numbers we keep rechecking because they seem so extravagant. He spends the rest of the morning on the phone trying to stress that we've hit another type of threshold here, that these are calamity-level numbers. It seems to him that everyone's *saying* they recognize the urgency of the new situation but that no one's *acting* like it. During lunch, a call comes in about the hinge and socket joint, itself five stories high, of one of the Maeslant doors. In order to allow the doors to roll with the waves, the joints are designed to operate like a human shoulder, swinging along both horizontal and vertical axes and transferring the unimaginable stresses to the joint's foundation. The maintenance engineers are reporting that the foundation block—all fifty-two thousand tons of it—is moving.

Finally, Kees flicks off his phone receptor and squeezes his eyes shut in despair. "Maybe our history's just the history of picking up after disasters like this," he tells me. "The Italians do pasta sauce and we do body retrieval."

After waiting a few minutes for updated numbers, I call Cato and fail to get through and then try my mother, who says she's soaking her corns. I can picture the enamel basin with the legend CONTENTED FEET around the rim. The image seems to confirm that we're all naked in the world, so I tell her to get some things together, that I'm sending someone out for her, that she needs to leave town for a little while.

It's amazing I'm able to keep trying Cato's numbers, given what's broken loose at every level of water management nationwide. Everyone's shouting into headpieces and clattering away at laptops at the same time. At the Delta stations, the situation has already triggered the automatic emergency procedures with their checklists and hour-by-hour protocols. Outside my office window, the canal is lined with barges of cows, of all things, awaiting their river pilot to transport them to safety. The road in front of them is a gypsy caravan of traffic piled high with suitcases and furniture and roped-down plastic bags. The occasional dog hangs from a car window. Those roads that can float should allow vehicular evacuation for six or seven hours longer than the other roads will. The civil defense teams at roundabouts and intersections are doing what they can to dispense biopacs and aquacells. Through the glass, everyone seems to be behaving well, though with a maximum of commotion.

I've got the mayor of Ter Heijde on one line saying he's up to his ass in ice water and demanding to know where the fabled Weak Links Project has gone when Cato's voice finally breaks in on the other.

"Where are you?" I shout, and the mayor shouts back "Where do you *think*?" I kill his line and ask again, and Cato answers, "What?" In just her one-word inflection, I can tell she heard what I said. "Is Henk with you?" I shout, and Kees and some of the others around the office look up despite the pandemic of shouting. I ask again and she says that he is. When I ask if she's awaiting evacuation, she answers that she's already in Berlin.

I'm shouting other questions when Kees cups a palm over my receptor and says, "Here's an idea. Why don't you sort out all of your personal problems now?"

After Cato's line goes dead, I can't raise her again, or she won't answer. We're engaged in such a blizzard of calls that it almost doesn't matter. "Whoa," Kees says, his hands dropping to his desk, and a number of our coworkers go silent as well, because the windows facing west are now rattling and black with rain. I look out mine, and bags and other debris are tearing free of the traffic caravan and sailing east. The rain curtain hits the cows in their barges and their ears flatten like mules and their eyes squint shut at the gale's power.

"Our ride is here," Kees calls, shaking my shoulder, and I realize that everyone's hurriedly collecting laptops and flash drives. There's a tumult heading up the stairs to the roof and the roar of the wind every time the door's opened, and the scrabbling sounds of people dragging something outside before the door slams shut. And then, with surprising abruptness, it's quiet.

My window continues to shake as though it's not double-pane but cellophane. Now that our land has subsided as much as it has, when the water does come, it will come like a wall, and each dike that stops it will force it to turn, and in its churning, it will begin to spiral and bore into the earth, eroding away the dike walls, until the pressure builds and that dike collapses and it's on to the next one, with more pressure piling up behind, and so on and so on until every last barrier falls and the water thunders forward like a hand sweeping everything from the table.

The lights go off, and then on and off again, before the halogen emergency lights in the corridors engage, with their irritated buzzing.

It's easier to see out with the interior lights gone. Along the line of cars, a man carrying a framed painting staggers at an angle, like a sailboat tacking. He passes a woman in a van with her head against the headrest and her mouth open in an *Oh* of fatigue.

I'm imagining the helicopter crew's negotiations with my mother, and their fireman's carry once those negotiations have fallen through. She told me once that she often recalled how long they drifted in the flood of 1953 through the darkness without the sky getting any lighter. When the sun finally rose, they watched the Navy drop food and blankets and rubber boats and bottles of cooking gas to people on roofs or isolated high spots, and when their boat passed a small body lying across an eave with its arms in the water, her father told her that it was resting. She remembered later that morning telling her mother, who'd grown calmer, that it was a good sign they saw so few people floating, and before her father could stop her, she answered that the drowned didn't float straightaway but took a few days to come up.

And she talked with fondness about how tenderly her father had tended to her later, after she'd been blinded by some windblown grit, by suggesting she rub one eye to make the other weep, like farmers did when bothered by chaff. And she remembered, too, the strangeness of one of the prayers her village priest recited once they were back in their old church, the masonry buttressed with steel beams and planking to keep the walls from sagging outwards any further: *I sink into deep mire, where there is no standing; I come into deep waters, where the floods overflow me.*

The window's immense pane shudders and flexes before me from the force of what's pouring out of the North Sea. Water's beginning to run its fingers under the seal on the sash. Cato will send me wry and brisk and newsy text updates whether she receives answers or not, and Henk will author a few as well. Everyone in Berlin will track the developments on the monitors above them while they shop or travel or work, the teaser heading reading something like THE NETHERLANDS UNDER SIEGE. Some of the more sober will think, *That could have been us.* Some of the more perceptive will consider that it soon might well be.

My finger's on the Cato icon on the screen without exerting the additional pressure that would initiate another call. What sort of person ends up with someone like me? What sort of person finds that *acceptable*, year to year? We went on vacations and fielded each other's calls and took turns reading Henk to sleep and let slip away the miracle that was there between us when we first came together. We hunkered down before the wind picked up. We modeled risk management for our son when instead, we could have embraced the freefall of that astonishing *Here, this is yours to hold.* We told each other *I think I know* when we should've said *Lead me farther through your amazing, astonishing interior.*

Cato was moved by my mother's flood memories but brought to tears only by the one she cherished from that year: the Queen's address to the nation afterwards, her celebration of what the crucible of the disaster had produced, and the return, at long last, of the unity the country had displayed during the war. My mother had years ago purchased a vinyl record of the speech, and later had a neighbor transfer it to a digital format. She played it once while we were visiting, and Henk knelt at the window spying on whoever was hurrying by. And my mother held the weeping Cato's hand and she held mine and Henk gave us fair warning of anything of interest on the street, while the Queen's warm and smooth voice thanked us all for working together in that one great cause, soldiering on without a thought for care, or grief, or inner divisions, and without even realizing what we were denying ourselves.

ABOUT THE AUTHOR

JIM SHEPARD is the author of six novels, including most recently *The Book of Aron*, and four story collections, including *You Think That's Bad*. His third collection, *Like You'd Understand, Anyway*, was a finalist for the National Book Award and won The Story Prize. His novel *Project X* won the 2005 Library of Congress/Massachusetts Book Award for Fiction, as well as the Alex Award from the American Library Association. His short fiction has appeared in, among other magazines, *Harper's*, *McSweeney's*, *The Paris Review*, *The Atlantic Monthly*, *Esquire*, *DoubleTake*, the *New Yorker*, *Granta*, *Zoetrope: All-Story*, and *Playboy*, and he was a columnist on film for the magazine *The Believer*. Four of his stories have been chosen for the Best American Short Stories, and one for a Pushcart Prize. He teaches at Williams College and in the Warren Wilson MFA program, and lives in Williamstown with his wife Karen Shepard, his three children, and two beagles.

THE PRECEDENT

SEAN McMULLEN

Even when the climate crime is so serious that death is not punishment enough, one still gets an audit. We were being taken to a mine in the desert to be audited, and a third of the tippers who had begun the journey had already died. Their bodies had been staked out by the roadside to desiccate. We pulled wagons that were loaded with our water and food, wagons that were SUVs stripped of their engines, doors, and seats. No fuel resources could be consumed on our journey.

There was no clear pattern to the deaths in our grisly and geriatric column. Some fat tippers died within the first ten miles, but others just got thinner and survived. I was quite fit to begin with, so I was better prepared than most. Red sand made the ground look red-hot and magnified my unending thirst. The surface of the road was appalling, but nobody tried to repair it. A good road would make it easier for us, and we were meant to be stressed. If some of us died, so much the better.

In the Midsouth Consolidation, they practiced desiccation. Once dead, the tippers were flayed open and left to dry in the sun. When there was only bone and dried flesh left, their remains were brought to the mines and buried. Thus the carbon of the guilty was returned to the Earth, rather than stressing the atmosphere.

*   *   *   *

At nightfall, we stopped where we were, shuffled to the roadside, and fell asleep. Each night, I had the same visitor. He was just a denser patch of darkness in the gloom with a pale oval for a face, yet his voice was perfectly clear.

"So you survived to the mine," he said.

"Not there yet," I replied, sitting up.

"You arrive tomorrow. The odds favor you."

"You talk as if this is good."

"What is wrong with being alive?"

"It's 2035 and vengeance is upon us; is that good? We tippers were born before the Millennium Year and so are guilty until pardoned. Is that good? I was born in 1955, so I'm guilty. For me, that's bad."

"You could plead guilty, then appeal for a merciful death."

"I intend to beat the audit."

"The Audit of Midsouth has a perfect record for tipper convictions."

"I'm used to standing alone."

Those of us who reached the mine had to camp in a vast holding ground of red sand, awaiting our turn to be audited. Some had been there a long time. These were the borderlines, those tippers who had difficult audits and were holding up the executions. Every execution meant a lessening of the burden on the ecosphere, so large numbers were important. Meantime, the borderlines were assigned to service, where they did the flaying, the desiccation, and the dropping of bodies down the mine shaft.

The miners were too guilty to die. They were lowered into the mine, there to live out what remained of their lives dragging corpses away from the drop shaft and packing them into the abandoned tunnels. Miners first class had no light; their only food was what they could gnaw from the corpses, and they had to drink the artesian water that seeped into the tunnels. It was a poor alternative to death.

Because those pending audit were already considered guilty, we were made to assist with disposals after executions. This began the day we arrived. Hot, parched, weary, and coated with red dust, we simply dropped our harnesses and joined the execution parade. The first convicted man was my age, and I was eighty. The executioner had been chosen by ballot from the pool of Wardens. She was about twenty and was lean and muscular. Her recreation was probably fitness, which was very climatically correct.

"What's your charges?" asked an older borderline as we shuffled along.

"Squandering and display," I replied mechanically.

"Yeah? Me, I got greed. The audit went for death, second class, but I got adjourned. Name's Chaz."

"I'm Jason; my audit's tomorrow."

The Wardens did not care if we tippers talked among ourselves. What we said was no longer important to anyone but us. The condemned man was walking with his hands tied behind his back. He turned as he heard us.

"I got denial, squandering, and greed," he announced proudly. "Death, second class on all three."

"What was your line?" I asked.

"Morels."

"As in the mushrooms?"

"Yeah, and I was good, too. Hunted them for a living back in the States. I just loved the wilderness. Used to teach folk the tricks, like how to get 'eyes on' in snow and burned pine forest, then to look for the 'pop-out' effect. That's when the morels suddenly start jumping out at you."

I was to hear that sort of spiel depressingly often in the fortnight to come. Tippers often tried to leave a little of their art or passion to those who might survive them. How to tune a motor, ways to score in a nightclub, tricks to beat the trend in a share market, or even the art of arranging Christmas lights. But there were no more gasoline motors, nightclubs and share markets had ceased to exist, and proof that you had ever displayed Christmas lights would get you death, second class.

"How does a mushroom hunter get denial, squandering, and greed?" asked Chaz.

"I drove an SUV to reach the best spots."

Denial, because he said he loved the wilderness yet drove an SUV. Squandering, merely because he drove an SUV. Greed, because he took from nature without giving back. Death, death, and death. Having spoken, he looked more relaxed, perhaps because he had left something of himself in our memories. Shepherded by the executioner, he walked out onto the tipping plank. The gallows were built of timber even though the old mine site was littered with steel pipes and beams. That was climatic symbolism. The Auditor General stood waiting.

"James Francis Harrington, you have been found guilty of denial, squandering, and greed," she declared. "For this you are sentenced to death by merciful means. As you did take from the Earth, so now you must give what remains to you back to the Earth. This by my tally, the twenty-fifth day of March, 2035. Wardens, reclaim his carbon."

The executioner arranged the noose to snap Harrington's neck as he stood on the tipping plank. This was a length of pinewood that extended out over the drop. The other end was held down by a pile of coal. Now a procession of Wardens filed past. Each took a lump of coal from the pile. The plank began to teeter. I counted fifteen seconds of teetering, during which Harrington's dignity and composure fled. He began to scream as the tipping point approached; he pissed his pants to try to lighten himself and gain a few more moments of life.

Relentlessly, the hands removed coal from the pile, as relentlessly as coal had once been dug out of the Earth and burned. Abruptly, the tipping point was reached, and a shower of coal catapulted over Harrington as he fell. The gallows creaked. The Wardens applauded.

"Now, that was a great piece of work," said Chaz. "Harrington didn't want to give the scream of repentance, but they got it out of him."

A long line of condemned tippers was waiting as we took the body down. A woman began to shriek and struggle. She was next. Her executioner was a youth of about seventeen, and he looked nervous. Nervous about killing someone, or nervous about screwing up? The Wardens collected the coal and piled it back onto the tipping plank.

The executions went on for a long time. The lumps of coal became coated with red sand, so that they seemed to glow hot. I was made to brush them, to keep the symbolism clear.

"So, what were you?" asked one of the few friendly Wardens as we were finally led away.

"I was a climatologist," I replied.

"A climate change denialist?" she gasped, as if I had just admitted to being the devil himself.

"No, a climate scientist. I was actually one of the first to warn about climate change, back in the 1980s."

She thought about this for a moment, then shook her head.

"Why would a climatologist get audited?" she asked.

"Every tipper gets audited," I replied.

This was the flaw that underlay the World Audit. Was any tipper innocent? Up to a point, the answer was easy. Everyone who had squandered resources for recreation or greed was guilty, but what about those who burned fossil fuels for a living? Not quite so clear, because these included cab drivers, airline pilots, and the like. Such cases were adjourned, but the backlog of marginal offenders was becoming quite a burden worldwide. Just what did make a tipper a climate criminal? A standard was needed.

"What was your line?" I asked the Warden.

"Name's Olivia; wanna do some climatically correct recreational sex?"

I put a hand to my face and shook my head.

"I meant your job before you became a Warden."

"Computers, systems administration. Then I got audited."

She lifted her kilt to show the brand on one thigh: S for squandering.

"It hurt like hell, but I deserved it."

I noticed Chaz staring at her thigh with as much admiration as someone in his seventies could manage.

"To me, that's squandering a mighty fine leg," he said, and the three of us laughed.

Sometimes, survival was who you knew, and Chaz went out of his way to be liked by the right people.

"Not many tippers beat the audit," I said.

"I was born in 2001, so I'm not a tipper," she explained.

"Ah, a victim."

"Yeah. We get leniency for climate crimes."

"What did you do?"

"I was two-sixty pounds back in 2023; can you believe it?"

"And you got squandering, not gluttony?"

"I wasn't greedy, just a slob living on Coke, turkey stuffing, and fries. Now I'm under one-thirty pounds. That's why I got just branded, second class. I was lucky. The Retributor wanted service, first class."

That night, I lay on my back, looking at the stars and thinking about how rapidly the world had changed. The victim riots had caught the authorities by surprise, but trends could grow exponentially thanks to the Internet. Going lateral was another movement that began on the Internet. The lateralists worked out that they could actually live way better by detaching themselves from the economic systems of derivatives, leverage, optionality, and toxic assets. In just months, the lateralists' ranks swelled from thousands to millions to hundreds of millions. This generated a crisis in confidence that triggered the biggest financial collapse in history, and very soon, the people who had formerly worked at generating meaningless wealth were out looking for real jobs. By then, it was too late because the climate was severely screwed, there were famines in Western democracies, the trillions of dollars based on derivatives and options were fast becoming meaningless, and economic growth was considered about as healthy as cancer.

Democracies did particularly badly against lateralism, because their politicians were working to very short agendas. They did nothing decisive to save the ecosphere, as everything had to be balanced to appease competing interests. Lateralism ignored wealth. Soon, there were only guards, goods, and obscenely rich people left in conventional economies. Dictatorships did not last long when entire populations became lateralist terrorists. What did citizens have to lose? They were starving and the world seemed to be ending, anyway. As the surviving nobles of Europe found out when the Black Death swept across their estates in the fourteenth century, however, you need peons as the foundation of any economy.

"You summoned me?" asked a familiar voice.

"I never summon you," I muttered.

"Of course you do. Enjoying the night sky?"

"The end of the world is close; the sky is all that's worth looking at."

"Not the end of *the* world, but *your* world," said my visitor. "The world will go on, but your world has been unsustainable for a long time."

"Funny, I thought the police and armies would hold things together for longer," I admitted.

"The World Audit promised order and organization, so the police and soldiers signed up very quickly. They annihilated the armed urban gangs and survivalist warlords. That earned a lot of support, almost as much as auditing and executing the rich."

"So, Death is an Auditor?"

"No, but an Auditor is Death."

"That makes no sense."

"It will, soon."

The most annoying thing about Death was that I kept catching myself agreeing with him. We seemed to have a lot in common. Did he want to be friends? I drifted into a proper sleep.

* * * *

Our audit consisted of eight Auditors and an Auditor General. They sat on a bench, each shaded by an umbrella held by a borderline. The Retributor, Advocate, and Wardens all wore top hats. This was highly symbolic. The indulgence generations had gloried in being casual and individual. Now was the age of formality, unity, and sacrifice. Black robes and black cloaks were the uniform. Black hats were for the important people, and black cowls for the really important. The latter were the Auditors. Just three decades ago, it would have looked ludicrous, but three decades ago, the Earth was three degrees cooler. The black robes were uncomfortable to wear in the merciless heat and symbolized the suffering that had been caused by the tippers who had burned too much fossil carbon.

We tippers sat exposed to the sun, whose effect we had enhanced so much. There were nine circles of tippers. Nine circles of hell. Nine degrees of warming that were predicted by 2100. We had been heating the world during a natural cooling cycle. When the next warming cycle kicked in, things went straight to hell in every sense.

The audits began as the sun's disk rose clear of the horizon. We were meant to suffer.

"Audit of Jason Hall, climatologist," the Clerk of the Audit announced.

There was a quota of audits for each day, so no more than minutes could be given to any one. For most, it was the work of less than a minute to confirm guilt and pass sentence. I was escorted to the dais by a Warden as the Retributor climbed the three steps to the lectern. Without using notes, he began.

"Worthy victims, I have records, confirmed by the defendant while wired to a veritor, proving that he squandered the resources of the Earth to acquire a second doctorate. I maintain that he did this for sheer vanity and so is guilty of display and squandering."

"Defendant?" asked the Auditor General.

"I did my second doctorate in history to get credibility. It was not display or squandering," I responded.

"Credibility for what?" the Retributor asked with smug confidence.

"I was studying links between the Little Ice Age and witch burnings from the fifteenth to the eighteenth centuries."

The Retributor opened his mouth to scoff, failed to find suitable words, and closed it again. He had been caught unprepared. A buzz of speculation rippled through the circles of tippers and borderlines, and even the auditors whispered among themselves.

"Ridiculous," said the Retributor, resorting to bluster. "The topic is frivolous."

"Not so: my research showed close parallels with the World Audit before—"

"Moving on to your use of motorcycles—"

"Objection!" called the Advocate. "My honorable colleague has made a statement but not allowed the defendant to refute it."

"Objection sustained," said the Auditor General. "The honorable Retributor must either withdraw his statement or allow the defendant to address it."

That was the first objection that had been decided in favor of a tipper within anyone's memory. Anger clouded the Retributor's face for a moment, then it cleared.

"I stand at your honor's pleasure," he said.

"Defendant, you will continue," said the Auditor General.

I now had the undivided attention of everyone. This was not just some boring accusation of SUV rallies or ten-kilowatt Christmas light displays.

"During the fifteenth century, around the time that the climatic event known as the Little Ice Age became really severe in Europe, the number of witch trials and burnings suddenly increased. Witches were said to call up storms, cause frosts, and induce other meteorological disasters."

"Point of clarification," said the Auditor General. "Are you suggesting that witches caused the Little Ice Age?"

"Absolutely not, but records show that people believed them to be responsible."

"Point taken. Proceed."

"As bad weather became more frequent and severe, people began to look for someone to blame. Supposed witches were plausible and vulnerable targets."

"Are you suggesting that audits such as yours, here, today, are witch trials?" asked the Auditor General.

"No, your honor."

For a moment, my life seemed to hang by a thread as she paused to discomfort me.

"Proceed."

"When I began my second PhD in 1997, I wanted to get credibility as an historian. As an expert in both history and climatology I thought my warnings would be taken more seriously."

"Warnings?"

"Warnings to polluters and squanderers that when human-induced climate change gripped the Earth, their descendants might want revenge. There would be whole generations of old tippers to provide guilty and vulnerable targets."

"Surely the Christian church initiated the medieval witch trials, not the general population?"

"Actually, most witch trials were secular and at the village level."

"Interesting. That is how the World Audit operates."

"True."

"Then what are you suggesting?"

"I am only relating history, your honor. My PhD was about instances of popular anger in response to severe weather. In the fifteenth century, anger was foolishly directed against witches. Popular anger has now revived, this time due to induced climate change. I make no judgment about whether it is just or unjust."

"Enough, enough," said the Auditor General. "You have demonstrated to my satisfaction that your second doctorate was in defense of the ecosphere. Retributor, do you have any further accusations?"

"Oh, yes, multiple accusations of squandering."

"Then I declare this audit of Jason Hall, climatologist, adjourned. Clerk of the Audit, what is the next audit?"

"Audit of Kieran Harley, who owned and operated a Jet Ski."

"For recreation?"

"Yes."

"Guilty as charged. Death, second class. Those in favor? Against? Confirmed. Next audit?"

My audit had been adjourned! I was borderline. I would join the ranks of those considered guilty but too difficult to waste time on. After all, millions of undeniably guilty tippers could be audited and executed easily.

Religious services were not as popular with the tippers and borderlines as one might have expected. Religion had not seriously challenged the World Audit, just as in the mid–twentieth century, the major religions had made no effective protests when American and Soviet politicians had threatened the world with thermonuclear annihilation. The World Audit promised action and revenge for what had been done to the planet. Unlike religions, it delivered.

Thus there were services to prepare people for death at the camp, but not much more. There was no shortage of entertainment, however.

Among the borderlines, there were tippers who had memorized their favorite movies and television shows, word for word. Over my two weeks in the adjourned backlog, I sat in the audience while episodes of *Cheers, Star Trek, Buffy*, and *Seinfeld* were acted out in the dusk and moonlight. The performances were a little stiff and arthritic, the props were minimal, and the theme music had to be hummed and whistled by an aged orchestra, but the dialogue seemed accurate.

On my second night, there was an extravaganza performance in the form of *The Rocky Horror Picture Show*. At the center of the stage space were the actors, along with those playing the parts of chairs, tables, doors, and a bed. Flanking them were a chorus of singers to the right and an orchestra of hummers to the left. Surrounding all this was the participating audience, who sang, danced, and called responses at the actors. The rest of us merely watched, although some tippers born after 1990 seemed a bit bewildered. The Wardens looked on, impassive.

Apparently, a suicide wave had been not only planned but coordinated with the Wardens. At the end of the show, the audience participators charged the Wardens, shouting lines from the show, hurling rocks, and waving walking sticks. Everyone else dropped and flattened themselves against the sand as the Wardens' assault rifles chattered into life and bullets whined overhead.

"Don't move," said the man beside me.

"Who's moving?"

"They're tippers facing greenhouse or mines. A bullet is way better than that."

The firing died down to the occasional sharp bark of a pistol shot.

"That's the Inspector of Wardens," said my companion. "He's finishing them off with a Smith & Wesson 1006. Beautiful gun, real classic."

A gun fancier. He was sure to be up for squandering, display, and possibly greed.

"Now, those Wardens, do you see what they got?"

The Wardens were carrying guns with curved magazines. They were very good at killing people, and that was about as much as I understood.

"Assault rifles?"

"Yeah, and they may be made in China, but they're still AK-47s."

"Er, that's Russian," I said, recalling television news items about terrorists and guerrillas from a lifetime ago.

"That's right, developed in the forties but perfected in nineteen fifty-nine. The M16, now, that was a better gun; the old AK couldn't shoot as fast or far. Mind, AKs could take way worse treatment and keep firing, and were cheap as chicken feed to make."

He kept talking, but my thoughts had already wandered. The AK-47 design was ninety years old, yet it still did the job. It also needed little maintenance and was cheap to build. That symbolized the modern world. Everything was merely good enough rather than optimized to have a slight edge. All things being equal, a slightly better range or rate of fire at twice the cost was no advantage because all things were never equal. The victims had new values, and better was seldom desirable. Good enough meant a softer ecological touch. The Chinese-made assault rifles designed in Russia were good enough, so good enough was perfect.

"All stand!"

The inspector's command meant that everyone was dead who was meant to be dead. I was put on a stretcher team, carrying away dead, bullet-riddled men and women painted with fishnet stockings and suspenders.

Hours later, I awoke beneath a sky that blazed coldly with stars. For someone who had spent so much of his life studying the atmosphere, I knew surprisingly little about the constellations above it. In desert skies, the stars are so numerous and intense that even the most familiar patterns are almost overwhelmed. I sat up and looked around.

Wardens patrolled the perimeter of the camp, no more than deeper shadows in the shadows and moonlight. The snores and wheezes from those nearby had stopped; in fact, all sounds had ceased.

Suddenly he was before me, a figure now in the black robes of a climate penitent. None of the Wardens reacted to him; perhaps he had no warmth for their thermal imagers to detect. I thought that I should be visible, but nobody paid me attention, either. Perhaps I was not alive when he came to see me.

"Don't try to say I summoned you," I snapped.

"Still, it's true."

"So now what?"

"Come along."

His voice was cold and remote but free of malice. I fell in beside him as he glided along through the darkness. The audit space was just a long bench for the Auditors, a lectern for the speaker, a dais for the accused, and a desk for the clerk. Everyone else sat in the sand, in the nine great circles.

"When does the audit begin?" I asked.

"This is not an audit."

"Then why bring me here?"

"You summoned me."

"I did not!"

"Everyone summons me, eventually."

"Everyone? Then you really are Death?"

"Close, but not quite."

"You keep denying it, but who else could you be?"

"That is for you to discover. Yesterday, how would you have audited James Harrington?"

"He was just a fool who never looked at his carbon footprint."

"But how would you have audited him—as an Auditor?"

"Death, second class. He chose to ignore the plight of the wilderness he loved. He was like a doctor fondling a woman's breast yet not telling her she has breast cancer."

"How would you audit him, this time as Jason Hall?"

"Service, second class, in wilderness restoration."

"What of Ellen Farmer, the woman who followed him onto the tipping gallows?"

"She built a fourteen-room house just to impress her friends and vacationed on cruise ships three months out of twelve. Guilty for aggravated display and squandering."

"How would you audit her—as Jason Hall?"

"Service, first class. Half a lifetime of healing the ecosphere in return for half a lifetime of screwing it."

And so it went. Two hundred people had faced the audit that day and the day before, but only a dozen cases had been adjourned. Mine was one. The specter knew every name, and so did I. I have a very good memory.

"Craig Brand?"

"He built supertuned engines for street racers and was a paid-up Climate Denier. Guilty, death, second class."

"Jason Hall?"

"Innocent."

"There is no such verdict. Pardoned is the most lenient."

"Then pardoned."

"You are less severe than the Retributor. Only three deaths in two hundred sentences. Do you feel compassion for them?"

"Yes."

"Why?"

"Most were fools, not monsters."

"The fool kills just as dead as the monster."

"True, but some fools are harmless. The audit has a perfect record; it's always death or mines for tippers, yet some deserve service, branding, or even pardoning."

"Many audits are adjourned. Yours was."

"And I'm eighty. I will probably die in the borderline backlog."

"Would you abolish the World Audit?"

"No. The Audit is all we have, but it must be seen to be fair; otherwise, the Auditors will look like a pack of Nazis."

"The Auditors think of themselves like the judges in the Nuremberg trials."

"Perhaps, but to them, *everyone* born before 2000 is an eco-Nazi, guilty of climate crimes."

Suddenly, I was alone. I felt no chill on the night air, and when I put my hand up, I could see stars through it. I would have been convinced that I was dead, yet I knew I would awake alive.

To everyone's surprise, I was called back to the audit the following morning. The Retributor said that I had commuted on a motorcycle when I could have used public transport. I quoted well-memorized figures proving that my motorcycle had a smaller carbon footprint per passenger mile than the public transport then available. Again, my audit was adjourned.

I was put on cart duty after the morning audits. Thirty of us were harnessed to a stripped-out SUV and made to draw it out to the north greenhouse fields. Death, first class, was performed here. Sector five was where we were going, but we had to pass through other sectors first. In sector two, they were performing executions.

Our team moved slowly. Ahead of us I saw a strong, fit-looking man of about fifty being forced to the ground by the Wardens. With the skill of much practice, they spread-eagled him on his back and chained him to a wooden frame in the shape of an *X*. All the while, he was shouting about his rights, demanding a retrial, telling the Wardens he had right of appeal, and calling for a proper lawyer.

"Your turn will come. You'll pay for this!" he screamed. "This is a concentration camp."

"You helped run the concentration camp called the global economy," replied a Warden. "You kept Mother Earth in there until she was a living skeleton."

They took two large glass panels and clamped them over him in a tent shape. We were level with them as they fitted a pair of glass triangles over the ends.

A greenhouse. For causing the greenhouse effect, death by greenhouse. It was a hideous way to die, roasted slowly in a glass oven. The unlucky ones lasted to evening, got the respite of night, then had to face a second day. As we trudged on, straining at our harnesses, we passed the glass tents that had already been set up. There were muffled screams and groans from these, but most were already weakening.

The next sector was at stage two of the greenhouse cycle. Here, teams of borderlines were slicing open the skin of the recently executed so that the sun could evaporate their bodily fluids. We moved on through the sector where bodies were drying out within their little glass tents. In sector five, the greenhouses were being dismantled and bodies stacked in neat piles. We stopped. Service borderlines loaded the desiccated dead into our SUV. The bodies were quite stiff, as if carved out of wood.

As we returned with our load, people began talking at last.

"Remember the old days?" said the man beside me.

"I've only been here two days."

"Yeah? In that case, welcome to hell. I been here since the start. I got service, second class."

"I didn't think tippers ever got off, except to be put in the backlog as a borderline."

"I'm a victim."

"Ah."

"Fifteen years to go."

"Fifteen years of this?" I said, shaking my head.

"It's job security. I'll be fifty when I'm released. Then I'm back to work."

"Back to work. What was your work?"

"Landscape gardening."

"And for that you got service, second class?"

"I drove a big off-roader. I got it free, so it seemed like a good deal back in twenty-nineteen."

"That was after the tipping year. Bad time to be seen in an off-roader."

"Yeah, but I was nineteen and stupid. The audit found that all my work was urban, so I should have driven a fuel-efficient utility."

"You were lucky. Not many people who drove off-roaders get less than death."

"I never drove mine recreationally; that was the trick. I love growing things, so gardening was all I ever did. Big demand for people who grow things now, so I got a future."

We trudged along in silence for a while. He had his sentence; mine was not decided. Because I was guilty until proven worthy of pardoning, I had to do service.

"Do you watch those nostalgia shows?" I asked presently.

"I just attend. All that toxic fast living, never liked it. I only watched renovation and gardening shows, and the environment docos. That counted when the audit examined me."

"I saw a nostalgia show last night. It was bizarre."

"You want a word of advice?"

"I'm listening."

"Go along, but try to look bored. You see, if you don't go, the borderlines will kill you for not being one of them. On the other hand, the Wardens watch you too. If you seem to be enjoying the shows, they'll report that to the Retributor. That gets you a verdict of guilty-and-unrepentant. You know what that means?"

"Death, first class?"

"Wrong. Mines, first class. That's way worse than dying."

Every morning, the audit would call me up for the first hearing of the day, and I would spend ten minutes refuting a new charge. Normally, the accused were made to bear the full force of the sun whose power they had enhanced so very much, but because I had established provisional doubt, I was now permitted to wear a broad wicker hat. This was also the source of much rumor among the borderlines and unaudited tippers.

The second-class executions were at noon and just before sunset. Until then, there was nothing to do but listen to the Retributor accuse people of taking Sunday afternoon drives, having central heating, using leaf blowers instead of brooms, and flying to Europe for annual vacations. All brought death. The really severe sentences were for the climate-change deniers. They got mines, first class.

"You beat the Retributor again."

I knew that I was asleep, I was always asleep when Death appeared.

"You must love this place. Do you claim all the souls of the condemned in person?"

"They are already mine."

"Then why are you here?"

"Because you call me, and you are important."

"Me? Important? My life's work was predicting climatic catastrophe—you know, most of China, Australia, and Africa turned into searing deserts, USA and Europe snap-frozen because the Gulf Stream is screwed, accelerated polar melting, sea level up two feet, and category seven hurricanes. In case you hadn't noticed, that's all happened, so I'm out of a job."

"You are important because you threaten the Auditors, Jason Hall. The currency of the century is position and power. You threaten their power."

"Me? Threaten the Auditors? Get a life."

"I get a great many lives. Do you know how very rich men used to become rich?"

"By third-level greed and second-level squandering."

"Not so. They just became good at gathering money. You don't have to *earn* money to accumulate it. Some means were legal, but few were ethical."

"So? Thanks to lateralism, wealth and growth are unfashionable."

"The Retributor is good at accumulating convictions, and he has a perfect record getting death or mine sentences. He is the new type of rich man, and the rich like to hold on to their riches."

The audit of Peggy-Anne was over very quickly. Records showing seven hundred thousand dollars in cosmetic surgery and implants were presented. Although in her late nineties, she looked less than forty, but when she moved she was slightly stiff. She was convicted of squander and display, and received a double death sentence, second class. Killing old people had once seemed abhorrent, but now it was considered just. The Earth had gone to the pack, and the victim generations wanted revenge on the squander generations for turning the pack loose.

Peggy-Anne got the tipping-point gallows. As the pile of coal diminished and the plank began to teeter, she started to cry. None of the

Wardens or Auditors seemed moved. Moments before the end, she began to pray. Hers were not formal prayers, just pleas to her god to end it all and have mercy on her. When the plank finally tipped, it was a profound relief for me.

"She was a lot of fun," said Chaz as we walked back.

"Nine decades of being a party girl," I observed. "It must have been like being immortal."

Chaz had shared Peggy-Anne's bedding the night before. I tried to tell myself that in a real sense, she had stopped living at some time during that night, in the arms of a man she had picked up during the show. The terrified, whimpering shell that had shuffled out onto the plank had not been Peggy-Anne.

There were car races at the camp that evening. Many wheelchairs had accumulated there, now superfluous to the needs of their owners. Names of famous models of cars were written on the sides along with brand names of long-defunct sponsors. Cardboard clappers were attached to make engine noises against the spokes, and with one man to drive and another to push, they were a faint but distinct echo of the squander decades.

The entire company of tippers and borderlines watched, most tippers cheering and clapping, as the fifteen wheelchairs were driven around an improvised track. There were pit stops for pusher changes, crashes, and even aged cheer squads. A few of us had the sense not to cheer. The Wardens looked on, scanning the audience for signs of enthusiasm among borderlines. The wheelchair pack rattled past, raising dust and cheered mightily by the crowd, then a pusher collapsed and fell dead in the dust. There were five such deaths from cardiac arrest during that race. Most participants were probably hoping for death on the raceway, because they were tippers facing serious charges. Dying of a heart attack was vastly preferable to death in the greenhouses or life in the mines.

The race ended with the winner and place-getters being presented with double rations of water in bottles that had held champagne decades earlier. This they splashed on each other and the onlookers in a defiant show of squandering, then there was a concert of Jan and Dean driving and surfing songs by various singers and a humming band. It was all pale and tenuous ghosts of cultures past, rude but futile gestures against the victim generations. I concluded that most of these people were actually beyond hope, help, or reason. They were not ashamed of what they had done, and they probably thought it very unreasonable of the Earth for running short of resources and warming so alarmingly fast.

By the end of the second week of my audit, I had broken all records for survival. The Retributor had exhausted any scope for finding serious climate crimes in my past, so he was pursuing me for minor neglect.

"Now explain why you did not do more," he said as the sun appeared on the eastern horizon for the fifteenth time.

All he could ask for now was branding, second class. I was holding out for pardoning.

"More relative to what?" I asked.

"More as in driving spikes into logs to be woodchipped, sabotaging oil rigs, smashing car windscreens, or spraying oil on auto race tracks?"

"I believed that such extreme actions alienated the public of the time from the message of climate change. Instead, I lived the sort of environmentally correct life that everyone could have managed. I turned off my television, DVD, microwave, stereo, and computer at the wall sockets when I was not using them, installed energy-efficient light globes, used solar cells and rechargeable batteries where I could, had two-minute showers, and washed my clothes in shower water. If everyone had lived like me, resource use would have dropped by sixty percent."

"That would not have saved the Earth."

"Not by itself, but it would have postponed the tipping year."

"You should have publicized what you were doing."

"I did! Whenever I spoke in conferences or to the media about climate change, I always talked about how I was moderating my personal behavior."

My trial was adjourned for the fifteenth time. The Retributor would check on everything I had said. He would send his research assistants to their solar-powered web portals to tweet, gryp, snatch, surf, scan, riffle, and drill for old power bills, conference proceedings, and even photographs taken in my apartment. I knew what they would find, so I was not worried.

Those who died while awaiting audit were declared guilty post mortem. There were many such deaths, mostly from exposure. We slept in the open, with blankets made from the discarded clothing of the dead. There was never a shortage of blankets. Aside from the big shows and races, we had to amuse ourselves without gadgets, so singing, storytelling, gossip, and dancing were very popular. By a couple of hours after sunset, the activities were reduced to sex, for those who could manage it. The Wardens made no attempt to stop any behavior that did not involve trying to escape.

"Way I see it, the woodlands near the coast been gettin' back to normal," said Chaz as we lay looking up at the stars on that fifteenth night.

"They were national parks before the tipping year," I replied blandly, ever wary of saying anything that might incriminate me.

"Full of game, as I hear."

"Probably due to the ban on hunting."

"You know, I saw this coming."

"So did I. I wrote a lot of articles about it."

"No, I mean I prepared. I buried some guns and three thousand rounds in the woods, all wrapped in grease and plastic. Old M16, a couple of Glock pistols, and a great hunting rifle. Figure we could live pretty well in the woods."

"That sort of talk would earn you death, first class for greed and squandering."

"So, you're not in?"

"I've heard nothing."

"But we'd be free."

"They would hunt us down in a day. Probably less."

"Hey, I'm a bushman. They'd never find us."

"There's no bush! We're in the desert, a thousand miles from the coast. Besides, the ranger Wardens have rifles, image enhancers, acoustic scopes, geopositioning, and satellite feed. Oh, and tracker dogs."

"Those greenie ferals don't cut it."

"Feral animals are great hunters, and they have a nasty bite. Victims still launch satellites and build weaponry gadgets, remember? They just do it with renewable tech."

"I'm serious, and I'm armed. I got a dozen twenty-two rounds, kept 'em up my arse during inspections. With all the metal scrap around here, it was a no-brainer to rig up a zip gun and silencer."

"I stay here."

"Listen, this isn't a sus proposition. I got a girl coming with me, that Warden with the brand."

"No."

"Why not?'

"Because I want to beat the Retributor."

"What planet are you on? Nobody's ever beaten him."

"Nobody's escaped from here, either. You fight your way, and I'll fight in mine."

He gave up on me around then. I knew he would be gone before dawn.

I awoke to the silky silence of Death's presence, and as I sat up, I saw the dark figure before me. I stood up uneasily, for I could never get used to the Wardens not being able to see me.

"I thought you would have been away, claiming Chaz," I said as we began to walk between the rows of sleeping bodies.

"I already have him."

That did not surprise me.

"Bushmen are so condescending about their enemies," I said. "They forget that victims also know bushcraft. Where did he try to get out?"

"A greenhouse desiccation field."

"Makes sense. Nobody alive, so no Wardens. Was he shot?"

"It was the woman he chose to escape with. She played along with him, then led him into a trap."

"Olivia?" I gasped, remembering how friendly she had seemed.

"Yes. She has been commended for preventing an escape without wasting a bullet. Do you really want to beat the Retributor?"

"Yes."

"Why?"

"It will save lives."

"Explain."

"In the last century, the Nazi Holocaust against the Jews was indiscriminate. The genocide of the Hutus against the Tutsis in Rwanda was indiscriminate too. Go back to the seventeen-nineties, and the French Terror guillotined aristocrats just for being what they were. The World Audit claims to be different. Everyone born before the tipping year is guilty, but everyone gets an audit. The problem is that the Retributors want tippers to get death, second class even for buying their kid a battery-powered Buzz Lightyear toy. That looks ridiculous, so the case is adjourned and the tippers become borderlines."

"There are millions of borderlines."

"Yes, all of them doing indefinite service. If there were a precedent, many could be pardoned, branded, or at least sentenced to a fixed period of service. I want to be that precedent. My audit has already set precedents for service and branding sentences. Some tippers of good will can be saved, and the Earth needs all the good will it can get."

"You are a hard act to follow, Jason Hall."

"Thank you."

When Death was with me, there were no sounds but our voices. The farts and bodily reeks of those around me vanished, fleas and lice no longer bit and itched, and my muscles did not ache with fatigue. There was only the desert night, cloudless, windless, and brilliant with stars. In a way, I enjoyed his visits, because I could step out of myself. Suddenly, I was thirty years in the past, servicing a remote observing station in the desert, enjoying the serenity of the night.

My companion's face was visible, even though there was nothing to illuminate it. One might have said that it was in daylight while everything else was smothered in night. Until now, it had been indistinct and unfocused, but suddenly it seemed to be resolving into clear lines. I noticed something very familiar about his features.

"You look like me," I remarked.

"Thank you."

It was true. Months ago, his face had just been an oval that floated above a greater blackness. He now defined himself to wear my robes and dust cloak. His manner of speech and tone of voice were even becoming echoes of mine. The transformation should have made him more familiar and agreeable, yet I found it disturbing.

"Do you always take the form of those you are about to claim?"

"No."

"Then why take my form?"

"You have two doctorates. Surely you can work it out."

To me it was not obvious, and I was not in a mood for games.

"The Retributor has no more charges, so tomorrow is the verdict," I said, steering the subject onto my own agenda. "Is that what you're here for?"

"No. You will get pardoned."

Pardoned. Even this word now carried a chill.

"You already know? Then why bother coming for me?"

"I am not here for you."

"Doctor Jason Hall, you are found pardoned of both squandering and display," declared the Auditor General.

For a moment, there was no sound at all, then came a huge, collective gasp for air. A mighty cheer rolled over the benches of the Auditors, across the greenhouse fields, and into the desert. Chaz had lost, but I had won.

I knew that the Retributor would not appeal. This was the sixteenth day of my audit, which was four times longer than any other since the World Audit itself had begun. To prolong it would attract a charge of squandering to him, and that was a very bad idea. I bowed to the Auditors on the bench, then waited to be dismissed.

"You are the standard that your age should have lived by," continued the Auditor General. "You lived as responsibly as an ordinary twentieth-century tipper could have. Had everyone else behaved as you did, minimizing their burden on the ecosphere and teaching others to do so, the world could have pulled back from the tipping year. Everyone born before the Millennium must be audited against your example. Members of the Audit, those of you in favor of appointing Doctor Jason Hall to the bench in the new position of Precedent, be upstanding."

The Auditor General got to her feet before my brain caught up with what was happening. To her right and left, the other members of the audit bench were standing up as well. At the extreme left, the Advocate stood, and to my surprise, at the other end of the bench, the Retributor was already on his feet by the time I turned.

I'll never escape! screamed in my mind.

"Doctor Hall, the bench has voted unanimously in favor of admitting you," the Auditor General concluded.

"But—but surely others are more worthy," I heard myself say. "Many environmental activists were far more extreme and militant."

"Not everyone needs to be a warrior; you have demonstrated that. You set a standard that all those born before the tipping year could have met, had they but bothered. In the audits to come in the days, months, and years ahead, you will provide the precedent to be met by everyone who stands before us, and even worldwide."

"But what about my work in climatology? Surely the Earth needs climatologists more than Auditors."

"The Earth needs both, to heal its wounds and punish the guilty. However, while there are now many climatologists, there are few good twentieth-century role models."

The Retributor was smiling. Now I was in his position. If I refused, I would be guilty of squandering a nonrenewable resource. Myself.

"I am honored to accept," I said, then bowed with my heart sinking.

"The precedents established in your audit have already been applied to all those in the national borderline database. Clerk of the Audit, have you run the program over the backlog of borderline audits as yet?"

"I have, your honor."

"Can you give us a summary of results?"

"Verdicts drawing sentences of death or mines have been returned in ninety-nine and three quarters of a percent of cases."

"Auditor Hall, it seems you are a hard act to follow," said the Auditor General, turning to me with a very sincere smile.

The rest of the day's audits were canceled. Ceremony and procedure were important in this new world, and there were few occasions more important than the appointment of a new Auditor. The entire encampment was assembled to watch. The hatred in the eyes of the two thousand borderline tippers glared hotter than the sun as I stood before them. Only five would get service, branding, or pardoning. Worldwide . . . my brain shut down when I tried to make an estimate. With a tipper on the bench, the audit became justice for the guilty, rather than mass slaughter.

I was dressed in the black robes of an Auditor by the Wardens, who also shaved my hair and beard. The Inspector of Wardens presented me with a pair of red leather gloves.

"From this day, the blood of the guilty will be on your hands," he said as he went down on one knee and raised the gloves on his upturned palms.

The Retributor now stood before me, bowed, and gave me a pair of sunshades.

"From this day, there will be no frailty, pity, or mercy in your eyes," he declared.

The Advocate had a staff, which she put into my hand.

"From this day, you will strike down the guilty but spare those tippers who are in truth victims."

Only one in four hundred passed through my mind.

Last of all was the Auditor General with my cowl.

"From this day you are an Auditor, shielded from the sun because you are without blame for its ravages."

That night, I was exhausted at many levels, yet dreading what would come with sleep. I was given a tent in the victims' enclosure, but I could not relax in it. I had slept in the open for too long, so now I went outside to try to sleep. The Wardens did not like the idea, but nobody argues with an Auditor.

Even lying on the sand beneath the new moon and first stars, I could not sleep. I got up and paced around my tent. At last I had the answer to the many puzzles that my dark visitor had been posing, yet he did not appear. A Warden came over and asked if I was all right. It was Olivia.

"Can't sleep," I replied curtly, now suspicious of her smiles and concern.

"I can call a counselor," she suggested.

"No. No, I . . . I'm just a bit edgy about being on the other side of the audit tomorrow."

"Why not rehearse?"

"Sorry?"

"Others do it. Walk down to the audit bench and sit there for a while. Practice speaking, like you're in a real audit."

"That's a good idea. Thank you."

"I'll make sure you're not disturbed. Just don't wander any farther out."

She escorted me out of the victims' enclosure and away to the audit space. She then left me and walked on to the outer perimeter to make sure that I went no farther. I was an Auditor and could go where I liked, but shadows in the wrong place got shot, no matter who they were. The bench was empty and unguarded. I sat down. Out in the glasshouse fields, someone was still alive and screaming. A figure in black came walking toward me from the victims' enclosure. As he got closer, I could see his face in the weak moonlight. As I expected, it was my face.

"So, do you understand yet?" I asked.

The figure nodded unhappily.

"Death was not coming for me; I was becoming Death," he said.

"True."

"Death will sit among the Auditors on the bench tomorrow. Jason Hall is Precedent, the standard by which they will audit. Jason Hall is Death."

"That is what you wanted—"

"No! I didn't realize that being Precedent means providing instant, brutal decisions. Instead of giving borderline tippers a proper hearing, the Auditors will just check if they measure up to Jason Hall. Thousands of borderlines who would have died of natural causes will now be re-audited and executed."

"Some will get service, branding, or pardoning."

"Handfuls out of thousands. Dozens out of millions. This is not what I wanted. I wanted to give hope to tippers."

"You have done that."

"You told me I was a hard act to follow. Now I understand. Hardly any tippers measure up against what I did. I can already see millions of frightened, desperate, pleading eyes staring at me."

The horned moon touched the western horizon, then sank out of sight. Jason became just a dark shape.

"I can't take it," he said. "I can't live with that."

"Can Death claim himself?" I asked.

"I can, and I will."

I now saw that he was merging with the shadows around him. His voice was becoming faint, and the white patch that was his face had lost focus.

"You fought so hard against the audit, but now you give up?" I said, suddenly afraid of losing him.

"This world is no place for tippers," said his fading voice. "Even those who are pardoned must kill themselves by abandoning their pasts, values, lifestyles, achievements, attitudes. . . ."

"Wait!" I called. "Without you, I will not be human."

There was no reply. He was already gone.

"Sir?"

It was Olivia's voice. I shook my head and looked up.

"Sir, you were asleep. We should get back to the victims' enclosure."

We began to walk through the darkness. Olivia's goggles were enhanced for night vision, so she guided me along the path.

"Did you rehearse well, sir?" she asked.

"Not really. I was thinking about tippers, and the danger that their story might soon be lost and forgotten."

"No bad thing, sir."

"Forgetting what the tippers did to the Earth means forgetting the lessons they left us, Warden. We need to remember what not to do, or it could all happen again."

She did not reply. The tippers had not left much to the world that was worthwhile, but they had to be remembered. The thought was not a palatable one, but the alternative was more terrifying than death.

ABOUT THE AUTHOR

SEAN MCMULLEN is an Australian author with twenty books and seven dozen stories published in over a dozen countries. He has won fifteen Australian and international awards for his fiction, and been nominated for the Hugo, BSFA, and Sidewise awards. He is best known for his neo-steampunk novel *Souls in the Great Machine* (1999), and his two most recent books are the collections *Colours of the Soul* (2013) and *Ghosts of Engines Past* (2013). For three decades Sean had a career in scientific computing in parallel with his science fiction and fantasy writing, but resigned to become a full time author in 2014. Before he began writing, Sean was a professional singer and actor, performing in venues as diverse as the Victorian State Opera and the folk-rock band Joe Wilson's Mates. He lives in Melbourne, and has one daughter, Catherine.

HOT SKY

ROBERT SILVERBERG

Out there in the chilly zone of the southern Pacific, somewhere between San Francisco and Hawaii, the sea was a weird goulash of currents, streams of cold stuff coming up from the Antarctic and coolish upwelling spirals out of the ocean floor and little hot rivers rolling off the sun-blasted continental shelf far to the east. Sometimes, you could see steam rising in places where cold water met warm. It was a cockeyed place to be trawling for icebergs. But the albedo readings said there was a berg somewhere around there, and so the *Tonopah Maru* was there too.

Carter sat in front of the scanner, massaging the numbers in the cramped cell that was the ship's command center. He was the trawler's captain, a lean thirtyish man, yellow hair, brown beard, skin deeply tanned and tinged with the iridescent greenish-purple of his armoring buildup, the protective layer that the infra/ultra drugs gave you. It was midmorning. The shot of Screen he'd taken at dawn still simmered like liquid gold in his arteries. He could almost feel it as it made its slow journey outward to his capillaries and went trickling cozily into his skin, where it would carry out the daily refurbishing of the body armor that shielded him against ozone crackle and the demon eye of the sun.

This was only his second year at sea. The company liked to move people around. In the past few years, he'd been a desert jockey in bleak, forlorn Spokane, running odds reports for farmers betting on the month the next rainstorm would turn up, and before that a cargo dispatcher for one of the company's L-5 shuttles, and a chip-runner before that. And one of these days, if he kept his nose clean, he'd be sitting in a corner office atop the Samurai pyramid in Kyoto. Carter hated a lot of the things he'd had to do in order to play the company game. But he knew that it was the only game there was.

"We got maybe a two thousand–kiloton mass there," he said, looking into the readout wand's ceramic-fiber cone. "Not bad, eh?"

"Not for these days, no," Hitchcock said. He was the oceanographer/navigator, a grizzled flat-nosed Afro-Hawaiian whose Screen-induced armor coloring gave his skin a startling midnight look. Hitchcock was old enough to remember when icebergs were never seen farther north than the latitude of southern Chile, and always glad to let you know about it. "Man, these days, a berg that's still that big all the way up here must have been three counties long when it broke off the fucking polar shelf. But you sure you got your numbers right, man?"

The implied challenge brought a glare to Carter's eyes, and something went curling angrily through his interior, leaving a hot little trail. Hitchcock never thought Carter had done anything right the first time. Though he often denied it—too loudly—it was pretty clear Hitchcock had never quite gotten over his resentment at being bypassed for captain in favor of an outsider. Probably he thought it was racism. But it wasn't. Carter was managerial track; Hitchcock wasn't. That was all there was to it.

Sourly, he said, "You want to check the screen yourself? Here. Here, take a look."

He offered Hitchcock the wand. But Hitchcock shook his head. "Easy, man. Whatever the screen says, that's okay for me." He grinned disarmingly, showing mahogany snags. On the screen, impenetrable whorls and jiggles were dancing, black on green, green on black, the occasional dazzling bloom of bright yellow. The *Tonopah Maru*'s interrogatory beam was traveling 22,500 miles straight up to Nippon Telecom's big marine scansat, which had its glassy unblinking gaze trained on the whole east-ern Pacific, looking for albedo differentials. The reflectivity of an iceberg is different from the reflectivity of the ocean surface. You pick up the differential, you confirm it with temperature readout, you scan for mass to see if the trip's worthwhile. If it is, you bring your trawler in fast and make the grab before someone else does.

This berg was due to go to San Francisco, which was in a bad way for water just now. The whole West Coast was. There hadn't been any rain along the Pacific seaboard in ten months. Most likely the sea around here was full of trawlers, Seattle, San Diego, LA. The Angelenos kept more ships out than anybody. The *Tonopah Maru* had been chartered to them by Samurai Industries until last month. But the trawler was working for San Francisco this time.

The lovely city by the bay, dusty now, sitting there under that hot soupy sky full of interesting-colored greenhouse gases, waiting for the rain that almost never came anymore.

Carter said, "Start getting the word around. That berg's down here, south-southwest. We get it in the grapple tomorrow, we can be in San Francisco with it by a week from Tuesday."

"If it don't melt first. This fucking heat."

"It didn't melt between Antarctica and here, it's not gonna melt between here and Frisco. Get a move on, man. We don't want LA coming in and hitting it first."

By midafternoon, they were picking it up optically, first an overhead view via the Weather Department spysat, then a sea-level image bounced to them by a Navy relay buoy. The berg was a thing like a castle afloat, stately and serene, all pink turrets and indigo battlements and blue-white pinnacles, rising high up above the water. The dry-dock kind of berg, it was, two high sides with a valley between, and it was maybe two hun-dred meters long, sitting far up above the water. Steaming curtains of fog shrouded its edges and the ship's ear was able to pick up the sizzling sound of the melt effervescence that was generated as small chunks of ice went slipping off its sides into the sea. The whole thing was made of glacial ice, which is compacted snow, and when it melted, it melted with a hiss. Carter stared at the berg in wonder. It was the biggest one he'd seen so far. For the last couple of million years, it had been perched on top of the South Pole, and it probably hadn't ever expected to go cruising off toward Hawaii like this. But the big climate shift had changed a lot of things for everybody, the Antarctic ice pack included.

"Jesus," Hitchcock said. "Can we do it?"

"Easy," said Nakata. He was the grapple technician, a sleek beady-eyed cat-like little guy. "It'll be a four-hook job, but so what? We got the hooks for it."

The *Tonopah Maru* had hooks to spare. Most of its long cigar-shaped hull was taken up by the immense rack-and-pinion gear that powered the grappling hooks, a vast, silent mechanism capable of hurling the giant hooks far overhead and whipping them down deep into the flanks of even the biggest bergs. The deck space was given over almost entirely to the great spigots that were used to spray the bergs with a sintering of melt-retardant mirror-dust. Down below was a powerful fusion-driven engine, strong enough to haul a fair-sized island halfway around the world.

Everything very elegant, except there was barely any room left over for the crew of five. Carter and the others were jammed into odd little corners here and there. For living quarters, they had cubicles not much bigger than the coffin-sized sleeping capsules you got at an airport hotel, and for recreation space, they all shared one little blister dome aft and a pacing area on the foredeck. A sardine-can kind of life, but the pay was good and at least you could breathe fresh air at sea, more or less, instead of the dense grayish-green murk that hovered over the habitable parts of the West Coast.

They were right at the mid-Pacific cold wall. The sea around them was blue, the sign of warm water. Just to the west, though, where the berg was, the water was a dark rich olive green with all the microscopic marine life that cold water fosters. The line of demarcation was plainly visible.

Carter was running triangulations to see if they'd be able to slip the berg under the Golden Gate Bridge when Rennett appeared at his elbow and said, "There's a ship, Cap'n."

"What you say?"

He wondered if he was going to have to fight for his berg. That happened at times. This was open territory, pretty much a lawless zone where old-fashioned piracy was making a terrific comeback.

Rennett was maintenance/operations, a husky, broad-shouldered little kid out of the Midwest dust bowl, no more than chest-high to him, very cocky, very tough. She kept her scalp shaved, the way a lot of them did nowadays, and she was brown as an acorn all over, with the purple glint of Screen shining brilliantly through, making her look almost fluorescent. Brown eyes bright as marbles and twice as hard looked back at him.

"Ship," she said, clipping it out of the side of her mouth as if doing him a favor. "Right on the other side of the berg. Caskie's just picked up a message. Some sort of SOS." She handed Carter a narrow strip of yellow radio tape with just a couple of lines of bright red thermoprint typing on it. The words came up at him like a hand reaching out of the deck. He read them out loud.

CAN YOU HELP US TROUBLE ON SHIP MATTER OF LIFE AND DEATH URGENT YOU COME ABOARD SOONEST KOVALCIK ACTING CAPTAIN CALAMARI MARU

"What the fuck?" Carter said. "*Calamari Maru*? Is it a ship or a squid?"

Rennett didn't crack a smile. "We ran a check on the registry. It's owned out of Vancouver by Kyocera-Merck. The listed captain is Amiel Kohlberg, a German. Nothing about any Kovalcik."

"Doesn't sound like a berg-trawler."

"It's a squid ship, Cap'n," she said, voice flat with a sharp edge of contempt on it. As if he didn't know what a squid ship was. He let it pass. It always struck him as funny, the way anybody who had two days more experience at sea than he did treated him like a greenhorn.

He glanced at the printout again. Urgent, it said. Matter of life and death. Shit. Shit shit shit.

The idea of dropping everything to deal with the problems of some strange ship didn't sit well with him. He wasn't paid to help other captains out, especially Kyocera-Merck captains. Samurai Industries wasn't fond of K-M these days. Something about the Gobi reclamation contract, industrial espionage, some crap like that. Besides, he had a berg to deal with. He didn't need any other distractions just now.

And then too, he felt an edgy little burst of suspicion drifting up from the basement of his soul, a tweak of wariness. Going aboard another ship out here, you were about as vulnerable as you could be. Ten years in corporate life had taught him caution.

But he also knew you could carry caution too far. It didn't feel good to him to turn his back on a ship that had said it was in trouble. Maybe the ancient laws of the sea, as well as every other vestige of what used to be common decency, were inoperative concepts here in this troubled, heat-plagued year of 2133, but he still wasn't completely beyond feeling things like guilt and shame. Besides, he thought, what goes around comes around. You ignore the other guy when he asks for help, you might just be setting yourself up for a little of the same later on.

They were all watching him, Rennett, Nakata, Hitchcock.

Hitchcock said, "What you gonna do, Cap'n? Gonna go across to 'em?" A gleam in his eye, a snaggly mischievous grin on his face.

What a pain in the ass, Carter thought.

Carter gave the older man a murderous look and said, "So, you think it's legit?"

Hitchcock shrugged blandly. "Not for me to say. You the cap'n, man. All I know is, they say they in trouble, they say they need our help."

Hitchcock's gaze was steady, remote, noncommittal. His blocky shoulders seemed to reach from wall to wall. "They calling for help, cap'n. Ship wants help, you give help, that's what I always believe, all my years at sea. Of course, maybe it different now."

Carter found himself wishing he'd never let Hitchcock come aboard. But screw it. He'd go over there and see what was what. He had no choice, never really had.

To Rennett he said, "Tell Caskie to let this Kovalcik know that we're heading for the berg to get claiming hooks into it. That'll take about an hour and a half. And after that, we have to get it mirrored and skirted. While that's going on, I'll come over and find out what his problem is."

"Got it," Rennett said, and went below.

New berg visuals had come in while they were talking. For the first time, now Carter could see the erosion grooves at the waterline on the berg's upwind side, the undercutting, the easily fractured overhangings that were starting to form. The undercutting didn't necessarily mean the berg was going to flip over—that rarely happened with big dry-dock bergs like this—but they'd be in for some lousy oscillations, a lot of rolling and heaving, choppy seas, a general pisser all around. The day was turning very ugly very fast.

"Jesus," Carter said, pushing the visuals across to Nakata. "Take a look at these."

"No problem. We got to put our hooks on the lee side; that's all."

"Yeah. Sounds good." He made it seem simple. Carter managed a grin.

The far side of the berg was a straight high wall, a supreme white cliff smooth as porcelain that was easily a hundred meters high, with a wicked tongue of ice jutting out into the sea in one place for about forty meters like a breakwater. That was what the *Calamari Maru* was using it for, too. The squid ship rode at anchor just inside that tongue.

Carter signaled to Nakata, who was standing way down fore, by his control console.

"Hooks away!" Carter called. "Sharp! Sharp!"

There came the groaning sound of the grapple-hatch opening, and the deep rumbling of the hook gimbals. Somewhere deep in the belly of the ship, immense mechanisms were swinging around, moving into position. The berg sat motionless in the calm sea.

Then the whole ship shivered as the first hook came shooting up into view. It hovered overhead, a tremendous taloned thing filling half the sky, black against the shining brightness of the air. Nakata hit the keys again and the hook, having reached the apex of its curve, spun downward with slashing force, heading for the breast of the berg.

It hit and dug and held. The berg recoiled, quivered, rocked. A shower of loose ice came tumbling off the upper ledges. As the impact of the hooking was transmitted to the vast hidden mass of the berg undersea, the whole thing bowed forward a little farther than Carter had been expecting, making a nasty sucking noise against the water, and when it pulled back again, a geyser came spuming up about twenty meters.

Down by the bow, Nakata was making his I-got-you gesture at the berg, the middle finger rising high.

A cold wind was blowing from the berg now. It was like the exhalation of some huge wounded beast, an aroma of ancient times, a fossil-breath wind.

They moved on a little farther along the berg's flank.

"Hook two," Carter told him.

The berg was almost stable again now. Carter, watching from his viewing tower by the aft rail, waited for the rush of pleasure and relief that came from a successful claiming, but this time it wasn't there. All he felt was impatience, an eagerness to get all four hooks in and start chugging on back to the Golden Gate.

The second hook flew aloft, hovered, plunged, struck, bit.

A second time the berg slammed the water, and a second time the sea jumped and shook. Carter had just a moment to catch a glimpse of the other ship popping around like a floating cork, and wondered if that ice tongue they found so cozy was going to break off and sink them. It would have been smarter of them to anchor somewhere else. But to hell with them. They'd been warned.

The third hook was easier.

"Four," Carter called. One last time, a grappling iron flew through the air, whipping off at a steep angle to catch the far side of the berg over the top, and then they had it, the whole monstrous floating island of ice snaffled and trussed.

Toward sunset, Carter left Hitchcock in charge of the trawler and went over to the *Calamari Maru* in the sleek little silvery kayak that they used as the ship's boat. He took Rennett with him.

The stink of the other ship reached his nostrils long before he went scrambling up the gleaming woven-monofilament ladder that they threw over the side for him: a bitter, acrid reek, a miasma so dense that it was almost visible. Breathing it was something like inhaling all of Cleveland at a single snort. Carter wished he'd worn a facelung. But who expected to need one out at sea, where you were supposed to be able to breathe reasonably decent air?

The *Calamari Maru* didn't look too good, either. At one quick glance, he picked up a sense of general neglect and slovenliness: black stains on the deck, swirls of dust everywhere, some nasty rust-colored patches of ozone attack that needed work. The reek, though, came from the squid themselves.

The heart of the ship was a vast tank, a huge squid-peeling factory occupying the whole mid-deck. Carter had been on one once before, long ago, when he was a trainee. Samurai Industries ran dozens of them. He looked down into the tank and saw battalions of hefty squid swimming in herds, big-eyed pearly phantoms, scores of them shifting direction suddenly and simultaneously in their squiddy way. Glittering mechanical flails moved among them, seizing and slicing, cutting out the nerve tissue, flushing the edible remainder toward the meat-packing facility. The stench was astonishing. The whole thing was a tremendous processing machine. With the one-time farming heartland of North America and temperate Europe now worthless desert, and the world dependent on the thin, rocky soil of northern Canada and Siberia for its crops, harvesting the sea was essential. But the smell was awful. He fought to keep from gagging.

"You get used to it," said the woman who greeted him when he clambered aboard. "Five minutes, you won't notice."

"Let's hope so," he said. "I'm Captain Carter, and this is Rennett, maintenance/ops. Where's Kovalcik?"

"I'm Kovalcik," the woman said.

His eyes widened. She seemed to be amused by his reaction.

Kovalcik was rugged and sturdy-looking, more than average height, strong cheekbones, eyes set very far apart, expression very cool and controlled, but strain evident behind the control. She was wearing a sack-like jumpsuit of some coarse gray fabric. About thirty, Carter guessed. Her hair was black and close-cropped and her skin was fair, strangely fair, hardly any trace of Screen showing. He saw signs of sun damage, signs of ozone crackle, red splotches of burn. Two members of her crew stood behind her, also women, also jumpsuited, also oddly fair-skinned. Their skins didn't look so good either.

Kovalcik said, "We are very grateful you came. There is bad trouble on this ship." Her voice was flat. She had just the trace of a European accent, hard to place.

"We'll help out if we can," Carter told her.

He became aware now that they had carved a chunk out of his berg and grappled it up onto the deck, where it was melting into three big aluminum runoff tanks. It couldn't have been a millionth of the total berg mass, not a ten millionth, but seeing it gave him a quick little stab of proprietary fury and he felt a muscle flicker in his cheek. That reaction didn't go unnoticed either. Kovalcik said quickly, "Yes, water is one of our problems. We have had to replenish our supply this way. There have been some equipment failures lately. You will come to the captain's cabin now? We must talk of what has happened, what must now be done."

She led him down the deck, with Rennett and the two crew women following along behind.

The *Calamari Maru* was pretty impressive. It was big and long and sleek, built somewhat along the lines of a squid itself, a jet-propulsion job that gobbled water into colossal compressors and squirted it out behind. That was one of the many low-fuel solutions to maritime transport problems that had been worked out for the sake of keeping CO_2 output down in these difficult times. Immense things like flying buttresses ran down the deck on both sides. These, Kovalcik explained, were squid lures, covered with bioluminescent photophores: you lowered them into the water and they gave off light that mimicked the glow of the squids' own bodies, and the slithery tentacular buggers came jetting in from vast distances, expecting a great jamboree and getting a net instead.

"Some butchering operation you got here," Carter said.

Kovalcik said, a little curtly, "Meat is not all we produce. The squid we catch here has value as food, of course, but also we strip the nerve fibers, we bring them back to the mainland; they are used in all kinds of biosensor applications. They are very large, those fibers, a hundred times as thick as ours. They are like single-cell computers. You have a thousand processors aboard your ship that use squid fiber, do you know? Follow me, please. This way."

They went down a ramp, along a narrow companionway. Carter heard thumpings and pingings in the walls. A bulkhead was dented and badly scratched. The lights down there were dimmer than they ought to be and the fixtures had an ominous hum. There was a new odor now, a tang of something chemical, sweet but not a pleasing kind of sweet, more a burnt kind of sweet than anything else, cutting sharply across the heavy squid stench the way a piccolo might cut across the boom of drums. Rennett shot him a somber glance. This ship was a mess, all right.

"Captain's cabin is here," Kovalcik said, pushing back a door hanging askew on its hinges. "We have drink first, yes?"

The size of the cabin amazed Carter after all those weeks bottled up in his little hole on the *Tonopah Maru*. It looked as big as a gymnasium. There was a table, a desk, shelving, a comfortable bunk, a sanitary unit, even an entertainment screen, everything nicely spread out with actual floor space you could move around in. The screen had been kicked in. Kovalcik took a flask of Peruvian brandy from a cabinet and Carter nodded, and she poured three stiff ones. They drank in silence. The squid odor wasn't so bad in here, or else he was getting used to it, just as she'd said. But the air was rank and close despite the spaciousness of the cabin, thick soupy stuff that was a struggle to breathe. *Something's wrong with the ventilating system too,* Carter thought.

"You see the trouble we have," said Kovalcik.

"I see there's been trouble, yes."

"You don't see half. You should see command room, too. Here, have more brandy, then I take you there."

"Never mind the brandy," Carter said. "How about telling me what the hell's been going on aboard this ship?"

"First come see command room," Kovalcik said.

The command room was one level down from the captain's cabin. It was an absolute wreck.

The place was all but burned out. There were laser scars on every surface and gaping wounds in the structural fabric of the ceiling. Glittering strings of program cores were hanging out of data cabinets like broken necklaces, like spilled guts. Everywhere, there were signs of some terrible struggle, some monstrous insane civil war that had raged through the most delicate regions of the ship's mind-centers.

"It is all ruined," Kovalcik said. "Nothing works any more except the squid-processing programs, and as you see those work magnificently, going on and on, the nets and flails and cutters and so forth. But every-thing else is damaged. Our water synthesizer, the ventilators, our navi-gational equipment, much more. We are making repairs but it is very slow."

"I can imagine it would be. You had yourselves one hell of a party here, huh?"

"There was a great struggle. From deck to deck, from cabin to cabin. It became necessary to place Captain Kohlberg under restraint, and he and some of the other officers resisted."

Carter blinked and caught his breath up short at that. "What the fuck are you saying? That you had a mutiny aboard this ship?"

For a moment, the charged word hung between them like a whirling sword.

Then Kovalcik said, voice flat as ever, "When we had been at sea for a while, the captain became like a crazy man. It was the heat that got to him, the sun, maybe the air. He began to ask impossible things. He would not listen to reason. And so he had to be removed from command for the safety of all. There was a meeting and he was put under restraint. Some of his officers objected and they had to be put under restraint too."

Son of a bitch, Carter thought, feeling a little sick. *What have I walked into here?*

"Sounds just like mutiny to me," Rennett said.

Carter shushed her. This had to be handled delicately. To Kovalcik he said, "They're still alive, the captain, the officers?"

"Yes. I can show them to you."

"That would be a good idea. But first, maybe you ought to tell me some more about these grievances you had."

"That doesn't matter now, does it?"

"To me it does. I need to know what you think justifies removing a captain."

She began to look a little annoyed. "There were many things, some big, some small. Work schedules, crew pairings, the food allotment. Everything worse and worse for us each week. Like a tyrant, he was. A Caesar. Not at first, but gradually, the change in him. It was sun poisoning he had, the craziness that comes from too much heat on the brain. He was afraid to use very much Screen, you see, afraid that we would run out before the end of the voyage, so he rationed it very tightly, for himself, for us too. That was one of our biggest troubles, the Screen." Kovalcik touched her cheeks, her forearms, her wrists, where the skin was pink and raw. "You see how I look? We are all like that. Kohlberg cut us to half ration, then half that. The sun began to eat us. The ozone. We had no protection, do you see? He was so frightened there would be no Screen later on that he let us use only a small amount every day, and we suffered, and so did he, and he got crazier as the sun worked on him, and there was less Screen all the time. He had it hidden, I think. We have not found it yet. We are still on quarter ration."

Carter tried to imagine what that was like, sailing around under the ferocious sky without body armor. The daily injections withheld, the unshielded skin of these people exposed to the full fury of the greenhouse climate. Could Kohlberg really have been so stupid or so looney? But there was no getting around the raw pink patches on Kovalcik's skin.

"You'd like us to let you have a supply of Screen, is that it?" he asked uneasily.

"No. We would not expect that of you. Sooner or later, we will find it where Kohlberg has hidden it."

"Then what is it you do want?"

"Come," Kovalcik said. "Now I show you the officers."

The mutineers had stashed their prisoners in the ship's infirmary, a stark, humid room far belowdeck with three double rows of bunks along the wall and some non-functioning medical mechs between them. Each of the bunks but one held a sweat-shiny man with a week's growth of beard. They were conscious but not very. Their wrists were tied.

"It is very disagreeable for us, keeping them like this," Kovalcik said. "But what can we do? This is Captain Kohlberg." He was heavyset, Teutonic-looking, groggy-eyed. "He is calm now, but only because we sedate him. We sedate all of them, fifty cc of omnipax. But it is a threat to their health, the constant sedation. And in any case, the drugs, we are running short. Another few days and then we will have none, and it will be harder to keep them restrained, and if they break free, there will be war on this ship again."

"I'm not sure if we have any omnipax on board," Carter said. "Certainly not enough to do you much good for long."

"That is not what we are asking either," said Kovalcik.

"What are you asking, then?"

"These five men, they threaten everybody's safety. They have forfeited the right to command. This I could show, with playbacks of the time of struggle on this ship. Take them."

"What?"

"Take them onto your ship. They must not stay here. These are crazy men. We must rid ourselves of them. We must be left to repair our ship in peace and do the work we are paid to do. It is a humanitarian thing, taking them. You are going back to San Francisco with the iceberg? Take them, these troublemakers. They will be no danger to you. They will be grateful for being rescued. But here they are like bombs that must sooner or later go off."

Carter looked at her as if she were a bomb that had already gone off. Rennett had simply turned away, covering what sounded like a burst of hysterical laughter by forcing a coughing fit.

That was all he needed, making himself an accomplice in this thing, obligingly picking up a bunch of officers pushed off their ship by mutineers. Kyocera-Merck men, at that. Aid and succor to the great corporate enemy? The Samurai Industries agent in Frisco would really love it when he came steaming into port with five K-M men on board. He'd especially want to hear that Carter had done it for humanitarian reasons.

Besides, where the fuck were these men going to sleep? On deck between the spigots? Should he pitch a tent on the iceberg, maybe? What about feeding them, for Christ's sake? What about Screen? Everything was calibrated down to the last molecule.

"I don't think you understand our situation," Carter said carefully. "Aside from the legalities of the thing, we've got no space for extra personnel. We barely have enough for us."

"It would be just for a short while, no? A week or two?"

"I tell you we've got every millimeter allotted. If God Himself wanted to come on board as a passenger, we'd have a tough time figuring out where to put Him. You want technical help patching your ship back together, we can try to do that. We can even let you have some supplies. But taking five men aboard—"

Kovalcik's eyes began to look a little wild. She was breathing very hard now. "You must do this for us! You must! Otherwise—"

"Otherwise?" Carter prompted.

All he got from her was a bleak stare, no friendlier than the green-streaked ozone-crisp sky.

"*Hilfe,*" Kohlberg muttered just then, stirring unexpectedly in his bunk.

"What was that?"

"It is delirium," said Kovalcik.

"*Hilfe. Hilfe. In Gottes Namen, hilfe!*" And then, in thickly accented English, the words painfully framed: "Help. She will kill us all."

"Delirium?" Carter said.

Kovalcik's eyes grew even chillier. Drawing an ultrasonic syringe from a cabinet in the wall, she slapped it against Kohlberg's arm. There was a small buzzing sound. Kohlberg subsided into sleep. Snuffling snores rose from his bunk. Kovalcik smiled. She seemed to be recovering her self-control. "He is a madman. You see what my skin is like. What his madness has done to me, has done to every one of us. If he got loose, if he put the voyage in jeopardy—yes, yes, we would kill him. We would kill them all. It would be only self-defense; you understand me? But it must not come to that." Her voice was icy. You could air-condition an entire city with that voice. "You were not here during the trouble. You do not know what we went through. We will not go through it again. Take these men from us, Captain."

She stepped back, folding her arms across her chest. The room was very quiet, suddenly, except for the pingings and thumpings from the ship's interior and an occasional snore out of Kohlberg. Kovalcik was completely calm again, the ferocity and iciness no longer visible. As though she were simply telling him: *This is the situation; the ball is now in your court, Captain Carter.*

What a stinking squalid mess, Carter thought.

But he was startled to find, when he looked behind the irritation he felt at having been dragged into this, a curious sadness where he would have expected anger to be. Despite everything, he found himself flooded with surprising compassion for Kovalcik, for Kohlberg, for all of them, for the whole fucking poisoned heat-blighted world. Who had asked for any of this, the heavy green sky, the fiery air, the daily need for Screen, the million frantic improvisations that made continued life on Earth possible? *Not us. Our great-great-grandparents had, maybe, but not us. Only they're not here to know what it's like, and we are.*

Then the moment passed. What the hell could he do? Did Kovalcik think he was Jesus Christ? He had no room for these people. He had no extra Screen or food. In any case, this was none of his business. And San Francisco was waiting for its iceberg. It was time to move along. *Tell her anything; just get out of here.*

"All right," he said. "I see your problem. I'm not entirely sure I can help out, but I'll do what I can. I'll check our supplies and let you know what we're able to do. Okay?"

Hitchcock said, "What I think, Cap'n, we ought to just take hold of them. Nakata can put a couple of his spare hooks into them, and we'll tow them into Frisco along with the berg."

"Hold on," Carter said. "Are you out of your mind? I'm no fucking pirate."

"Who's talking about piracy? It's our obligation. We got to turn them in, man, is how I see it. They're mutineers."

"I'm not a policeman, either," Carter retorted. "They want to have a mutiny, let them goddamn go and mutiny. I have a job to do. I just want to get that berg moving east. Without hauling a shipload of crazies along. Don't even think I'm going to make some kind of civil arrest of them. Don't even consider it for an instant, Hitchcock."

Mildly, Hitchcock said, "You know, we used to take this sort of thing seriously, once upon a time. You know what I mean, man? We wouldn't just look the other way."

"You don't understand," Carter said. Hitchcock gave him a sharp scornful look. "No. Listen to me, and listen good," Carter snapped. "That ship's nothing but trouble. The woman that runs it, she's something you don't want to be very close to. We'd have to put her in chains if we tried to take her in, and taking her in's not as easy as you seem to think, either. There's five of us and I don't know how many of them. And that's a Kyocera-Merck ship there. Samurai isn't paying us to pull K-M's chestnuts out of the fire."

It was late morning now. The sun was getting close to noon height, and the sky was brighter than ever, fiercely hot, with some swirls of lavender and green far overhead, vagrant wisps of greenhouse garbage that must have drifted west from the noxious high-pressure air mass that sat perpetually over the midsection of the United States. Carter imagined he could detect a whiff of methane in the breeze. Just across the way was the berg, shining like polished marble, shedding water hour by hour as the mounting heat worked it over. Back in San Francisco, they were brushing the dust out of the empty reservoirs. Time to be moving along, yes. Kovalcik and Kohlberg would have to work out their problems without him. He didn't feel good about that, but there were a lot of things he didn't feel good about, and he wasn't able to fix those, either.

"You said she's going to kill those five guys," Caskie said. The communications operator was small and slight, glossy black hair and lots of it, no bare scalp for her. "Does she mean it?"

Carter shrugged. "A bluff, most likely. She looks tough, but I'm not sure she's that tough."

"I don't agree," Rennett said. "She wants to get rid of those men in the worst way."

"You think?"

"I think that what they were doing anchored by the berg was getting ready to maroon them on it. Only, we came along, and we're going to tow the berg away, and that screwed up the plan. So, now she wants to give them to us instead. We don't take them, she'll just dump them over the side soon as we're gone."

"Even though we know the score?"

"She'll say they broke loose and jumped into the ship's boat and escaped, and she doesn't know where the hell they went. Who's to say otherwise?"

Carter stared gloomily. *Yes,* he thought, *who's to say otherwise.*

"The berg's melting while we screw around," Hitchcock said. "What'll it be, Cap'n? We sit here and discuss some more? Or we pull up and head for Frisco?"

"My vote's for taking them on board," said Nakata.

"I don't remember calling for a vote," Carter said. "We've got no room for five more hands. Not for anybody. We're packed as tight as we can possibly get. Living on this ship is like living in a rowboat as it is." He was feeling rage beginning to rise in him. This business was getting too tangled: legal issues, humanitarian issues, a lot of messy stuff. The simple reality underneath it all was that he couldn't take on passengers, no matter what the reason.

And Hitchcock was right. The berg was losing water every minute. Even from here, bare eyes alone, he could see erosion going on, the dripping, the calving. The oscillations were picking up, the big icy thing rocking gently back and forth as its stability at waterline got nibbled away.

Later on, the oscillations wouldn't be so gentle. They had to get that berg sprayed with mirror-dust and wrapped with a plastic skirt at the waterline to slow down wave erosion, and start moving. San Francisco was paying him to bring home an iceberg, not a handful of slush.

"Cap'n," Rennett called. She had wandered up into the observation rack above them and was shading her eyes, looking across the water. "They've put out a boat, cap'n."

"No," he said. "Son of a bitch!"

He grabbed for his 6x30 spyglass. A boat, sure enough, a hydrofoil dinghy. It looked full up: three, four, five. He hit the switch for biosensor boost and the squid fiber in the spyglass went to work for him. The image blossomed, high resolution. Five men. He recognized Kohlberg sitting slumped in front.

"Shit," he said. "She's sending them over to us. Just dumping them on us."

"If we doubled up somehow—" Nakata began, smiling hopefully.

"One more word out of you and I'll double you up," said Carter. He turned to Hitchcock, who had one hand clamped meditatively over the lower half of his face, pushing his nose back and forth and scratching around in his thick white stubble. "Break out some lasers," Carter said. "Defensive use only. Just in case. Hitchcock, you and Rennett get out there in the kayak and escort those men back to the squid ship. If they aren't conscious, tow them over to it. If they are, and they don't want to go back, invite them very firmly to go back, and if they don't like the invitation, put a couple of holes through the side of their boat and get the hell back here fast. You understand me?"

Hitchcock nodded stonily. "Sure, man. Sure."

Carter watched the whole thing from the blister dome at the stern, wondering whether he was going to have a mutiny of his own on his hands now, too. But no. No. Hitchcock and Rennett kayaked out along the edge of the berg until they came up beside the dinghy from the *Calamari Maru*, and there was a brief discussion, very brief, Hitchcock doing the talking and Rennett holding a laser rifle in a casual but businesslike way. The five castoffs from the squid ship seemed more or less awake. They pointed and gestured and threw up their arms in despair. But Hitchcock kept talking and Rennett kept stroking the laser, casual but businesslike, and the men in the dinghy looked more and more dejected by the moment. Then the discussion broke up and the kayak headed back toward the *Tonopah Maru*, and the men in the dinghy sat where they were, no doubt trying to figure out their next move.

Hitchcock said, coming on board, "This is bad business, man. That captain, he say the woman just took the ship away from him, on account of she wanted him to let them all have extra shots of Screen and he didn't give it. There wasn't enough to let her have so much, is what he said. I feel real bad, man."

"So do I," said Carter. "Believe me."

"I learn a long time ago," Hitchcock said, "when a man say *Believe me*, that's the one thing I shouldn't do."

"Fuck you," Carter said. "You think I wanted to strand them? But we have no choice. Let them go back to their own ship. She won't kill them. All they have to do is let her do what she wants to do and they'll come out of it okay. She can put them off on some island somewhere, Hawaii, maybe. But if they come with us, we'll be in deep shit all the way back to Frisco."

Hitchcock nodded. "Yeah. We may be in deep shit already."

"What you say?"

"Look at the berg," Hitchcock said. "At waterline. It's getting real carved up."

Carter scooped up his glass and kicked in the biosensor boost. He scanned the berg. It didn't look good. The heat was working it over very diligently.

This was the hottest day since they'd entered these waters. The sun seemed to be getting bigger every minute. There was a nasty magnetic crackling coming out of the sky, as if the atmosphere itself was getting ionized as it baked. And the berg was starting to wobble. Carter saw the oscillations plainly, those horizontal grooves filling with water, the sea not so calm now as sky/ocean heat differentials began to build up and conflicting currents came slicing in.

"Son of a bitch," Carter said. "That settles it. We got to get moving right now."

There was still plenty to do. Carter gave the word and the mirror-dust spigots went into operation, cannoning shining clouds of powdered metal over the exposed surface of the berg, and probably all over the squid ship and the dinghy, too. It took half an hour to do the job. The squid ship was still sitting at anchor by the ice tongue, and it looked like some kind of negotiation was going on between the men in the dinghy and the people on board. The sea was still roughening, the berg was lolloping around in a mean way. But Carter knew there was a gigantic base down there out of sight, enough to hold it steady until they could get under way, he hoped.

"Let's get the skirt on it now," he said.

A tricky procedure, nozzles at the ship's waterline extruding a thermoplastic spray that would coat the berg just where it was most vulnerable to wave erosion. The hard part came in managing the extensions of the cables linking the hooks to the ship, so they could maneuver around the berg. But Nakata was an ace at that. They pulled up anchor and started around the far side. The mirror-dusted berg was dazzling, a tremendous mountain of white light.

"I don't like that wobble," Hitchcock kept saying.

"Won't matter a damn once we're under way," said Carter.

The heat was like a hammer now, pounding the dark cool surface of the water, mixing up the thermal layers, stirring up the currents, getting everything churned around. They had waited just a little too long to get started. The berg, badly undercut, was doing a big sway to windward, bowing like one of those round-bottomed Japanese dolls, then swaying back again. God only knew what kind of sea action the squid ship was getting, but Carter couldn't see them from this side of the berg. He kept on moving, circling the berg to the full extension of the hook cables, then circling back the way he'd come.

When they got around to leeward again, he saw what kind of sea action the squid ship had been getting. It was swamped. The ice tongue they'd been anchored next to had come rising up out of the sea and kicked them like a giant foot.

"Jesus Christ," Hitchcock murmured, standing beside him. "Will you look at that. The damn fools just sat there all the time."

The *Calamari Maru* was shipping water like crazy and starting to go down. The sea was boiling with an armada of newly liberated squid, swiftly propelling themselves in all directions, heading anywhere else at top speed. Three dinghies were bobbing around in the water in the shadow of the berg.

"Will you look at that," Hitchcock said again.

"Start the engines," Carter told him. "Let's get the fuck out of here."

Hitchcock stared at him, disbelievingly.

"You mean that, Cap'n? You really mean that?"

"I goddamn well do."

"Shit," said Hitchcock. "This fucking lousy world."

"Go on. Get 'em started."

"You actually going to leave three boats from a sinking ship sitting out there in the water full of people?"

"Yeah. You got it. Now start the engines, will you?"

"That's too much," Hitchcock said softly, shaking his head in a big slow swing. "Too goddamn much."

He made a sound like a wounded buffalo and took two or three shambling steps toward Carter, his arms dangling loosely, his hands half cupped. Hitchcock's eyes were slitted and his face looked oddly puffy. He loomed above Carter, wheezing and muttering, a dark massive slab of a man. Half as big as the iceberg out there was how he looked just then.

Oh, shit, Carter thought. *Here it comes. My very own mutiny, right now.*

Hitchcock rumbled and muttered and closed his hands into fists. Exasperation tinged with fear swept through Carter and he brought his arm up without even stopping to think, hitting Hitchcock hard, a short, fast jab in the mouth that rocked the older man's head back sharply and sent him reeling against the rail. Hitchcock slammed into it and bounced. For a moment, it looked as if he'd fall, but he managed to steady himself. A kind of sobbing sound but not quite a sob, more of a grunt, came from him. A bright dribble of blood sprouted on his white-stubbled chin.

For a moment, Hitchcock seemed dazed. Then his eyes came back into focus and he looked at Carter in amazement.

"I wasn't going to hit you, Cap'n," he said, blinking hard. There was a soft stunned quality to his voice. "Nobody ever hits a Cap'n, not ever. Not ever. You know that, Cap'n."

"I told you to start the engines."

"You hit me, Cap'n. What the hell you hit me for?"

"You started to come at me, didn't you?" Carter said.

Hitchcock's shining bloodshot eyes were immense in his Screen-blackened face. "You think I was coming at you? Oh, Cap'n! Oh, Jesus, Cap'n. Jesus!" He shook his head and wiped at the blood. Carter saw that he was bleeding too, at the knuckle, where he'd hit a tooth. Hitchcock continued to stare at him, the way you might stare at a dinosaur that had just stepped out of the forest. Then his look of astonishment softened into something else, sadness, maybe. Or was it pity? *Pity would be even worse,* Carter thought. *A whole lot worse.*

"Cap'n—" Hitchcock began, his voice hoarse and thick.

"Don't say it. Just go and get the engines started."

"Yeah," he said. "Yeah, man."

He went slouching off, rubbing at his lip.

"Caskie's picking up an autobuoy SOS," Rennett called from somewhere updeck.

"Nix," Carter yelled back furiously. "We can't do it."

"What?"

"There's no fucking room for them," Carter said. His voice was as sharp as an icicle. "Nix. Nix."

He lifted his spyglass again and took another look toward the oncoming dinghies. Chugging along hard, they were, but having heavy weather of it in the turbulent water. He looked quickly away before he could make out faces. The berg, shining like fire, was still oscillating. He thought of the hot winds sweeping across the continent to the east, sweeping all around the belly of the world, the dry, rainless winds that forever sucked up what little moisture could still be found. It was almost a shame to have to go back there. Like returning to hell after a little holiday at sea, is how it felt. It was worst in the middle latitudes, the temperate zone, once so fertile. Rain almost never fell at all there now. The dying forests, the new grasslands taking over, deserts where even the grass couldn't make it, the polar icepacks crumbling, the lowlands drowning everywhere, dead buildings sticking up out of the sea, vines sprouting on freeways, the alligators moving northward. *This fucking lousy world,* Hitchcock had said. Yeah. This berg here, this oversized ice-cube, how many days' water supply would that be for San Francisco? Ten? Fifteen?

He turned. They were staring at him, Nakata, Rennett, Caskie, everybody but Hitchcock, who was on the bridge setting up the engine combinations.

"This never happened," Carter told them. "None of this. We never saw anybody else out here. Not anybody. You got that? This never happened."

They nodded, one by one.

There was a quick shiver down below as the tiny sun in the engine room, the little fusion sphere, came to full power. With a groan, the engine kicked in at high. The ship started to move away, out of the zone of dark water, toward the bluer sea just ahead. Off they went, pulling eastward as fast as they could, trying to make time ahead of the melt rate. It was afternoon now. Behind them, the other sun, the real one, lit up the sky with screaming fury as it headed off into the west. That was good, to have the sun going one way as you were going the other.

Carter didn't look back. What for? So you can beat yourself up about something you couldn't help?

His knuckle was stinging where he had split it punching Hitchcock. He rubbed it in a distant, detached way, as if it were someone else's hand. *Think east*, he told himself. *You're towing two thousand kilotons of million-year-old frozen water to thirsty San Francisco. Think good thoughts. Think about your bonus. Think about your next promotion. No sense looking back. You look back, all you do is hurt your eyes.*

ABOUT THE AUTHOR

ROBERT SILVERBERG—four-time Hugo Award winner, five-time winner of the Nebula Award, Science Fiction and Fantasy Writers of America Grand Master, Science Fiction and Fantasy Hall of Fame honoree—is the author of nearly five hundred short stories, nearly one hundred-and-fifty novels, and is the editor of in the neighborhood of one hundred anthologies. Among his most famous works are *Lord Valentine's Castle, Dying Inside, Nightwings,* and *The World Inside.* Learn more at majipoor.com.

THAT CREEPING SENSATION

ALAN DEAN FOSTER

"Code four, code four!"

Sergeant Lissa-Marie nodded to her partner and Corporal Gustafson acknowledged the alarm. It was the fourth code four of what had long since turned into a long hot one—both temperature-wise and professionally. She checked a floating readout: It declared that the temperature outside the sealed, climate-controlled truck cab was ninety-six degrees Fahrenheit at two in the afternoon. Happily, the humidity was unusually low, floating right around the eighty-percent mark.

"Gun it," she snapped. From behind the wheel, Gustafson nodded and floored the accelerator. Supplying instant torque, the electric motors mounted above each of the panel truck's four wheels sent it leaping forward. As the sharp acceleration shoved her back into her seat, she directed her attention to the omnidirectional pickup mounted in the roof. "What is it this time?" she asked.

"Bees." The human dispatcher's reply was as terse as it was meaningful. "Nobody dead, but two teens on their way to Metro Emergency."

"They're getting smarter." Gustafson chewed his lower lip as he concentrated on his driving.

"Manure," she shot back. "You're anthropomorphizing. That's dangerous in a business like ours."

Her younger subordinate shook his head as much as his contoured seat would allow. "It's true." He refused to drop the contention. "They're getting smarter. You can sense it. You can see it. They don't just crawl around and wait to be smoked anymore. They react earlier. They're . . ." He glanced over at her. "They're anticipating."

She shrugged and returned her gaze forward, out the armored windshield. "Just drive. If you insist, we can continue with your insane speculations after we've finished the job."

The streets of Atlanta's outer ring were nearly deserted. Few people chose to spend money on an expensive personal vehicle anymore. Not when public transportation was so much cheaper and a steady stream of workers kept the rails and tunnels free of the insects that obscured windshields and clogged wheel wells after barely twenty minutes of driving. The lack of traffic certainly made things easier for the exterminator branch of the military to which the two people in the truck belonged. Lissa was musing on the vilm she had been reading when a sudden swerve by Gustafson caused her to lurch and curse. Her partner was apologetic.

"Sorry. Roaches," he explained.

She nodded her understanding and relaxed anew. One three-foot roach wouldn't damage the specially armored truck, but if they'd hit it full on, they would have had to explain their carelessness to the cleanup crew back at base.

As they neared their destination, she lifted her reducer off its hook and made sure it fit snugly over her nose and mouth. Like everyone else, she hated having to wear the damn things. No matter how much they improved and miniaturized the integrated cooling system, you still sweated twice as much behind the device. But it was necessary. It wouldn't do to consistently suck air that was nearly forty percent oxygen and still rising. That might have been tolerable if the runaway atmosphere hadn't also grown hotter and distinctly more humid.

At least she'd never been in a fire, she told herself. Like most people, she shuddered at the thought. Given the current concentration of oxygen in the atmosphere, the smallest fire tended to erupt into an inferno in no time. *Leave those worries to the fire brigades,* she told herself. The multinational she worked for had enough to do trying to keep ahead of the bugs.

As studies of the Carboniferous Era, the climate in Earth's history nearest to that of the present day, had shown, the higher the oxygen content of the air, the bigger bugs could grow. Mankind's loathing of the arthropods with whom he was compelled to share the planet had grown proportionately.

"We're here." Gustafson brought the truck to a halt outside the single-family home.

They didn't have to look for the bees. They were all over the one-story residence they intended to appropriate. A cluster of civilian emergency vehicles was drawn up nearby. Occasionally, a crack would sound from one of the tightly sealed police cruisers and a six-inch bee would go down, obliterated by a blast of micro bugshot. Operating in such piecemeal fashion, the cops could deal with the bees, but only by expending a lot of expensive ammunition and at the cost of causing serious collateral damage to the immediate neighborhood. Buttoned up in their cruisers and guarding the perimeter they had established around the home, they had hunkered down to await the arrival of military specialists.

That would be me and Gustafson, she knew.

Already half dressed for the extirpation, she wiggled around in the truck cab as she donned the rest of her suit. An ancient apiarist would have looked on in amazement as she zipped up the one-piece reinforced Kevlar suit, armorglass helmet, and metalized boots. Once dressed, individual cooling systems were double-checked. Ten minutes trapped inside one of the sealed suits in the current heat and humidity would bring even a fit person down. The coolers were absolutely necessary, as were the tanks of poison spray the two exterminators affixed to their back plates. When both had concluded preparations, they took care to check the seals of each other's suits. A few stings from the six-inch-long bees contained more than enough venom to kill.

"Let's go," she murmured. Gustafson shot her a look, nodded, and cracked the driver's-side door.

The bees pounced on them immediately. Exhibiting a determination and aggression unknown to their smaller ancestors, several dozen of them assailed the two bipedal figures that had started toward the house. The swarm covered that edifice entirely. From decorative chimney to broken windows, it was blanketed by a heaving, throbbing, humming scrum of giant bees. Lissa grunted as one bee after another dove to fruitlessly slam its stinger into her impenetrable suit. Walking toward the house through such a persistent swarm was like stumbling around the ring with a boxer allowed to hit you from any and every angle.

As they reached the front of the overrun house, a nervous voice sounded on an open police channel on Lissa's helmet communicator.

"We think the queen's around back, near the swimming pool."

"Thanks." She didn't have to relay the information to Gustafson. The corporal had picked up the same transmission.

Working their way around to the back, they found the swarm there even thicker than what they had encountered out front. Surrounded by increasingly agitated workers, the queen had settled herself into a corner of the house where workers were already preparing hexagonal wax tubes to receive the first eggs. She never got the chance to lay them.

"You know the routine," she muttered into her helmet pickup.

"Start with the queen; work back to front."

Holding his sprayer, her partner nodded even as he opened fire.

The killing mist that would render the house uninhabitable began to send bees tumbling off the walls, roof, and one another. Most staggered drunkenly for a few seconds before collapsing in small black-and-orange heaps. Lissa kicked accumulating piles of plump, boldly striped bodies aside as she and Gustafson finished up in the back yard and started working their way around to the front.

"'Ware ten o'clock!" she yelled as she raised the muzzle of her sprayer.

The trio of foot-long yellow jackets, however, were only interested in taking a few of the now panicky live bees. Natural predators of such hives, they were the human's allies in extirpation. Though even more formidable than the giant honeybees, they had no interest in the two suited humans. Which was a good thing, Lissa knew. A yellow jacket's stinger could punch into an unprotected human like a stiletto.

As she and the corporal worked their way through the swarm, she reflected on the unexpected turn of history. When the greenhouse effect had begun to set in, scientists had worried about the presumed surplus of carbon dioxide that was expected to result. They had failed to account for Earth's astonishing ability to adapt to even fast-changing circumstances.

With the increased heat and humidity, plant life had gone berserk. Rainforests like those of the Amazon and Congo that had once been under threat expanded outward. Loggers intent on cutting down the big, old trees paid no attention to the fecund explosion of ferns, cycads, and soft-bodied plants that flourished in their wake. A serious problem in temperate times, vines and creepers like the ubiquitous kudzu experienced rates of growth approaching the exponential.

The great sucking sound which resulted was that of new vegetation taking carbon dioxide out of the atmosphere and dumping oxygen in its wake. Their size restricted for eons by the inability of their primitive respiratory systems to extract enough oxygen from the atmosphere, arthropods responded to the new oxy-rich air by growing to sizes not seen since similar conditions existed more than 300 million years ago. Short-lived species were the first to adapt, with each new generation growing a little larger than its predecessor as it feasted on the increasingly oxygen-rich atmosphere.

There had been no bees in the Carboniferous, she knew, because there had been no flowers. But modern plants had adapted to the radical climate change as eagerly as their more primitive ancestors. The result was fewer and increasingly less workable beehives as bigger bees crowded out smaller competitors.

Changes occurred with such startling rapidity that in little over a hundred years, insects, spiders, and their relatives had not only matched but in some cases surpassed the dimensions attained by their ancient relatives. This made for an increasingly uncomfortable coexistence with the supposedly still-dominant species on the planet, but a very good living for Lissa and her hastily constituted branch of the military. Nearing fifty, she could remember when her company, one of many that had appeared in the wake of the Runaway, had been able to offer its enlisted personnel predictable hours and regular furloughs. Such downtime still existed, of course, but she was making so much combat pay that she felt unable to turn down the assignments that came her way.

Sure enough, scarcely moments after they had finished their work and a pair of city front-loaders had begun the odious task of scooping up the thousands of dead bee bodies, the truck's com whistled for attention.

"We got a 42B." Gustafson had removed his reducer and was leaning out the open door. The oxygen-dense air might be dangerous for steady breathing, but it was great for making a quick recovery after a bit of heavy physical exertion. One just had to be careful not to rely on it too long. "Boy stepping on scorpion."

She shook her head as she approached the truck. "That's 42A. 42B is scorpion stepping on boy."

Fortunately, the yard-long arthropod they trapped and killed half an hour later in the public playground hadn't stung anyone. Nocturnal by nature, it had been disturbed by children who had been building a fort. They stood around and watched wide-eyed as the two exterminators hauled the chelatinous carcass away. The scorpion wasn't such a big stretch, Lissa knew. Nine-inch-long predecessors had thrived in equatorial rainforests as recently as the twenty-first century. It hadn't taken much of an oxygen boost to grow them to their present frightening size.

They were finishing coffee when the code two red call came in. Looks were exchanged in lieu of words. It was one call neither of them wanted to answer. As senior operative, it fell to Lissa.

"Why us?" she spoke tersely into her tiny mouth pickup. "We've been hot on it all morning."

"Everyone's been hot on it all morning." The dispatcher on duty at the Atlanta Metropolitan Command Center sounded tired. He would not be moved, Lissa knew. "You're the best, Sergeant Sweetheart. Take care of this one and I'll let you break for the rest of the day."

She looked over at Corporal Gustafson, who was hearing the same broadcast. Inside the sealed restaurant equipped with its own industrial-strength reducers, they had no need for their face masks. She checked her chronometer. If they wrapped up the call early, they would each gain a couple of hours of paid free time.

"All right." She was grumbling as she rose from the table. Other patrons regarded the two uniformed specialists with the respect due their unpleasant and dangerous calling. "But not because you called me the best, Lieutenant. Because you called me Sweetheart."

"Don't let it go to your head," the officer finished. "Take care on this one."

A single descendant of *Meganeura* shadowed their truck as they sped through the city streets and out into the suburbs. Since this was an emergency call, they had their lights and sirens on, but they didn't dissuade the dragonfly. Its four-foot wingspan flashed iridescent in the heavy, humid air until, finally bored with riding in the truck's airflow, it flashed off toward a nearby office building. Going after a goliath fly, Lissa mused as she let Gustafson focus on his driving. Or one of the city's rapidly shrinking and badly overmatched population of pigeons. Unable to compete with the increasingly large and powerful insects, birds had suffered more than any other group under the Runaway.

The family that had put in the emergency call was grateful for the arrival of the exterminator team but refused to emerge from the house's safe room where they had taken refuge.

"It's in the basement." On the small heads-up display that floated in front of Lissa's face, the mother looked utterly terrified. So did the two children huddled behind her. "We've had break-ins before. Ants mostly, when they can get across the electrical barrier, and roaches my son can handle with his baseball bat. But this is a first for us."

"Take it easy, ma'am. We're on it."

Looking none too reassured, the woman nodded as the transmission ended. Lissa checked her gear and made sure her reducer was tight on her face before nodding at Gustafson.

"This'll be your first time dealing with a chilopod, won't it?" Her partner nodded slowly. "Watch your chest. They always go for the chest."

Donning helmets, they exited the car and headed for the single-family home. No sprays this time. Not for this afternoon's quarry. Both of them hefted pump guns.

The front door had been left open, not to greet the arriving exterminators but in the forlorn hope that the invader might depart of its own volition. Not much chance of that, Lissa knew. Chilopoda favored surroundings that were dark and damp. Eying the family compound and the looming, nearby trees, she sighed. If people were going to live in the woods in this day and age . . .

As they entered the basement, the house's proximity lights flicked on. A good sign. It meant that their quarry wasn't moving. Gun barrel held parallel to the floor, she was first down the stairs. The basement was filled with the usual inconsequential detritus of single-family living: crates of goods meant to be given away that would remain in place forever, a couple of old electric bikes, lawn furniture, the home O_2 reducer that allowed residents to move freely about the sealed building without having to don face masks, heavy-duty gardening gear, and more.

A sound made her raise her left hand sharply in warning.

Whispering into her mask, she pointed toward a far, unilluminated corner. Gustafson nodded and, without waiting, started toward it.

"I'll take care of it, Lissa. You just . . ."

"No! Flanking movement or . . . !"

Too late.

The six-foot-long centipede burst from its hiding place to leap straight at her startled companion. Its modern Amazonian ancestors had jumped into the air to catch and feed on bats. This oxygen-charged contemporary monster had no difficulty getting high enough off the ground to go straight for Gustafson's throat. If it got its powerful mandibles into his neck above his shirt and below his helmet and started probing with the poison claws that protruded from its back end . . .

She raised her gun and fired without thinking.

Guts and goo sprayed everywhere as the pumper blew the monster in two. Still, it wasn't finished. As both halves twitched and jerked independently, she approached them with care. Two more shots shattered first the dangerous anterior claws and then the head containing the powerful, snapping mandibles.

Turning, she found her partner on the ground, seated against a trunk still holding his weapon and staring. Walking over to him, she bent slightly as she extended a hand to help him up.

"I . . ." He didn't look at her. "I'm sorry, Lissa. It came out so fast that I . . ."

She cut him off curtly. "Forget it. First encounter with a chilopod; no need for excuses."

He stared at her. "You warned me. You said they were fast. The class manual talks about their quickness. But I didn't . . ." His voice trailed away.

She gave him a reassuring pat on the back. "Like I said, forget it. Visuals and words in a manual are one thing. Having it jump you in a basement is a little different. They make a tiger seem slow and an insurgent unarmed. Next time, you'll be ready."

He nodded somberly, and they climbed the stairs. The basement was a mess, but that was a job for a city or private cleanup crew. Back in the truck, she kept expecting to be assigned another job as soon as they reported in that they had successfully completed this one. Surprisingly, the officer on duty seemed inclined to keep his word. The bugband stayed silent.

As a chastened Gustafson headed the truck back toward the military base on the outskirts of the city, she leaned forward to have a look at the sky through the windshield. Overcast, as always. The usual tepid rain on tap for the evening. Other than that, the weather report was promising. Temperatures in the low nineties and humidity down to seventy-five percent. Things were a lot worse the closer one got to the now nearly uninhabitable tropics, she knew. The tech journals were full of reports of new threats emerging from the depths of the impenetrable Amazon. Ten-foot carnivorous beetles. Deadlier scorpions. Six-inch-long fire ants . . .

Home and business owners might fret over giant centipedes and spiders with three-foot leg spans, but as a military-trained specialist, she worried far more about the ants. All ants. Not because they were prolific and not because they could bite and sting, but because they cooperated. Cooperation could lead to bigger problems than any sting. In terms of sheer numbers, the ants had always been the most successful species on the planet. Let them acquire a little of the always-paranoid Gustafson's hypothetical intelligence to go with their new size and . . .

She checked the weather a last time. Atmospheric oxygen was up to forty-one percent, give or take a few decimals. It was continuing its steady rise, as it had over the preceding decades. How big would the bugs get if it reached forty-five percent? Or fifty? How would the fire brigades cope with the increasingly ferocious firestorms that had made wooden building construction a relic of the past?

Rolling down her window, she removed her mask and stuck her head outside, into the lugubrious wind. Gustafson gave her a look but said nothing and stayed with his driving. Overhead and unseen, another giant dragonfly dropped lower, sized up the potential prey, and shot away. A human was still too big for it to take down. But if its kind kept growing . . .

Lissa inhaled deeply of the thick, moist air. It filled her lungs, the oxygen boost reinvigorating her after the confrontation in the basement. Drink of it too much and she would start feeling giddy. There were benefits to the increased oxygen concentration. Athletes, at least while performing in air-conditioned venues, had accomplished remarkable feats.

Humanity was adapting to the changed climate. It had always done so. It would continue to do so. And in a radically changed North America, at least, the military would ensure that it would be able to do so.

As an exterminator noncom charged with keeping her city safe, her only fear was that something else just might be adapting a little faster.

ABOUT THE AUTHOR

ALAN DEAN FOSTER is the bestselling author of more than a hundred and twenty novels, and is perhaps most famous for his Commonwealth series, which began in 1971 with the novel *The Tar-Aiym Krang*. His most recent series is the transhumanism trilogy The Tipping Point. Foster's work has been translated into more than fifty languages and has won awards in Spain and Russia in addition to the U.S. He is also well-known for his film novelizations, the most recent of which is *Star Trek Into Darkness*. He is currently at work on several new novels and film projects.

TRUTH AND CONSEQUENCES

KIM STANLEY ROBINSON

From 40 Signs of Rain

The light under the thunderheads had gone dim. Cloud bottoms were black, and splotches like dropped water balloons starred the sidewalk pavement. Charlie started hurrying and got to Phil's office just ahead of a downpour.

He looked back out through the glass doors and watched the rain hammer down the length of the Mall. The skies had really opened. Raindrops remained large in the air, as if hail the size of baseballs had coalesced in the thunderheads and then somehow been melted back to rain again before reaching the ground.

Charlie watched the spectacle for a while, then went upstairs. There he found out from Evelyn that Phil's flight in had been delayed, and that he might be driving back from Richmond instead.

Charlie sighed. No conferring with Phil today.

He read reports instead, went down to clear his mailbox. Evelyn's office window faced south, with the Capitol looming to the left, and across the Mall the Air and Space Museum. In the rainy light the big buildings took on an eerie cast, like the cottages of giants.

Then it was past noon, and Charlie was hungry. The rain seemed to have eased a bit since its first impact, so he went out to get a sandwich at the Iranian deli on C Street, grabbing an umbrella at the door.

Outside, it was raining steadily but lightly. The streets were deserted. Many intersections had flooded to the curbs, and in a few places well over the curbs, onto the sidewalks.

Inside the deli, the grill was sizzling, but the place was almost empty. Two cooks and the cashier were standing under a TV that hung from a ceiling corner, watching the news. When they recognized Charlie, they went back to looking at the TV. The characteristic smell of basmati rice enfolded him.

"Big storm coming," the cashier said. "Ready to order?"

"Yeah, thanks. I'll have the usual, pastrami sandwich on rye."

"Flood too," one of the cooks added.

"Oh, yeah?" Charlie replied. "What, more than usual?"

The cashier nodded, still looking at the TV. "Two storms and high tide. Upstream, downstream, and middle."

"Oh, my."

Charlie wondered what it would mean. He stood watching the TV with the rest of them. Satellite photos showed a huge sheet of white pouring across New York and Pennsylvania. Meanwhile, the tropical storm was spinning past Bermuda. It looked like another perfect storm might be brewing. Not that it took a perfect storm these days to make the mid-Atlantic states seem like a literal name, geographically speaking. A far-less-than-perfect storm could do it. The TV spoke of eleven-year tide cycles, of the strongest El Niño ever recorded. "It's a fourteen thousand square mile watershed," the TV said.

"It's gonna get wet," Charlie observed.

The Iranians nodded silently. Five years earlier, they would probably have been closing the deli, but this was the fourth perfect storm in the last three years, and like everyone else, they were getting jaded. It was Peter crying wolf at this point, even though the previous three storms had all been major disasters at the time, at least in some places. But never in DC. Now people just made sure their supplies and equipment were okay and then went about their business, umbrella and phone in hand. Charlie was no different, he realized; here he was, getting a sandwich and going back to work. It seemed the best way to deal with it.

The Iranians finished his order, all the while watching the TV images: flooding fields, apparently in the upper Potomac watershed.

"Three meters," the cashier said as she gave him his change, but Charlie wasn't sure what she meant. The cook chopped Charlie's wrapped sandwich in half, put it in a bag. "First one is worst one."

Charlie took it and hurried back through the darkening streets. He passed an occasional lit window occupied by people working at computer terminals, looking like figures in a Hopper painting.

Now it began to rain hard again, and the wind was roaring in the trees and hooting around the building corners. The curiously low-angle nature of DC made big patches of lowering clouds visible through the rain.

Charlie stopped at a street corner and looked around. His skin was on fire. Things looked too wet and underlit to be real; it looked liked stage lighting for some moment of ominous portent. Once again, he felt that he had crossed over into a space where the real world had taken on all the qualities of a dream, being just as glossy and surreal, just as stuffed to a dark sheen with ungraspable meaning. Sometimes, just being outdoors in bad weather was all it took.

Back in the office, he settled at his desk and ate while looking over his list of things to do. The sandwich was good. The coffee from the office's coffee machine was bad. He wrote a memo for Phil, urging him to follow up on the elements of the bill that seemed to be dropping into cracks.

His phone rang and he jumped a foot.

"Hello!"

"Charlie! Are you all right?"

"Hi, babe; yeah, you just startled me."

"Sorry, oh, good. I was worried, I heard on the news that downtown is flooding, the Mall is flooding."

"The what?"

"Are you at the office?"

"Yeah."

"Is anyone else there with you?"

"Sure."

"Are they just sitting there working?"

Charlie peered out of his carrel door to look. In fact, his floor sounded empty. It sounded as if everyone was gathered down in Evelyn's office.

"I'll go check and call you back," he said to Anna.

"Okay, call me when you find out what's happening!"

"Okay. Call you back in a second."

He went into Evelyn's office and saw people jammed around the south window or in front of a TV set on a desk.

"Look at this," Andrea said to him, gesturing at the TV screen.

"Is that our door camera?" Charlie exclaimed, recognizing the view down Constitution. "That's our door camera!"

"That's right."

"My God!"

Charlie went to the window and stood on his tiptoes to see past people. The Mall was covered by water. The streets beyond were flooded. Constitution Avenue was floored by water that looked to be at least two feet deep, maybe deeper.

"Incredible, isn't it."

"Shit!"

"Look at that."

"Will you look at that!"

"Why didn't you guys call me?" Charlie cried, shocked by the view.

"Forgot you were here," someone said. "You're never here."

Andrea added, "It just came up in the last half hour. It happened all at once, it seemed like. I was watching." Her voice quivered. "It was like a hard downburst, and the raindrops didn't have anywhere to go, they were splashing into a big puddle everywhere, and then it was there, what you see."

"A big puddle everywhere."

Constitution looked like the Grand Canal in Venice. Beyond it the Mall was like a rain-beaten lake. Water sheeted equally over streets, sidewalks, and lawns. Charlie recalled the shock he had felt many years before, leaving the Venice train station and seeing water right there outside the door. A city floored with water. Here it was quite shallow, of course. But the front steps of all the buildings came down into an expanse of brown water, and the water was all at one level, as with any other lake or sea. Brown-blue, blue-brown, brown, gray, dirty white—drab urban tints all. The rain pocked it into an infinity of rings and bounding droplets, and gusts of wind tore cats' paws across it.

Charlie maneuvered closer to the window as people milled around. It seemed to him that the water in the distance was flowing gently toward them; for a moment, it looked (and even felt) as if their building had cast anchor and was steaming westward. Charlie felt a lurch in his stomach, put his hand to the windowsill to keep his balance.

"Shit, I should get home," he said.

"How are you going to do that?"

"We've been advised to stay put," Evelyn said.

"You're kidding."

"No. I mean, take a look. It could be dangerous out there right now. That's nothing to mess with—look at that!" A little electric car floated or rather was dragged down the street, already tipped on its side. "You could get knocked off your feet."

Charlie wasn't quite convinced, but he didn't want to argue. The water was definitely a couple of feet deep, and the rain was shattering its surface. If nothing else, it was too weird to go out.

"How extensive is it?" he asked.

Evelyn switched to a local news channel, where a very cheerful woman was saying that a big tidal surge had been predicted, because the tides were at the height of an eleven-year cycle. She went on to say that this tide was cresting higher than it would have normally because Tropical Storm Sandy's surge was now pushing up Chesapeake Bay. The combined tidal and storm surges were moving up the Potomac toward Washington, losing height and momentum along the way but meanwhile impeding the outflow of the river like a kind of moving dam. The Potomac, which had a watershed of "fourteen thousand square miles," as Charlie had heard in the Iranian deli—dammed. A watershed experiencing record-shattering rainfall. In the last four hours, ten inches of rain had fallen in parts of the watershed. Now all that water was pouring downstream and encountering the tidal bore, right in the metropolitan area. The four inches of rain that had fallen on Washington during the midday squall, while spectacular in itself, had only added to the larger problem, which was that there was nowhere for any of the water to go. All this the reporter explained with a happy smile.

Outside, the rain was falling no more violently than during many a summer shower. But it was coming down steadily and striking water when it hit.

"The trains will be stopped for sure."

"What about the Metro? Oh, my God."

"I've gotta call home."

Several people said this at once, Charlie among them. People scattered to their desks and their phones. Charlie said, "Phone, get me Anna."

He got a quick reply: "All circuits are busy. Please try again." This was a recording he hadn't heard in many years, and it gave him a bad start. Of course it would happen at a moment like this: everyone would be trying to call someone, and towers and lines would be down. But what if it stayed like that for hours—or days? Or even longer? It was a sickening thought; he felt hot, and the itchiness blazed anew across his broken skin. He even felt dizzy, as if a limb were being threatened with immediate amputation—his sixth sense, in effect, which was his link to Anna. All of a sudden, he understood how completely he took his state of permanent communication with her for granted. They talked a dozen times a day, and he relied on those talks to know what he was doing, sometimes literally.

Now he was cut off from her. Judging by the voices in the offices, no one's connection was working. They regathered; had anyone gotten an open line? No. Was there an emergency phone system they could tap into? No.

TV told them what was going on. One camera on top of the Washington Monument gave a splendid view of the extent of the flooding around the Mall, truly breathtaking. The Potomac had disappeared into the huge lake it was forming on the Mall, all the way up to the steps of the White House and the Capitol, both on little knolls, the Capitol's higher. The entirety of Southwest was floored by water, though its big buildings stood clear; the broad valley of the Anacostia looked like a reservoir. It seemed the entire city south of Pennsylvania Avenue was a building-studded lake.

And not just there. Flooding had filled Rock Creek to the top of its deep but narrow ravine, and now water was spilling over at the sharp bends the gorge took while dropping through the city to its confluence with the Potomac. Cameras on the bridges at M Street caught the awesome sight of the Creek roaring around its final turn west, upstream from M Street, and pouring over Francis Junior High School and straight south on 23rd Street into Foggy Bottom, where it joined the lake covering the Mall.

Then on to a different channel, a different camera. The Watergate Building was indeed a curving water gate, like a remnant of a broken dam. The wave-tossed spate that indicated the Potomac looked as if it could knock the Watergate down. Likewise the Kennedy Center just south of it. The Lincoln Memorial, despite its pedestal mound, appeared to be flooded up to about Lincoln's feet. Across the Potomac the water was going to inundate the lower levels of Arlington National Cemetery. Reagan Airport was completely gone. A voice on the TV said that ten million acre-feet of water were converging in the metropolitan area, and more rain was predicted.

Out the window, Charlie saw that people were already taking to the streets around them in small water craft, despite the wind and drizzle. Kayaks, a waterski boat, canoes, rowboats. Then as the evening wore on, and the dim light left the air below the black clouds, the rain returned with its earlier intensity. It poured down in a way that surely made it dangerous to be on the water. Most of the small craft had appeared to be occupied by men who it did not seem had any good reason to be out there. Out for a lark—thrillseekers, already!

"It looks like Venice," Andrea said, echoing Charlie's earlier thought.

"Wow. What a mess."

"Shit, I got here by Metro."

Charlie said, "Me too."

They thought about that for a while. Taxis weren't going to be running.

"I wonder how long it takes to walk home."

But then again, Rock Creek ran between the Mall and Bethesda.

Sometime during that second night, the rain stopped, and though dawn of the third morning arrived sodden and gray, as the day progressed the clouds scattered, flying north at speed. By nine, the sun blazed down onto the flooded city between big puffball clouds. The air was breezy and unsettled.

Helicopters and blimps had already taken to the air in great numbers. Now all the TV channels in the world could reveal the extent of the flood from on high, and they did. Much of downtown Washington DC remained awash. A giant shallow lake occupied precisely the most famous and public parts of the city; it looked like someone had decided to expand the Mall's reflecting pool beyond all reason. The rivers and streams that converged on this larger tidal basin were still in spate, which kept the new lake topped up. In the washed sunlight the flat expanse of water was the color of caffè latte, with foam.

Standing in the lake, of course, were hundreds of buildings-become-islands, and a few real islands, and even some freeway viaducts, now acting as bridges over the Anacostia Valley. The Potomac continued to pour through the western edge of the lake, overspilling its banks both upstream and down whenever lowlands flanked it. Its surface was studded with floating junk, which moved slower the farther downstream it got. Apparently, the ebb tides had only begun to allow this vast bolus of water out to sea.

As the morning wore on, more and more boats appeared. The TV shots from the air made it looked like some kind of regatta—the Mall as water festival, like something out of Ming China. Many people were out on makeshift craft that did not look seaworthy. Police boats on patrol were even beginning to ask people who were not doing rescue work to leave, one report said, though clearly they were not having much of an impact. The situation was still so new that the law had not yet fully returned. Motorboats zipped about, leaving beige wakes behind. Rowers rowed, paddlers paddled, kayakers kayaked; swimmers swam; some people were even out in the blue pedal boats that had once been confined to the Tidal Basin, pedaling around the Mall in majestic mini-steamboat style.

Although these images from the Mall dominated the media, some channels carried other news from around the region. Hospitals were filled. The two days of the storm had killed many people, no one knew how many; and there were many rescues as well. In the first part of the third morning, the TV helicopters often interrupted their overviews to pluck people from rooftops. Rescues by boat were occurring all through the Southwest district and up the Anacostia basin. Reagan Airport remained drowned, and there was not a single passable bridge over the Potomac all the way upstream to Harpers Ferry. The Great Falls of the Potomac was no more than a huge turbulence in a nearly unbroken, gorge-topping flow. The President had evacuated to Camp David, and now he declared all of Virginia, Maryland, and Delaware a federal disaster area, the District of Columbia, in his words, "worse than that."

LOOSED UPON THE WORLD

Then there came yells from down the hall.

A police motor launch was at the second-floor windows, facing Constitution, ready to ferry people to dry ground. This one was going west, and, yes, would eventually dock in Georgetown if people wanted off there. It was perfect for Charlie's hope to get west of Rock Creek and then walk home.

And so when his turn came, he climbed out of a window, down into a big boat. A stanza from a Robert Frost poem he had memorized in high school came back to him suddenly:

> *It went many years, but at last came a knock,*
> *And I thought of the door with no lock to lock.*
> *The knock came again, my window was wide;*
> *I climbed on the sill and descended outside.*

He laughed as he moved forward in the boat to make room for other refugees. Strange what came back to the mind. How had that poem continued? Something something; he couldn't remember. It didn't matter. The relevant part had come to him after waiting all these years. And now he was out the window and on his way.

The launch rumbled, glided away from the building, turned in a broad curve west down Constitution Avenue. Then left, out onto the broad expanse of the Mall. They were boating on the Mall.

The National Gallery reminded him of the Taj Mahal—same water reflection, same gorgeous white stone. All the Smithsonian buildings looked amazing. No doubt they had been working inside them all night to get things above flood level. What a mess it was going to be.

Charlie steadied himself against the gunwale, feeling so stunned that it seemed he might lose his balance and fall. That was probably the boat's doing, but he was, in all truth, reeling. The TV images had been one thing, the actual reality another; he could scarcely believe his eyes.

White clouds stood overhead in the blue sky, and the flat brown lake was gleaming in the sunlight, reflecting a blue glitter of sky, everything all glossy and compact—real as real, or even more so. None of his poison-ivy visions had ever been as remotely real as this lake was now.

Their pilot maneuvered them farther south. They were going to pass the Washington Monument on its south side. They puttered slowly past it. It towered over them like an obelisk in the Nile's flood, making all the watercraft look correspondingly tiny.

The Smithsonian buildings appeared to be drowned to about ten feet. Upper halves of their big public doors emerged from the water like low boathouse doors. For some of the buildings, that would be a catastrophe. Others had steps or stood higher on their foundations. A mess any way you looked at it.

Their launch growled west at a walking pace. Trees flanking the western half of the Mall looked like water shrubs in the distance. The Vietnam Memorial would of course be submerged. The Lincoln Memorial stood on its own little pedestal hill, but it was right on the Potomac and might be submerged to the height of all its steps; the statue of Lincoln might even be getting his feet wet. Charlie found it hard to tell, through the shortened trees, just how high the water was down there.

Boats of all kinds dotted the long brown lake, headed this way and that. The little blue paddle boats from the Tidal Basin were particularly festive, but all the kayaks and rowboats and inflatables added their dots of neon color, and the little sailboats tacking back and forth flashed their triangular sails. Brilliant sunlight filled the clouds and the blue sky. The festival mood was expressed even by what people wore—Charlie saw Hawaiian shirts, bathing suits, even Carnival masks. There were many more black faces than Charlie was used to seeing on the Mall. It looked as if something like Trinidad's Mardi Gras parade had been disrupted by a night of storms, but was re-emerging triumphant in the new day. People were waving to each other, shouting things (the helicopters overhead were loud); standing in boats in unsafe postures, turning in precarious circles to shoot three-sixties with phones and cameras. It would only take a water-skier to complete the scene.

Charlie moved to the bow of the launch and stood there soaking it all in. His mouth hung open like a dog's. The effort of getting out the window had reinflamed his chest and arms; now he stood there on fire, torching in the wind, drinking in the maritime vision. Their boat chugged west like a vaporetto on Venice's broad lagoon. He could not help but laugh.

"Maybe they should keep it this way," someone said.

A Navy river cruiser came growling over the Potomac toward them, throwing up a white bow wave on its upstream side. When it reached the Mall, it slipped through a gap in the cherry trees, cut back on its engines, settled down in the water, continued east at a more sedate pace. It was going to pass pretty close by them, and Charlie felt their own launch slow down as well.

Then he spotted a familiar face among the people standing in the bow of the patrol boat. It was Phil Chase, waving to the boats he passed like the grand marshal of a parade, leaning over the front rail to shout greetings. Like a lot of other people on the water that morning, he had the happy look of someone who had already lit out for the territory.

Charlie waved with both arms, leaning over the side of the launch. They were closing on each other. Charlie cupped his hands around his mouth and shouted as loud as he could.

"HEY, PHIL! Phil Chase!"

Phil heard him, looked over, saw him.

"Hey, Charlie!" He waved cheerily, then cupped his hands around his mouth too. "Good to see you! Is everyone at the office okay?"

"Yes!"

"Good! That's good!" Phil straightened up, gestured broadly at the flood. "Isn't this amazing?"

"Yes! It sure is!" Then the words burst out of Charlie: "So, Phil! Are you going to do something about global warming now?"

Phil grinned his beautiful grin. "I'll see what I can do!"

From Fifty Degrees Below

They came down on Reykjavík just before dawn. The surface of the sea lay around the black bulk of Iceland like a vast sheet of silver. By then, Diane was awake; back in DC, this was her usual waking hour, unearthly though that seemed to Frank, who had just gotten tired enough to lean his head on hers. These little intimacies were shaken off when seatbacks returned to their upright position. Diane leaned across Frank to look out the window; Frank leaned back to let her see. Then they were landing, and into the airport. Neither of them had checked luggage, and they weren't there long before it was time to join a group of passengers trammed out to a big helicopter. On board, earplugs in, they rose slowly and then chuntered north over empty blue ocean.

Soon after that, passengers with a view were able to distinguish the tankers themselves, long and narrow, like Mississippi river barges but immensely bigger. The fleet was moving in a rough convoy formation, and as they flew north and slowly descended, there came a moment when the tankers dotted the ocean's surface for as far as they could see in all directions, spread out like iron filings in a magnetic field, all pointing north. Lower still: black syringes, lined in rows on a blue table, ready to give their "long injections of pure oil."

They dropped yet again, toward a big landing pad on a tanker called the *Hugo Chavez*, an Ultra Large Crude Carrier with a gigantic bridge at its stern. From this height, the ships around them looked longer than ever, all plowing broad white wakes into a swell from the north that seemed miniature in proportion to the ships but began to look substantial the lower they got. Hovering just over the *Hugo Chavez's* landing pad, it became clear from the windcaps and spray that the salt armada was in fact crashing through high seas and a stiff wind, almost a gale. Looking in the direction of the sun the scene turned black-and-white, like one of those characteristically windblown chiaroscuro moments in *Victory At Sea*.

When they got out of the helo, the wind blasted through their clothes and chased them upstairs to the bridge. There a crowd of visitors larger than the crew had a fine view over a broad expanse of ocean, crowded with immense ships. As the director of the US National Science Foundation, and therefore the person most responsible for gathering this fleet and making this effort, Diane was the star of the show.

Looking away from the sun the sea was like cobalt, a deep Adriatic blue.

The *Hugo Chavez* from its bridge looked like an aircraft carrier with the landing deck removed. The quarterdeck or sterncastle that held the bridge at its top was tall but only a tiny part of the craft; the forecastle looked like it was a mile away. The intervening distance was interrupted by a skeletal rig that resembled a loading crane but also reminded Frank of the giant irrigation sprayers one saw in California's central valley. The salt in the hold was being vacuumed into this device, then cast out in powerful white jets, a couple hundred meters to both sides. The hardrock salt had been milled into sizes ranging from table salt grains to bowling balls. In the holds, it looked like dirty white gravel and sand. In the air, it looked almost like dirty water or slush, arching out and splashing in a satisfyingly broad swath. Between the salt fall and the ship's wakes, and the whitecaps, the deep blue of the ocean surface was infinitely mottled by white. Looking aft, in the direction of the sun, it turned to silver on pewter and lead.

Diane watched the scene with her nose almost on the glass, deeply hooded in a blue heavy jacket. She smiled at Frank. "You can smell the salt."

"The ocean always smells like this."

"It seems like more today."

"Maybe so." She had grown up in San Francisco, he remembered. "It must smell like home." She nodded happily.

They followed their hosts up a metal staircase to a higher deck of the bridge, a room with windows on all sides. It was this room that made the *Hugo Chavez* the designated visitor or party ship, and now the big glass-walled room was crowded with dignitaries and officials. Here they could best view the long ships around them, all the way to the horizon. Each ship cast two long curving jets out to the sides from its bow, like the spouts of right whales. Every element was repeated so symmetrically that it seemed they had fallen into an Escher print.

The tankers flanking theirs seemed nearer than they really were because of their great size. They were completely steady in the long swells. The air around the ships was filled with a white haze. Diane pointed out that the diesel exhaust stayed in the air while the salt mist did not. "They look so dirty. I wonder if we couldn't go back to sails again, just let everything go slower by sea."

"Labor costs," Frank suggested. "Uncertainty. Maybe even danger."

"Would they be more dangerous? I bet you could make them so big and solid they wouldn't be any more dangerous than these."

"These were reckoned pretty dangerous."

"I don't hear of many accidents that actually killed people. It was mostly leaking oil when they hit something. Let's look into it."

They moved from one set of big windows to the next, taking in the views.

"It's like the San Joaquin Valley," Frank said. "There are these huge irrigation rigs that roll around spraying stuff."

Diane nodded. "I wonder if this will work."

"Me too. If it doesn't . . ."

"I know. It would be hard to talk people into trying anything else."

Around the bridge they walked. Everyone else was doing the same, in a circulation like any other party. Blue sky, blue sea, the horizon ticked by tiny wavelets, and then the fleet, each ship haloed by a wind-tossed cloud of white mist. Frank and Diane caught each other by the shoulder to point things out, just as they would have in Optimodal. A bird; a fin in the distance.

Then another group arrived in the room, and soon they were escorted to Diane: the Secretary-General of the UN; Germany's environmental minister, who was the head of their Green Party and a friend of Diane's from earlier times; lastly, the prime minister of Great Britain, who had done a kind of Winston Churchill during their hard winter, and who now shook Diane's hand and said, "So this is the face that launched a thousand ships," looking very pleased with himself. Diane was distracted by all the introductions. People chatted as they circled the room, and after a while, Diane and Frank stood in a big circle, listening to people, their upper arms just barely touching as they stood side by side.

After another hour of this, during which nothing varied outside except a shift west in the angle of the sun, it was declared time to go; one didn't want the helicopters to get too far from Reykjavík, and there were other visitors waiting in Iceland for their turns to visit, and the truth was, they had seen what there was to see. The ship's crew therefore halted the *Hugo Chavez's* prodigious launching of salt, and they braved the chilly blast downstairs and got back in their helo. Up it soared, higher and higher. Again, the astonishing sight of a thousand tankers on the huge burnished plate spreading below them, instantly grasped as unprecedented: the first major act of planetary engineering ever attempted, and by God, it looked like it. They were salting the ocean to restart the Gulf Stream, to rescue the world's climate. The hubris implied by that was astonishing— or maybe it was the desperation.

But then the helo pilot ascended higher and higher, higher and higher, until they could see a much bigger stretch of ocean, water extending as far as the eye could see, for hundreds of miles in all directions—and all of it blank, except for their now-tiny column of ships, looking like a line of toys. And then ants. In a world so vast, could anything humans do make a difference?

From Sixty Days and Counting

It was Diane who suggested that Frank string all his necessary trips together in a quick jaunt around the world, dropping in on Beijing, the

Takla Makan, Siberia, and England. He could start with San Diego, and the White House travel office could package it so it would only take him ten days or so. So he agreed, and then the day of his departure was upon him, and he had to dig out his passport and get his visas and other documents from the travel office, and put together a travel bag and jump on the White House shuttle out to Dulles.

As soon into his flight as he could turn on his laptop, he checked out a video from Wade Norton. The little movie even had a soundtrack, a hokey wind and bird-cry combination, even though the sea looked calm and there were no birds in sight. The black rock of the coastline was filigreed with frozen white spume, a ragged border separating white ice and blue water. Summer again in Antarctica. The shot must have been taken from a helicopter, hovering in place.

Then Wade's voice came over the fake sound. "See, there in the middle of the shot? That's one of the coastal installations."

Finally, Frank saw something other than coastline: a line of metallic blue squares. Photovoltaic blue. "What you see covers about a football field. The sun is up 24-7 right now. Ah, there's the prototype pump, down there in the water." More metallic blue: in this case, thin lines, running from the ocean's edge up over the black rocks, past the field of solar panels on the nearby ice, and then on up the broad, tilted road of the Leverett Glacier toward the polar cap.

"Heated pumps and heated pipelines. It's the latest oil tech, developed for Alaska and Russia. And it's looking good, but now we need a lot more of it. And a lot more shipping. The pipes are huge. You probably can't tell from these images, but the pipes are like sewer mains. They're as big as they could make them and still get them on ships. Apparently, it helps the thermal situation to have them that big. So, they're taking in like a million gallons an hour and moving it at about ten miles an hour up the glacier. The pipeline runs parallel to the polar overland route; that way they have the crevasses already dealt with. I rode with Bill for a few days on the route; it's really cool. So, there's your proof of concept. It's working just like you'd want. They've mapped all the declivities in the polar ice, and the oil companies are manufacturing the pumps and pipes and all. They're loving this plan, as you can imagine. The only real choke points in the process now are speed of manufacture and shipping and installation. They haven't got enough people who know how to do the installing. You need some thousands of these systems to get the water back up onto the polar plateau."

Here Frank got curious enough to get on the plane's phone and call Wade directly. He had no idea what time it was in Antarctica, he didn't even know how they told time down there, but he figured Wade must be used to calls at all hours by now and probably turned his phone off when he didn't want to get them.

But Wade picked up, and their connection was good, with what sounded like about a second in transmission delay.

"Wade, it's Frank Vanderwal, and I'm looking at that e-mail you sent with the video of the prototype pumping system."

"Oh, yeah, isn't that neat? I helo'ed out there day before yesterday."

"Yeah, it's neat," Frank said. "But tell me, does anyone down there have any idea how frozen sea water is going to behave on the polar cap?"

"Oh, sure. It's kind of a mess. You know, when water freezes, the ice is fresh and the salt gets extruded, so there are layers of salt above and below and inside the new ice, so it's kind of slushy or semi-frozen. So, the spill from the pumps really spreads flat over the surface of the polar cap, which is good, because then it doesn't pile up in big domes. Then the salt kind of clumps and rises together, and gets pushed onto the surface, so what you end up with is a mostly solid freshwater ice layer with a crust of salt on top of it, like a little devil's golf course–type feature. Then the wind will blow that salt down the polar cap and disperse it as a dust. So, back into the ocean again! Pretty neat, eh?"

"Interesting," Frank said.

"Yeah. If we build enough of these pumping systems, it really will be kind of a feat. I mean, the west Antarctic ice sheet is definitely going to fall into the ocean. No one can stop that now. But we might be able to pump the water back onto the east Antarctic ice sheet."

"So, what about the desert basins in the north thirties?" Frank said. "A lot of those are being turned into salt lakes. It'll be like a bunch of giant Salton Seas."

"Is that bad?"

"I don't know; what do you think about that?"

"They'll hydrate the areas downwind, don't you think?"

"Would that be good?"

"More water? Probably good for people, right? I mean, it wouldn't be good for arid desert biomes. But maybe we have enough of those. I mean, desertification is a big problem in some regions. If you were to create some major lakes in the western Sahara, it might slow down the desertification of the Sahel. I think that's what the ecologists are talking about now anyway. They're loving all this stuff. I sometimes think they love it that the world is falling apart. It makes the earth sciences all the rage. They're like atomic scientists in World War Two."

"I suppose they are. But on the other hand . . ."

"Yeah, I know. Better if we didn't have to do all this stuff. Since we do, though, it's good we've got some options."

"I hope this doesn't give people the feeling that we can just silver-bullet all the problems and go on like we were before."

"No. Well, we can think about crossing that bridge if we get to it."

"True."

"Have to hope the bridge is still there at that point."

"True."

Short and unhumorous laughs from both of them, and they signed off.

In San Diego, Frank rented a van and drove up to UCSD, checking in at the department, then walking up North Torrey Pines Road to RRCCES.

The new labs were fully up and running, crowded, not messy but busy.

A functioning lab was a beautiful thing to behold. A bit of a Fabergé egg: fragile, rococo, needing nurturance and protection. A bubble in a waterfall. Science in action. In these, they changed the world. And now—

Yann came in. "You have to go to Russia."

"I am."

"Oh! Good. The Siberian forest is amazing. It's so big even the Soviets couldn't cut it down. We flew from Chelyabinsk to Omsk and it went on and on."

"And your lichen?"

"It's way east of where we spread it. The uptake has been amazing. It's almost scary."

"Almost?"

Yann laughed defensively. "Yeah, well, given the problems I see you guys are having shifting away from carbon, a little carbon drawdown overshoot might not be such a bad thing, right?"

Frank shook his head. "Who knows? It's a pretty big experiment."

"Yeah, it is. Well, you know, it'll be like any other experimental series in that sense. We'll see what we get from this one and then try another one."

"The stakes are awfully high."

"Yeah, true. Good planets are hard to find." Yann shrugged. "But maybe the stakes have always been high, you know? Maybe we just didn't know it before. Now we know it, and so maybe we'll do things a little more . . ."

"Carefully? Like by putting in suicide genes or other negative feedback constraints? Or environmental safeguards?"

Yann shrugged, embarrassed. "Yeah, sure."

He changed the subject, with a look heavenward as if to indicate that what the Russians had done was beyond his control.

After that, Asia. First a flight to Seattle, then a long shot to Beijing. Frank slept as much as he could, then got some views of the Aleutians, followed by a pass over the snowy volcano-studded ranges of Kamchatka.

The Beijing meeting, called Carbon Expo Asia, was interesting. It was both a trade show and a conference on carbon emissions markets, sponsored by the International Emissions Trading Association. Carbon was a commodity with a futures market (like Frank himself). With Phil Chase in office, the value of carbon emissions had soared. Now, however, futures traders were beginning to wonder if carbon might become so sharply capped, or the burning of it become so old-tech that emissions would so radically decrease that their futures would lose all value in a market collapse. So, there were countervailing pressures coming to bear on the daily price and its prognosis, as in any futures market.

All these pressures were on display for Frank to witness. Naturally, Chinese traders were prominent, and the Chinese government appeared to be calling the shots. They were trying to bump the present value up by holding China's potential coal-burning over everyone else's head as a kind of giant environmental terrorist threat. By threatening to burn their coal, they hoped to create all kinds of concessions and essentially get their next generation of power plants paid for by the rest of the global community. Or so went the threat. The Chinese bureaucrats wandered the halls looking fat and dangerous, as if explosives were strapped to their waists, implying that if their requirements were not met, they would explode their carbon and cook the world.

The United States, meanwhile, still had the second biggest carbon burn ongoing and from time to time could threaten to claim that it was proving harder to cut back than they had thought. So, all the big players had their cards, and in a way it was a case of mutually assured destruction all over again. Everyone had to agree on the need to act, or it wouldn't work for any of them. So, everyone was dealing, the Americans as much as anyone. It was like a giant game of chicken. And in a game of chicken, everyone thought the Chinese would win. They were bloody-minded hardball players, and only a hundred guys there had to hold their nerve, rather than three hundred million; that was a magnitude-seven difference and should have guaranteed China could hold firm the longest. If you believed the theory that the fewer were stronger in will than the many.

It was an interesting test of America's true strength. Did the bulk of the world's capital still reside in the US? Yes. Did the US's military strength matter in this world of energy technology? Maybe. Was it a case of dominance without hegemony, as some were describing it, so that in the absence of a war, America was nothing but yet another decrepit empire, falling by history's wayside? Hard to say. If America stopped burning 25 percent of the total carbon burned every year, would that make the country geopolitically stronger or weaker? Probably stronger. One would have to measure many disparate factors that were not usually calculated together. It was a geopolitical mess to rival the end of World War Two, and the negotiations establishing the UN.

Then the meeting was over, with lots of trading done but little accomplished toward a global treaty. That was becoming the usual way with these meetings, the American rep told Frank wearily at the end. Once you were making what could be called progress (meaning inventing another way to make money, it seemed to Frank), no one was inclined to push for anything more.

Frank then caught a Chinese flight down to the Takla Makan desert, in far western China, and landed at Khotan, an oasis town on the southern edge of the Tarim Basin. There he was loaded with some Hungarian civil engineers into a mini-bus and driven north, to the shores of the new salt sea. Throughout the drive they saw plumes of dust, as if from a volcanic explosion, rising in the sky ahead of them. As they approached, the yellow wall of rising dust became more transparent and finally was revealed as the work of a line of gigantic bulldozers heaving a dike into place on an otherwise empty desert floor. It looked like the Great Wall was being reproduced at an order-of-magnitude-larger scale.

Frank got out at a settlement of tents, yurts, mobile homes, and cinder block structures, all next to an ancient dusty tumbledown of brown brick walls. He was greeted there by a Chinese-American archeologist named Eric Chung, with whom he had exchanged e-mails.

Chung took him by jeep around the old site. The actual dig occupied only a little corner of it. The ruins covered about a thousand acres, Chung told him, and so far, they had excavated ten.

Everything in sight, from horizon to horizon, was a shade of brown: the Kunlun Mountains rising to the south, the plains, the bricks of the ruin, and in a slightly lighter shade, the newly exposed bricks of the dig.

"So, this was Shambala?" Frank said.

"That's right."

"In what sense, exactly?"

"That was what the Tibetans called it while it existed. That arroyo and wash you see down the slope was a tributary of the Tarim River, and it ran all year round because the climate was wetter and the snowpack on the Kunluns was thicker, and there were glaciers. They're saying that flooding the Tarim Basin may mean this river would run again, which is one of the reasons we have to get the dig at the lower points done fast. Anyway, it was a very advanced city, the center of the kingdom of Khocho. Powerful and prominent in that time. It was located on a precursor of the Silk Road, and was a very rich culture. The Bön people in Tibet considered it to be the land of milk and honey, and when the Buddhist monasteries took over up there on the plateau, they developed a legend that this was a magical city. Guru Rinpoche then said it was a magic city that could move from place to place, and that started their Shambala motif."

"And now you have to move it again."

"Well, it's already moved on, from what I understand. But if we're going to protect these ruins from the flooding of the Takla Makan, we'll have to act fast."

Frank shook his head. Another salt sea, created on purpose to keep sea level itself from rising too much; it was hard to believe it would work. But this dry basin in central Asia was so large that filling it with sea water would take something like five to ten percent of all the water that would otherwise devastate the coastal cities of the world. It was geo-engineering again, and God knew what would happen there and downwind from there, but the Chinese were willing to do it, and so it was getting done. Hubris, desperation; could anyone tell which was which anymore? Had they ever been different?

An Aeroflot flight then, during which he caught sight of the Aral Sea, which apparently was already twice as big as before its flooding project had begun, thus almost back to the size it had been before people began diverting its inflow a century before. All kinds of landscape restoration experiments were being conducted by the Kazakhs and Uzbeks around the new shoreline, which they had set legally in advance and which now was almost achieved. From the air, the shoreline appeared as a ring of green, then brown, around a lake that was light brown near the shoreline, shading to olive, then a murky dark green, then blue. It looked like a big vernal pool.

Later, the plane landed and woke Frank. He got off and was greeted by an American and Russian from Marta and Yann's old company. It was cold, and there was a dusting of dirty snow on the ground. Winter in Siberia! Although in fact, it was not that cold and seemed rather dry and brown.

They drove off in a caravan of four long gray vans, something like Soviet Land Rovers, it seemed, creaky like the plane but warm and stuffy. They progressed over a road that was not paved but did have fresh pea gravel spread over it, and a coating of frost. The vehicles had to keep a certain distance from each other to avoid having their windshields quickly pitted.

Not far from the airport, the road led them into a forest of scrubby pines. It looked like Interstate 95 in Maine, except that the road was narrower and unpaved, and the trees therefore grayed by the dust thrown up by passing traffic. They were somewhere near Cheylabinsk-56, someone said. You don't want to go there, a Russian added. One's of Stalin's biggest messes. Somewhere southeast of the Urals, Frank saw on a phone map.

Their little caravan stopped in a gravel parking lot next to a row of cabins. They got out, and locals led them to a broad path into the woods. Quickly, Frank saw that the roadside dust and frost had obscured the fact that all the trees in this forest had another coating: not dust but lichen.

It was Small Delivery System's lichen. Frank saw now why Marta had been not exactly boasting, nor abashed, nor exuberant, nor defensive, but some strange mixture of all these. The lichen was obviously doing well, to the point where a balance had clearly been lost; lichen plated everything, trunk, branches, twigs—everything but the pine needles themselves. Such a thorough cloaking looked harmful. A shaft of sunlight cut through the clouds and hit some trees nearby, and their cladding of lichen made them gleam like bronze.

The Small Delivery people were sanguine about this. They did not think there would be a problem. They said the trees were not in danger. They said that even if some trees died, it would only be a bit of negative feedback to counter the carbon drawdown. If a certain percentage took on lignin so fast they split their trunks or had roots rupture underground, then that would slow any further runaway growth of lichen. Things would then eventually reach a balance.

Frank wasn't so sure. He did not think this was ecologically sound. Possibly, the lichen could go on living on dead trees; certainly, it could spread at the borders of the infestation to new trees. But these were not the people to talk to about this possibility.

The new lichen started out khaki, it appeared, and then caked itself with a layer that was the dull bronze that eventually dominated. As with the crustose lichen of the high Sierra that you saw everywhere on granite, it was quite beautiful. The little bubbles of its surface texture had an insec-tile sheen. That was the fungus. Frank recalled a passage in Thoreau: "The simplest and most lumpish fungus has a peculiar interest to us, because it is so obviously organic and related to ourselves; matter not dormant, but inspired, a life akin to my own. It is a successful poem in its kind."

Which was true; but to see it take over the life it was usually symbiotic with was not good. It looked like the parts of Georgia where kudzu had overgrown everything.

"Creepy," Frank remarked, scraping at an individual bubble.

"It is, kind of, isn't it?"

"How do the roots look?"

"Come see for yourself." They took him to an area where the soil had been removed from beneath some sample trees. Here they saw both before and after roots, as some trees had been girdled and killed and their roots exposed later, to give them baseline data. Near them, some living trees, or trees in the process of being killed by the exposure of their roots, were standing in holes balanced on their lowest net of fine roots, leaving most of the root balls exposed. The root balls were still shallow, in the way of evergreens, but the lichen-infested trees had roots that were markedly thicker than the uninfested trees.

"We started by treating an area of about a thousand square kilometers, and now it's about five thousand."

"About the size of Delaware, in other words."

Meaning some tens of million trees had been affected, and thus tens of millions of tons of carbon had been drawn down. Say a hundred million tons for the sake of thinking—that was about one percent of what they had put into the atmosphere in the year since the lichen was released.

Of course, if it killed the forest, a lot of that carbon would then be eaten by microbes and respired to the atmosphere, some of it quickly, some over years, some over decades. This, Frank's hosts assured him, given the situation they were in, was a risk worth taking. It was not a perfect nor a completely safe solution, but then again, none of them were.

Interesting to hear this reckless stuff coming from the Russians and the Small Delivery Systems people about equally, Frank thought. Who had persuaded whom was probably irrelevant; now it was a true *folie à deux*.

He had once stood a thousand feet tall, it had seemed, on the floor of the Atlantic, while in a simulator in La Jolla; now it looked like he had been miniaturized and was threading his way through the mold in a Petri dish. "Really creepy," he declared.

Certainly time to declare limited discussion. It was impossible to tease out the ramifications of all this; they depended so heavily on what happened to the various symbioses feeding each other, eating each other. There would need to be some kind of Kenzo modeling session, in which the whole range of possibilities got mapped, then the probabilities of each assessed. Feedback on feedback. It was probably incalculable, something they could only find out by watching what happened in real time. Like history itself. History in the making, right out there in the middle of Siberia.

Then it was on to London by way of Moscow, which he did not see at all. In his London hotel after the flights, he was jetlagged into some insomniac limbo and couldn't sleep. He checked his e-mail and then the internet, clicking to Emersonfortheday.com, where searching using the word *traveling* brought up this:

"Traveling is a fool's paradise. Our first journeys discover to us the indifference of places. At home I dream that at Naples, at Rome, I can be intoxicated with beauty and lose my sadness. I pack my trunk, embrace my friends, embark on the sea and at last wake up in Naples, and there beside me is the stern fact, the sad self, unrelenting, identical, that I fled from. I seek the Vatican and the palaces. I affect to be intoxicated with sights and suggestions, but I am not intoxicated. My giant goes with me wherever I go."

From "Self-Reliance." Frank laughed, then showered and went to bed, and in the midst of his giant's buzzing, the luxury of lying down took him away.

The conference he was attending was in Greenwich, near the Observatory, so that they could inspect in person the Thames River Barrier.

Witness the nature of the beast. The barrier was up permanently these days, forming a strangely attractive dam, composed of modular parts in a curve like a longbow. Ribbed arcs. The arcs only came down to the level of the surface of the river, which still ran out underneath them, and so they blocked any higher water than that from flooding areas upstream. One could therefore walk to its end on the north bank of the river, up onto a platform, see that the seaward side of the river was a plane of water distinctly higher than the plane of water on the London side. It reminded Frank of the view from the dike surrounding Khembalung, right before the monsoon had drowned the island.

Now he walked in a state of profound jet lag: sandy-eyed, mouth hung open in sleepy amazement, prone to sudden jolts of emotion. It was not particularly cold out, but the wind was raw; that was what kept him awake. When the group went back inside and took up the work on the sea level issues, he fell asleep, unfortunately missing most of a talk he had really wanted to see on satellite-based laser altimetry measurements. An entire fleet of satellites and university and government departments had taken on the task of measuring sea level worldwide. Right before Frank fell asleep, the speaker said something about how the sea level rise had been slowing down lately, meaning their first pumping efforts might be having an effect, because other measurements showed the polar melting was continuing apace in a feedback loop many considered unstoppable. This was fascinating, but Frank fell asleep anyway.

When he woke up, he was chagrinned but realized he could see the paper online. The general upshot of the talk seemed to have been that they could only really stem the rise by drawing down enough CO_2 to get the atmosphere back to around 250 parts per million, levels last seen in the Little Ice Age from 1200–1400 AD. People were murmuring about the nerviness of the speaker's suggestion that they try for an ice age, but as was pointed out, they could always burn some carbon to warm things if they got too cold. This was another reason to bank some of the oil that remained unburned.

"I can tell you right now my wife's going to want you to set the thermostat higher," someone prefaced his question, to general guffaws. They all seemed much more confident of humanity's terraforming abilities than seemed warranted. It was a research crowd rather than a policy crowd, and so included a lot of graduate students and younger professors. The more weathered faces in the room were looking around and catching each other's eyes, then raising their eyebrows. Hubris? Desperation? Both at once? The older faces recognized the looks they saw in each other: it was the pinch of fear.

ABOUT THE AUTHOR

KIM STANLEY ROBINSON is the bestselling author of sixteen novels, including three series: the Mars trilogy, the Three Californias trilogy, and the Science in the Capitol trilogy. He is also the author of about seventy short stories, much of which has been collected in the retrospective volume *The Best of Kim Stanley Robinson*. He is the winner of two Hugos, two Nebulas, six Locus Awards, the World Fantasy Award, the British Science Fiction Award, and the John W. Campbell Memorial Award. His latest novels are *Aurora*, *Shaman*, *Galileo's Dream* and *2312*.

ENTANGLEMENT

VANDANA SINGH

...*Flapping Its Wings*...

... and flying straight at her. She ducked, averting her eyes. The whole world had come loose: debris flying everywhere; the roar of the wind. Something soft and sharp cannoned into her belly—she looked up to see the monster rising into the clouds, a genie of destruction, yelled—"Run! Run! Find lower ground! Lower ground!"

She woke up. The boat rocked gently; instrument panels in the small cabin painted thin blue and red lines. Outside, the pale arctic dawn suffused the sky with orange light. Everything was normal.

"Except I hadn't been asleep, not really," she said aloud. Her morning coffee had grown cold. "What kind of dream was that?"

She rubbed the orange bracelet. One of the screens flickered. There was a fragmented image for a microsecond before the screen went blank: a gray sky, a spinning cloud, things falling. She sat up.

Her genie appeared in a corner of the screen.

"Irene, I just connected you to five people around the world," it said cheerfully. "Carefully selected, an experiment. We don't want you to get too lonely."

"Frigg," she said, "I wish you wouldn't do things like that."

There were two messages from Tom. She thought of him in the boat three hundred kilometers away, docked to the experimental iceberg, and hoped he and Mahmoud were getting along. Good, he had only routine stuff to report. She scrolled through messages from the Arctic Science Initiative, the Million Eyes project, and three of her colleagues working off the northern coast of Finland. Nothing from Lucie.

She let out a long, slow breath. Time to get up, make fresh coffee. Through the tiny window of the boat's kitchenette, the smooth expanse of ocean glittered in the morning light. The brolly floated above it like a conscientious ghost, not two hundred meters away. Its parachute-like top was bright in the low sun, its electronic eyes slowly swiveling as the intelligent unit in the box below drank in information from the world around it. Its community of intelligences roved the water below, making observations and sending them back to the unit so that it could adjust its behavior accordingly. She felt a tiny thrill of pride. The brolly was her conception, a crazy biogeochemist's dream, brought to reality by engineers. The first prototype had been made by Tom himself in his first year of graduate school. Thinking of his red thatch of hair framing a boyish face, she caught herself smiling. He was such a kid! The first time he'd seen a seal colony, he'd almost fallen off the boat in his enthusiasm. You'd think the kid had never even been to a zoo. He was so Californian, it was adorable. Her own upbringing in the frozen reaches of northern Canada meant she was a lot more cold-tolerant than him—he was always overdressed by her standards, buried under layers of thermal insulation and a parka on top of everything. Some of her colleagues had expressed doubts about taking an engineering graduate student to the arctic, but she'd overruled them. The age of specialization was over; you had to mix disciplinary knowledge and skills if you wanted to deal intelligently with climate change, and who was better qualified to monitor the brollies deployed in the region? Plus, Mahmoud would make a great babysitter for him. He was a sweet kid, Tom.

She pulled on her parka and went out on deck to have her coffee the way she liked it, scalding hot. Staring across the water, she thought of home. Baffin Island was not quite directly across the North Pole from her station in the East Siberian Sea, but this was the closest she had come to home in the last fifteen years. She shook her head. Home? What was she thinking? Home was a sunny apartment in a suburb of San Francisco, a few BART stops from the university, where she had spent ten years raising Lucie, now twenty-four, a screenwriter in Hollywood. It had been over a year since she and Lucie had had a real conversation. Her daughter's chatty e-mails and phone calls had given way to a near silence, a mysterious reserve. In her present solitude, that other life, those years of closeness, seemed to have been no more than a dream.

Over the water the brolly moved. There was a disturbance not far from the brolly—an agitation in the water, then a tail. A whale maybe five meters in length swimming close to the surface popped its head out of the water—a beluga! Well, she probably wasn't far from their migration route. Irene imagined the scene from the whale's perspective: the brolly like an enormous, airborne jellyfish, the boat, the human craft, and a familiar sight.

The belugas were interested in the brolly. Irene wondered what they made of it. One worry the researchers had was that brollies and their roving family units would be attacked and eaten by marine creatures. The brolly could collapse itself into a compact unit and sink to the seabed or use solar power to rise a couple of meters above the ocean surface. At the moment, it seemed only to be observing the whales as they cavorted around it. Probably someone, somewhere, was looking at the ocean through the brolly's electronic eyes and commenting on the internet about a whale pod sighting. Million Eyes on the Arctic was the largest citizen science project in the world. Between the brollies, various observation stations, and satellite images, more than two million people could obtain and track information about sea ice melt, methane leaks, marine animal sightings, and ocean hot spots.

It occurred to Irene that these whales might know the seashore of her childhood, that they might even have come from the north Canadian archipelago. A sudden memory came to her: going out into the ocean north of Baffin Island with her grandfather in his boat. He was teaching her to use traditional tools to fish in an icy inlet. She must have been very small. She recalled the rose-colored arctic dawn, her grandfather's weathered face. When they were on their way back with their catch, a pod of belugas had surfaced close enough to rock their boat. They clustered around the boat, popping their heads out of the water, looking at the humans with curious, intelligent eyes. One large female came close to the boat. "*Qilalugaq*," her grandfather said gently, as though in greeting. The child Irene—no, she had been Enuusiq then—Enuusiq was entranced. The Inuit, her grandfather told her, wouldn't exist without the belugas, the caribou, and the seals. He had made sure she knew how to hunt seals and caribou before she was thirteen. Memories surfaced: the swish of the dog sled on the ice in the morning, the waiting at the breathing holes for the seals, the swift kill. The two of them saying words of apology over the carcass, their breath forming clouds in the frigid air.

Her grandfather died during her freshman year of high school. He was the one who had given her her Inuk name, Enuusiq, after his long-dead older brother, so that he would live again in her name. The name held her soul, her *atiq*. "Enuusiq," she whispered now, trying it on. How many years since anyone had called her that? She remembered the gathering of the community each time the hunters brought in a big catch, the taste of raw meat with a dash of soy. How long had it been since those days? A visit home fifteen years ago when her father died (her mother had died when she was in college)—after that, just a few telephone conversations and internet chats with her cousin Maggie in Iqaluit.

The belugas moved out of sight. Her coffee was cold again. She was annoyed with herself. She had volunteered to come here partly because she wanted to get away—she loved solitude—but in the midst of it, old memories surfaced; long-dead voices spoke.

The rest of the morning, she worked with a fierce concentration, sending data over to her collaborators on the Russian research ship *Kolmogorov*, holding a conference call with three other scientists, politely declining two conference invitations for keynote speaker. But in the afternoon, her restlessness returned. She decided she would dive down to the shallow ocean bed and capture a clip for a video segment she had promised to the Million Eyes project. It was against protocol to go down alone without anyone on the boat to monitor her—but it was only twenty-two meters, and she hadn't got this far by keeping to protocol.

Some time later she stood on the deck in her dry suit, pulled the cap snugly over her head, checked the suit's computer, wiggled her shoulders so the oxygen tank rested more comfortably on her back, and dove in.

That was why she was there. This falling through the water was like falling in love, only better. In the cloudy blue depths, she dove through marine snow, glimpsing here and there the translucent fans of sea butterflies, a small swarm of krill, the occasional tiny jellyfish. A sea gooseberry with a glasslike two-lobed soft body winged past her face. Some of these creatures were so delicate, a touch might kill them—no fisherman's net could catch them undamaged. You had to be here, in their world, to know they existed. Yet there was trouble in this marine paradise. Deeper and deeper she went, her dry suit's wrist display clocking time, temperature, pressure, oxygen. The sea was shallow enough at twenty-two meters that she could spend some time at the bottom without worrying about decompression on the way up. It was darker there on the seaweed-encrusted ocean floor; she turned on her lamp and the camera. Swimming along the seafloor toward the array of instruments, she startled a mottled white crab. It was sitting on top of one of the instrument panels, exploring the device with its claws. Curiosity . . . well, that was something she could relate to. The crab retreated as she swam above it, then returned to its scrutiny. Well, if her work entertained the local wildlife, that was something.

A few meters away she saw the fine lines of the thermoelectric mesh on the seabed. There were fewer creatures in the methane-saturated water.

Methane gas was coming up from the holes in the melting permafrost on the seabed—there were even places you could see bubbles. Before her a creature swam into focus: a human-built machine intelligence, one of the brolly's family unit. Its small cylindrical body, with its flanges and long snout, looked like a fish on an alien planet. It was injecting a rich goo of nutrients (her very own recipe) for methane-eating bacteria. She was startled by how natural it looked in the deep water. "Eat well, my hearties," she told her favorite life-forms. Methanotrophs were incredibly efficient at metabolizing methane, using pathways that were only now being eluci- dated. Most of the processes could not be duplicated in labs. So much was still unknown—hell, they'd found five new species of the bacteria since the project had started. Methanotrophs, like most living beings, didn't exist in isolation but in consortia. The complex web of interdependencies determined behavior and chemistry.

"If methane-eating bacteria sop up most of the methane, it will help slow global warming," she said into the recorder. "It will buy time until humanity cuts its carbon dioxide emissions. Methane is a much more potent greenhouse gas than CO_2. Although it doesn't stay in the atmo- sphere as long, too much methane in the atmosphere might excite a posi- tive feedback loop—more methane, more warming, more thawing of permafrost, more methane . . . a vicious cycle that might tip the world toward catastrophic warming." Whether that could happen was still a point of argument among scientists, but the methane plumes now known to be coming off the seabed all over the shallow regions of the arctic were enough to worry anyone whose head wasn't buried in the sand.

Maybe her bacteria could help save the world. With enough nutrients, they and their communities of cooperative organisms might take care of much of the methane; in the meantime, the thermoelectric mesh was an experiment to see whether cooling down the hot spots might slow the outgassing. The energy generated by the mesh was captured in batteries, which had to be replaced when at capacity. The instrument array mea- sured biogeochemical data and sent it back to the brolly.

Her dry suit computer beeped. It was time to return to the surface—or else she would run out of oxygen. She turned off the camera-recorder and swam slowly and carefully toward the light. "Message from Tom," her genie said. "Not urgent but interesting. Two messages from Million Eyes, one to you, asking about the video, the other a news item. A ballet dancer in Estonia saw an illegal oil and gas exploration vessel messing around the Laptev Sea. There's a furor. Message from your cousin Maggie in Iqaluit, marked Personal. She's in San Francisco, wondering where you are."

Damn. Hadn't she told Maggie she was going on an expedition? Maggie hardly ever left Canada, so the trip to San Francisco must be something special.

"I'm coming up," she said, just as she felt a numbing pain sear into her left calf. The cold was coming in through a leak, a tear in the suit; her dry suit computer beeped a warning. Her leg cramped horribly. She looked up, willing herself not to panic—the surface seemed impossibly far away, and the cold was filling her body, making her chest contract with pain. She moved her arms as strongly as she could. She must get up to the surface before the cold spread—she had had a brush with hypothermia before. But as she went up with excruciating slowness, she knew at once that she was going to die here, and a terror came upon her. *Lucie*, she said. *Lucie, forgive me, I love you, I love you.* Her arms were tired, her legs like jelly, and the cold was in her bones, and a part of her wanted simply to surrender to oblivion. Frigg was chirping frantically in her ear—calling for rescue, not that there was anyone in the area who could get to her in time—and then a voice cut in, and her grandmother said, "Bless you and be careful up there; I'm praying for you." This was really odd because her grandmother was dead, and the accent was strange. But the voice spoke with such clarity and concern, and there was such an emphasis on "be careful"—and weren't there kitchen sounds in the background, a pan banging in the sink, so incongruously ordinary and familiar?—that she was jolted from the darkness of spirit that had descended on her. Her arms seemed to be the only part of her body still under her control, and although they felt like lead, she began to move them again.

Tom's voice cut in, frantic. "I'm coming, I'm coming as fast as I can; hold on," and Mahmoud said, more calmly, "I've contacted the *Kolmogorov* for their helicopter—and the Coast Guard." But the helicopter had been sent over to a station in Norway that very afternoon. She saw her death before her with astonishing clarity. Then she felt something lift her bodily—*how could Tom get here so soon?*—an enormous white shadow loomed, a smile on the bulbous face—a whale. A *beluga*? She felt the solid body of the whale below her, tried to get ahold of the smooth flesh, but she needn't have worried, because it was pushing her up with both balance and strength, until she broke the water's surface near the boat. Hauling herself up the rungs of the ladder proved to be impossible: she was shaking violently, and her legs felt numb. The whale pushed her up until all she had to do was to tumble over the rail onto the deck. She collapsed on the deck, pulled off her mask, sobbing, breathing huge gulps of cold air. Her suit beeped shrilly.

"Get dry NOW," Frigg said in Mahmoud's voice, or maybe it was Mahmoud. She half crawled into the cabin, peeled everything off, and huddled under a warm shower until the shivering slowed. A searing pain in both legs told her that blood was circulating again. There was a frayed tear in the dry suit—had it caught on a nail as she was pulling it out of the cupboard? So much for damning protocol, something she never did if a colleague or student was involved. Her left calf still ached, and the tears wouldn't stop. At last, she toweled off and got into warm clothes, with warm gelpacks under her armpits and on her stomach. The medbot checked her vital signs while hot cocoa bubbled.

"Frigg, tell Tom and Mahmoud not to come; my vitals are fine," she said, but her voice shook. "Tell them to call off the rescue." Her chest still ached, but as she sipped the cocoa, she started to feel more normal. After a while, she could stand without feeling she was going to fall over.

She stepped gingerly out on the deck. The sun, already low in the sky, was falling slowly into the ocean like a ripe peach. The first stars sequined the coming arctic night. The belugas swam around the boat. She finished her cocoa in a few gulps and felt a shadow of strength return to her. A whale popped its head out of the water next to her boat and looked at her with friendly curiosity.

She put her arms between the railing bars and touched the whale's head. It was smooth as a hard-boiled egg. "*Qilalugaq*," she whispered, and tears ran down her cheeks, and her shoulders shook. "Thank you, thank you for saving my life. Did Ittuq send you?" She realized she was speaking Inuktitut, the familiar syllables coming back as though she had never left home. "Ittuq," she whispered. She had been too young when her grandfather died, too shocked to let herself mourn fully. Now, thirty-nine years later, the tears flowed.

At last she stood, leaning against the rail, spent, and waved to the pod as it departed.

Later that night, when she had eaten her fill of hot chicken soup, she talked to Tom on video. He was touchingly grateful that she was all right and excited about the whale rescue. Irene said, "Don't go around broadcasting it, will you?" She had no desire to see her foolishness go viral on the internet. Fortunately, Tom had something exciting of his own to share.

"Look!" he said. "This is from this afternoon." A photo appeared on the side of the screen. There lay the enormous bulk of the artificial iceberg to which his boat was docked. An irregular heap lay atop it.

"Polar bear," he said, grinning. "Must have been swimming for a while, looking for a rest stop. Poor guy's sleeping off a late lunch. I tossed him my latest catch of fish."

"Stay away from him!" Irene said sharply. "Wild animals aren't cute house pets—remember your briefing!"

"You're a fine one to talk, Irene." He grinned again, and then, anticipating her protests, said, "Yes, yes, I know; don't worry. If I go aboard the berg with the bear on it, some kid somewhere is going to notice and send me a message. This morning, I stepped out without my snow goggles and a twelve-year-old from Uzbekistan messaged my genie. Thanks to Million Eyes you can hardly take a shit in peace. . . . Er, sorry . . ."

"It's not that bad." She couldn't help smiling. Good for the kid in Uzbekistan. Tom could be absentminded. The screen image of the fake berg was impossibly white. It was coated with a high-albedo nano-structured radiative paint that sent infrared right back into the atmosphere while leaving the surface cool to the touch.

"Another interesting thing happened today," he said, with the kind of casualness that betrayed suppressed excitement. "You know we have eight brollies on Big Lump?" Big Lump was the largest iceberg in a flotilla about fifty kilometers north of Tom's station. "They've been screening meltwater pools on the berg from the sun, refreezing them before they have a chance to melt deeply enough to make cracks. Well, three nomad brollies arrived from Lomonosov Station—just left their posts of their own accord and came over and joined them. Mahmoud just reported."

"Very interesting," she said.

It was not surprising that brollies were making their own decisions. It meant that as learning intelligences, intimately connected to their environment and to one another, they had gone on to the next stage of sophistication. Her own brolly continuously monitored the biogeo-chemical environment, knowing when to feed the methanotroph con-sortia their extra nutrients, and when to stop. Her original conception of linked artificial intelligences with information-feedback loops was based on biomimicry, inspired by natural systems like ecosystems and endo-crine systems. Her brolly was used to working as a community of minds, so she imagined that facility could be scaled up. Each brolly could com-municate with its own kind and was connected to the climate databases around the world, giving as well as receiving information, and capable of learning from it. She had a sudden vision of a multilevel, complexly interconnected grid, a sentience spanning continents and species, a kind of Gaiaweb come alive.

"How much time before they become smarter than us?" she said, half jokingly. "This is great news, Tom."

Afterward, she watched the great curtains of the aurora paint the sky. She sat in her cabin, raising her eyes from the data scrolling down her screen. Temperature was dropping in the ocean seabed—the methane fizzler had perceptibly slowed since the project began. It was a minute accomplishment compared to the scale of the problem, but with two million pairs of eyes watching methane maps of the Arctic, maybe they could get funding to learn how to take care of the worst areas that were still manageable. Partly, the methane outgassing was a natural part of a thousands-years process, but it was being exacerbated by warming seas. Didn't science ultimately teach what the world's indigenous peoples had known so well—that everything is connected? A man gets home from work in New York City and flips a switch, and a little more coal is burned, releasing more warming carbon dioxide into the atmosphere. Or an agribusiness burns a tract of Amazon rain forest, and a huge carbon sink is gone, just like that. Or a manufacturer in the United States buys palm oil to put in cookies, and rain forests vanish in Southeast Asia to make way for more plantations. People and their lives were so tightly connected across the world that it would take a million efforts around the globe to make a difference.

She touched the orange wristlet and the screen came on. "Frigg, call Maggie."

"Irene, Irene?" Maggie had more gray in her hair, but her voice was as loud as before. Demanding. "Where have you been? They told me at your campus you were in the Arctic, and I thought, dammit, she's come home at last, but I hear you're somewhere in Siberia?"

"Don't you keep up?" Irene said, growling, trying not to grin in delight and failing. She blinked tears from her eyes. "Siberia is where it's at. I'm in a boat, running an experiment on the seabed. Trying to stop methane outgassing, you know, save the world, all in a day's work."

"Great, great, but I hate coming all the way here and finding you gone.

I have to tell you, I saw Lucie. Yes, you heard me right. She's going into documentary filmmaking—expedition to Nepal—"

Nepal!

"Well, I am glad she's talking to you," Irene said after a moment. "Is she . . . is she all right?"

"She's fine! Irene, she just needs to find her own way—you two have been by yourselves for so long. . . ."

"By ourselves! In the middle of the empty streets of the Bay Area!"

"You know what I mean. Big cities can be terribly lonely. Why do you think I came back after college? Listen, Irene, nuclear families suck, and single-parent nuclear families suck even more. People need other people than just their parents. My kids have issues with being here in Iqaluit, but at least they are surrounded by uncles and aunts and cousins and grandparents—"

"How are your parents? How is everyone?"

"Waiting for you to come home. Come and visit, Irene. It's been too long. We all thought you were the one who was going to stay because of everything you learned about the old ways from Grandfather."

"The last time I came, when my father died . . . your mother threw a fish at me and told me to gut it."

Maggie laughed.

"Which I think you did pretty well. Surprised me. Now you have to come on up, Irene! Or down, I should say. Come talk to my boy. Peter's part of a collaboration between Inuit high schoolers and scientists. Hunters, too. Going out with GPS units, recording information about ice melting and wildlife sightings."

Irene wanted to say, *Maggie, I almost died today, but* Qilalugaq *gave me the gift of life, and that means I have to change how I live. I need your help.* The words wouldn't come out. She said, instead, "Maggie, I got to go. Let's talk tomorrow. . . . We have to talk."

"Irene, are you all right? Irene?"

"Yes . . . no, I can't talk about it now. Tomorrow? If . . . if you see Lucie again, tell her—give her my love."

"I'm seeing her Friday for lunch before she leaves. I will, don't worry. Tomorrow, for sure, then. Hang in there, girl!"

She waved good-bye and the screen went blank. The lights of the aurora reflected off the walls and desk in the darkened room. The boat swayed gently—out there, the pale top of the brolly floated. Something splashed out at sea, a smooth back. She remembered the small house in Iqaluit where she'd grown up with her parents and grandfather and two aunts and cousins. The great sky over the ice, sky reflecting ice reflecting sky in an endless loop. Her grandfather had been an immensely practical man, but he had also taught her to pay attention to intangible things, things you couldn't quantify, like the love you could feel for a person, or the land, or the whale. She had been rescued by a whale, a whale from home. What more of a sign did she need? She had stayed away first because it was inconvenient to go all the way, and then because she had been so busy, doing important work—and later, because she was confused and ashamed. How to face them all, knowing that despite her successes she had lost her way, wandered off from her own self? How to return home without Lucie, knowing herself a failure in so many ways? Now she saw that the journey home was part of her redemption, and as the belugas migrated, traveling in great closed loops in the still-frigid waters of the Arctic, visiting and revisiting old ground, so must she. *Enuusiq*, she whispered, practicing. She thought of her daughter's eager, tender face in childhood as she listened to a story, and the bittersweet delight when Lucie went off to college, so young and beautiful, intelligence and awareness in her eyes, at the threshold of adulthood. She thought of herself as a small child, watching her mother weaving a pattern on the community loom: the sound, the rhythm, the colors, her mother's hands. The world she loved was woven into being every moment through complex, dynamic webs of interaction: the whales in their pods, the methanotrophs and their consortia, the brollies and their family units, the Million Eyes of eager young people trying to save the world.

"*Ittuq*," she said aloud, "I'm coming home."

. . . In the Amazon . . .

. . . There is a city in the middle of the rain forest: Manaus. This year, there is a drought. The rains are scant. When they fall, they fall kilometers downwind of the city. . . .

In the heat, outside the glitzy hotels and bars, there is the smell of rotting fruit, fish, garbage, flowers, exhaust. Rich and poor walk the streets with their cell phones or briefcases or Gucci handbags or baskets of jenipapo or camu camu, and among them prowls the artist. He's looking for a blank wall, the side of a building. Any smooth, empty surface is a canvas to him.

His favorite time is the early morning. In that pale light when the bugio monkeys and the birds begin to call, he is there with black oil chalk and a ladder, drawing furiously in huge arm strokes, then filling in the fine-detail work. He never knows what animal will emerge from the wall—the first stroke tells him nothing, nor the next, or the next, but each stroke limits the possibilities until it is clear what spirit has possessed him, and then it emerges. When it is a jaguar, he, the artist, feels the bark of the tree limb; he flickers through the jungle on silent, padded feet. When a manatee emerges from the blank wall, the artist knows the watery depths of the river, the mysterious underwater geography. When it is a bird, he knows the secret pathways of the high jungle canopy.

Then he is done. He looks around, and there is nobody, and he breathes a sigh of relief. He slips away through the sleeping streets to another self, another life.

Fernanda stared out from the airplane window at the city that was her home. It was a bright splash of whiteness in the green of the Amazon rain forest. *Urban heat island, indeed,* she thought. The city had grown enormously in the last decade, with the boom in natural gas and high-tech manufacturing—returning to it was always a surprise—a populous, economically vigorous human habitation in the middle of the largest forest in the world. Despite the urban forests that made green pools in the white sea of concrete, it lay before her like scar tissue in the body of the jungle. The Rio Negro was languid as an exhausted lover—the water was lower than she could remember since the last drought. She hadn't forgotten what it had been like, as a child, to stand on the dry bed of the river during the big drought, feeling like the world was about to end. Bright rooftops came up toward her as the plane dipped, and she tried to see if there were any green roofs—hard to tell from this height. Never mind; she would know soon enough, when she joined the new project.

"Been on holiday?" the man next to her said pleasantly.

Fernanda was caught off guard. She had spent three months in the coastal jungle studying the drought, counting dead trees, making measurements of humidity, temperature, and rainfall, and, on one occasion, fighting a forest fire started by an agricultural company to clear the forest. Her left forearm still hurt from a burn. The team had camped in the hot, barren expanse, and after two months, she and Claudio had broken up, which was why she was coming back alone. They'd established beyond doubt that barren wasteland was hotter than healthy forest, and that less rain fell here, and that it was similar to an urban heat island. Far from being able to regrow the forest, they had to fight greedy marauders to prevent more of it from being destroyed. Claudio remained behind with the restoration team, and the rest of them had trekked through the deep coolness of the remaining healthy forest until they had got to civilization. She had grown silent as the forest muttered, called, clucked, and roared around her, had felt its rhythms in some buried ancestral part of her, and her pain had quieted to a kind of soft background noise. Now she looked at the man in his business suit and his clean-shaven, earnest face, the shy smile, the hint of a beer belly, and thought how alien her own species seemed whenever she returned from the forest.

"Business," she said coldly, hoping he wouldn't inquire any further. The plane began its descent.

The city was the same and not the same. She found out within the next few days that the cheerful family gatherings at Tia Ana's, which she'd always enjoyed, were a lot more difficult without Claudio, mostly because of the questions and commiserations. Tia Ana had that look in her eye that meant she was already making matchmaking plans. Her mother had tickets for two for a performance of *Aida* at the Teatro Amazonas, no less, which was something to look forward to. Inevitably, she thought about that last fight with Claudio, when he accused her of being more sexual with her saxophone than with him. Not that she'd brought her sax into the rain forest—but she hadn't been able to take it out of its case as yet.

What was different was that there wasn't enough rain. When the clouds did gather, there might be a scant shower over the city, but most of the rain would fall about fifty kilometers downwind. Meanwhile the humans sweltered in their concrete and wooden coops—those who had air conditioning cranked it up—the poor on the city's east side made do without, some falling victim to heat exhaustion. But for the most part, the lives of the middle and upper classes went on much the same, apart from the occasional grumbling. It seemed peculiar to Fernanda that even in this self-consciously eco-touristy city, people whom she knew and loved could live such oblivious lives, at such a remove from the great, dire warnings the biosphere was giving them.

The other thing that was different was the artist.

An anonymous graffiti artist had hit the streets of Manaus. Sides of buildings, or walls, were transformed by art so startling that it slowed traffic, stopped conversations. She heard about all this with half an ear and didn't pay attention until she went running the day before her new project began. White shorts and tank top, her black hair flying loose, along the harborway, through the crowded marketplaces with their bright awnings and clustering tourists, she ran through the world of her species, trying to know it again. She paused at a fruit stand, good-naturedly fending off the flirtations of two handsome youths while she drank deeply of buriti juice. There were ferries as usual on the Rio Negro, and the water was as she remembered it, dark and endless, on its way to its lover's tryst with the Solimões to form the Amazon, the Amazon she had known and loved all her life.

She turned onto a side street and there was a jaguar about to leap at her from the windowless side of a building. She stopped and stared. It was abstract, rendered in fluid, economical brushstrokes, but the artist knew which details were essential; whoever it was had captured the spirit of the beast, the fire in its eyes, what Neruda had called its phosphorescent absence. For a moment, she stood before it, enthralled, the jungle around her again.

After that, she looked for more of the work, asking at street corners and market stalls. The drawings were everywhere—a flight of macaws, a sloth on a tree branch, or an anaconda about to slide off a wall onto the street. Wherever they were, there was a crowd. The three-dimensionality of the drawings was astounding. The ripple of muscle, the fine lines of feathers, the spirit come alive in the eye. She was contemplating a particularly stunning rendering of a sauim-de-coleira that a real monkey would be forgiven for mistaking for its relative, when a car full of university freshmen went by, loudly playing what passed for music among the young (she was getting old and jaded at twenty-seven!). The car stopped with a screech of brakes and the youngsters piled out, silenced, and Fernanda thought in triumph: *This is the answer to the oblivious life. Art so incredible that it brings the jungle back into the city, forces people to remember the nations of animals around us.*

But the next day, looking at the data from her rooftop lab, she was not encouraged. The city's pale roofs were glaring back at the sun. What impact did the city's heat island have on the local climate, compared to the drought-ridden sections of the forest? The drought was mostly due to large-scale effects connected with warming oceans and coastal deforestation, but she was interested in seeing whether smaller-scale effects were also significant and, by that logic, whether small-scale reparations at the right scale and distribution might make some difference. It was still a controversial area of research. She spent days poring over maps on her computer screen, maps generated by massive computer models of climate, local and regional. Could the proposed green-roofing experiment be significant enough to test the models? How to persuade enough people and institutions to install green roofs? Scientists were notoriously bad at public relations. Tia Ana would say they weren't good at other kinds of relationships either, although that wasn't strictly true. Her former advisor, Dr. Aguilar, had been happily married to his wife for half a century.

There was a private home in the Cidade Nova area that was already green-roofed according to the design—native plants, chosen for their high rates of evapotranspiration, mimicking the radiative properties of the rainforest canopies. If they could get enough city officials, celebrities, and so on to see a green roof in action, maybe that would popularize the idea. The home was in a wealthy part of town, and the owner, one Victor Gomes, was connected to the university. She went to see it one hot afternoon.

It was quite wonderful to stand in a rooftop garden with small trees in pots, shrubs in raised beds arranged with a pleasing lack of respect for straight lines, and an exuberance of native creepers that cascaded lushly over the walls. There were fruits and vegetables growing between the shrubs. This was the same model that the restoration team was using in the drought-ridden portions of the Atlantica forest—organically grown native forest species with room for small vegetable gardens and cacao, rubber, and papaya trees, inspired by the *cabruca* movement: small-scale agriculture that fed families and preserved the rain forest. Fernanda looked over the railing and saw that the foliage covered almost the entire side wall of the house. A misting sprayer was at work, and a concealed array of instruments on poles recorded temperature, humidity, and radiative data. It felt much cooler here. Of course, water would be a problem, with the rationing that was being threatened. Damn the rains, why didn't they come?

But she was encouraged. On her way back, her smartphone beeped. There was a message from Claudio that the initial plantings had been completed in the experimental tract in the drought-ridden forest, and that the local villagers were tending to the saplings. The grant would help pay for the care of the trees, and when the trees were older, they would bear fruit and leaves for the people. There were only a few cases worldwide where rain forests had been partially restored—all restoration was partial because you couldn't replicate the kind of biodiversity that happened over thousands of years—but it was astonishing how things would grow if you looked after them in the initial crucial period. Only local people's investment in the project would ensure its success.

Claudio sounded almost happy. Perhaps healing the forest would heal him, too.

The heat wave continued without respite. Fernanda saw people out in the streets staring up at the sky now, looking at the few clouds that formed above as though beseeching them to rain. The river was sullen and slow. Everyday life seemed off—the glitter of the nightlife was faded too and the laughter of the people forced. She spent an evening with her cousins Lila and Natalia at the Bar do Armando, where the literati and glitterati seemed equally subdued. The heat seemed to have gotten to the mysterious artist too, since there had been no new work for several days.

Fernanda found herself making the rounds of the graffiti art in the evenings. There were tourist guides who would take visitors to the exhibits. Small businesses sprouted up near these, selling street food and souvenirs. There was outrage when one store painted out the drawing of macaws on its side walls. Each time Fernanda went to see the artwork, there would be people standing and staring, and cameras clicking, and groups of friends chattering like monkeys in the jungle. Once, she bumped into the man she had sat next to on the plane. He was standing with his briefcase balanced against his legs while he tried to take a picture. She thought of saying hello, apologizing for her coldness on the plane, but he didn't look her way.

She noticed him on three other occasions at different parts of the city, clicking away at the graffiti with his camera. He was photographing the crowds as much as the graffiti. Just a businessman with a hobby, she told herself. But one day, he dropped his briefcase and papers flew open. There were sheets of accounts, tiny neat numbers in rows, a notepad, a notebook computer, a badly wrapped half-eaten sandwich, and a piece of black chalk. The chalk rolled near where Fernanda was standing. The people near the man were solicitously bending over and picking up his things, but he looked around at the ground wildly. Without thinking, Fernanda put her foot over the piece of chalk. She dropped her bag, bent down to retrieve it, and got the chalk in her purse with a fluidity that surprised her. It was hard and oily, not at all like ordinary chalk. There was a loose sheet of paper not far from her that the crowd had missed—she picked it up, hurriedly scribbled an address on it, put her business card and the chalk behind the sheet, and gave the whole thing to the man, looking at him with what she hoped was the innocent gaze of a good citizen. She saw recognition leap into his eyes. Obrigado. He averted his gaze and hurried off.

She spent the rest of the day feeling restless. If only she could reassure him! She wasn't going to give him away. She'd seen the name of the company where he worked on top of the sheets. Now if only . . .

At home, she touched her wristpad, turning on her computer. She scrolled through the news. The tornado in an eastern state of India. Arguments in the United States Senate about the new energy strategy. Floods here, droughts there, the fabric of the biosphere tearing. She thought of the Amazon rain forest, so often called the earth's green lung. Even some tourist guides in the city, taking their mostly North American charges into the jungle, used that term. Did anyone know what those words *meant*? She thought of the predictions of several models, that the great forest, currently a massive carbon dioxide sink, might turn into a *source* of CO_2 if it was stressed enough by drought and tree-cutting. What would happen then? "Hell on earth," she said aloud. She wondered how many people looked up into the sky and imagined, as she did, the invisible river of moisture, the Rios Voadores, roaring in over the

Amazon from the Atlantic coast. It thrilled her to think of it: flying river, the anaconda of the sky, carrying as much water as the Amazon, drawn in and strengthened by the pull of the forest so that it flowed across Brazil, hit the Andes, turned south, bringing rain like a benediction. What had human foolishness done to it that there was drought in the *Amazon*? The green lung had lung cancer. She remembered Claudio's face in the lamplight at camp, speaking passionately about the violated Atlantica forest, the mutilated Mato Grosso, the fact that nearly seven thousand acres of forest were cleared every year.

"What do *you* think—are we a stupid species, or what?" she asked the lizard on the wall. The lizard gave her an enigmatic look.

She rested her head on her arms, thinking of Claudio, his physical presence, his kindness. The work they had been doing had drawn them together—maybe the relationship had never been more than that. And yet . . . the work was important. To know whether such reparations would make a difference was crucial. She was usually so positive, so determined despite the immensity of the task. Perhaps it was the drought, the lack of rain when it should be raining buckets every day, that was making her feel like this. "What shall I do to bring the rain?" she asked aloud. The wristpad beeped, and then there was a kid's voice, distorted by electronic translation software. On the computer screen, he was sitting in a hospital bed, his dark, thin face earnest. His ears stuck out.

Sing, he said. Behind the translation she could hear the kid's real voice speaking an unfamiliar language. He sounded tired. What had he said? *Sing*, he said again. *Sing for the clouds, for the rain.* He started to sing in an astonishingly musical voice. She could tell he was untrained, even though the musical style was unfamiliar. But it was strangely uplifting, this music that would bring the rain. She wanted his voice to go on and on, even though the translation software was off-key. Then, abruptly, the screen went dark.

Where had the kid come from? She had signed on to an experimental social network software device at a friend's urging, but the kid wasn't in her list of contacts. The connections were really bad most of the time. She hoped he was all right.

The next day, the idea of music bringing the rain still haunted her. Of course, such things didn't happen in the real world—as a scientist, she knew better. The vagaries of the climate were still beyond them, and the reparations, the stitches in the green fabric of the jungle, had just begun. The trouble with repairing the forest was that it would never be enough without a million other things happening too, like the work at the polar icecaps, and social movements, ordinary people pledging to make lifestyle changes, and governments passing laws so that children and grandchildren could have a future. The crucial thing was to get net global carbon dioxide emissions down to zero, and that would take the participation of nearly everyone. The days of the Lone Ranger were gone; this was the age of the million heroes.

Still, she opened her saxophone case the next day and caressed the cool metal. It drew her, the music she had put away from her. She hadn't answered her bandmates' e-mails. Now she had to run to the lab—*maybe this evening*, she told her saxophone. *We'll have a date, you and I.*

But she never got to the lab, because her colleague Maria called her, excited. As a result, she went straight to the home in Cidade Nova with the experimental green roof. She went around the house to the side wall, where a crowd had already gathered. People were getting out of cars, and there was even a TV truck. From behind the foliage cascading down the wall of the house peered a jaguar, a gentle jaguar, sleepy even, at peace with the world. Fernanda let out a long breath. The artist had understood her message. The owner of the house, elderly Victor Gomes, was standing with the crowd, his mouth agape.

Within a few hours, the news spread and the crowd swelled until the traffic became a problem. Sensing an opportunity, she talked briefly and urgently to Victor Gomes, and he gave an impromptu tour of the rooftop garden. Suddenly, everyone was talking about green roofs. Imagine, if you went ahead and got one (and there was a grant to help you out with costs if you couldn't afford it), not only did your air-conditioning bills go down, but maybe, just maybe, the artist would come paint the side of your house.

Two days later, there was a gala fund-raiser and awareness event at the Hotel Amazonas. Fernanda played with her old band. She put her lips to her saxophone and into each note she poured her yearning for the rain, for a world restored. The music spilled out, clear as light, smooth as flowing water, and she sensed the crowd shift and move with the sound, with her breath. During a break, when she leaned against the side wall of the stage, watching Santiago's fingers ripple over the piano keyboard, a waiter came up to her and handed her an envelope. Curious, she opened it, and inside was a paper napkin, and an Amazonian butterfly drawn on it, so vivid she half expected it to rise off the napkin. She searched for him in the crowd but there were too many people. Her wristpad beeped. "A butterfly," she whispered, and she felt the wings of change beating in the light-filled air around her.

" . . . Can Cause a Tornado . . ."

" . . . but scientists now know more than they did only five years ago. We will now speak to an expert. . . ." Can you please turn off the TV? I can't bear to see anything more about the storm. . . . It was the same program this morning.

I am too sad to tell this story. You'll have to wait a moment.

I am sad because my grandfather, the professor, died. He was not really my grandfather, but he treated me like I was his own. I called him Dadaji. He let me sleep on the verandah of his bungalow, on a little cot. I felt safe there. I cleaned and cooked for him, and he would talk to me and tell me about all kinds of things. He taught me how to read and write. From the place where I slept, I could look down a low incline to the village, my village.

Are you translating this into English? Does that mean I'll be famous all over India?

I want to help my village. I want people to know about it, even though it is only a Harijan basti sitting on stony ground. I want to make sure the world knows that we did something good.

Let me tell you about my village. The river is many hours' walk from us, but the floods are getting worse. Last year during the monsoons, the water came into the huts and the fields and drowned everything except what we could carry. The ground where the village sits is very stony, and things don't grow well. We don't have fields of our own, not really. We are *doms*—most of us work in town, or for the big Rajput village—Songaon— two miles away. We do all the dirty work—sweeping and cleaning privies, that sort of thing. Me, I am lucky because the professor employs me and takes care of me and treats me as though I were not a *dom*. He doesn't observe caste even though he is a Rajput himself—he says it is already dying out in the towns and cities. He says the government laws protect people like us, but I don't know about those things because if the Rajputs are angry, then they can do what they like to us and nobody can stop them. But the professor, he is a different kind of person—a *devata*. He even has me cook his food, and pats my head when I do my lessons well— and when there is a festival, we share a plate of sweets together.

See this thing I am wearing around my wrist, like a watch? The professor gave it to me. He has been teaching me the computer and this thing makes it come on and we can see and talk to people from around the world. Once, I spoke to a man all the way in Chennai—it was very exciting. It was really like magic, because the man didn't know Bhojpuri or Hindi and the computer translated his words and mine so we could both understand. The translator voices were funny. Mine didn't sound like me at all.

What I love most is music. In the early morning when the mist lies on the river, the first thing I hear is the birds in the bougainvillea bush. When I bring the tea out on the verandah and we have drunk the first cup, the professor gives me his tanpura to tune. Then he starts to sing *Bhairav*, which is a morning raga. Listening to him, I feel as though I am climbing up and down mountain ranges of mist and cloud. I feel I could fly. I sing with him, as though my voice is a shadow following his voice. He tells me I have a good ear. It isn't the same kind of singing as in the movies—it is something deeper that calls to your soul. When I told the professor that, he looked pleased and said that good music makes poets of us. I never thought that just anybody could be a poet.

From his house, I can see all the way to the river far beyond the village. In the last few years, we have either had drought or flood. This year seems to be a dry year. Always there is some difficulty we have to deal with. But we have been changing too, ever since the professor came and began to live in his house. He has problems with his sons; they don't get along, so he lives alone except for me. He and some other people have been working with our basti. The other people are also dalits like us, but they can read and write, and they know how to make the government give them their rights. They have traveled all over the country, telling villages like ours that the climate is changing, and we must change too, or we won't survive. So, now we have a village panchayat, and there are three women and two men who speak for all of us. You see, new times are coming, difficult times, when Dharti Mai herself is against us because instead of treating her like a mother, human beings have treated her like a slave. Most of those people who did this are in America and places like that, but they are here too, in the big cities. It is strange because at first, we used to think places like that were the best in the world, because of what we saw on TV, but the professor explained that living like that, with no regard for Dharti Mai, comes with costs. Why doesn't Dharti Mai punish *them*, then? I asked him that once. Why is she punishing us poor people, who have done nothing to cause the problem? The professor sighed and said that Dharti Mai was punishing everyone. So, people ask him all the time, what can we do? This makes the professor happy because he says that earlier most people in our basti just accepted their lot—after all, for thousands of years, it has been our lot to suffer. He is pleased because now we want to do something to save ourselves and make the world better. If all those rich, upper-caste people and all the *goras* have been wrong all this time about how they should live, maybe they're wrong about us, too. Maybe our time has come.

But Bojhu kaku—he's the one who took me in when my parents died—he says what's the good in pointing fingers? Even the *goras* are changing how they live. The question is what can we do to heal Dharti Mai? How can we help each other survive the terrible times that are upon us? So, in the village, people take turns being lookouts when there is a bad weather forecast, and they help each other more, and they've got a teacher to come twice a week to teach them how to read and write. They sent Barki kaki off to the town to be trained by a doctor—she's the midwife—so that she can help us all be healthier. You should have seen her when she came back, she was so proud—she got to see how they work in the big hospital and she came back with pink soap for everyone. We now have our own hand pump and don't have to drink river water. All this is because of the professor, and because of people like Bojhu kaku, and Barki kaki—and Dulari mai, even though most people are scared of her temper. The professor and I are treated like royal guests whenever we go to visit. The professor studies people—anthropology—and even though he is retired, he hasn't stopped. He goes around all the local villages, tap-tapping with his cane—he's got a bad leg—and he tells people about the world.

Which is how we know about how the world is getting hotter, and even the *goras* are burning up in their big cities with all those cars and TVs. But that is not all. You know there is a big coal-mining company that wants to buy all the land around us? The professor gets angry whenever the coal company is mentioned, so angry he can hardly get a word out. It is burning coal and oil that is making the world hotter, and Dharti Mai so angry with us. He says the government, instead of finding ways to use other things, is mining more coal and making more coal plants so that the people in the big cities can have electricity and cars and TVs, which warm the world even more. It sounds to me like when Dhakkan kaka gets drunk, he wants to keep on drinking. So, maybe the way the rich people of the world live is like a sickness where they can't make themselves stop. Also, most people in my village don't want to give up their ancestral land for the coal company, small and poor and stony though it might be, even though the government has promised compensation. That tiny piece of earth is all we have. But some of the young men think that the money would be good, and they can go to the big city and make it big. The professor told them that there are already too many people trying to make it in the city, but behind his back, they grumble and talk about the good life they could have. It's mostly people like Jhingur kaka's older son, who is a malcontent. The Rajput village—Songaon—doesn't like the coal-mining idea either, and the professor persuaded them to let us join a protest delegation in the town, although we had to keep our distance behind them. The professor sat with us and argued against the coal company from the back. You should have seen how furious the Rajputs were! They respect him for his education and his caste, even though he doesn't keep caste, but his ways upset them. Later, when we were walking back, one of them told him, "If you weren't an old man, and learned too, I would take my stick to you for the example you are setting to our children." I know, because I heard him. It was Ranbir Singh. He is the one with the biggest mustache, and the biggest, stoutest sticks, and the biggest temper. His mood changes so quickly, everyone is afraid of him. He even has guns. The professor just said quietly that if Ranbir Singh did that with every Rajput in the country who had broken caste, he would run out of sticks pretty quickly.

The day it all happened, in the morning, we were listening to the classical program on the radio because the professor wanted to hear a new *bandish* that was playing. There were clouds in the sky but no sign of rain. Just then we heard a roaring sound. The radio crackled and the announcer said something about an unusual cloud formation. The sound of the wind became so strong that we couldn't hear the radio. The sky became dark, even though over the river, it was still light. There was a tapping sound over our heads: hail! I was very excited. Hail has fallen only once in my village in my lifetime. I ran down the verandah steps to collect some, and then I saw the storm.

I had never seen anything like it. I saw a whirling monster towering in the fields behind the house, like a top spun out of clouds and wind. The professor looked alarmed. He said he had heard of things like this in other lands, and that it was called a *tur-nado*. He said we would be all right in a pukka house like his, but then he stared out into the distance toward my village. People were coming out of their homes and getting ready to walk to Songaon or the town for the long day of work.

"Bhola," he said to me, "I am going to check on the computer what we should do. Get ready to run down to the village and warn people."

"Dadaji, will you be all right?" He's an old man, and lame, too. But he pushed me impatiently off, saying of course he would be fine. That's the last thing he said to me.

I ran down toward the village. The wind was strong, and I saw a crow in the sky struggling to keep its wings under control. It swooped down in a big arc and came right at me, flapping its wings, and hit me in the stomach. I grabbed it and held it to my chest—a full-grown crow. I thought it was dead, but I couldn't just throw it away. So I held it to my chest and I ran.

The sky darkened and the wind howled in my ears. I looked behind me at the house. The tur-nado was over it. The verandah was so dark, I couldn't see the professor. I saw the lit screen of the computer disappearing as he went into the house. Above us, the tur-nado looked like a monster. I have never been so scared. Then my wrist strap beeped. A woman's voice said out of nowhere, "Find low ground, low ground," and "Run! Run!" I wanted to see if the professor was all right, but he had told me to warn the village. So, I ran.

There is a narrow ravine not far from the village. Old people say that it is a crack that opened in the earth during an earthquake. In the monsoons it fills with water, but right now it is dry, full of thorny bushes and rocks. The goats like it there. That was the only low place I could think of. I began to shout as I got closer, yelling to people to stop gawking and trying to lead them to the ravine. I couldn't hear my own voice because of the wind, but Dulari mai started to scream at people and gather them and point them to the ravine. Everyone worked quickly; they are afraid of her temper. There was even someone carrying Joti ma, old Gobind-kaka's mother, on his back, the terrified children were all holding hands, some were carrying the babies. Behind me, the tur-nado danced across the fields, ripping up everything in its path. It picked its way across the land. I saw people rushing toward the ravine, some carrying bundles with them. There was a lot of shouting but everyone was moving. I thought: *I'm not needed here; I could have stayed with the professor.* I thought I should see if I could go around the tur-nado and get to his house. I made my way back across the fields, keeping a careful eye on the storm.

When I was halfway there, I saw the children. It was Ranbir Singh's younger daughter and son, returning from school on the footpath through the fields. Usually someone takes them from Songaon to the town and back by bicycle, but they were walking home. She is older than me, maybe fourteen, and he is only about five years old. Her father once had Bojhu kaku's son beaten because he said he—Kankariya bhai—dared to raise his eyes and look at his daughter. Before I was born, there was trouble that nobody talks about and the Rajputs came and burned down some of our huts, and three people died. That's what I mean when I say they can do anything to us. I hesitated, because if I said anything to the children they didn't like, their father could have me thrashed and the village burned down.

The children looked scared. The girl was trying to use her mobile but she gave up and put it in her schoolbag, looking upset. They looked at me and looked away, and the older sister said to the boy, "Come," urgently, and pulled on his arm. He was tired and about to cry.

I thought: *Why should I try to help them?* But I pointed to the tur-nado raging behind us:

"Sister, that is a bad *toofan*. The professor told me we have to hide. We are all at the ravine near my basti. I can take you there."

I took extra care to be polite. I didn't want her to accuse us later on and get the whole village in trouble. She hesitated. The little boy said, "Why are you holding a dead crow?"

The girl came to a decision. She said, "Show me where this place is."

They followed me. There were leaves and branches flying around, and I saw the thatched roof lift off a hut and vanish. A brick came hurtling through the air and missed us by two spans of my hand. I didn't dare look back—we were racing over the fields. The little boy stumbled, and the girl picked him up. Panting, she followed me. It would have been faster if I'd carried the child, but she wasn't going to let a *dom* boy touch her brother. Then she half stumbled. She said, "*Wait!*" I almost didn't hear her but when I looked back, she was crying. She thrust her brother at me. Her breath was coming in sobs. He was crying too.

"You want me to carry him? Your father will break my neck!"

She was wailing and shaking her head, and the tur-nado was very close, so I put the child on one hip and handed her the still-warm body of the crow.

"I'm not going to hold that," she said, scowling.

"Then take your brother back," I said, losing my temper. "This crow is a *vahan* of Shani Deva, and we must not disrespect it. Don't you keep pigeons?"

She wrinkled her nose but took the crow in her dupatta, and we ran the rest of the way until we were at the ravine.

It was dark inside, because the low, thorny bushes growing on the top edges of the ravine blocked the sky. Wind screamed over our heads and we heard the most terrible sounds, as though the world was being torn apart.

And then silence.

We all looked at each other. Bojhu kaku and the others saw that I was holding Ranbir Singh's son in my arms, and his daughter was standing next to me, holding the body of a crow in her dupatta, her eyes wide with fear.

"Bhola, what have you done?" someone said. Maybe it was Barki kaki. People gasped.

"I couldn't leave them to die," I said. The boy wriggled out of my grasp and went to his sister. She handed me the crow and held her brother close. Tears ran down her face.

Bojhu kaku said to the girl, "We will see you home. Come, there is nothing to be scared of."

So, the children were escorted to Songaon by the crowd. If Bojhu kaku went by himself, he might have to bear the brunt of Ranbir Singh's mood. There was no telling whether he'd be grateful or angry. So Barki kaki said she would go, and then Dulari Mai (and we had to tell her no because she would insult even the gods if she lost her temper, and where would we all be then?). So, about fifteen people went.

We climbed out of the ravine. The village was smashed flat. There were pots and pans scattered about the fields, and bricks also. The bargad tree that has stood at the crossing on the way to Songaon for two hundred years was completely uprooted. The pathway was covered with big tree branches. Our homes were gone. You might say, *What's a mud-and-thatch house? It is nothing.* But to a poor person, it is home. Our hands shape it; our hands weave the *bhusa*. It is where our hopes live. When you have very little, everything you have becomes more precious. We wept and, in the same breath, we thanked the gods for sparing our lives.

I didn't go with them. My duty was to my Dadaji now, and I had a terrible fear growing inside me. I went to the house on the hill. Midway, the crow stirred in my arms, and I saw that it was only stunned, not dead. I stopped in the field and found a pocket of moisture where some hail-stones had fallen, and let a few drops trail from my fingers into its throat. Suddenly, it struggled and flapped its wings. I opened my hands and it flew. It was unsteady at first, but it got stronger as it flew, making two big circles over my head before it went off. Then I went up to what was left of the house.

The windows and doors were gone, and I could see the sky through the roof. Two walls were down. I thought, *This is a* pukka *house, how could this have happened? How could brick and mortar come down like this?* There was dust in the air. It made me cough. There were pages and pages torn from his books, fallen everywhere like leaves. I saw that his computer had fallen under his desk and was all right. Bricks fell as I walked around. I fell too, and broke my arm, and hurt my leg. That's why I'm in hospital.

I was the one who found him. He was near the drawing room window, under a pile of bricks.

He was my grandfather, no matter what anyone says about caste and blood. He gave me everything I have—he was like a god to me. I would have given my life for him, but instead, he is the one who is gone. He said I would grow up to be a learner and a singer—someone who could change the world. A *dom* boy like me—nobody has ever told me such things. I'm telling you, he was my Dadaji; I don't care what anyone says.

His sons came for his body. I'm not allowed to be there for the last rites. But I know, and he knows, that I should be there. He used to tell me that if you look at things on the surface, you don't know their true nature. You also have to look with your inner eye. He looked at me with his inner eye. He was my Dadaji and he's gone.

That's his computer on the table. His sons didn't ask about it.

Nobody has come to see me and I am scared.

What is that you say? Half of Songaon is destroyed? That is a terrible thing. Seven people dead!

I am glad Ranbir Singh's children gave a good account of us. It is strange for him to be in our debt.

Earlier today, there was a TV program about the tur-nado. They interviewed an expert. He said that although a tur-nado is strong, it is also delicate. I think I know what he means. Before it is born, the tur-nado is a confusion of cloud and wind. It takes only a little touch here and there to turn the cloud and wind into a monster that can destroy houses. Even once it is made, you can't tell where it is going to go, because it is

so delicate a thing that maybe one leaf on one tree might persuade it to go this way instead of that. Or one breath from one sleeping farmhand in the field.

When I leave the hospital, I'm going to help rebuild my village. And I'm going to collect all the pages of Dadaji's books that are scattered all over the fields. I imagine I will find the thoughts of a scientist or philosopher, or the speeches of a poet, stuck in a tree's branches, or blowing in the wind with the dust. I will pick up every page I find and put it together.

I have to find out how I can keep learning. Dadaji was going to teach me so that I could be a learned man like him when I grow up. How is it possible for a tur-nado to be so powerful and so delicate at the same time? How do we tell Dharti Mai we are sorry? How do we stop the mining company that wants to take our land? Please print that in your newspaper—we cannot let them mine and burn more coal, because that is destroying the world. Please tell the big people in the cities like Delhi and in faraway places like America. They won't care about someone like me, but ask them if they care about their own children. I saw just yesterday that it is not just the poor who will suffer in this new world they are making. Tell them to stop.

I have been seeing crows at the window all afternoon. They land on the sill and caw. The orderly says Shani Deva has shown me grace because of the crow I saved. Everyone fears Shani Deva because he brings us difficult times. But crows remember, and they tell each other who is a friend, and maybe the crows will help us. It's their world, too.

I'm very tired. In one day, I lost my grandfather, hid my people from the tur-nado, saved two Rajput children, and became a friend of crows.

Something strange happened after dinner. I was half asleep. I heard a woman saying very sadly, "What shall I do to bring the rain?" Then I saw it wasn't a dream, because there was this young woman on the computer screen, a foreigner. I thought she must be one of the people who used to talk to the professor. She looked sad and tired. I told her, "You have to

sing to the clouds. You have to sing the rain down." Between the radio and my Dadaji's lessons, I have learned a little of the raga—*Malhaar*, the rain-calling raga. I sang a line or two for her before the connection broke.

Dadaji told me once that sound is just a tremble in the air. A song is a tremble that goes from the soul into the air, and thus to the eardrums of the world. The tur-nado is a disturbance of the air, but it is like an earth-quake. Perhaps it is the song of the troubled earth, our mother Dharti Mai. One day, I will compose a song to soothe her.

. . . In Texas . . .

. . . It was the kind of day Dorothy Cartwright's husband wouldn't have allowed. Wasn't it just a year and a half ago he'd gotten so mad at the heat wave at Christmastime that he'd cranked up the air conditioning until she had to go find a sweater? But they'd had the traditional Christmas evening fire in the fireplace, and weather be damned. It was nowhere near Christmas day, being March, but it was hotter than it should be, the kind of day when Rob would have had the AC going and the windows closed. Closed houses always made her feel claustrophobic, no matter that her old home had been over four thousand square feet—just the two of them after their son, Matt, grew up and left home. But now Rob was dead of a heart attack more than a year ago, and Dorothy lived in a little two-room apartment in an assisted-living facility. She could open the windows if she felt like it. She did so, and turned on the fans, and checked the cup-cakes baking in the oven. There was a cool breeze, no more than a breath. The big magnolia tree in the front lawn made a shade so deep, you could be forgiven for thinking evening had come early. She arranged the chairs in the living room for the fifth time and glanced at the clock. Fifteen minutes and they would be here.

As she was taking the cupcakes out, the phone rang. She nearly dropped

LOOSED UPON THE WORLD

the tray. Shaking, she set it on the counter and picked up the phone. It was Kevin.

"Gramma! Guess where your favorite grandson's calling from?"

He was cheerful in the faked way he had when he was upset. Which meant—

"I'm in rehab, and this time, I'm going to quit for good."

"Of course, hon," she said. Who could believe the kid when he'd been in and out of rehab six times in two years? She remembered Rob's cold fury the last time the boy had been over. Her grandson was adrift, and she was helpless and useless. The other day, she'd watched a show on PBS about early humans and how the human race wouldn't have survived without old people, other people than the parents, to help raise the young and transmit the knowledge of earlier generations. Grandmothers in particular were important. That was all very well, but in this day of books and computers and all, who needed grandmothers? They lived in retirement homes or in huge, echoing houses, at the periphery of society, distracting themselves, waiting for death. Times had changed. Kevin was beyond anyone's help. She gripped the edge of the counter with her free hand. An ache shot through her chest. She felt a momentary dizziness.

"I'll send you some cupcakes," she said. All she had been able to do for the people she loved was to offer them food, as though the trouble in the world could be taken away by sugar and butter and chocolate. She said good-bye, feeling hopeless.

He had sent her an orange wristlet, rather pretty. It had jewel-like white buttons on it that allowed her to communicate with her new notebook computer (a gift from her son) with a touch. She looked at it and thought how nice Kevin was to get her a present. She touched the button and her notebook computer lit up, and there was an image of a woman in a diving suit suspended in murky blue water, her arms working, and a reedy electronic voice like a cartoon character saying something about cold arctic waters and repeating a name, Dr. Irene Ariak, Irene Ariak. Surely she had heard the name in some show or other. A scientist working in the Arctic. What a dangerous thing to do, to go up there in the cold and dark. "Bless you and be careful up there; I'm praying for you," she said. The cartoon voice said, *Mrs. Cartwright, thank you!* And the screen went blank. Dorothy wondered if she'd heard right. Well, this was a new world, to be sure.

The doorbell rang as she was setting the cupcakes on a plate. Patting her hair, glancing at the small oval mirror over by the little dining table (her lipstick was just right), she went to the door.

There they all were, smiling. Rita, with her defiantly undyed white hair in a braid tied with rainbow-colored ribbons (Rob would have thought them loud), said, "How nice of you to host the meeting, Dorothy!" and planted herself in the comfortable armchair. The others, Mary-Ann, Gerta, Lawrence, Brad, Eva, and three women she didn't know, crowded into the small living room. Dorothy handed around cupcakes and poured tea and coffee and felt as awkward as a new wife hosting her first dinner party. She scolded herself: *Now, then, you've known these people for eight months, and you've hosted more parties in your life than you can remember!* This was about reinventing herself. Stretching outside her comfort zone, learning new things. Rob would have never allowed these people in their house—there was something not done about their passionate intensity. "Aging hippies," Rob would have said. He would have told her what was wrong with each of them, and she would never have invited them again. Once she'd had a local mothers' group over for tea; Rob came home early. He'd been pleasant enough greeting them and had gone upstairs. The women were upset about the firing of the principal at the local elementary school, and one of them had raised her voice emphatically, making her point. Rob had banged the bedroom door so hard upstairs that the reverberation made the windows rattle. She'd never invited those women over again.

She sat down and let the conversation swirl around her, trying to ignore the tightness in her chest. Keeping up the smile was becoming difficult.

"Well," Rita said, "Our energy-saving campaign has been successful beyond anything we expected. Management has stopped grumbling. We've saved them $14,504 in energy bills annually!"

"New light bulbs and more insulation, and cranking down the AC so it isn't freezing in the middle of summer, and one set of solar panels . . . Who'd a' thought it?"

"Our see-oh-two emissions are down by . . . let's see . . . 18 percent . . ."

"Multiply individual actions by millions or billions, and you're looking at real global difference . . ."

It was one of the new women, a blonde with intense blue eyes. Not from the apartment complex. Dorothy had already forgotten her name. Now the woman was smiling at her a little uncertainly.

"Mrs. Cartwright, we need to recruit people for the protest. The pipeline is coming to us. Janna Helmholtz's land is being *violated*—they got a court order to cut a corridor through her woods to bring the oil pipes through, and we're going to protest. Can we count on you?"

"Yes, yes, of course," Dorothy said, feeling foolish. What had she agreed to?

". . . they say fracking for shale oil and gas is going to reduce carbon dioxide emissions, but can you believe they base that on completely ignoring the methane emissions from the fracking?"

"Methane is twenty times worse than see-oh-two . . . cooking the planet . . ."

"My objection to fracking is entirely on another plane—see, less coal burned here means coal prices fall, and it gets exported elsewhere, so coal usage will go up somewhere else if fracking happens here in the United States—idiots don't understand the meaning of 'global' . . ."

"Yes, but there's also the issue, I told him that, I told him just because you work for Texas O&G, try to have an open mind, for fuck's sake—I told him, think about switching to green energy. Fracking for oil and gas just means putting off what we need to do. Like, you know, you need to fucking quit, not go from cocaine to . . . to meth!"

Rob wouldn't approve of the f-word, either. Dorothy told herself to stop thinking about Rob. Rob used the f-word as much as he liked, but he couldn't stand women swearing. Generally, he said that meant that either they were common or they needed a good lay. *Shut up about Rob,* she told herself.

"Well, Mrs. Cartwright?"

She cleared her throat. What had they been talking about?

"I don't know," she said. What could she do? Her life behind her . . . She felt a sudden wave of utter misery.

"What can I do? I'm not trained . . ."

"Dorothy, you don't need training for this," Rita said, in her proselytizing voice. Rita was a You-nitarian You-niversalist, as Eva had once said in mincing tones—*Rita, there's so much You in UU; where's the room for God?* They'd had quite a spat about it, but they stayed friends. Rob had always said you could only be friends with people who thought like you.

"Honey, there are retired people all over the country like you and me who care about the world we are leaving our grandchildren—"

"—hell, everyone thinks we are old fogies, useless relics, and I say we are a totally untapped resource, a revolution waiting to happen. . . ."

Lawrence ("not Larry") nodded. "We have experience, and knowledge of human nature—Dorothy, just by being who you are you can make a difference—"

She found herself signing up to recruit five people and be at the meeting place today in three hours. Janna Helmholtz had called to say the earthmovers were going to be on her property ripping up the trees her granddaddy had planted and she needed them to be there. Three hours! (*Well, the fracking company doesn't wait at our convenience, honey. Besides, imagine if you were in the middle of the workday; you wouldn't be able to make it. But we have the time and the determination! So be there or be a quadrilateral!* This from Eva, retired math teacher at Pine Tree Elementary.)

After they had all left, Dorothy found herself putting the dirty dishes by the sink in a mood of despair. How was she going to go to wing five and recruit five people? She couldn't imagine being able to convince anyone. Talking to people was difficult anyway, especially when they didn't wear their hearing aids or were taking a nap. She heard Rob's voice: *You're being a fool, Dottie. We Cartwrights don't get into other people's business. Do you really think you can make a difference?*

It was hard to remember that she had been second valedictorian at her school, and that she had got into a prestigious college and been on a debating team. After she met Rob—he'd chased and flattered her relentlessly—she had seen the possibility of another life, the kind that she'd only glimpsed through the iron lattice gates of rich acquaintances— a life of going to theater and art museums and raising children to send off to the best schools. Who in the world would love her like Rob? She remembered when they were both young, and he had lost his first job, how much he'd looked up to her, needed her. She began to scrub the baking tray, thinking of Rob's love for her cooking. He'd always praised her culinary skills to his business friends whenever there was a party. She sighed. He would not have been pleased about her involvement with this cause. But she'd given her word—what had made her agree to talk to five strangers? She wiped her sudsy hands absently on the towel, and her wristlet beeped. "I'm no use to anyone," she said aloud. "I don't know what to do." And she heard a voice from the little computer on the mantelpiece say, with the utmost conviction, "Something good will happen to you today." Very clear English, but a strange accent. She went and picked up the computer but the screen had gone dark.

She rearranged her hair and put on fresh lipstick and went deter- minedly down the hall to wing five. There were several people in the lounge. She told herself *second valedictorian* and made herself smile and say hello. By the end of an hour, she had recruited eight people. Would have been nine if Molly hadn't had her annual physical that afternoon. *Damn, you're good*, Rita said, when she called and told her, and Dorothy thought, with pleased surprise, *Yes*.

In an hour, they were loading into cars, driving over the long, empty roads soon to be filled with rush-hour traffic, over to Janna's place. Janna had a big house on a hundred acres, and there was already a crowd in the middle of a field, and at least half a dozen cars, and my goodness, was that a TV truck? There was Janna, with a new perm and her big smile, waving to the newcomers walking over to her. The sun was hot. Along one side of the field ran a dark line of woodlands, presumably the place where the pipeline was going through. Dorothy walked over determinedly, ignoring the odd breathlessness that caught her at moments, gritting her teeth, closing her ears against Rob's voice. *That woman should never wear shorts, her legs are too fat, and that one, dressed like a slut, tells you what she wants. These wannabe hippies are a laugh. Can barely walk and they want to change the world!* Well, that bit was true of some of the protesters, old ladies with walkers and even a man in a wheelchair. There was Rita, high-fiving him. Dorothy found herself standing at the edge of the crowd, grateful for her hat. There were the earthmovers roaring up in front of them. A young man at the helm of each, one of them grinning, the other one nervous. The sun glinted off the windshields.

A black woman was making a speech. Eva nudged Dorothy and whispered, "Myra Jackson, professor over at the university."

"It's not just about land," the woman said. "Global warming is real, and we have to do something about it now, not tomorrow. Shale gas only puts off what we really need, which is green energy, and a new alternative energy–based economy. Germany's already ahead of us in solar energy. We need a Marshall Plan for the ecological-economic crisis!"

There were cheers.

Now they could hear police sirens getting louder. The protesters began to shout slogans. Dorothy's heart began to beat thunderously in her ears. What had she gotten herself into?

There was Janna, yelling above the noise. "Y'all pack up your equipment and get outta here; we're not gonna let you clear my family's woods! No more fracking!"

There were signs now going up, and cameras flashing, and people yelling, "Don't frack Texas!" and the big yellow machines kept coming, although slowly. The professor woman jumped off the table—she was too young and fit to be one of the oldies—and someone moved the table away. The cops arrived, waving the protesters to the side so that the machinery could get to the trees. The crowd shifted and surged without backing away. The man in the wheelchair waved his stick at a policeman and yelled something. Handcuffs clicked, cameras rolled. The giant machines kept inching forward. Dorothy found herself ignored by everyone, even the cops. She felt the cool air of the woods at her back through her thin cotton dress. She was just in front of one of the machines. She stared at the young man in the driver's seat. He looked like Kevin. She wondered why his face was set—goodness, the boy was nervous! She thought of him suddenly as a sacrifice, like all the young men in her life, her son gone to the army, returned a silent shadow of his former self, her grandson beset by demons, all that youth and strength turned wrong. She thought of the poor woman out in the bottom of the ocean in the Arctic trying to save the world so that her grandchild, Dorothy's grandchild, and all, everyone's grandchild could live in the world. And she thought how cruel the world that makes young men hold the guns against their own temples, the knives at their own throats, so that their own hands poison the earth and its creatures that the good Lord made—and Rob said in her mind, *Dottie, you're talking like a fool*—and something broke inside her.

She was standing with a Tupperware box of cupcakes—stupidly, she waved it in front of the boy like an offering. She walked toward him, her own face set, as though she could save him, as though she, Dorothy Cartwright, BA, MRS, could do anything. The kid's eyes went wide, and he waved frantically at her, and she turned around and saw the great yellow arm of the other machine swing, and the horrified face of the other man, who saw her only at the last minute—then it hit her shoulder, and the side of her head, and then she was falling, and cupcakes falling everywhere.

She awoke in the hospital. The light was too bright. Someone drew the curtains across the window. She could hear some kind of hubbub outside her door. She slept.

Hours later, she woke feeling better. A lantern-jawed doctor who looked like a very tired Clint Eastwood told her she had a mild concussion and a cracked bone in her shoulder. The man at the bulldozer had turned the thing off just in time; it was the momentum that had gotten her. Otherwise, she might be dead. She was really lucky. All the scans were clear, but they were going to keep her overnight for observation. After that, six weeks of rest for her shoulder.

"I can see you're a wild young rebel, Mrs. Cartwright, but promise me you won't be up to those shenanigans for a while," he said, smiling.

She told him, smiling back, surprising herself, "You do your job; I'll do mine."

Her son called. Matt was driving over the next day. He sounded more bemused than anything. She thought with satisfaction that she had finally managed to surprise someone.

And then Molly was there, praising her like she had done something heroic.

"Wish I could have been there," she said wistfully. "Rita and Eva are in jail, and that black professor too, and about ten other people. They're probably going to charge you as soon as you are well."

Dorothy couldn't imagine going to jail—but Molly made it sound like it was the thing to do. Well, it had been some day. She decided not to worry. Over the doctor's objections, she let two journalists interview her and take pictures. Her mother used to call her a chatterbox, a trait that had disappeared with time and Rob, and now she couldn't stop talking.

"When my husband was still alive," she said, "he used to tell me how impractical it was to worry about the environment. Practical people run the economy, make sure things work. That attitude, combined with greed, has ruined the earth to a degree that threatens our grandchildren. I'm only a housewife, but I know that we need good, fresh air to breathe, and trees to grow, and we need the wild things around us. As a grandmother, I can't think of one single grandparent who wouldn't want to do the best for their grandchildren. That's why I believe we need to protect what the good Lord gave us, this blessed Earth, else how can we live? And what's more practical than that?"

After they had all gone, in the silence of the room, she lay back against the pillows, spent. An incredulity rose in her. What had she done? The whole day she had been putting herself forward, Rob would say. The elation subsided. She hid her face in the pillows.

Then the phone rang. This time it was Kevin.

"Gramma! I saw you on TV! You kicked ass!"

She laughed. It was so very nice of him to call. They talked for half an hour, until the nurse came and frowned at her.

"Gramma, I'm going to get clean this time," Kevin said. Dorothy took a deep breath.

"Kev, soon as they let me out of here, I'm going to come see you. This time, you will get clean, love. You've got a life to live."

And so do I, she thought after she hung up.

Lying back in the darkened room, she saw from the digital clock on the side table that it was nearly midnight on March 16. Heavens, no wonder Rob had been haunting her all day—it was his birthday! And she had forgotten. Well, at least she had baked his favorite cupcakes. She thought about how her life had changed in one day, and the work left to be done. It wasn't going to be easy, and she had no illusions that she was any kind of heroine, or that her few minutes of fame were going to lead to any major changes. But Molly had told her that the phone lines of No Fracking Texas were swamped with calls from other assisted-living facilities and retired people's associations. It seemed the old ones, the forgotten ones, were coming out of the woodwork. In times gone by, the old were the ones to whom the young turned for advice. Now the old had to bear responsibility for ruining the earth, but they also, by the same logic, bore the responsibility for setting things right. The press was calling it the Suspender Revolution. The Retirees' Spring. Kind of disrespectful, but they'd show them. And she, Dorothy Cartwright, had helped it come about. *Viva la revolución*, and poor Rob, rest in peace, and happy birthday.

The End

The Story Begins

Or does it end here?

It ends, the young man thinks, as he climbs the last mountain, emerging into the last alpine valley. It ends with his own life winding down as he climbs to the roof of the world. The strength that has allowed him to leave the busy streets of Shanghai and journey to this remote place in the Himalayas is like the sudden flaring of the moth caught in the flame. Lately, he's had a vision of simply lying down in the tall green meadow grass and falling asleep, and feeling the grass stalks growing through his body, a thousand tiny piercings, until he is nothing but a husk.

He pauses to catch breath against the rocky wall of the cliff. His breath forms clouds of condensation in the cold air. His rucksack feels heavier now. He can't remember when he last ate. Probably at the village he left in the morning. He takes out a flask of water, drinks, and finds a small bag with trail mix and walks again.

When he emerges from the narrow pass, he finds himself at a vertiginous height. Below him, lost in mist and distance, is a rocky, arid valley through which a silver river winds. On the other side, the mountains are gaunt and bare, the white tongues of melting glaciers high on the slopes. But the place he seeks is immediately to his right, where the path leads. The stone facade of the monastery comes into view, a rocky aerie impossible to conceive of—how could anyone build here, halfway up to the sky?—but it is solid, it is there. So, he walks on, up the narrow path, to the great flight of steps. The tiers of windows above him are empty, and there is an enormous hole in the roof of the entrance hall, through which he can see a lammergeier circling high in the blue sky. Could it be that the last refuge is destroyed after all? He had dreamed of a great university hidden deep in the Himalayas, a place where people like him could gather to weave the web that would save the dying world. He had dreamed of its destruction too, at the hands of greed and power. Can it have happened already?

Wearily, he sinks down on the dusty floor at the top of the steps. In the silence he hears his own breath coming fast and the faint trickle of water in the distance. He is conscious of being watched.

A man is standing on a fallen column. He is tall, dressed in rough black robes. There is some kind of small animal on his shoulder, brown, with a long, bushy tail—a squirrel, perhaps, or a mongoose?

Yuan bows, clears his throat.

"I dreamed of this place," he says in English, hoping the monk can understand him. "I came here to try to do something before I die. But it's too late, I see."

The monk gestures to him, and Yuan stumbles over broken pieces of stone, follows him around a corner into a small, high courtyard open to sun and sky.

"Sit," the monk says, indicating a low wooden seat. There is tea in a black kettle, steaming over a small fire. "Tell me about your dream of this place." There is white stubble on his shaven chin, and deep lines are etched on the brown face. His English is fluent, with an accent that is vaguely familiar. Yuan clears his throat, speaks.

"It was a monastery first, then a university. It was a place for those who sought to understand the world in a new way and to bring about its resurrection. I saw the humblest people come here to share what they knew, and the learned ones listened. It didn't have the quietude of the monastery it had once been—at every corner, in every gathering, I heard arguments and disagreements, but true peace is dynamic, not static, and rests on a thousand quarrels.

"It wasn't a secret, although not many people knew about it. It was rumor and it was real, because at the university where I studied in Shanghai, there was a woman—a scientist from Nigeria—who spoke of this place. She came and taught for five days and nights. After that, we were all changed. I got a new idea, and even though I was dying, I made sure it came to light. Then I thought I needed to find her, my teacher, and this place. Here and there I heard rumors that it had been destroyed— because there are people who will try to hasten the end of the world so they can make a profit. And this place stood in their way.

"It was the hope of the world. I heard that there were branches in a few other places. There was an idea about connecting it through small-world architecture to webs of information, webs of knowledge and people, to generate new ideas and, through redundancy, ensure their survival. If it hadn't been destroyed before that hope was made real, its disappearance may not have mattered so much."

His voice fades as he slumps to the ground. The monk gathers him up and carries him effortlessly through long corridors into a room of stone, where there is a rough bed. He wakes from his faint to see the wild creature sitting on a wooden stool by the bed, staring at him with dark, round eyes. The monk helps him up so he can sip hot yak-butter tea, rich and aromatic. Then Yuan sleeps.

Over five days and nights they talk, the monk and Yuan, sometimes in this room with its narrow windows, sometimes in the high, sunny courtyard.

"This place was destroyed in an avalanche," the monk tells him, pointing to the mountain behind them, from the high spur on which the monastery perches. "The glacier melted and brought down half the mountain with it. It rained boulders. Many were killed, and the place abandoned. I live here alone, except for the odd scientific team that comes to study the glacier."

Yuan is silent. So much for the university that would save the world. But how could his dreams be so vivid if they weren't true?

When he feels a little better, Yuan goes with the monk to a high terrace from which he has the best view of the glacier. The terrace is broken in places—holes have been torn out of it, and the room below is littered with massive stones. The still-intact portions of the floor make a zigzag safe pathway across the terrace.

The terrace is open to wind and sun, and the immensity of the mountain overwhelms him for a moment. Squinting, he looks up at it and nearly loses his balance. The monk steadies him.

Far above them, what remains of the glacier is a bowl of snow above sheer rocky walls. A great, round boulder bigger than a house stands guard at the edge of the bowl, rimmed with white.

"Don't worry," the monk says. "If that falls, it will fall right here and finish off this terrace and what's left of the western wing. The part of the monastery where we sleep is not going to be affected—see that ridge?"

Yuan sees a ridge of rock high above and to his right, rising out of the steep incline of the mountain. A fusillade of snow, ice, and boulders falling down the slope would be deflected by it just enough to avoid the eastern edge of the monastery, which is why it is still intact.

Yuan begins to shake. The monk guides him silently across the broken floor, and they return to the room. He sinks onto the bed.

"Why do you remain in this terrible place?" he cries.

The monk brings him tea.

"Thirty-three died in the avalanche," he says, "my teacher among them. So, I stay here. The others left to join another monastery."

Yuan is thinking how this does not answer his question. He is beginning to wonder about this monk and his excellent English. After a pause the monk says, "Tell me about yourself. You said you came up with an idea."

Yuan rummages in his rucksack, which is at the foot of the bed. He draws out a handful of orange wristlets. Each has a tiny screen on it, and some are encrusted with cheap gems.

"I am a student of computer engineering," he says. "In my university in Shanghai, I was working toward some interesting ideas in network communications. Then she came—Dr. Amina Ismail, my teacher—and changed everything I knew about the world.

"Most of us think there is nothing we can do about climate disruption. So, we live an elaborate game of denial and pretend—as though nothing was about to happen, even though every day there are more reports of impending disaster, and more species extinctions, and more and more climate refugees. But what I learned from my teacher was that the world is an interconnected web of relationships—between human and human, and human and beast and plant, and all that's living and nonliving. I used to feel alone in the world after my parents died, even when I was with friends or with my girlfriend, but my teacher said that aloneness is an illusion created by modern urban culture. She said that even knowledge had been carved up and divided into territorial niches with walls separating them, strengthening the illusion, giving rise to overspecialized experts who can't understand each other. It is time for the walls to come down and for us to learn how to study the complexity of the world in a new way. She had been a computer scientist, but she taught herself biology and sociology so she could understand the great generalities that underlie the different systems of the world."

"She sounds like a philosopher," the monk says.

"They used to call scientists natural philosophers once," Yuan says. "But anyway, I learned from her that whether we know it or not, the world and we are interconnected. As a result, human social systems have chaotic features, rather like weather. You know Lorenz's metaphor—the butterfly effect?"

"I've heard of it," says the monk.

Yuan pauses.

"She said—Dr. Ismail—that we may not be able to prevent climate change because we've not acted in time—but perhaps we can prevent catastrophic climate change, so that in our grandchildren's future—my teacher has two grandchildren—in that future, maybe things will start turning around. Maybe the human species won't go extinct.

"I'm connected right now to seven other people, seven strangers. The connection is poor, but sometimes I hear their voices or see them on my notebook screen. On the way here, I stopped at a grassy meadow crisscrossed by streams, a very beautiful place. The reception must have been good because all at once, I saw an old woman on my computer screen. She was standing at a kitchen counter feeling like she had nothing to give to the world. Helpless, useless, because she was old. So, I told her—I didn't know what to tell her, because I felt her pain—but finally, I told her something clichéd, like a fortune from a fortune cookie. I said, 'Something good will happen to you today.' I don't know if that turned out to be true. I don't even know who she is, only that she's from another country and culture and religion, and I felt her pain like it was my own."

The monk listens very carefully, leaning forward. The little creature has gone to sleep on his lap.

"Perhaps you suffer from an excess of empathy," he says.

"Is that a bad thing? I suppose it must be, because of how I've ended up. As you grow up, you are supposed to get stronger and harder, and wiser, too. But I seem to be less and less able to bear suffering—especially the suffering of innocents. I saw a photo of a dead child in a trash heap; I don't know where. The family was part of a wave of refugees, and the locals didn't want them there. There was violence. But what could these people do? Their homeland had been flooded by the sea. They were poor.

"I once saw a picture of a dead polar bear in the arctic. It had died of starvation. It was just skin and bone, and quite young. The seals on which it depended for food had left because the ice was gone.

"There are people who don't care about dead polar bears, or even dead children in trash heaps. They don't see how our fates are linked. Everything is connected. To know that truth, however, is to suffer. Each time there is the death of innocents, I die a little myself."

"Is that why you are so sick?" the monk says harshly. "What good will it do you to take upon yourself the misery of the world? Do you fancy yourself a Buddha, or a Jesus?"

"So, one day I was walking through the streets, very upset because my girlfriend and I had just broken up, and I didn't look where I was going. I got hit by a motor scooter. The man who was driving it yelled at me. I wasn't seriously hurt—mostly bruises and a few cuts—but he didn't even stop to ask and went on his way. I dragged myself to the curb. People kept walking around me as though I was nothing but an obstacle. I thought— why should I go on with my life? Then a man came out of a shop. He bent over me, helped me to my feet. In his shop, he attended to my cuts, and he gave me hot noodle soup and wouldn't let me pay. I stayed there until I was well enough to go home.

"That incident turned me away from my dark thoughts. I realized that although friends and family are crucial, sometimes the kindness of a stranger can change our lives.

"So, I came up with this device that you wear around your wrist, and it can gauge your emotional level and your mood through your skin. It can also connect you, via your genie, to your computer or mobile device, specifically through software I designed."

He sighed.

"I designed it at first as a cure for loneliness. I had to invent a theory of loneliness, with measures and quantifiers. I had to invent a theory of empathy. The software enables your genie to search the internet for people who have similar values of certain parameters . . . and it gauges security and safety as well. When you most need it, based on your emotional profile at the time, the software will link you at random to someone in your circle."

"Does it work?" said the monk.

"It's very buggy," Yuan says. "There are people working on it to make it better. The optimal network architecture isn't in place yet. My dream is that one day, it can help us raise our consciousness beyond family and friend, neighborhood and religion, city and country. Throughout my journey, I've been giving it away to people. In every town and village."

He taps the plain orange wristlet on his left arm.

Yuan is startled. He shakes his head.

"I've no such fancies. I'm not even religious. I'm only trying to learn what my teacher called the true knowledge that teaches us how things are linked. My sickness has nothing to do with all this. The doctors can't diagnose it—low-grade fever, systemic inflammation, weight loss—all I know is that no treatment has worked. I am dying."

The monk walks out of the room.

Yuan sits up weakly, finds the cooling yak-butter tea by the bedside, and takes a sip. He is bewildered. Why is the monk so upset?

Later, the monk returns.

"Since the third day you came here," he says, "you haven't had a fever. Once your strength returns, you should go back, down into the world. You have things to do there."

Yuan is incredulous.

"Even if what you say is true," he says after a while, with some bitterness, "how can I trust myself? My vision of this place—remember? The university I dreamed of—the hope of the world. My reason to keep going. It was all false."

"Maybe it was a vision of the future," the monk says gently. "After all, your teacher was real. If she mentioned this place to you, then that must mean that others are dreaming the same dream. Go back down. Do your work. This malady, I think it is nothing but what everyone down there has. Most of the time, they don't even know it."

He gestures savagely toward the world below and falls silent.

Yuan has not allowed himself to feel hope for so long that at first, he doesn't recognize the feeling. But it rises within him, an effervescence. He looks at the monk's averted face, the way the animal on his shoulder nestles down.

"If I am cured, then you have saved my life. You took me in and nursed me back to health. The kindness of strangers. I am twice blessed."

The monk shakes his head. He goes out of the room to attend to their next meal.

As Yuan's condition improves, he begins to explore the ruined monastery. There are rooms and rooms in the east wing that are still intact. The meltwater from the avalanche has filled the lower chambers of the west wing. In that dark lake, there are splashes of sunlight under the holes in the roof.

"We got all the bodies out," the monk says.

Then one afternoon, when he is exhausted from exploring and has taken to his bed, Yuan is woken by the monk's little pet. The animal is scrabbling frantically at Yuan's shoulder, whimpering. Sitting up, Yuan looks around for the monk, but there is no sign of him. There is a great, deep rumble that appears to come from the earth itself.

At first Yuan thinks there is an earthquake, because the mountain is shaking. Then he realizes what it is. He rushes out of the room, conscious of the little creature's scampering feet on the stone floor behind him. He runs up the stone stairway to the broken terrace that lies directly in the glacier's path.

The monk is standing on the terrace, gazing upward, his black robes billowing behind him. The enormous boulder that was poised at the lip of the glacier has loosened and is thundering down the mountainside, gathering snow and rocks with it.

"What are you doing?" Yuan yells, grabbing the man. "Get away from here—you'll be killed!"

He grabs the man's robe near the throat, shakes him. The monk's eyes are wild. With great difficulty, Yuan pulls him across the shaking, broken terrace floor, toward the stairs.

"You die here, I die here too!" he yells.

At last, they are half falling down the steps, running down the broken corridors, over to the east wing. When they get to the terrace, there is a sound like an explosion, and the ground shakes. It seems to Yuan that the whole monastery is going to go down, but after what seems like a long, endless moment, the shaking stops. They look around and see that the east wing is still standing. The small creature leaps up the monk's robe and trembles on his shoulder. The monk caresses it.

There are tears in his eyes, making tracks down the lined face. Yuan sits him down on the low wooden seat. The kettle has fallen over. He brings water from the great stone jar, pours some into the kettle, gets the fire going.

When the first cup of tea has been made and drunk, when the monk has stopped shaking, he starts to speak:

"I'm not a monk. I'm only the caretaker. They took me in when I came in as sick as you, but where the world made you feel like you would die of grief, it made me burn with anger. I was a city man, living what I thought was the only way to live, the good life. Then some things happened and my life unraveled. I lost everything, everyone. I ran away up here so that I wouldn't hear the voices in my head. I was full of anger and pain. My sickness would have killed me if the monks hadn't calmed it, slowed me down. Instead, thirty-three of them died when the avalanche came—my teacher among them. And I lived."

"So, you were waiting for that last rock to come down," Yuan says slowly, "so you'd have your death."

The man starts to say something, but his eyes fill with tears, and he wipes them with the back of his hand. The creature on his shoulder chitters in agitation.

"Your little animal needs you to live," Yuan says. "He came and called me. That is why you are alive."

The man is holding the animal against his cheek as the tears flow.

"Life is a gift," Yuan says. "You gave me mine; I gave you yours. That means we are bound by a mutual debt, the kind you can't cancel out. Come back with me when I return."

Several days later, much recovered, Yuan made his way back the way he had come. His companion had decided to stay in the village nearest the monastery. There, under a sky studded with stars, Yuan heard the man's story. Yuan left with him an orange wristlet, even though the satellite connection was intermittent there. When they parted, it was with the expectation of meeting again.

"In the future that you dreamed of," said his friend, "don't be too long!"

"I'll be back before you know it," Yuan said.

After he had passed through the high mountain desert, Yuan descended into the broad alpine meadow. He lay down in the deep, rich grass and felt his weight, the gentle tug of gravity tethering him to the earth. Around him, the streams sang in their watery dialect. Sleep came to him then, and dreams, but they weren't about death. His wristlet pinged, and he woke up. He must be back in satellite range. He heard, faintly, music, and the sound of a celebration. A woman's voice spoke to him, a young voice, excited. Two words.

" . . . A Butterfly . . ."

ABOUT THE AUTHOR

VANDANA SINGH is an Indian science fiction writer living in the Boston area. She has a Ph.D. in theoretical particle physics and teaches physics full-time at a small and lively state university. Her recent short fiction includes "Sailing the Antarsa" in the anthology *The Other Half of the Sky*. Many of her stories have been reprinted in Year's Best anthologies, and she is a winner of the Carl Brandon Parallax Award. Recent work includes a novella, "Entanglement," in the anthology *Hieroglyph* (November 2014). She has a new website at vandana-writes.com and a blog at vandanasingh.wordpress.com.

STAYING AFLOAT

ANGELA PENROSE

Just past eleven o'clock at night, the rain pressed hard against Paula Casillas's back, forcing her to lean into the storm to keep her balance. It felt like she was being shot by a steady hail of tiny bullets—tiny, cold, splashing bullets that soaked her jeans and trickled down the neck of her heavy rain jacket.

The maize field she stood next to was well enough established that the rain wasn't damaging the plants directly, but the soil was saturated, and what'd been a slight rise in the middle of the dirt road ninety minutes earlier was now a shallow stream creeping up around her ankles.

Lightning lit the sky, painting the experimental field with a blinding flash. Paula counted three seconds before thunder boomed.

To the west, the land rose into steep and unstable hills. Too many hills were unstable now, with the rain pouring down ten months of the year, harder than ever before. Who would have thought that the farmers of the altiplano would have ever had to worry about too much water? Paula remembered her Abuelo Jimenez muttering about drought in the many years when the rains were light and brief, but he'd never complained of too much water. But since the mid-twenty-first century, the old farmers spoke of drought years with what almost sounded like nostalgia.

"Here it comes." José Orozco pointed upslope with his flashlight, picking out a sparkle that wasn't just wet soil. Paula nodded and whispered a prayer. The water was coming down, rushing out of the mountains, and the field was in its way. And between the maize field and the coming flood was a fence of bright orange plastic that she and her grad student had assembled and installed just two days earlier.

"It will hold," said José. He took a few steps closer to the slope, clearly visible even in the dark and the rain. Unlike most graduate students Paula knew (or had been, in her day), José had a social life, and had come out to meet her after the awaited rain interrupted him at some club. His white pants and shirt practically glowed in the dismal night; the smart grey jacket didn't dim the effect much.

Youngsters. Paula was only forty-two, but sometimes José made her feel old. Luckily, he did it in a way that she didn't mind too much.

Paula nodded to his back and repeated to herself, *It will hold*. Maybe if they asserted it often enough, it would be true.

It should hold. The plastic, an American product pushed by smiling blond spokesmen in expensive "casual" suits who promised miracles every time they opened their mouths, called it "Tufflon." Twenty-eight times stronger than spider silk, it was light and cheap, and was one of the wonder products being sold all over the world as an essential part of the climate warrior's toolkit.

Practical applications—practical from the point of view of the people being battered by the changing world, and who did not have the bank account or credit line of the average American—were harder to come by. Yes, it could help keep soil from washing away in a heavy rain on a perfectly flat field, but when the problem was flooding, that wasn't so helpful. It was good for covering windows before one of the too-common hurricanes, and cheaper than plywood, but while useful, that was hardly a revolutionary development.

The leading edge of the floodwater hit the plastic barrier. Paula played her flashlight across it and could see the inverted-V shape channeling water into the drainage ditches on both sides of the field.

Paula and José had spent an entire day up on that slope, pounding wooden support stakes usually used for wire fences, stretching and securing the plastic, moving the stakes to get the angles correct and let a single long strip of the stuff—shaped with a dart held with duct tape—stand up straight with its lower edge hugging the ground. Once it was set, they secured the bottom, poking holes with nails and pushing sharp twigs into the ground to pin the edge down, because if the water just swept under the plastic, they might as well not have bothered. Then they'd had to pull up most of the twigs and re-secure the bottom edge using other twigs with bends or forks in them, so the plastic wouldn't just lift off with the wind.

A little leakage was acceptable. Unavoidable. But if the orange plastic dam would hold, would it channel most of the water away? This was something any farmer could afford, could install on his own to protect a field at the base of a hill, or actually up on a slope, as so many Mexican farms were.

Lightning flashed again, casting a white glare over the sodden field. The *crack-rumble* of thunder was less than two seconds behind. The rain kept falling, and more water poured down the hill.

"Profesora!" José waved his flashlight off to one side, then went scramble-splashing up the slope. Paula squinted after him and, after a moment of straining to resolve the dark, rain-fuzzed shapes, saw one of the wooden stakes tipping.

By the time José reached the tilted stake, the two stakes on either side of it were beginning to tip as well.

Longer stakes, thought Paula. *Pound them deeper next time.*

Unless they were breaking? She hadn't heard the wood cracking, but between the rain and the thunder, the sound wouldn't carry far. If they were, then what? Steel stakes? They were expensive. She'd thought of rebar—cheap to buy new, and even cheaper if reclaimed—but José had pointed out that it was made to bend and would never stand up under the weight of the water. Wooden fence posts would eventually rot but were the best compromise between utility and economics.

But only if they'd hold . . .

Another stake on the opposite side of the V was leaning, succumbing to the pressure. It wasn't going to work.

José was trying to straighten the first stake, pounding at it with . . . something, maybe a rock? Whatever it was, it wasn't going to work.

She shouted, "José! This isn't working; come down!" but before she could finish the sentence, the entire plastic line started moving. Not falling over but moving—the hillside was sliding underneath them.

"José!" There wasn't time for more than that. He lost his footing and came sliding down the hill on his stomach with the stakes, the plastic, a field's worth of mud, and a pond's worth of water.

Paula waded in, her heart slamming and her brain stuck on "frantic." The wave of water and earth surged past her, sending her to hands and knees to keep from being knocked backward off the hill. She crawled up, fighting through the liquid mud, terrified that José had been buried.

Struggling to her feet, she pointed her flashlight beam over the ground, back and forth, while climbing. There! Those ridiculous white trousers—one leg from foot to knee was exposed, and the rain washed the mud clear.

It took a minute of hard, skin-tearing digging with her hands to expose José's face. She turned him onto his stomach, straddled his hips, and did an awkward maneuver that Dr. Heimlich probably wouldn't have recognized, but it got José coughing and that was what mattered.

He heaved and spat out mud and water, struggled for air, coughed again, sucked in more air. Paula pulled out her phone and called for help.

José recovered enough to control his panicked tears before the ambulance arrived, and they both calmed down enough for Paula to stare down at the tangle of orange plastic and wooden stakes and mud covering half the experimental field.

Catastrophic failure. Looking at how much of the hill had slumped, they'd never have been able to—no farmer working by hand would be able to—sink the stakes deep enough to prevent the slide. They needed something else. If only she had any idea what that could be.

*　*　*　*

Two months later, nothing. Plenty of ideas, and arguments enough to take them all well into the next century, but nothing that made everyone, or even a significant subset, go "Aha!"

Profesor Rivera thought the answer was flood-resistant plant varieties, grains or other starch crops that could thrive even under half a meter of water, with roots deep enough not to wash off a hillside. Paula explained, again, exactly how deep that would have to be, but he still kept muttering about taproots.

Taproots? On annual grasses? Three-quarters of the plant's energy would be wasted growing roots; there'd be nothing left to develop seed heads.

Profesora Sanchez-Gallegos thought Paula had the right idea, but the wrong materials. "Stronger," she said. "Walls instead of flimsy fences. Earthworks or rock walls. It will take longer to install, but it will last."

"No!" said Paula, waving her mostly empty grapefruit soda at Sanchez. "I should have recorded a vid because you're not understanding; none of you are. The *entire hillside* slid. Unless you dig or pound foundations down to bedrock, nothing you build on the surface will stand up to the water, the mud." She huffed out her frustration and finished her soda.

They all knew. In actuality, they all understood. No one had been able to think of anything that would work, anything practical, anything cheap enough for the farmers who would have to implement it. They were running in circles, digging a circular ditch deeper and deeper into the earth that had turned against them.

The university café was full of bustling, chatting students and faculty. Sun shone through the windows, making the shabby room more cheerful. Everyone knew there was a crisis—a complex of crises all over the world—but people could only be grim for so long before they either sank into depression or pushed the problems away. The students, laughing and calling and tossing the occasional tamale at each other, had pushed away anything that wasn't an imminent exam, and most of them likely weren't even thinking about those.

Profesora Zavala crumpled the paper wrappers from her lunch and stood. "I have a seminar," she said. "We'll try again next week, yes? I know someone in Israel who's working on water control there—I'll mail him and see if he wants to exchange problems and ideas. If we all did that, brought more people in? Maybe someone will have a new idea. We might be able to help them too. Fresh eyes on everyone's problems, yes?"

Paula muttered assent along with the others. It was nothing they hadn't done before. Everyone had their own problems, and suggestions from someone who didn't have all the information was rarely as helpful as it was in feel-good movies.

Everyone at the table started shuffling and gathering to leave when Paula's phone buzzed. She sat back down and pulled it out.

Abuelo Jimenez had sent her a text. Why her abuelo couldn't just leave a voice message or an avatar vid like everyone else, or even a proper letter if he wanted to write, she didn't know. But he was old, and seemed proud of his turn-of-the-century habits.

RM RDY 4 U C U SOON

Paula squinted at the string of characters and slowly deciphered it. *Room ready for you, see you soon.*

She smirked at the message, then put her phone away. She hadn't been looking forward to the visit and had actually been planning to find some excuse to put it off. She knew her abuelo would be disappointed, but she'd expected—hoped—to be busy that weekend.

What she actually was, was tired. Exhausted in her heart. A weekend, maybe even a long weekend, at Abuelo Jimenez's place by the lake sounded wonderfully relaxing. Even if he was still puttering around in his vegetable garden, the last remnant of the farm he'd labored on for seventy-some years, a plot of beans or squash or whatever he was growing that year might help her remember why she'd devoted her life to agricultural technology—to gardening, at the heart of it—in the first place.

She tapped the VID button and said, "Looking forward to seeing you too, 'Buelo. Be ready to feed me!" Her current avatar, a little cartoon woman in a campesina's rough trousers and blousy work shirt, with an old-fashioned hard hat on her head, spoke the words back to her, shifting her weight and moving her hands. Paula had chosen the mannerisms mode that fit her personality, then tweaked it a little, back when she'd changed to this avatar. It looked fine, and she sent it off.

Abuelo always wanted to feed people from his garden, so the last bit would make him happy.

She stuffed her trash into the recycling bins and headed across the sun-dusted campus back to her office. She had a meeting with José about his own research into alleviating soil compaction with amendments, then a seminar of her own to lead before she could head up to Abuelo's place.

It was raining again by the time she left town. The car's fat, nubbed tires handled the wet and mud better than the old flat-surface tires ever had, but Paula still drove carefully up the winding road. Once she left the highway, with eight kilometers still to go, the road was packed dirt and gravel, and the wet weather had turned it into a stewed mess.

Abuelo Jimenez's house was a bright island of beckoning comfort in the rainy night by the time she pulled her car up next to his ancient truck. She grabbed her bag and splashed up the squishy path to the front door, slipping inside quickly to keep the heat in.

"There you are! I thought you'd fallen into the lake!" He gave her a quick hug, ignoring her soaked coat, then pointed her to the door she knew perfectly well. "Go put on something dry. I'll get supper on the table."

"Yes, 'Buelo." Paula smiled at his retreating back and headed into his workroom, where she would sleep on the studio couch amid his tools and clutter. She didn't mind at all. She'd slept in a similar room whenever she visited his farm as a child. The tools had been fascinating—they'd made her plastic toys look like cheap baby things. Abuelo's projects, wood and metal and wires, had drawn her in, teased her with their promise of revealing how the world worked. How to make things, *real* things that people could use.

She was an engineer because of Abuelo Jimenez's workroom.

While getting changed, she looked over the semi-ordered clutter on the big wooden bench. Her abuelo was the opposite of a specialist; he always seemed to be doing something different. Among the more common broken lamp to be fixed and cracked hoe handle to be replaced, there was always something new he was trying out or fiddling with.

The central project on the bench that evening was some kind of partially complete woven basket.

Paula pulled a warm sweater on over her head, slipped on a dry pair of shoes, and went to the bench for a closer look while toweling her hair.

The basket he was working on was odd, to say the least. The base seemed to be a half-crushed pad of thick, twiggy brush. Willow strips were woven through it, loosely—it wouldn't hold anything much smaller than an egg—and built up around the sides to form a long, narrow, rectangular basket. A handspan of willow ends stuck up, so it probably wasn't finished, but Paula had no idea what such a basket would be used for even when finished.

Warm, savory smells drew her out to the main room, where Abuelo was setting a cast-iron pot on the table. Paula sat down and he spooned a hearty stew onto her plate—haunch of goat cooked tender (well, almost) with peppers and onions and chunks of orange squash, and some cilantro on top. It was one of her favorites, and she knew he had made it just for her.

They caught up a bit during dinner, exchanging news, but mostly eating in comfortable silence. It wasn't until after, when Paula was finishing up the dishes, that she thought to ask about the weird basket.

"Hah, that," said Abuelo. He was sitting in his chair with a bottle of after-dinner beer, which he said helped him sleep. "I had a thought last month, while it was raining. The flat fields flood, and the sloped fields slide into the lake. You spoke of this problem."

Paula nodded and turned to face him, leaning back against the counter while drying the cast-iron pot.

"Our ancestors built fields that floated. On the lakes around Tenochtitlan? We all learned this in school. If we could duplicate the old floating fields, it wouldn't matter how much it rains or whether it floods."

"But the chinampas didn't actually float," Paula protested.

"Says who?" he demanded. "Abbe Francésco said they did. I read his account online. He would have had to be a ridiculously stupid man not to know the difference between a field built up from the bottom of a lake and a field that could float about on the surface of a lake."

Paula didn't voice the obvious conclusion. Instead, she said, "It'd be interesting if it were true. Have you made any progress?"

Abuelo scowled. "Some. No. I've tried several basket types, tight-woven and loose-woven. And different materials. The Abbe says brush and willow, but if he was looking at what floats at the top, he might not have known for sure. Maybe he spoke to someone who didn't want to give away the secret, or maybe he didn't understand the names of the plants and guessed, or substituted things he was familiar with when he wrote it all down? I keep trying, though. I know it will work eventually."

He'd said the same thing about many projects over the years, from a can opener to a whole tractor, and he'd succeeded more often than he'd failed. Paula wasn't sure about this one, though.

Every schoolchild knew the chinampas hadn't really floated. They had been wonderfully fertile, though, filled with rich soil dredged from the lake bottoms and kept constantly moist by water seeping in through the woven sides. It might be worth pursuing, at least on a small scale. If the containment walls were tall enough to keep out the rising lake water? But rainwater would fill the containment unless there were drainage holes, and simple drainage would let rising lake water in. Pumps would be expensive; if the farmers could afford enough powerful pumps, they could protect the fields they already had.

Paula put away the iron pot and picked up a bowl to dry. Her abuelo sipped his beer and rambled on about his chinampas.

"The problem is getting the densities right," he said, staring across the room at a dark-mirrored window. "Water mass is one gram per cubic centimeter. The chinampa needs a lower density, in total, basket and soil and plants all together. Most soils, even good farming dirt, are one-point-three to one-point-six. Some is one-point-two or even a bit lower, but that's not good enough. The Aztecs must have had a way of lightening it."

Paula pondered that. She hadn't realized it was so close. "What if they used some kind of hollow cane to make the basket? Something with enough buoyancy?"

"It would collapse when woven. If it were strong enough to hold its shape, it would be too rigid to weave."

"Are we sure they wove it?"

"Ehhh . . ." He frowned in thought for a moment. "Even if we had bamboo or something similar, it wouldn't be enough." He pulled out his phone and tapped for a minute, then shook his head. "It would help, but to support soil and crops? They planted trees on the chinampas. Some of the farmers built houses and lived on one. We need a *large* margin of density."

Paula put away the last of the utensils and sat on a stool near him. "We don't need enough buoyancy for a house," she pointed out. "Or even a tractor. These things weren't that big, and most of the small farmers still use hand tools anyway, or animals."

"So, enough for an ox, then, and a couple of men. With a good safety margin. That's still more buoyancy than we'd get even with bamboo, unless we built it like an iceberg, with ninety percent of its bulk under the water."

"It won't work." Paula had been getting interested, but it was getting too complicated. "We need something a small farmer could do." She laughed and shook her head. "As it is, expecting a small farmer to weave a basket the size of a field? It's a fun idea, but not practical."

"Not for the Americans, maybe, with their thousands of acres and twenty-ton combines. Small farmers in *third-world countries*"— he sneered at the English phrase—"are not afraid to work with their hands. Our ancestors wove baskets the size of a field *and* built pyramids, all with hand labor. The Egyptians built their pyramids. The Chinese built their Great Wall. It might take a long time, but we could do this. And every field that does not flood or slide down the hill is that much more security for the farmer, or his children and grandchildren. It would be worth the time and the labor—*if* we could show that it would work."

"If we could." She could agree that far.

Abuelo grunted and finished his beer. "Work tomorrow," he said. "Let's play for a while tonight, then bed."

Paula nodded and got up to get the pirinola, the top used to play toma todo. Even very young children learned to recognize the instructions written on the sides of the top and do what they said, putting coins into the pile or taking coins out; Paula had played with Abuelo since she was three. He'd cheated terribly to let her win then, but when she got older, he'd clean her out with no mercy. She always brought a full jar of peso coins with her when she came to visit; sometimes she left with more, and sometimes she left with less.

On one visit, after Abuelo had retired, she'd tried to "cheat" to let him win, the way he had when she was small. She had a good job and thought she could pass a bit of money back to him in his old age.

She had never tried that again.

The next morning, there were tomatoes to pick, squash to weed, and chickens to feed. Paula had to laugh when she saw the chicken houses— Abuelo had separated his old chicken house into four smaller ones and set them on top of old oil drums on their sides, six drums together in a wooden frame to support each small chicken house. The chickens strutted up and down the ramps between the doors and the ground, apparently unaware that their homes would float in a flood.

Or maybe they did know?

"Have the chickens had a sea voyage yet, Abuelo?"

He grunted out a laugh. "Four times. They are old salts now. Some of them will even run for their house when the rain begins."

"You should tether the houses to something so they don't wash away. A stake—" She cut herself off. *No, estupida, that wouldn't work at all.* "A tree, maybe? A high branch, in case the water rises that far?"

Abuelo shook his head. "If there were a strong current or heavy wind, the chicken houses would break apart jerking against a rope. I'd rather they wash away whole, so I could find them later. Or at least someone could find them and have the use of them. If a storm is that bad, whoever finds them will need them. They do me no good drowned and buried in mud."

"You could put a GPS transmitter in each one," she pointed out. "They're cheap, and you'd be able to find them if they washed away."

She got another grunt, that one with a nod. "A good idea. I'll order them this evening."

Floating chicken houses with GPS tracking could be useful for any small chicken farmer. Paula's work didn't involve livestock, but she knew others whose did. She pulled out her phone and posted the idea to a couple of agricultural and weather-related groups so it could be spread further.

With both of them working, they finished in time for a late lunch. Paula took a shower first, and by the time she went to the kitchen to forage, Abuelo was fiddling with one of his baskets, out in his chair in deference to decency.

"Workroom is yours again, 'Buelo."

He nodded and hauled his things back to the other room. Paula found leftover beans, squash, cheese, and tortillas, and rolled up a couple of quick burritos. She made herself sit to eat them, since indigestion later wouldn't help anything, then headed back to see what Abuelo was doing.

Hunched over a half-finished basket, he was fiddling with wood and glue. Paula peered over his shoulder and saw he was fitting a deck into the bottom of the basket.

"Air space," said Abuelo. "A sealed chamber for air would give it the buoyancy it needs."

"Yes, but . . ." She frowned and tried to think of how it would scale up.

"Aye, but. You're right—I could make it airtight on a model but never on something full size. A factory could do it, but it would be too expensive for the size we need."

Air space. Buoyancy. Soil density.

It was a good idea but didn't have to be all in one chamber. Maybe small balloons?

Or not even balloons. They didn't need actual air pockets; pockets of lower density, greater than air but significantly less than water—that would do.

Paula remembered José's project, adding amendments to the soil to lighten it. That was exactly what they needed. But it didn't have to be anything fancy or special-made; anything light, nontoxic, breakable into small bits, and not easily crushed in the soil—even when wet—would work.

"Junk—I need to look through your junk!" Paula dashed out of the room, heading for the junk heap behind the house.

Abuelo always had a junk heap—piles of stuff he saved for some day when it might come in handy. Leftovers, scraps, things he collected, things that were broken, all sorts of things lived in a good junk heap. A mature junk heap could produce parts for a water pump or a wheelbarrow or a sink or a computer. What she needed was simpler than that.

Paula dug through it, tossing things right and left, digging through the refuse, looking for something she just knew Abuelo had to have. . . .

"If you told me what you needed—"

"Aye! Here!" Paula pulled up a chunk of dirty white Styrofoam. It looked like it'd come packed in a box as protection for whatever had been shipped in it. Once you unpacked your new whatever, the Styrofoam was useless; there was tons of it in junk heaps all over the world, and considering how light the stuff was, that was *a lot*.

"Packing foam?" Abuelo frowned, then nodded. "We could put a layer of the stuff on the bottom of the basket. That might work."

Paula took her chunk of foam and dashed past him, toward the garden. "Better!" she called. She grabbed a bucket and knelt in the dirt, scooping soil up with a trowel, filling the bucket about two-thirds. "The basket, one of your finished baskets! We're going to float a plant!"

Abuelo grunted but headed inside. By the time he got back with a basket, she had the Styrofoam chopped into nut-sized chunks. "It should be smaller," she said. "We'll have to think of a way to get it smaller, about the size of lemon seeds, or even a bit smaller than that. But this will work for now."

She mixed the foam bits into the soil, using the trowel like a spatula, folding the bits into the soil like nuts into cake batter.

A layer of the foam-studded soil went into the basket, about three fingers deep, then she carefully transplanted a young comino, filling the space around it with more foam-dotted soil.

"There. Shall we launch it?" She beamed up at her abuelo and got a lined smile in return.

"Aye, let's try it. To the lake."

They went down to the lakeshore, a quiet arm of a larger body that bordered his land. Ridges and markings in the soil, rock, and foliage showed where the lake had risen in the recent past. It was also probably higher than usual because of the previous night's rain. It was quiet now, but when it stormed, the little lake could turn into a monster, devouring land and anything else in its path.

If Paula had accounted for all the variables, it would never devour this tiny "field."

Crouching on the lakeshore, she set the small basket into the water. She held it for a few moments, testing its buoyancy, waiting to see whether the water soaking in would change anything. It shouldn't, but "shouldn't" wasn't always so; that was what experimentation was for.

"Well, let it go. Let's see what it does."

Paula nodded and released the basket. She stood up to watch.

It floated.

The basket itself, the willow or whatever Abuelo had used for this one, was darkening as it absorbed water. The soil was surely absorbing water as well. It shouldn't matter, though; the soil was light and loose, and the foam bits should take the average density down well below that of the water, even after water seeped in wherever it could.

They watched it for a few minutes, then Abuelo said, "It would be easier to just put a chunk of Styrofoam in the bottom."

"Easier, yes," said Paula. "But it's more stable with the buoyancy spread over the entire soil depth. It would be more likely to flip with all the foam at the bottom."

Abuelo grunted assent.

They watched for a while longer, then he said, "Mixing small pellets of foam into the soil also gives the soil more depth for the roots. It doesn't matter with maize, a few others, but some plants want to send their roots deeper. Mixing the foam in lets us get deeper soil without having to weave a deeper basket."

"Another good point," Paula said.

Still, weaving a basket the size of a field? Even a small one? The chinampas weren't exactly forty acres, but still . . .

"How were you planning to weave a field-size basket once you were done with your models?"

"I thought I would weave the basket on land, then launch it like a boat. Fill it with soil once it was in the water." He frowned down at the little basket, still floating. "Our ancestors dredged dirt off the bottom of the lake. Very rich and fertile, but also heavy, and difficult to bring up. More difficult than just shoveling in dry dirt."

"Maybe use dirt from landslides to begin? Dirt will probably sift slowly out of the basket—you'll have to top up each year anyway, yes? Use lake dirt for that."

"Could work," said Abuelo.

"It looks like it's soaked through," said Paula. "It's still floating." She couldn't stop smiling, and although her abuelo was not a demonstrative man, she gave him a big hug and a kiss on the cheek anyway. "This is it; the principle works. If it scales up, if the farmers can do it, if it's cheap enough? I think we have an answer."

"Not immediately, even if it works. This is a long-term answer."

"Large problems always have large answers. You taught me that."

"I'm glad you were listening." He gave a grunt that was as close as she'd ever heard to a laugh out of him. "So, the work gets harder, yes? Now we have to build one full size."

Paula came back the next five weekends. On the first weekend, she found that Abuelo had built a frame out of reclaimed beams. They spent two days trying to weave willow wands among the beams, but it didn't work well, even with adding more support structure. And there weren't enough willow trees in the area, anyway.

The second weekend, she brought José and his girlfriend Martina, who was an anthropology major. Martina seemed to be more excited than any of them, even when Paula hauled five rolls of bright orange plastic from the trunk of her car.

"Strong, light, and cheap!" she declared to Abuelo. He grunted, and they wove with the plastic. After the first hour, they gave up on trying to keep it flat and just let it crinkle up however it wanted. By Sunday afternoon, they had an ugly orange basket, twelve meters wide by fifty meters long and three meters deep.

After that, they spent their weekends filling it. On the third weekend, they launched the basket. It didn't float very well by itself, but they pushed on, and Paula, Martina, and José dumped dirt into it bucket by bucket while Abuelo chopped up the Styrofoam he'd scrounged during the week. The basket sank to the bottom by midafternoon; luckily, the water was shallow and the top half stuck up into the air, making it look like a tiny, fenced-off swimming area.

The fourth week, they had plenty of Styrofoam bits, and all four of them mixed and hauled and heaved dirt. By midafternoon Sunday, even Martina was less enthusiastic, but just before they quit for the evening, Abuelo stared at the basket, then gave it a shove. "It's floating," he said.

And he was right.

The fifth week, Paula's department head, Profesor Nuñez, came along. He gaped at the basket, the size of a home vegetable garden, floating serenely in the lake.

"It rained on Wednesday," said Abuelo. "Very hard. I had to swim out with a rope long enough to go around the whole thing, then tow it back to shore with my truck. But it's still floating."

Profesor Nuñez stared at him for a moment, then back at the basket, the chinampa, then nodded. "How long did it take you to make it?"

Paula had already told him, but she let Abuelo repeat it. While she and Abuelo and the two students got to work hauling dirt, Profesor Nuñez got out his phone. He took video and sent it around, with excited messages Paula didn't hear clearly because she was working. But the next day, Profesor Nuñez came back with the Minister of Agriculture and the smiling, blond Tufflon spokesman in his expensive casual suit. He took a video of his own, smiling even wider.

"They'll come out with special 'extra buoyant' plastic and raise the price; you just watch," muttered José.

"We had rolls of plastic before they came," Abuelo said with a shrug. "We'll use the old stuff again if theirs gets too expensive.

Paula nodded and filled another bucket. She had no doubt that someone would market special Styrofoam pellets, too. Some people would probably use them, but the thrifty farmers would get theirs from trash barrels and junk heaps, chop it up themselves, and have it for free. Poor people were fiercely practical that way.

They finished filling the chinampa, leaving about half a meter empty to form a barrier against the lake. It wasn't watertight, but it would prevent rough waves from rolling across the crops during storms.

Paula came alone the next weekend. Abuelo already had the whole chinampa planted—she recognized the scattered sprouts as maize—and a group of farmers come by to stare at it. Older people, mostly, Abuelo's friends. They were all talking, arguing, gesturing.

One silver-haired woman was trying to figure out how to build them on dry land to protect against flooding but not need a lake to float on. That was an interesting problem too—keeping roots from anchoring the thing to the soil it sat on would be the key issue, Paula thought.

They'd go away still talking, and the chinampas would spread. Not next week or next month or even next year, but more and more, there'd be crops that lasted through the storms and floods.

She wondered what the people in countries where farming was huge and industrialized would do. She and Abuelo had talked of that, and she still couldn't see someone used to driving a combine around thousands of acres, with radio and air conditioning, building a chinampa.

That wasn't their worry, however. The small farmers in the poor countries would grow more and prosper, and their people would eat.

ABOUT THE AUTHOR

Angela Penrose lives in Seattle with her husband. She writes in several genres, but F&SF is her first love. She likes writing for anthologies for the variety, and the challenge of creating to a theme. You can find her at angelapenrosewriter.blogspot.com.

EIGHTH WONDER

CHRIS BACHELDER

1

When they came, they destroyed.

2

They came swimming, paddling, rowing with lumber. Shocked by storm, they rushed in like the water. They broke the locked doors of offices, closets, skyboxes. They splintered wood and smashed glass. The dome roared with de-creation. Bodies floated in the water. Blood tarnished the handles of doors. Drawings and messages covered the walls. Prayers and threats. Parents searched for their children and children searched for their pets. The nights were worse than the days. They rose to the upper decks and hid from one another in the dark. They took refuge. All night, there was crying and barking and the squeak of wet soles running. There was a storm outside the dome and a storm inside. The water, all day and night, splashed softly down the concrete stairs. Fifty thousand seats encircled the calm dark lake.

3

It was a Fast Fact that the level of the dome floor was lower than the level of the street. It was a Fun Trivia that the game scheduled for June 15, 1976, was postponed because of a flood.

4

It was early spring. The last of the four storms stalled, churned, departed slowly. Some swam away from the dome but many stayed. They formed clans along the club level. Clan membership provided protection but required precious supplies. The food that was found was eaten. The water that was found was drunk. They left the dome for food and supplies but often did not return. There were pirates on Kirby, on 610. There were pirates on the Old Spanish Trail. Swimming was perilous. They still thought of themselves as refugees. The dome, and life itself, seemed temporary.

5

What are human beings like? How are they inclined to act? These humans ate dogs, stole one another's shoes, struck each other with the sharpened legs of chairs. They were vicious and frightened. They drank urine and salt water. They lost their minds with grief and despair and privation. They walked the narrow catwalks along the roof of the dome and then jumped. It was a Fast Fact that it was like jumping from an eighteen-story building. Beneath the dark shallow water was concrete, ruined turf. These humans took care of their babies. They gave food and solace to strangers. They made a chapel in Section 749, an infirmary in Section 763, a nursery in Section 733. They built a long, fast waterslide in one of the external pedestrian ramps. The children waited in line, then slid, screaming.

6

They sat in colorful seats and looked down at the event of the water. They lived in the air, and they felt themselves perched high in the heavy dome, suspended by it. They had dim light but no sun. Their skin grew waxy and pallid; their eyes ached with strain. The water did not recede as the refugees believed it would. This would take some time to understand. They thought the water concealed the damage. But the water was the damage.

7

It was a Fast Fact that the dome covered nine and a half acres, and yet the sound of the violin carried through the darkness to each section and level. Every night, it was clear and distant. The people cursed and shouted for it to stop. They lay in nests and strained to hear it. Then one night, it stopped. Many days passed. It was not difficult for the people to imagine the destruction of the violin, so small and fragile. Another dead and broken thing, floating. But after a time, it began again, just as suddenly as it had stopped, the same violin or perhaps another one, small sound expanding to fill its container. A pulse, resuming.

8

In Section 435, near the water, the electrician lay in the dark and imagined. In the mornings, he woke early and walked the dome, learning it. He passed through even the dangerous sections. He moved lightly, like a thought. He was tall, thin, quiet. His large hands hung nearly to his knees. He did not seem quite real and so no violence came to him. He carried a notebook and a pen. His books were stashed in secret places. Like all electricians, he was awake to the power of the invisible.

9

They were still refugees, not residents, so the dome was squalid. The hallways were strewn with trash, excrement, the bones of animals. The still heat was horrible; the stench was worse. The street-fed lake beneath them was filled with broken furniture, rusted metal, floating fish. Boys dropped heavy things from the low sections, hooted at the splash. Some even dived. They swam to the bottom, looking for treasure. Every room had been turned over. In many rooms, the electrician found slashed cardboard boxes spilling glossy programs. He took them, organized them, stashed them. He created a library. He read them at night with a candle he received in exchange for a candy bar. He read the Fast Facts, the Fun Trivia, the Dome History. It was a Dome History that Judge Roy Hofheinz enjoyed watching minor league baseball with his daughter, Dene. After a rainout in the summer of 1952, the disappointed girl asked her father, "Why can't they play baseball inside?" Hofheinz, the son of a laundry truck driver, was inspired by the Colosseum in Rome, the enormous velaria that protected spectators from the sun. The dome was completed in November 1964. It was the first of its kind. The Eighth Wonder of the World, Hofheinz called it. The electrician blew out his candle. He did not clutch a weapon. Before sleep, he tried to make his mind as large as the dome. The ceiling was 710 feet in diameter. He tried to make the space where something might occur. He had noticed the catwalks. He had noticed the rising water, halfway up the doors of the lobbies, flowing through the hallways of the first level and down the concrete stairs to the dark lake.

10

Parents brought their sick children to the infirmary. This is not the infirmary, they were told. The infirmary is in Section 763. The parents looked about. They turned to leave, then turned back. *Then what is this?* they asked. *This is the nursery,* they were told.

11

Other instruments joined the violin at night. A flute, a clarinet, a French horn. They tried to make something simple and beautiful, but there was too much acreage, too much space between them. They could not synchronize. The concerts were discordant, disconcerting. The electrician lay still and considered it. The musicians stopped or were stopped.

12

Others must have read what the electrician read. The soggy programs were scattered throughout the dome. It was a Dome History that the original floor was dirt, the playing field was grass. It was Tifway-419 Bermuda. The grass had been tested in a specially constructed greenhouse at a university. The ceiling was made of 4,796 semitransparent plastic panels to allow sunlight. Grass grew in the dome. The fielders could not catch fly balls because of the sun's glare off the plastic panels. Outfielders wore sunglasses and batting helmets. Orange baseballs did not solve the problem. The team went on a long road trip while workers painted the ceiling panels a translucent white. The glare was reduced, but the grass died. The team played on dirt that was painted green. The baseballs rolled through the outfield and turned green. A chemical company invented grass made of nylon. The team went on a long road trip while workers installed it over the dirt. The electrician carefully removed the pages and hid them. He had a deep gash across his palm. He tried to keep it clean and wrapped. He blew out his candle. He understood that the dome was the space where the dome could be dreamed.

13

Birds lived there, too, in the spaces between beams. They flew through the deep sunless sky. People looked up to watch, but they grew dizzy and had to sit.

14

The dome had its first baby. Everyone could hear the birth in the skybox and they felt part of it. There were plenty of doctors. Gifts arrived. Someone made a sturdy crib. Someone made a mobile of feathers. For two days, nobody leaped, nobody fired a gun. Something was wrong with the baby. It didn't make a sound. It was small and its color was wrong. When it died, even the doctors went to stare into the lake. They had strong assumptions about human life, which they were prepared to have confirmed. Other babies were born and others were conceived. This was either heroic or foolish, and the parents had no way, except time, to know which. For the babies, the dome was home. At night, between fitful naps, the electrician sketched the dome, the gentle curve of the roof, the cross-hatch of catwalk. To save candles, he occasionally drew in the dark, blind, and he awoke in the light to odd lines, impossible arcs. It was a Dome History that people wondered whether clouds would form beneath the roof. He stashed his notebook, ate crackers from plastic packages. He walked, searching for a shoelace, a belt.

15

The electrician found a discarded weapon, a hollow metal pole, roughly three feet long, roughly three inches in diameter at its ends. For one day, he pounded the end of the pole with the marble base of a trophy he found in an office closet. The top of the trophy was a gold man riding a gold bull. The end of the pole became flat and sharp. The electrician took the pole and climbed the catwalk to the top of the ceiling. The catwalk was narrow, its railings low. The electrician's legs grew weak and he struggled for air. He lay down and closed his eyes. He crawled, trying not to look at the water below. Near the top he saw the leapers' tokens, the notes and letters, photographs, keys, gold bands. A hat, a doll, a child's shoe. The electrician was careful not to disturb the objects. When he got to the top of the dome, he lay on his back and looked up at the skylight panels. The ceiling side had not been painted. There was a short ladder leading to a small hatch in the roof, just as the electrician knew there would be. He climbed the ladder, opened the hatch, and emerged onto the roof of the dome, squinting. The sun was too bright, too close, too hot. He had not been outside since arriving. He was on top of the sky and beneath it. He did not see another person. The water extended to every horizon. Beside the dome, to the west, was the other stadium, its light stanchions snapped or swaying. In the distance, to the north, was downtown, silver buildings rising from the water, their windows glowing with sun. To the east was ocean, dotted with billboards. Out near Fannin the electrician could see the large helicopter of a relief organization, capsized and nearly submerged. To the south, the overpasses on 610 arched over the flood, crowded with abandoned cars. He walked out onto the roof, onto a rectangular panel, roughly six feet by four feet. The pitch was less steep than the electrician had imagined, though he knew the Fast Fact that the roof of the dome, the dome itself, was built flatter than its original plans. The electrician squatted, and with the flat, sharp end of his metal pole, he began scraping the surface of the white panel. The paint did not peel or chip. He stood and moved to another panel. He squatted and scraped. He moved to another panel. He stood in the heat and wiped his face with his shirt. It was a Dome History that a man on a motorcycle jumped over thirteen cars on January 9, 1971. That a woman beat a man in tennis on September 20, 1973. The electrician returned to the original panel. He went to his hands and knees. Eventually, he scraped a thin white layer of dust. He leaned down and blew it away. The electrician's body remembered working on his grandfather's house, twenty years earlier. The same motion, sound. The same patience. Eventually, the tool created a small hole in the paint. He had scraped down to the transparent plastic panel. This—it was a Fast Fact—was Lucite. He put his forehead on the panel and cupped his hands around his eyes. He peered through the small hole into the dome but could only make out a dark blur. He scraped from inside the hole, working outward, making it larger, chipping away larger pieces of paint from the plastic panel. It occurred to him that it would be useful to have a set of scrapers of various widths. He had to squint against the glare. He saw spots. He could feel the sun burning the back of his neck. His sweat dripped into his work. He had no water for his thirst. He smacked mosquitoes, smeared his own blood across his skin. In three hours, he had finished a panel. He was dizzy, delirious. The pole slipped from his hands. Later, he would not remember climbing back into the hatch, walking the catwalks. That night he lay in his nest, shivering and vomiting. He awoke in the infirmary, staring at the ceiling.

16

Many of the poems survive. The poetry of the dome is distinguished by its resignation, its rejection of nostalgia, its ambivalence toward the structure, the treatment of humans as animals, and its careful observation of startling juxtaposition and conjunction.

17

The electrician returned to the roof. He worked in the mornings and evenings. In a week, he had scraped eight panels. His hands were blistered.

The gash in his palm had reopened, bloodying the rags he bound it with. The dome leaked light. A beam moved daily down the seats, across the water, up the seats. It marked the days; it returned the dome to the natural world. The beam was salutary. People sat in the hot bright seats, eyes closed. Others looked upward for the source, squinting and shading their eyes. Many took credit for the sun. The electrician hunted for metal to make more tools. He pounded flat, sharp ends until his neighbors hollered. He was regarded as suspicious, dangerous, making so many sharp things. He stashed the tools with his books and programs. When he visited the clans along the club level, his voice was too quiet. They asked him to speak louder and when he did, they laughed or shouted threats. He wore a yellow construction helmet. He cupped his hands in front of him as he spoke, as if holding something that might leap out. He walked a circle around the dome.

18

One morning at dawn, three men were waiting on the roof when the electrician emerged through the hatch. The men held clubs or knives. The catwalk was the electrician's only escape, but the height still terrified him. He often had to lie down, crawl. He would not be able to run. He was surprised by his terror, his attachment to this life. *Please*, he said quietly, *I just want to work.* In the dim light, he could not see them well. What he had thought to be clubs or knives were tools. The next morning, there were nine more, six men and three women. One of the workers attached a wooden handle to his metal scraper, then held the scraping end in the flame of a torch. Others constructed large screens to block the sun. *Velaria*, thought the electrician. More workers arrived each day. They emerged through the hatch like ants from an anthill. Many did not even know why they were scraping, what they were building, nor did they care. They were happy to feel useful. Many had worked for years before the water and had never felt useful. One good worker could finish two to three panels per day. Several workers were burned by hot steel, several collapsed in the heat, several were sliced by splinters of wood or steel. One man lost an eye. Fights erupted and workers were badly injured by the scrapers. The paint dust blew across the roof and covered their skin and clothes. Those who scraped paint by day could be heard coughing at night. It was a Fast Fact that one worker had died constructing the dome. The poets wrote about Michelangelo on his scaffold. Rain came and washed away the dust and chips of paint. The electrician watched the water flow down the panels of the roof. The panels gradually became clean and clear, and the dome filled with light.

19

The yacht salesman stared at the electrician's drawings of the platform. He nodded, though the sketch was poor and implausible. He left the dome, scouting wood in a yellow raft. He paddled past the other stadium, then north along Kirby. When he tied his raft to a telephone pole, he got a splinter in the tip of his finger. He pulled out the splinter and then looked up at the pole. They were everywhere, they stretched away forever, and yet they had been invisible to him. The heat was nearly unendurable. Paddling back to the dome, the yacht salesman saw the dome in the distance behind the other stadium. He saw the workers spread out across the white hemisphere of the roof. The workers heard a distant buzz in the sky. They all stood, shielded their eyes with their dusty hands. They saw the speck of the airplane to the west. Then it was gone and they knelt again on the panels.

20

It was a Fast Fact that the dome's air conditioning system could circulate 2.5 million cubic feet of air per minute. It was a Fun Trivia that dome engineers claimed they could make it snow.

21

The electrician often could not sleep. One night, after meeting with the yacht salesman and the translator, he sat in Section 452, low down by the lake, listening to the soft splash and trickle, the cries of babies. Above, the disk of the full moon was fuzzy through the Lucite. Upper-deck candles looked like stars. There was movement on the catwalk, near the hatch. He thought he saw the hatch open. When he crawled through, clutching a scraper, there was nobody there. Then, in the light of the moon, he saw a head above the distant slope of the roof. For a week, someone had been darkening the panels. Everyone had assumed that the vandal was a teenage boy or a group of teenage boys. But here was a man in his fifties, a former librarian, rubbing a panel with sticky black syrup. He looked up at the electrician but did not stop until he finished the panel. He had covered four. The black material, when dry, had proven more difficult to scrape than the white paint. The librarian stood and said, *There*. The electrician said, *That's enough*. The librarian said, *I hate watching you fools. I can't stand it. All you busy fools.* The electrician did not say anything. He led the librarian back to the hatch, and down. He speculated that the librarian had had a good life before the water. It was those who had been content that had the most trouble in the dome.

22

The summer storms came without warning or names. Lobby doors collapsed and the dark lake grew deeper. Stores of food grew thin. The sun's heat entered the dome and did not leave. Its light was too bright off the water. Those in the upper decks descended because of the heat. Those on the lower decks rose because of the water. The club level became crowded, loud, filthy. The infirmary filled, expanded. The sick sat in cushioned seats or lay on thin sheets on the concrete. Through their dry lips, they cursed the electrician.

23

Beyond Dome History, after it, the dome was empty. A new stadium was built beside it. The dome was a problem. It could become something or nothing. It could be a shopping center, a parking garage, a museum. It could be demolished. It could implode, crumble in on itself. The pieces could be hauled away to make a parking lot. A monument could be erected there. Engineers worried that even the most cautious demolition might harm surrounding structures. It could be a movie studio, a luxury hotel.

24

The yacht salesman led six boats out on Fannin, steering a line beneath the thick wires strung between telephone poles. Their boats were made from conference tables and large blocks of Styrofoam. The world outside was still and flat and quiet. Faded pictures of food peeled away from half-submerged billboards. The sailors used long poles and makeshift oars to guide the boats along the street. On low rooftops they could see scattered clothes, plastic bags, suitcases. Some thought they saw faces from the second-story windows of stores and offices. They turned occasionally to look back at the dome behind them. It seemed to float or hover like a ghost ship. It was a Dome History that a press release in 1965 compared the dome to the Eiffel Tower. The yacht salesman stopped and pointed up at a telephone pole. The other boats kept their distance, spread out, kept watch. One sailor climbed up the pole. With a rope, he pulled up a rusty saw. He hesitated before cutting the wires. *Zap,* the sailors yelled, laughing. The sailor on the top of the pole did not laugh. His hand was shaking. He cut through the wires, lowered the saw, climbed down. Three sailors took turns swinging the axe at the telephone pole. The pole, when it fell, shattered a streetlight, nearly cleaved the yacht salesman's boat. The waves rocked the boats, soaked the sailors. They cheered and slapped each other's backs. They took down another, then tied ropes to the poles. The six boats turned back to the dome, dragging the lumber. There was a loud shot and a sailor fell, bleeding from the shoulder. The sound did not fade from the air. *Leave the poles,* the yacht salesman shouted. The sailors paddled back to the dome, their boats nearly full of water. The injured sailor was carried to the infirmary. The other sailors were concerned but not surprised. They had all felt, so recently, the impulse to unmake.

25

It was either a Fast Fact, Fun Trivia, or Dome History that a no-hitter was thrown on September 25, 1986. Only three balls were hit out of the infield. Only three players reached base. The yacht salesman had been there with his uncle. The old scoreboard, nearly five hundred feet wide, showed fireworks and six-shooters. The ticket stub was still in the yacht salesman's wallet and his wallet was long lost.

26

The platform would require miles of telephone poles. The yacht salesman and the banker took the sailors back out. Each boat had a gun, each gun pointed at passing windows, rooftops. One morning, a sailor crawled through the second-floor window of a small office building. He was gone a long time. The yacht salesman considered whether to leave or to send someone after him. Then the man was at the window, beckoning the others to come in. They tied their boats to gargoyles and ducked through the window. The sailor led them down a hallway, through a smashed door, and into a large carpeted room with couches and chairs. On a bar, there were a dozen large bottles. They drank all day. They ate food from small plastic pouches. They saved nothing. They cleared a space in the middle of the room to dance and wrestle, then they fell asleep on the couches and carpet.

27

New people arrived at the dome daily, bringing ideas, guns, illness, strength, food, and hunger. The electrician rowed a small raft around the perimeter of the dome. He saw them coming. He saw them swimming or paddling their leaky boats. *Go away,* he thought. *Please go.* Often, they were injured. Often, their eyes did not work anymore except to see. He helped them into the lobbies and up the ramps to dry ground. The lobbies had become treacherous with water and flotsam. The electrician walked circles around the dome, ducking beneath the clotheslines. Frequently, his arms and cheeks brushed the hanging clothes, the cotton and polyester, cool and damp against his skin. The electrician stared up and back down. He opened his notebook. They could use domemade sledgehammers to smash holes on the second level of the external pedestrian walkways. The holes would need to be large enough to load in the wood, the soil. They could build floating docks for boats. The docks could rise with the water and so, for a time, could they. It was a Dome History that the original name was the Harris County Domed Stadium. The electrician admired that name for its modesty, its accuracy. It seemed to him a true and accommodating name.

28

Boys fished the dome lake. One of them caught a giant turtle. There was great commotion as they pulled it in, placed it on its back, argued about the best way to destroy it. With plywood scraps, the boys built a ramp down the stairs between Sections 259 and 260. They took turns riding the two bicycles down the ramp and into the water. The bicycles rusted, their tires went flat, the wheel rims bent. The translator watched the boys from a skybox. The boys were her problem. The lake had to be cleaned before the platform could be built. *If you clear the lake,* the translator said to the boys, *I'll get you another bike.* The boys looked as if they might set upon her. They were barefoot, shirtless, and they dripped water on the concrete. A few had patchy beards. *Five bikes,* one said. *Four,* she said. The boys called and whistled as she walked away. They swam into the water and began to haul out the suitcases, tires, chairs, bottles, cans, knives, clothing, birds, stuffed animals, flashlights, books, programs, boxes, computers, phones, strollers, blankets, guns, dogs. Two boys swam down to tie a rope around a heavy wooden box resting on the turf. Five boys pulled the box up out of the lake. Inside the box were hundreds of little domes.

29

There once had been (Fun Trivia) shoeshine stands located on the lower level behind home plate. The children who heard the story could not understand. Shiny shoes. Shoeshine. The world before seemed strange to them. Snow in the dome, and grass, and men who walked on shoes that shone. They played games, kneeled at each other's feet, pretended they had shoes, pretended their shoes were too bright to behold.

30

The yacht salesman's dreams were horrors. He stayed awake for days, until his waking life was a dream, and then he swam away from the dome.

31

The banker went out at dawn with eight boats. He had grown up on a lake. He remembered the sudden plunge of the bobber, the dragonflies that settled on the ends of the rods. He lived in a skybox (19) and the sailors did not like him, but they did what he said. They brought down more telephone poles, cut 2×4s and 2×6s out of stores and houses, pulled plywood from storm-boarded offices. The lumber for the platform was stored in dry passageways above the lower level. Late at night, one of the guards would allow the insurance executive and his daughter to take pieces of wood to build coffins. The coffins were crude flat boats with small ornate boxes for candles, dried flowers, letters, toys, or jewelry. The coffins were stacked, large to small, several levels up in an external pedestrian walkway. The banker noticed the missing wood. One night, he hid in the passageways. He saw the insurance executive nod to the guard. He saw him select his pieces and carry them, with his daughter, back to the pedestrian walkway. They walked quickly through the dark. The banker followed them up the ramps. He lit a torch and walked along the long row of stacked coffins, touching them lightly. He kneeled down to look at some unfinished boxes. He picked up the woodworking tools and held them close to his face. The insurance executive and his daughter sat in the shadows. The banker stood and walked back down the ramps.

32

Whatever story the poets wanted to tell, the dome contained it. Nature was proven, and so was nurture. Altruism and selfishness were proven. Community and individual, chaos and order, art and shit, tool and weapon, freedom and gene, God and void—everything was proven and true, filling the dome like music. And every person was a dome too. *But won't the telephone poles float?* asked the limousine driver. The electrician stared at him. *I need you to figure that out,* he said. The limousine driver sat and thought for days. Once the platform was built, the poles would be weighted down, but the problem was how to begin, how to plant and secure the poles on the turf, partially submerged in the water. When his son would not stop crying, the limousine driver held the infant up by his ankle and shook. He climbed to Section 909, high above the lake. His notebook was full of strange sketches, smudged by his sweat. He felt constrained by the elements and conditions of the dome, the physical laws of the planet. He stared across the dome at tattered clothes on taut lines. There was nothing, and then from nothing there was something, elegant and correct. He would need some kind of drill and great lengths of strong cable.

33

What are the rights of humans? One morning, the boys caught the librarian urinating in the lake. They had all urinated in the lake many times, occasionally as a contest. When they ran at him, he did not try to escape. They picked him up and threw him into the water. Broken-necked, he floated, and the boys swam in to pull his body out.

34

The platform was a large rectangle of plastic-wrapped plywood sheets resting on top of hundreds of telephone poles cut to the same length. It stood ten feet above the water, centered in the lake. The platform workers were vulnerable to objects dropped from the catwalks. In late fall and winter, the dome cooled. The platform workers erected tall, thick sides around the perimeter of the platform. The outside of the platform walls had painted messages from the city from long ago. HELP. NEED WATER. NEED INSULIN. TIMMY WAIT HERE. THIS BILDING PROTECTED BY GUN. GOD IS WATCHING. EAT ME. SAVE ME, NASA. There were three kinds of workers: those who deliberately concealed the writing by facing it inward, those who deliberately displayed the writing by facing it outward, and those who both concealed and displayed because they did not notice or care about the writing. There were arguments and all of the positions were sound. Wooden walkways spanned the water between the platform and the sections of the lower deck.

35

Twenty-one boats sailed northeast, over the Old Spanish Trail, past the medical center until they saw Sam Houston's horse standing on the water. That was Hermann Park. Then it was slow and dangerous, diving to bring up soil in buckets, baskets, boxes, hands. At the end of the day, tiny piles dotted the enormous platform. How many days just to cover the platform floor. The carts, barrows, and chutes. The soccer coach didn't believe in it. He dreamed of killing the electrician, burying him alive, but he kept sailing to the park, diving for dirt. When others complained, he talked them into believing in something foolish. He stood in his wobbly boat and exhorted. *Let's go,* the soccer coach shouted. *What's your plan? That's what I thought. It's a bountiful planet. It gives and gives. Bring it out of the water. We're soil men. Brown gold. Come on. Get the dirt.*

36

It was a Fun Trivia that the dome was, at the millennial turn, the nation's 134th favorite structure.

37

Even the pirates had given up. The soilers could work all day. They took dirt from the Japanese Gardens, the golf course. Twice a day, the soccer coach would take off his shirt and dive with the others. When he came back up, he tipped his small load into the dirt raft and sat on the edge of the boat with his feet in the water. He could not see his toes. He did not know what month it was. The sun dried his back and hair. If he had cigarettes, he would hand them out, one each. They would all sit, still breathing heavily, staring into the water. If the dirt raft was more than half full, someone might say something. *The water's warm. Like it is in the Gulf. Like it was.* The soccer coach would nod. He had lain on a raft, his arm dangling over the edge. He had gotten stung by something. All he had seen was a dark ripple. Others nodded and pointed to places on their bodies. Most of them had been stung long ago by something in the Gulf.

38

The historian says, *They brought soil to the dome, filled the platform.* The sentence makes a bridge over time. Beneath the bridge are the minutes, the bodies, the glare off the water, the dead cranes floating. The golf balls and dark quarters the divers brought back for children. The aching lungs, flaking skin, the infections that never healed. Someone had painted the flank of Sam Houston's horse. It said PTSD DADDY. One day, a soiler, catching his breath, pointed at the statue and said, *He's the only person ever to serve as governor of two different states.* The soccer coach was up on the horse with Sam Houston like a lifeguard or emperor. *Let's go now,* he said. *Come on. Cut the small talk. Soil time.*

39

The veterinarian, the florist, the animal researcher, the data enterer, the consultant, the editor, the lab technician, the classics professor, the actuary, the hotline volunteer, the sculptor, the traffic engineer, the detective, the door and window installer, the plumber, the landscaper, the gambler, the architect, the quilter, the taxidermist, the nurse, the accountant—none of them returned with seeds. The mechanic thought he had something, but it turned out he did not. The historian builds a bridge over a year, says, *That was the worst time imaginable.* The storms came, the food ran out, the heat increased, the water rose. Despair became violence. Many died and many swam away. The boys tore down the walls of the platform and soil slid into the lake. The coffin maker's hands were swollen and splintered. His daughter died and he pushed her lightly from the floating dock. The violin stopped and did not start again. The historian knows how it turned out. The people in the dome did not know. This is the end of the story because they considered it the end, the very worst they could imagine.

40

They would eventually find seeds. Eventually, there would be vegetables, rice, cotton, but initially wheat and corn. They repaired the wooden walls of the farm, replaced the lost soil. They planted and waited. They gripped the sides of the platform, peeking over. The sunlight through the roof coated the soil, turned it gold. Then the tiny green stalks pushed through the dirt and into the dome. One morning, the electrician woke up early. He saw a sleeping guard, a deer in the corn. It looked like a dream, but it wasn't. He watched it for some time. The electrician would have a life precisely bisected. The harvest would be meager, the corn salty. They would fry fish, dance, play music. They would have a feast beneath the blurry moon. They would plant again, rotate crops, trap rainwater on the roof. The electrician would walk circles around the dome, listening. His hand would be amputated. He would meet with the residents one section at a time. *We could try to remove some of the ceiling panels to allow sunlight and rain,* a woman in Section 433 would say. *We could use gutters and spouts to funnel rainwater down into the dome,* a man in Section 638 would say. *We could plant saltbush to desalinate the soil,* an elderly man in Section 928 would say. *We'll have to raise and extend the platform,* a woman in Section 767 would say. *We have to get air in here,* a man in Section 722 would say. A boy in Section 600 would stand and speak quietly. Louder, son, people would say. *Why can't this whole dome float?* the boy would repeat. The electrician would stare at the boy's drawing. Some of the residents would laugh but many of the residents would not.

ABOUT THE AUTHOR

CHRIS BACHELDER is the author of the novels *Bear v. Shark*, *U.S.!*, and *Abbott Awaits*. He teaches writing at the University of Cincinnati.

EAGLE

GREGORY BENFORD

The long, fat freighter glided into the harbor at late morning—not the best time for a woman who had to keep out of sight.

The sun slowly slid up the sky as tugboats drew them into Anchorage. The tank ship, a big, sectioned VLCC, was like an elephant ballerina on the stage of a slate-blue sea, attended by tiny, dancing tugs.

Now off duty, Elinor watched the pilot bring them in past the Nikiski Narrows and slip into a long pier with gantries like skeletal arms snaking down, the big pump pipes attached. They were ready for the hydrogen sulfide to flow. The ground crew looked anxious, scurrying around, hooting and shouting. They were behind schedule.

Inside, she felt steady, ready to destroy all this evil stupidity.

She picked up her duffel bag, banged a hatch shut, and walked down to the shore desk. Pier teams in gas workers' masks were hooking up pumps to offload, and even the faint rotten egg stink of the hydrogen sulfide made her hold her breath. The Bursar checked her out, reminding her to be back within twenty-eight hours. She nodded respectfully, and her maritime ID worked at the gangplank checkpoint without a second glance. The burly guy there said something about hitting the bars and she wrinkled her nose. "For breakfast?"

"I seen it, ma'am," he said, and winked.

She ignored the other crew, solid merchant marine types. She had only used her old engineer's rating to get on this freighter, not to strike up the chords of the Seamen's Association song.

She hit the pier and boarded the shuttle to town, jostling onto the bus, anonymous among boat crews eager to use every second of shore time. Just as she'd thought, this was proving the best way to get in under the security perimeter. No airline manifest, no Homeland Security ID checks. In the unloading, nobody noticed her, with her watch cap pulled down and baggy jeans. No easy way to even tell she was a woman.

Now to find a suitably dingy hotel. She avoided Anchorage center and kept to the shoreline where small hotels from the TwenCen still did business. At a likely one on Sixth Avenue, the desk clerk told her there were no rooms left.

"With all the commotion at Elmendorf, ever' damn billet in town's packed," the grizzled guy behind the counter said.

She looked out the dirty window, pointed. "What's that?"

"Aw, that bus? Well, we're gettin' that ready to rent, but—"

"How about half price?"

"You don't want to be sleeping in that—"

"Let me have it," she said, slapping down a fifty-dollar bill.

"Uh, well." He peered at her. "The owner said—"

"Show it to me."

She got him down to twenty-five when she saw that it really was a "retired bus." Something about it she liked, and no cops would think of looking in the faded yellow wreck. It had obviously fallen on hard times after it had served the school system.

It held a jumble of furniture, apparently to give it a vaguely homelike air. The driver's seat and all else was gone, leaving holes in the floor. The rest was an odd mix of haste and taste. A walnut Victorian love seat with a medallion backrest held the center, along with a lumpy bed. Sagging upholstery and frayed cloth, cracked leather, worn wood, chipped veneer, a radio with the knobs askew, a patched-in shower closet, and an enamel basin toilet illuminated with a warped lamp completed the sad tableau. A generator chugged outside as a clunky gas heater wheezed. Authentic, in its way.

Restful, too. She pulled on latex gloves the moment the clerk left, and took a nap, knowing she would not soon sleep again. No tension, no doubts. She was asleep in minutes.

Time for the recon. At the rental place she'd booked, she picked up the wastefully big Ford SUV. A hybrid, though. No problem with the credit card, which looked fine at first use, then erased its traces with a virus that would propagate in the rental system, snipping away all records.

The drive north took her past the air base but she didn't slow down, just blended in with late-afternoon traffic. Signs along the highway now had to warn about polar bears, recent migrants to the land and even more dangerous than the massive local browns. The terrain was just as she had memorized it on Google Earth, the likely shooting spots isolated, thickly wooded. The internet maps got the seacoast wrong, though. Two Inuit villages had recently sprung up along the shore within Elmendorf, as one of their people, posing as a fisherman, had observed and photographed. Studying the pictures, she'd thought they looked slightly ramshackle, temporary, hastily thrown up in the exodus from the tundra regions. No need to last, as the Inuit planned to return north as soon as the Arctic cooled. The makeshift living arrangements had been part of the deal with the Arctic Council for the experiments to make that possible. But access to post schools, hospitals, and the PX couldn't make this *home* to the Inuit, couldn't replace their "beautiful land," as the word used by the Labrador peoples named it.

So, too many potential witnesses there. The easy shoot from the coast was out. She drove on. The enterprising Inuit had a brand-new diner set up along Glenn Highway, offering breakfast anytime to draw odd-houred Elmendorf workers, and she stopped for coffee. Dark men in jackets and jeans ate solemnly in the booths, not saying much. A young family sat across from her, the father trying to eat while bouncing his small, wiggly daughter on one knee, the mother spooning eggs into a gleefully unco-operative toddler while fielding endless questions from her bespectacled, school-aged son. The little girl said something to make her father laugh, and he dropped a quick kiss on her shining hair. She cuddled in, pleased with herself, clinging tight as a limpet.

They looked harried but happy, close-knit and complete. Elinor flashed her smile, tried striking up conversations with the tired, taciturn workers, but learned nothing useful from any of them.

Going back into town, she studied the crews working on planes lined up at Elmendorf. Security was heavy on roads leading into the base, so she stayed on Glenn. She parked the Ford as near the railroad as she could and left it. Nobody seemed to notice.

At seven, the sun still high overhead, she came down the school bus steps a new creature. She swayed away in a long-skirted yellow dress with orange Mondrian lines, her shoes casual flats, carrying a small orange handbag. Brushed auburn hair, artful makeup, even long, artificial eye-lashes. Bait.

She walked through the scruffy district off K Street, observing as care-fully as on her morning reconnaissance. The second bar was the right one. She looked over her competition, reflecting that for some women, there should be a weight limit for the purchase of spandex. Three guys with gray hair were trading lies in a booth and checking her out. The noisiest of them, Ted, got up to ask her if she wanted a drink. Of course she did, though she was thrown off by his genial warning, "Lady, you don't look like you're carryin.'"

Rattled—had her mask of harmless approachability slipped?—she made herself smile and ask, "Should I be?"

"Last week, a brown bear got shot not two blocks from here, goin' through trash. The polars are bigger, meat-eaters, chase the young males out of their usual areas, so they're gettin' hungry and mean. Came at a cop, so the guy had to shoot it. It sent him to the ICU, even after he put four rounds in it."

Not the usual pickup line, but she had them talking about themselves. Soon, she had most of what she needed to know about SkyShield.

"We were all retired refuel jockeys," Ted said. "Spent most of thirty years flyin' up big tankers full of jet fuel so fighters and B-52s could keep flyin', not have to touch down."

Elinor probed. "So, now you fly—"

"Same aircraft, most of 'em forty years old—KC Stratotankers, or Extenders—they extend flight times, y'see."

His buddy added, "The latest replacements were delivered just last year, so the crates we'll take up are obsolete. Still plenty good enough to spray this new stuff, though."

"I heard it was poison," she said.

"So's jet fuel," the quietest one said. "But it's cheap, and they needed something ready to go now, not that dust-scatter idea that's still on the drawing board."

Ted snorted. "I wish they'd gone with dustin'—even the traces you smell when they tank up stink like rotten eggs. More than a whiff, though, and you're already dead. God, I'm sure glad I'm not a tank tech."

"It all starts tomorrow?" Elinor asked brightly.

"Right, ten KCs takin' off per day, returnin' the next from Russia. Lots of big-ticket work for retired duffers like us."

"Who're they?" she asked, gesturing to the next table. She had overheard people discussing nozzles and spray rates. "Expert crew," Ted said. "They'll ride along to do the measurements of cloud formation behind us, check local conditions like humidity and such."

She eyed them. All very earnest, some a tad professorial. They were about to go out on an exciting experiment, ready to save the planet, and the talk was fast, eyes shining, drinks all around.

"Got to freshen up, boys." She got up and walked by the tables, taking three quick shots in passing of the whole lot of them, under cover of rummaging through her purse. Then she walked around a corner toward the rest rooms, and her dress snagged on a nail in the wooden wall. She tried to tug it loose, but if she turned to reach the snag, it would rip the dress further. As she fished back for it with her right hand, a voice said, "Let me get that for you."

Not a guy, but one of the women from the tech table. She wore a flattering blouse with comfortable, well-fitted jeans, and knelt to unhook the dress from the nail head.

"Thanks," Elinor said, and the woman just shrugged, with a lopsided grin.

"Girls should stick together here," the woman said. "The guys can be a little rough."

"Seem so."

"Been here long? You could join our group—always room for another woman up here! I can give you some tips, introduce you to some sweet, if geeky, guys."

"No, I . . . I don't need your help." Elinor ducked into the women's room.

She thought on this unexpected, unwanted friendliness while sitting in the stall and put it behind her. Then she went back into the game, fishing for information in a way she hoped wasn't too obvious. Everybody likes to talk about their work, and when she got back to the pilots' table, the booze worked in her favor. She found out some incidental information, probably not vital, but it was always good to know as much as you could. They already called the redesigned planes "Scatter Ships" and their affection for the lumbering, ungainly aircraft was reflected in banter about unimportant engineering details and tales of long-ago combat support missions.

One of the big guys with a wide grin sliding toward a leer was buying her a second martini when her cell rang.

"Albatross okay. Our party starts in thirty minutes," said a rough voice. "You bring the beer."

She didn't answer, just muttered, "Damned salesbots," and disconnected.

She told the guy she had to "tinkle," which made him laugh. He was a pilot just out of the Air Force, and she would have gone for him in some other world than this one. She found the back exit—bars like this always had one—and was blocks away before he would even begin to wonder.

Anchorage slid past unnoticed as she hurried through the broad, deserted streets, planning. Back to the bus, out of costume, into all-weather gear, boots, grab some trail mix and an already-filled backpack. Her thermos of coffee she wore on her hip.

She cut across Elderberry Park, hurrying to the spot where her briefing said the trains paused before running into the depot. The port and rail lines snugged up against Elmendorf Air Force Base, convenient for them and for her.

The freight train was a long, clanking string and she stood in the chill gathering darkness, wondering how she would know where they were. The passing autorack cars had heavy shutters, like big steel venetian blinds, and she could not see how anybody got into them.

But as the line clanked and squealed and slowed, a quick laser flash caught her, winked three times. She ran toward it, hauling up onto a slim platform at the foot of a steel sheet.

It tilted outward as she scrambled aboard, thudding into her thigh, nearly knocking her off. She ducked in and saw by the distant streetlights vague outlines of luxury cars. A Lincoln sedan door swung open. Its interior light came on and she saw two men in the front seats. She got in the back and closed the door. Utter dark.

"It clear out there?" the cell phone voice asked from the driver's seat.

"Yeah. What—"

"Let's unload. You got the SUV?"

"Waiting on the nearest street."

"How far?"

"Hundred meters."

The man jigged his door open, glanced back at her. "We can make it in one trip if you can carry twenty kilos."

"Sure," though she had to pause to quickly do the arithmetic, forty-four pounds. She had backpacked about that much for weeks in the Sierras. "Yeah, sure."

The missile gear was in the trunks of three other sedans, at the far end of the autorack. As she climbed out of the car the men had inhabited, she saw the debris of their trip—food containers in the back seats, assorted junk, the waste from days spent coming up from Seattle. With a few gallons of gas in each car, so they could be driven on and off, these two had kept warm running the heater. If that ran dry, they could switch to another.

As she understood it, this degree of mess was acceptable to the railroads and car dealers. If the railroad tried to wrap up the autoracked cars to keep them out, the bums who rode the rails would smash windshields to get in, then shit in the cars, knife the upholstery. So, they had struck an equilibrium. That compromise inadvertently produced a good way to ship weapons right by Homeland Security. She wondered what Homeland types would make of a Dart, anyway. Could they even tell what it was?

The rough-voiced man turned and clicked on a helmet lamp. "I'm Bruckner. This is Gene."

Nods. "I'm Elinor." Nods, smiles. Cut to the chase. "I know their flight schedule."

Bruckner smiled thinly. "Let's get this done."

Transporting the parts in via autoracked cars was her idea. Bringing them in by small plane was the original plan, but Homeland might nab them at the airport. She was proud of this slick work-around.

"Did railroad inspectors get any of you?" Elinor asked.

Gene said, "Nope. Our two extras dropped off south of here. They'll fly back out."

With the auto freights, the railroad police looked for tramps sleeping in the seats. No one searched in the trunks. So, they had put a man on each autorack, and if some got caught, they could distract from the gear. The men would get a fine, be hauled off for a night in jail, and the shipment would go on.

"Luck is with us," Elinor said. Bruckner looked at her, looked more closely, opened his mouth, but said nothing.

They both seemed jumpy by the helmet light. "How'd you guys live this way?" she asked, to get them relaxed.

"Pretty poorly," Gene said. "We had to shit in bags."

She could faintly smell the stench. "More than I need to know."

Using Bruckner's helmet light, they hauled the assemblies out, neatly secured in backpacks. Bruckner moved with strong, graceless efficiency. Gene too. She hoisted hers on, grunting.

The freight started up, lurching forward. "Damn!" Gene said.

They hurried. When they opened the steel flap, she hesitated, jumped, stumbled on the gravel, but caught herself. Nobody within view in the velvet, cloaking dusk.

They walked quietly, keeping steady through the shadows. It got cold fast, even in late May. At the Ford, they put the gear in the back and got in. She drove them to the old school bus. Nobody talked.

She stopped them at the steps to the bus. "Here, put these gloves on."

They grumbled but they did it. Inside, heater turned to high, Bruckner asked if she had anything to drink. She offered bottles of vitamin water but he waved it away. "Any booze?"

Gene said, "Cut that out."

The two men eyed each other and Elinor thought about how they'd been days in those cars and decided to let it go. Not that she had any liquor, anyway.

Bruckner was lean, rawboned, and self-contained, with minimal movements and a constant, steady gaze in his expressionless face. "I called the pickup boat. They'll be waiting offshore near Eagle Bay by eight."

Elinor nodded. "First flight is nine a.m. It'll head due north, so we'll see it from the hills above Eagle Bay."

Gene said, "So, we get into position . . . when?"

"Tonight, just after dawn."

Bruckner said, "I do the shoot."

"And we handle perimeter and setup, yes."

"How much trouble will we have with the Indians?"

Elinor blinked. "The Inuit settlement is down by the seashore. They shouldn't know what's up."

Bruckner frowned. "You sure?"

"That's what it looks like. Can't exactly go there and ask, can we?"

Bruckner sniffed, scowled, looked around the bus. "That's the trouble with this nickel-and-dime operation. No real security."

Elinor said, "You want security, buy a bond."

Bruckner's head jerked around. "Whassat mean?"

She sat back, took her time. "We can't be sure the DARPA people haven't done some serious public relations work with the Natives. Besides, they're probably all in favor of SkyShield anyway—their entire way of life is melting away with the sea ice. And by the way, they're not 'Indians'; they're 'Inuit.'"

"You seem pretty damn sure of yourself."

"People say it's one of my best features."

Bruckner squinted and said, "You're—"

"A maritime engineering officer. That's how I got here and that's how I'm going out."

"You're not going with us?"

"Nope, I go back out on my ship. I have first engineering watch tomorrow, oh-one-hundred hours." She gave him a hard, flat look. "We go up the inlet, past Birchwood Airport. I get dropped off, steal a car, head south to Anchorage, while you get on the fishing boat; they work you out to the headlands. The bigger ship comes in, picks you up. You're clear and away."

Bruckner shook his head. "I thought we'd—"

"Look, there's a budget and—"

"We've been holed up in those damn cars for—"

"A week, I know. Plans change."

"I don't like changes."

"Things change," Elinor said, trying to make it mild.

But Bruckner bristled. "I don't like you cutting out, leaving us—"

"I'm in charge, remember." She thought, *He travels the fastest who travels alone.*

"I thought we were all in this together."

She nodded. "We are. But Command made me responsible, since this was my idea."

His mouth twisted. "I'm the shooter; I—"

"Because *I* got you into the Ecuador training. Me and Gene, we depend on you." Calm, level voice. No need to provoke guys like this; they did it enough on their own.

Silence. She could see him take out his pride, look at it, and decide to wait a while to even the score.

Bruckner said, "I gotta stretch my legs," and clumped down the steps and out of the bus.

Elinor didn't like the team splitting and thought of going after him. But she knew why Bruckner was antsy—too much energy with no outlet. She decided just to let him go.

To Gene she said, "You've known him longer. He's been in charge of operations like this before?"

Gene thought. "There've *been* no operations like this."

"Smaller jobs than this?"

"Plenty."

She raised her eyebrows. "Surprising."

"Why?"

"He walks around using that mouth while he's working?"

Gene chuckled. "'Fraid so. He gets the job done, though."

"Still surprising."

"That he's the shooter, or—"

"That he still has all his teeth."

While Gene showered, she considered. Elinor figured Bruckner for an injustice collector, the passive-aggressive loser type. But he had risen quickly in the LifeWorkers, as they called themselves, brought into the inner cadre that had formulated this plan. Probably because he was willing to cross the line, use violence in the cause of justice. Logically, she should sympathize with him because he was a lot like her.

But sympathy and liking didn't work that way.

There were people who soon would surely yearn to read her obituary, and Bruckner's too, no doubt. He and she were the cutting edge of environmental activism, and these were desperate times indeed. Sometimes, you had to cross the line and be sure about it.

Elinor had made a lot of hard choices. She knew she wouldn't last long on the scalpel's edge of active environmental justice, and that was fine by her. Her role would soon be to speak for the true cause. Her looks, her brains, her charm—she knew she'd been chosen for this mission, and the public one afterwards, for these attributes as much as for the plan she had devised. People listen, even to ugly messages, when the face of the messenger is pretty. And once they finished here, she would have to be heard.

She and Gene carefully unpacked the gear and started to assemble the Dart. The parts connected with a minimum of wiring and socket clasps, as foolproof as possible. They worked steadily, assembling the tube, the small recoilless charge, snapping and clicking the connections.

Gene said, "The targeting antenna has a rechargeable battery; they tend to drain. I'll top it up."

She nodded, distracted by the intricacies of a process she had trained for a month ago. She set the guidance system. Tracking would first be infrared only, zeroing in on the target's exhaust, but once in the air and nearing its goal, it would use multiple targeting modes—laser, IR, advanced visual recognition—to get maximal impact on the main body of the aircraft.

They got it assembled and stood back to regard the linear elegance of the Dart. It had a deadly, snakelike beauty, its shiny white skin tapered to a snub point.

"Pretty, yeah," Gene said. "And way better than any Stinger. Next generation, smarter, near four times the range."

She knew guys liked anything that could shoot, but to her it was just a tool. She nodded.

Gene sniffed, caressed the lean body of the Dart, and smiled.

Bruckner came clumping up the bus stairs with a fixed smile on his face that looked like it had been delivered to the wrong address. He waved a lit cigarette. Elinor got up, forced herself to smile. "Glad you're back; we—"

"Got some 'freshments," he said, dangling some beers in their six-pack plastic cradle, and she realized he was drunk.

The smile fell from her face like a picture off a wall.

She had to get along with these two, but this was too much. She stepped forward, snatched the beer bottles, and tossed them onto the love seat. "No more."

Bruckner tensed and Gene sucked in a breath. Bruckner made a move to grab the beers and Elinor snatched his hand, twisted the thumb back, turned hard to ward off a blow from his other hand—and they froze, looking into each other's eyes from a few centimeters away.

Silence.

Gene said, "She's right, y'know."

More silence.

Bruckner sniffed, backed away. "You don't have to be rough."

"I wasn't."

They looked at each other, let it go.

She figured each of them harbored a dim fantasy of coming to her in the brief hours of darkness. She slept in the lumpy bed and they made do with the furniture. Bruckner got the love seat—ironic victory—and Gene sprawled on a threadbare comforter.

Bruckner talked some but dozed off fast under booze, so she didn't have to endure his testosterone-fueled patter. But he snored, which was worse.

The men napped and tossed and worried. No one bothered her, just as she wanted it. But she kept a small knife in her hand, in case. For her, sleep came easily.

After eating a cold breakfast, they set out before dawn, two thirty a.m., Elinor driving. She had decided to wait till then because they could mingle with early-morning Air Force workers driving toward the base. This far north, it started brightening by three thirty, and they'd be in full light before five. Best not to stand out as they did their last reconnaissance. It was so cold, she had to run the heater for five minutes to clear the windshield of ice. Scraping with her gloved hands did nothing.

The men had grumbled about leaving absolutely nothing behind. "No traces," she said. She wiped down every surface, even though they'd worn medical gloves the whole time in the bus.

Gene didn't ask why she stopped and got a gas can filled with gasoline, and she didn't say. She noticed the wind was fairly strong and from the north, and smiled. "Good weather. Prediction's holding up."

Bruckner said sullenly, "Goddamn *cold*."

"The KC Extenders will take off into the wind, head north." Elinor judged the nearly cloud-free sky. "Just where we want them to be.

They drove up a side street in Mountain View, and parked overlooking the fish hatchery and golf course, so she could observe the big tank refuelers lined up at the loading site. She counted five KC-10 Extenders, freshly surplussed by the Air Force. Their big bellies reminded her of pregnant whales.

From their vantage point, they could see down to the temporarily expanded checkpoint set up just outside the base. As foreseen, security was stringently tight this near the airfield—all drivers and passengers had to get out, be scanned, IDs checked against global records, brief-cases and purses searched. K-9 units inspected car interiors and trunks. Explosives-detecting robots rolled under the vehicles.

She fished out binoculars and focused on the people waiting to be cleared. Some carried laptops and backpacks, and she guessed they were the scientists flying with the dispersal teams. Their body language was clear. Even this early, they were jazzed, eager to go, excited as kids on a field trip. One of the pilots had mentioned there would be some sort of preflight ceremony honoring the teams that had put all this together. The flight crews were studiedly nonchalant—this was an important, high-profile job, sure, but they couldn't let their cool down in front of so many science nerds. She couldn't see well enough to pick out Ted or the friendly woman from the bar.

In a special treaty deal with the Arctic Council, they would fly from Elmendorf and arc over the North Pole, spreading hydrogen sulfide in their wakes. The tiny molecules of it would mate with water vapor in the stratospheric air, making sulfurics. Those larger, wobbly molecules reflected sunlight well—a fact learned from studying volcano eruptions back in the TwenCen. Spray megatons of hydrogen sulfide into the strato-sphere, let water turn it into a sunlight-bouncing sheet—SkyShield—and they could cool the entire Arctic.

Or so the theory went. The Arctic Council had agreed to this series of large-scale experiments, run by the USA since they had the in-flight refu-elers that could spread the tiny molecules to form the SkyShield. Small-scale experiments—opposed, of course, by many enviros—had seemed to work. Now came the big push, trying to reverse the retreat of sea ice and warming of the tundra.

Anchorage lay slightly farther north than Oslo, Helsinki, and Stockholm, but not as far north as Reykjavík or Murmansk. Flights from Anchorage to Murmansk would let them refuel and reload hydrogen sulfide at each end, then follow their paths back over the pole. Deploying hydrogen sul-fide along their flight paths at 45,000 feet, they would spread a protective layer to reflect summer sunlight. In a few months, the sulfuric droplets would ease down into the lower atmosphere, mix with moist clouds, and come down as rain or snow, a minute, undetectable addition to the acidity already added by industrial pollutants. Experiment over.

The total mass delivered was far less than that from volcanoes like Pinatubo, which had cooled the whole planet in 1991–92. But volcanoes do messy work, belching most of their vomit into the lower atmosphere. This was to be a designer volcano, a thin skin of aerosols skating high across the stratosphere.

It might stop the loss of the remaining sea ice, the habitat of the polar bear. Only ten percent of the vast original cooling sheets remained. Equally disruptive changes were beginning to occur in other parts of the world.

But geoengineered tinkerings would also be a further excuse to delay cutbacks in carbon dioxide emissions. People loved convenience, their air conditioning and winter heating and big lumbering SUVs. Humanity had already driven the air's CO_2 content to twice what it was before 1800, and with every developing country burning oil and coal as fast as they could extract them, only dire emergency could drive them to abstain. To do what was right.

The greatest threat to humanity arose not from terror but error. Time to take the gloves off.

She put the binocs away and headed north. The city's seacoast was mostly rimmed by treacherous mudflats, even after the sea kept rising. Still, there were coves and sandbars of great beauty. Elinor drove off Glenn Highway to the west, onto progressively smaller, rougher roads, working their way backcountry by Bureau of Land Management roads to a sagging, long-unused access gate for loggers. Bolt cutters made quick work of the lock securing its rusty chain closure. After she pulled through, Gene carefully replaced the chain and linked it with an equally rusty padlock, brought for this purpose. Not even a thorough check would show it had been opened, till the next time BLM tried to unlock it. They were now on Elmendorf, miles north of the airfield, far from the main base's bustle and security precautions. Thousands of acres of mudflats, woods, lakes, and inlet shoreline lay almost untouched, used for military exercises and not much else. Nobody came here except for infrequent hardy bands of off-duty soldiers or pilots, hiking with maps red-marked UXO for "Unexploded Ordnance." Lost live explosives, remnant of past field maneuvers, tended to discourage casual sightseers and trespassers, and the Inuit villagers wouldn't be berry-picking till July and August. She consulted her satellite map, then took them on a side road, running up the coast. They passed above a cove of dark blue waters.

Beauty. Pure and serene.

The sea level rise had inundated many of the mudflats and islands, but a small rocky platform lay near shore, thick with trees. Driving by, she spotted a bald eagle perched at the top of a towering spruce tree. She had started bird-watching as a Girl Scout and they had time; she stopped.

She left the men in the Ford and took out her long-range binocs. The eagle was grooming its feathers and eyeing the fish rippling the waters offshore. Gulls wheeled and squawked, and she could see sea lions knifing through fleeing shoals of herring, transient dark islands breaking the sheen of waves. Crows joined in onshore, hopping on the rocks and pecking at the predators' leftovers.

She inhaled the vibrant scent of ripe, wet, salty air, alive with what she had always loved more than any mere human. This might be the last time she would see such abundant, glowing life, and she sucked it in, trying to lodge it in her heart for times to come.

She was something of an eagle herself, she saw now, as she stood looking at the elegant predator. She kept to herself, loved the vibrant natural world around her, and lived by making others pay the price of their own foolishness. An eagle caught hapless fish. She struck down those who would do evil to the real world, the natural one.

Beyond politics and ideals, this was her reality.

Then she remembered what else she had stopped for. She took out her cell phone and pinged the alert number.

A buzz, then a blurred woman's voice. "Able Baker."

"Confirmed. Get a GPS fix on us now. We'll be here, same spot, for pickup in two to three hours. Assume two hours."

Buzz buzz. "Got you fixed. Timing's okay. Need a Zodiac?"

"Yes, definite, and we'll be moving fast."

"You bet. Out."

Back in the cab, Bruckner said, "What was that for?"

"Making the pickup contact. It's solid."

"Good. But I meant, what took so long?"

She eyed him levelly. "A moment spent with what we're fighting for."

Bruckner snorted. "Let's get on with it."

Elinor looked at Bruckner and wondered if he wanted to turn this into a spitting contest just before the shoot.

"Great place," Gene said diplomatically.

That broke the tension and she started the Ford.

They rose farther up the hills northeast of Anchorage, and at a small clearing, she pulled off to look over the landscape. To the east, mountains towered in lofty gray majesty, flanks thick with snow. They all got out and surveyed the terrain and sight angles toward Anchorage. The lowlands were already thick with summer grasses, and the winds sighed southward through the tall evergreens.

Gene said, "Boy, the warming's brought a lot of growth."

Elinor glanced at her watch and pointed. "The KCs will come from that direction, into the wind. Let's set up on that hillside."

They worked around to a heavily wooded hillside with a commanding view toward Elmendorf Air Force Base. "This looks good," Bruckner said, and Elinor agreed.

"Damn—a bear!" Gene cried.

They looked down into a narrow canyon with tall spruce. A large brown bear was wandering along a stream about a hundred meters away.

Elinor saw Bruckner haul out a .45 automatic. He cocked it.

When she glanced back, the bear was looking toward them. It turned and started up the hill with lumbering energy.

"Back to the car," she said.

The bear broke into a lope.

Bruckner said, "Hell, I could just shoot it. This is a good place to see the takeoff and—"

"No. We move to the next hill."

Bruckner said, "I want—"

"Go!"

They ran.

One hill farther south, Elinor braced herself against a tree for stability and scanned the Elmendorf landing strips. The image wobbled as the air warmed across hills and marshes.

Lots of activity. Three KC-10 Extenders ready to go. One tanker was lined up on the center lane and the other two were moving into position.

"Hurry!" she called to Gene, who was checking the final setup menu and settings on the Dart launcher.

He carefully inserted the missile itself in the launcher. He checked, nodded, and lifted it to Bruckner. They fitted the shoulder straps to Bruckner, secured it, and Gene turned on the full arming function. "Set!" he called.

Elinor saw a slight stirring of the center Extender and it began to accelerate. She checked: right on time, oh-nine-hundred hours. Hard-core military like Bruckner, who had been a Marine in the Middle East, called Air Force the "saluting Civil Service," but they did hit their markers. The Extenders were not military now, just surplus, but flying giant tanks of sloshing liquid around the stratosphere demands tight standards.

"I make the range maybe twenty kilometers," she said. "Let it pass over us, hit it close as it goes away."

Bruckner grunted, hefted the launcher. Gene helped him hold it steady, taking some of the weight. Loaded, it weighed nearly fifty pounds. The Extender lifted off, with a hollow, distant roar that reached them a few seconds later, and Elinor could see media coverage was high. Two choppers paralleled the takeoff for footage, then got left behind.

The Extender was a full extension DC-10 airframe and it came nearly straight toward them, growling through the chilly air. She wondered if the chatty guy from the bar, Ted, was one of the pilots. Certainly, on a maiden flight the scientists who ran this experiment would be on board, monitoring performance. Very well.

"Let it get past us," she called to Bruckner.

He took his head from the eyepiece to look at her. "Huh? Why—"

"Do it. I'll call the shot."

"But I'm—"

"Do it."

The airplane was rising slowly and flew by them a few kilometers away.

"Hold, hold . . ." she called. "Fire."

Bruckner squeezed the trigger and the missile popped out—*whuff!*— seemed to pause, then lit. It roared away, startling in its speed—straight for the exhausts of the engines, then correcting its vectors, turning, and rushing for the main body. Darting.

It hit with a flash and the blast came rolling over them. A plume erupted from the airplane, dirty black.

"Bruckner! Re-sight—the second plane is taking off."

She pointed. Gene chunked the second missile into the Dart tube. Bruckner swiveled with Gene's help. The second Extender was moving much too fast, and far too heavy, to abort takeoff.

The first airplane was coming apart, rupturing. A dark cloud belched across the sky.

Elinor said clearly, calmly, "The Dart's got a max range about right, so . . . *shoot*."

Bruckner let fly and the Dart rushed off into the sky, turned slightly as it sighted, accelerated like an angry hornet. They could hardly follow it. The sky was full of noise.

"Drop the launcher!" she cried.

"What?" Bruckner said, eyes on the sky.

She yanked it off him. He backed away and she opened the gas can as the men watched the Dart zooming toward the airplane. She did not watch the sky as she doused the launcher and splashed gas on the surrounding brush.

"Got that lighter?" she asked Bruckner.

He could not take his eyes off the sky. She reached into his right pocket and took out the lighter. Shooters had to watch, she knew.

She lit the gasoline and it went up with a *whump*.

"Hey! Let's go!" She dragged the men toward the car.

They saw the second hit as they ran for the Ford. The sound got buried in the thunder that rolled over them as the first Extender hit the ground kilometers away, across the inlet. The hard clap shook the air, made Gene trip, then stagger forward.

She started the Ford and turned away from the thick column of smoke rising from the launcher. It might erase any fingerprints or DNA they'd left, but it had another purpose, too.

She took the run back toward the coast at top speed. The men were excited, already reliving the experience, full of words. She said nothing, focused on the road that led them down to the shore. To the north, a spreading dark pall showed where the first plane went down.

One glance back at the hill told her the gasoline had served as a lure. A chopper was hammering toward the column of oily smoke, buying them some time.

The men were hooting with joy, telling each other how great it had been. She said nothing.

She was happy in a jangling way. Glad she'd gotten through without the friction with Bruckner coming to a point, too. Once she'd been dropped off, well up the inlet, she would hike around a bit, spend some time bird-watching, exchange horrified words with anyone she met about that awful plane crash—*No, I didn't actually see it; did you?*—and work her way back to the freighter, slipping by Elmendorf in the chaos that would be at crescendo by then. Get some sleep, if she could.

They stopped above the inlet, leaving the Ford parked under the thickest cover they could find. She looked for the eagle but didn't see it. Frightened skyward by the bewildering explosions and noises, no doubt. They ran down the incline. She thumbed on her comm, got a crackle of talk, handed it to Bruckner. He barked their code phrase, got confirmation.

A Zodiac was cutting a V of white, homing in on the shore. The air rumbled with the distant beat of choppers and jets, the search still concentrated around the airfield. She sniffed the rotten-egg smell, already here from the first Extender. It would kill everything near the crash, but this far off should be safe, she thought, unless the wind shifted. The second Extender had gone down closer to Anchorage, so it would be worse there. She put that out of her mind.

Elinor and the men hurried down toward the shore to meet the Zodiac. Bruckner and Gene emerged ahead of her as they pushed through a stand of evergreens, running hard. If they got out to the pickup craft, then suitably disguised among the fishing boats, they might well get away.

But on the path down, a stocky Inuit man stood. Elinor stopped, dodged behind a tree.

Ahead of her, Bruckner shouted, "Out of the way!"

The man stepped forward, raised a shotgun. She saw something compressed and dark in his face.

"You shot down the planes?" he demanded.

A tall Inuit racing in from the side shouted, "I saw their car comin' from up there!"

Bruckner slammed to a stop, reached down for his .45 automatic— and froze. The double-barreled shotgun could not miss at that range.

It had happened so fast. She shook her head, stepped quietly away. Her pulse hammered as she started working her way back to the Ford, slipping among the trees. The soft loam kept her footsteps silent.

A third man came out of the trees ahead of her. She recognized him as the young Inuit father from the diner, and he cradled a black hunting rifle. "Stop!"

She stood still, lifted her binocs. "I'm bird-watching; what—"

"I saw you drive up with them."

A deep, brooding voice behind her said, "Those planes were going to stop the warming, save our land, save our people."

She turned to see another man pointing a large-caliber rifle. "I, I, the only true way to do that is by stopping the oil companies, the corporations, the burning of fossil—"

The shotgun man, eyes burning beneath heavy brows, barked, "What'll we do with 'em?"

She talked fast, hands up, open palms toward him. "All that SkyShield nonsense won't stop the oceans from turning acid. Only fossil—"

"Do what you can, when you can. We learn that up here." This came from the tall man. The Inuit all had their guns trained on them now. The tall man gestured with his and they started herding the three of them into a bunch. The men's faces twitched, fingers trembled.

The man with the shotgun and the man with the rifle exchanged nods, quick words in a complex, guttural language she could not understand. The rifleman seemed to dissolve into the brush, steps fast and flowing, as he headed at a crouching dead run down to the shoreline and the waiting Zodiac.

She sucked in the clean sea air and could not think at all. These men wanted to shoot all three of them and so, she looked up into the sky to not see it coming. High up in a pine tree with a snapped top, an eagle flapped down to perch. She wondered if this was the one she had seen before.

The oldest of the men said, "We can't kill them. Let 'em rot in prison."

The eagle settled in. Its sharp eyes gazed down at her and she knew this was the last time she would ever see one. No eagle would ever live in a gray box. But she would. And never see the sky.

ABOUT THE AUTHOR

GREGORY BENFORD is a professor of physics at the University of California, Irvine. He is a Woodrow Wilson Fellow, was a Visiting Fellow at Cambridge University, and in 1995 received the Lord Prize for contributions to science. In 2007, he won the Asimov Award for science writing. His 1999 analysis of what endures, *Deep Time: How Humanity Communicates Across Millennia*, has been widely read. A fellow of the American Physical Society and a member of the World Academy of Arts and Sciences, he continues his research in astrophysics, plasma physics, and biotechnology. His fiction has won many awards, including the Nebula Award for his novel *Timescape*.

OUTLIERS

NICOLE FELDRINGER

Fix your climate model! Join scientists in digging through climate model output from more than thirty international research centers. Your mission: Decide whether each file contains interesting information, and identify the key factors contributing to global warming.

Some simulations will be control runs to create a historical baseline. Others will be generated from emissions scenarios with varying burdens of greenhouse gases and aerosols, reflecting alternative socioeconomic pathways.

Complexities in our cloud microphysics scheme are potentially producing unphysical realizations. And who knows what else may turn up? By validating models against actual observations, citizen scientists like yourself will help us better predict, and plan for, climate change where you live!

Esme Huybers-Smith resents taking on the work of some drudge graduate student who should have made better life choices, but her fingers keep flexing to navigate back to the browser tab. The ad, copied to the gamer message board she frequents, is festooned with enough university logos that she thinks maybe they ponied up money for good designers. Could be a slick game. In her apartment, her leg jitters in anticipation; without a full haptic suit, the motion doesn't register on her avatar. She isn't sold on saving the world—isn't sure what that world would look like. The talking heads on the media outlets wax nostalgic about plenty, prosperity, and stretches of peaceful coastline that sound like bullshit to Esme. But a game . . . well, she'll try any game once.

Esme closes windows to clear real estate on her display. She has a vague feeling that she's forgetting to be somewhere, but the Play Now button beckons, and anyway, it's the weekend. She shakes off the feeling and dives into the tutorial.

Gameplay centers around comparing model output ("simulation") with satellite observations ("data").

Step 1: A simulated climate field (temperature, humidity, etc.) will be plotted on the left.

Step 2: Compare the simulation to real-world satellite data automatically loaded on the right.

Step 3: In the comment form, make any specific observations about why the data deserve further scrutiny. Look for areas where the simulation disagrees with the data: Water droplets that are too big or too small, or icy where they should be liquid. Rain that is too heavy or too drizzly. Temperatures that are too cold or too warm. Clouds that form in the wrong place. Links to extensive satellite data archives can be found under the menu bar.

You also have the option to fix the climate model of the nearest modeling center by entering your postal code. Or hit "random."

Esme types in her postal code and is surprised to find a modeling center in New Jersey. There's an FAQ on how climate models work too, with an eye-numbing list of equations. Maybe she'll read over it later.

She's about to pull up her first simulation when a jingle erupts in her earbud. Esme's gaze flicks to the notification icon. Her father. She ignores it, but the ringtone trills a second time. Esme taps to accept.

"Dad, I'm a little busy right now."

"Because you're on the train?"

"What? No."

He continues as if she hasn't said anything. "You're busy because you're on the train to your brother's wedding. Your mother is waiting at the station to pick you up." His voice is dangerously even.

"Ah, about that . . . I'm not going to make the wedding after all."

She listens to him breathe on the other end of the connection. They both know that if she hasn't left by now, she's already missed the wedding. The high-speed train down the coast is six hours minimum. "Jacob will be so busy, he won't even notice I'm—"

"Attending virtually," he interrupts.

"But—"

"Nonnegotiable if you want a second chance with Huybers-Smith. Your family deserves better and so does your new brother-in-law. Wear something nice."

That's rich. She opens her mouth to say she's not particularly inclined to give *him* a second chance, but he's already logged out of chat. She worked for the family corporation out of college, but her father wanted an assistant, and Esme isn't assistant material. To say they butted heads is an understatement.

Esme shrinks the game window to a thumbnail. She pulls up the wedding invitation (re-sent by her father so she couldn't claim she lost it) and taps the door icon in the corner.

Her avatar materializes at her brother's wedding extravaganza on St. Pete Island. She thinks she looks just fine in black jeans and a ripped tank—otherwise, how will her brother recognize her? She makes a concession to the occasion by painting on some lipstick. Her aunts' inane greetings wash over her. Esme provides the aunts with equally inane responses. It must be so nice in New Jersey, they say.

Esme imagines her apartment. Her body, visored and gloved and sprawled across rumpled bed sheets. The slit of a window, curtains drawn tight to keep out the glare even though it makes her room stuffy as hell. When the apartment was subdivided decades ago, the contractors ran drywall down the middle of the window so each unit got a bit of natural light. They bisected the shower as well, not that she has the water rations to use it. Balanced on the windowsill and nearly buried by curtain is a withered jade plant that Esme's been meaning to trash for weeks.

"How's the beach?" she asks instead of answering. As long as the aunts don't start in on Jacob's latest triumph at the corporation, maybe she'll survive the family gathering. He always did play well with others. She loves her brother. It's the rest of them who lack subtlety.

"We have an amazing view from the dome, and the margaritas are divine. It's too bad you couldn't make it here for the ceremony." They wear sweaters tossed over their shoulders, the dome's climate control being another unspoken selling point. Esme licks the salt from her upper lip.

Sure, she could have gone to Florida. But the idea of touristing on the broken back of a hurricane-slammed economy makes her feel like a vampire. In the corner of her display, *Fix Your Climate Model!* beckons.

The guests file into rows of white folding chairs, their avatars auto-tracking their devices for the benefit of Esme and those too infirm to attend in person. NPCs fill out the back rows. Up near a palm tree arbor, Esme's father scans the crowd. Esme waggles her fingers at him. He frowns when he takes in her appearance.

When the minister clears his throat, Esme toggles the windows, bringing up the game and shrinking the wedding to a thumbnail.

She links her hands over her head to stretch, checking the wedding progress bar. The vows are over; the reception has begun. Sunlight sparkles on the Gulf beyond and below the dome, and the tarps of a distant shanty-town flap in the breeze. Esme tries to remember if she's ever met her brother's boyfriend—husband—outside of a chat room but draws a blank.

On the game, she hits start and is presented with her first climate simulation. A colorful, meaningless plot fills the window. Satellite data appears on the right side of the window with the same height-latitude axes. The two plots look the same, near as she can tell. Esme swipes for the next image and hopes that the difficulty setting ramps up.

It's soothing, she decides, like listening to music. She scans through ten in rapid succession. Then twenty. She gets points for every simulation she looks at, and double points for submitting comments.

"Esme?"

At the top of the display, her name populates the bottom of the high score board. The first stirrings of game obsession flutter in her chest.

"*Esme?*"

Her gaze snaps down to the wedding thumbnail, and she hastily maximizes it. A sea of avatar faces stare back at her from a shining, air-conditioned dome overlooking the sea. Esme squints. They all hold champagne flutes aloft. Her father, still trim and rather dapper—at least according to his avatar—stares at her steadily. Her brother, sitting before a gargantuan cake, tugs at their father's coat sleeve, already seeing how this will play out and trying to stop it.

"Esme, the toast?"

Shit. Esme chews her lip, considering whether she can make something up on the fly. Her father's frown deepens, and she shrugs helplessly at her brother.

Days later, boxes of empty Cheez-Its and rehydration packets surround her bed like shrapnel as Esme swipes through simulation after simulation. With her paychecks cleared from the last couple of freelance jobs, she can afford to devote herself to the hunt for the elusive outlier.

She likes outliers. She identifies with outliers.

Unfortunately, the game developers, or climate modelers, don't.

She's been monitoring outlier frequency. The game is converging. If she's right, soon all the models will be tuned to produce the same cookie-cutter output, and extreme weather events won't even be projected. Which means the game can't be won the way Esme plays it.

It also means the other players are being duped. Perhaps they wouldn't care. With each simulation taking less than a minute to complete, the game is obviously designed to appeal to do-gooders in their spare moments. But the unfairness of it burns in Esme.

The data formats have become more familiar to her than family. Eight times daily instantaneous, monthly mean, lat-lon, lat-height, 500 millibar pressure level. For most players, the game probably begins and ends at pattern recognition, but Esme makes a point of paying attention to the plot axes. In a separate window, the satellite data archives are open and ready, in case she wants to double-check the simulation against yet more data.

Her gaze zeros in on a wash of magenta, and she checks the values on the color bar. She barely glances at the data and already she can tell the ice droplet concentration is too high, and the cloud too deep. Esme flags the simulation, typing a quick note in the comment box. As she hits submit, her gaze is trained on the scoreboard. She scowls when her user-name doesn't budge. Second place. Always the bridesmaid.

She broods at the name above hers: dc2100.

Esme knows she's good. A folder on her desktop is filled with screen captures of her best finds. If someone is scoring higher than she is, they must be following a different MO, flagging minutiae on simulations that Esme skips and racking up double points that way.

She's already mentally composing the message she'll leave on the gamer boards—blowing the whistle on the rigged game. But if the project is canned, what then? No more climate forecasting and it's all on her? No, thank you.

Esme pulls up the About page, this time reading more carefully. She considers the contact form but isn't in the mood to wait out a reply. The project scientist is listed as Dr. Derya Çok. A moment later, Esme has accessed her webpage at the nearby lab, complete with contact information.

She'll just call her up and straighten this out.

Esme considers her skin inventory. Her hand hovers over her white male avatar, her go-to when it doesn't suit her to be underestimated. On the other hand, Derya Çok is a woman, and not senior staff. Authenticity could go a long way. With a sigh, Esme pulls off her VR headset and haptic gloves. She leverages herself out of bed and rummages around in her closet for a nice shirt. While her outdated laptop boots, she kicks food wrappers out of the camera field of view and initiates the connection as herself.

As she waits for Dr. Çok to accept or reject the call, Esme hopes she won't have to track her down in person. The streets are clogged with refugees, and they make her feel helpless. Meanwhile, ads tout romantic gondola rides around the flooded streets of Atlantic City, or cruises out to the storm-surge barriers. She avoids leaving her apartment.

To Esme's surprise, someone picks up.

"This is Derya Çok." She pronounces it like choke. Her expression is serious and composed.

Esme straightens. "Hello, Dr. Çok. I'm contacting you about *Fix Your Climate Model!*"

Dr. Çok raises her brows in silent inquiry.

Esme forges on. "I've identified a bug. Initially, whenever I flagged a good outlier, my score would go up, and the game would get harder. But lately, I'm barely seeing any game adjustment at all. It's like the outliers are being tuned away."

Dr. Çok smiles reassuringly. "We have a graduate student who's addressing each report submitted by the public."

"But my score doesn't go up."

"We appreciate your participation. To be clear, you're upset that you haven't won?"

Yes. "No. I'm upset because the game is rigged to reward conservative thinking."

"The game is *designed* to reduce uncertainty in climate change projections. This is what the funding agencies want and the policymakers demand. A single number, or as close as we can give them. Not a wide range that governments can use to argue for inaction. Given the opportunity, they would happily bank on the slim chance that the low estimate is the right one, and leave later generations in the lurch."

"Precise doesn't mean accurate."

Patience has fled Dr. Çok's voice. "I am well aware of the distinction," she says. "*Fix Your Climate Model!* isn't just a game, and winning is not just about one individual. I'm sorry if that offends your aesthetics. For decades, we've struggled to get a handle on cloud variability, and we're actually making progress now."

"But you're preconditioning to predict the answer you want," Esme says.

"It's not about what I want." Dr. Çok makes an arrested motion, as if to pinch the bridge of her nose. "I have a meeting to attend. Good day."

Esme lounges in her chair and steeples her fingers. The image of Dr. Derya Çok lingers on her screen until she keystrokes out of the program.

Should have gone with the avatar, she thinks as she spins in a circle.

Esme needs a hacker.

She doesn't have the computer skills to do what needs doing, and she doesn't have the people skills to convince a random person (or project scientist) to help. Which leaves family. Her father's out of the question. She logs into her private chat room and pings Jacob.

"Hey, bro," she says when his avatar materializes. "I need a hacker."

He mills around the sectional sofa and quirks an eyebrow at the media screen that covers most of one wall. "And you're telling me this why?"

"More specifically, I need your husband."

"I need my husband too," he says. "Too bad you made a scene at our wedding."

She checks to make sure she didn't actually call her father. "You don't really care about that, do you? Toasts are lame. Better that I talked too little—"

"Try not at all."

"—than too much. I saved you the embarrassment."

"That's really not how I . . ." He sighs. "When are you going to stop playing games and grow up, Esme?"

"What do you care how I spend my time, anyway? You have your pretty apartment and your pretty husband. Isn't that enough to keep you occupied?"

"It would be, if not for Dad," he says. "I'm sick of being the responsible heir. Take some of the fucking pressure off me for once."

"Reality is one big game to Dad. At least I'm honest about what I'm doing."

An orange tabby leans into Jacob's leg. Jacob starts, then bends over to scratch the cat behind its ears. The beast starts to purr. Esme programmed it to put her guests at ease.

Esme relents. "If you help me with this," she says, "I'll do my best to make up with Dad."

"Deal. If Manuel agrees, of course."

"I agree," a cheery voice calls, picked up by the mic in Jacob's headset.

"You had us on *speaker*?" Esme says in disgust.

"Just grant Manuel access." Jacob logs off, and Manuel appears a moment later.

"So, I'm pretty?" Manuel settles on the sofa, and the cat jumps into his lap.

"Sure, but can you code?"

They share a grin, and Manuel cracks his knuckles.

"Do you know where the code repository is?" He pulls up a window in the space in front of him and leaves it visible to her.

"The lab in New Jersey."

"Give me the address. Let me run a pentest on it." His hands flex in a flurry of keystrokes, and a moment later, he groans. "This is a government computer."

"Technically, it's a government-*funded* computer. Nonessential, non-defense."

"I don't think they see the distinction."

Esme thinks of Dr. Çok. "They never do."

Manuel lowers his voice. "Do you know any staff account usernames?"

Esme's gaze strays to the open window of *Fix Your Climate Model!* hidden from Manuel's view. The scoreboard taunts her. "Try dc2100."

"I'll attempt to brute-force the password first. Give me a minute."

"Does my father know you can do this?" Esme says.

"He hired me."

Smart. Sense of humor. Maybe Jacob landed a good one after all.

She leaves off pondering her brother's love life when Manuel's hands still. "I have write access. Tell me how you want the game to work."

Esme explains about the convergence. She gets pissed off all over again thinking about it.

"So they're weighting entries more heavily that fall within some preferred range? And then the models are tuned to those outputs and provide more of the same?" Manuel asks.

"Exactly that," Esme says, grateful he grasps the problem immediately. "I don't want to break the physics of the models. I just want them to sample the full range of variability."

"I think I can reset the thresholds."

He makes it sound so easy. Esme shakes her hands nervously, and her stomach grumbles. "How long is this going to take?"

"Don't know," he says without looking away from the window.

"Do you mind if I grab something to eat?"

Manuel gives a distracted nod and Esme puts her avatar on standby. As she slips out of VR, she plucks her sweat-soaked shirt away from her skin and fans herself. It's only three o'clock but she grabs a box of noodle soup and switches on the hotplate. By the time Manuel resurfaces, she's licked the bowl clean.

"I uploaded the patch," he says. "You know network security might question dc2100 and clue in to the backdoor?"

Esme restarts *Fix Your Climate Model!* "As long as they don't catch it till Monday. I have a game to win."

Manuel glances to the side, presumably to a hidden display. "Jacob sent me some articles. . . . This game has sparked a wave of climate mitigation policies. It's a good thing they're doing," he says softly. "You're not out to destroy the world, are you?"

Esme recalls what Dr. Derya Çok said. How the policymakers want an answer, and it doesn't so much matter if the answer is right or wrong as long as they're seen trying to do something. It's not good enough.

"I'm *fixing* the world."

She's nervous to resume the game. What if Manuel's patch didn't fix the problem? What if an overzealous network tech was paying attention and undid the changes to the source code? Esme gives her display the side eye as she selects the first simulation.

It's a boring one. She swipes through the output until she finds something worth flagging.

Chills run along her spine, and she knows Manuel's hack worked.

The image spread before her is a surface map, which is her favorite, because continents. Most of the simulations in the game focus on cloudy skies up in the troposphere, but the problem with big data—the reason the global community of scientists crowdsourced gamers to troll through it in the first place—is that there's too much of it and it's too complex to winnow automatically. And occasionally, she runs across surface maps.

It takes her a moment to identify what's different about this particular simulation, a sweep of blues across the whole northeast quadrant of North America. Esme squints at the color bar, then finds New Jersey for reference. It's *colder*. By about five degrees C, and the temperature gradient between the equator and pole is out of whack. From hours spent playing *Fix Your Climate Model!*, Esme knows the warming pattern has a profound effect on the circulation of the atmosphere, the distribution of clouds, the intensity of rain. The boundaries of deserts.

She stares at the display. With the original thresholds back in place, this find will send her to the top of the scoreboard, but so what? Who does that help other than her own ego? Not the homeless encampments up and down the Eastern seaboard.

Esme's hand flexes in an aborted keystroke. If only she had a way to pull up the matching precipitation file, or the emissions cocktail, or the daily extremes. She wants access beyond that doled out by the game, the kind of access that no one will grant a gamer. She also has more resources than most, much as she hates to admit it.

Dr. Derya Çok was right about one thing. Fixing the game world is the lesser goal. Esme scares herself, a little, even contemplating manipulating the actual climate. Engineering hurdles don't daunt her but unintended consequences do. As does the ethical dilemma of optimizing one region's climate at the expense of another's, and what does "optimize" even mean? But it would be irresponsible not to study these cases. If some models are simulating more amenable climates, she wants to know why and if that can be replicated in the real world.

Esme sends a chat request to her father. If her family wants her back in the fold, they'll have to take her on her own terms.

Her father is quiet for a long moment after she makes her proposition. "How do I know you won't bail on this project, too?"

"I didn't leave last time," Esme says, encouraged that he hasn't said no outright. "You pushed me out."

"I expected you to want to learn the ropes from me, not try to take over."

Esme shrugs. "I had my own ideas. I *have* my own ideas."

She finishes the conversation with her father and turns her attention back to *Fix Your Climate Model!* Into the comment box, she types:

Dear Derya/dc2100,

I know you'll tell me it's way more complex than I realize. That this one (awesome) simulation spit out by one climate model doesn't represent a panacea. That's okay.

But if there's one outlier, there can be another. It's beautiful, what's out here in the fringe.

I'm involved in a new geoengineering working group at Huybers-Smith, and we could use your expertise. I've already okayed your consulting fees.

The more I think about it, the more I wonder if you seeded that simulation for someone to find. Either way, I'm pretty sure shilling your precisely accurate predictions to the government gets old, though I've done what I can to alleviate that. Besides, where's the fun if you're always in first place?

Esme Huybers-Smith

ABOUT THE AUTHOR

NICOLE FELDRINGER holds a PhD in Atmospheric Sciences from the University of Washington and a Master's degree in Geological Sciences. In 2011, she attended the Viable Paradise Writer's Workshop, and her first published short story appeared in the *Sword & Laser Anthology*. She currently lives in Los Angeles where she is a research fellow at the California Institute of Technology. Find her on Twitter @nicofeld.

QUIET TOWN

JASON GURLEY

She was in the laundry room, bent over a basket of Benjamin's muddy trousers and grass-stained T-shirts and particularly odorous socks, when a rap sounded on the screen door. She didn't hear at first; she'd noticed, bent over there, a cluster of webbed, purplish veins just below her thigh, beside her knee. She didn't like seeing them. They were like a slow-moving car wreck, those veins, a little darker, a little more severe each time she looked.

The front porch creaked, and the screen door rattled on its hinges as the knock came again.

Bev eased up to standing, still clutching a mound of laundry against her middle. She pinned the clothes with one hand and, with the other, looped the hair out of her eyes.

"Yeah?" she called over her shoulder.

"Me," the answer came.

Bev took in a long breath, let it fill up her lungs, and raised her voice to a tone one might reasonably mistake for pleasant.

"Come on in, Ezze," she hollered. "Coffee cake on the table, you want some."

The screen door complained a bit, and not for the first time Bev made a mental note to oil the damn thing. But she knew she'd forget between now and the next time Ezze hobbled over. The door banged shut, followed by the scuff of the dining chair being pulled out, the expulsion of breath as Ezze dropped, too heavily, onto it. The chair wouldn't take such abuse forever. Bev sometimes wished it would give out, and then felt guilty for thinking such things. Beneath her gravel and bluster, Ezze was just lonely.

Bev stuffed the clothes into the wash and spun the old machine up. It rocked agreeably, knocking with a small clatter into the dryer beside it. She leaned against the wall, just for a second, just to take a few breaths before going in to the kitchen. The back door was open, its own screen door shut. Gray light spilled through the window, leaked through the uneven gaps in the door jamb. She could see the pale, lumbering clouds that scraped the tops of the houses around hers. Most of those houses were empty now.

Just me and Benji, Bev thought.

From the kitchen, a smacking sound, the clink of a serving knife against the platter.

Just me and Benji and Ezze, Bev corrected.

She didn't like the wind out there today. The Aparicios had left laundry on the line when they moved out—in a hurry, like everybody these past few weeks—and almost all of it was scattered around the neighborhood now, T-shirts and pantyhose and thermal underwear caught up in bare tree branches, soaked and plastered in gutters. Almost all of it, except for the heavy quilt, heavier now from all the rain, that dragged the laundry line low. The wind caught even that, lifted it nearly horizontal, a cheerful, soggy flag.

"A bit dry, dear," came Ezze's voice.

Bev turned away from the screen door. Cold air breathed around it, pushing through the gaps, and Bev shivered. But she left the inner door open for Benjamin and went into the kitchen.

"How's the hip?" Bev asked, ignoring Ezze's comment.

Ezze groaned theatrically. "I'd give anything for a new one," she said. "But who's got money for that?"

Her gray cane rested against the table beside her, tipped up on two of its four stubby feet. The rubber nubs on the end of each were damp and clumped with gray earth and grit. Bev sighed and picked up the cane and carried it onto the porch. Ezze didn't say anything. Bev cranked the spigot attached to the house. It choked and sputtered, coughing up a weak stream. Bev rinsed the cane, then propped it against the house and went back inside.

Ezze regarded her irritably as Bev spritzed a paper towel with Windex, then wiped up the mud the cane had left behind.

"That's for windows, dear," Ezze said, watching Bev from beneath her glasses.

Bev didn't say anything, just balled up the towel and dropped it into the wastebasket. The plastic lid swung twice, stopped.

"That's why it's called Windex," Ezze went on. "*Windows. Win*-dex." She wrinkled her slug of a nose and squinted up at the ceiling thoughtfully. "Don't know where the '-ex' part came from, though."

Bev went into the kitchen, her hands searching for tasks. Perhaps if she appeared to be busy, Ezze would leave. But the countertops were tidy, the sink free of dishes.

"Your linoleum's soft," Ezze said. Bev looked up to see the woman bouncing lightly in the chair. Beneath her, the linoleum bowed. "It's cheap stuff. I've got the same in my place."

"Well, stop making it worse," Bev said.

Ezze laughed as if this was funny. "You should see mine," she said. "Sagging all over the place."

I wonder why, Bev thought.

Ezze took another bite of coffee cake, then made a show of gagging on crumbs. "Water," she croaked, putting one damp hand to the loose skin around her throat. "Water."

Bev filled a glass from the tap, then put it down in front of Ezze, who stared at it in horror, her stage act forgotten.

"Dear," Ezze said. "You're not drinking it, are you? There's a warning. It's all over the TV."

"We don't have a TV," Bev said flatly. "What warning?"

"Contaminated supply or something. I don't know." Ezze waved her hand about. "Real problem is what I came over to tell you about, though. You're not going to believe it."

Bev took the glass of water away from Ezze, crossed back into the kitchen, and dumped it aggressively into the sink. Then the fight faded from her, just as quickly as it seemed to have risen up. Ezze didn't mean any harm, she reminded herself again. She was old; she was alone. It wasn't her fault, none of it. Can't fight age. Can't make people stay.

"What's that?" Bev asked, brushing her hair back again. "Believe what?"

The back screen door banged open then, and Benji clattered into the kitchen like a runaway shopping cart. He was out of breath, his pants rolled up to his knees. He held his tennis shoes in one hand, but whatever he'd gotten into, he'd taken them off too late. They were caked with gray mud, and his legs were splashed with it.

Ezze looked at Benji, who gasped like a fish, trying to get some words out.

"*He* knows," Ezze said. "Don't you, boy."

Bev looked wide-eyed at Ezze, then back at Benjamin. "Knows what? Benjamin, you're filth—"

Benjamin shook his head and held up a hand, working on just breathing.

"Oh, fine," Ezze said. "I'll tell her."

"Tell me what?" Bev asked. "What the hell is going on?"

Benjamin, cheeks strawberry-colored against his pale skin, said, "Water—water—"

Bev turned to fill her glass again, but Benji lurched forward and grabbed her hand.

"No," he said, chest heaving. "Water's— The water—"

"Oh, for Pete's sake," Ezze said. "The water's here, Bev."

* * * *

What was it Gordy had said?

"When ice melts, the glass don't spill over."

Bev had leaned against him in the porch swing, comforted by his disbelief, while he told her about a column he read when they were in college, by that brainy woman who answered people's letters. Someone wrote in and asked the woman if you were to fill a glass with ice cubes, then run tap water right up to the rim of the glass, what would happen when the ice melted? And the brainy woman's reply had been something about melting ice cubes displacing the same amount of water as the frozen ice.

It's not my fault, Bev thought now. *It's his fault, not mine. His.*

She wasn't the fool. It was him. He was.

But that wasn't fair. Gordy hadn't taken the news seriously, but at the time, nobody had. They'd been on the porch, listening to the radio while the neighborhood noisily settled in for the night. Benjamin had been scrambling around in the front yard, kicking dried-out pinecones around like footballs.

"You remember the oddest things," Bev had said, and Gordy had laughed. There had been plenty of laughter in those days. *Those days,* that's how Bev thought of them. As in: those days when life was good. Those days when there were still people around. When the sun blazed and they called it a nice summer day, not an ice-melter like everyone did now. Those days. When Gordy was still around.

But Gordy had been wrong. The brainy woman had been wrong. The radio warning all those years ago, when Benji was small, had been wrong. Fifty years, they'd said. In fifty years, the coastlines will be different. Your homes will be underwater. Fifty years.

They'd listened to the talk shows afterward, the pundits arguing that nobody knew what the next ten years would look like, much less the next fifty. It's all a farce, they argued. It's a campaign strategy. A ploy. Fifty years—ha!

It had happened in five.

Gordy went and died before it got serious, and on summer evenings, when the skies went purple and orange, Bev and Benjamin and some-times Ezze, even, would wander down to the seawall with the rest of the town, and they'd all stand on the wall and look down at the water level. When they couldn't see the high-water mark, somebody would motor out in a rubber boat and spray a new line of paint on the wall.

Soon enough, someone could just lean over the rail and spray that new line. The water kept rising. When it was a few inches from the top of the wall, people started leaving town. In a month's time, the village had emptied.

Ezze scooped up her cane and went heavily down the porch steps. Benji tugged on Bev's hand. He held it tightly as they walked, following the older woman as she puffed along. Bev barely registered his grip until it was too tight, and she yelped.

"Sorry, Mama," he said.

She saw Gordy in Benji's eyes. They weren't a child's eyes anymore. Benji was nearly thirteen, and already his eyes were narrow slots. He and Gordy both had a Clint Eastwood squint, and she could see the boy's jawline, his cheekbones, sharpening. His hair was already drawing back on his head, though. She didn't dare break his heart by telling him now, but he'd lose most of it by twenty, probably, just like his father.

The thought that he might not see twenty was a block of ice in her gut.

"I knowed about it when Pippa came home with a crab shell in her mouth," Ezze said, huffing as she waddled ahead. "Came right on home with it. No place else she could've gotten it. Had to have washed up over the wall. Fresh, too. She'd pulled half the meat out, but I swear the thing was still twitching."

The street was gritty under their feet. Bev padded along in her flip-flops, and as Ezze fell silent, Bev's shoes *pock-pock*ed like tennis balls. There was a sound she hadn't heard in a long time. Used to be a court down by the high school, and on quiet days, you could hear the distant sound of rackets *pock*ing the balls, back and forth, back and forth. The sharp shriek of tennis shoes on the clay, too. People grunting and shouting excitedly.

Quiet town.

"I saw your Rascal," Benji said. "I tried to fix it, but . . ."

He trailed off.

"Your Rascal?" Bev asked.

Ezze stopped for a moment, breathing heavily. "Yeah," she admitted, bending over a bit, leaning on the cane. "I rode down there on it with Pippa to see for myself. Battery died right up at the wall. There were some boys putting down sandbags, and they tried to help me with it, but it's just dead. One of them walked me back home. Nice kid. I don't know whose kid. Not many left, you know."

Benji said, "It's still where you left it. There's some seagull shit on it, but—"

"Benjamin Howard Marsh," Bev said sharply.

"Never mind that," Ezze said loudly. She pounded the rubber feet of her cane on the concrete. "Look."

They all looked down to see a thin ribbon of water. It cascaded between their feet, and they all watched in a hush as it passed them by, gathering up bits of leaves and fine gravel. The water kept going, making its way down the street until they couldn't quite make out its leading edge. It was here now, Bev thought.

"Oh, Jesus," Ezze cried. She high-stepped around her cane as another rivulet ran through the yellowed grass on the shoulder of the road. And in the quiet then they could hear it: the water, its thousand narrow fingers, creeping through the dead lawns and over the bleached asphalt. They could see it, stream after stream of it moving across empty driveways, splitting around the stop sign post, and then the thousand fingers of it bled together until the water was a blue-gray sheet, rippling along beneath the darkening sky, claiming the land for its own.

"Mama," Benji said.

The water spilled around their feet, thin but *here*.

"Mama," he said again, tugging Bev's hand. She looked up at him, then at Ezze, whose stern features had folded into a new shape, a softer, more honest mask, a fearful one.

"Mama, we gotta go," Benjamin said.

Such a fool, Bev thought to herself again. *What would Gordy have done?* But it didn't matter what he would do now. It mattered what he had done then, and what he had done then was laugh, then die.

We should've had a TV, she thought absurdly.

She looked at Ezze. The fading sun caught the faint whiskers on Ezze's cheeks, turning them into tiny glowing filaments. Benji stared at her, his narrow eyes still fierce with hope and promise, his skin rosy where it faced the sunset, and dusky purple on the opposite side, in shadow, as if he was already dead, and there was no way around it.

ABOUT THE AUTHOR

JASON GURLEY is the author of *Eleanor*, *The Man Who Ended the World*, *Deep Breath Hold Tight*, and the bestselling novel *Greatfall*, among other books. He lives with his family in the Pacific Northwest, and can be found at jasongurley.com.

THE DAY IT ALL ENDED

CHARLIE JANE ANDERS

Bruce Grinnord parked aslant in his usual spot and ran inside the DiZi Corp headquarters. Bruce didn't check in with his team or even pause to glare at the beautiful young people having their toes stretched by robots while they sipped macrobiotic goji-berry shakes and tried to imagine ways to make the next generation of gadgets cooler-looking and less useful. Instead, he sprinted for the executive suite. He took the stairs two or three at a time, until he was so breathless he feared he'd have a heart attack before he even finished throwing his career away.

DiZi's founder, Jethro Gruber—*Barron's* Young Visionary of the Year five years running—had his office atop the central spire of the funhouse castle of DiZi's offices, in a round glass turret. Looking down on the employee oxygen bar and the dozen gourmet cafeterias. If you didn't have the key to the private elevator, the only way up was this spiral staircase, which climbed past a dozen Executive Playspaces, and any one of those people could cockblock you before you got to Jethro's pad. But nobody seemed to notice Bruce charging up the stairs, fury twisting his round face, even when he nearly put his foot between the steps and fell into the Moroccan Spice Café.

Bruce wanted to storm into Jethro's office and shout his resignation in Jethro's trendy schoolmaster glasses. He wanted to enter the room already denouncing the waste, the stupidity of it all—but when he reached the top of the staircase, he was so out of breath, he could only wheeze, his guts wrung and cramped. He'd only been in Jethro's office once before: an elegant goldfish bowl with one desk that changed shape (thanks to modular pieces that came out of the floor), a few chairs, and one dot of maroon rug at its center. Bruce stood there, massaging his dumb stomach and taking in the oppressive simplicity.

So, Jethro spoke first, the creamy purr Bruce knew from a million company videos. "Hi, Bruce. You're late."

"I'm . . . I'm what?"

"You're late," Jethro said. "You were supposed to have your crisis of conscience three months ago." He pulled out his Robo-Bop and displayed a personal calendar, which included one entry: "Bruce Has a Crisis of Conscience." It was dated a few months earlier. "What kept you, man?"

It started when Bruce took a wrong turn on the way to work. Actually, he drove to the wrong office—the driving equivalent of a Freudian slip.

He was on the interstate at seven thirty, listening to a banjo solo that he hadn't yet learned to play. Out his right window, every suburban courtyard had its own giant ThunderNet tower, just like the silver statue in Bruce's own cul-de-sac—the sleek concave lines and jet-streamed base like a 1950s Googie space fantasy. To his left, almost every passing car had a Car-Dingo bolted to its hood, with its trademark sloping fins and whirling lights. And half the drivers were listening to music, or making Intimate Confessions on their Robo-Bops. Once on the freeway, Bruce could see much larger versions of the ThunderNet tower dotting the landscape, from shopping-mall roofs as well as empty fields. Plus everywhere he saw giant billboards for DiZi's newest product, the Crado—emptyfaced, multicultural babies splayed out in a milk-white, egg-shaped chair that monitored the baby's air supply and temperature in some way that Bruce still couldn't explain.

Bruce was a VP of marketing at DiZi—shouldn't he be able to find something good to say about even one of the company's products?

So, this one morning, Bruce got off the freeway a few exits too soon. Instead of driving to the DiZi offices, he went down a feeder road to a dingy strip mall that had offices instead of dry cleaners. This was the route Bruce had taken for years before he joined DiZi, and he felt as though he'd taken the wrong commute by mistake.

Bruce's old parking spot was open, and he could almost pretend time had rolled back, except that he'd lost some hair and gained some weight. He found himself pushing past the white balsawood-and-metal door with the cheap sign saying ECO GNOMIC and into the offices, and then he stopped. A roomful of total strangers perched on beanbags and folding chairs turned and stared, and Bruce had no explanation for who he was or why he was there. "Uh," Bruce said.

The Eco Gnomic offices looked like crap compared to DiZi's majesty, but also compared to the last time he'd seen them. Take the giant Intervention Board that covered the main wall: When Bruce had worked there, it'd been covered with millions of multicolored tacks attached to scraps of incidents. *This company is planning a major polluting project, so we mobilize culture-jammer flash mobs here and organize protesters at the public hearing there.* Like a giant multidimensional chess game covering one wall, deploying patience and playfulness against the massive corporate engine. Now, though, the Intervention Board contained nothing but bad news, without much in the way of strategies. Arctic shelf disintegrating, floods, superstorms, droughts, the Gulf Stream stuttering, extinctions like dominos falling. The office furniture teetered on broken legs, and the same computers from five years ago whined and stammered. The young woman nearest Bruce couldn't even afford a proper Mohawk—her hair grew back in patches on the sides of her head, and the stripe on top was wilting. None of these people seemed energized about saving the planet.

Bruce was about to flee when his old boss, Gerry Donkins, showed up and said, "Bruce! Welcome back to the nonprofit sector, man." Bruce and

Gerry wound up spending an hour sitting on crates, drinking expired Yoo-hoo. "Yeah, Eco Gnomic is dying," said Gerry, giant mustache twirling, "but so is the planet."

"I feel like I made a terrible mistake," Bruce said. He looked at the board and couldn't see any pattern to the arrangement of ill omens.

"You did," Gerry replied. "But it doesn't make any difference, and you've been happy. You've been happy, right? We all thought you were happy. How is Marie, by the way?"

"Marie left me two years ago," Bruce said.

"Oh," Gerry said.

"But on the plus side, I've been taking up the banjo."

"Anyway, no offense, but you wouldn't have made a difference if you'd stayed with us. We probably passed the point of no return a while back."

Point of no return. It sounded sexual, or like letting go of a trapeze at the apex of its arc.

"You did the smart thing," said Gerry, "going to work for the flashiest consumer products company and enjoying the last little bit of the ride."

Bruce got back in his Prius and drove the rest of the way to work, past the rows of ThunderNet towers and the smoke from far-off forest fires. This felt like the last day of the human race, even though it was just another day on the steep slope. As Bruce reached the lavender glass citadel of DiZi's offices, he started to go numb inside, like always. But instead, this time, a fury took him, and that's when he charged inside and up the stairs to Jethro's office, ready to shove his resignation down the CEO's throat.

"What do you mean?" Bruce said to Jethro, as his breath came back. "You were *expecting* me to come in here and resign?"

"Something like that." Jethro gestured for Bruce to sit in one of the plain white, absurdly comfortable teacup chairs. He sat cross-legged in the other one, like a yogi in his wide-sleeved linen shirt and camper pants.

In person, he looked slightly chubbier and less classically handsome than all his iconic images, but the perfect hipster bowl haircut and sideburns, and those famous glasses, were instantly recognizable. "But like I said: late. The point is, you got here in the end."

"You didn't *engineer* this. I'm not one of your gadgets. This is real. I really am fed up with making pointless toys when the world is about to choke on our filth. I'm done."

"It wouldn't be worth anything if it wasn't real, bro." Jethro gave Bruce one of his conspiratorial/mischievous smiles that made Bruce want to smile back in spite of his soul-deep anger. "That's why we hired you in the first place. You're the canary in the coal mine. Here, look at the org chart."

Jethro made some hand motions, and one glass surface became a screen, which projected an org chart with a thousand names and job descriptions. And there, halfway down on the left, was Bruce's name, with *CANARY IN THE COAL MINE*. And a picture of Bruce's head on a cartoon bird's body.

"I thought my job title was junior executive VP for product management," Bruce said, staring at his openmouthed face and those unfurled wings.

Jethro shrugged. "Well, you just resigned, right? So, you don't have a title anymore." He made another gesture, and a bright-eyed young thing wheeled a minibar out of the elevator and offered Bruce beer, whiskey, hot sake, coffee, and Mexican Coke. Bruce felt rebellious, choosing a single-malt whiskey, until he realized he was doing what Jethro wanted. He took a swig and burned his throat and eyes.

"So, you're quitting; you should go ahead and tell me what you think of my company." Jethro spread his hands and smiled.

"Well." Bruce drank more whiskey and then sputtered. "If you really want to know . . . Your products are pure evil. You build these sleek little pieces of shit that are designed with all this excess capacity and redundant systems. Have you ever looked at the schematics of the ThunderNet towers? It's like you were *trying* to build something overly complex. And it's the ultimate glorification of form over function—you've been able to convince everybody with disposable income to buy your crap, because people love anything that's ostentatiously pointless. I've had a Robo-Bop for years, and I still don't understand what half the widgets and menu options are for. I don't think anybody does. You use glamour and marketing to convince people they need to fill their lives with empty crap instead of paying attention to the world and realizing how fragile and beautiful it really is. You're the devil."

The drinks fairy had started gawking halfway through this rant, then she seemed to decide it was against her pay grade to hear this. She retreated into the elevator and vanished around the time Bruce said he didn't understand half the stuff his Robo-Bop did.

Bruce had fantasized about telling Jethro off for years, and he enjoyed it so much, he had tears in his eyes by the end. Even knowing that Jethro had put this moment on his Robo-Bop calendar couldn't spoil it.

Jethro was nodding, as if Bruce had just about covered the bases. Then he made another esoteric gesture, and the glass wall became a screen again. It displayed a PowerPoint slide:

DIZI CORP. PRODUCT STRATEGY
+ Beautiful Objects That Are Functionally Useless
+ Spare Capacity
+ Redundant Systems
+ Overproliferation of Identical But Superficially Different Products
+ Form Over Function
+ Mystifying Options and Confusing User Interface

"You missed one, I think," Jethro said. "The one about overproliferation. That's where we convince people to buy three different products that are almost exactly the same but not quite."

"Wow." Bruce looked at the slide, which had gold stars on it. "You really are completely evil."

"That's what it looks like, huh?" Jethro actually laughed as he tapped on his Robo-Bop. "Tell you what. We're having a strategy meeting at three, and we need our canary there. Come and tell the whole team what you told me."

"What's the point?" Bruce felt whatever the next level below despair was. Everything was a joke, *and* he'd been deprived of the satisfaction of being the one to unveil the truth.

"Just show up, man. I promise it'll be entertaining, if nothing else. What else are you going to do with the rest of your day, drive out to the beach and watch the seagulls dying?"

That was exactly what Bruce had planned to do after leaving DiZi. He shrugged. "Sure. I guess I'll go get my toes stretched for a while."

"You do that, Bruce. See you at three."

The drinks fairy must have gossiped about Bruce, because people were looking at him when he walked down to the main promenade. If there'd been a food court in *2001: A Space Odyssey*, it would have looked like DiZi's employee promenade. Bruce didn't have his toes stretched. Instead, he ate two organic calzones to settle his stomach after the morning whiskey. The calzones made Bruce more nauseated. The people on Bruce's marketing team waved at him in the cafeteria but didn't approach the radioactive man.

Bruce was five minutes early for the strategy meeting, but he was still the last one to arrive, and everyone was staring at him. Bruce had never visited the Executive Meditation Hole, which also doubled as Jethro's private movie theater. It was a big bunker under the DiZi main building with wall carpets and aromatherapy.

"Hey, Bruce." Jethro was lotus-positioning on the dais at the front, where the movie screen would be. "Everybody, Bruce had a Crisis of Conscience today. Big props for Bruce, everybody."

Everyone clapped. Bruce's stomach started turning again, so he put his face in front of one of the aromatherapy nozzles and huffed calming scents. "So, Bruce has convinced me that it's time for us to change our product strategy to focus on saving the planet."

"You what?" Bruce pulled away from the soothing jasmine puff. "Are you completely delusional? Have you been surrounded by yes-men and media sycophants for so long that you've lost all sense of reality? It's way, way too late to save the planet, man." Everybody stared at Bruce until Jethro clapped again. Then everyone else clapped too.

"Bruce brings up a good point," Jethro said. "The timetable is daunting, and we're late. Partly because your Crisis of Conscience was months behind schedule, I feel constrained to point out. In any case, how would we go about making this audacious goal? Enterprise audacity being one of our corporate buzzsaws, of course. And for that, I'm going to turn it over to Zoe. Zoe?"

Jethro went and sat in the front row, and a big screen appeared up front. A skinny woman in a charcoal-gray suit got up and used her Robo-Bop to control a presentation.

"Thanks, Jethro," the stick-figure woman, Zoe, said. She had perfect Amanda Seyfried hair. "It really comes down to what we call product versatility." She clicked onto a picture of a nice midrange car with a swooshy device bolted to its roof. "Take the Car-Dingo, for example. What does it do?"

Various people raised their hands and offered slogans like, "It makes a Prius feel like a muscle car," or "It awesomizes your ride."

"Exactly!" Zoe smiled. She clicked the next slide over, and proprietary specs for the Car-Dingo came up. They were so proprietary, Bruce had never seen them. Bruce struggled to make sense of all those extra connections and loops going right into the engine. She pulled up similar specs for the ThunderNet tower, full of secret logic. Another screen showed all those nonsensical Robo-Bop menus, suddenly unlocking and making sense.

"Wait a minute." Bruce was the only one standing up, besides Zoe. "So, you're saying all these devices were dual-function all this time? And in all the hundreds of hellish product meetings I've sat through, you never once mentioned this fact?"

"Bruce," Jethro said from the front row, "we've got a little thing at DiZi called the Culture of Listening. That means no interrupting the presentation until it's finished, or no artisanal cookies for you."

Bruce sighed and climbed over someone to find a seat and listened to another hour of corporate "buzzsaws." At one point, he could have sworn Zoe said something about "end-user velocitization." One thing Bruce did understand in the gathering haze: even though DiZi officially frowned on the cheap knockoffs of its products littering the Third World, the company had gone to great lengths to make sure those illicit copies used the exact same specs as the real items.

Just as Bruce was passing out from boredom, Jethro thanked Zoe and said, "Now let's give Bruce the floor. Bruce, come on down." Bruce had to thump his own legs to wake them up, and when he reached the front, he'd forgotten all the things he was dying to say an hour earlier. The top echelons of DiZi management stared, waiting for him to say something.

"Uh." Bruce's head hurt. "What do you want me to say?"

Jethro stood up next to Bruce and put an arm around him. "This is where your Crisis of Conscience comes in, Bruce dude. Let's just say, as a thought embellishment, that we could fix it." ("Thought embellishment" was one of Jethro's buzzsaws.)

"Fix . . . it?"

Jethro handed Bruce a Robo-Bop with a pulsing Yes/No screen. "It's all on you, buddy. You push yes, we can make a difference here. There'll be some disruptions, people might be a mite inconvenienced, but we can ameliorate some of the problems. Push no, and things go on as they are. But bear in mind—if you push yes, you're the one who has to explain to the people."

Bruce still didn't understand what he was saying yes to, but he hardly cared. He jabbed the yes button with his right thumb. Jethro whooped and led him to the executive elevator so they could watch the fun from the roof.

"It should be almost instantaneous," Jethro said over his shoulder as he hustled into the lift. "Thanks to our patented 'snaggletooth' technology that makes all our products talk to each other. It'll travel around the world like a wave. It's part of our enterprise philosophy of Why Not Now."

The elevator lurched upward, and in moments, they had reached the roof. "It's starting," Jethro said. He pointed to the nearest ThunderNet tower. The sleek lid was opening up like petals, until the top resembled a solar dish. And a strange haze was gathering over the top of it.

"This technology has been around for years, but everybody said it was too expensive to deploy on a widespread basis," Jethro said with a wink. "In a nutshell, the tops of the towers contain a photocatalyst material, which turns the CO_2 and water in the atmosphere into methane and oxygen. The methane gets stored and used as an extra power source. The tower is also spraying an amine solution into the air that captures more CO_2 via a proprietary chemical reaction. That's why the ThunderNets had to be so pricey."

Just then, Bruce felt a vibration from his own Robo-Bop. He looked down and was startled to see a detailed audit of Bruce's personal carbon footprint—including everything he'd done to waste energy in the past five years.

"And hey, look at the parking lot," Jethro said. All the Car-Dingos were reconfiguring themselves, snaking new connections into the car engines. "We're getting most of those vehicles as close to zero emissions as possible, using amines that capture the cars' CO_2. You can use the waste heat from the engine to regenerate the amines." But the real gain would come from the car's GPS, which would start nudging people to carpool whenever another Car-Dingo user was going to the same destination, using a "packet-switching" model to optimize everyone's commute for greenness. Refuse to carpool, and your car might start developing engine trouble—and the Car-Dingos, Bruce knew, were almost impossible to remove.

As for the Crados? Jethro explained how they were already hacking into every appliance in people's homes, to make them energy-efficient whether people wanted them to be or not.

Zoe was standing at Bruce's elbow. "It's too late to stop the trend or even reverse all the effects," she said over the din of the ThunderNet towers. "But we can slow it drastically, and our most optimistic projections show major improvements in the medium term."

"So, all this time—all this hellish time—you had the means to make a difference, and you just . . . sat on it?" Bruce said. "What the fuck were you thinking?"

"We wanted to wait until we had full product penetration." Jethro had to raise his voice now; the ThunderNet towers were actually thundering for the first time ever. "And we needed people to be ready. If we had just come out and told the truth about what our products actually did, people would rather die than buy them. Even after Manhattan and Florida. We couldn't give them away. But if we claimed to be making overpriced, wasteful pieces of crap that destroy the environment? Then everybody would need to own two of them."

"So, my crisis of conscience—" Bruce could only finish that sentence by wheeling his arms.

"We figured the day when you no longer gave a shit about your own future would be the day when people might accept this," Jethro said, patting Bruce on the back like a father, even though he was younger.

"Well, thanks for the mind games." Bruce had to shout now. "I'm going to go explore something I call my culture of drunkenness."

"You can't leave, Bruce," Jethro yelled in his ear. "This is going to be a major disruption, everyone's gadgets going nuts at once. There will be violence and wholesale destruction of public property. There will be chainsaw rampages. There may even be Twitter snark. We need you to be out in front on this, explaining it to the people."

Bruce looked out at the dusk, red-and-black clouds churning as millions of ThunderNet towers blasted them with scrubber beams. Even over that racket, the chorus of car horns and shouts as people's Car-Dingos suddenly had minds of their own started to ring from the highway. Bruce turned and looked into the gleam of his boss's schoolmaster specs. "Fuck you, man," he said. Followed a moment later by "I'll do it."

"We knew we could count on you." Jethro turned to the half-dozen or so executives cluttering the roof deck behind him. "Big hand for Bruce, everybody." Bruce waited until they were done clapping, then leaned over the railing and puked his guts out.

ABOUT THE AUTHOR

CHARLIE JANE ANDERS's story "Six Months Three Days" won a Hugo Award and was shortlisted for the Nebula and Theodore Sturgeon Awards. Her writing has appeared in *Mother Jones*, *Asimov's Science Fiction*, *Lightspeed*, *Tor.com*, *Tin House*, *ZYZZYVA*, *The McSweeney's Joke Book of Book Jokes*, *The End Is Nigh*, and elsewhere. She's the managing editor of *io9.com* and her first novel, *All the Birds in the Sky*, is forthcoming in early 2016. More info at charliejane.net.

THE SMOG SOCIETY

CHEN QIUFAN
TRANSLATED BY CARMEN YILING YAN AND KEN LIU

Lao Sun lived on the seventeenth floor facing the open street, nothing between him and the sky. If he woke in the morning to darkness, it was the smog's doing for sure.

Through the murky air outside the window, he had to squint to see the tall buildings silhouetted against the yellow-gray background like a sandy-colored relief print. The cars on the road all had their high beams on and their horns blaring, crammed one against the other at the intersection into one big mess. You couldn't tell where heaven and earth met, and you couldn't tell apart the people, either. Passels of pedestrians, dusty-faced under filter masks that made them look like pig-faced monstrosities, walked past the jammed cars.

Lao Sun washed, dressed, and got his kit. Before he left, he made sure to give the picture frame on the table a wipe.

He greeted the elevator girl, and the girl greeted him back behind a layer of mesh gauze. "It's twelve degrees Celsius today with the relative humidity at sixty-four percent. Visibility is less than two kilometers, and the Air Quality Index of six-eighty indicates severe smog. Long-distance travelers, please be careful. Young children, the elderly, and those with respiratory illnesses, please remain indoors . . ."

Lao Sun smiled, put on his mask, and stepped out of the elevator.

On his light electric bike, he nimbly wove through the gaps between the crawling traffic. There were plenty of children banging on car windows, hawking newspapers and periodicals, but no cleaners. This smog was there to stay for another couple of weeks. No point in cleaning cars now.

Through the goggles on his mask, he could just barely see the road for a couple dozen meters ahead. It was as if someone was standing above the city, pouring dust down endlessly. The sky was darker than the ground, dirty and sticky. Even with the filter mask, you felt as if the smog could worm its way through everything, through dozens of layers of polymer nanomaterial filter membrane and into your nostrils, your pores, your alveoli, your blood vessels, and swim all over your body from there; stuff your chest full until you couldn't breathe; and turn your brain into a drum of concrete too thick to stir or spin.

People were like parasites burrowed into the smog.

On these occasions, Lao Sun always thought of old times with his wife.

"Oh, Lao Sun, can't you drive slower? There's no rush."

"Mm."

"Lao Sun, stop at that store ahead; I'll buy a bottle of water for you."

"Mm."

"Lao Sun, why aren't you saying anything? How about I sing you a song? You used to like singing."

"Mm."

Lao Sun parked his bike at the roadside and entered the fancy big skyscraper with all the fancily dressed men and women going in and out. They were all wearing filter masks, saving them the trouble of greeting him. The building manager was polite to him, though. He told him one of the public elevators was broken, so the others were crowded. He should use the freight elevator in the back, although it meant climbing a few more floors.

Lao Sun smiled and said it was fine, although the manager couldn't see that, of course.

He took the freight elevator to the twenty-eighth floor, then climbed the stairs to the open platform on the top floor. It made him pant and puff a little, but no matter. From the top of the skyscraper, he could better see the smog; the aerosolized particles that engulfed the city hung thick like protoplasm, motionless.

Lao Sun began to unpack his bag, taking out and assembling each intricate scientific instrument. He wasn't clear on how they worked, but he knew how to use them to record temperature, pressure, humidity, visibility, particulate matter density, and so on. The devices were spruced-up versions of civilian-use models, less precise but much more portable.

He glanced northwest. He should have been seeing grand palaces and shining white pagodas, but today, there was only the same murk as everywhere else.

He remembered how it looked in the fall, the red leaves dyeing the hillsides layer by layer, trimming the clear blue sky. The white towers and the falling leaves all reflected in the lake's emerald surface: a tranquil airiness through which the cooing of pigeons drifted.

On that day, the two of them had sat in a boat at the center of the lake, rowing slow circles. The oars drew ripples that washed aside the fallen leaves.

Golden sunlight spilled on the water, glittering. She was covered in golden light too.

"A rare thing, to have a peaceful day like this. Sun, sing something!"

"Haven't sung in a long time."

"I remember we went rowing here twenty years ago. A whole twenty years ago."

"That's right, Lao Li's son is almost the age we'd been."

". . ."

"I—I didn't mean it that way."

"I know what you meant."

"I really didn't."

"This is pointless."

"All right, if it's boring, we'll go back."

"He would have been ten by now."

"Didn't you say not to talk about this?"

"Sun, I still want to hear you sing."

"Forget it; let's go back."

At the designated time, Lao Sun recorded the data, and then started packing up. He knew that at that moment, there were more than a hundred individuals like him in each and every corner of this city, doing the same thing. They belonged to a civilian environmental organization, officially registered as the "Municipal Smog Research and Prevention Society," unofficially known by the catchier moniker of "The Smog Society." Their logo was a yellow window with a sponge wiping out a patch of cerulean blue.

The Smog Society wasn't as radical as some green groups, but it wasn't the government's cheering squad, either. Its official status was unclear, its work low-key, its membership slowly and steadily growing. They sometimes appeared in the media, but only quietly and cautiously.

All groups had their own worldview and style, but not all viewpoints were acceptable.

The Smog Society only espoused what was acceptable: Aside from the biological dangers, smog also caused psychological harm—easily overlooked, but with far greater and longer-lasting consequences.

Lao Sun hurried to the next sampling location. On his way, he saw some people with bare faces—manual laborers unable to afford masks. Their skin was much dimmer and grayer than the sky, suffused with an inky gleam like coarse sandpaper. They were constructing a completely enclosed skywalk to connect the whole of the central economic district together seamlessly so people wouldn't have to go outside.

Lao Sun knew that antioxidant facial films were all the rage right now. Many women would apply a thirty-nanometer-thick layer of imported facial spray before putting on their masks. It blocked UV radiation and toxins, and would naturally shed with the skin. Of course, not everyone had a face precious enough.

If the facial spray had appeared a few years earlier, he would have bought it for his wife for sure. Just a few years earlier.

He shook his head. It felt as if his old wife was once again sitting behind him.

"Ai, Lao Sun, do you think the weather will get better tomorrow?"

"Mm."

"This awful weather makes me feel all stifled—like there's a rope choking me, getting tighter bit by bit."

"Mm."

"Lao Sun, how about we move somewhere else? Leave this place?"

"Should have left early, then. We're standing by the coffin's side by now. Where are we supposed to go?"

"That's true; we should have left early. We should have left early if we were going to leave."

" . . ."

He stopped the bike. This was a large stock exchange center, where every day a mix of young and old and of every color congregated to stare at the huge LCD screens suspended in midair, their expressions shifting with the rise and fall of graphs and numbers. It was a giant gambling den, where everyone thought themselves a winner or a soon-to-be winner.

As usual, Lao Sun climbed onto the roof and began his measurements.

Lao Sun vaguely knew some of the Smog Society's philosophy, but not well. Maybe his rank wasn't high enough. He'd joined the Smog Society for simple reasons—giving some purpose to his monotonous post-retirement life. Of course, by the time you lived to his age, you tended to understand that having a purpose in life wasn't any more important than living itself.

One afternoon, he'd been dragged to some so-called psychological counseling course located on the tenth floor of a rundown building where the elevator doors squeaked. He wasn't interested, but he'd caved under his old coworker's pleading and gone with him. At first, he'd thought it was some Buddhist or Daoist lecturer spouting philosophy to con people into giving him money, but he discovered otherwise.

He first filled out a quiz that indicated that his depression level scored 73 out of 100. Out of all the attendees, he counted as below average.

The speaker smoothly drew his audience in. Some began to sob and wail, some threw chairs, others hugged each other tightly and revealed their most deeply hidden little secrets. Lao Sun had never seen anything like it. He didn't know what to do. Someone patted his shoulder: a lady of about thirty, who could be considered beautiful, though not beautiful enough to move someone Lao Sun's age.

"Sorry to bother you, but I saw your answer sheet. You mentioned the weather as a factor."

"Mm. The smog."

She introduced herself as the administrator of the Municipal Smog Research and Prevention Society. He didn't remember her name.

"You don't seem to like talking. Something on your mind?"

"Mm."

"Our association is recruiting volunteers right now. Maybe you'd be interested. Here's our flyer."

He'd wanted to say no, but he glanced at the flyer and a few words caught his eye. He accepted it.

"Maybe we can provide you with a new view of smog."

"Mm?"

Lao Sun wanted to ask more, but she'd hurried away already. A specter flashed in front of his eyes at that moment: his wife's. He looked at the flyer again. *Smog Causes an Increase in City Residents' Depression Rates.*

So it began.

The current consensus holds smog to be the product of industrial pollution combined with natural weather patterns. Automobile exhaust, industrial waste gas, and other forms of man-made particulate matter are caught in thermal inversions where the temperature of the air decreases with altitude, cold on top and hot on the bottom. An inversion layer forms a hundred meters from the surface and closes over the ground like the lid of a pot. With no wind, pollutants in the city disperse too slowly and become concentrated near the surface. Combined with lack of precipitation, strong sunlight, and low humidity, the conditions promote photochemical reactions between pollutants to form smog.

As of now, there are no methods of prevention.

For Lao Sun, aside from bronchitis, acute emphysema, asthma, pharyngitis, strokes, and the other physical ailments, the most immediate consequence of smog was the sense of removal from the world. Whether you were dealing with people or things, you felt as though you were separated by a layer of frosted glass. No matter how hard you tried, you couldn't really see or touch.

That the masks meant to protect from smog added a second layer was especially ironic. The detachment, the numbness, the estrangement, and the apathy now all had an obvious physical excuse for existing.

The city was cocooned. The people were cocooned.

As Lao Sun rode his bike, the highway overpasses wound overhead like giant dragons, alternating light and shadow. They widened the roads every year, but the traffic still grew more and more congested. Even so, all these people remained willing to squeeze themselves into their little cars, watch the endless lines crawl forward inch by inch. They hid in their four- or five-square-meter metal cans and kept a safe distance from the world and other people.

And so the air pollution worsened, too.

At last he reached his final destination, a daycare called Sunflower.

Sunflower Daycare was built on a raised railway platform and looked like a giant glass greenhouse with children studying and playing on each floor. They didn't need masks; the parents had to foot the bill for the expensive air circulation systems, but even so, looking at those healthy, rosy, bare faces crying or laughing, it seemed worth it.

At least they were still genuine. At least they still had hope.

Each time, Lao Sun would hungrily gaze at the children behind the glass, losing track of time. As he looked at these exposed souls romping and frolicking, another voice would sound, so close it seemed right next to him, so far it seemed decades in the past.

"I know what you're thinking."

"No, you don't."

"I know."

"No. You. Do. Not."

"Fine, fine, let's not argue. I promise you, five more years."

"Five years! Can I still bear a child in five years?"

"There're plenty of thirty-year-olds having kids nowadays. Our finances are only so-so, and with our surroundings a dirty mess like this, it would be unfair to the kid. We'll work hard for another few years, and then we'll go somewhere better to have a child, let them grow up somewhere nice."

"You're talking pie-in-the-sky; you always do."

"Being able to do it well is a skill too. We'll go to the doctor's in the afternoon."

"I want to hear you sing."

"Sure! Whatever you want to hear."

Lao Sun tasted salt in the corner of his mouth. Something had trickled down his face and between his lips.

Strange how the present seemed so blurry, when he could see and hear everything from his memories so clearly. Sometimes, they'd play over and over in his mind. No wonder they said old people got nostalgic.

That conversation was decades old. When you're young, money is important, a house is important, a car is important—everything is important—and yet you still end up neglecting the most important things of all. By the time you earn all your money and get all the things you ought to have, some things are lost forever. Lao Sun understood now, but he was already old.

And so far, no one had invented a time machine, or a pill to take away regret.

Lao Sun had to submit his recordings to the Smog Society headquarters' data analysis center, but he didn't know how to use the internet, so he had to find Xiao Wang, one of his "smog buddies." That was how members referred to each other.)

Xiao Wang had joined the society half a year earlier than Lao Sun. He had a job during the day and spent his free time with the society. They were from the same hometown, so they ended up close to each other.

Xiao Wang seemed somewhat excited as he led Lao Sun to his office and had his secretary pour a cup of water. Then he asked, "So, you still don't know?"

Lao Sun shook his head, confused. "Know what?"

"Our association sent in the report to the government."

"What report?"

"The research report about the smog!"

"Oh. Well, it's not like we'll get to see it."

"Hey, I spend my spare time helping the Smog Society process data. I know the gist of the report. Just don't go spreading it around."

"Don't worry. Who would I talk to?"

"You know the Smog Society's central statement, right?"

"The thing about smog and mental illness? Who doesn't?"

"Most people only know about the correlation between smog and mental illness, not the causation."

"What do you mean?"

"Did you think you were just weather-watching, Lao Sun?"

Xiao Wang began to lay out the deeper theory. The Smog Society's monitoring had three components. Lao Sun participated in the basic weather monitoring. In addition, at each sampling location, the psychological states of the relevant people were monitored. The exact method was unclear: maybe with miniature RFID chip sampling, maybe with the entrance security systems or networks, maybe using free goodies with questionnaires attached. Of course, the easiest and most accurate way was to pay the target population to download software that displayed survey questions to be answered at specific times. Either way, they managed. More secretly, they conducted laboratory experiments researching aerosol distribution in the atmosphere, the electrosensitivity of organic hydrocarbons, bioelectric fields, physical manifestations of psychological conditions under different environmental circumstances, and other similar topics.

A tenet of statistics is using large quantities of long-term data to eliminate sampling biases and other sources of error.

All of this effort had one goal: creating a mathematical model of smog to examine the connection between aerosol systems and human psychological state, controlling for weather conditions.

They discovered that the bioelectrical fields generated by groups displayed coherence: The overlay of peaks and valleys caused the bioelectric field within a certain area to approach constancy. It was like the folk wisdom that fair and foul moods were both infectious. And these large-scale bioelectric fields, in turn, affected the distribution of aerosolized particles. Generally, the lower the psychological health score, the greater the density of particulate matter and the more stable their formation—in other words, the thicker the smog, the slower it dispersed.

They also found that within the PM distribution system were bands of greater density like ocean currents, mostly located along thoroughfares with severely congested traffic, flowing sluggishly, dissipating once the traffic eased to congregate toward nearby areas with high population density.

The sampling locations in the central economic district and high-density residential areas showed PM densities significantly higher than the average in other sampling locations. These areas had the lowest psychological health scores as well. In contrast, areas with dense populations of teenagers and children had higher psychological health scores, and the air quality tended to be better. And at large stock exchanges, the psychological health score, the air quality rating, and the stock prices were all closely correlated.

Causation also went the other way: The smog lowered people's psychological health scores. Therefore, barring major changes in weather, marauding cold fronts, or an increase in wind, the smog would continue to strengthen its grip.

Lao Sun listened dazedly to Xiao Wang's explanation. He felt like he understood a little and not at all at the same time. Finally, he said, "So, smog is caused by how we feel."

Xiao Wang clapped his hands. "I spouted all that drivel, and you summed it up in a sentence. Wow!"

Lao Sun said, "We used to love talking about the heart, not the brain. It's the other way around nowadays."

"We've modernized. We use science now."

"Anyway, we won't need to record the weather anymore?"

"Not necessarily. We have to see how the government responds."

Lao Sun said goodbye to Xiao Wang and returned home. There were still leftovers in the refrigerator, ready to heat and eat.

Ready to heat and eat. In that moment, he felt like he'd returned to that hot, humid night. The two of them lay side by side, unable to sleep.

"Lao Sun, do you think tomorrow will be a good day?"

"Mm."

"I've had a couple of strange days. I keep dreaming about things from before, when we just met."

"Mm?"

"The sky was always blue back then, and the clouds were white. There weren't so many buildings. There were big paulownia trees on either side of the road, and when the wind blew, their leaves would rustle, sha sha. You'd take me nice places on your bike. There weren't so many cars back then, either. The roads were so wide and open, you could see all the way from one side to the other. The sun wasn't nasty. There were birds and cicadas. We'd ride to the city outskirts and lay down on the grass wherever we liked. It felt so good. Lao Sun, you remember, right?"

"Mm."

"I also remember that you had so many entertaining tricks back then. You juggled, you played the harmonica, and you always wanted to sing me songs. I didn't want to listen, and you'd chase after me singing, singing— what was that song again?"

"..."

"That's right, I remember now. 'Young Friends Gather,' wasn't it? Ha-ha."

"..."

"Lao Sun, tomorrow morning, I want to go out for a while. I've put breakfast in the fridge for you; just heat and eat. Are you asleep?"

"..."

The next day, when Lao Sun woke, his wife had already left. He took out the meal from the fridge, heated it, and ate. The laundry from the night before still hung on the balcony. The sky was still gray.

She never came back.

Lao Sun suddenly panicked like he'd never panicked before. He hadn't panicked like this back then when he first saw her.

He remembered how he'd dug through his heart to find things to say, back then, while she replied so carelessly. He'd felt as frantic as an ant on a hot pot. Then they were going out, and there was no end to the back-and-forth. Then they married. Each attending to their own career, they'd had less time together and less to say. They said a bit more only when they fought. His career alternately rose and fell, and she missed her best childbearing years. She started to nag; he started to hold his tongue. They fought, and they threatened divorce, but in the end, neither of them could leave the other.

One nagging, the other silent, they'd passed so many years. It seemed that both of them had gotten used to it. If you weren't meant to love each other, you wouldn't be together, Lao Sun had thought. It wouldn't be a half-bad life, to be like this till the end. But almost at the finish line, she left.

Lao Sun felt like his heart emptied in that moment, deflated to nothing, like a burst balloon.

A week later, the Smog Society disbanded. Some people from the government invited Lao Sun to have tea and "talk" but allowed him to leave afterward.

Several of the organization leaders had disappeared, and the core members had also been "called in to talk." When they returned, they said nothing. When they met smog buddies, they looked at them like strangers.

Rumors spread after that. Some said that the smog above the city was actually an enemy country's new climate-altering weapon, while others said it was a side effect of their own country's new secret weapon tests gone wrong. There was an even bolder theory claiming that the smog was really a massive gaseous life form. It—or maybe they—lumbered over the city, subsisting on industrial waste gas and the nitric acid, sulfuric acid, and hydrocarbon particles from automobile exhaust. They were slowly dissolving the calcium in human bones. In time, people would become afflicted with osteoporosis and rickets. Children and the elderly would easily break bones, even become paralyzed.

Of course, the rumors were quickly debunked. After investigation, the calcium-sucking monster story was tracked back to a calcium supplement manufacturer. Its unscrupulous marketing practices were punished as they deserved. The government vowed to formulate a five-year plan to return blue skies to the people.

As for that report, it was as if it never existed.

Today was smoggy again. Lao Sun got up early as usual, washed, dressed, and got his travel things. Before he left, he made sure to give the picture frame on the table a wipe. The woman in the frame smiled at him.

That photo was more than ten years old by now.

He smiled at the elevator girl. The elevator girl saw the mask he carried and smiled back.

Lao Sun put on his mask and got on his light electric bike. It was festooned with lights and streamers of every color and played chipper music. All along his journey, passers-by in pig-snouted masks watched him, pointed at him. His bike was like a Brazilian parrot zipping through a desert, brilliant, colorful, and noisy.

He went straight to Sunflower Daycare, got off the bike, and stood in front of the massive glasshouse.

Lao Sun opened his bag and scooped out his strange little knick-knacks. First, he filled some helium balloons and let them float high. The children stopped their games and ran to the window to watch this man in the clown mask. The music continued to play from the bike's speakers. He followed the rhythm, slowly and comically contorting his body, and began to juggle.

"See, I can juggle three oranges at once. Watch!"

". . ."

"You won't watch? Then I'll play the harmonica for you. I don't even need my hands. I can change pitch with just my tongue."

". . ."

"Then I'll sing for you. What song do you want to hear? I know them all!"

"..."

Lao Sun was breathing heavily. Something had trickled down his face and into his mouth, salty. The little pixies were wide-eyed, their faces pressed against the window, pink and white. They were laughing, showing their teeth, some of them clutching their bellies, even. The caretakers were laughing too.

"I know what song you'll like. I'll sing it for you right now...."

"No way you know!"

"I know. Listen, if you don't believe me."

"You're all talk!"

An old song played from the speakers.

... Young friends, us young friends, are gathering today

Rowing the boats as the warm wind blows....

Flowers sweet, birds a-tweet, spring sun to get you drunk

And laughter flies 'round the clouds in circles....

The melody, which was so cheerful that it verged on the absurd, pierced the glass. The children began to move to the music, following the clown in his gymnastics. They laughed unabashedly, singing, dancing, crowing, every bare face shining golden.

Lao Sun looked up at the sky. The smog seemed to be thinning too.

ABOUT THE AUTHOR

CHEN QIUFAN (a/k/a Stanley Chan) was born in Shantou, Guangdong province. Chan is a science fiction writer, columnist, script writer, and a technology start-up CMO. Since 2004, he has published over thirty stories in *Science Fiction World*, *Esquire*, *Chutzpah!*, many of which are collected in *Thin Code*. His debut novel, *The Waste Tide*, was published in January 2013 and was praised by Liu Cixin as "the pinnacle of near-future SF writing." Chan is the most widely translated young writer of science fiction in China, with his short works translated into English, Italian, Japanese, Swedish, and Polish, and published in *Clarkesworld*, *Interzone*, and *F&SF*. He has won Taiwan's Dragon Fantasy Award, China's Galaxy and Nebula Award, and a Science Fiction & Fantasy Translation Award along with Ken Liu. He lives in Beijing.

ABOUT THE TRANSLATORS

KEN LIU (http://kenliu.name) is an author and translator of speculative fiction, as well as a lawyer and programmer. A winner of the Nebula, Hugo, and World Fantasy Awards, he has been published in *The Magazine of Fantasy & Science Fiction*, *Asimov's*, *Analog*, *Clarkesworld*, *Lightspeed*, and *Strange Horizons*, among other places. He lives with his family near Boston, Massachusetts. Ken's debut novel, *The Grace of Kings*, the first in a silkpunk epic fantasy series, was released in April 2015. Saga will also publish a collection of his short stories later in 2015.

CARMEN YILING YAN was born in China and currently attends UCLA. Since starting out as an amateur translator, her translation work has been published by *Clarkesworld*, *Lightspeed*, and *Galaxy's Edge*. Her writing has been published in *Daily Science Fiction*. Her other interests include drawing, mineralogy, and ancient Chinese history.

RACING THE TIDE

CRAIG DeLANCEY

"Gramma Tara, we gonna get a new house today?"

Tara looked at her granddaughter, who sat on the edge of the front deck, dangling her feet over the water. Her toes could just touch the sea as she swung her legs back and forth. The flow of the ocean swirled around the house's support beams as the tide hurried in. The water would touch the deck soon. A good wave would curl right over into the living room. No doubt about it: The house was sinking. Or the sea level was still rising. Probably both.

"No, Emma," she said. "That's gonna take a long time. The company is just sending out an engineer today to talk with us."

"But we won't have to move up north? We can stay?"

"That's the plan."

"And my room won't be wet? There was water in there yesterday. My shoes got squishy."

Tara looked back through the screen door at the hallway floor, trying to assess the slope of it. The back of the house was lower than the front. "The company has big machines on barges that'll put down big pillars, real deep. Then they'll bring our houses out on barges, too, and just set them on the pillars, way up high off the water."

Emma peered to the northeast, squinting, as if hoping to see a barge out there now, already on its way. Shimmering water stretched to the horizon, broken only by the gray spires of drowned trees. Nothing moved out there but the languid flapping of herons and the white wake of a single boat moving north. Probably a fisherman.

"Gramma," Emma said very softly. She looked down at her feet. "Tommy called."

Tara froze, mouth open. After a while, she managed to ask, "What did he say?"

"I didn't talk to him. He left a message."

Tara nodded, relieved.

"Can he come over?" Emma asked, her voice pleading. "Is he coming over? Let's call him. Please, Gramma."

Tara sighed. "I can't call Tommy now, honey. I just can't."

"Why not?" Emma asked.

Because I'm exhausted, Tara thought. *Because I'm done with him, even if he is my son and your father. Because he can't be helped. Because he never takes advice; he only takes money. Because he can't make a good choice, only a bad one.*

But what she said was "Because the company people are coming." She pointed. A wake parted on the horizon, and a boat skipped on its edge, speeding toward them.

"You stay here, honey. I've got to go over to the barge. Be good. Aunt Grace is gonna check up on you soon."

Tara turned and backed a rung down the deck's ladder. Her phone began to buzz on her wrist, but she ignored it as she took the long step into the bow of their boat, which had turned to point at the rising tide.

Tara recognized immediately that the approaching boat was bringing them trouble. It was a cigarette boat, long and lean and ostentatiously pre-flood, with a thundering engine burning gasoline. The woman sitting by the captain looked old-school Florida: blonde, with sun-dried skin and a too-tight dark suit. Tara caught the rope tossed by the captain and tied a clove hitch over one of the barge's bollards. The woman hurried forward, heels clacking on the fiberglass bow. She leapt to the barge.

"Mayor Orton?" she asked, offering her hand. After they shook, she passed Tara a card that read KELLY LUCY, JD. In her other hand she held an aluminum tube of the kind people use to protect blueprints or maps.

Tara frowned. "Just call me Tara. The company had promised to send an engineer."

The woman nodded. Behind her, the boat went silent. The fumes of its engines drifted over them.

"Mayor, we have a proposal."

Tara sighed. "You want to dredge."

"How did you know?"

Tara walked over to the southern edge of the barge. The lawyer followed. Hand on the safety line, Tara said, as calmly as she could manage, "No. We won't dredge. There are engineers among us. I'm an engineer. We've thought very hard about this; we pooled our money—and we don't have any money, let me tell you, so that wasn't easy, but we pooled our money and we had a study done. Our plan will work. We don't have to dredge."

"Mayor Orton, I'm convinced that you'll agree with us that our plan is better, if you can just hear me out, learn all its details. You see, you're ten miles across water from the Big Bridge." The "Big Bridge" is what they were now calling the project to elevate I-95 above the water. They'd finished connecting all the way to what remained of Miami, and extended it down a bit farther south, to serve the homes still above water in Kendall and Cutter.

The lawyer pointed east. "No spur is going to come out here, not for thirty-seven houses up on stilts."

Tara nodded. "That's why our village has to be self-sustaining. Ms. Lucy, if you're not willing to do the work as we want, then we'll just hire someone else."

"You know, many municipalities have been disbanded by their counties for being too small," the lawyer said. She turned and leaned back against the safety line so that she faced the houses that stood on ramshackle supports formed of cinder blocks or heaped stones or hastily dropped concrete pillars. "Some had twice as many homes as you have here."

"Are you threatening us?" Tara asked.

"No," the woman said. She did not take offense. Her tone remained matter-of-fact. "No. But nearly a million homeowners in Florida will file claim to Rising Waters Disaster Funds. Here you have thirty-seven houses, ten miles across water from anything—that's not how they want to hear the relief funds are being spent. They could force on you a buyout and spend the savings elsewhere, hoping to accomplish something."

"We consider this something," Tara said. "This will all be the Everglades in a dozen years. And we'll live in it."

The woman nodded. "Okay. But you can do that on an island, right?"

Tara pointed down at the water. "You make a sandbar here, you'll have to dig a trench all around it to get the sand to pile up. Any island you make is going to sit in a lake."

The lawyer paused, considering the course of her argument. Finally, she held up the tube. "Please, just look at the plans."

Tara sighed. She looked at the municipal building, which sat at the center of the barge. Inside, Pat Cosby, the town secretary, pressed against the glass door, shamelessly gawking at them both. Tara would like to send the lawyer away and call another company. Perhaps she should. But they both knew that there were few contractors willing to work this far out. And she owed it to the people of her town to hear the whole pitch. "Let's go in," Tara said.

The phone on Tara's wrist began to buzz incessantly.

"If you need to take that," the lawyer said, smiling, "I won't mind. I can wait for you inside."

"No," Tara said. "It's just my son, calling to tell me he's dying again, and that only I can save him."

＊　＊　＊　＊

"You busy?" Pat asked Tara.

Tara sat, staring at the wall, as she listened to the calls recorded on her phone. She moved her hand back and forth over the maps that the lawyer had left spread out on the table. All but one of the messages had been left by her son. His voice seemed to warble like a bird. In broken phrases, he pled for money and promised to pay her back. There was also a single calm message from a nurse at the clinic where Tommy lived now, leaving an address.

Tara tapped her watch to stop the playback. "I'm done, Pat; thanks."

Pat pointed at the maps. It was only an hour after noon, and the sun fell from the skylight and down on the table, making the maps seem to glow. "Well. What d'ya think?"

Tara frowned. The last vote had been contentious. And before the vote, everyone in town had argued for weeks, argued on front decks as the sun set over the water, argued across the bows of boats tethered together while they fished, argued in tentative but loud voices at the weekly town meetings. It had not been easy to come to a decision. Of the fifty-five residents of voting age, only thirty-two had supported her plan in the end. The others wanted to pay for a dredge, to have a sandbar built. They wanted to set their feet on dry land once in a while. And who could blame them?

"I think it's bad news," Tara said. "This is going to start the whole debate over again."

And not in their wildest dream had they imagined this: a huge dredging project, to create not a sandbar out here but an island. A big island. Too big.

"Only if people see these plans . . ." Pat said.

"You let people in to look it all over, whoever wants to look. It's gotta be done." Tara stood. "Listen, Pat. I gotta go to Orlando tomorrow. You think your boy Pauly would be willing to sail me out to the train stop on the Big Bridge?"

"I'm sure he would," Pat said.

"Well. You'll have to try to keep things together here while I'm away."

"You need someone to watch Emma?"

"I might. I was going to ask Grace to keep Emma for the night tomorrow. But I'll tell Grace she can count on you to help out, if that's okay. Thanks."

"It's for Tommy, isn't it?" Pat asked, her voice soft. "You going to see another doctor? Some kind of expert?"

"None of them are experts," Tara said bitterly. "They're just tinkering. Using up brains the way we used to burn up the oil."

It took the whole morning to tack to the Big Bridge. She and Pauly sat in the cockpit of the boy's six-meter sailboat. The lines rang against the aluminum mast. Pauly was fifteen, quiet to the point of brooding, but proud of his skill on the water. He watched the telltales on the sail and kept the boat moving as fast as the winds allowed. Finally, the bridge rose before them, and Pauly trimmed a tight beam reach that shot them under the dark shade of the two highways. A little building hung down between the lanes, and a strip of sunlight fell through, seeming somehow dirtied by the sound and smell of the cars that roared overhead. Pauly dropped sails and deftly turned, stalling right next to the small dock. Tara thanked the boy for the lift. They did not bother to tie up. With only a nod, Pauly lifted his mainsail as soon as she stepped off. It snapped taut with wind, and the boat leaned away toward open waters.

Tara climbed the stairs to the train stop, just a row of benches between the two train tracks, flanked by the lanes of I-95. She sat alone in the shade of a big sign showing endless advertisements. After an hour of cringing from the roar of passing trucks, she saw the train loom in the distance. She waved, afraid it might pass by if she didn't show them that someone waited. It squealed to a stop, as if pained to be forced to slow, and Tara leapt through a door that shuddered open reluctantly.

She ignored the other passengers who tried to strike up a conversation with her—the South would always remain the South, she thought, polite and conversational. But she didn't have the energy for it. She only smiled sadly and turned back to the glass, to watch the tide back out into the Atlantic. Patches of ground, some black with cracked tarmac, others still holding up the cinder block wall of some box store or fast food joint, peeked up through the shallower places. But that wasn't land. The land was gone. The sea had taken it. Florida had shrunk to a narrow, blunted knife of sand and trees.

The train climbed up away from the sparkling water when they neared Port St. Lucie. Tiredness overcame her then, as if the green-and-brown land lay heavily on her. She watched, half asleep, while the train passed hotel after hotel, their parking lots fringed by pools and swing sets.

Two hours brought her to Daytona Beach. She wrestled with the clunky municipal internet to navigate incomprehensible bus schedules. Eventually, she discovered a way to string together three trips to get to her destination in Orlando. She bought an exchange ticket online and boarded a noisy, dirty bus waiting in a covered lot behind the station. Two hours later, bus doors parted with a sigh and she clomped down before a brick building with GRACE CLINIC printed over its entrance.

She did not go in immediately. An old bench stretched out beside the door, its wood slats carved all over with inscrutable graffiti. Exhausted and bone weary, she flopped down on it. She had thought the air on the bus oppressive and close, but now she discovered it was just the land-locked air, still and hot. Her body longed for the ocean breeze.

She turned on her phone and told it to call home. "Emma?" she shouted, feeling she needed to be loud to reach across the distance.

"Gramma?"

"How are you, honey?"

"Are you with Tommy?"

"Not yet, honey. But I'm almost there. I'll see him soon."

"Call me back and turn on the camera," she said.

"Honey, I been meaning to tell you. Your daddy might be asleep. Okay? So, he might not be able to talk on the phone. Sick people have to sleep a lot sometimes."

"Wake him up," Emma said. "Shake him so he wakes."

"We'll just have to see. I'll call you when I know."

When she passed inside, she realized that she had come in a side door, or a rear door, of the clinic. It was crowded and busy inside. A long hall with a scratched but shining floor stretched to big glass doors in the distance that parted again and again as people came and went. Stretchers lined the halls, with patients sleeping on them or just lying there, staring at the ceiling and gasping in the close heat. The smell was a mixture of harsh antiseptics and urine.

Tara passed rooms filled with rows of beds, some of them bunks. She understood then that it was not much more than a homeless shelter. A shelter for the indigent ill. At the end of the long hallway, she came to a desk where a nurse stood, impatiently swiping at an old tablet computer with a sputtering screen.

"Excuse me; I'm looking for Tommy Ortey."

"And you are?"

"I'm his mother."

The nurse nodded, paged through screens, and poked at the pad vindictively, and finally said, "Room 154. That way."

"Thank you."

It was one of the rooms that she had passed. Inside, six beds were arranged in a space not much wider than the hall. Tommy lay in the bed against the far wall. Walking sideways, Tara worked her way to him, squeezing between the beds. Tommy lay on his back, sweating atop the covers, eyes closed, breath uneven. He wore a pale aqua gown, and his naked limbs were thin, like sticks, so that his knees and elbows were knobs. Fresh scars left pale lines on his shaved head. He twitched while he slept.

"Tommy?" she said softly. He did not open his eyes. A chart hung on the end of his bed. She lifted it and read, but nothing there meant anything to her.

The room lacked any chairs. She gently lowered herself on the corner of his bed and let her weight sink down into the mattress. He did not stir, other than his frequent twitches.

"Tommy?" she said, a little more loudly. "Tommy? Tommy?" She touched him. His skin was hot.

Tommy opened his eyes. He looked around in panic for a second, then focused on her. The twitching grew worse. He lifted a shaking hand, dropped it back onto the bed. "Mama?" he warbled.

She nodded, trying not to cry.

"I can . . . har . . . har . . . hardly . . . talk," he said.

"That's okay, Tommy; that's okay. You don't have to talk."

But that upset him more. His limbs shook violently now. He lifted his hand but seemed uncertain about what to do next.

"I . . . I . . . I . . ." he said. "I . . . I . . . I . . ."

"Shh. I'll talk to your doctor. Okay? I'll talk to your doctor."

He trembled a long time, and she sat with him till his eyes closed again and he fell asleep.

After a long time, hours, maybe, someone touched her shoulder.

"Mrs. Ortey?"

She looked up. Her eyes had been closed. In another minute, she might have lain back across the foot of the bed and slept there.

A man stood over her, a portly black man with sad eyes and a cleanly shaven face. He wore a white doctor's smock, and sweat had stained the underarms. "Mrs. Ortey?" he repeated.

"Yes," she said, whispering.

"I'm Doctor Armstrong. I'm the psychiatrist here at the clinic. Would you like to come to my office?"

She looked down at Tommy but he did not stir. She got up and followed the psychiatrist without saying a word. It was a long walk down the hall and up another to his office, a little cubicle with a buzzing neon light and a single window looking out on a dirty brick wall just two meters away. The psychiatrist offered her coffee and she gladly accepted.

"You're from down south, end of the old five."

"Yes," she said.

"You lost your home, your whole town, your son told me."

"Not the whole town. Some of us are still left. We're the crazy holdouts who can't leave our land, even if it is underwater. We just love the sea and the 'Glades too much."

The doctor nodded. "Tommy has fond memories of his childhood. His memory is better than some of the people I see here who took rewrite."

"And what's the matter with him now? What is it you want to do?"

"I don't want to do anything." He sighed. "I mean, I'm not in a position to do anything. Please understand; I'm a community medicine doctor. We're a clinic for patients that the hospitals won't take, including a lot of psychiatric patients. Your son landed on our doorstep. I've done my best to stabilize him. But I can't help him. The only thing that I know of that might help him is a course of properly tuned biogenetic machine implants."

"More machines," she said bitterly.

He nodded. "I know how you feel. I've seen other patients like him. He started with the drugs—I mean, lots of drugs, right, not just rewrite?"

"He thought they were going to make him smarter," Tara said. "He started when he was a teenager. 'Mom,' he said, 'I wanna code and if you code you gotta compete with every kid in China, you gotta compete against every kid in India, and there are millions of them, not to mention all the white kids in California, and every one is taking the brainhacks, they're taking the enhancers.' So he started on the drugs, different drugs. But he never really worked at his computer again. The drugs ruined him."

The doctor nodded. "We saw a lot of patients with the side effects from rewrite and the other early mental-enhancement drugs: memory loss, tardive dyskinesia, and worse."

"He got the wires next," she said. "He thought that would fix the damage of the drugs and also make him smarter. He spent all day reading internet posts from hundreds of programmers who claimed the wires had made them lightning-fast thinkers."

The psychiatrist nodded. "But the wires caused acquired epilepsy."

He'd had this conversation before, Tara realized. But she could not help but feel a small satisfaction to get it all out, to someone who understood. The doctor's sad eyes fixed on her, pleading that she continue.

"So, then he got the machines," she said.

"Microrobotic neural control units."

"I paid for it. Spent my entire 401(k). Everything I had left."

"I'm very sorry," he said.

"Well, it didn't work."

"It worked," he said. "Your son has had no seizures, he tells me. And I believe him: He's had no seizures here, as far as we can tell. But after a year or more, a significant number of the patients with the neural control units develop Parkinson's-like symptoms and some ataxia symptoms because the units begin to interfere with the striatum and the cerebellum."

She nodded.

"There is no known treatment," the doctor said. "But there is a possibility. A clinic is experimenting with a new kind of neural control unit. Smaller, faster, less harmful. They are actually mostly grown out of organic molecules. I mean, out of, well, molecules that—"

"I was a bioengineer," she interrupted.

"Sorry. You never know what's clear, what's not. So, these new units can be used to disassemble, in place, the implants he currently has. Then they take over their function in a reduced and, supposedly, less harmful way."

"And if he doesn't get it?"

"He's getting worse. His speech functions have started to fail just in the last twenty-four hours. It looks likely that the damage will soon impede autonomic function."

"He'll stop breathing, you mean."

The doctor nodded.

"How did we get here?" she said, looking out his window at the bleak wall beyond. In the cramped office, that view was worse than if there had been no window. It seemed to say, *There is nowhere to go. No future.*

"Mrs. Ortey?"

"How did we get on this rat race?"

The doctor sighed. "When I went to medical school, I imagined that I would work in a clinic like this, and I would cure people, people from neighborhoods like my own. But really, much of the time, it seems I just . . . move them a little farther down their road. One drug has this side effect, so we switch to another drug, and then another. Some treatment does such-and-such damage, so we add this other additional treatment to fix that and find yet more side effects. I wish I could make your son a boy again, before he ever started down this road. But I can't. No one can."

Tears welled in her eyes. She came prepared to fight. But this man was not one of the corporate drones that she'd met in every one of the clinics, their humanity completely consumed by greed, their every sentence a PowerPoint bullet meant to sell the idea. Faced with human decency, her resistance failed completely.

"How much would it cost?" she asked.

"I'm sorry, but because it's experimental, the state won't help."

"It's always experimental," she said. "How much?"

She held her breath and he named a huge number.

She got back to Daytona Beach late that evening, ate a stale bagel at the station's dreary coffee shop, and then bought a ticket on the night train. She waited hours outside, watching the moon creep overhead, until the train came out of the dark, pushing dirty air and drawing so much power, the lights all around her flickered. Again, she found a seat against the window. Face pressed against the cool glass, she managed to sleep the two hours till sunrise.

When she leaned back, her joints creaked and cracked, sore from sleeping all hunched up. Outside, there was only water. She was nearly home.

She logged into the train's internet, put on her net glasses, and began a search of municipal filings and SEC filings. It took her only minutes to prove her suspicions.

She took the lawyer's business card from her pocket and touched it to her phone. It rang only once before the lawyer answered, "This is Kelly."

"Ms. Lucy, this is Tara Ortey."

"Mayor Ortey," she said, her voice becoming forced with brightness.

"I've been doing some research."

"Yes."

"And I see that you have a project five miles northeast of us."

"Yes. We have several projects underway."

"Just that one, as far as I can tell. But you have filings to represent several hundred households in the areas south and west of us."

"Yes." She sounded wary now.

"A straight line from our location to the nearest train station at the Big Bridge would go right through the other island you're making. If you organized some land swaps and then made our island big—big enough for hundreds of homes—you could convince the state to run a spur to the island."

Silence hung on the other end of the line.

"You need us to agree, however," she said. "We get say over what is done with our land, even if we won't own all of it after you make the island."

Still the silence hung. Tara pictured the lawyer calculating furiously, wondering what she could say or deny without endangering their plans.

"My town will have another vote," Tara said. "It's inevitable. What I want from you is a bonus to my people."

"A bonus?" She could not help keep the sound of relief from her voice.

"They'll still vote, understand. I can't say how that vote will go. But I want this in writing. A payment to each household if you build the island."

"How much would you consider . . . equitable?"

Tara named a number. The same number that the doctor had quoted her for Tommy's treatment.

"That's a lot of money."

"It would be for us. But not for you, not for your kind of people, Ms. Lucy. Not at all."

"I'll need time to discuss this. To make a counteroffer."

"No counteroffer. That's the amount. Take it or leave it."

She hung up.

The barge listed as the entire town all gathered on one side. People slapped at mosquitos and talked in voices that they tried and failed to keep hushed. But silence fell when Tara spoke up.

"Excuse me!" she called. "Excuse me!"

Everyone turned and faced her. She stood in one corner with the dark southeastern sky behind her. The smooth water reflected the first stars of evening.

She looked out at the faces. These were people she knew for many years now. Their children—children she had watched grow—pushed to the front and stared up at her; even they gave her their attention for a minute, though she knew they'd slip away soon to go chase each other across the deck.

"We had our debate about what to do, and I thought it was ended. But the company has come with a new offer, so it seems we need to reconsider. You've all seen the maps."

"I haven't!" shouted Bess Howe from the back of the crowd.

"Well," Tara shouted back. "Go inside and look in a minute. Patsy will show you. Now, most of you have seen the maps, the plans. They want to make an island here. A big island."

"And money," Paul Cosby shouted. He was Pat's husband, and Pauly's father, a big man who still fished and somehow managed to find fish.

"That's right, Paul. I managed to get them to promise some extra money."

"A lot of money," Grace murmured from the front of the crowd. And somehow, her voice carried. Others nodded and murmured in agreement.

"Yes," Tara agreed. "They agreed to a lot of money. This is relatively high land here. Besides, you know the rules: Around here, if you abandon your land, it goes to the National Park. And most folks have abandoned their land. So, the company needs our land, and they need us to support some complicated land swap deals too before they can build."

She took a deep breath. "It's up to you all, of course. But here's what I want to say. Mayor's prerogative, I get to talk first.

"I'm going to suggest we vote no." She let that hang in the air.

"But the money," someone called. "You forced them. . . ."

"Yes. I'd like money too, you know. But . . . Well, all I can do is repeat what I said before. When we voted before."

She turned slightly to face southwest. The sky was mostly dark, the sun a flattened red orb near the horizon. She gestured over the water. "We got ourselves—I mean everyone, all of us, the whole world—we got ourselves in this mess by rushing ahead with things that we knew couldn't last. At any time, we could have stopped, found a better way to live—slower, maybe, and less easy, okay, but better. We could have saved Florida, and Bangladesh, and all the other places that are sunk now.

"Well, in that sense, nothing has changed. We can choose to live better now or just keep trying to fix things after they get worse. The Everglades are coming back here. The mangroves are coming south. We could live in this place, in a way that won't make things worse. The new prefab elevated houses are strong—with solar roofs and walls tough enough to take a wave right against them, and with their own desalination plants. They'll work. It wouldn't be an easy life. But it would be a life that could last.

"Or . . . Or we could live here in a way that's easier now, for a while, but that will require a bigger fix later, down the road. Because how long is any island going to last? A decade? Five years? They'll be back dredging every year, trying to restore the sand that the winter tides take away.

"I say, let's stick with our plan. Let's say no to this company, and find another company, and do it right." She dropped her hands so that they slapped against her thighs, a clear sign she was finished.

The people started talking all at once, first in a murmur, but the conversations soon rose to a roar. Tara did not stop them; she did not demand that they have a formal debate. There were only fifty-five of them. They could talk amongst themselves for an hour, even two, before she called order. She stepped back and let them talk.

The voting started at midnight. Pat passed around squares of scrap paper she'd cut up for ballot slips, and she told everyone, "Write 'YES' if you want to build the island and take the money! Write 'NO' if you want to stick with our original plan, and get new houses, up on pillars, brought out here!"

"Which one is no?" someone shouted. Pat moved into the crowd, passing out ballots, repeating herself.

It took only a few minutes for people to vote, and then twenty minutes for Pat to count and Grace to double-check her addition, the two of them huddled under a little LED lamp at a picnic table set out on the deck.

"Twenty-seven yes," Pat said quietly.

"What?" someone shouted.

"Twenty-seven yeses!" she called. "And twenty-seven nos!"

They had lit torches, and the moon was up and nearly full. Tara could see all the eyes turn toward her.

"It's up to you, Tara," Grace said. "The mayor has to make the tie-breaking vote."

Tara held her breath. The phone on her wrist began to buzz, buzz, buzz.

Tara and Emma got back home very late. Emma lay asleep in the back of the boat, and after Tara tied to the house, she lifted Emma up to the deck, where the girl stood, wobbling and half conscious. The tide had only just started to retreat, so it was still high, and Tara took a single step up to the deck. She lifted Emma into her arms. She walked to the back of the house, not turning on any lights but feeling her way.

But when she stepped into Emma's bedroom, her feet splashed on the floor. There was an inch of seawater in the room. She cursed and carried Emma to her own room. She laid the girl on her bed, pulled off her shoes, and climbed in next to her.

Emma snuggled up against her. A wave of relief rushed through Tara. Emma had been so angry with her when she'd come home. Grace had told Tara how the girl had waited, phone in hand, all the previous day. But Tara had never called to put Tommy on the line.

How could I? Tara thought. *How could I show her that?* Her father shriveled up, legs as thin as an egret's, arms shaking, barely able to talk. So Tara had told Emma that it was not good to wake sick people when they were asleep. Somehow, Emma had known she was lying.

Now all seemed forgiven. "Will we get our house tomorrow?" Emma whispered.

"No, not tomorrow, honey," Tara said. "They're going to come very soon, though, with huge barges and big machines. They're going to make an island, a big island, and put our house on that. You can run, like other kids, on the sand."

"Will we still have a boat?"

"Yes," Tara whispered. "We'll have a boat parked by the beach. You can take it out whenever you want."

"Will Tommy come? Will my daddy live with us?"

Tara hesitated a long while, staring into the dark. Finally, she said, "I don't know, honey. He's got to go to a special doctor for a while. Then, well, we'll see."

"Why doesn't he live with us, Gramma?"

"Your father . . . he had an illness, and they fixed that a little, but then another illness came from that, and then another, and he just runs ahead, just races a few steps ahead of the last disease. That takes all his time. Like how some people with a house by the water, they just keep moving their house back, and then back again, while the water keeps coming closer and closer. You see? Your father—he's racing the tide."

Emma's soft breath told Tara that the girl had fallen asleep. Tara felt the exhaustion of her trip sink down in her. She could sleep for days. For a week. Of course, she had to make calls to doctors, get second opinions, and then call that psychiatrist; she had to do a hundred other things, but tomorrow. After she slept.

But sleep did not come. As the soft light of dawn seeped into the room, she lay with her eyes open, listening. Somewhere, a fish splashed. An engine puttered alive and then disappeared in the distance—Paul Cosby heading southwest to his fishing grounds. Atop a nearby house, two gulls began to screech at each other. Other gulls took up the chorus. And through it all, water gurgled around the support beams beneath her house as the sea pulled away from their little village. The tide was retreating. For a little while.

ABOUT THE AUTHOR

CRAIG DELANCEY is a writer and philosopher. He has published dozens of short stories in magazines like *Analog, Cosmos, Shimmer, The Mississippi Review Online,* and *Nature Physics.* His novel *Gods of Earth* is available now with 47North Press. He also writes plays, many of which have received staged readings and performances in New York, Los Angeles, Sydney, Melbourne, and elsewhere. His stories have also appeared in translation in Russia and China, and his writing has garnered numerous awards. Born in Pittsburgh, PA, he now makes his home in upstate New York and, in addition to writing, teaches philosophy at Oswego State, part of the State University of New York (SUNY).

THE MUTANT STAG
AT HORN CREEK

SARAH K. CASTLE

I remember when I first saw it. Those were damn good days. Maybe the best, but I was younger then.

They'd just started closing the Grand Canyon down. They didn't do it all at once, of course. It started with the canyons that had been mined. Horn Creek was one of them.

One of the good things about global warming was it made the Southwest wetter than it had been since the Pleistocene. But all that rain meant the Grand Canyon's mines filled with water. The old adits and shafts from the 1800s filled up and stayed full. The water soaked in and leached out what was left of the metals. After a while, the mines overflowed. They became springs and spawned little creeks in side canyons that didn't usually have water.

You can't tell a national park hiker not to mess with a stream in the Canyon. It still seemed like desert to most people. The humidity just made the sun seem hotter. After a day hiking across the Tonto Plateau, baking like a cookie on a shale oven sheet, a hiker would see a turquoise pool rimmed with brilliant orange in a shady canyon bottom, and you couldn't keep 'em out of it. I know. I tried.

I remember a couple who showed up with special suits. Covered them from toes to fingertips. Left heads and necks bare. They knew the risks. They just thought they could beat 'em.

"Why don't you tie plastic bags over your heads?" I asked them. "Less painful if we get to the emergency part before you get in the water." I could tell that fabric wouldn't protect them. It wasn't even waterproof. Wishful thinking and technology; put 'em together and city folk believe they can do anything they want. I've never been able to tolerate that attitude. There is such a thing as common sense, though I'm not saying you should never question it.

The guy smiled at me like I was a fool. "Honey, we want to get wet," he said. "That's the point."

I stayed around until they asked me to call the rescue 'copter. That water was acid. Swimmers didn't notice until they started itching. By then, the damage was already done. To drink it meant sulfate or lead poisoning, depending on the mine. Sometimes, worse than that.

There were only five backcountry rangers in those days. I was one of 'em. Five people to patrol more than a million acres. On foot. Budget cuts hit the park hard. I guess Congress figured it was in the middle of nowhere. We patrolled alone a lot. I came to prefer it. In a world full of nine billion people, you appreciate every chance you get to be alone in nature with plenty of space and time.

So, I was patrolling up Horn Creek with twenty pounds of water on my back. You didn't want to drink anything coming out of the ground in that canyon. While the mine there had started out chasing copper, it ended up in high-grade uranium. They mined it just after World War II, back when atom bombs weren't just in the movies. In those days, there wasn't a place on Earth they wouldn't have mined uranium.

I always carried a pulaski then. A ranger didn't just patrol. We did quite a bit of trail maintenance, though it wasn't required of us. Besides, all the older rangers carried 'em strapped to their packs. Hell if I wasn't going to carry one, too.

I saw the herd a long ways off. I'd just rounded Dana Butte, coming out of the part of Salt Creek Canyon they call "The Inferno." I watched those deer for half an hour as I hiked toward them. They grazed the plateau's flattest part, right near the edge where the cliffs dropped off into the Canyon's Inner Gorge. I counted forty does at least and was damn impressed. One stag for all those does. The sucker had a huge rack. Huge. I couldn't exactly see the shape from that far off, but I had a sense the guy had a regular horn thicket up there on his head.

I took my pack off and snuck toward them. I wanted a better look. You've got to move smooth and quiet around deer or you'll scare 'em off. God only knows why, but I'd grabbed my pulaski. I carried it low, with both hands, at my waist.

No, I take that back. God didn't have anything to do with it. It was what I'd seen so far of that damned rack.

I got pretty close before the does smelled me. They started moving, quick and orderly, down into a little side canyon that led to the Inner Gorge. Their hooves clattered on the rock as they descended out of sight. The buck stood guard as his herd departed, keeping an eye on me and them both. I stayed low in the sagebrush. I crushed some as I pushed through it. It might've been that sharp sage nip that tipped them off about me.

The closer I got, the weirder his rack struck me. Now I could see it was tangled. The horns didn't branch out straight from each other. They twisted and bent in every direction. A couple bits had flattened out, more like what you'd see on a moose. I was just close enough to see it was strange, but not exactly how strange, when he followed the last doe over the cliff into that drainage.

I strained my ears. His hooves *clip-clopped* just a couple times after he dropped out of sight. They were waiting down there, not more than a couple hundred flat feet away and maybe ten or twenty feet down in the side canyon. They wanted me to pass. That was all. They wanted to come back up on the plateau to continue their easy grazing. I'd let them. But I wanted a closer look at that buck first.

I crept up to the canyon edge, quiet as I could, stepping toes first on the soft dirt between the shrubs and slowly lowering my heels. I wonder now if I held my breath. Maybe I was a little dizzy when I looked over the edge. That would explain a lot.

Because when I did look over, I saw the stag all right. He stood not twenty feet away on a narrow sandstone shelf just below the notch he knew I'd peer over. I didn't see what was in his eyes at first because, good God, I was looking at that rack!

It was something from a nightmare of warped bone plates and twisted, sharpened spears. I couldn't take my eyes off it until he snorted and kind of barked at me. Then I saw his face.

His brown eyes were bugged out. They blazed. His lips peeled back.

My legs went weak. I swear to this day I saw fangs in his mouth. Big ones, almost like the tusks on a javelina, two on top and two sticking up from its lower jaw. I screamed, loud and high, in such a way I'm embarrassed to admit to it.

That buck took it as a threat. Any creature would have. He reared back on his haunches. Even in my advanced state of inexperience, I could see he was going to spring at me. It wasn't hard to imagine that wicked rack smashing into my face, because that's what it was about to do.

Without thinking, I threw my pulaski like a boomerang. I remember the damned tool, all hardwood handle, steel axe, and adze, spinning through the air. It hit with a clunk and a splinter. The stag's head whipped to the side. Its body twisted after it. That was all I saw, because then I turned and ran.

First, I went and got my pack. Then, I ran all the way out of the Canyon, twelve miles on rough trail climbing two thousand, five hundred feet. I ran the whole way.

I never forgot that day. Thirty years later, I still think about it probably once a month, sometimes more often if something reminds me. They closed Horn Creek to everybody shortly thereafter. A big flood tore it up the following year. Radioactive mud got sloshed all over. Before the flood, a couple other rangers saw the stag, but nobody got as close as I did that day.

They used to tease me about the teeth, so I quit talking about it. But I always wondered what happened to that stag. I didn't want to believe I'd hurt it. It had twisted to catch itself, that's all. I'd scared it a little, maybe. Certainly, I'd knocked it off balance. Anyone would believe I'd done what I did in self-defense, but I hated to think I'd hurt a creature just being itself, protecting its herd, only because I'd been rash.

I always wanted to go back to look for that stag. It vexed me that nature would create something so . . . distorted. I guess that's the word I'm looking for. It didn't make sense. I felt then as I feel now: nature makes sense. A person can't always figure it, but you can learn something if you try. I know radiation damages things, but that stag was not sick. It was as strong and full of fight as any critter I'd ever seen. God only knows what would change a creature that way.

I take that back. I just didn't know and couldn't figure it. It bugged me. The Canyon had created it. Humanity had helped, of course, by being careless with our concentrated radiation, but there had to be some reason the ecosystem reacted the way it did. I wanted to know what it was.

Two years ago, they lifted the Horn Creek travel restrictions for rangers. They'd flown a couple drones down there to check for radiation. It had taken thirty years, but all that mud had finally washed away. The stag himself couldn't have lived more than another decade, but I still felt drawn to go have a look at the Horn Creek herd. I talked to Steve Mokiyesva, the park superintendent, about me going in.

"I want to check on the deer population down there," I told him. "I studied it a bit when I first started here." Steve had been around long enough to know that wasn't strictly true.

I mean, we made counts of the critters we saw on our patrols. We even entered the numbers in a computer, but interest in "wildlife resources" was dying down.

"You can go down there, Sue," Steve said, "but not by yourself. And I don't have anybody to spare to send with you." He'd heard about the mutant stag. "It would be good to see who's down there, how they're doing."

Steve never called any creature a "wildlife resource." He was of the Hopi deer clan, and flute clan, too. He nodded. "I tell you what. You can go down Horn Creek for your final patrol." He looked me hard in the eye. My stomach turned sour. "You know it's time. They need help at the outreach center. They'd fix your hip."

The outreach center is where they send old rangers to ease them out of the service. They keep us working as long as they can to get some labor from that pension money. It's up in that goddamned city where they need people to talk to folks who can't make it to the parks themselves. People to tell stories and show pictures. Technology and wishful thinking. I'd have spat on the ground if we'd been standing outside.

I got the message. My hip was slowing me down. Growing up in the gas fields had left me with asthma. It got worse every year. There were junior rangers who needed a promotion. It couldn't happen until a senior slot came open. "All right," I told him. "I'll let you know when I'm ready." It took another two years.

In those two years, a backcountry ranger didn't have much to do. They'd completely closed the Canyon to casual hikers by then. A massive flash flood swept two tourist mule trains and forty-seven hikers off Bright Angel Trail. Eighty-two people killed, all total. One of 'em was famous, so the Park Service took it more seriously. It was that guy who started the pay-per-view home movie site. Any person could put their movie up there. The more people who watched it, the more expensive it got, but he kept the top price below five bucks so most people could still afford it. He made a lot of people rich and got rich himself. His site still makes people rich today. Anyway, after that flood, tourists were only allowed below the rim on guided tours.

It was for their own protection.

Wolves had come back in from the north rim. The rattlesnakes were bigger, fatter, and more defensive. All the rain made for meaty mice, but they were harder for a snake to catch. Tourists needed a guide and a babysitter. Danger and beauty be damned, they looked more at their devices than they looked around, even here! No, I wasn't the tour guide type. That was what the park needed then.

Steve left me in a tough place, so it served him right to have to wait. He wanted me to take someone with me so he'd be sure I wouldn't just lie down to die out there like old Bruce Tanaka had. If I didn't have anybody, I guess he wanted to know that, too. He was a man sensitive to family ties. So much so, I'd have bet he knew I had trouble with mine. Steve would never go to the outreach center. He had family right here, people to care for him.

I didn't think again about my final patrol until I heard from my niece Katy. I'd met her a couple times when she was still a kid, maybe twelve or thirteen years old. We'd gotten along okay then. My sister even left her with me for a couple weeks once when she took off after some new dude. Katy had been a wide-eyed critter, ready to go anywhere and do everything. I'd gotten a real kick out of her.

Katy had just turned eighteen. I knew because she sent me a birthday card on her birthday to catch me up on her life. Her mother had moved to that goddamned city. Katy had finished school. She wanted to come see me, wondered if I could get her a special trip below the rim. Something different than what everyone else sees. I smiled real big when I read that.

So, there I was, on March eighteenth, waiting for Katy's bus to arrive at Grand Canyon Village. I admit I was looking for a kid dressed in a T-shirt and cutoff shorts in the line of people filing off the bus. Longer legs and arms, sure, but still the pony-tailed critter who'd trailed me around five years ago, watching me like I was the most interesting thing she'd seen in her whole life.

Katy was taller, all right, and topless, though that was hardly strange anymore. What struck me were the bright green tattoos all over her shaved head. They split and spread over her cheeks like tendrils creeping from a vine. Her shoulders, chest, and stomach were blotched with them.

When she got closer, I saw they were fuzzy, like patches of moss. Vein-like stringers connected the patches. Looking at them made my skin crawl. I'd seen the style on other tourists, but I'll admit it shocked me to see it on Katy. It was photosynthesizing nanotech embedded in the skin and left to grow. For what purpose besides style, I didn't know.

I did know the look on her face. Same as when she was a kid. Tears welled in my eyes. I got a knot in my throat. I didn't trust my voice, so I just opened my arms to her.

"Aunt Sue!" She dropped her backpack on the ground and hugged me close.

I wasn't sure I wanted to touch the tats, but it seemed rude not to return the gesture. The green stuff on her back felt like a mild rash: bumpy but not swollen or warm with irritation. The fuzz felt like hairs standing up on goose bumps. She smelled like fresh-cut grass. "Good to see you, gal. I'm so glad you came." I stepped back to get a better look at her. She pushed her glasses up on her head and wiped her eyes with a knuckle.

She looked plenty strong to carry lots of water, and she'd brought a sturdy backpack, which showed she was ready and willing to do it. My heart felt full for the first time since Sergei left, ten years ago. It was kind of . . . instant love, and it turned me to water.

This must be what it's like to have people, a clan, I thought, and it broke my heart the way dreams do when they come true. I wiped my eyes, but the tears kept coming. I admitted to myself I hoped to the heavens she'd love it here as I had and that she'd stay. That we would stay.

Katy brought her glasses back down, smiled, and gave a little shrug. She sniffed and then swallowed. Her expression changed to one like you'd see in the movies, all puppy love and excitement. "When do we leave?"

"Since you're ready, we'll take off this afternoon." I'd gotten the food and everything ready the day before.

"What will we see?" she asked, but it was like she asked herself more than me.

The question seemed strange. She'd been here before. I hadn't told her about the mutant stag. After more than thirty years, I didn't expect we'd see him, but I would no longer be surprised to see something equally as strange. I watched, waiting for her to say more, but she didn't. She just looked at me with that same set expression. "The Canyon," I said after a bit. Shouldn't have to say anything else.

Then I noticed her glasses' frames were kind of thick. Two tiny lenses shone at their upper outside corners. All of a sudden, I wasn't even sure she was talking to me.

I pointed to the glasses. "Data specs?"

She nodded quickly, like a dog wags its tail. "Stereoscopic." She took them off and handed them to me. "Lightest, toughest pair on the market."

I held them in my hand. They were indeed light.

"Got them just for this trip," she said. "This too." She brushed her fingertips across the green fuzzy tats on her breasts, and smiled, again like she had as a kid. She wanted me to like her, to be proud.

"What for, exactly?"

She looked around, checking to be sure nobody was close enough to hear. Then she looked back to me, eyes shining like they had the time I taught her to catch lizards with a lasso made from a grass strand.

"Killer content, Aunt Sue. You're taking me to a place no one's seen for thirty years. We're going to get some KC."

That shook me a little. I thought she'd come mostly to see me. "What does 'KC' do for you?"

"Makes me a rich and famous movie producer." Like that was all anyone would ever want. As she talked, she touched the green tats, fingers brushing and circling around on her belly and then shoulders.

"What do *they* do for you?" I asked, pointing my chin towards the spot she stroked on her shoulder.

She dropped her hand, embarrassed. "Sorry, I can't stop touching it. It's only two months old." She said this like it was her baby. "It charges the specs. Enough to get through a day if it's sunny out."

I bit my lip to keep my mouth shut. I hadn't thought about her taking that kind of tech down with us. I would take a camera, but that was it. Just a slight tilt of my hand and the specs would fall to the ground, where they would get quickly crushed under my boot. I took a deep breath. I knew that wasn't the way to handle it. Not if I wanted her to think about making a life here.

"These things are expensive, aren't they?" I asked, determined not to be an old-fashioned ass.

She nodded, as if impressed with herself. "Them and the phototats cost me my college fund."

That stunned me. I wanted to believe she was smart, someone the park would hire. The park only hired people with degrees. She held her hand out for the specs. Couldn't wait to get them back on. She was still just a kid—full of hope and wonder. It wasn't her fault she lived in a world where an eighteen-year-old could lawfully spend her whole college fund on tech that would be obsolete in less than ten years.

I handed her the specs, thinking back to the guy who'd started this craze, the one buried under tons of sand and stone somewhere in Bright Angel Canyon. He probably hadn't been paying attention either. People had lived through that flood.

I could imagine "killer content" was rare. It might be worth more than all the metal ever mined in this state if you could get a good fraction of nine billion people to pay for it. The chances she'd get KC out of the canyon were much better than one in nine billion. It might work out.

I didn't tell her that if we saw anything really strange down there, she couldn't upload it to any public site. There was no law against it, but I wouldn't allow it. Not until Superintendent Mokiyesva gave his okay. Media drones swarming the place would upset the Canyon's natural quiet, disturb the critters and the visitor experience. We'd learned that after the big Bright Angel flood.

We spent the first night down at Indian Gardens near the old rangers' bunkhouse. We slept under the stars. Katy wouldn't have it any other way after she saw the Milky Way stretched like a smoky road from one Canyon rim to the other. She'd seen it before. I know because I showed it to her. But after five years under city streetlights, I let her think it was the first time.

She took the specs off to go to sleep, but she still stared up, head resting on both hands, elbows open to the sky.

"Stars aren't KC?" I asked.

She laughed, "Not like that, standing still. I've seen stars fly circles around the sky and constellations we can't even see from Earth."

"Keep watching," I told her. "This ain't the movies."

She did for about five minutes. "What will I see? Shooting stars?"

"Maybe, but if you watch long enough, you'll see time. Watch it pass."

"Couldn't you watch the sun and see the same thing?"

"Sure, but stars are easier on the eyes." We lay in silence for a long while before her breathing got deep.

The next morning, I woke to her sleeping bag's rustle. I opened my eyes. She was propped on her elbows, looking at me with a funny little smile. "Did you see it?" I asked.

She nodded. "It was faster than I thought."

I laughed a little. "You're at a good age to learn that."

She rubbed her green head with one hand. "Not fast enough to make KC. If I speed it up, it's like everything else. If I don't, no one will watch it long enough to see."

"You ever wonder what else they're missing?"

She got out of the sleeping bag, stretched her arms overhead, and bent from side to side. The sky was already bright, though the sun hadn't come over the canyon rim yet. Pale yellow light filtered through the cottonwoods' tender green leaves. They leafed out so early now.

She shrugged. "Whatever it is, let's get it on disk."

Not the answer I was looking for. I wanted her to recognize the beauty for its own sake, outside what money it could bring. I held out my hand. I hadn't slept on the ground in an age. My hip was so stiff, I could hardly bend it.

She saw what I needed right away. I guess when you live in a city, you learn to pay attention to people. She helped me up, and I hoped she saw how I needed her.

"You got enough signal to upload stuff from down here?" I asked as I stood.

"No. I think the Canyon walls are too high, and I can't find a local network."

I put my hands on her shoulders and shook them playfully, like I used to do when she was a kid. "Then don't use the specs. I've watched tourists for years. They think about framing their shots, what their friends will think of the pics, everything but the reality around them and how they fit into it." I said the last five words one at time, so she'd know how important it was. Then I let her go and laughed, not wanting to come on too heavy.

She gave me a hard look. It made me feel like I'd come close to preaching. "I came here to get KC."

I looked right back at her, my heart beating fast. I couldn't believe how much what I wanted to say scared me. I said it anyway. "I thought you came to see me."

Her mouth fell open a little and her eyes got wide. "I didn't mean . . . Shit, I did come to see you, but . . . You know."

I wasn't sure I did. We stood there staring at each other. She seemed honestly embarrassed by what she'd said. Stepping up to give her a hug would've been the right thing to do, but I didn't want to touch the tats again. My heart rate started to settle down, but only because I'd put a chill on it.

The sun appeared at the Canyon's eastern rim. We both turned to look. Its edge arched skyward until the full circle blazed down on us. Katy watched it until it cut loose from the horizon. She didn't wear the specs and glanced sideways at me to see I noticed. I smiled to let her know I did, but it was hard to let go of the hurt I'd felt. I didn't know if she was sincere or just acting that way. I shook myself out, got ready to hike. The warmth greased my hip now, but the sun would scald later in the afternoon. Katy slathered herself in sunscreen and we got going.

We turned west on the Tonto Trail and headed off across the plateau. The Tonto Plateau is a huge shelf about halfway down the Canyon. It's the broadest flat area below the rim. The four-legged animals loved it. Even bighorn sheep liked to hang out on the Tonto's gentle slopes now and then. And they climb things on hoof I wouldn't try without a rope. It was a restful place, even more so now that no hikers crossed it. A hot breeze seared my ears and dried my throat.

Katy hiked fast, nipping at my heels. She covered ground like most city folk who wanted to check "Hike Grand Canyon" off their list of things to do: like doing laps at a track. I kept my own pace, let her nip. For all the years she'd spent in the city, nothing about the Canyon seemed to impress her now. Maybe she was trying to impress me that she could keep up. Maybe she'd seen it all in a movie already. More likely, nothing yet had jumped out as KC material, and she wanted to walk hard until she found some. I found myself walking slower and slower, hoping she'd look around more.

I was glad I hadn't told her about the mutant stag. She'd probably have broken out in a run to look for it. No, I wanted her behind me, where she wouldn't scare off every living thing with slamming footsteps. I hoped we would talk, maybe straighten out the morning's misunderstandings, but I couldn't bring myself to start the conversation. I sure as hell kept my eyes open. I didn't expect to see the old stag himself, but I was alert for clues as to what had changed down here that might've made him what he'd been.

We crossed the plateau in the hours before noon. Floods had scraped out many of the deeper dips in the trail, leaving steep-sided gullies with bare rock or gravel-raveling slopes. Decades of rain had ravaged and ripped the place. It was as if the clouds themselves had decided to rinse it clean by lingering here more often.

We came to a place where water had scoured the trail completely away. "This is what happens to a trail when no one's around to care for it." I patted my pulaski's handle, where it was strapped to my pack's side. "You ever think about doing trail-building work?"

"I didn't even know it was a job."

"It is," I said, "and a damn good one." Her expression let me know she wasn't sure she believed it.

I took the lead, showing Katy how to skid down the gravel parts and down-climb the rock. We scrambled up the gully's other side. The sun stayed sharp, the air, hazy. The dust we kicked up joined the sweat salt stuck on my skin. I felt gritty as sandstone. I smiled. A hike's second day was always when I started to feel more part of the Canyon and less a visitor.

I pulled myself over the ledge at the gully's top. I'd taken a few steps when I saw a big, greenish-gray slash out of the corner of my eye. I focused quick. A Mojave green rattlesnake, thick and blunt as a man's severed arm and twice as long, lay stretched out in the sun. I was still in shock to see it this far east in the Canyon, when Katy came up from behind and stepped past me.

The snake whip-curled, rattling so fast it buzzed. It advanced on us, its head high and ready to strike. I grabbed Katy, but it took a yank to get her moving.

When we got a couple meters away, the snake calmed down and I stopped.

"Rattlesnake?" Katy asked, eyes alive behind her specs.

"Mojave green. One of the tougher snakes." I couldn't believe she hadn't startled at the rattle and backed off like any person with sense would've. My heart pounded. "How's that for KC?"

She shrugged. "We'd have to go back to get more footage, something more threatening."

My eyes almost popped out in disbelief. I realized she just didn't know the danger. "You have no idea. They can strike half their body's length. Neurotoxins in their venom will leave you in pain and prickly for months. They've got hemotoxins that will rot living muscle and leave an orange-sized dent in your leg."

She looked at me now but focused about a foot past my head. I realized she was filming me, or worse, some "me" she thought would make killer content.

"Stop it," I said, quietly. "Please."

"Perfect," she said, under her breath. "I will," she said, louder. "I did."

I wondered what she saw in me, what she'd been looking at all morning. A stringy old woman, walking funny on a bad hip, now with eyes bugged out and terrified. If the snake didn't scare viewers on its own, maybe my reaction would. Or make them laugh out loud. I wondered if she'd ask my permission to upload it. I wondered if I'd give it.

"What will you do with all this money you hope to get?" I asked.

She thought for a while, looking back toward the snake. Finally, she answered me. "I won't have to work. I could do whatever I wanted."

"What would you do?"

She thought hard on that too, which impressed me. "Come up with more KC. Hang out, relax."

"With who?"

"Cool people." She shrugged. "Everybody wants to hang out with people who make KC. They're more interesting." She looked down and smiled faintly. "I'd be more interesting."

I nodded, but the answer made me sad, somehow. Attention was likely hard to come by if you're competing with nine billion people, but there ought to be something else out there worth working for.

We walked on, hiking on the slope above the gully's head to avoid any more surprises. I had a heightened awareness for anything linear and green-colored. It didn't serve me well.

The farther we got towards Horn Creek, the stranger the prickly pear cactus got. Prickly pear usually had succulent pads, the size of salad plates, standing tall in upraised branches. The ones here were wrinkled up like giant prunes. Their branches lay on the ground in shriveled green chains as if they didn't have enough strength to stand up anymore. It made the place look like it crawled with snakes.

We came to a gully that had eaten into solid rock at its head, creating a cliff we could not pass. The rock was loose and crumbly, impossible to climb.

"Is this it?" Katy asked. "Do we have to go back now?"

It pleased me to hear her disappointed at the possibility. I eyed the gully downstream, where there were slopes of softer material. They were too steep, loose, and long to walk down safely, but we could get down by cutting ledges and digging a path in a couple key places. I took off my pack and unstrapped the pulaski. "Let's build some trail, girl."

She looked at me in disbelief.

"A rough one, just a foot wide."

We walked back to where the slope was less steep, a soft spot in the shale. I cut the first bit, showing Katy how to set her back and swing the tool, always keeping it at or below the shoulder. Katy took over after a while. She was clumsy at first but finally got the rhythm. Swing and heft, swing and heft. She smiled and hummed as she worked. I'd have sworn she liked it. The crumbly rock was easy to work through, and we made a neat path to the bottom and back up in two hours.

We got to the top. I took my pack off and enjoyed the cool of the sweat-soaked shirt on my back. Katy wiped her brow. Her tattoos glistened with sweat like dew-covered moss. She smelled green like cut grass again. The scent seemed alien. Most of the shrubs and grasses were gone, replaced by cactus that could live with the cycles of short, hard rains followed by long, brutally hot and dry spells. I wondered about forage for the deer. The shriveled, prickly cactus pads would not be edible to anything with a tender tongue.

We looked back down our trail. It was a thin thing, a couple ledges cut into the hard places and a narrow platform dug into the soft parts. Katy looked from me, to it, and back again.

"We did that," she said. "We built it."

I smiled. "It'll be there for us when we come back, for the critters and any hikers or rangers who come this way after us. This is good work."

Katy saw what I was getting at. "My videos will stay around, Aunt Sue.

People will watch them over and over again if I do them right. They might change the way people think."

What she said was true, but I thought it over, because it missed something. Finally, I came around to it. "What a person thinks is only important if it changes what they do."

Her expression went sour. I knew I'd done wrong. She'd taken what I'd said as criticism, and it had hurt her.

"The next big rain will take this trail out," she said, striking back at me.

I kept my voice as gentle as I could. "And then we'll need somebody to come rebuild it." I reached over and touched her cheek lightly. "Someone like you." I patted the green leaf shape ingrained in her face. Her expression changed gradually. It got softer but touched with worry. She saw what I was really getting at for the first time: I wanted her to stay here with me, get a job at the park, and all that came with it.

"Let's get going," I said. I wanted her to think it over for a while. I wouldn't ask her to stay straight out unless I thought she'd say yes. "I want to camp at Horn Creek tonight."

We walked on, and I stayed sharp-eyed. The Canyon has nooks, cracks, and caves aplenty to hide in. I searched the ground and sky. The snake and the cactus spooked me, but I kept the possible dangers to myself. I wanted her to see the beauty here and the peace of it.

A couple California condors soared so high above us, they looked small against the Canyon's walls. The trail dropped into a little side canyon along a stone ledge too hard to get washed out. Three condors stood together on the ground down there.

I put an arm out to hold Katy back. They looked like a group of bald, feathered kids. That's how big they were. The two bigger ones turned their black, beady eyes our direction. The smaller one kept its face to some carcass they'd all been picking at.

"Vultures?" asked Katy. She stared avidly through her specs.

"Condors," I told her. I was proud she'd made a good guess, but worried about how intent she seemed. Not paying attention; more like working on buying it for herself. "Be aware. Condors are carrion eaters, but I've seen them fight over carcasses. They have a young one with them, which might make them defensive. Stay close. Don't move fast unless I do." She nodded, eyes still stuck on the condors.

I took Katy's hand and walked real slow down the trail. I figured we could get past them if we didn't make any fast moves or get too much closer. Our footsteps, quiet as they were, echoed around the little canyon like sharp whispers. The place stank with the rotten-fish scent of flesh long dead. I swallowed against a gag and pinched my nose shut with my other hand.

"Bob?" the biggest condor said. The name gurgled up from deep in its throat.

I froze, shocked to hear a word from its big, hooked beak. My mind spun on it. Bob Patchett was the only man left in the California condor captive breeding program. He'd been alone up there at Vermillion Cliffs for decades, hand-feeding every baby bird until it was old enough to hunt for itself. I'd heard rumors he even chased the parents off sometimes so the little critters would still need him. I had no trouble believing they were smarter than parrots, given similar training.

"Bob?" the condor said again, louder this time. "Bob?" It took two hops toward us, each one long enough to shame any human broad-jumper. "Bob?" It sounded hopeful. I noticed the carcass they shared: a wolf. The condors in comparison made it look mighty small.

Katy squeezed my hand tighter each time it hopped. A condor won't usually attack a person, but they've got beaks and talons evolved to pluck tendons from dead mammoths and smilodons. They can do serious damage just poking around, being curious. The creature was close, no more than thirty feet off. I shuffled sideways down the trail, keeping my eyes on the condor. Katy stuck with me, her palm slick with sweat on mine.

The bird saw our retreat and took another desperate hop forward, a really big one this time. It flared its wings to catch a little glide. I swear those big, black wings touched the canyon walls on both sides. They could've wrapped around the two of us twice. The long feathers at its wingtips spread out like too many fingers. The damn thing was way too close. In seconds, it could start pecking at our hands, looking for a treat. I thought fast and remembered the one thing that made Bob Patchett really mad. He'd been married once. The woman had been last to leave the program up there. I searched for her name.

"Diane!" I shouted. "Diane!" I launched a curse-laden tirade against this woman I'd never met.

The condor knew the name. He jumped backward twice and ruffled up the feather frill at the base of its bald neck. Just as I'd suspected, thinking about Diane had put Bob out of the nurturing mood, probably every time.

I pulled Katy along with me. We made quick time up the canyon's other side. I continued cussing Diane as we climbed. When we got back up on the plateau, I felt safer. A condor wouldn't hop after us this whole way, and they weren't built to attack from the air.

Katy looked at me wide-eyed. "What is a condor, and who's Diane?"

"California condors. We saved 'em. When I was your age, there weren't more than a couple hundred left."

"How'd you save them?" She looked at me, honestly interested.

I laughed. "I didn't do it myself, honey. We did it. As in us human beings." I explained about Bob and all the people who'd gone before him, caring for those birds. Then I told her about Diane, and how it was a good thing these condors were teaching their youngster how to feed on its own. Bob had gone further than anyone knew to make the birds dependent on him. It was a bad kind of interference, like feeding bears in your backyard, and there were laws against it.

She watched me closely the whole time, looking interested, excited even. Then too excited. Her expression changed from wonder-struck kid to the phony movie-actor face she'd made by the bus yesterday. The more I noticed it, the less I wanted to say. So, I shut up.

Her face relaxed into a wide, wide grin. She thought I'd finished talking—didn't notice the change in my attitude. "Killer!" she said, grinning wide. Her eyes twitched around behind the specs. She was already editing.

My heart went cold in my chest. The little lenses in the spec's frames looked blacker and beadier than the condors' eyes.

I put a finger to my lips, mainly to get my hand in range of her face. It surprised her. She watched, waiting for me to say something.

"How are those specs attached to the tats?" I asked, like it was the most interesting fact in the world.

"Oh!" Now she smiled naturally. She really was proud of that stuff. She folded her right ear forward and turned it toward me a little. "These little nano pads behind the ears are different. The specs' arms rest there, and the current goes through a conductive patch. . . ."

Good. No nasty skin-penetrating jacks. I snatched the specs off her face.

"You can't upload a minute of that." I folded the specs up and put them in my thigh pocket, wanting to avoid my instinct to throw them down and crush them under my boot.

"You put this up now, and those condors could end up dead," I said.

Katy looked from me to my thigh pocket, not saying a word and pissed off as hell. I would've been, too, had it been my stuff.

"This could be it for me, Aunt Sue. It would at least get my investment back."

I shook my head.

She waited a while, though I could tell she knew what she wanted to say. Finally, she came to it. "You care more for condors than me?"

Now she could wait. I didn't want to say the first thing that came to mind, so I kept my mouth shut and gave her the goddamn eye. She kept her back up, but her mouth twitched a couple times.

"That was mean," I said. "But you asked it, so I'll answer you straight. I do care more about them than you. They rip through hides too tough for vultures. Smaller scavengers eat the torn-up bodies they leave behind.

Bears and wolves can do the same thing, but how many more of those do we want around? I know it's different in the city. Bodies don't lie around there. Out here, when something dies, it just lays down under the big, blue sky. We want condors around to clean 'em up. They're better than the alternatives."

I thought it was sinking in. Katy's eyes had gotten softer.

I pressed on. "If the media swarms these birds, they won't make it. Condors might be used to people, but news drones would drive 'em crazy. They'd stop eating, stop raising their young right. We call 'em a recovered species, but there aren't more than two thousand of them. Every one still counts."

That caught her attention. *Every one still counts.* Katy looked up from the ground, which she'd been staring at. In a world of nine billion people . . . My heart went out to her a little bit. She looked sorry, but she hadn't said it yet. "You understand me?"

She nodded in a way that disposed me to believe her.

I took the specs from my pocket and put them on. The lenses were clear, but tinted gray like sunglasses. I saw no data display. "Iris recognition?" I asked.

"Yeah," she said. "The data display only works when they're on my face."

"How about the recording functions?"

"They stay on until I turn them off."

So, the specs had saved my whole lecture, along with the view inside my pocket. It still recorded. I took the glasses off and weighed them in my hand.

Katy sniffed and then swallowed. She looked me right in the eye. "I'm sorry, Aunt Sue. I swear I'll delete it."

I waited for her to say she'd then give the specs back to me afterward, but she didn't. The girl knew how to stand her ground.

The sun moved a millimeter across the sky.

I was impressed, but I put the specs back in my pocket. "I'm sorry, but I won't risk it."

"You're never going to give them back?" Her face went red behind the green tats. Regret turned to rage so fast, I knew I'd done the right thing.

"Only if I can find a tech I can trust to access the memory and erase these parts."

She looked at me differently, like I was something more than a stringy old woman. I was someone to be reckoned with. "You don't trust me."

I nodded. "Sorry to say."

She took a deep breath and looked me up and down. I stood my ground. "You can head out now," I told her, "if you're no longer interested." Now I'd learn what she was really here for. I kept my hand on my pocket. If she tried to take the specs back by force, I'd crack 'em in half and pitch the pieces over a cliff. If she was that kind of person, I wanted to know it.

She steamed over it for a while, looking from me to the Canyon's south rim. I got tired of waiting. "Trust has to be earned, girl." I pointed down the trail toward Horn Creek. "Let's get going."

She gave me a look. Whether it was calculating or compassionate, I couldn't quite tell. She did stay, though. "You go ahead," I said. "It's different when you're the one leading." She sighed and took off in the direction I pointed.

There's nothing like walking out on a trail and seeing no one ahead of you, even when you can see for twenty miles. You know you're not the first. You've got a trail beneath your feet, right? But it sure can feel like it.

I wasn't sure Katy appreciated it. Where before she nipped at my heels, now she never got more than fifty meters ahead. Every time she'd stop to enjoy a view, she'd glance back, making sure I saw her appreciate it.

Part of me thought it sweet. For all she was a strong young woman, brave enough to shoot herself up with tech that would grow under her skin, she craved attention like a little kid.

Another part of me felt uneasy about it.

"Aunt Sue?"

I stopped and looked where she pointed. I'd been more caught up in my thoughts than was appropriate for the situation.

"A turtle?" she asked. She took a few steps through the cactus chains. I scanned the space, looking for the snake she might not see. My gaze fell on the creature. She crouched down to look at it. The scaly legs and blunt face were as familiar to me as an old friend.

"It's a tortoise, honey. A desert tortoise. These are new here." Its shell was something else altogether. It had grown spikes all around the edges, each one an inch or two long. Despite the heat, I suddenly felt cold.

"How's it new?" she asked. She reached forward, real slow. The tortoise tucked up. She stroked its shell with one finger. She didn't know it was any different. I didn't see any need to point it out. I hoped it was a fluke, unique to this one animal.

I spoke carefully, not sure how much I wanted to reveal. "Back in the days when they covered the Mojave Desert with solar panels, some crazed conservation biologists set a bunch of tortoises loose here. They figured the environment would be friendly for 'em and no one could put up solar panels in the park. The damn things thrived. Now you can't hardly walk a trail without tripping over one."

"They're damned?" she asked.

I smiled a little, but she didn't see it. She watched the tortoise. I decided to tell. "Damned lucky. It's against the law to move an endangered species, but we did. We were right to do it. You can't find a desert tortoise in the Mojave Desert these days. They're all here or in roadside zoos, far as I know."

She turned to face me, all attention. "'We' as in us human beings?"

"As in me. My first job out of college, I did desert tortoise surveys for utility right-of-ways. Years before I came here."

I could tell she was impressed. She looked back to the tortoise, her eyes running over it and the ground around it. "It's been eating these cactus." She pointed to nibble marks on the prickly pears' new growth. "Its little mouth can bite between the thorns, huh?"

"You're right." I fingered the specs through the fabric over my pocket. It wouldn't hurt to let her record this. She couldn't upload until we got above the rim, anyway. I pulled the specs out and handed them to her. "Here, get some video."

She gave me a solid, thoughtful look and then took them from me. As she slid them past her ears, she shivered.

"You okay?" It was a strange thing to see, as hot as it was.

"Yeah. The tats start to tingle when they build up too much charge. Feels good to let it bleed off into the specs' batteries."

The thought made me itch. All those tiny machines, vibrating under her skin. "I'd gladly lend you a shirt to cover up." I wouldn't let her keep the specs just on that account, if that's what she was thinking. At the moment, she didn't appear to be thinking about me at all. She filmed the tortoise carefully from several angles and distances. I had to smile a little. I wanted people to know somebody cared enough to save these tortoises.

"I did this," I said to Katy. "Saved a species. No amount of video could've hidden those critters in the back of a van and brought them across the state line. A billion people thinking about it couldn't have carried them as gently as we did to bring them here, alive and ready to thrive in a place we knew would suit them."

Katy looked at me seriously, but I couldn't tell if she was thinking hard about what I'd said or only half paying attention as she recorded. "Wow," she finally said. "That's . . . It's . . ."

I cringed, afraid she would label me "killer" and wondering how I'd deal with it.

"It's really cool, Aunt Sue." She rested her palm on the tucked-up tortoise's shell. "That is really cool."

I smiled big then, because I believed she meant it. "You can keep the glasses on for a while, but I'll want them back tonight."

"I'll hand them over anytime you ask."

It was the right thing to say. Maybe too right, but I had to give her a chance to earn my trust. It would be cruel to withhold it without reason.

We saw a dozen more tortoises that afternoon. Seven were alive. Five were dead, their shells shattered. They all had the spiked fringe around their shells. My gut wrenched each time I saw it.

"Do the condors smash them?" Katy asked. "Maybe they drop them from up high."

"I doubt it. Condors don't think to kill."

"Condors don't talk, either."

I didn't have any answer for that, but she watched me, waiting. "They eat what's dead," I said. "They could pry a tortoise open but would only do it if they smelled something dead inside."

"What else would do it?"

I just shook my head. I still hadn't told her the spikes were something new. "A wolf wouldn't have a big-enough mouth," I said. "Stay closer, okay?"

The whole thing gave me a bad feeling. I tried to make myself feel better, told myself the tortoises were better off than if they'd gone extinct. We'd thought the move through as carefully as we could. Playing God is a tough role, but in this case, somebody had to do it.

We slept that night at Horn Creek, just above where the trail crosses it. You still don't want to get too close to the creek. I insisted on a tent. Ever since we'd come into this drainage, I'd felt like something watched us. Once, I heard a rustle and crunch off to the trail's right. Way out across the plateau, I thought I saw something moving out there between the desert thorn and wolfberry. Horn thickets. Whatever they were, they would go still whenever I looked right at 'em, like stealthy things will do. Same thing happens when your imagination runs wild, so I didn't mention it to Katy. It was probably just some critter out there minding its own business. No need for both of us to be paranoid.

I woke in the dark to the sound of hoofs, clattering on rock in the next gulch over, distant and echoing. For a while, I wondered if I dreamt it, or if maybe that stag still walked the canyon as a ghost. Maybe the damned thing was still alive. The sound faded. I stared at the tent's fabric overhead for a good long while, listening and hearing nothing else. The moon was half full and bright. The branches of a dead cottonwood tree cast twisted shadows on the tent. I rolled to my side.

Katy's eyes were wide open, shining in the dark with reflected moonlight. She looked over at me. She'd heard it too. Neither of us said a word. We just lay there together. The creek's splash and trickle finally lulled me.

I must've fallen hard asleep, because when I woke up, Katy was gone. You can only be so quiet getting out of a sleeping bag and tent with the zippers and all. I was proud she'd done it so well, but worried about where she'd gone. I pulled my pants on and found she'd taken her specs out of my pocket.

I got out of the tent and looked around. The sky was the gray-blue color it turns just before dawn. I hated to think what a wolf could do in this light. I wanted to shout for Katy and hear her yell right back. I did not. It would be a wrong thing to stir up every animal in Horn Creek just because I was worried. Hell, it could call a wolf right in and scare the deer into hiding from here to Salt Creek.

Instead, I looked around. It was hard to stay quiet. On a still morning, the Canyon can seem like a big, empty room, all walls and echoes. My breath sounded too loud. My feet crunched on the sand. I stopped every couple steps to listen and looked sharp all around.

I had to because the Canyon is not a big, empty room—ever or anywhere. Far from it. Even the Tonto Plateau only looked flat compared to the eight-hundred-foot-tall Redwall cliffs. Here where we'd camped, rounded hills fifty to a hundred feet high from creek bed to crest surrounded us. A critter could easily hide close enough to hear every step and smell you sweat. I scanned the ground and hills as if Katy's life depended on it.

The scuffmarks put me on to her: little drag marks in the silt on the rock ledge next to the creek. Then I saw footprints in the sand. The tread marks were familiar. I'd followed them down the trail for hours yesterday. It was Katy for sure. She'd gone exploring like young people will do. Like I had done and still do. I followed her trail up the drainage a ways before I saw her.

She stood almost halfway up the hill slope on the creek's other side. She saw me and waved big, swinging her arm wide overhead. She kept doing it, afraid I wouldn't see. God only knows why she didn't shout.

No, I take that back. God had nothing to do with it. She didn't shout because she had an instinct for quiet. Maybe living in a goddamned city with millions of people hones that instinct. I hurried up the slope, sensing she had something to show me.

She sure as hell did. Just at her feet, beneath a narrow shale ledge on the hillside, sat that stag's skull. That stag. There was absolutely no doubt about it, because my pulaski was still stuck in its rack. I could read my name etched on the damn handle.

So, I had killed it. Not that day but before the season had ended and it could shed its horns. Life couldn't have been easy with a pulaski stuck to its head. A couple horns on that side were broken, like it had bashed its rack against things to try to knock it loose.

I knelt down and set my hand on what would've been its snout. The skull still had some dried skin and fur stuck to it, but it was mostly covered with a patchy light green moss. The rest of the bones were scattered and gone, but even the wolves and coyotes wouldn't touch that creature's crazy head.

I bowed my head and let out a long breath.

"I'm sorry," I whispered. Some things need to be said out loud, no matter what.

Katy stood by, silent and respectful. She had the specs on, of course, but I didn't give a damn.

Besides, it was her moment, too. I hadn't told her what I'd been looking for on this trip, and here she'd found it. Exactly it. It made the hair on my arms stand up. She looked from me to the skull with eyebrows pushed together. Without a word, she knelt down. She stroked each long, sharp incisor once with her index finger. Anybody could see there was something wrong about those teeth.

"I'm sorry too," she said. Then she looked sideways at me to see if she'd done the right thing.

I almost cried. I closed my eyes and swallowed it. She had a sense for people. It was the right thing to say, but it hurt me. It was hard not to take it as criticism.

The sky was now bright. The sun had risen somewhere, but we still stood in the shadows of the Canyon's eastern walls. I let out a breath and turned away from the skull.

A couple of quick *clops*. A clatter. Katy's eyes got wide. Mine bugged out too. The sounds came from the west, from the hill's other side. More *clip-clops* and scraping sounds.

Katy took off, running quick and quiet, toward the hilltop. I opened my mouth to shout, but clamped it shut real quick. It would be better not to surprise whatever was over there. I clearly remembered the look on that stag's face, so many years ago, when I dared follow its herd to where it had gone to protect them.

I turned back to my old friend. I grabbed a horn with my right hand and then stomped on the aged antlers. One strong blow shattered them to pieces. I grabbed my old pulaski from the pile of shattered bone.

Katy was halfway up the hill. I ran to follow, slowed by my hip and the pulaski. I kept my head down, watching the ground carefully to make time and still stay quiet. Just short of the hill's crest, I looked up. Katy was nowhere to be seen. She'd gone over to the other side. I got to the hillcrest and lay on my belly, heart pounding, to have a look around.

The critters caught my eye first. It wasn't a whole herd. There were six bucks down there in the stream bottom, two bigger and older than the others. They all had those crazy racks. None had grown quite as big as my old friend's, but they all had a couple of warped, flattened plates like moose, and crooked bone spears bristling out with no rhyme or reason. I looked around but didn't see or hear Katy. There were plenty of places to hide. She must've been using them wisely. My eyes were drawn back to the bucks.

I couldn't see their faces at first. The two bigger critters stood in the drainage's bottom on rock scoured clean by past floods. They looked up at their younger brothers, who ranged across the hillside opposite, their backs to me. I couldn't make out the mouths on the smaller ones further away. It was quiet for a while. Those little deer knew all they needed to about stealthy travel.

One started bucking and kicking at the slope. Dirt and gravel flew and *tickety-ticked* down the hill. Then something big came sliding down. I thought it was a just a big rock. Then I recognized it. A tortoise. My guts twisted.

I could make out the shell's broad curve and the flat part on its belly. The young buck stopped digging. He knew what he'd gotten. He jumped and turned. He chased the tortoise downhill to where it had stopped. With a whip of its head, it tossed it down toward its elders.

The tortoise hit the rock bottom with a thunk and a scrape. The two elder stags danced around it for a full minute or two, swinging their heads and grunting. I squinted, stared, and wished for binoculars, but I still couldn't get a good look at their mouths.

I did get a good look at Katy. More than halfway down the slope, she peered out from behind a boulder, pointing those damn specs at the fighting bucks. I eased over the hillcrest. Quiet as I could, I made my way down to her. She didn't even turn to look when she felt my breath on her neck. She reached a hand out and grabbed my wrist after a quick fumble across my belly. It made me angry. I could've been a bear or wolf, and she hadn't even turned to look.

It turned out to be a play fight. The bigger buck took the prize without striking a blow on the smaller one. It nosed the tortoise along the ground for a bit, shoving it up next to a step in the rock. It struck the shell with three tough chops from one of the bony plates in its rack. The tortoise stayed tucked up tight. The hits must've rung the tortoise like a bell, put it right out of its senses.

Katy let me go and took off again, slower this time and still quiet, but we were too damn close already. I cursed silently and followed her to the next boulder. We were close enough now to hear the critters breathe. I couldn't help myself. I leaned out to look around Katy to see what was going on.

The big stag walked around the tortoise to get a better angle on it, I guess. Then I saw them: four giant incisors. The top two were like awls, the bottom two like chisels. It pulled its lips back and opened its mouth wider than I'd have thought possible. I'd swear it drooled on that tortoise's shell.

I grabbed Katy's arm and squeezed hard. It was all I could do to keep from screaming. That's how terrifying a sight it was. Katy gasped, but those bucks didn't hear it. They were too busy watching their headman tear the tortoise apart.

And I'll be goddamned if they didn't eat it. They'd gone carnivorous.

No, I won't take that back. I will be goddamned. To make it worse, I felt a cold thrill over it. The Canyon and the radiation had both surely played a part in this, but by bringing in the tortoises, so had I. The deer's usual forage had been lost to the changing weather. They couldn't eat the cacti themselves. The radiation allowed a series of freak mutations that let them eat critters that could chomp on the prickly pear.

We watched them find and eat two more tortoises in a similar fashion. They shared each meal to some extent. The shell-cracker took his share first, but he left some for the littler ones. Another medium-sized buck came over the opposite hill, dragging a jackrabbit by its neck like a mountain lion would do. Blood dripped from its fangs when it dropped its prize at its fellows' feet. The biggest buck lowered its head and took the choice cut. It tore the rabbit's head off with a chomp and a quick twist of the neck.

That was too much. My legs went weak and my shoulders trembled. I must've lost my grip, because in a second, Katy had twisted loose. She took long steps to get closer to the stags.

In my horror, to my horror, I shouted after her, "No!"

The word came out as a breathy squeak. Every one of those animals raised their heads and turned their bloody mouths our direction. Their eyes blazed. Nostrils flared. The biggest stag lowered its head and pointed its wicked rack toward Katy.

Katy saw the threat. She stopped in her tracks, as frozen now as I'd been wobbly a moment before. She needed to back away, cede the territory to its obvious owner, but she didn't know it.

The stag snorted and scraped a hoof on the rock. He took a step forward, putting himself between Katy and the others. He was just protecting his young and defending the food they needed. All Katy had to do was start walking backward. She didn't do it, and I had no way to tell her. A word spoken then could startle the stag into a charge. I thought hard and fast, determined not to act rashly. The pulaski hung heavily in my hands. I suddenly knew what to do.

I swung the steel head back to my shoulder. The movement felt as natural as walking after years of using the tool. The next motion would be the sideways swing forward to bring the axe to bear on a standing tree, but I kept the blades high, next to my shoulder, with my forearm across my body. I walked forward slowly, with short, smooth strides. I put myself between Katy and the stags.

The big one raised its head a bit and stared, bug-eyed at me and that pulaski. It took a long, deep breath and then shot it out on the exhale, like a wave crashing in on the tide. Either me, the tool, or both had made it think twice. I stepped back, bumping into Katy.

She got the message and took a step back, waited a moment, and then took another. The stag held its ground but let its head rise a bit with each step we took backward, becoming less and less ready to charge. They kept their eyes on us until we got to the hillcrest. We stopped there and watched them back.

When the sun came over the hill and hit the ground down in the drainage, the biggest stag tossed his head around, proudly displaying his antlers as if showing off his lineage. He kept his eyes on me, so I raised the pulaski overhead, punching it toward the sky. That seemed to settle him down. He kept his head up, but I swore he gave me a quick nod before they all headed upstream toward the Redwall cliffs, to some secret place in deeper shade.

It gave me a good feeling. It was like the Canyon, with its ways and wiles, had made him and me both.

I felt breath on my cheek. Katy looked at me, really looked at me, but still through the specs. She saw my face now, but she'd also seen my expression as I'd watched those stags do their work. She likely had it recorded. You've got to know I was ashamed.

No, I take that back. I was mortified. Mortified at my role in what had happened to these critters and at the thrill of pride I'd felt about it.

I did this must've been written all over my face. Katy turned away, aiming her specs back at the now-empty canyon. If this wasn't killer content, I didn't care what was.

"Here," I said, holding the pulaski out to Katy. "Do you want it?" My heart pounded and my eyes were wet. The damned tool weighed more than two kilos, and we both still had big water loads we needed to get us out of the Canyon. She would not be able to take it on the bus. I was asking her if she'd stay, but I wasn't sure she understood the question.

She took it but held it like it was an artifact, not a tool she'd ever use again. She glanced at me with something in her eyes I hadn't seen yet. Respect.

I swore her shadow shrank a centimeter as we both stood there, still and quiet. The sun's heat built on my back.

I started to feel scared and sad. Finally, I asked, "You going to upload that?" It was an offer and a hard one to make.

She looked up at me. Her chin trembled. She looked nervous. She looked scared . . . and hopeful. My heart dropped.

"The media would swarm you. They'd swarm the deer, but they could probably do it in a way the deer wouldn't mind."

Not so for me. She knew that.

I wiped my eyes with the back of my hand and then took a big breath and stood up straight. "It wouldn't be so hard to take if I knew you'd use the money to go back to school. I believe you'd keep your word if you promised me."

She looked at me with a face full of wonder. Wonder on the verge of joy.

"Finish school before you upload it, is what I mean. I'll front you the money from what I make at the outreach center." That threw her through a loop, but I could see she considered it. "Maybe when you're done, you'd consider a job down here in the Canyon. Mokiyesva could use someone with tech like yours to keep an eye on the backcountry." It took a long time for tech to get obsolete in the Park Service. We didn't have money to upgrade very often.

Katy smiled. She pushed the specs back onto her head and looked around. The rising sun lit the Canyon with a warm, golden light. "Maybe I would."

She shifted the pulaski to a more comfortable position, holding it low at her waist, and started down the hill toward our camp. I let her get ahead. I stopped to see the skull on my way back. I knelt next to it and rested my hand on his head between the shattered antlers. To the best of my ability, I blessed it with a prayer about good intentions and unintended consequences. I prayed Katy would give attention before she decided what work she wanted to do to receive it.

It disturbed me that these peaceful grazers had mutated into eaters of living flesh, but I wasn't ready to talk about it yet. Not with her. She was a young woman, starting out on life in a world gone so cruel that deer grew fangs and tortoises styled spikes. It was her world, our world, a world largely changed by us, and now I couldn't deny my hand in it.

Her tattoos and way of looking past me through the specs still disturbed me quite a bit too. I spent more than a few silent miles trying to figure it. Maybe all this virtual communication was as much a defense mechanism as fangs or spikes. In a world of nine billion people, I could imagine a person might need a social buffer in the absence of having true physical space.

I wasn't sure it made sense, but I determined to spend at least a few years at the outreach center trying to figure it. I'd at least learn something if I tried.

On the hike back out, I noticed Katy looked around sharper than she had before. Once in a while, she'd stop there in front of me. She'd hold up a hand for quiet, push her specs back, and we'd just watch and listen together.

I hoped she noticed the way light and shadow played across the Canyon's walls, highlighting its fractal complexity. I wanted her to read the history written in its rockfall scars and imagine the full-flood glory of its ephemeral waterfalls. To the inattentive eye, the Canyon is just rock walls and river, but to those who watch carefully, it's a temple made of living earth. You can't make a person see it. They have to come to it themselves, each in their own way.

ABOUT THE AUTHOR

SARAH K. CASTLE has published short fiction in *Analog Science Fiction and Fact*, *Nature*, and *Helix*. She received both her BS and MS in Geology from Northern Arizona University. In her career as an environmental scientist, she's worked as a geologist and environmental scientist in national forests, oil fields, and a landfill. She lives with her family in Durango, CO, where she works as an air quality specialist.

HOT RODS

CAT SPARKS

The winds blow pretty regular across the dried-up lake. Traction's good—when luck's on your side, you can reach three hundred KPH or faster. Harper watches the hot rods race on thick white salt so pure and bright, the satellites use it for colour calibration.

Harper doesn't care about souped-up hot rods. Throwdowns, throwbacks, who can go the longest, fastest, hardest. But there's not much else to do in Terina Flat. She used to want to be a journalist, back when such professions still existed. Back when the paper that employed you didn't own you. Back when paper still meant paper. Back before the world clocked up past three degrees and warming. Back when everybody clamoured for Aussie coal and wheat and sheep. The sheep all died when the topsoil blew away in a dust cloud stretching almost five hundred K. Ships still come for the uranium. Other countries bring their own land with them. Embassies, fenced off and private, no one in or out without a pass. Cross the wire and they get to shoot you dead.

Harper thinks about her boyfriend Lachie Groom as the racers pick up speed. The future plans they've made between them. How they're gonna get the hell out of Terina, score work permits for Sydney or Melbourne. They say white maids and pool boys are in high demand in the walled suburban enclaves. Only, Lachie couldn't wait. Said they needed the money now, not later.

The racers purpose-build their dry lake cars from whatever they can scavenge. Racers used to care about the look; these days, it's all about the speed. There's nothing new, no paint to tart things up. No juice to run on except for home-strained bio-D. You need the real stuff for startup and shutdown. The racers pool their meagre cash, score black-market diesel from a guy who hauls it in by camel train.

She can hear them coming before she sees them kicking up thick clouds of salty dust. The pitch drops dramatically as they pass; she takes a good long look as the cars smudge the horizon. Hot rods, classics and jalopies, streamliners and old belly tankers, all the side windows and gaps taped firm against the salt. It gets into everything: your clothes, your hair, your skin. Nothing lives or grows upon it. No plants, no insects, not a single blade of grass.

The short racecourse is five K long, the long one near to twelve. King of the short run is Cracker Jack, Lachie's cousin—plain Cracker to his mates. Obsessed with Dodges. Today's pride and joy is a 1968 Dodge Charger, automatic, gauges still intact. Purpose-built for the super speedway, veteran of Daytona and Darlington.

He loves those cars like nothing else alive. Spends everything he has on keeping them moving. Harper has come to envy the racing regulars: Bing Reh, Lucas Clayton, Scarlett Ottico. Others. There's enough on the salt flats to keep them focused. Enough to get them out of bed in the morning.

Cracker nods at Harper; she throws him half a smile. Checks out his sweat-slicked, salt-encrusted arms. "I'll take you out there," he says, wiping his forehead. No need to specify *where* out there. She knows he's talking about the American Base—and Lachie.

She doesn't say no but he gauges her expression. "After sundown. The others don't have to know."

Unfortunately, in towns like Terina Flat, everyone knows everybody else's business.

"Was a stupid plan," she tells him. "We never should have . . ."

Cracker dusts salt flecks off his arms. "It was a fucken' *awesome* plan. 'Bout time we got a look behind that wire. Found out what all the bullshit is about."

She shrugs. Her and Lachie's "plan" had sounded simple. Just two people trying to keep in touch. Inching around a Base commandment that seems much harsher than it ought to be.

Cracker tried to talk Lachie out of taking the job at all. Too late. By then, Base medics had tested his blood, piss, and spit. He'd signed away his rights on the dotted line.

Lachie's been gone almost a week—the full week if you're counting Sunday, which Harper is because she's counting days, hours, minutes, seconds. Segregating Sundays is for the churchy folks. Whole town's riddled with true believers since the heavens clammed and the good soil blew away.

"'S'no trouble," says Cracker.

Harper shakes her head. Her eyes are focused on the middle distance. On Janny Christofides and that beat up 1968 Ford Mk 2 Cortina she loves more than most girls love their boyfriends. Janny's boyfriend's been on Base six months. She never wins a race but she keeps on trying.

Lachie's not so far away, just over the wire on newly foreign soil— American, although it could just as easily have been China or India or Russia.

Once past that wire, you don't come back until your contract's through. Money comes out, sometimes with a message. Stuff like *I miss you honey* and *I love you* and *tell grandma not to worry* and *its OK in here, the food is pretty good.*

The whole town knows about that food. They watch it trucking in by convoy, trucks long enough to fit houses in them. Refrigerated, loaded up with ice cream. Bananas from the Philippines, prime beef barely off the hoof. They stand there salivating in the hot red dust. Whole town's been on starvation rations since before the last town council meeting proper, the one where Mr Bryce got shot in the leg.

Crude jokes about Lachie circulate, not quite out of earshot. Somehow everyone found out about their ribbon secret. Voices carping on about how he's probably too distracted. Too busy shagging those hot chick Growler pilots. Boeing EA-18Gs—sleek and fast—have been burning across the blanched blue sky all week.

She ignores them, watches as a flecked and rusted 1936 Plymouth sedan tailgates a '58 Chevrolet Apache that once used to be red, apple rosy.

Cracker tries to shift the subject. Says those 18Gs were manufactured in Missouri—what's left of it. Mumbles something about future threats across the electromagnetic spectrum.

Harper recalls peculiar ads on free-to-air: The smiling lady saying shit like *Stealth is perishable; only a Growler provides full-spectrum protection.* Making *stealth* sound like a brand of sunscreen. What use could there be for *stealth* in Terina Flat? Nothing but more sky than anyone can handle laced with impotent wisps of cloud.

The racers pass, wave, whoop, and holler, some of the vehicles dis-integrating in motion, belching smoke and farting acrid fumes. People used to think that only topless roadsters could hit top speeds. Back when Lake Gairdner was the only lake to race on. Back before the Bases and the droughts. Back before a lot of things that changed this country into someplace you'd barely recognise.

Harper turns her back on them all and starts walking toward home.

Cracker runs to catch up with her. "Those guys don't mean nothing by it. Half of 'em's gonna be taking Base contracts themselves."

She keeps walking.

"Wanna ride?"

"Nope."

"You really gonna hoof it all the way?"

She nods. Walking gives her time to think. Time to run through all the reasons she's not going back to the Base. Not tonight—or any other night. Not even with Cracker, who she trusts more than she's ever trusted anyone aside from Lachie.

Eventually, the salty crunch gives way to russet dirt. Her boots disturb the road's powdery dust. No salt here, just brown on brown. Crooked fence posts, barbed wire curling in the sun.

Not everything is dead or dying. She admires the millet, still holding its own, but the sorghum fields have seen far better days. There used to be rice, but rice needs irrigation, and for irrigation, you need rain. No decent rainfall three years running, which is how come council got desperate enough to call in a priest-of-the-air. Prayer vigils week in, week out have altered nothing.

Apparently, a flying priest worked miracles in Trundle, scoring them forty millimeters three days in a row. Not just hearsay; plenty of Terina locals were present when the heavens opened. Plastic buckets clutched against their chests, praising Jesus and the man in the yellow Cessna.

When the downpour ceased, a flock of black-and-white banded birds descended. Whole sky was thick with them. Stilts, reportedly confused, as if they had been expecting something other than Trundle mud at the end of their epic journey.

A year on now and prayer vigils have all dried up. Terina passed the hat around, everybody kicking in what they can scrounge.

Harper's toes are blistered and her shirt is soaked with sweat. Things come in threes—or so folks say. Three days of rain for Trundle in a row. Three nights was how long Lachie managed to tie a bit of ribbon to the fence. Low so the Hellfighter spotlights wouldn't catch it. Nothing fancy. No messages attached. But from the fourth night onwards, there was no ribbon. Nothing.

Lachie is as close to family as she has. Dad's long gone; there's only her and Mum. Mum was all for him taking that contract job.

Dusk is falling by time she makes it back. Still hot but tempered by gentle breaths of wind. A warm glow pulsing from the big revival tent. She knows her mother will be in there alongside all the other mothers. She knows she ought to go inside and grab a bite to eat if nothing else.

Beyond the fraying canvas flap lies a warm enveloping glow; a mix of lantern light and tallow candle. Town still has plenty of functioning generators but they made a lot of smoke and noise.

The overpowering tang of sweat mixed in with cloying, cheap perfume. Still hot long after the sun's gone down, women fanning their necks with outdated mail order catalogues. Out of their farming duds and all frocked up, like Sunday church, not plain old Thursday evening. Scones and sticky Anzac biscuits piled high on trestle tables. Offerings. Harper's stomach grumbles at the sight.

Reg Clayton has the microphone. He's telling some story she's sure she's heard before about nitrogen and ploughing rotted legumes.

Her mother claps and cheers from second row. Dry dirt has got inside her head. Made her barking mad as all the others. Farmers with their fallow stony fields, rusted-up tractors, and heat-split butyl tires. All for praying for the rains to come. They really believe that praying makes a difference.

The big tent puts some hope back in the air—Harper gives it that much credit even if she doesn't buy their Jesus bullshit. Jesus isn't coming and he isn't bringing rain. Jesus and his pantheon of angels have snubbed their town before moving on to bigger, better things.

She lets the tent flap fall again before anyone catches sight of her. Not everyone in the tent is old, but most of them are. Old enough to believe in miracles. To believe that flying in some Jesus freak from Parkes might make it rain.

When the singing starts, it's sudden as a thunderclap.

> When peace like a river,
> attendeth my way,
> When sorrows like sea billows roll . . .

Three years have passed since any of them clapped eyes on the dirty trickle that was once the proud Killara river. Sea billows—whatever the hell they are, seem more than a million miles from Terina Flat.

Harper jumps when a firm hand presses upon her shoulder. It's only Cracker and he jumps back in response.

"Didn't mean to startle ya. Coming out to Base with me or what?"

She shies away from the tent flap, away from the candied light. He lopes after her like a giant puppy.

"Not going back out there again," she stops and says at last. "What would be the point of it? There's nothing to see but wire and towers—and what if we get caught? You know what they say happens to trespassers. Those two guys from Griffith that—"

"Those two bastards buggered off to Sydney."

"Cracker, nobody knows what happened to those guys."

The swell of hymns gets louder, the voices enunciating clearly.

He sends the snow in winter,
The warmth to swell the grain,
The breezes and the sunshine,
And soft, refreshing rain.

Cracker grunts at the mention of snow. "Not bloody lately, he doesn't."

Harper almost smiles.

The two of them bolt when the tent flap flies open, taking cover behind the shadowy row of trucks and cars that reek of sour corn pulp and rancid vegetable oil. Cracker barely spares the cars a glance. He has no interest in vehicles whose sole purpose is to ferry occupants from A to B.

"Yer mum in with that lot?" he asks.

"Yup."

"Mine too."

She nods. All the mums and dads are in the tent, banging tambourines and clapping hands. All the folks who yell at the younger ones for frittering their time and cash on hot rods.

They wait until the coast is clear, then climb the tufty knob of ground that offers a clear view across the dried-up river. All the way to the American Base. Harper can't see that riverbed without picturing Lachie, boasting about the time he and his brother dug a rust-red 1936 Ford Model 48 up out of the silt. How they had to scrape out twenty-six inches of dirt from firewall to tailpan.

The Base has a glow to it, a greeny-ochre luminescence. The kind of colour mostly seen in long-exposure borealis photos.

Behind that wire and the machine gun–guarded towers lies a big rectangular grid: A forty-eight-element high-frequency antenna array. Beyond it stands a power generation building, imaging riometer, and a flat-roofed operations centre built of cinder blocks. They all know this; it's no kind of secret. Base PR admits to investigating the potential for developing ionospheric enhancement technology for radio communications and surveillance. It supports a cluster of ELF wave transmitters slamming 3.6 million watts up at the ionosphere. There have been whispers of other things such as successful moon-bounce experiments—whatever that means. New kinds of weapons for new kinds of war, still in experimental phases. What weapons and what war are never specified.

The tent hymns fade, absorbed by other forms of background noise. Cracker stuffs his hands into his pockets, closes his eyes, feels the warm breeze on his face. When he opens them, Harper's staring at the Base and pointing.

Above it, the sky has shifted burgundy, like dried blood. Lightning bolts, ramrod straight—not jagged, strike the ground, then thicken, changing colour, and slowly fade.

"What the . . ."

"Did you just see that?"

She's fidgeting, running her thumb along the friendship bracelet knotted on her right wrist. Three blue ribbons tightly braided. Three wishes for bringing her Lachie safe back home.

The plane appears like a lonesome dove, winging its way to Terina Flat bringing with it salvation in the form of a priest decked out like Elvis Presley. Elvises aren't unusual in these parts, what with Terina being so close to Parkes and its famous Elvis festival. Back in January, fifty thousand tourists flooded in to celebrate the King's hundredth birthday.

Harper has never seen one of them up close. The Elvis who lands on the blistered tarmac is dusty and kind of faded. Paunchy, but not in the proper Elvis way. A golden cross hangs around his neck. A knife tucked into his boot if he's smart. A pistol hooked through his belt if he's even smarter.

Town folks skip right past the rhinestones and move straight to calling him Father. Press around him like bleating sheep. Harper doesn't plan on making contact. She cringes as the shrivelled biddies primp and fuss and preen. Flirting with the sly old dog, promising him pumpkin scones and carrot cake—all chokos with artificial flavour added, if truth be known, although you won't catch any of them admitting such a thing. Lamingtons run soft and gooey from the broiling sun. Local piss-weak beer to wash it down with.

The Elvis plane, though, that's something else. An ancient Beech A60 Duke, knocked up and turbocharged—Cracker was mouthing off about that plane before the sunlight hit its yellow sides, planes being the one thing capable of distracting him from Dodges.

Harper waits until the fuss dies down. Elvis shoos his flock away from the landing strip towards the revival tent. Promises to be joining them just as soon as he's checked his luggage. Once the parents and grandparents have moved off, small children run to place their grubby palms on the fuselage.

"Piss off, you little buggers," spits Darryl Quiggen, charged with checking the battered old bird over, hand-rolled cigarette dangling from his pinched white lips. Used to be some kind of expert once. The tang of avgas hangs in the air—the good stuff, not the crap distilled from corn.

Quiggen pays Harper no attention. He's never had much luck with women, finds it preferable to pretend they don't exist. She makes sure she's out of his line of sight, inching as close as she can get away with to examine the peculiar assortment of religious symbols painted across the plane's canary yellow casing.

Jesus—rendered clear as day, hands pressed together in prayer. Surrounding his head, a thick halo of icons: an egg with a cross, a flaming heart with barbed wire wrapped across its middle. A snake and an anchor. Some poorly rendered birds. A hand with an eye set into its palm. A star made of two triangles. A crescent moon and a tiny little star. Some writing that looks like it might be Hindu—not that she'd know a Hindu from a Sikh.

There's something strange underneath the wings. Bulging clusters of attachments reminiscent of wasp nests. She steps up closer but she isn't game to touch. Up closer still, she can see the welds and other bodged repairs beneath paint blisters. Paint costs a fortune. There must be something well worth hiding under there.

She peers in through the grimy windows until Quiggen shoos her off. The rear cabin's stuffed with all kinds of junk. Looks like maybe Elvis sleeps in it.

The plane serves well as a distraction. She's trying not to think about the Base's empty wire, the thick red lightning, and the sickly green light rippling over everything the night before. The Base is locked down, nothing unauthorised in or out—not even bits of ribbon tied to wire. "Earn good money" was what they said, money they were all in need of. They were desperate or curious, all the ones that took up contract offers. Three months on. No worries. She'll be right. But how often three months extended to six or twelve. How often at the end of it, they climbed into one of those Blackhawks and disappeared.

She's sheltering beneath the concrete shade of what remains of a Shell service station. Hard to believe people used to drive right up and pump petrol into their tanks.

Dusty Elvis saunters over, his jaw working over a wad of gum. "Like the look of my equipment, now, do ya? Give you a private tour if you come back later." He winks.

Harper straightens up and inches back. "You oughta be ashamed of yourself," she says. "These people don't have much to spare. Drought's taken everything the wheat rust missed the first time through."

"Mind your own goddamned business," he spits, forcing her back with the bulk of his rhinestoned, jumpsuited bulk, fiddling with a bunch of keys attached to his belt. Reaches into his pocket for mirror shades, the kind with wire frames. He somehow looks bigger—meaner—with them on. He leans his shoulder against the crumbling concrete wall, looks her up and down until she itches. Tugs a packet of cigarettes from another pocket. Tailor-mades—they cost a bloody fortune. Sticks one on his lower lip, lights it with a scratched and battered Zippo.

"Girl like you oughta be thinking of her future," he says. Rhinestones sparkle in the stark midmorning light. The scent of tobacco curls inside her nose. "I was you, I'd be fucking my way up and out of this dustbowl shithouse." He jams the cigarette between fat lips and smiles.

"Lucky you're not me, then," she says drily. Waiting. Not wanting to give him the satisfaction. He keeps on smoking, smiling, leering, his BO permeating the plumes of tobacco smoke. She turns on her heel and walks away, angry but keeping it bottled up like she's learned to do with guys who stare at her like hungry dogs.

"Don't wait too long," he calls after her. "Yer not that far off yer use-by date, you know."

Harper avoids the revival tent and its excited, anticipatory believers. She heads for the crowd amassing in Whitlam Park, which still boasts two functioning wooden picnic tables not too warped and cracked from years of exposure. Young people cluster around a battered laptop, taking turns to log on through the Base's web page portal.

Janny looks up when she sees Harper coming. "There's one for you," she calls across their heads.

Harper almost doesn't want to read it. She already fears what it isn't going to say. Four simple words: *pet Cooper for me*. There isn't any dog called Cooper. Lachie created the imaginary pooch when he filled in his application form. Cooper is their private code meaning everything's okay. No mention of Cooper means everything isn't.

The message on screen supposedly from Lachie is bland and cold. Words that could have been written from anybody to anybody.

"They still eating like kings in there?" calls someone from behind.

She nods in silence and hits the delete key.

By sundown, everyone is drunk. Rain is the only topic of conversation. Anecdotes stretching from Lightning Ridge all the way down to the Eden coast.

Outside the tent, it's hard to tell at what point prayer vigil descends into full-bore hootenanny. Night wears on and the music gets louder. Clapping and shouting and stomping for rain, fuelled by Ray Clayton's palm-heart toddy, what they drink when they're out of everything else. Songs for Jesus, dancing for him too, work boots and sun-cracked plastic sandals thumping hard on the warped and weathered dance boards.

With a blast of laughter, a couple of Country Women's Association stalwarts burst their way out through the tent flaps. "Just as hot out here as 'tis inside," says one, fanning her bright pink face—frowning when she notices Harper, a look that screams, *Girl, you oughta be throwing your lot in with the righteous.*

Because everyone who's anyone in Terina Flat is stomping and shrieking and hollering, both inside and outside the revival tent—social niceties be damned. Priest-Elvis has prepared his song list well: "Kentucky Rain" for openers, following on with "How Great Thou Art." Short-verse speeches in between, paving the way to "I Shall Not Be Moved."

In the pauses between numbers, conversational buzz drones like the chittering of cicadas. A few stray blasts of it swim towards Harper through the heat. Nothing she doesn't already know: that entrance to the revival tent is by gold-coin donation; that the way-past-their-bedtimes children scampering underfoot have been encouraged to write to God on precious scraps of multicoloured paper (the remaining dregs of the school's once-vibrant art department). At the crack of dawn tomorrow, smoke-lipped Elvis is going to hit the skies. Fly up high as close as he dares to deliver God their messages, extra personal.

Yeah, right.

As "It's Now or Never" starts up, Harper's surprised to catch old Doc Chilby slipping out through the tent flap. The women exchange suspicious glances. Doc Chilby nods, so Harper returns the favour. Doc Chilby delivered her into this world. She deserves respect even if she's thrown her lot in with the Bible-thumpers.

Up on the knoll, the racers admire the Base lit up like Christmas squared, same as every other night, but this night, there's something extra in the air. The town itself emits barely a glow. Night skies dark enough to drown the Milky Way in all its glory.

There's talk of cars and trade in missing parts. Who needs what and what they're going to barter for it. How the camel guy is late again. How someone's cousin's investigating other sources.

Janny Christofides saunters over, sipping on a can of something warm and flat. "Saw you checking out that Jesus plane. A cloud-seeder for sure."

"Didya get a look at it up close?" says Harper.

Janny shakes her head. "Didn't have to."

Harper continues. "It's got these bulges under the wings like wasp nests."

Janny nods, enthusiasm causing her to spill a couple of splashes from her can. "Dispensers holding fifty-two units apiece. Flares built into the wings themselves. Avoids resistance. As little drag as possible." Her eyes are shining.

"How'd ya know all this?"

"Old man used to do crop-dusting, don't forget."

"But dusting's different. Seeding's illegal—"

"*Dusting's* illegal—there's nothing left to dust. Everything's illegal, unless you're frackers or big foreign money or those massive fuckoff land barges dumping toxic shit deep into cracks."

"We oughta report him," Harper says bitterly, remembering Elvis grinding his cigarette butt into Terina dirt.

"Like anybody's gonna give two shits." Janny cocks her head back in the direction of the revival tent. The singing has long since become incoherent. Songs mashing into one another, Presley numbers indistinguishable from hymns. "How much you reckon we're paying that—"

She doesn't get to finish her sentence. Somebody calls out, "Lightning!"

Janny looks up, startled, points to the empty airspace above the Base. Racers stand there frozen, jam jars of fermented melon hooch clutched in their hands.

"I don't see any—"

"Wait—there it is again!"

This time, they see and hear it too, a cracking split. Like thunder but not. Thick spikes stabbing at the fallow dirt. Aftershocks of colour, green and red.

There's a scrabble for phones as a volley of sharp, thick beams shoot upwards from the Base. High-pitched whining that fades, then swells, then fades. A sonic boom followed by overbearing silence. The town dogs start barking and howling all at once. Nothing to see now. No more laser lights. The racers stuff their phones into pockets and head for their cars.

Cracker's already seated behind the wheel of his precious Dodge Charger. Harper runs up to cadge a lift.

"Stay here," he warns as he's revving up his engine.

"Are you shitting me?"

But he's got this serious look on his face and he's not going to give her a ride. No matter. She waits till he takes off, then climbs in beside Bing Reh in his 1951 Ford Five-Star pickup. The racers are heading to the salt, their vehicles overloaded. Everyone's in a hurry to get out there.

The Base has fallen still and silent. No more lasers. No more lightshow. No Blackhawks either, which seems odd, considering.

There's more light than there ought to be, all coming from a suspicious patch of sky above the salt.

More lightning strikes drown out the growl of engines.

"Looks dangerous!" says Harper. Bing nods, eyes on the road. Half drunk or not, they have to go check it out.

Her heart pounds, thinking, *Lachie, please stay under cover; whatever you do, stay away from that chain link fence.*

Things are not as they had seemed when viewed from the edge of town. The lightning's localised, not spread across the sky—they got that right, but it isn't striking anywhere close to Base. The salt flats are soaking up the brunt of it. Singed salt particles fling themselves at Harper's nose. She sneezes, half expecting blood. Too dark to tell what she wipes across her jeans.

There's no stopping Cracker. He aims his Dodge straight out into the thick of it. Looks like he's deciding to play chicken with the lightning. Bing slows down. Harper knows what that means; he's giving her the opportunity to get out. And she *should* get out, because not doing so is crazy, but instead, she nods and the pickup's engine roars and surges.

She can smell that smell no one ever smells anymore, that heady, moody tang just before a thunderhead lets rip. Plant oil sucked from dry rocks and soil mixed up with ozone and spores. Chemical explanations half remembered from biology class, never dreaming back then how rare the experience of rain would become in future times.

They gather, staring at the crazy lights.

"Red sprite lightning," says Bing, "Or something like it."

Nobody argues. They've all seen strange stuff above and around the Base. Clouds that didn't look like clouds when no clouds hung in any other patch of sky. Lenticular shapes like UFOs, only insubstantial. Ephemeral, like ghost residue of clouds. Not made of metal like anything you'd expect.

"Check it out!"

Sharp intakes of breath all round as a thick red lightning bolt travels horizontally from one cloud to another. Hits the second hard like there's something solid at its core, shatters into separate fragments, which coagulate into orbs.

Balls of crackling light drift down, hover, pause, pink neon glow emanating from their centre mass. Pulsing. Like the crackling orbs are breathing.

"Man, I don't like the—"

"Shhh."

More crackling, louder, like automatic weapons fire. They cover their ears and duck, only it's not ammo. It's coming from the glowing orbs, close to the ground now, pulsing with red and light. A high-to-low-pitched whistle, almost musical.

A blood-red cloudshape jellyfish emerges, dangles tentacles of pure blue light. Drags across the surface of the salt. Almost moves like a living, breathing creature.

The air hangs thick with acrid ozone stench. Some of those lightning stabs are getting close.

Beneath the cloudshape, thick swirling coils writhe like a nest of snakes. Pale clouds forming angry faces, elongated skulls, animals with jagged teeth.

Somehow, some way, they lose track of time. Dawn is so insipid by comparison, they almost miss it when it finally arrives. Their eyes are dazed from the flash and flare. Colours dancing across their inner vision.

Harper isn't the one who first spots Lachie. She's staring in the opposite direction. Up into a pink-and-orange sky at the dark gnat wobbling across its luminescent swathe. Elvis in his patched-up plane, heaven-bound with a hangover, she hopes, of Biblical proportions. A plane packed tight with cigarette-size sticks of silver iodide if Janny's right. Cold rain. Pyrotechnic flares. At best it's alchemy; at worst, yet another hick-town scam. Perhaps he will coax moisture from the wispy cirrus. Not enough to make a difference. Just enough to make sure he gets paid.

"Harper!"

Cracker's voice. She turns around as, dazed and moaning, three figures stagger across the salt. Somebody's got binoculars. They shout the names out: Lachie, Danno, Jason. Staggering like zombies, only this isn't some kind of joke. They get back in their vehicles and race out to intercept the scarecrow men. Clothing torn up, singed, and smoking. Eyes wide and shit-scared sightless.

Harper's screaming, *Lachie Lachie Lachie,* when she comprehends the state he's in. He doesn't react. Doesn't even look at her. Doesn't stare at anything. Just ahead.

All three are hurt bad. Jason is the worst.

Everybody's shouting at everybody else. Eventually, Lachie cocks his head at the sound of Harper's voice. She goes to fling her arms around his neck but Janny grabs her wrist and holds on tight. "Needs Doc Chilby," she says grimly. Harper slaps her hand away but she doesn't dare touch Lachie, because Janny's right.

"Base's got a hospital," says Lucas Clayton, son of Reg. "State of the art."

Nobody else says anything, but everybody's thinking it. If they take the injured boys back to the Base, they'll never be seen again. That lightning was not the natural kind. Whatever just happened here is Base-related.

A siren wails in the far off distance. The sound makes everybody jump.

"Doc Chilby will know what to do," says Bing.

Lachie and Danno get loaded into the back of Bing's pickup. Harper spreads down a blanket first, a ratty old thing balled up and wedged beside the tool kit. She tries not to wince at the sight of those burns. Keeps saying, "Everything's gonna be okay," although it isn't.

The third guy, Jason, is laid gently across the back seats of a Holden Torana. Softly moaning like an animal, he seems the most out of it of the three.

They don't notice the Blackhawks until too late. The cars split up—a reflex action—fanning in all directions, two vehicles heading for Doc Chilby's by different routes, the others planning to drive decoy all over until they're apprehended or run out of juice.

Harper presses her back against the cabin, crouches, hanging on with one hand to the pickup's battered side. The ride is reasonably smooth until they reach the limits of the salt. Each bump and pothole sets the injured men off moaning.

By time they reach the town's outskirts, Lachie is delirious and screaming. Impossible to keep the salt out of their wounds. He tries to sit up but the passage is too ragged. Harper holds her breath, heart thumping painfully against her ribs. *Hang on, Lachie. Hang on till we get there.*

The sky is streaked with morning glow, the Jesus plane now the size of a lonely bird. A few clouds scudding, clumping stickily together. More than usual.

Any minute now the pickup will get intercepted by soldiers in full combat gear. Or a hazmat team in an unmarked van—they've all seen that in movies on TV.

But the streets are empty. Everyone's still clustered around the revival tent or passed out on the ground. All necks are craned, all eyes on the Jesus plane looping and threading its way through a puff of clouds like a drunken gnat. Rosaries muttered, beads looped tightly around arms and wrists. Clutched in hands, pressed against hearts and lips. Holy Mary, Mother of—Jesus, is that rain?

Thick, fat drops smack the dusty ground.

Proper rain for the first time in three long years. Rain coaxed from clouds not even in sight when the plane began its journey.

Looks like Elvis is no charlatan after all. Elvis is the real deal. Elvis can talk to Jesus and make it pour.

And then they're dancing, arms flung into the air. Laughing and shrieking and praising the heavenly host. "Ave Maria" as bloated splats drill down upon their heads, soaking their shirts and floral print dresses, muddying up the packed-dirt hospital car park. Mud-splattered boots and trouser legs.

There'll be time for Jesus later. Harper stays by Lachie's side as the injured men are unloaded off the pickup. Straight through to Emergency; lucky such an option still exists. Terina Community Hospital once boasted fifty beds; now only ten of them are still in operation. The place was supposed to have closed a year ago. They're all supposed to drive to Parkes if an accident takes place. Supposed to use the Base if it's life or death.

One of the racers must have thought to phone ahead. Two nurses stand tentatively inside the sterile operating theatre. Waiting for Doc Chilby to scrub up. Waiting for something. Harper doesn't find out what—she's hustled into another room and made to fill out forms. Their Medicare numbers—how the fuck is she supposed to know? Didn't they have their wallets in their pants?

"Don't call the Base," she says, but it's too late. That helicopter stopped chasing them for a reason—there's only one place in town they can go for help.

An hour of waiting before a nurse brings her a cup of tea. Two biscuits wrapped in cellophane and a magazine with blonde models on the cover. The magazine's two years old, its recipes ripped roughly out of the back.

"Is Lachie gonna be okay?" she asks.

The nurse is about her age or maybe a few years older. Nobody Harper knows or went to school with. The hospital has trouble keeping staff. They rotate young ones from the bigger towns, but they never stay for more than a couple of months.

"That other boy died," the nurse says eventually. "I'm not supposed to tell you."

Harper knows the nurse means Jason even though she didn't say his name. He'd been in the worst shape of all three.

"Were they all from the Base?"

"Yeah, reckon." The nurse doesn't seem to think anything of the fact. Definitely not a local, then. To her, the Base is nothing more than it seems.

The nurse chews on her bottom lip. "Never seen anything like it. Multiple lightning strikes each one, poor things. Left its mark on them, it did. Tattoos like blood-red trees." She points to the base of her own neck by way of demonstration. "What were they doing out there on the salt in the middle of the night?"

Harper doesn't have an answer. The nurse is not expecting one, not even wild speculation. She wanders over to the window and lifts the faded blue and purple blind. "Still raining, I see. "Least that's something."

Still raining. Words that take awhile to sink in. Harper unfolds her legs from underneath her, heaves up out of the sagging beige settee.

The nurse's heels *clip-clop* against linoleum as she leaves.

The opened blind reveals a world awash with mud and gloom. Water surges along the gutters like a river. Slow-moving cars plough through, their wheels three-quarters covered. More water than Harper has seen in a long, long time.

"When can I see Lachie?" she calls after the nurse. Too late. The corridor is empty.

Harper slips the crinkly biscuit packet into her pocket, hops down the fire escape two steps at a time.

The water in the car park is brown and up to her knees already. A couple of men in anoraks wade out in an attempt to rescue their cars.

The rain keeps falling, too hard, too fast. Main Street is barely recognisable. Whole families clamber up onto roofs, clinging to spindly umbrella stems—and each other. Half drenched dogs bark up a storm. Nobody's singing songs of praise to Jesus.

She pictures the revival tent swept away in a tsunami of soggy scones and lamingtons, trampled as panic sets in, random and furious as the rain itself.

The deluge is too much, too quick for the ground to cope with. Hard-baked far too many months to soak it up. There's nowhere for the surge to slosh but up and down the streets. Vehicles bob along like corks and bottles.

She doesn't want to think about the cattle in the fields. Dogs chained up in unattended backyards. Children caught in playgrounds.

She's wading waist-deep in filthy swell when a wave breaks over her head. A wave on Main Street, of all unlikely things. Next thing she knows, she's going under, mouth full of mud and silt. Scrabbling for a slippery purchase, bangs her shins on something hard, unseen. This can't be happening. The rain keeps falling, mushing everything to brown and grey.

Her leg hurts but she keeps on moving, half swimming, half wading, crawling her way to higher ground. To the knoll. She doesn't recognise it at first. Not until she stands and checks the view. A line of lights snaking out from the Base and heading in her direction.

She's shaking, either from the cold or shock. Bit by bit, the sky is clearing, bright blue peering through grey rents and tears. Clouds the colour of dirty cotton wool break up. Voices shout from rooftop to rooftop. A sound that might be a car backfiring—or a gunshot.

She wipes grit from her eyes with the heel of her palm. Hugs her shoulders, slick hair plastered against her face.

"Leg's bleeding."

It's Janny. She glances down at red rivulets streaking her muddy calf.

"It's nothing."

"Can you walk?"

She nods.

"Better get you up to the hospital, then."

Steam rises from the rapidly warming sludge. A cloying smell like rotting leaves and sewage. Damp human shapes mill about, disorganised. Unanchored.

She watches three men in anoraks attempt to right a car. Others stand staring stupidly at the mess. Like they don't know where to start or what to do.

She limps back up to the hospital with Janny by her side. Only two army trucks are parked out the front of it. Doc Chilby stands her ground in a sodden coat, arms folded across her chest. Four soldiers briskly unload boxes, stacking them up on the verandah out of the mud.

Doc Chilby argues with another soldier. "We didn't ask for anything. You're not taking anyone out of here—that's final."

The soldier has his back to Harper; she can't hear what he's saying. Only that the doc is getting flustered, flinching every time a Blackhawk thunders close. She repeats herself but the soldier isn't listening.

The nurse who told Harper that Jason had died stands smoking on the verandah.

Loud voices emanate from inside the building, then a sudden surge of soldiers swarm. That nurse starts shouting, Doc Chilby too. Three stretchers are borne swiftly down wooden stairs. Weapons raised. Threats issued. The steady thrum of Blackhawk blades drowning out all attempts at negotiation.

The Base has come for its wounded contract workers. Wounded doing what, exactly? Harper has been watching without comprehending. Now wide awake, she adds her own voice to the shouting. Ignores the nurse signalling frantically from the verandah, the ache in her leg and the Blackhawk's thudding blades. She runs after one of the trucks—too late, it's out of reach. Picks up a rock and throws it. The rock bounces harmlessly off the taut khaki canvas. She almost trips as she reaches for something else to throw. The road's sticky and slippery from rain.

The convoy lumbers like a herd of beasts. A minute later and she's standing helpless in the middle of the road, a chunk of rock gripped tightly in her hand.

Her bleeding leg gets sprayed with mud as a car pulls up beside her. Cracker in a rattling old army Dodge from his collection. The M37 convertible minted 1953. Same colour as the green-grey mud. Dented. Spotted with rust and a couple of bullet holes. Thick treads built to handle difficult terrain.

Neither of them says anything. The crazed glint in his eyes fills her with hope. She climbs into the passenger seat. He floors it, following close behind the trucks at first, then lagging. The old Dodge putters and chokes, but it holds its own.

A bright new day. Sun and daylight are banishing the nighttime landscape's sinister cast. Red-and-blue jellyfish lightning seems like another world ago.

Cracker races, slams his palm down on the horn. The convoy of army trucks ignores him. He keeps his foot pressed to the accelerator. Harper keeps her gaze fixed on the Base.

They can't get in. They'll be turned back at the front gate. Threatened with whatever trespassers get threatened with. Whatever happens, she's ready for it. So is Cracker.

The Base's electronic gates do not slide open. The truck convoy halts. Cracker stops too but keeps the engine purring. Just in case.

A soldier gets out of the truck ahead and slams the cabin door. He's armed but he hasn't drawn his weapon. She's still gripping that rock chunk in her hand.

"Get out of the vehicle," booms a megaphone voice.

"Not fucken' likely," says Cracker.

"I repeat: Get out of the vehicle."

Nothing happens. Nobody moves. The Dodge keeps grunting and grumbling like a big old dog.

Harper turns the door handle, slides out of the passenger seat. "You can't just do whatever you like," she shouts. She's shaking hard and she knows she'd better drop the rock, not give them any reason. She's waiting for that soldier to draw his gun. "You've got no right," she repeats, softer this time.

He approaches, one arm raised. "Ma'am, this country is at war." The walkie-talkie on his shoulder crackles but he doesn't touch it.

"Which country?" she says, squinting through harsh sunlight. "Which war?"

He gives her a half-arsed smirk but doesn't answer. Mumbles into the electronic device. Turns his back, gets back in the truck.

She lets the rock fall to the dusty road. *Dusty.* It appears the rain didn't reach this far. Not the strangest thing she's seen in recent times. "Lachie," she says, but it's too late. Too late for Lachie, too late for her and Cracker. The gates slide open with electronic precision. Trucks pass through, one by one, Cracker's Dodge amongst them—too late for turning back. A voice behind commands her to keep moving. Not to turn. Not to pick up any rocks. Not to make any sudden movements.

She looks up just in time to catch a speck in the wide blue sky. A wedge-tailed eagle, coasting on the updraft, its diamond-shaped tail unmistakable. Those birds partner up for life—something else she learned in school. They fly together, perform acrobatics, but she cannot spot the other one, its mate. When she cranes her neck and shades her eyes, a soldier twists her arm behind her back. Pushes her forwards through the steel Base gates. Metal grates as they snap and lock behind her.

ABOUT THE AUTHOR

CAT SPARKS (catsparks.net) is a multi-award-winning author, editor, and artist whose former employment has included: political and archaeological photographer, graphic designer, and manager of Agog! Press among other (much less interesting) things. She's currently fiction editor of Australia's *Cosmos Magazine* while simultaneously grappling with a PhD on YA climate change fiction.

THE TAMARISK HUNTER

PAOLO BACIGALUPI

A big tamarisk can suck 73,000 gallons of river water a year. For $2.88 a day, plus water bounty, Lolo rips tamarisk all winter long.

Ten years ago, it was a good living. Back then, tamarisk shouldered up against every riverbank in the Colorado River Basin, along with cotton-woods, Russian olives, and elms. Ten years ago, towns like Grand Junction and Moab thought they could still squeeze life from a river.

Lolo stands on the edge of a canyon, Maggie the camel his only companion. He stares down into the deeps. It's an hour's scramble to the bottom. He ties Maggie to a juniper and starts down, boot-skiing a gully. A few blades of green grass sprout neon around him, piercing juniper-tagged snow clods. In the late winter, there is just a beginning surge of water down in the deeps; the ice is off the river edges. Up high, the mountains still wear their ragged snow mantles. Lolo smears through mud and hits a channel of scree, sliding and scattering rocks. His jugs of tamarisk poison gurgle and slosh on his back. His shovel and rockbar snag on occasional junipers as he skids by. It will be a long hike out. But then, that's what makes this patch so perfect. It's a long way down, and the riverbanks are largely hidden.

It's a living; where other people have dried out and blown away, he has remained: a tamarisk hunter, a water tick, a stubborn bit of weed.

Everyone else has been blown off the land as surely as dandelion seeds, set free to fly south or east or, most of all, north where watersheds sometimes still run deep and where even if there are no more lush ferns or deep cold fish runs, at least there is still water for people.

Eventually, Lolo reaches the canyon bottom. Down in the cold shadows, his breath steams.

He pulls out a digital camera and starts shooting his proof. The Bureau of Reclamation has gotten uptight about proof. They want different angles on the offending tamarisk, they want each one photographed before and after, the whole process documented, GPS'd, and uploaded directly by the camera. They want it done on site. And then they still sometimes come out to spot-check before they calibrate his headgate for water bounty.

But all their due diligence can't protect them from the likes of Lolo. Lolo has found the secret to eternal life as a tamarisk hunter. Unknown to the Interior Department and its BuRec subsidiary, he has been seeding new patches of tamarisk, encouraging vigorous brushy groves in previously cleared areas. He has hauled and planted healthy root balls up and down the river system in strategically hidden and inaccessible corridors, all in a bid for security against the swarms of other tamarisk hunters that scour these same tributaries. Lolo is crafty. Stands like this one, a quarter mile long and thick with salt-laden tamarisk, are his insurance policy.

Documentation finished, he unstraps a folding saw along with his rockbar and shovel, and sets his poison jugs on the dead salt bank. He starts cutting, slicing into the roots of the tamarisk, pausing every thirty seconds to spread Garlon 4 on the cuts, poisoning the tamarisk wounds faster than they can heal. But some of the best tamarisk, the most vigorous, he uproots and sets aside for later use.

$2.88 a day, plus water bounty.

It takes Maggie's rolling, bleating camel stride a week to make it back to Lolo's homestead. They follow the river, occasionally climbing above it onto cold mesas or wandering off into the open desert in a bid to avoid the skeleton sprawl of emptied towns. Guardie choppers buzz up and down the river like swarms of angry yellow jackets, hunting for porto-pumpers and wildcat diversions. They rush overhead in a wash of beaten air and gleaming National Guard logos. Lolo remembers a time when the guardies traded potshots with people down on the riverbanks, tracer-fire and machine-gun chatter echoing in the canyons. He remembers the glorious hiss and arc of a Stinger missile as it flashed across red rock desert and blue sky and burned a chopper where it hovered.

But that's long in the past. Now, guardie patrols skim up the river unmolested.

Lolo tops another mesa and stares down at the familiar landscape of an eviscerated town, its curving streets and subdivision cul-de-sacs all sitting silent in the sun. At the very edge of the empty town, one-acre ranchettes and snazzy five-thousand-square-foot houses with dead-stick trees and dust-hill landscaping fringe a brown-tumbleweed golf course. The sand traps don't even show anymore.

When California put its first calls on the river, no one really worried. A couple towns went begging for water. Some idiot newcomers with bad water rights stopped grazing their horses, and that was it. A few years later, people started showering real fast. And a few after that, they showered once a week. And then people started using the buckets. By then, everyone had stopped joking about how "hot" it was. It didn't really matter how "hot" it was. The problem wasn't lack of water or an excess of heat, not really. The problem was that 4.4 million acre-feet of water were supposed to go down the river to California. There was water; they just couldn't touch it.

They were supposed to stand there like dumb monkeys and watch it flow on by.

"Lolo?"

The voice catches him by surprise. Maggie startles and groans and lunges for the mesa edge before Lolo can rein her around. The camel's great padded feet scuffle dust, and Lolo flails for his shotgun where it nestles in a scabbard at the camel's side. He forces Maggie to turn, shotgun half drawn, holding barely to his seat and swearing.

A familiar face, tucked amongst juniper tangle.

"Goddamnit!" Lolo lets the shotgun drop back into its scabbard. "Jesus Christ, Travis. You scared the hell out of me."

Travis grins. He emerges from amongst the junipers' silver bark rags, one hand on his gray fedora, the other on the reins as he guides his mule out of the trees. "Surprised?"

"I could've shot you!"

"Don't be so jittery. There's no one out here 'cept us water ticks."

"That's what I thought the last time I went shopping down there. I had a whole set of new dishes for Annie and I broke them all when I ran into an ultralight parked right in the middle of the main drag."

"Meth flyers?"

"Beats the hell out of me. I didn't stick around to ask."

"Shit. I'll bet they were as surprised as you were."

"They almost killed me."

"I guess they didn't."

Lolo shakes his head and swears again, this time without anger. Despite the ambush, he's happy to run into Travis. It's lonely country, and Lolo's been out long enough to notice the silence of talking to Maggie. They trade ritual sips of water from their canteens and make camp together. They swap stories about BuRec and avoid discussing where they've been ripping tamarisk and enjoy the view of the empty town far below, with its serpentine streets and quiet houses and shining, untouched river.

It isn't until the sun is setting and they've finished roasting a magpie that Lolo finally asks the question that's been on his mind ever since Travis's sun-baked face came out of the tangle. It goes against etiquette, but he can't help himself. He picks magpie out of his teeth and says, "I thought you were working downriver."

Travis glances sidelong at Lolo, and in that one suspicious, uncertain look, Lolo sees that Travis has hit a lean patch. He's not smart like Lolo. He hasn't been reseeding. He's got no insurance. He hasn't been thinking ahead about all the competition and what the tamarisk endgame looks like, and now he's feeling the pinch. Lolo feels a twinge of pity. He likes Travis. A part of him wants to tell Travis the secret, but he stifles the urge. The stakes are too high. Water crimes are serious now, so serious Lolo hasn't even told his wife, Annie, for fear of what she'll say. Like all of the most shameful crimes, water theft is a private business, and at the scale Lolo works, forced labor on the Straw is the best punishment he can hope for.

Travis gets his hackles down over Lolo's invasion of his privacy and says, "I had a couple cows I was running up here, but I lost 'em. I think something got 'em."

"Long way to graze cows."

"Yeah, well, down my way, even the sagebrush is dead. Big Daddy Drought's doing a real number on my patch." He pinches his lip, thoughtful. "Wish I could find those cows."

"They probably went down to the river."

Travis sighs. "Then the guardies probably got 'em."

"Probably shot 'em from a chopper and roasted 'em."

"Californians."

They both spit at the word. The sun continues to sink. Shadows fall across the town's silent structures. The rooftops gleam red, a ruby cluster decorating the blue river necklace.

"You think there's any stands worth pulling down there?" Travis asks.

"You can go down and look. But I think I got it all last year. And someone had already been through before me, so I doubt much is coming up."

"Shit. Well, maybe I'll go shopping. Might as well get something out of this trip."

"There sure isn't anyone to stop you."

As if to emphasize the fact, the *thud-thwap* of a guardie chopper breaks the evening silence. The black-fly dot of its movement barely shows against the darkening sky. Soon, it's out of sight and cricket chirps swallow the last evidence of its passing.

Travis laughs. "Remember when the guardies said they'd keep out looters? I saw them on TV with all their choppers and Humvees and them all saying they were going to protect everything until the situation improved." He laughs again. "You remember that? All of them driving up and down the streets?"

"I remember."

"Sometimes, I wonder if we shouldn't have fought them more."

"Annie was in Lake Havasu City when they fought there. You saw what happened." Lolo shivers. "Anyway, there's not much to fight for once they blow up your water treatment plant. If nothing's coming out of your faucet, you might as well move on."

"Yeah, well, sometimes I think you still got to fight. Even if it's just for pride." Travis gestures at the town below, a shadow movement. "I remember when all that land down there was selling like hotcakes and they were building shit as fast as they could ship in the lumber. Shopping malls and parking lots and subdivisions, anywhere they could scrape a flat spot."

"We weren't calling it Big Daddy Drought back then."

"Forty-five thousand people. And none of us had a clue. And I was a real estate agent." Travis laughs, a self-mocking sound that ends quickly. It sounds too much like self-pity for Lolo's taste. They're quiet again, looking down at the town wreckage.

"I think I might be heading north," Travis says finally.

Lolo glances over, surprised. Again, he has the urge to let Travis in on his secret, but he stifles it. "And do what?"

"Pick fruit, maybe. Maybe something else. Anyway, there's water up there."

Lolo points down at the river. "There's water."

"Not for us." Travis pauses. "I got to level with you, Lolo. I went down to the Straw."

For a second, Lolo is confused by the non sequitur. The statement is too outrageous. And yet Travis's face is serious. "The Straw? No kidding? All the way there?"

"All the way there." He shrugs defensively. "I wasn't finding any tamarisk, anyway. And it didn't actually take that long. It's a lot closer than it used to be. A week out to the train tracks, and then I hopped a coal train and rode it right to the interstate, and then I hitched."

"What's it like out there?"

"Empty. A trucker told me that California and the Interior Department drew up all these plans to decide which cities they'd turn off when." He looks at Lolo significantly. "That was after Lake Havasu. They figured out they had to do it slow. They worked out some kind of formula: how many cities, how many people they could evaporate at a time without making too much unrest. Got advice from the Chinese, from when they were shutting down their old communist industries. Anyway, it looks like they're pretty much done with it. There's nothing moving out there except highway trucks and coal trains and a couple truck stops."

"And you saw the Straw?"

"Oh, sure, I saw it. Out toward the border. Big old mother. So big you couldn't climb on top of it, flopped out on the desert like a damn silver snake. All the way to California." He spits reflexively. "They're spraying with concrete to keep water from seeping into the ground and they've got some kind of carbon-fiber stuff over the top to stop the evaporation. And the river just disappears inside. Nothing but an empty canyon below it. Bone dry. And choppers and Humvees everywhere, like a damn hornets' nest. They wouldn't let me get any closer than a half mile on account of the eco-crazies trying to blow it up. They weren't nice about it, either."

"What did you expect?"

"I dunno. It sure depressed me, though: They work us out here and toss us a little water bounty, and then all that water next year goes right down into that big old pipe. Some Californian's probably filling his swimming pool with last year's water bounty right now."

Cricket song pulses in the darkness. Off in the distance, a pack of coyotes starts yipping. The two of them are quiet for a while. Finally, Lolo chucks his friend on the shoulder. "Hell, Travis, it's probably for the best. A desert's a stupid place to put a river, anyway."

Lolo's homestead runs across a couple acres of semi-alkaline soil, conveniently close to the river's edge. Annie is out in the field when he crests the low hills that overlook his patch. She waves but keeps digging, planting for whatever water he can collect in bounty.

Lolo pauses, watching Annie work. Hot wind kicks up, carrying with it the scents of sage and clay. A dust devil swirls around Annie, whipping her bandana off her head. Lolo smiles as she snags it; she sees him still watching her and waves at him to quit loafing.

He grins to himself and starts Maggie down the hill, but he doesn't stop watching Annie work. He's grateful for her. Grateful that every time he comes back from tamarisk hunting, she is still here. She's steady. Steadier than the people like Travis who give up when times get dry. Steadier than anyone Lolo knows, really. And if she has nightmares sometimes, and can't stand being in towns or crowds, and wakes up in the middle of the night calling out for family she'll never see again, well, then it's all the more reason to seed more tamarisk and make sure they never get pushed off their patch like she was pushed.

Lolo gets Maggie to kneel down so he can dismount, then leads her over to a water trough, half full of slime and water skippers. He gets a bucket and heads for the river while Maggie groans and complains behind him. The patch used to have a well and running water, but like everyone else, they lost their pumping rights and BuRec stuffed the well with Quikrete when the water table dropped below the Minimum Allowable Reserve. Now he and Annie steal buckets from the river, or, when the Interior Department isn't watching, they jump up and down on a foot pump and dump water into a hidden underground cistern he built when the Resource Conservation and Allowable Use Guidelines went into effect.

Annie calls the guidelines "ReCAUG" and it sounds like she's hawking spit when she says it, but even with their filled-in well, they're lucky. They aren't like Spanish Oaks or Antelope Valley or River Reaches: expensive places that had rotten water rights and turned to dust, money or no, when Vegas and LA put in their calls. And they didn't have to bail out of Phoenix Metro when the Central Arizona Project got turned off and then had its aqueducts blown to smithereens when Arizona wouldn't stop pumping out of Lake Havasu.

Pouring water into Maggie's water trough, and looking around at his dusty patch with Annie out in the fields, Lolo reminds himself how lucky he is. He hasn't blown away. He and Annie are dug in. Calies may call them water ticks, but fuck them. If it weren't for people like him and Annie, they'd dry up and blow away the same as everyone else. And if Lolo moves a little bit of tamarisk around, well, the Calies deserve it, considering what they've done to everyone else.

Finished with Maggie, Lolo goes into the house and gets a drink of his own out of the filter urn. The water is cool in the shadows of the adobe house. Juniper beams hang low overhead. He sits down and connects his BuRec camera to the solar panel they've got scabbed onto the roof. Its charge light blinks amber. Lolo goes and gets some more water. He's used to being thirsty, but for some reason, he can't get enough today. Big Daddy Drought's got his hands around Lolo's neck today.

Annie comes in, wiping her forehead with a tanned arm. "Don't drink too much water," she says. "I haven't been able to pump. Bunch of guardies around."

"What the hell are they doing around? We haven't even opened our headgates yet."

"They said they were looking for you."

Lolo almost drops his cup.

They know.

They know about his tamarisk reseeding. They know he's been splitting and planting root clusters. That he's been dragging big, healthy chunks of tamarisk up and down the river. A week ago, he uploaded his claim on the canyon tamarisk—his biggest stand yet—almost worth an acre-foot in itself in water bounty. And now the guardies are knocking on his door.

Lolo forces his hand not to shake as he puts his cup down. "They say what they want?" He's surprised his voice doesn't crack.

"Just that they wanted to talk to you." She pauses. "They had one of those Humvees. With the guns."

Lolo closes his eyes. Forces himself to take a deep breath. "They've always got guns. It's probably nothing."

"It reminded me of Lake Havasu. When they cleared us out. When they shut down the water treatment plant and everyone tried to burn down the BLM office."

"It's probably nothing." Suddenly, he's glad he never told her about his tamarisk hijinks. They can't punish her the same. How many acre-feet is he liable for? It must be hundreds. They'll want him, all right. Put him on a Straw work crew and make him work for life, repay his water debt forever. He's replanted hundreds, maybe thousands of tamarisk, shuffling them around like a cardsharp on a poker table, moving them from one bank to another, killing them again and again and again, and always happily sending in his "evidence."

"It's probably nothing," he says again.

"That's what people said in Havasu."

Lolo waves out at their newly tilled patch. The sun shines down hot and hard on the small plot. "We're not worth that kind of effort." He forces a grin. "It probably has to do with those enviro crazies who tried to blow up the Straw. Some of them supposedly ran this way. It's probably that."

Annie shakes her head, unconvinced. "I don't know. They could have asked me the same as you."

"Yeah, but I cover a lot of ground. See a lot of things. I'll bet that's why they want to talk to me. They're just looking for eco-freaks."

"Yeah, maybe you're right. It's probably that." She nods slowly, trying to make herself believe. "Those enviros, they don't make any sense at all.

Not enough water for people, and they want to give the river to a bunch of fish and birds."

Lolo nods emphatically and grins wider. "Yeah. Stupid." But suddenly, he views the eco-crazies with something approaching brotherly affection. The Californians are after him, too.

Lolo doesn't sleep all night. His instincts tell him to run, but he doesn't have the heart to tell Annie or to leave her. He goes out in the morning hunting tamarisk and fails at that as well. He doesn't cut a single stand all day. He considers shooting himself with his shotgun but chickens out when he gets the barrels in his mouth. Better alive and on the run than dead. Finally, as he stares into the twin barrels, he knows that he has to tell Annie, tell her he's been a water thief for years and that he's got to run north. Maybe she'll come with him. Maybe she'll see reason. They'll run together. At least they have that. For sure, he's not going to let those bastards take him off to a labor camp for the rest of his life.

But the guardies are already waiting when Lolo gets back. They're squatting in the shade of their Humvee, talking. When Lolo comes over the crest of the hill, one of them taps the other and points. They both stand. Annie is out in the field again, turning over dirt, unaware of what's about to happen. Lolo reins in and studies the guardies. They lean against their Humvee and watch him back.

Suddenly, Lolo sees his future. It plays out in his mind the way it does in a movie, as clear as the blue sky above. He puts his hand on his shotgun. Where it sits on Maggie's far side, the guardies can't see it. He keeps Maggie angled away from them and lets the camel start down the hill.

The guardies saunter toward him. They've got their Humvee with a .50 caliber on the back, and they've both got M-16s slung over their shoulders. They're in full bulletproof gear and they look flushed and hot. Lolo rides down slowly. He'll have to hit them both in the face. Sweat trickles between his shoulder blades. His hand is slick on the shotgun's stock.

The guardies are playing it cool. They've still got their rifles slung, and they let Lolo keep approaching. One of them has a wide smile. He's maybe forty years old and tanned. He's been out for a while, picking up a tan like that. The other raises a hand and says, "Hey there, Lolo."

Lolo's so surprised he takes his hand off his shotgun. "Hale?" He recognizes the guardie. He grew up with him. They played football together a million years ago, when football fields still had green grass and sprinklers sprayed their water straight into the air. Hale. Hale Perkins. Lolo scowls. He can't shoot Hale.

Hale says. "You're still out here, huh?"

"What the hell are you doing in that uniform? You with the Calies now?"

Hale grimaces and points to his uniform patches: Utah National Guard.

Lolo scowls. Utah National Guard. Colorado National Guard. Arizona National Guard. They're all the same. There's hardly a single member of the "National Guard" that isn't an out-of-state mercenary. Most of the local guardies quit a long time ago, sick to death of goose-stepping family and friends off their properties and sick to death of trading potshots with people who just wanted to stay in their homes. So, even if there's still a Colorado National Guard, or an Arizona or a Utah, inside those uniforms with all their expensive night-sight gear and their brand-new choppers flying the river bends, it's pure California.

And then there are a few like Hale.

Lolo remembers Hale as being an okay guy. Remembers stealing a keg of beer from behind the Elks Club one night with him. Lolo eyes him. "How you liking that Supplementary Assistance Program?" He glances at the other guardie. "That working real well for you? The Calies a big help?"

Hale's eyes plead for understanding. "Come on, Lolo. I'm not like you. I got a family to look after. If I do another year of duty, they let Shannon and the kids base out of California."

"They give you a swimming pool in your back yard, too?"

"You know it's not like that. Water's scarce there, too."

Lolo wants to taunt him, but his heart isn't in it. A part of him wonders if Hale is just smart. At first, when California started winning its water lawsuits and shutting off cities, the displaced people just followed the water—right to California. It took a little while before the bureaucrats realized what was going on, but finally someone with a sharp pencil did the math and realized that taking in people along with their water didn't solve a water shortage. So, the immigration fences went up.

But people like Hale can still get in.

"So, what do you two want?" Inside, Lolo's wondering why they haven't already pulled him off Maggie and hauled him away, but he's willing to play this out.

The other guardie grins. "Maybe we're just out here seeing how the water ticks live."

Lolo eyes him. This one, he could shoot. He lets his hand fall to his shotgun again. "BuRec sets my headgate. No reason for you to be out here."

The Calie says, "There were some marks on it. Big ones."

Lolo smiles tightly. He knows which marks the Calie is talking about. He made them with five different wrenches when he tried to dismember the entire headgate apparatus in a fit of obsession. Finally, he gave up trying to open the bolts and just beat on the thing, banging the steel of the gate, smashing at it, while on the other side he had plants withering. After that, he gave up and just carried buckets of water to his plants and left it at that. But the dents and nicks are still there, reminding him of a period of madness. "It still works, don't it?"

Hale holds up a hand to his partner, quieting him. "Yeah, it still works. That's not why we're here."

"So, what do you two want? You didn't drive all the way out here with your machine gun just to talk about dents in my headgate."

Hale sighs, put-upon, trying to be reasonable. "You mind getting down off that damn camel so we can talk?"

Lolo studies the two guardies, figuring his chances on the ground. "Shit." He spits. "Yeah, Okay. You got me." He urges Maggie to kneel and climbs off her hump. "Annie didn't know anything about this. Don't get her involved. It was all me."

Hale's brow wrinkles, puzzled. "What are you talking about?"

"You're not arresting me?"

The Calie with Hale laughs. "Why? 'Cause you take a couple buckets of water from the river? 'Cause you probably got an illegal cistern around here somewhere?" He laughs again. "You ticks are all the same. You think we don't know about all that crap?"

Hale scowls at the Calie, then turns back to Lolo. "No, we're not here to arrest you. You know about the Straw?"

"Yeah." Lolo says it slowly, but inside, he's grinning. A great weight is suddenly off him. They don't know. They don't know shit. It was a good plan when he started it, and it's a good plan still. Lolo schools his face to keep the glee off and tries to listen to what Hale's saying, but he can't; he's jumping up and down and gibbering like a monkey. They don't know—

"Wait." Lolo holds up his hand. "What did you just say?"

Hale repeats himself. "California's ending the water bounty. They've got enough Straw sections built up now that they don't need the program. They've got half the river enclosed. They got an agreement from the Department of the Interior to focus their budget on seep and evaporation control. That's where all the big benefits are. They're shutting down the water bounty payout program." He pauses. "I'm sorry, Lolo."

Lolo frowns. "But a tamarisk is still a tamarisk. Why should one of those damn plants get the water? If I knock out a tamarisk, even if Cali doesn't want the water, I could still take it. Lots of people could use the water."

Hale looks pityingly at Lolo. "We don't make the regulations; we just enforce them. I'm supposed to tell you that your headgate won't get opened next year. If you keep hunting tamarisk, it won't do any good." He looks around the patch, then shrugs. "Anyway, in another couple years, they were going to pipe this whole stretch. There won't be any tamarisk at all after that."

"What am I supposed to do, then?"

"California and BuRec is offering early buyout money." Hale pulls a booklet out of his bulletproof vest and flips it open. "Sort of to soften the blow." The pages of the booklet flap in the hot breeze. Hale pins the pages with a thumb and pulls a pen out of another vest pocket. He marks something on the booklet, then tears off a perforated check. "It's not a bad deal."

Lolo takes the check. Stares at it. "Five hundred dollars?"

Hale shrugs sadly. "It's what they're offering. That's just the paper codes. You confirm it online. Use your BuRec camera phone, and they'll deposit it in whatever bank you want. Or they can hold it in trust until you get into a town and want to withdraw it. Any place with a BLM office, you can do that. But you need to confirm before April 15. Then BuRec'll send out a guy to shut down your headgate before this season gets going."

"Five hundred dollars?"

"It's enough to get you north. That's more than they're offering next year."

"But this is my patch."

"Not as long as we've got Big Daddy Drought. I'm sorry, Lolo."

"The drought could break any time. Why can't they give us a couple more years? It could break any time." But even as he says it, Lolo doesn't believe. Ten years ago, he might have. But not now. Big Daddy Drought's here to stay. He clutches the check and its key codes to his chest.

A hundred yards away, the river flows on to California.

ABOUT THE AUTHOR

PAOLO BACIGALUPI is the bestselling author of the novels *The Windup Girl, Ship Breaker, The Drowned Cities, Zombie Baseball Beatdown,* and the collection *Pump Six and Other Stories.* He is a winner of the Michael L. Printz, Hugo, Nebula, Locus, Compton Crook, and John W. Campbell Memorial awards, and was a National Book Award finalist. A new novel for young adults, *The Doubt Factory,* came out in 2014, and a new science fiction novel dealing with the effects of climate change, *The Water Knife,* was published in May 2015.

MITIGATION

TOBIAS S. BUCKELL & KARL SCHROEDER

Chauncie St. Christie squinted in the weak 3 a.m. sunlight. *No, two degrees higher.* He adjusted the elevation, stepped back in satisfaction, and pulled on a lime-green nylon cord. The mortar burped loudly, and seconds later, a fountain of water shot up ten feet from his target.

His sat phone vibrated on his belt and he half reached for it, causing the gyroscope-stabilized platform to wobble slightly. "Damn it." That must be Maksim on the phone. The damn Croat would be calling about the offer again. Chauncie ignored the reminder and reset the mortar. "How close are they?"

His friend Kulitak stood on the rail of the trawler and scanned the horizon with a set of overpowered binoculars. "Those eco response ships are throwing out oil containment booms. Canuck gunboats're all on the far side of the spill."

"As long as they're busy." Chauncie adjusted the mortar and dropped another shell into it. This shot hit dead-on, and the CarbonJohnny™ blew apart in a cloud of Styrofoam, cheap solar panel fragments, and chicken wire.

Kulitak lowered his binoculars. "Nice one."

"One down, a million to go," muttered Chauncie. The little drift of debris was already sinking, the flotsam joining the ever-present scrim of trash that peppered all ocean surfaces. Hundreds more CarbonJohnnies dotted the sea all the way to the horizon, each one a moronically simple mechanism. A few bottom-of-the-barrel cheap solar panels sent a weak current into a slowly unreeling sheet of chicken wire that hung in the water. This electrolyzed calcium carbonate out of the water. As the chicken wire turned to concrete, sections of it tore off and sank into the depths of the Makarov Basin. These big reels looked a bit like toilet paper and unraveled the same way, a few sheets at a time: hence the name CarbonJohnny. Sequestors International (NASDAQ symbol: SQI) churned them out by the shipload with the noble purpose of sequestering carbon and making a quick buck from the carbon credits.

Chauncie and his friends blew them up and sank them almost as quickly. "This is lame," Kulitak said. "We're not going to make any money today." "Let's pack up, find somewhere less involved."

Chauncie grunted irritably; he'd have to pay for an updated satellite mosaic and look for another UN inspection blind spot. Kulitak had picked this field of CarbonJohnnies because overhead, somewhere high in the stratosphere, a pregnant blimp staggered through the pale air dumping sulfur particulates into a too-clean atmosphere to help block the warming sun. But in the process it also helpfully obscured some of the finer details of what Chauncie and Kulitak were up to. Unfortunately, the pesky ecological catastrophe unfolding off the port bow was wreaking havoc with their schedule.

A day earlier, somebody had blown up an automated U.S. Pure Waters, Inc. tug towing a half cubic kilometer of iceberg. Kulitak thought it was the Emerald Institute who'd done it, but they were just one of dozens of ecoterrorist groups who might have been responsible. Everybody was protesting the large-scale "strip mining" of the Arctic's natural habitat, and now and then somebody did something about it.

The berg had turned out to be unstable. As Chauncie'd been motoring out to this spot he'd heard the distant thunder as it flipped over. He hadn't heard the impact of the passing supertanker with its underwater spur three hours later; but he could sure smell it when he woke up. The news said three or four thousand tonnes of oil had leaked out into the water, and the immediate area was turning into a circus of cleanup crews. Media, Greenpeace, oil company ships, UN, government officials—they would all descend soon enough.

"There's money in cleanup," Chauncie commented; he smiled at Kulitak's grimace.

"Money," said Kulitak. "And forms. And treaties you gotta watch out for; and politics like rat traps. Let's find another Johnny." The Inuit radicals who had hired them were dumping their own version of the CarbonJohnny into these waters. Blowing up SQI's Johnnies was not, Chauncie's employer had claimed, actually piracy; it was merely a diversion of the carbon credits that would otherwise have gone to SQI—and at $100 per tonne sequestered, it added up fast.

He shrugged at Kulitak's impatient look, and bent to stow the mortar. Broken Styrofoam, twirling beer cans, and plush toys from a container-ship accident drifted in the trawler's wake; farther out, the Johnnies bobbed in their thousands, a marine forest through which dozens of larger vessels had to pick their way. On the horizon, a converted tanker was spraying a fine mist of iron powder into the air—fertilizing the Arctic Ocean for another carbon sequestration company, just as the blimps overhead were smearing the sky with reflective smog to cut down global warming in another way. Helicopters crammed with biologists and carbon-market auditors zigged and zagged over the waters, and yellow autosubs cruised under them, all measuring the effect.

Mile-long oil supertankers cruised obliviously through it all. Now that the world's trees were worth more as carbon sinks than building material, the plastics industry had taken off. Oil as fuel was on its way out; oil for the housing industry was in high demand.

And in the middle of it all, Chauncie's little trawler. It didn't actually fish. There were fish enough—the effect of pumping iron powder into the ocean was to accelerate the Arctic's already large biodiversity to previously unseen levels. Plankton boomed, and the cycle of life in the deep had exploded. The ocean's fisheries no longer struggled, and boats covered the oceans with nets and still couldn't make a dent. Chauncie's fishing nets were camouflage. Who would notice one more trawler picking its way toward a less-packed quadrant of CarbonJohnnies?

Out in relatively clearer ocean Chauncie sat on the deck as the Inuit crew hustled around, pulling in the purposefully holed nets so that the trawler could speed up.

In this light the ocean was gunmetal blue; he let his eyes rest on it, unaware of how long he stood there until Kulitak said, "Thinking of taking a dip?"

"What? Oh, heh—no." He turned away. There was no diving into these waters for a refreshing swim. Chauncie hadn't known how precious such a simple act could be until he'd lost it.

Kulitak grunted but said nothing more; Chauncie knew he understood that long stare, the moments of silent remembrance. These men he worked with cultivated an anger similar to his own: their Arctic was long gone, but their deepest instincts still expected it to be here, he was sure, the same way he expected the ocean to be a glitter of warm emeralds he could cup in his hand.

Losing his childhood home, the island of Anegada, to the global climate disaster had been devastating, but sometimes Chauncie wondered whether Kulitak's people hadn't gotten the worse end of the disaster. As the seven seas became the eight seas and their land literally melted away, the Inuit faced an indignity that even Chauncie did not have to suffer: seeing companies, governments, and people flood in to claim what had once been theirs alone.

He found it delicious fun to make money plinking at CarbonJohnnies for the Inuit. But it wasn't big money—and he needed the big score.

He needed to be able to cup those emeralds in his hands again. On rare occasions he'd wonder whether he was going to spend the rest of his life up here. If somebody told him that was his fate, he was pretty sure he'd take a last dive right there and then. He couldn't go on like this forever.

"Satellite data came back," said Kulitak after a while. "The sulfur clouds are clearing up." Chauncie glanced up and nodded. They couldn't hide the trawler from satellite inspection right now. It was time to head back to port. As the ship got under way, Chauncie checked the sat phone.

Maksim had indeed called. Five times.

Kulitak saw his frown. "The Croat?"

Chauncie clipped the sat phone back to his waistband. "You said it was a slow day; we're not making much. And with the spill, it's going to be a zoo. We could use a break."

His friend grimaced. "You don't want to work with him. There's money, but it's not worth it. You come in the powerboat with me, the satellites can't see our faces, we hit more CarbonJohnnies. I'll bring sandwiches."

There was no way Chauncie was going to motor his way around the Arctic in a glorified rowboat. They'd get run over. By a trawler, a tanker, or any other ship ripping its way through the wide-open lanes of the Arctic Ocean. There was just too much traffic.

"I'll think about it," Chauncie said as the sat phone vibrated yet again.

Late the next evening, Chauncie entered the bridge of a rusted-out container ship that listed slightly to port. Long shadows leaned across the docks and cranes of Tuktoyaktuk, their promise of night destined to be unfulfilled.

"Hey Max," he said, and sat down hard on the armchair in the middle of the bridge. Chauncie rubbed his eyes. He hadn't stopped to sleep yet. An easy error in the daylong sunlight. Insomnia snuck up on you, as your body kept thinking it was day. Run all-out for forty-eight hours and forget about your daily cycle, and you'd crash hard on day three. And the listing bridge made him feel even more off-balance and weary.

"Took you damn long enough. I should get someone else, just to spite you." Maksim muttered his reply from behind a large, ostentatious, and extraordinarily expensive real wooden desk. He was almost hidden behind the nine screens perched on it.

Maksim was a slave to continuous partial attention: his eyes flicked from screen to screen, and he constantly tapped at the surface of the desk or flicked his hands at the screens. In response, people were being paid, currencies traded, stocks bought or sold.

And that was the legitimate trade. Chauncie didn't know much about Maksim's other hobbies, but he could guess from the occasional exposed tattoo that Maksim was Russian Mafia.

"Well, I'm here."

Maksim glanced up. "Yes. Yes you are. Good. Chauncie, you know why I give you so much business?"

Chauncie sighed. He wasn't sure he wanted to play this game. "No, why?"

Maksim sipped at a sweaty glass of iced tea with a large wedge of lemon stuck on the rim. "Because even though you're here for dirty jobs, you like the ones that let you poke back at the big guys. It means I understand you. It makes you a predictable asset. So I have a good one for you. You ready for the big one, Chauncie, the payday that lets you leave to do whatever it is you really want, rather than sitting around with little pop-guns and Styrofoam targets?"

Chauncie felt a weird kick in his stomach. "What kind of big, Max?"

Maksim had a small smile as he put the iced tea down. "Big." He slowly turned a screen around to face Chauncie. There were a lot of zeros in that sum. Chauncie's lips suddenly felt dry, and he nervously licked them.

"That's big." He could retire. "What horrible thing will I have to do for that?"

"It begins with you playing bodyguard for a scientist."

Uh-oh. As a rule, scientists and Russian Mafia didn't mix well. "I'm really just guarding her, right?"

Maksim looked annoyed. "If I wanted her dead, I wouldn't have called *you.*" He pointed out the grimy windows. A windblown, ruddy-cheeked woman wrapped in a large "Hands around the World" parka stood at the rail. She was reading something off the screen of her phone.

"That's the scientist? Here?"

"Yes. That is River Balleny. Was big into genetic archeology. She made a big find a couple years ago and patented the DNA for some big agri-corporation for exotic livestock. Now she mainly verifies viability, authenticity, and then couriers the samples to Svalbard for various government missions out here."

"And she's just looking for a good security type, in case some other company wants to hijack a sample of what she's couriering? Which is why she came out to this rusted-out office of yours?"

Maksim grinned over his screens. "Right."

Chauncie looked back at the walkway outside the bridge. River looked back, and then glanced away. She looked out of place, a moonfaced little girl who should be in a lab, sequencing bits and pieces sandwiched between slides. Certainly she shouldn't be standing in the biting wind on the deck of thousands of tons of scrap metal. "So I steal what she'll be couriering? Is that the big payday?"

"No." Maksim looked back down and tapped the desk. Another puppet somewhere in the world danced to his string pulls. "She'll be given some seeds we could care less about. What we care about is the fact that she can get you into the Svalbard seed vault."

"And in there?"

Maksim reached under his desk and gently set a small briefcase on the table. "This is a portable sequencer. Millions of research and development spent so that a genetic archeologist in the field could immediately do out on the open plains what used to take a lab team weeks or months to do. Couple it with a fat storage system, and we can digitize nature's bounty in a few seconds."

Chauncie stared down at the case. "You can't tell me those seeds haven't already been sequenced. Aren't they just there for insurance, in case civilization collapses totally?"

"There are unique seeds at Svalbard," said Maksim, shaking his head. "One-of-a-kind from extinct tropical plants; paleo-seeds. Sequencing them destroys the seed, and lots of green groups ganged up about ten years ago in a big court case to stop the unique ones being touched. Bad karma if the sequencing isn't perfect, you know; you'd lose the entire species. Sequencing is almost foolproof now, but the legislation is . . . hard to reverse.

"We want you to get into the seed vault and sequence as many of those rare and precious seeds as you can. They have security equipment all over the outside, but inside, it's just storage area. No weapons, just move quick to gather the seeds and control the scientist while you gather the seeds. The more paleo-seeds the better. When you leave, with or without her, you get outside. You pull out the antenna, and you transmit everything. You leave Svalbard however you wish—charter a plane to be waiting for you, or the boat you get there with. We do not care. Once we have the information, we pay you. You leave the Arctic, find a warm place to settle down. Buy a nice house, and a nice woman. Enjoy this new life. Okay, we never see each other again. I'll be sad, true, but maybe I'll retire too, and neither of us cares. You understand?"

Chauncie did. This was exactly the score he'd been looking for.

He looked at the windblown geneticist and thought about what Maksim might not be telling him. Then he shook his head. "You know me, Max, this is too big. Way out of my comfort level. I'll become internationally wanted. I'm not in that league."

"No, no." Maksim slapped the table. "You are big-league now, Chauncie. You'll do this. I know you'll do this."

Chauncie laughed and leaned back in the chair. "Why?"

"Because if you don't"—Maksim also leaned back—"if you don't, you will never forgive yourself when military contractors occupy Svalbard in two weeks, taking over the seed vault and blackmailing the world with it."

"You've got to be joking." The idea that someone might trash Svalbard was ridiculous. Svalbard was the holiest of green holies, a bank for the world's wealth of seeds, stored away in case of apocalypse. "That would be like bombing the Vatican."

"These are Russian mercenaries, my friend. Russia is dying. They never were cutting edge with biotech, ever since Lysenkoism in the Soviet days. The plague strains that ripped through their wheat fields last year killed their stock, and Western companies have patented nearly everything that grows. Russian farms are hostage to Monsanto patents, so they have no choice but to raid the seed bank. They can either sequence the unique strains themselves, in hopes of making hybrids that won't get them sued for patent infringement in the world market, or they may threaten to destroy those unique seeds unless some key patents are annulled. I don't know which exactly—but either way, the rare plants are doomed. They'll sequence the DNA, discard everything but the unique genes . . . or burn the seed to put pressure on West. Either way—no more plant."

"Whereas if we do it . . ."

"We take whole DNA of plant. Let them buy it from us; in twenty years we give whole DNA back to Svalbard when it's no longer worth anything. It's win-win—for us and plant."

"It's the Russians behind the mercenaries? And no one knows about this."

"No one. No one but us." Maksim laughed. "You will be hero to many, but more importantly, rich."

Chauncie sucked air through his teeth and mulled it all over. But he and Maksim already knew the answer.

"What about travel expenses?"

Maksim laughed. "You're friends with those Indians—"

"First Nations peoples—"

"Whatever. Just get permission to use one of their trawlers. The company she's couriering for is pretty good about security. They drop in by helicopter when you're in transit to hand over the seeds. They'll call with a location and time at the last minute, as long as you tell them what your course will be. A good faith payment is . . ." Maksim tapped a screen. ". . . now in your account. You can afford to hire them. Happy birthday."

"It's not my birthday."

"Well, with this job, it is. And Chauncie?"

"Yes, Max?"

"You fuck it up, you won't see another."

Chauncie wanted to say something in return, but it was no use. He knew Maksim wasn't kidding. Anyway, Maksim had already turned his attention back to his screens. Chauncie was already taken care of, in his mind.

For a moment, Chauncie considered turning Maksim down, still. Then he glanced out the windows, at a sea that would never be the right color—that would never cradle his body and ease the sorrow of his losses.

He hefted the briefcase and stepped outside to introduce himself to River Balleny.

The trawler beat through heavy seas, making for Svalbard. The sun rolled slowly around a sky drained of all but pastel colors, where towering clouds of dove gray and mauve hinted at a dusk that never came. You covered your porthole to make night for yourself, and stepped out of your stateroom seemingly into the same moment you had left. After years up here Chauncie could tell himself he was as used to the midnight sun as he was to heavy seas; but the new passenger, who was much on his mind, stayed in her cabin while the seas heaved.

After two days the swells subsided, and for a while the ocean became calm as glass. Chauncie woke to a distant crackle from the radio room, and as he buttoned his shirt Kulitak pounded on his door. "I heard, I heard."

"It's not just the helicopter," Kulitak hissed. "The elders just contacted me over single sideband radio. We think Maksim's dead."

"Think?" Chauncie looked down the tight corridor between the trawler's cabins. The floorboards creaked under their feet as the ship twisted itself over large waves.

"Several tons of sulfur particulates, arc welded into a solid lump, dropped from the stratosphere by a malfunctioning blimp. So they say. There's nothing left of Maksim's barge. It's all pieces."

"Pieces . . ." Chauncie instinctively looked up toward the deck, as if expecting something similar to destroy them on the spot.

"I told you, you don't get involved with that man. You're out here playing a game that will get you killed. Get out now."

Chauncie braced himself in the tiny space as the trawler lurched. "It's too late now. They don't let you back out this late in the game." He thought about the private army moving out there somewhere, getting ready to take over the vault. All at the behest of another nation assuming it could just snatch that which belonged to all.

They still had time.

"Come on, let's get that package. She'll fall overboard if we don't help her out."

They stepped on deck to find River Balleny already there. She was staring up at the dragonfly shape of an approaching helicopter, which was framed by rose-tinted puffballs in the pale, drawn sky. She said nothing, but turned to grin excitedly at the two men as the helicopter's shuddering voice rose to a crescendo.

The wash from its blades scoured the deck. Kulitak, clothes flapping, stepped into the center of the deck and raised his hands. Dangling at the bottom of a hundred feet of nylon rope, a small plastic drum wrapped in fluorescent green duct tape swung dangerously past his head, twirled, and came back. On the third pass he grabbed it and somebody cut the rope in the helicopter. The snaking fall of the line nearly pulled the drum out of Kulitak's hands; by the time he'd wrestled his package loose the helicopter was a receding dot. River walked out to help him, and after a moment's hesitation, Chauncie followed.

"The fuck is this?" The empty drum at his feet, Kulitak was holding a small plastic bag up to the sunlight. River reached up to take it from him.

"It's your past," she said. "And our future." She took the package inside without another glance at the men.

They found her sitting at the cleaver-hacked table in the galley, peering at the bag. "Those seem to mean a lot to you," he said as he slid in opposite her.

Opening the bag carefully, River rolled a couple of tiny orange seeds onto the tabletop. "Paleo-seeds," she mused. "It looks like mountain aven, but according to the manifest"—she tapped a sheet of paper that had been tightly wadded and stuffed into the bag—"it's at least thirty thousand years old."

Chauncie picked one up gingerly between his fingertips. "And that makes it different?"

She nodded. "Maybe not. But it's best to err on the side of caution. Have you ever been to the seed vault?" He shook his head.

"When I was a girl I had a model of Noah's ark in my bedroom," she said. "You could pop the roof open and see little giraffes and lions and stuff. Later I thought that was the dumbest story in the Bible—but the seed vault at Svalbard really *is* the ark. Only for plants, not animals."

"Where'd you grow up?"

"Valley, Nebraska," she said. "Before the water table collapsed. You?"

"British Virgin Islands: Anegada."

She sucked in a breath. "It's gone. Oh, that must have been terrible for you."

He shrugged. "It was a slow death. It took long enough for the sea to rise and sink the island that I was able to make my peace with it; but my wife . . ." How to compress those agonizing years into some statement that would make sense to this woman, yet not do an injustice to the complexity of it all? All he could think of to say was, "It killed her." He looked down.

River surprised him by simply nodding, as if she really did understand. She put her hand out, palm up, and he laid the seed in it. "We all seem to end up here," she mused, "when our lands go away. Nebraska's a dust bowl now. Anegada's under the waves. We come up here to make sure nobody else has to experience that."

He nodded; if anybody asked him flat out, Chauncie would say that Anegada hadn't mattered, that he'd come to the Arctic for the money. Somehow he didn't think River would buy that line.

"Of course it's a disaster," she went on, "losing the Arctic ice cap, having the tundra melt and outgas all that methane and stuff. But every now and then there's these little rays of hope, like when somebody finds ancient seeds that have been frozen since the last glaciation." She sealed the baggie. "Part of our genetic heritage, maybe the basis for new crops or cancer drugs or who knows? A little lifeboat—once it's safely at Svalbard."

"Must be quite the place," he said, "if they only give the keys to a few people."

"It's the Fortress of Solitude," she said seriously. "You'll see what I mean when we get there."

Svalbard was a tumble of dollhouses at the foot of a giant's mountain. Even in the permanent day of summer, snow lingered on the tops of the distant peaks, and the panorama of ocean behind the docked trawler was wreathed in fog as Chauncie and River stepped down the gangplank. Both wore fleeces against the cutting wind.

A thriving tourist industry had grown up around the town and its famed fortress. Thriving by northern standards, that is—the local tourist office had three electric cars they rented out for day trips up to the site. Two were out; Chauncie rented the third. He was counting out bills when his sat phone vibrated. He handed River the cash and stepped across the street to answer.

"Chauncie," said a familiar Croatian voice. "You know who it is, don't answer, we must be careful, the phones have ears, if you know what I mean. Listen, after my office had that unfortunate incident I've been staying with . . . a friend. But I'm okay.

"That big event, that happens soon by your current location, I regret to say we think it has been moved up. They know about our little plan. We don't know when they attack, so hurry up. We still expect your transmission, and for you to complete your side of the arrangement. Our agreement concerning success . . . and failure, that still stands.

"Good luck."

Chauncie jumped a little at the dial tone. River waited next to the little car, and in a daze Chauncie put the briefcase behind his seat, took control, and they followed the signs along a winding road by the sea.

River was animated, pointing out local landmarks and chattering away happily. Chauncie did his best to act cheerful, but he hadn't slept well, and his stomach was churning now. He kept seeing camouflaged killers lurking in every shadow.

"There it is!" She pointed. It took him a moment to see it, maybe because the word *fortress* had primed him for a particular kind of sight. What Chauncie saw was just a grim mountainside of scree and loose rock, patched in places with lines of reddish grass; jutting eighty or so feet out of this was a knife blade of concrete, twenty-five feet tall but narrow, perhaps no more than ten feet wide. There was a parking lot in front of it where several cars were parked, but that, like Svalbard itself, seemed absurd next to the scale of the mountain and the grim darkness of the landscape. The cars were all parked together, as though huddling for protection.

Chauncie pulled up next to them and climbed out into absolute silence. From here you could see the bay, and distant islands capped with white floating just above the gray mist.

"Magnificent, isn't it?" said River. He scowled, then hid that with a smile as he turned to her.

"Beautiful." It was, in a bleak and intimidating way—he just wasn't in the mood.

The entrance to the global seed vault was a metal door at the tip of the concrete blade. River was sauntering unconcernedly up to it; Chauncie followed nervously, glancing about for signs of surveillance. Sure enough, he spotted cameras and other, subtler sensor boxes here and there. Maksim had warned him about those.

The door itself was unguarded; River's voice echoed back as she called, "Hallooo." He hurried in after her.

The inside of the blade was unadorned concrete lit by sodium lamps. There was only one way to go, and after about eighty feet the concrete gave over to a rough tunnel sheathed in spray-on cement and painted white. The chill in here was terrible, but he supposed that was the point; the vault was impervious to global warming, and was intended to survive the fall of human civilization. That was why it was empty of anything worth stealing—except its genetic treasure—and was situated literally at the last place on Earth any normal human would choose to go.

Six tourists wearing bright parkas were chatting with a staff member next to a set of rooms leading off the right-hand side of the tunnel. The construction choice here was unpainted cinderblock, but the tourists seemed excited to be here. River politely interrupted and showed her credentials to the guide, who nodded them on. Nobody looked at his briefcase; he supposed they would check it on the way out, not on the way in.

"We're special," she said, and actually took his arm as they continued on down the bleak, too-brightly lit passage. "Normally nobody gets beyond that." About twenty feet farther on, the tunnel was roped off. Past it, a T-intersection could be seen where only one light glowed.

These were the airlocks. Strangely, the doors were just under five feet high. Chauncie and River had to duck to step inside the right one.

The outer door shut with a clang. He was in. He'd made it.

When the inner door opened it was into a cavern some 150 feet long. Shelves filled with wooden boxes lined the interior like an industrial wholesale store. The boxes were stenciled with black numbers.

It was a polar library of life.

Chauncie pulled a small, super-spring-loaded chock out of his pocket. He surreptitiously dropped it in front of the door and kicked it firmly underneath. It had a five-second count after his fingerprint activated it.

After the count the door creaked as it was wedged firmly shut. It was a preventative mechanism to keep River in more than anyone out.

River brought out her foil packet. It nestled, very small, in the palm of her hand. "They're amazing, seeds. All that information in that one tiny package: tough, durable, no degradation for almost a century in most cases. Just add water. . . ."

She led them to a row at the very back of the vault, reading off some sort of Dewey Decimal System for stored genetic material that Chauncie couldn't ascertain.

Here they were.

With a slight air of reverence in her careful, deliberate movements, she slid a long box off the shelf. She set it carefully on the ground and opened the lid.

Inside were hundreds of glittering packets. Treasure, Chauncie thought, and the idea must have hovered in the air, because she said it as well. "It's a treasure, you know, because it's rarity that makes something valuable. There used to be hundreds of species of just plain apples in the U.S. Farmers standardized down to just a dozen. . . . Somewhere in here are thousands more, if we ever choose to need them."

She seemed fascinated. As she crouched and started flipping through foil packets Chauncie retreated down the rows. He turned a corner out of her sight and pulled out the sheet of paper with Maksim's list of the rarest seeds.

Matching the code next to the list with where to find the seeds was slightly awkward; he wasn't familiar with it like River was. But by wandering around he found his first box, and opened it to find the appropriate packet with three seeds inside.

He flipped the briefcase open to reveal a screen, a pad, and a small funnel in the right-hand side. All he had to do was dump a couple seeds in the funnel and press a button. The tiny grinder reduced the seeds to pulp and extracted the DNA.

After it whirred and spat dust out the side of the briefcase a long dump of text scrolled down the screen, with small models of DNA chains popping up in the corners. Not much more than pretty rotating screensavers for Chauncie.

All he cared was that it seemed to be working.

But he was going to have to pick up the pace. That had taken several minutes. He cradled the briefcase, leaving the box on the floor as he strode along looking for the next item on the list.

There. This time the foil packet only had a single seed. Chauncie sat with it in the palm of his hand and stared at it. It was even more precious than River's paleo-seeds, because this was the only one of its kind in existence.

Suppose the machine wasn't working?

He shook his head and dropped the single seed in and listened to the grinding. More text scrolled down the screen. Success, a full sequence.

Chauncie blew out his held breath; it steamed in the freezing air.

"Just what the hell are you doing?" River asked. Her voice sounded so shocked it had modulated itself down into almost baritone.

There was another foil packet with two seeds in it nearby. It matched the list. Chauncie had hit a box full of rare and unique paleo-seeds stored here by a smaller government prospecting in the Arctic, or maybe a large and paranoid corporation. He dumped the seeds in and the briefcase whirred.

"Jesus Christ," River looked around him at the briefcase. "That's a sequencer. Chauncie, those seeds are one-of-a-kind."

He nodded and kept working. "Listen." River stayed oddly calm, her breath clouding the air over his head. "That might be a good sequencer, but even the best ones have an error rate. You're going to be losing some data. This is criminal. You have to stop, or I'm going to get someone in here to stop you."

"Go get someone." The chock would keep her occupied for a while.

She ran off, and Chauncie finished the box. He ticked the samples off his list, then started hunting for the next one along the shelves. It was taking too long.

There. He cracked open the new box and dumped the seeds in. River had caught back up to him, though, giving up on the door faster than he'd anticipated.

"Listen, you can't do this," she said. "I'm going to stop you."

He glanced over his shoulder to see that she'd pulled pepper spray out of the ridiculous little pouch she kept strapped to her waist in lieu of a purse.

Chauncie slid one hand into a pocket. He had what looked like an inhaler in there; one forcibly administered dose from it and he could knock her out for twenty-four hours. But he didn't want to leave River passed out among the boxes for the mercenaries to find. And if he left without her, he'd have to deal with the security guards as well.

He really couldn't live with victimizing any of them. River was a relatively naïve and noble refugee, caught up in a vicious world of international fits over genetic heritage and ecological policy. He was not going to leave her for the sharks. "Look, River, a private army-for-hire is about to land on Svalbard and do exactly what I'm doing—only not as carefully."

She hesitated, the pepper spray wavering. "What?"

"Overengineered agristock and plague. I'm told the Russians are pretty damn hell-bent on regaining control of un-copyrighted genetic variability for robustness. And to reboot their whole agricultural sector. They've hired a private army to come here; it gives them some plausible deniability on the world stage. But here's the thing: plausible deniability also means cutting up the DNA data into individual genes—scrambling it— so nobody can tell where they got them later on. All they want is the genes for splicing experiments, so they may preserve the data at the gene level, but they're going to destroy the record of the whole plant so they can't be traced. I've been sent to get what I can out of the vault before they get here."

River paused. "And who are *you* working for?"

Chauncie bit his lip. He hated lying. In this situation, she might as well hear the truth; he didn't have time to lay down anything believable anyway. "The Russian Mafia, they're connected enough to have gotten a heads-up. They think they can get some serious coin selling the complete sequences to companies across the world."

She stared at him. "You swear?"

"Why the hell would I make this up?"

He watched as she opened the zipper on the hip pouch and pocketed the pepper spray. She grabbed her forehead and leaned against the nearest shelf. "I can't fucking believe this. I need to think."

"It's a crazy world," Chauncie mumbled, and tipped a new pouch of seeds into the sequencer as she massaged her scalp and swore to herself.

The sequence returned good, and he stood up, looking for the next box. "What are you doing?"

"Looking for the next item on the list."

She walked over, and Chauncie tensed. But all she did was snatch the list from him. "There are a few missing they should have," she said.

"Like?"

"Like the damn seed I just brought here." River looked up at the shelves. "Look, you're wandering around like a lost kid in here. Let me help you."

He took the sheet of paper back from her. "And why would you do that?"

"Because until five minutes ago, I thought the vault was the best bank box, and seeds the best storage mechanism. You just blew that out of the water, Chauncie. As a scientist, I have to go with the best solution available to me at the time. If these mercenaries are going to invade and hold the seeds, then we need to get that genetic diversity backed up, copied, and kicked out across the world. Selling it to various companies and keeping copies in a criminal organization is . . . an awful solution, but we *have* to mitigate the potential damage. We have to make sure the seeds can be re-created later on."

He'd expected her to ask for a cut of the profit. Instead, she was offering to help out of some scientific rationalism. "Okay," he said, slowly. "Okay. But the list stays here, and you bring back the foil packets, sealed, to me."

"So that you can see that I'm not bringing back the wrong seeds, and so I don't rip up your list."

Chauncie smiled. "Exactly."

Plinking CarbonJohnnies was a lot more fun. And a hell of a lot easier. He felt ragged and frayed. Screw retirement; he just wanted out of this incredibly cold, eerie environment and the constant expectation that armed men would kick in the airlock door and shoot him.

But things moved quicker now. River ranged ahead, snagging the foil packets he needed and those he didn't even know he needed. For the next forty minutes he made a small mountain of pulped seed around him as the briefcase processed sample after sample, resembling more a small portable mill than an advanced piece of technology.

His sat phone beeped, an alarm he'd set back on the boat.

Chauncie closed the briefcase, and River walked around a shelf corner with a foil packet. "What?"

"It's time to go," Chauncie said. "We don't have much time."

"But . . ." Like any other treasure hunter, she looked around the cavern. So many more precious samples that hadn't been snagged.

But Chauncie had a suspicion that what River valued was not necessarily what the market valued. They had what they needed—best not push it any further. "Come on. We do not want to be standing here when these people arrive."

Chauncie bent over and rolled his fingerprint on the chock, and it slowly cranked itself down into thinness again. He placed it back in his pocket, and they cycled through the airlocks, again ducking under the unusually low entranceways.

They walked up the slight slope of the tunnel, the entrance looking small and brightly lit in the distance. The tourists were gone. As they passed the offices on their left one of the guards looked up and smiled. "All good? You were in there a long while. Sir, may I inspect your briefcase?"

Chauncie let him open it on a metal table while the other man carefully checked his coat lining and patted them both down. The briefcase contained nothing but empty foil packets; he'd left the sequencer under a shelf in the vault.

"What's this?" The guard drew out the sequencer's Exabyte data chip from Chauncie's pocket. He tensed.

But River smiled. "Wedding photos. Would you like to see them?"

The guard shook his head. "That's okay, ma'am." These guys probably didn't know DNA sequencers had shrunk to briefcase size. They'd been trained to think their job was to make sure no seeds left the vault;

Chauncie was pretty sure the idea of them being digitized hadn't been in the course.

River shrugged with a smile, and they passed on. Chauncie breathed out heavily.

"Hey," the guard said. "If you're in town, take a few shots of that fleet of little boats out there. They're doing some serious exercises, wargaming some sorta Arctic defense scenario for the oil companies or other. They're all around Svalbard. Just amazing to see all those ships."

Chauncie's mood died.

They entered the mouth of the tunnel, shielding their eyes from the sun.

Chauncie took a high-throughput satellite antenna out of the car's trunk and put it on the roof. He plugged his sat phone into it, then the Exabyte core into that. The sat phone's little screen lit up and said hunting . . . . "Damn it, come on," he muttered.

"Uh, Chauncie?"

"Just wait, wait! It'll just take a second—" But she'd grabbed his arm and was pointing. Straight up.

He craned his neck, and finally spotted the tiny dot way up at the zenith. The sat phone said *hunting . . . hunting . . . hunting . . .* and then, *No Signal.*

"You've been jammed," River said, quite unnecessarily.

Chauncie cursed and slammed the briefcase. "And there!" She grabbed his arm again. Way out in the sky over the bay, six corpse-gray military blimps were drifting toward them with casual grace.

"We're out of time." No way they'd outrun those in a bright yellow electric car. Chauncie looked around desperately. Hole up in the vault? Fortress of Solitude it might be, but it wouldn't keep the mercenaries out for more than a minute. Run along the road? They'd be seen as surely as if they were in the car.

He popped up the hatch of the car and rummaged around in the back. As he'd hoped, there was a cardboard box there crammed with survival gear—a package of survival blankets, flares, and heat packs standard for any far-northern vehicle. He grabbed some of the gear and slammed the hatch. "Run up the hill," he said. "Look for an area of loose scree behind some boulders. We're going to dig in and hide."

"That's not a very good plan."

"It's not the whole plan." He pulled Maksim's list out and rummaged in the car's glove compartment. "Damn, no pen."

"Here." She fished one out of her pocket.

"Ah, scientists." Quickly, he wrote the words *scanned* and *uploaded* at the top of the first page, above and to the right of the list. He underlined them. Then he made two columns of checkmarks down the page, next to each of the seeds on the list. "Okay, come on."

They ran back to the vault. Chauncie threw the list down just outside the door; then they started climbing the slope beside the blade. The oncoming blimps were on the other side; if there were men watching, it would look like Chauncie and River had gone back into the vault. He hoped they were too confident to be that attentive. After all, the vault was supposedly unguarded.

"Over there!" River dragged him away from the concrete blade, toward a flat shelf fronted by a low pile of black rocks. The slope rose above it at about thirty degrees, a loose tumble of dark gravel and fist-sized stone where a few hardy grasses clung.

"Okay, get down." She hunkered down, and he wrapped her in a silvery survival blanket, then began clawing at the scree with his bare hands, heaping it up around her. The act was a kind of horrible parody of the many times he'd buried his sister in the sand back home.

Awkwardly, he made a second pile around himself, until he and River were two gravel cones partially shielded by rock. "You picked a good spot," he commented; they had a great view of the parking lot and the ground just in front of the entrance. He'd wedged the briefcase under the shielding stones; his eyes kept returning to it as the mercenary force came into view over the flat roof of the vault.

The blare of the blimps' turboprops shattered the valley's serene silence.

They swiveled into position just below the parking lot, lowered down, touched, and men in combat fatigues began pouring out. Chauncie and River ducked as they scanned the hillside with binoculars and heat-sensing equipment.

"I'm cold," said River.

"Just wait. If this doesn't work we'll give up."

After a few minutes Chauncie raised his head so he could peer between two stones. The mercenaries had pulled the security guards out of the vault and had them on their knees. Someone was talking to them. The rest of them seemed satisfied with their perimeter, and now a man in a greatcoat strode up the hillside. The coat flew out behind him in black wings as one of the soldiers ran up holding something small and white. "Jackpot!" muttered Chauncie. It was Maksim's list.

"What's happening?"

"Moment of truth." He watched as the commander flipped through the list. Then he went to talk to the security guards, who looked terrified. The commander looked skeptical and kept shaking his head as they spoke. It wasn't working!

Then there was a shout from the doorway. Two soldiers came down to the commander, one carrying Chauncie's sequencer, the other a double handful of open foil packets.

Chauncie could see the commander's mouth working: cursing, no doubt. He threw down the list and pulled a sat phone out of his coat.

"He thinks we got the data out," said Chauncie. "There's nothing left for them to steal." The commander put away the sat phone and waved to his men. Shaking his head in disgust, he walked away from the vault. The bewildered soldiers followed, knotting up into little groups to mutter amongst themselves.

"I don't believe it. It worked."

"I can't see anything!"

"They think Maksim's got the data on the unique seeds. It's pretty obvious that we destroyed those in processing them. So these guys have exactly nothing now, and they know it. If they stay here they'll just get rounded up by the UN or the Norwegian navy."

"So you've won?"

"We win." The blimps were taking off. One of the guards was climbing into a car as the other ran back into the vault. Doubtless the airwaves were still jammed, and would be for an hour or so; the only way to alert the army camp at Svalbard would be to drive there.

"It's still plunder, Chauncie." Stones rattled as River shook them off. "Theft of something that belongs to all of us. Besides, there's one big problem you hadn't thought of."

He frowned at her. "What?"

"It's just that those guys are now Maksim's best customers. And the deal they'll be looking for is still the same: the unique gene sequences, not the whole plant DNA. Plausible deniability, remember? And Maksim would be a fool to keep the whole set after he's sold the genes. It would be incriminating."

He stood up, joints aching, to find his toes and ears were numb. Little rockfalls tumbled down the slope below him. "Listen," River continued, "I don't think you ever wanted to do this in the first place. The closer we got to Svalbard the unhappier you looked. You know it was wrong to steal this stuff to begin with. And look at the firepower they sent to get it! It was always a bad deal, and it's a hot potato and you'd best be rid of it."

"How?" He shook his head, scowling. "We've already scanned the damned things. Maksim . . ."

"Maksim will know the mercenaries got here while we were here. We just tell him they got here *before* us. That they got the material."

"And this?" He hefted the Exabyte storage block.

"We give it to that last guard; hey, he'll be a hero, he might as well get something for his trouble. So the DNA goes back into the vault—virtually, at least, after they back it up to a dozen or so off-site locations."

He thought about it as they trudged down the hillside. Truth to tell, he had no idea what he'd do if he retired now anyway. Probably buy a boat and come back to plink CarbonJohnnies. He wanted the emerald sea; he wanted those waters back. But now they were battered with hurricanes, the islands themselves depopulated and poor now that tourism had left, and the beaches had been destroyed by rising tides and storms.

From behind him she said, "It's an honorable solution, Chauncie, and you know it." They reached the level of the parking lot and she stopped, holding out her hand. "Here. I'll take it in. I've got my pepper spray if he tries to keep me there. And you know, now that the Russians have tried this they'll put real security on this place. Keep it safe for everybody. The way it was meant to be."

He thought about the money, about Maksim's wrath; but he was tired, and damn it, when during this whole fiasco had he been free to make his own choice on anything? If not now . . .

He handed her the data block. "Just be quick. The whole Norwegian navy is going to descend on this place in about an hour."

She laughed, and disappeared into the dark fortress with the treasure of millennia in her hand.

Night was falling at last. Chauncie stood on the trawler's deck watching the last sliver of sun disappear. Vast purple wings of cloud rolled up and away, like brushes painting the sky in delicate hues of mauve, pale peach, silver. There were no primary colors in the Arctic, and he had to admit that after all this time, he'd fallen in love with that visual delicacy.

The stars began to come out, but he remained at the railing. The trawler's lights slanted out, fans of yellow crossing the deck, the mist of radiance from portholes silhouetting the vessel's shape. The air was fresh and smelled clean—scrubbed free of humanity.

He wondered if River Balleny was watching the fall's first sunset from wherever she was. They had parted ways in Svalbard—not exactly on friendly terms, he'd thought, but not enemies either. He figured she was satisfied that he'd done the right thing, but disappointed that he'd gotten them into the situation in the first place. Fair enough; but he wished he'd had a chance to make it up to her in some way. He'd probably never see her again.

Kulitak's voice cut through his reverie. "Sat phone for you!" Chauncie shot one last look at the fading colors, then went inside.

"St. Christie here."

"Chauncie, my old friend." It was Maksim. Well, he'd been expecting this call.

"I can't believe you sent us into that meat grinder," Chauncie began. He'd rehearsed his version of events and decided to act the injured party, having barely escaped with his life when the mercenaries came down on the vault just as he was arriving. "I'm lucky to be here to talk to you at—"

"Oh, such sour grapes from a conquering hero!" That was odd. Maksim actually sounded *pleased*.

"Conquering? They—"

"Have conceded defeat. You uploaded the finest material, Chauncie; our pet scientists are in ecstasy. So, as I'm a man of my word, I've wired the rest of your payment to the new account number you requested."

"New acc—" Chauncie stopped himself just in time. "Ah. Uh, well thank you, Maksim. It was good, uh, doing—"

"Business, yes! You see how business turns out well in the end, my friend? If you have a little faith and a little courage? Certainly I had faith in you, and justly so! I'd like to say we must do it again someday, but I know you'll vanish back to your beloved Caribbean now to lounge in the sunlight—and I'd even join you if I didn't love my work so much." Maksim prattled happily on for a minute or two, then rang off to deal with some of his other hundreds of distractions. Chauncie laid down the sat phone and collapsed heavily onto the bench beside the galley table.

"Something wrong?" Kulitak was staring at him in concern.

"Nothing, nothing." Kulitak shot him a skeptical look and Chauncie said, "Go on. Go find us some CarbonJohnnies to bomb or something. I need a moment."

After Kulitak had left, Chauncie went to his cabin and woke up his laptop. An email waited from one of the online payment services he'd tied to his Polar Consulting Services Web site.

Twenty-five thousand dollars had just been transferred to him, according to the email, from an email address he didn't recognize—a tiny fraction of the number Maksim had promised him. Chauncie had no doubt that it was a tiny fraction of the amount Maksim had actually paid out.

His inbox pinged. A strange sense of fated certainty settled on Chauncie as he opened the mail program and saw a videogram waiting. He clicked on it.

River Balleny's windburnt face appeared on the screen. Behind her was bright sunlight, a sky not touched in pastels. She was wearing a T-shirt, and appeared relaxed and happy.

"Hi, Chauncie," she said. "I swore to myself I wouldn't contact you—in case they got to you somehow—but it just seemed wrong to leave you in the lurch. I had to do something. So . . . well, check your email. A little gift from me to you.

"You know . . . I really wasn't lying when I told you I think the seed data belongs to all of mankind. I walked back into the vault seriously intending to leave it there. But then I realized that it wouldn't solve anything. We'd still have all our eggs in one basket, so to speak. As long as the seed data was in one place, stored in only one medium—whether it was as seeds or bits on a data chip—it would be *scarce*. And anything that's scarce can be bought, and sold, and hoarded, and killed for.

"The guard wasn't around; he'd run down to the vault. So I just put the data core in an inner pocket and hung around for a minute. After we parted, I uploaded the data to Maksim; it wasn't hard to get an ftp address from the guy who'd introduced me to him in the first place. And, yeah, I gave Maksim my own bank account number." She chuckled. "Sorry—but I was never the naïve farmgirl you and Kulitak seemed to think I was."

Chauncie swore under his breath—but he couldn't help smiling too.

"As long as the genetic code of those seeds was kept in one place, it remained scarce," she said again. "That gave it value but also made it vulnerable. Now Maksim has it; but so do I. I made copies. I backed it up. And someday—when Maksim and the Russians have gotten what they want out of it and it's ceasing to be scarce anyway—someday I'll upload it all onto the net. For everyone to use.

"We all have to make hard choices these days, Chauncie—about what can be saved, and what we have to leave behind. Svalbard will always be there, but its rarest treasure is out now, and with luck, it won't be rare for long. So everybody wins this time.

"As to me personally, I'm retiring—and no, I'm not going to tell you where. And I've left you enough for a really good vacation. Enjoy it on me. Maybe we'll meet again someday."

She smiled, and there was that naïve farmgirl look, for just a second. "Good-bye, Chauncie. I hope you don't think less of me for taking the money."

The clip ended. Chauncie sat back, shaking his head and grinning. He walked out onto the deck of the trawler and looked out over the sea. The sun had just slightly dipped below the horizon, bringing a sort of short twilight. It would reemerge soon, bringing back the perpetual glare of the long days.

Stars twinkled far overhead.

No, not stars, Chauncie realized. There were far too many to be stars, and the density of them increased. Far overhead a heavy blimp was dumping tiny bits of chaff glued to little balloons. Judging by the haze, they'd dumped the cloud into a vast patch of sulfur particulates. Both parties would be in court soon to fight over who would get the credit for blocking the sun's rays as it climbed back over the horizon.

The sulfur haze had caused the remaining sun's rays to flare in a full hue of purples and shimmering reds, and the chaff glittered and sparkled overhead.

It was so beautiful.

ABOUT THE AUTHORS

TOBIAS S. BUCKELL is a Caribbean-born speculative fiction writer who grew up in Grenada, the British Virgin Islands, and the U.S. Virgin Islands. He has written several novels, including the *New York Times* bestseller *Halo: The Cole Protocol*, the Xenowealth series, and *Arctic Rising* and *Hurricane Fever*. His short fiction has appeared in magazines such as *Lightspeed, Analog, Clarkesworld,* and *Subterranean,* and in anthologies such as *Armored, All-Star Zeppelin Adventure Stories, Under the Moons of Mars, Operation Arcana,* and *The End Is Nigh.* He currently lives in Ohio with a pair of dogs, a pair of cats, twin daughters, and his wife.

KARL SCHROEDER (kschroeder.com) was born into a Mennonite community in Manitoba, Canada, in 1962. He started writing at age fourteen, following in the footsteps of A. E. van Vogt, who came from the same Mennonite community. He moved to Toronto in 1986, and became a founding member of SF Canada (he was president from 1996–97). He sold early stories to Canadian magazines, and his first novel, *The Claus Effect* (with David Nickle) appeared in 1997. His first solo novel, *Ventus,* was published in 2000, and was followed by *Permanence and Lady of Mazes.* His most recent work includes the Virga series of science fiction novels (*Sun of Suns, Queen of Candesce, Pirate Sun,* and *The Sunless Countries*) and hard SF space opera *Lockstep.* He also collaborated with Cory Doctorow on *The Complete Idiot's Guide to Writing Science Fiction.* Schroeder lives in East Toronto with his wife and daughter.

TIME CAPSULE FOUND ON THE DEAD PLANET

MARGARET ATWOOD

1. In the first age, we created gods. We carved them out of wood; there was still such a thing as wood then. We forged them from shining metals and painted them on temple walls. They were gods of many kinds, and goddesses as well. Sometimes they were cruel and drank our blood, but also they gave us rain and sunshine, favourable winds, good harvests, fertile animals, many children. A million birds flew over us then, a million fish swam in our seas.

Our gods had horns on their heads, or moons, or sealy fins, or the beaks of eagles. We called them All-Knowing, we called them Shining One. We knew we were not orphans. We smelled the earth and rolled in it; its juices ran down our chins.

2. In the second age, we created money. This money was also made of shining metals. It had two faces: on one side was a severed head, that of a king or some other noteworthy person, on the other face was something else, something that would give us comfort: a bird, a fish, a fur-bearing animal. This was all that remained of our former gods. The money was small in size, and each of us would carry some of it with him every day, as close to the skin as possible. We could not eat this money, wear it, or burn

it for warmth; but as if by magic, it could be changed into such things. The money was mysterious, and we were in awe of it. If you had enough of it, it was said, you would be able to fly.

3. In the third age, money became a god. It was all-powerful, and out of control. It began to talk. It began to create on its own. It created feasts and famines, songs of joy, lamentations. It created greed and hunger, which were its two faces. Towers of glass rose at its name, were destroyed, and rose again. It began to eat things. It ate whole forests, croplands, and the lives of children. It ate armies, ships, and cities. No one could stop it. To have it was a sign of grace.

4. In the fourth age we created deserts. Our deserts were of several kinds, but they had one thing in common: nothing grew there. Some were made of cement, some were made of various poisons, some of baked earth. We made these deserts from the desire for more money and from despair at the lack of it. Wars, plagues, and famines visited us, but we did not stop in our industrious creation of deserts. At last, all wells were poisoned, all rivers ran with filth, all seas were dead; there was no land left to grow food.

Some of our wise men turned to the contemplation of deserts. A stone in the sand in the setting sun could be very beautiful, they said. Deserts were tidy, because there were no weeds in them, nothing that crawled. Stay in the desert long enough, and you could apprehend the absolute. The number zero was holy.

5. You who have come here from some distant world, to this dry lake-shore and this cairn, and to this cylinder of brass, in which on the last day of all our recorded days I place our final words:

Pray for us, who once, too, thought we could fly.

MARGARET ATWOOD

ABOUT THE AUTHOR

MARGARET ATWOOD was born in 1939 in Ottawa, and grew up in northern Ontario and Quebec, and in Toronto. She received her undergraduate degree from Victoria College at the University of Toronto and her master's degree from Radcliffe College. She is the author of more than forty volumes of poetry, children's literature, fiction, and non-fiction, but is best known for her novels, which include *The Edible Woman*, *The Handmaid's Tale*, *The Robber Bride*, *Alias Grace*, and *The Blind Assassin*, which won the prestigious Booker Prize in 2000. Her latest work is a book of short stories called *Stone Mattress: Nine Tales*. Her newest novel, *MaddAddam*, is the final volume in a three-book series that began with the Man-Booker Prize–nominated *Oryx and Crake* and continued with *The Year of the Flood*. She is also the author of *In Other Worlds: SF and the Human Imagination*, a collection of non-fiction essays, and the non-fiction book, *Payback: Debt and the Shadow Side of Wealth*, which was adapted for the screen in 2012. Ms. Atwood's work has been published in more than forty languages.

AFTERWORD:
SCIENCE SCARIER THAN FICTION

RAMEZ NAAM

Mount Rainier looms over Seattle. Look south and east toward downtown from the Queen Anne neighborhood, and you can see the mountain, sixty miles away but still gigantic, as tall as any skyscraper, even from this distance, five times as wide on the horizon, its upper flanks permanently covered in white, even more impressive since it rises from nearly sea level, no other mountains around the big volcano.

I climbed it for the first time in 2000. It was the toughest, wildest, most gorgeous thing I'd done. We hiked on a long but safe snowfield up to Camp Muir at about 10,000 feet of elevation, napped for a few hours, then rose at midnight. Under the moonlight, we roped ourselves together, strapped metal-pronged crampons to our boots, pulled out our ice axes, and finished the much more dangerous part of the climb, stepping or jumping over crevasses in the ice beneath our feet, or going around them if they were too wide, until we reached the summit at 14,411 feet. I couldn't believe I'd made it.

I've been back almost every year, at least to hike the Muir Snowfield up to Camp Muir. So, I can tell you from firsthand experience: It's melting.

In 2007, crevasses—cracks in the ice, uncovered by melting of the snow above them—opened up on that long, generally safe snowfield below 10,000 feet. The rangers had never seen anything like it.

It happened again in 2012.

And again in 2014.

Rainier is a friend of mine. I know that mountain. I love that mountain. And it's melting. Numbers tell the tale. Mount Rainier isn't quite the tallest mountain in the lower forty-eight states, but it's the biggest. A quarter of the glacier area of the lower forty-eight sits on its flanks. And that area shrank by around twenty-five percent in the twentieth century. It's sure to shrink more in the twenty-first.

Soar up into space. Watch the Earth recede beneath you until we're looking down on it like a globe. And then follow me as we zoom down south, to where the real ice is: Antarctica.

You've seen *Game of Thrones*? (Or read the books?) You know the Wall, the giant construction of ice that guards the north? Imagine standing at the base of it, and looking up. Seven hundred feet high—as tall as a skyscraper—three hundred miles wide.

That's nothing.

The Antarctic ice sheet is an average of seven *thousand* feet thick. In some places, it's *fifteen thousand* feet thick—three vertical miles of ice. It goes on for more than a thousand miles—not just wide but deep as well.

And it, too, is melting. Faster and faster and faster.

In 1995, the Larsen A ice shelf—ice that had clung to Antarctica for four thousand years—unexpectedly disintegrated. In 2002, the much larger Larsen B ice shelf, stable for the last 12,000 years, disintegrated over the course of a few days. Larsen B is floating ice, but it's massive. It was an ice sheet two hundred and twenty meters thick . . . or as thick as the Wall in *Game of Thrones*. And it was huge—more than twelve hundred square miles in area—as large as the state of Rhode Island.

Now even the Larsen C ice sheet—ten times larger than Larsen B, larger than nine out of fifty US states—is at risk of breaking up. It could go at any time. Perhaps it will be gone by the time you read this.

Those ice shelves are floating ice. Their breakup doesn't raise sea levels. They're inherently more fragile than the miles-thick ice on land. But that, too, is melting. In the last year, West Antarctica lost almost *two hundred billion* tons of ice from land.

All of Mount Everest only weighs one hundred and sixty billion tons.

Yet the ocean is vast. All that melt has added just a fraction of an inch to sea ice in the last twenty years. Over the course of this century, if Antarctica keeps melting at its current pace, it will add just inches to the world's sea level, out of an overall rise of three feet, or perhaps a bit more—most of that caused by thermal expansion of the oceans. At that rate, it would take thousands of years for Antarctica's ice cap to melt entirely (and a good thing, too, as that would raise sea levels by a catastrophic two hundred feet).

But the melt won't continue at its current pace. It's accelerating. In another ten years, if the acceleration continues, Antarctica will be losing ice weighing *two* Mount Everests each year. And after that?

Well, even the *rate of acceleration* is speeding up. The arc is bending faster and faster downward. But how fast will it go? Will we someday be losing ten Everests' worth of ice from Antarctica each year? One hundred?

How fast can ice destabilize?

Here's the thing, despite all our tools, our satellite observations, our hypersensitive gravity sensors that can measure ice mass, our super-computer models of the ice and the water and the wind: We just don't know for sure. Events keep happening faster than we predict them.

This planet can still surprise us.

Zoom back up, then north, until we reach the other end of the Earth: The Arctic. The North Pole.

The Arctic is the opposite of the Antarctic. It's not just north vs. south; where Antarctica is a vast piece of land covered in miles-thick ice, then surrounded by ocean, the Arctic is the inverse. It's a polar ocean, covered by a floating layer of ice just a few feet thick, and bounded all around by land—Russia, Canada, Alaska.

In 2007, the IPCC, the international body that reports on climate change, predicted that the Arctic ice cap wouldn't completely melt for more than a century—sometime around 2150 or so.

But they were wrong.

The Arctic ice shrinks each summer as conditions warm, then regrows in winter. At its summer minimum, it's now hitting areas less than half of those it saw in the 1980s. And the ice is also *thinner*, more fragile. It's often just two or three feet thick in summer now, where often it was five or six feet thick. So, the total volume is down even more—down to a fifth of what it was in the 1980s.

It now looks like we'll see our first ice-free Arctic summer a century ahead of schedule. We may see it even sooner than that: perhaps by 2030. Some models even show an ice-free summer day in the Arctic by 2020.

The melt of floating ice doesn't raise sea levels. But as the Arctic thaws, it'll kick off more warming for the rest of the world. Ice is bright white. It reflects up to 90 percent of the sunlight that hits it back into space. Arctic water is dark and absorbs almost 90 percent. The melting Arctic becomes darker. The planet becomes darker and starts to warm faster. How much faster? If all the Arctic sea ice were gone in the sunniest months of May and June and July, the planet might warm *twice as fast*, just from the extra sunlight absorbed by those dark waters.

Now, we're a long way from that. The first ice-free day will be late in September when the sun is low on the horizon. But bit by bit, that ice-free period will get longer and stretch out further in the year, until one day it will be a year-round polar ocean (as in the story "Mitigation" by Tobias S. Buckell and Karl Schroeder).

Then there's the methane, a greenhouse gas that captures a hundred times more heat than CO_2. The permafrost all around the Arctic is dense with vegetation. As the whole area warms—speeded by heat being captured in those seas—the permafrost thaws. Vegetation that rots under the soil releases its carbon as methane. There's a trillion tons of it in Arctic soil. Enough that a tenth of it going up would triple our rate of warming for the next twenty years. And there's an estimated *six trillion tons* of methane captured in icy slush at the Arctic sea floor. The last time all of that was in the atmosphere, fifty-eight million years ago, tropical trees and crocodile-like reptiles thrived on Antarctica.

So, that's your worst-case scenario. An explosive release of methane from a rapidly thawing world, bringing forward a rapid surge of warming, far faster than we've expected, accelerating superstorms and crop losses, melting ice faster, speeding the thermal expansions of the ocean, bringing both the mega-rains of Kim Stanley Robinson's *Forty Signs of Rain* and the decades-long mega-droughts like the ones that feature in Paolo Bacigalupi's and Nancy Kress's stories in this collection.

It wouldn't be *Waterworld*. But it wouldn't be pretty.

Is that going to happen?

Oh, probably not. The methane slush at the bottom of the Arctic has been stable for millions of years. It even survived a period eight thousand or so years ago that might have seen ice-free summers. And the thawing permafrost in Canada and Siberia probably won't go all at once—it'll probably stretch out over decades, spreading out and muting its effect.

Climate change will probably keep coming the way it has been, bit by bit, the weather growing more intense, droughts growing more frequent and longer in the west, flood rains growing harder elsewhere, seas growing more acidic, stressing corals. But those changes will probably happen over decades, over generations, over time that we at least have a chance of adapting to, rather than in the snap of a year or three.

Probably.

Then again, the planet does like to surprise us. As in Nicole Feldringer's story, "Outliers," it's the extreme events that matter just as much as the central prediction. The outliers are what get you. Indeed, history shows that the climate is far less stable than we like to think. At the end of the last ice age—the Younger Dryas—temperatures slowly crept higher for hundreds of years, then shot up by nine degrees Fahrenheit in the span of just a decade and a half.

Nine degrees. That's the difference between a summer high of one hundred and a summer high of one-oh-nine. And that wasn't a one-time spike. That was the new normal.

Nine degrees would be a very unwelcome surprise indeed. That's the kind of outlier that our planet is capable of.

I don't raise these possibilities to depress you, dear reader. I am, in fact, one of the more optimistic people on the topic of climate change that I know. I believe we'll turn the corner on this challenge, as gigantic as it is, just like we turned the corner on ozone depletion, on acid rain, and on a host of other things.

But we won't do that passively. We'll do it because we're highly motivated. What I love most about this collection of stories is that it brings to life real possibilities of the future. It turns the future into something you can see through the eyes of people you empathize with. That's what motivates us: People. Their stories.

And the stories here almost universally show people fighting. That's what we do. Whether it's at the intensely human scale of women and men fighting for their livelihood—a theme that shows up over and over again—or the planetary-scale fight to survive with every tool in our arsenal: iron-seeding the seas to take up carbon, reflective aerosols in the sky to reflect sunlight over the Arctic, giant engineering efforts to stabilize ice sheets or rebuild the Arctic ice cap—we fight to survive.

Many of the most science-fictional tools to fight climate change are untested, are almost impossible to truly test at planetary scale—we only have one planet, after all. We're better off cutting our emissions so we *don't need them*. But one way or another, when our back is up against the wall, we humans rally. We innovate. We face realities we previously ignored. And we hustle like we never did before.

We fight.

There are scars on our planet. There are scars in the natural world—species lost, half our forests cut down, soil degraded, oceans acidified. We're going to take deeper scars before this is over. We're going to lose more species, acidify the oceans more, do damage that it will take millions of years—if not longer—to unwind. Exactly how much damage will we do? How deep will those scars run? We don't know yet. But we will turn the ship. Just like the characters in this collection, we're fighters.

I'd never want to bet against that.

ABOUT THE AUTHOR

RAMEZ NAAM wrote about climate, energy, and how to overcome our challenges in his nonfiction book *The Infinite Resource*. He's also the author of the award-winning Nexus trilogy (*Nexus*, *Crux*, and *Apex*) of science fiction novels. He lives in Seattle.

ACKNOWLEDGMENTS

Publisher/Editor: Joe Monti, for acquiring the book (and suggesting I do it in the first place!), and to managing editor Bridget Madsen, designer Michael McCartney, production manager Elizabeth Blake-Linn, and the rest of the team at Saga Press.

Agent: Seth Fishman for being awesome and supportive (writers: you'd be lucky to have Seth in your corner).

Mentors: Gordon Van Gelder and Ellen Datlow, for being great mentors and friends.

Colleagues: Ben Bova, Eric Choi, Ed Finn, Kathryn Cramer, Kristine Kathryn Rusch, Gabrielle Gantz, Jordan Bass, Vaughne Hansen, Emily Hockaday, Trevor Quachri, Sean Williams, and Suzanna Porter.

Family: My amazing wife, Christie; my mom, Marianne; and my sister, Becky, for all their love and support. Also, of course, my stepdaughter, Grace, to whom this book is dedicated.

Writers: Everyone who had stories included in this anthology, and in all of my other projects.

Readers: Everyone who bought this book, or any of my other anthologies, and who make it possible to do books like this.

Climate Scientists: Thanks most of all to all of the scientists working to help halt and/or reverse the effects of climate change. I really hope we can save this planet; it's where I keep all my stuff.

ABOUT THE EDITOR

JOHN JOSEPH ADAMS is the series editor of *Best American Science Fiction and Fantasy*, published by Houghton Mifflin Harcourt. He is also the bestselling editor of many other anthologies, such as *The Mad Scientist's Guide to World Domination, Armored, Brave New Worlds, Wastelands*, and *The Living Dead*. Recent projects include *Operation Arcana, Press Start to Play*, and The Apocalypse Triptych, consisting of *The End Is Nigh, The End Is Now*, and *The End Has Come*. Called "the reigning king of the anthology world" by Barnes & Noble, John is a winner of the Hugo Award (for which he has been nominated nine times) and is a six-time World Fantasy Award finalist. John is also the editor and publisher of the digital magazines *Lightspeed* and *Nightmare* and is a producer for WIRED's *The Geek's Guide to the Galaxy* podcast. Find him online at johnjosephadams.com and @johnjosephadams.